Rosa's

Room

To my friend with the kite
—B. B.

In loving memory of my mom, Dorothy
—B. S.

Rosa's Room

Written by

Barbara Bottner

Illustrated by

Beth Spiegel

Ω

PEACHTREE

ATLANTA

Rosa had a new room in a new house.

It seemed empty.

On Monday, Rosa took out her crayons
and put them in a drawer in her desk.

She hung her clothes in her closet.
She unpacked her doll, Maria, and laid her on the bed.

On Tuesday, Rosa found her treasure box,
the one her father had made. She placed it on her desk.

Then she unwrapped her teapot,
while her cat Concertina looked on.

Rosa looked around.
Her room was still too empty.

That night, as Rosa went to sleep,
she wondered what else she could do to decorate her room.

On Wednesday, Rosa's new teacher gave her
a poster for Book Day. It fit perfectly on Rosa's wall,
just between the door and the bookcase.

On Thursday, Rosa's mother took her to the library.
Rosa borrowed five new books.
She placed them around her room.

On Friday, when Rosa was in the park,
she thought about her room some more.

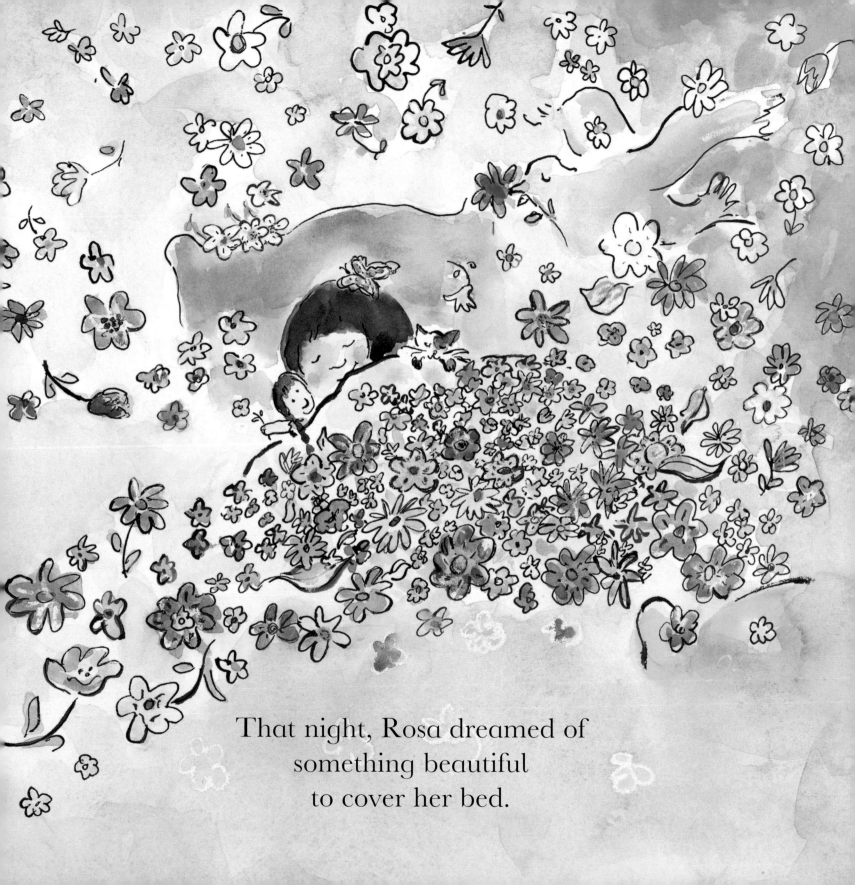

That night, Rosa dreamed of
something beautiful
to cover her bed.

On Saturday, Rosa's mother bought some flowered material,
and together they made a bedspread that fit just right.

"My room looks better," Rosa whispered to Concertina.
But Concertina sat in the middle of the room.
"More," the cat seemed to say.

On Sunday, when Rosa was drawing
a picture, she saw a girl outside.
That gave her an idea.

"My name is Lili," said the girl with the kite.
Rosa invited her to come see her room.

Lili loved kites, butterflies, and drawing. She loved Maria,
Concertina, and every single thing that was in Rosa's room.

Especially Rosa.

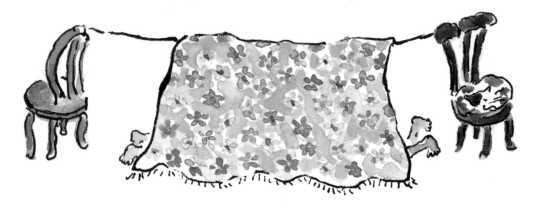

Ω

Published by
PEACHTREE PUBLISHERS
1700 Chattahoochee Avenue
Atlanta, Georgia 30318-2112
www.peachtree-online.com

10 9 8 7 6 5 4 3 2 1
First Edition

Printed in China

Art direction by Loraine M. Joyner
Composition by Melanie Ives
Title calligraphy by Liz Manera

Paintings created in watercolor, gouache, and India ink on acid-free 100% rag paper
Text typeset in Baskerville Infant

Library of Congress Cataloging-in-Publication Data

Bottner, Barbara.
Rosa's room / written by Barbara Bottner; illustrated by Beth Spiegel.-- 1st ed.
p. cm.
Summary: Rosa searches for things that will fill her room in her new home,
but it feels empty until she discovers exactly what is missing.

ISBN 1-56145-302-1
[1. Bedrooms--Fiction. 2. Moving, Household--Fiction. 3. Friendship--Fiction.]
I. Spiegel, Beth, 1957- ill.   II. Title.
PZ7.B6586 Ro 2004

[E]--dc22   2003016837

Humvees

By E. S. Budd

The Child's World®, Inc.

Published by The Child's World®, Inc.
PO Box 326
Chanhassen, MN 55317-0326
800-599-READ
www.childsworld.com

Design and Production:
The Creative Spark, San Juan Capistrano, CA

Photos: © 2002 David M. Budd Photography

We thank the personnel at Fort Carson (Colorado Springs, CO)
for their help and cooperation in preparing this book.

Library of Congress Cataloging-in-Publication Data

Budd, E. S.
Humvees / by E.S. Budd.
        p. cm.
ISBN 1-56766-983-2 (library bound)
1. Hummer truck—Juvenile literature.
2. Military trucks—United States—Juvenile literature.
[1. Hummer truck. 2. Vehicles, Military.]   I. Title.
UG618 .B83 2001
623.7'4722—dc21
                                    2001000340

Contents

On the Job

On the job, humvees take soldiers where they need to go. "Humvee" is a nickname for "High **Mobility** Multipurpose Wheeled **Vehicle.**"

Humvees have very big tires. The tires
make humvees sit high off the ground.

Large springs make the ride smoother.

Humvees also have a powerful **engine.**

These things help humvees travel over

rough, rocky land.

A humvee can travel up and down

steep hills.

A humvee has a **hitch.** It is used to pull heavy **trailers.**

The military uses humvees for

many things. Sometimes humvees

are used to carry **troops.** The

troops sit in the back.

Other humvees are used to

carry **cargo.**

A humvee can be used as an ambulance. It takes injured soldiers to safety.

Humvees have many parts. They

have headlights just like a car.

They also have a blackout light. This special light helps soldiers travel at night without being seen. The blackout light is not as bright as the headlights. It has a cover. The cover aims the light at the ground.

The driver can take the doors off

of a humvee. This makes it easy

to get in and out of the **cab.**

The driver doesn't need a key to start the engine. A special switch turns the engine on and off.

Climb Aboard!

Would you like to see where the driver sits? A humvee has a steering wheel, just like a car. The driver uses **controls** to drive the humvee. The cab has seats for the driver and three **passengers.**

Up Close

The inside

1. The driver's seat

2. The engine switch

3. The steering wheel

4. The controls

5. The passenger's seat

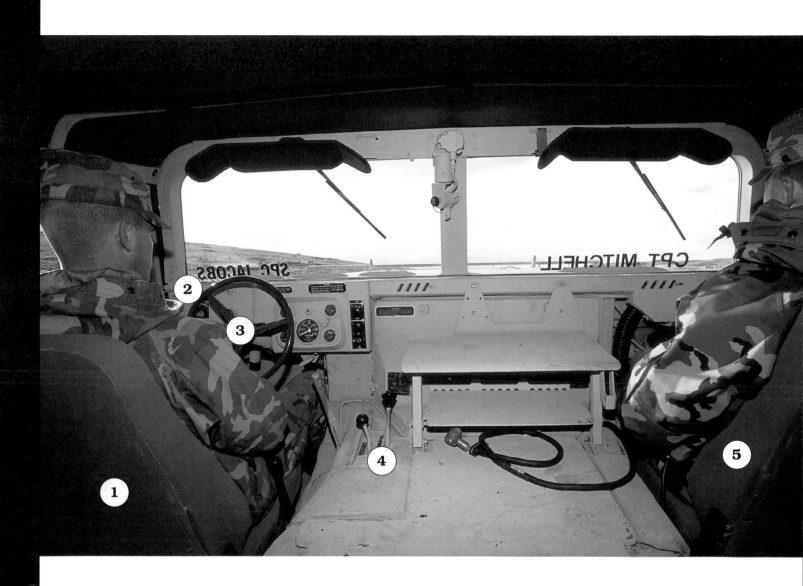

Outside

1. The lights

2. The tires

3. The blackout light

4. The cab

5. The troop and cargo area

6. The spring

Glossary

cab (KAB)
A cab is the part of a vehicle where the driver and passengers sit. A humvee has a cab.

cargo (KAR-goh)
Cargo is a load of goods carried by a vehicle. A humvee can carry cargo.

controls (kun-TROHLZ)
Controls are buttons, switches, and other tools that make a machine work. A driver uses controls to drive a humvee.

engine (EN-jen)
Engines are motors that use energy to make machines move or run. A humvee has a powerful engine.

hitch (HITCH)
A hitch is a hook used to attach one thing to another. A humvee has a hitch for pulling a trailer.

mobility (moh-BIL-ih-tee)
Mobility is the ability to move. Humvees are built for mobility on rough roads.

passengers (PASS-en-jerz)
Passengers are people who travel in vehicles. A humvee's cab has seats for three passengers.

trailers (TRAY-lerz)
Trailers are vehicles that are used to carry things. A trailer is usually pulled by another vehicle, such as a humvee.

troops (TROOPS)
Troops are soldiers. A humvee can carry troops from place to place.

vehicle (VEE-hih-kul)
A vehicle is a machine that takes people or things from one place to another. A humvee is a vehicle.

...ke Mearls, Jeremy Crawford

...Christopher Perkins
...t: Chris Sims, Rodney Thompson,

...Robert J. Schwalb, Matt Sernett,
...James Wyatt
...eremy Crawford
...gerald Gray
...lsland

...ate Irwin, Dan Gelon, Jon Schindehette,
...sky, Melissa Rapier, Shauna Narciso
...gners: Bree Heiss, Emi Tanji, Barry Craig
...ator: Raymond Swanland
...strators: Tom Babbey, Daren Bader, John-Paul
...Mark Behm, Eric Belisle, Michael Berube, Zoltan
...Christopher Bradley, Aleksi Briclot, Filip Burburan,
...opher Burdett, Sam Burley, Mike Burns, Wesley Burt,
...oj Ćeran, Jedd Chevrier, Conceptopolis, Adam Danger
..., Julie Dillon, Dave Dorman, Jesper Ejsing, Emrah
...asli, Wayne England, Mike Faille, Toma Feizo Gas,
...ily Fiegenschuh, Tomas Giorello, E.M. Gist, Lars Grant-
...est, E.W. Hekaton, jD, Jon Hodgson, Ralph Horsley, Kurt
...Huggins and Zelda Devon, Lake Hurwitz, Tyler Jacobson,
...ance Kovacs, Daniel Landerman, Lindsey Look, Daniel
Ljunggren, Raphael Lübke, Titus Lunter, Slawomir Maniak,
Andrew Mar, Brynn Metheney, Christopher Moeller, Mark
Molnar, Marco Nelor, Jim Nelson, Mark A. Nelson, Hector
Ortiz, Ryan Pancoast, Adam Paquette, Jim Pavelec, Kate
Pfeilschiefter, Steve Prescott, Vincent Proce, Darrell Riche,
Ned Rogers, Scott Roller, Jasper Sandner, Mike Sass, Marc
Sasso, Ilya Shkipin, Carmen Sinek, Craig J Spearing, Annie
Stegg, Zack Stella, Matt Stewart, Raymond Swanland,
Justin Sweet, Anne Stokes, Matias Tapia, Cory Trego-
Erdner, Autumn Rain Turkel, Cyril Van Der Haegen, David
Vargo, Franz Vohwinkel, Richard Whitters, Sam Wood, Ben
Wootten, Kieran Yanner, Min Yum, Mark Zug

Additional Contributors: Bruce R. Cordell, Kim Mohan, Chris
Dupuis, Tom LaPille, Miranda Horner, Jennifer Clarke Wilkes,
Steve Winter, Chris Youngs, Ben Petrisor, Tom Olsen,
R.A. Salvatore

Project Management: Neil Shinkle, Kim Graham, John Hay
Production Services: Cynda Callaway, Brian Dumas,
Jefferson Dunlap, David Gershman, Matt Knannlein,
Anita Williams

Brand and Marketing: Nathan Stewart, Liz Schuh,
Chris Lindsay, Shelly Mazzanoble, Hilary Ross,
Laura Tommervik, Kim Lundstrom, Trevor Kidd

Based on the original game created by
E. Gary Gygax and Dave Arneson,
with Brian Blume, Rob Kuntz, James Ward, and Don Kaye
Drawing from further development by
J. Eric Holmes, Tom Moldvay, Frank Mentzer, Aaron Allston,
Harold Johnson, David "Zeb" Cook, Ed Greenwood,
Keith Baker, Tracy Hickman, Margaret Weis, Douglas Niles,
Jeff Grubb, Jonathan Tweet, Monte Cook, Skip Williams,
Richard Baker, Peter Adkison, Bill Slavicsek, Andy Collins,
and Rob Heinsoo

Playtesting provided by
over 175,000 fans of D&D. Thank you!
Additional feedback provided by
Robert Alaniz, Anthony Caroselli, Josh Dillard, Curt Duval,
Sam E. Simpson Jr., Adam Hennebeck, Sterling Hershey,
Paul Hughes, Doug Irwin, Ken J. Breese, Yan Lacharité, Tom
Lommel, Jonathan Longstaff, Rory Madden, Matt Maranda,
Paul Melamed, Mike Mihalas, David Milman, Daren Mitchell,
Claudio Pozas, John Proudfoot, Karl Resch, M. Sean Molley,
Sam Sherry, Pieter Sleijpen, David "Oak" Stark, Vincent
Venturella, Fredrick Wheeler, Arthur Wright

ON THE COVER
Raymond Swanland illustrates the Xanathar
ambushing explorers in the darkest depths
of Undermountain, proving that the beholder
crime lord's interests run deep beneath the
city of Waterdeep.

*Disclaimer: Any similarities between monsters depicted in this
book and monsters that actually exist are purely coincidental.
That goes double for mind flayers, which absolutely, utterly, and
completely do not exist, nor do they secretly run the D&D team.
Do we really need a disclaimer to tell you that? You shouldn't use
your brain to consider such irrational thoughts. They only make
the mind cluttered, confused, and unpleasantly chewy. A good
brain is nice, tender, and barely used. Go ahead, put down this
book and watch some reality TV or Internet cat videos. They're
really funny these days. You won't regret it. We say this only
because we love you and your juicy, succulent gamer brain.*

620A9218000001 EN
ISBN: 978-0-7869-6561-8
First Printing: September 2014   (This printing includes corrections.)

13 12 11 10 9

MONSTER M

CREDITS

D&D Lead Designers: Mi

Monster Manual Lead:
Stat Block Developm
Peter Lee
Story Development:
Steve Townshend
Managing Editor:
Editing: Scott Fitz
Producer: Greg F

Art Directors:
Mari Kolkov
Graphic Desi
Cover Illustr
Interior Illu
Balmet,
Boros,
Christ
Miliv
Coo
Elm
Er
W

CONTENTS

INTRODUCTION

his bestiary is for storytellers and world-builders. If you have ever thought about running a DUNGEONS & DRAGONS game for your friends, either a single night's adventure or a long-running campaign, this tome contains page after page of inspiration. It's your one-stop shop for creatures both malevolent and benign.

Some of the creatures that inhabit the worlds of D&D have origins rooted in real-world mythology and fantasy literature. Other creatures are D&D originals. The monsters in this book have been culled from all previous editions of the game. Herein you'll discover classic critters such as the beholder and the displacer beast next to more recent creations such as the chuul and the twig blight. Common beasts mingle with the weird, the terrifying, and the ridiculous. In collecting monsters from the past, we've endeavored to reflect the multifaceted nature of the game, warts and all. D&D monsters come in all shapes and sizes, with stories that not only thrill us but also make us smile.

If you're an experienced Dungeon Master (DM), a few of the monster write-ups might surprise you, for we've gone into the *Monster Manuals* of yore and discovered some long-lost factoids. We've also added a few new twists. Naturally, you can do with these monsters what you will. Nothing we say here is intended to curtail your creativity. If the minotaurs in your world are shipbuilders and pirates, who are we to argue with you? It's your world, after all.

How to Use This Book

The best thing about being a DM is that you get to invent your own fantasy world and bring it to life, and nothing brings a D&D world to life more than the creatures that inhabit it. You might read a monster's entry and be spurred to create an adventure revolving around it, or you might have an awesome idea for a dungeon and need just the right monsters to populate it. That's where the *Monster Manual* comes in handy.

The *Monster Manual* is one of three books that form the foundation of the DUNGEONS & DRAGONS game, the other two being the *Player's Handbook* and the *Dungeon Master's Guide*. The *Monster Manual*, like the *Dungeon Master's Guide*, is a book for DMs. Use it to populate your D&D adventures with pesky goblins, stinky troglodytes, savage orcs, mighty dragons, and a veritable horde of creepy crawlies.

Guidelines for creating encounters with monsters can be found in the *Dungeon Master's Guide*. That book also contains wandering monster tables and other goodies to help you use the monsters in this book in interesting ways, as well as advice for modifying monsters and creating your own.

If you've never run a D&D adventure before, we recommend that you pick up the DUNGEONS & DRAGONS *Starter Set*, which demonstrates how to take a bunch of monsters and build an exciting adventure around them.

What Is a Monster?

A monster is defined as any creature that can be interacted with and potentially fought and killed. Even something as harmless as a frog or as benevolent as a unicorn is a monster by this definition. The term also applies to humans, elves, dwarves, and other civilized folk who might be friends or rivals to the player characters. Most of the monsters that haunt the D&D world, however, are threats that are meant to be stopped: rampaging demons, conniving devils, soul-sucking undead, summoned elementals—the list goes on.

This book contains ready-to-play, easy-to-run monsters of all levels, and for nearly every climate and terrain imaginable. Whether your adventure takes place in a swamp, a dungeon, or the outer planes of existence, there are creatures in this book to populate that environment.

Where Do Monsters Dwell?

If you are new to the D&D game, you might not be familiar with the weird and wondrous places where monsters can be found and fought.

Dungeons

When most people think of a dungeon, images of dark cells with iron bars and shackles spring to mind. In the D&D game, the word "dungeon" takes on a broader meaning to include any enclosed, monster-infested location. Most dungeons are sprawling underground complexes. Here are a few other examples:

- A ruined wizard's tower atop a lonely hill riddled with goblin-infested tunnels
- A pharaoh's pyramid filled with haunted crypts and secret treasure vaults
- A lost city in the jungle, overgrown with vines and overrun with demons and demon-worshiping cultists
- The icy tomb of a frost giant king
- A filthy, labyrinthine sewer system controlled by a gang of wererats

The Underdark

There is no greater dungeon than the Underdark, the underworld beneath the surface world. It is a vast subterranean realm where monsters accustomed to darkness dwell. It is a place filled with lightless caverns connected by tunnels that wind ever downward. One could spend a lifetime (however brief!) exploring the Underdark and find such places as the following:

- A mind flayer prison or asylum, filled with mindless thralls and raving lunatics
- A lost dwarven necropolis containing row after row of dusty tombs waiting to be plundered
- A fortified outpost bristling with armaments, guarding the way to a magnificent drow city
- A subterranean rift filled with giant fungi and ruled by a megalomaniacal beholder or mad fomorian king
- A chain of rocky islands on a vast, sunless sea that's home to aboleths and insane kuo-toa

THE WILDERNESS

Not all monsters lurk underground. Many of them inhabit deserts, mountains, swamps, canyons, forests, and other natural settings. The wilderness can be just as dangerous as any dungeon, particularly when there's nowhere to hide! Some wilderness locations are just as memorable as any dungeon:

- A roc's nest made of shattered ship hulls, built atop a lonely mountain or rocky hill
- A vast arctic tundra that serves as a hunting ground for berserkers and yeti
- A primeval forest protected by treants or corrupted by demon-worshiping gnolls
- A fog-shrouded swamp haunted by lizardfolk that worship a vile black dragon
- A jungle island inhabited by dinosaurs and human tribal warriors

TOWNS AND CITIES

Some of the best adventures unfold in the cradles of civilization. Urban settings afford adventurers the chance to rub shoulders with the rich and powerful, butt heads with the dregs of society, and peel back the veneer of civility to see the monstrous evil lurking beneath. Within a medieval town or city are places as deadly as any dungeon:

- A clock tower that serves as a base for a guild of kenku rogues and assassins
- A slavers' den hidden in an orphanage run by a rakshasa disguised as the headmaster
- A wizard's academy rife with corruption and practitioners of the necromantic arts
- A noble's manor where rich, devil-worshiping cultists gather to perform sacrifices
- A temple, vault, or museum watched day and night by animated constructs

UNDERWATER

Not all adventures take place on land. This book casts light on several creatures that haunt the oceans of the world, from the devilish sahuagin to the peaceful aquatic elves who loathe them. Within this aquatic domain are many surprising adventure locations:

- A graveyard of sunken ships haunted by sharks, aquatic ghouls, and angry ghosts
- A storm giant's coral castle, beautiful yet foreboding
- A lost city on the sea floor, encased in a magic bubble of air and ruled by a medusa queen
- A kraken's cave or bronze dragon's cavernous lair, filled with ancient treasures
- A sunken temple of Sekolah, evil god of the sahuagin

THE PLANES OF EXISTENCE

The Abyss. The Nine Hells. The City of Brass. Such faraway places beckon high-level adventurers to their doorsteps, defying the brave and the foolhardy to overthrow their evil masters and unlock their hidden mysteries. Many powerful, weird creatures live on other planes of existence, from orderly modrons to murderous demons. When it comes to interesting adventure locations, not even the sky is the limit when you pass beyond the boundaries of the world:

- A pit fiend's stronghold on Avernus, the first layer of the Nine Hells
- A haunted castle in the Shadowfell that serves as a shadow dragon's lair
- An elf queen's tomb in the Feywild
- A djinni's palace on the Elemental Plane of Air, filled with marvelous stolen treasures
- A lich's secret demiplane, where the undead archmage hides its phylactery and spellbook

See the *Dungeon Master's Guide* for more information on the planes of existence.

What Monsters to Use?

Many monsters inhabit dungeons, while others live in deserts, forests, labyrinths, and other environments. Regardless of which environment a monster traditionally calls home, you can place it anywhere you want. After all, "fish out of water" stories are memorable, and sometimes it's fun to surprise players with gricks hiding under the desert sands or a dryad living in a giant mushroom in the Underdark.

Statistics

A monster's statistics, sometimes referred to as its **stat block**, provide the essential information that you need to run the monster.

Size

A monster can be Tiny, Small, Medium, Large, Huge, or Gargantuan. The Size Categories table shows how much space a creature of a particular size controls in combat. See the *Player's Handbook* for more information on creature size and space.

Size Categories

Size	Space	Examples
Tiny	2½ by 2½ ft.	Imp, sprite
Small	5 by 5 ft.	Giant rat, goblin
Medium	5 by 5 ft.	Orc, werewolf
Large	10 by 10 ft.	Hippogriff, ogre
Huge	15 by 15 ft.	Fire giant, treant
Gargantuan	20 by 20 ft. or larger	Kraken, purple worm

Modifying Creatures

Despite the versatile collection of monsters in this book, you might be at a loss when it comes to finding the perfect creature for part of an adventure. Feel free to tweak an existing creature to make it into something more useful for you, perhaps by borrowing a trait or two from a different monster or by using a **variant** or **template**, such as the ones in this book. Keep in mind that modifying a monster, including when you apply a template to it, might change its challenge rating.

For advice on how to customize creatures and calculate their challenge ratings, see the *Dungeon Master's Guide*.

Type

A monster's type speaks to its fundamental nature. Certain spells, magic items, class features, and other effects in the game interact in special ways with creatures of a particular type. For example, an *arrow of dragon slaying* deals extra damage not only to dragons but also other creatures of the dragon type, such as dragon turtles and wyverns.

The game includes the following monster types, which have no rules of their own.

Aberrations are utterly alien beings. Many of them have innate magical abilities drawn from the creature's alien mind rather than the mystical forces of the world. The quintessential aberrations are aboleths, beholders, mind flayers, and slaadi.

Beasts are nonhumanoid creatures that are a natural part of the fantasy ecology. Some of them have magical powers, but most are unintelligent and lack any society or language. Beasts include all varieties of ordinary animals, dinosaurs, and giant versions of animals.

Celestials are creatures native to the Upper Planes. Many of them are the servants of deities, employed as messengers or agents in the mortal realm and throughout the planes. Celestials are good by nature, so the exceptional celestial who strays from a good alignment is a horrifying rarity. Celestials include angels, couatls, and pegasi.

Constructs are made, not born. Some are programmed by their creators to follow a simple set of instructions, while others are imbued with sentience and capable of independent thought. Golems are the iconic constructs. Many creatures native to the outer plane of Mechanus, such as modrons, are constructs shaped from the raw material of the plane by the will of more powerful creatures.

Dragons are large reptilian creatures of ancient origin and tremendous power. True dragons, including the good metallic dragons and the evil chromatic dragons, are highly intelligent and have innate magic. Also in this category are creatures distantly related to true dragons, but less powerful, less intelligent, and less magical, such as wyverns and pseudodragons.

Elementals are creatures native to the elemental planes. Some creatures of this type are little more than animate masses of their respective elements, including the creatures simply called elementals. Others have biological forms infused with elemental energy. The races of genies, including djinn and efreet, form the most important civilizations on the elemental planes. Other elemental creatures include azers, invisible stalkers, and water weirds.

Fey are magical creatures closely tied to the forces of nature. They dwell in twilight groves and misty forests. In some worlds, they are closely tied to the Feywild, also called the Plane of Faerie. Some are also found in the Outer Planes, particularly the planes of Arborea and the Beastlands. Fey include dryads, pixies, and satyrs.

Fiends are creatures of wickedness that are native to the Lower Planes. A few are the servants of deities, but many more labor under the leadership of archdevils and demon princes. Evil priests and mages sometimes summon fiends to the material world to do their bidding. If an evil celestial is a rarity, a good fiend is almost inconceivable. Fiends include demons, devils, hell hounds, rakshasas, and yugoloths.

Giants tower over humans and their kind. They are humanlike in shape, though some have multiple heads (ettins) or deformities (fomorians). The six varieties of true giant are hill giants, stone giants, frost giants, fire giants, cloud giants, and storm giants. Besides these, creatures such as ogres and trolls are giants.

Humanoids are the main peoples of the D&D world, both civilized and savage, including humans and a tremendous variety of other species. They have language and culture, few if any innate magical abilities (though most humanoids can learn spellcasting), and a bipedal form. The most common humanoid races are the ones most suitable as player characters: humans, dwarves, elves, and halflings. Almost as numerous but far more savage and brutal, and almost uniformly evil, are the races of goblinoids (goblins, hobgoblins, and bugbears), orcs, gnolls, lizardfolk, and kobolds.

A variety of humanoids appear throughout this book, but the races detailed in the *Player's Handbook*—with the exception of drow—are dealt with in appendix B. That appendix gives you a number of stat blocks that you can use to make various members of those races.

Monstrosities are monsters in the strictest sense— frightening creatures that are not ordinary, not truly natural, and almost never benign. Some are the results of magical experimentation gone awry (such as owlbears), and others are the product of terrible curses (including minotaurs and yuan-ti). They defy categorization, and in some sense serve as a catch-all category for creatures that don't fit into any other type.

Oozes are gelatinous creatures that rarely have a fixed shape. They are mostly subterranean, dwelling in caves and dungeons and feeding on refuse, carrion, or creatures unlucky enough to get in their way. Black puddings and gelatinous cubes are among the most recognizable oozes.

Plants in this context are vegetable creatures, not ordinary flora. Most of them are ambulatory, and some are carnivorous. The quintessential plants are the shambling mound and the treant. Fungal creatures such as the gas spore and the myconid also fall into this category.

Undead are once-living creatures brought to a horrifying state of undeath through the practice of necromantic magic or some unholy curse. Undead include walking corpses, such as vampires and zombies, as well as bodiless spirits, such as ghosts and specters.

Tags

A monster might have one or more tags appended to its type, in parentheses. For example, an orc has the *humanoid (orc)* type. The parenthetical tags provide additional categorization for certain creatures. The tags have no rules of their own, but something in the game, such as a magic item, might refer to them. For instance, a spear that is especially effective at fighting demons would work against any monster that has the demon tag.

Alignment

A monster's alignment provides a clue to its disposition and how it behaves in a roleplaying or combat situation. For example, a chaotic evil monster might be difficult to reason with and might attack characters on sight, whereas a neutral monster might be willing to negotiate. See the *Player's Handbook* for descriptions of the different alignments.

The alignment specified in a monster's stat block is the default. Feel free to depart from it and change a monster's alignment to suit the needs of your campaign. If you want a good-aligned green dragon or an evil storm giant, there's nothing stopping you.

Some creatures can have **any alignment**. In other words, you choose the monster's alignment. Some monster's alignment entry indicates a tendency or aversion toward law, chaos, good, or evil. For example, a berserker can be any chaotic alignment (chaotic good, chaotic neutral, or chaotic evil), as befits its wild nature.

Many creatures of low intelligence have no comprehension of law or chaos, good or evil. They don't make moral or ethical choices, but rather act on instinct. These creatures are **unaligned**, which means they don't have an alignment.

Armor Class

A monster that wears armor or carries a shield has an Armor Class (AC) that takes its armor, shield, and Dexterity into account. Otherwise, a monster's AC is based on its Dexterity modifier and natural armor, if any. If a monster has natural armor, wears armor, or carries a shield, this is noted in parentheses after its AC value.

Hit Points

A monster usually dies or is destroyed when it drops to 0 hit points. For more on hit points, see the *Player's Handbook*.

A monster's hit points are presented both as a die expression and as an average number. For example, a monster with 2d8 hit points has 9 hit points on average ($2 \times 4\frac{1}{2}$).

A monster's size determines the die used to calculate its hit points, as shown in the Hit Dice by Size table.

Hit Dice by Size

Monster Size	Hit Die	Average HP per Die
Tiny	d4	2½
Small	d6	3½
Medium	d8	4½
Large	d10	5½
Huge	d12	6½
Gargantuan	d20	10½

A monster's Constitution modifier also affects the number of hit points it has. Its Constitution modifier is multiplied by the number of Hit Dice it possesses, and the result is added to its hit points. For example, if a monster has a Constitution of 12 (+1 modifier) and 2d8 Hit Dice, it has 2d8 + 2 hit points (average 11).

Speed

A monster's speed tells you how far it can move on its turn. For more information on speed, see the *Player's Handbook*.

All creatures have a walking speed, simply called the monster's speed. Creatures that have no form of ground-based locomotion have a walking speed of 0 feet.

Some creatures have one or more of the following additional movement modes.

Burrow

A monster that has a burrowing speed can use that speed to move through sand, earth, mud, or ice. A monster can't burrow through solid rock unless it has a special trait that allows it to do so.

Climb

A monster that has a climbing speed can use all or part of its movement to move on vertical surfaces. The monster doesn't need to spend extra movement to climb.

Fly

A monster that has a flying speed can use all or part of its movement to fly. Some monsters have the ability to **hover**, which makes them hard to knock out of the air (as explained in the rules on flying in the *Player's Handbook*). Such a monster stops hovering when it dies.

Swim

A monster that has a swimming speed doesn't need to spend extra movement to swim.

Ability Scores

Every monster has six ability scores (Strength, Dexterity, Constitution, Intelligence, Wisdom, and Charisma) and corresponding modifiers. For more information on ability scores and how they're used in play, see the *Player's Handbook*.

Saving Throws

The Saving Throws entry is reserved for creatures that are adept at resisting certain kinds of effects. For example, a creature that isn't easily charmed or frightened might gain a bonus on its Wisdom saving throws. Most creatures don't have special saving throw bonuses, in which case this section is absent.

A saving throw bonus is the sum of a monster's relevant ability modifier and its proficiency bonus, which is determined by the monster's challenge rating (as shown in the Proficiency Bonus by Challenge Rating table).

Proficiency Bonus by Challenge Rating

Challenge	Proficiency Bonus	Challenge	Proficiency Bonus
0	+2	14	+5
1/8	+2	15	+5
1/4	+2	16	+5
1/2	+2	17	+6
1	+2	18	+6
2	+2	19	+6
3	+2	20	+6
4	+2	21	+7
5	+3	22	+7
6	+3	23	+7
7	+3	24	+7
8	+3	25	+8
9	+4	26	+8
10	+4	27	+8
11	+4	28	+8
12	+4	29	+9
13	+5	30	+9

Skills

The Skills entry is reserved for monsters that are proficient in one or more skills. For example, a monster that is very perceptive and stealthy might have bonuses to Wisdom (Perception) and Dexterity (Stealth) checks.

A skill bonus is the sum of a monster's relevant ability modifier and its proficiency bonus, which is determined by the monster's challenge rating (as shown in the Proficiency Bonus by Challenge Rating table). Other modifiers might apply. For instance, a monster might have a larger-than-expected bonus (usually double its proficiency bonus) to account for its heightened expertise.

Vulnerabilities, Resistances, and Immunities

Some creatures have vulnerability, resistance, or immunity to certain types of damage. Particular creatures are even resistant or immune to damage from nonmagical attacks (a magical attack is an attack delivered by a spell, a magic item, or another magical source). In addition, some creatures are immune to certain conditions.

Senses

The Senses entry notes a monster's passive Wisdom (Perception) score, as well as any special senses the monster might have. Special senses are described below.

Blindsight

A monster with blindsight can perceive its surroundings without relying on sight, within a specific radius.

Creatures without eyes, such as grimlocks and gray oozes, typically have this special sense, as do creatures with echolocation or heightened senses, such as bats and true dragons.

If a monster is naturally blind, it has a parenthetical note to this effect, indicating that the radius of its blindsight defines the maximum range of its perception.

Darkvision

A monster with darkvision can see in the dark within a specific radius. The monster can see in dim light within the radius as if it were bright light, and in darkness as if it were dim light. The monster can't discern color in darkness, only shades of gray. Many creatures that live underground have this special sense.

Tremorsense

A monster with tremorsense can detect and pinpoint the origin of vibrations within a specific radius, provided that the monster and the source of the vibrations are in contact with the same ground or substance. Tremorsense can't be used to detect flying or incorporeal creatures. Many burrowing creatures, such as ankhegs and umber hulks, have this special sense.

Truesight

A monster with truesight can, out to a specific range, see in normal and magical darkness, see invisible creatures and objects, automatically detect visual illusions and succeed on saving throws against them, and perceive the original form of a shapechanger or a creature that is transformed by magic. Furthermore, the monster can see into the Ethereal Plane within the same range.

Languages

The languages that a monster can speak are listed in alphabetical order. Sometimes a monster can understand a language but can't speak it, and this is noted in its entry. A "—" indicates that a creature neither speaks nor understands any language.

Telepathy

Telepathy is a magical ability that allows a monster to communicate mentally with another creature within a specified range. The contacted creature doesn't need to share a language with the monster to communicate in this way with it, but it must be able to understand at least one language. A creature without telepathy can receive and respond to telepathic messages but can't initiate or terminate a telepathic conversation.

A telepathic monster doesn't need to see a contacted creature and can end the telepathic contact at any time. The contact is broken as soon as the two creatures are no longer within range of each other or if the telepathic monster contacts a different creature within range. A telepathic monster can initiate or terminate a telepathic conversation without using an action, but while the monster is incapacitated, it can't initiate telepathic contact, and any current contact is terminated.

A creature within the area of an *antimagic field* or in any other location where magic doesn't function can't send or receive telepathic messages.

Challenge

A monster's **challenge rating** tells you how great a threat the monster is. An appropriately equipped and well-rested party of four adventurers should be able to defeat a monster that has a challenge rating equal to its level without suffering any deaths. For example, a party of four 3rd-level characters should find a monster with a challenge rating of 3 to be a worthy challenge, but not a deadly one.

Monsters that are significantly weaker than 1st-level characters have a challenge rating lower than 1. Monsters with a challenge rating of 0 are insignificant except in large numbers; those with no effective attacks are worth no experience points, while those that have attacks are worth 10 XP each.

Some monsters present a greater challenge than even a typical 20th-level party can handle. These monsters have a challenge rating of 21 or higher and are specifically designed to test player skill.

Experience Points

The number of experience points (XP) a monster is worth is based on its challenge rating. Typically, XP is awarded for defeating the monster, although the DM may also award XP for neutralizing the threat posed by the monster in some other manner.

Unless something tells you otherwise, a monster summoned by a spell or other magical ability is worth the XP noted in its stat block.

The *Dungeon Master's Guide* explains how to create encounters using XP budgets, as well as how to adjust an encounter's difficulty.

Experience Points by Challenge Rating

Challenge	XP	Challenge	XP
0	0 or 10	14	11,500
1/8	25	15	13,000
1/4	50	16	15,000
1/2	100	17	18,000
1	200	18	20,000
2	450	19	22,000
3	700	20	25,000
4	1,100	21	33,000
5	1,800	22	41,000
6	2,300	23	50,000
7	2,900	24	62,000
8	3,900	25	75,000
9	5,000	26	90,000
10	5,900	27	105,000
11	7,200	28	120,000
12	8,400	29	135,000
13	10,000	30	155,000

SPECIAL TRAITS

Special traits (which appear after a monster's challenge rating but before any actions or reactions) are characteristics that are likely to be relevant in a combat encounter and that require some explanation.

INNATE SPELLCASTING

A monster with the innate ability to cast spells has the Innate Spellcasting special trait. Unless noted otherwise, an innate spell of 1st level or higher is always cast at its lowest possible level and can't be cast at a higher level. If a monster has a cantrip where its level matters and no level is given, use the monster's challenge rating.

An innate spell can have special rules or restrictions. For example, a drow mage can innately cast the *levitate* spell, but the spell has a "self only" restriction, which means that the spell affects only the drow mage.

A monster's innate spells can't be swapped out with other spells. If a monster's innate spells don't require attack rolls, no attack bonus is given for them.

SPELLCASTING

A monster with the Spellcasting special trait has a spellcaster level and spell slots, which it uses to cast its spells of 1st level and higher (as explained in the *Player's Handbook*). The spellcaster level is also used for any cantrips included in the feature.

The monster has a list of spells known or prepared from a specific class. The list might also include spells from a feature in that class, such as the Divine Domain feature of the cleric or the Druid Circle feature of the druid. The monster is considered a member of that class when attuning to or using a magic item that requires membership in the class or access to its spell list.

A monster can cast a spell from its list at a higher level if it has the spell slot to do so. For example, a drow mage with the 3rd-level *lightning bolt* spell can cast it as a 5th-level spell by using one of its 5th-level spell slots.

You can change the spells that a monster knows or has prepared, replacing any spell on its spell list with a spell of the same level and from the same class list. If you do so, you might cause the monster to be a greater or lesser threat than suggested by its challenge rating.

PSIONICS

A monster that casts spells using only the power of its mind has the psionics tag added to its Spellcasting or Innate Spellcasting special trait. This tag carries no special rules of its own, but other parts of the game might refer to it. A monster that has this tag typically doesn't require any components to cast its spells.

ACTIONS

When a monster takes its action, it can choose from the options in the Actions section of its stat block or use one of the actions available to all creatures, such as the Dash or Hide action, as described in the *Player's Handbook*.

MELEE AND RANGED ATTACKS

The most common actions that a monster will take in combat are melee and ranged attacks. These can be spell attacks or weapon attacks, where the "weapon" might be a manufactured item or a natural weapon, such as a claw or tail spike. For more information on different kinds of attacks, see the *Player's Handbook*.

Creature vs. Target. The target of a melee or ranged attack is usually either one creature or one target, the difference being that a "target" can be a creature or an object.

Hit. Any damage dealt or other effects that occur as a result of an attack hitting a target are described after the "*Hit*" notation. You have the option of taking average damage or rolling the damage; for this reason, both the average damage and the die expression are presented.

Miss. If an attack has an effect that occurs on a miss, that information is presented after the "*Miss:*" notation.

MULTIATTACK

A creature that can make multiple attacks on its turn has the Multiattack action. A creature can't use Multiattack when making an opportunity attack, which must be a single melee attack.

AMMUNITION

A monster carries enough ammunition to make its ranged attacks. You can assume that a monster has 2d4 pieces of ammunition for a thrown weapon attack, and 2d10 pieces of ammunition for a projectile weapon such as a bow or crossbow.

REACTIONS

If a monster can do something special with its reaction, that information is contained here. If a creature has no special reaction, this section is absent.

LIMITED USAGE

Some special abilities have restrictions on the number of times they can be used.

X/Day. The notation "X/Day" means a special ability can be used X number of times and that a monster must finish a long rest to regain expended uses. For example, "1/Day" means a special ability can be used once and that the monster must finish a long rest to use it again.

Recharge X–Y. The notation "Recharge X–Y" means a monster can use a special ability once and that the ability then has a random chance of recharging during each subsequent round of combat. At the start of each of the monster's turns, roll a d6. If the roll is one of the numbers in the recharge notation, the monster regains the use of the special ability. The ability also recharges when the monster finishes a short or long rest.

For example, "Recharge 5–6" means a monster can use the special ability once. Then, at the start of the

monster's turn, it regains the use of that ability if it rolls a 5 or 6 on a d6.

Recharge after a Short or Long Rest. This notation means that a monster can use a special ability once and then must finish a short or long rest to use it again.

EQUIPMENT

A stat block rarely refers to equipment, other than armor or weapons used by a monster. A creature that customarily wears clothes, such as a humanoid, is assumed to be dressed appropriately.

You can equip monsters with additional gear and trinkets however you like, using the equipment chapter of the *Player's Handbook* for inspiration, and you decide how much of a monster's equipment is recoverable after the creature is slain and whether any of that equipment is still usable. A battered suit of armor made for a monster is rarely usable by someone else, for instance.

If a spellcasting monster needs material components to cast its spells, assume that it has the material components it needs to cast the spells in its stat block.

LEGENDARY CREATURES

A legendary creature can do things that ordinary creatures can't. It can take special actions outside its turn, and it might exert magical influence for miles around.

If a creature assumes the form of a legendary creature, such as through a spell, it doesn't gain that form's legendary actions, lair actions, or regional effects.

LEGENDARY ACTIONS

A legendary creature can take a certain number of special actions—called legendary actions—outside its turn. Only one legendary action option can be used at a time and only at the end of another creature's turn. A creature regains its spent legendary actions at the start of its turn. It can forgo using them, and it can't use them while incapacitated or otherwise unable to take actions. If surprised, it can't use them until after its first turn in the combat.

A LEGENDARY CREATURE'S LAIR

A legendary creature might have a section describing its lair and the special effects it can create while there, either by act of will or simply by being present. Such a section applies only to a legendary creature that spends a great deal of time in its lair.

LAIR ACTIONS

If a legendary creature has lair actions, it can use them to harness the ambient magic in its lair. On initiative count 20 (losing all initiative ties), it can use one of its lair action options. It can't do so while incapacitated or otherwise unable to take actions. If surprised, it can't use one until after its first turn in the combat.

REGIONAL EFFECTS

The mere presence of a legendary creature can have strange and wondrous effects on its environment, as noted in this section. Regional effects end abruptly or dissipate over time when the legendary creature dies.

GRAPPLE RULES FOR MONSTERS

Many monsters have special attacks that allow them to quickly grapple prey. When a monster hits with such an attack, it doesn't need to make an additional ability check to determine whether the grapple succeeds, unless the attack says otherwise.

A creature grappled by the monster can use its action to try to escape. To do so, it must succeed on a Strength (Athletics) or Dexterity (Acrobatics) check against the escape DC in the monster's stat block. If no escape DC is given, assume the DC is 10 + the monster's Strength (Athletics) modifier.

Aarakocra

Aarakocra range the Howling Gyre, an endless storm of mighty winds and lashing rains that surrounds the tranquil realm of Aaqa in the Elemental Plane of Air. Making aerial patrols, these birdlike humanoids guard the windy borders of their home against invaders from the Elemental Plane of Earth, such as gargoyles, their sworn enemies.

Enemies of Elemental Evil. In service to the Wind Dukes of Aaqa, aarakocra scout the planes in search of temples of Elemental Evil. They spy on malign elemental creatures and then either take the fight to those creatures or report back to the Wind Dukes.

On the Material Plane, aarakocra create aeries atop the highest mountains, especially peaks near portals to the Elemental Plane of Air. From such heights, aarakocra watch for signs of elemental incursions, as well as for nascent threats to their home plane. Aarakocra prefer to live their lives like the wind—unburdened and ever moving—yet they watch over a region for years if that's what it takes to guard against the incursions of Elemental Evil.

Aarakocra have no concept of political borders or property ownership, and the value of gems, gold, and other precious materials means little to aarakocra. In their eyes, a creature should use what is necessary and then cast what is left on the wind for others to use.

Search for the Seven Shards. The Wind Dukes of Aaqa come from a race of elemental beings called the vaati, which once ruled many worlds. A creature known as the Queen of Chaos arose and initiated an interplanar war against vaati rule. To combat the threat, seven vaati heroes combined their powers to create the mighty *Rod of Law*. In a battle against the queen's greatest general, Miska the Wolf Spider, a vaati killed Miska by thrusting the rod into him like a spear. The rod shattered into seven shards that scattered across the multiverse. Aarakocra seek signs of the pieces' locations in order to rebuild what is now known as the *Rod of Seven Parts*.

Aarakocra

Medium humanoid (aarakocra), neutral good

Armor Class 12
Hit Points 13 (3d8)
Speed 20 ft., fly 50 ft.

STR	DEX	CON	INT	WIS	CHA
10 (+0)	14 (+2)	10 (+0)	11 (+0)	12 (+1)	11 (+0)

Skills Perception +5
Senses passive Perception 15
Languages Aarakocra, Auran
Challenge 1/4 (50 XP)

Dive Attack. If the aarakocra is flying and dives at least 30 feet straight toward a target and then hits it with a melee weapon attack, the attack deals an extra 3 (1d6) damage to the target.

Actions

Talon. *Melee Weapon Attack:* +4 to hit, reach 5 ft., one target. *Hit:* 4 (1d4 + 2) slashing damage.

Javelin. *Melee or Ranged Weapon Attack:* +4 to hit, reach 5 ft. or range 30/120 ft., one target. *Hit:* 5 (1d6 + 2) piercing damage.

Summoning Air Elementals

Five aarakocra within 30 feet of each other can magically summon an air elemental. Each of the five must use its action and movement on three consecutive turns to perform an aerial dance and must maintain concentration while doing so (as if concentrating on a spell). When all five have finished their third turn of the dance, the elemental appears in an unoccupied space within 60 feet of them. It is friendly toward them and obeys their spoken commands. It remains for 1 hour, until it or all its summoners die, or until any of its summoners dismisses it as a bonus action. A summoner can't perform the dance again until it finishes a short rest. When the elemental returns to the Elemental Plane of Air, any aarakocra within 5 feet of it can return with it.

Aboleth

Large aberration, lawful evil

Armor Class 17 (natural armor)
Hit Points 135 (18d10 + 36)
Speed 10 ft., swim 40 ft.

STR	DEX	CON	INT	WIS	CHA
21 (+5)	9 (–1)	15 (+2)	18 (+4)	15 (+2)	18 (+4)

Saving Throws Con +6, Int +8, Wis +6
Skills History +12, Perception +10
Senses darkvision 120 ft., passive Perception 20
Languages Deep Speech, telepathy 120 ft.
Challenge 10 (5,900 XP)

Amphibious. The aboleth can breathe air and water.

Mucous Cloud. While underwater, the aboleth is surrounded by transformative mucus. A creature that touches the aboleth or that hits it with a melee attack while within 5 feet of it must make a DC 14 Constitution saving throw. On a failure, the creature is diseased for 1d4 hours. The diseased creature can breathe only underwater.

Probing Telepathy. If a creature communicates telepathically with the aboleth, the aboleth learns the creature's greatest desires if the aboleth can see the creature.

Actions

Multiattack. The aboleth makes three tentacle attacks.

Tentacle. *Melee Weapon Attack:* +9 to hit, reach 10 ft., one target. *Hit:* 12 (2d6 + 5) bludgeoning damage. If the target is a creature, it must succeed on a DC 14 Constitution saving throw

or become diseased. The disease has no effect for 1 minute and can be removed by any magic that cures disease. After 1 minute, the diseased creature's skin becomes translucent and slimy, the creature can't regain hit points unless it is underwater, and the disease can be removed only by *heal* or another disease-curing spell of 6th level or higher. When the creature is outside a body of water, it takes 6 (1d12) acid damage every 10 minutes unless moisture is applied to the skin before 10 minutes have passed.

Tail. *Melee Weapon Attack:* +9 to hit, reach 10 ft. one target. *Hit:* 15 (3d6 + 5) bludgeoning damage.

Enslave (3/Day). The aboleth targets one creature it can see within 30 feet of it. The target must succeed on a DC 14 Wisdom saving throw or be magically charmed by the aboleth until the aboleth dies or until it is on a different plane of existence from the target. The charmed target is under the aboleth's control and can't take reactions, and the aboleth and the target can communicate telepathically with each other over any distance.

Whenever the charmed target takes damage, the target can repeat the saving throw. On a success, the effect ends. No more than once every 24 hours, the target can also repeat the saving throw when it is at least 1 mile away from the aboleth.

Legendary Actions

The aboleth can take 3 legendary actions, choosing from the options below. Only one legendary action option can be used at a time and only at the end of another creature's turn. The aboleth regains spent legendary actions at the start of its turn.

Detect. The aboleth makes a Wisdom (Perception) check.
Tail Swipe. The aboleth makes one tail attack.
Psychic Drain (Costs 2 Actions). One creature charmed by the aboleth takes 10 (3d6) psychic damage, and the aboleth regains hit points equal to the damage the creature takes.

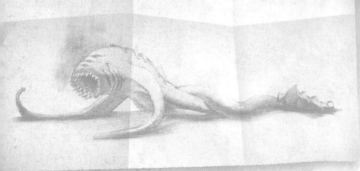

"COULD IT BE THAT ABOLETHS ARE OLDER THAN
THE GODS ... THAT BEFORE THE DIVINE ONES CAME
TO BE, SUCH HORRORS SHAPED THE MULTIVERSE?
NOW THERE'S A CHILLING THOUGHT."

—VAQIR ZEKH'R, GITHZERAI PHILOSOPHER AND
AUTHOR OF THE FAR REALM: REAL YET UNREAL

ABOLETH

Before the coming of the gods, aboleths lurked in primordial oceans and underground lakes. They reached out with their minds and seized control of the burgeoning life-forms of the mortal realm, making those creatures their slaves. Their dominance made them like gods. Then the true gods appeared, smashing the aboleths' empire and freeing their slaves.

Aboleths have never forgotten.

Eternal Memories. Aboleths have flawless memories. They pass on their knowledge and experience from generation to generation. Thus, the injury of their defeat by the gods remains perfectly preserved in their minds.

Aboleths' minds are treasure troves of ancient lore, recalling moments from prehistory with perfect clarity. They plot patiently and intricately across eons. Few creatures can conceive of the extent of an aboleth's plan.

Gods in the Lake. Aboleths dwell in watery environments, including ocean abysses, deep lakes, and the Elemental Plane of Water. In these domains and the lands that adjoin them, aboleths are like gods, demanding worship and obedience from their subjects. When they consume other creatures, aboleths add the knowledge and experiences of their prey to their eternal memories.

Aboleths use their telepathic powers to read the minds of creatures and know their desires. An aboleth uses this knowledge to gain a creature's loyalty, promising to fulfill such wants in exchange for obedience. Within its lair, the aboleth can further use its powers to override senses, granting creatures, such as its followers, the illusion of promised rewards.

Enemies of the Gods. The aboleths' fall from power is written in stark clarity on their flawless memories, for aboleths never truly die. If an aboleth's body is destroyed, its spirit returns to the Elemental Plane of Water, where a new body coalesces for it over days or months.

Ultimately, aboleths dream of overthrowing the gods and regaining control of the world. Aboleths have had untold eons to plot and to prepare their plans for perfect execution.

AN ABOLETH'S LAIR

Aboleths lair in subterranean lakes or the rocky depths of the ocean, often surrounded by the ruins of an ancient, fallen aboleth city. An aboleth spends most of its existence underwater, surfacing occasionally to treat with visitors or deranged worshipers.

LAIR ACTIONS

When fighting inside its lair, an aboleth can invoke the ambient magic to take lair actions. On initiative count 20 (losing initiative ties), the aboleth takes a lair action to cause one of the following effects:

- The aboleth casts *phantasmal force* (no components required) on any number of creatures it can see within 60 feet of it. While maintaining concentration on this effect, the aboleth can't take other lair actions. If a target succeeds on the saving throw or if the effect ends for it, the target is immune to the aboleth's *phantasmal force* lair action for the next 24 hours, although such a creature can choose to be affected.
- Pools of water within 90 feet of the aboleth surge outward in a grasping tide. Any creature on the ground within 20 feet of such a pool must succeed on a DC 14 Strength saving throw or be pulled up to 20 feet into the water and knocked prone. The aboleth can't use this lair action again until it has used a different one.
- Water in the aboleth's lair magically becomes a conduit for the creature's rage. The aboleth can target any number of creatures it can see in such water within 90 feet of it. A target must succeed on a DC 14 Wisdom saving throw or take 7 (2d6) psychic damage. The aboleth can't use this lair action again until it has used a different one.

REGIONAL EFFECTS

The region containing an aboleth's lair is warped by the creature's presence, which creates one or more of the following effects:

- Underground surfaces within 1 mile of the aboleth's lair are slimy and wet and are difficult terrain.
- Water sources within 1 mile of the lair are supernaturally fouled. Enemies of the aboleth that drink such water vomit it within minutes.
- As an action, the aboleth can create an illusory image of itself within 1 mile of the lair. The copy can appear at any location the aboleth has seen before or in any location a creature charmed by the aboleth can currently see. Once created, the image lasts for as long as the aboleth maintains concentration, as if concentrating on a spell. Although the image is intangible, it looks, sounds, and can move like the aboleth. The aboleth can sense, speak, and use telepathy from the image's position as if present at that position. If the image takes any damage, it disappears.

If the aboleth dies, the first two effects fade over the course of 3d10 days.

ANGELS

An angel is a celestial agent sent forth into the planes to further its god's agenda for weal or woe. Its sublime beauty and presence can drive awestruck onlookers to their knees. Yet angels are destroyers too, and their appearance portends doom as often as it signals hope.

Shards of the Divine. Angels are formed from the astral essence of benevolent gods and are thus divine beings of great power and foresight.

Angels act out the will of their gods with tireless devotion. Even chaotic good deities command lawful good angels, knowing that the angels' dedication to order best allows them to fulfill divine commands. An angel follows a single driving purpose, as decreed by its deity. However, an angel is incapable of following commands that stray from the path of law and good.

An angel slays evil creatures without remorse. As the embodiment of law and good, an angel is almost never mistaken in its judgments. This quality can create a sense of superiority in an angel, a sense that comes to the fore when an angel's task conflicts with the goals of another creature. The angel never acquiesces or gives way. When an angel is sent to aid mortals, it is sent not to serve but to command. The gods of good therefore send their angels among mortals only in response to the most dire circumstances.

Fallen Angels. An angel's moral compass grants it a sense of infallibility that can sometimes spell its undoing. Angels are usually too wise to fall for a simple deception, but sometimes pride can lead one to commit an evil act. Whether intentional or accidental, such an act is a permanent stain that marks the angel as an outcast.

Fallen angels retain their power but lose their connection to the deities from which they were made. Most fallen angels take their banishment personally, rebelling against the powers they served by seeking rulership over a section of the Abyss or a place among other fallen in the hierarchy of the Nine Hells. Zariel, the ruler of the first layer of the Nine Hells, is such a creature. Rather than rebel, some fallen angels resign themselves to an isolated existence on the Material Plane, living in disguise as simple hermits. If they are redeemed, they can become powerful allies dedicated to justice and compassionate service.

Immortal Nature. An angel doesn't require food, drink, or sleep.

DEVA

Devas are angels that act as divine messengers or agents to the Material Plane, the Shadowfell, and the Feywild and that can assume a form appropriate to the realm they are sent to.

Legend tells of angels that take mortal form for years, lending aid, hope, and courage to goodhearted folk. A deva can take any shape, although it prefers to appear to mortals as an innocuous humanoid or animal. When circumstances require that it cast off its guise, a deva is a beautiful humanoid-like creature with silvery skin. Its hair and eyes gleam with an unearthly luster, and large feathery wings unfurl from its shoulder blades.

DEVA

Medium celestial, lawful good

Armor Class 17 (natural armor)
Hit Points 136 (16d8 + 64)
Speed 30 ft., fly 90 ft.

STR	DEX	CON	INT	WIS	CHA
18 (+4)	18 (+4)	18 (+4)	17 (+3)	20 (+5)	20 (+5)

Saving Throws Wis +9, Cha +9
Skills Insight +9, Perception +9
Damage Resistances radiant; bludgeoning, piercing, and slashing from nonmagical attacks
Condition Immunities charmed, exhaustion, frightened
Senses darkvision 120 ft., passive Perception 19
Languages all, telepathy 120 ft.
Challenge 10 (5,900 XP)

Angelic Weapons. The deva's weapon attacks are magical. When the deva hits with any weapon, the weapon deals an extra 4d8 radiant damage (included in the attack).

Innate Spellcasting. The deva's spellcasting ability is Charisma (spell save DC 17). The deva can innately cast the following spells, requiring only verbal components:

At will: *detect evil and good*
1/day each: *commune, raise dead*

Magic Resistance. The deva has advantage on saving throws against spells and other magical effects.

ACTIONS

Multiattack. The deva makes two melee attacks.

Mace. *Melee Weapon Attack:* +8 to hit, reach 5 ft., one target. *Hit:* 7 (1d6 + 4) bludgeoning damage plus 18 (4d8) radiant damage.

Healing Touch (3/Day). The deva touches another creature. The target magically regains 20 (4d8 + 2) hit points and is freed from any curse, disease, poison, blindness, or deafness.

Change Shape. The deva magically polymorphs into a humanoid or beast that has a challenge rating equal to or less than its own, or back into its true form. It reverts to its true form if it dies. Any equipment it is wearing or carrying is absorbed or borne by the new form (the deva's choice).

In a new form, the deva retains its game statistics and ability to speak, but its AC, movement modes, Strength, Dexterity, and special senses are replaced by those of the new form, and it gains any statistics and capabilities (except class features, legendary actions, and lair actions) that the new form has but that it lacks.

A

Planetar

Planetars act as the weapons of the gods they serve, presenting a tangible representation of their deities' might. A planetar can call down rain to relieve a drought, or can loose an insect plague to devour crops. A planetar's celestial ears detect every falsehood, and its radiant eyes see through every deception.

Planetars are muscular and hairless and have opalescent green skin and white-feathered wings. They tower over most humanoids, brandishing immense swords with grace. Sometimes sent to aid powerful mortals on important tasks for good, planetars are especially fond of missions that involve battling fiends.

Planetar
Large celestial, lawful good

Armor Class 19 (natural armor)
Hit Points 200 (16d10 + 112)
Speed 40 ft., fly 120 ft.

STR	DEX	CON	INT	WIS	CHA
24 (+7)	20 (+5)	24 (+7)	19 (+4)	22 (+6)	25 (+7)

Saving Throws Con +12, Wis +11, Cha +12
Skills Perception +11
Damage Resistances radiant; bludgeoning, piercing, and slashing from nonmagical attacks
Condition Immunities charmed, exhaustion, frightened
Senses truesight 120 ft., passive Perception 21
Languages all, telepathy 120 ft.
Challenge 16 (15,000 XP)

Angelic Weapons. The planetar's weapon attacks are magical. When the planetar hits with any weapon, the weapon deals an extra 5d8 radiant damage (included in the attack).

Divine Awareness. The planetar knows if it hears a lie.

Innate Spellcasting. The planetar's spellcasting ability is Charisma (spell save DC 20). The planetar can innately cast the following spells, requiring no material components:

At will: *detect evil and good, invisibility* (self only)
3/day each: *blade barrier, dispel evil and good, flame strike, raise dead*
1/day each: *commune, control weather, insect plague*

Magic Resistance. The planetar has advantage on saving throws against spells and other magical effects.

Actions

Multiattack. The planetar makes two melee attacks.

Greatsword. *Melee Weapon Attack:* +12 to hit, reach 5 ft., one target. *Hit:* 21 (4d6 + 7) slashing damage plus 22 (5d8) radiant damage.

Healing Touch (4/Day). The planetar touches another creature. The target magically regains 30 (6d8 + 3) hit points and is freed from any curse, disease, poison, blindness, or deafness.

Solar

A solar is godlike in its glory and power. On the battlefield, the solar's sword flies into the fray on its own, and a single arrow from a solar's bow can strike a target dead on contact. So great is a solar's celestial might that even demon princes shrink at its resonant commands.

It is said that only twenty-four solars exist. The few solars that are known are stewards of specific deities. The others rest in a state of contemplation, waiting for the time when their services are needed to stave off some cosmic threat to the cause of good.

Solar

Large celestial, lawful good

Armor Class 21 (natural armor)
Hit Points 243 (18d10 + 144)
Speed 50 ft., fly 150 ft.

STR	DEX	CON	INT	WIS	CHA
26 (+8)	22 (+6)	26 (+8)	25 (+7)	25 (+7)	30 (+10)

Saving Throws Int +14, Wis +14, Cha +17
Skills Perception +14
Damage Resistances radiant; bludgeoning, piercing, and slashing from nonmagical attacks
Damage Immunities necrotic, poison
Condition Immunities charmed, exhaustion, frightened, poisoned
Senses truesight 120 ft., passive Perception 24
Languages all, telepathy 120 ft.
Challenge 21 (33,000 XP)

Angelic Weapons. The solar's weapon attacks are magical. When the solar hits with any weapon, the weapon deals an extra 6d8 radiant damage (included in the attack).

Divine Awareness. The solar knows if it hears a lie.

Innate Spellcasting. The solar's spellcasting ability is Charisma (spell save DC 25). It can innately cast the following spells, requiring no material components:

At will: *detect evil and good, invisibility* (self only)
3/day each: *blade barrier, dispel evil and good, resurrection*
1/day each: *commune, control weather*

Magic Resistance. The solar has advantage on saving throws against spells and other magical effects.

Actions

Multiattack. The solar makes two greatsword attacks.

Greatsword. *Melee Weapon Attack:* +15 to hit, reach 5 ft., one target. *Hit:* 22 (4d6 + 8) slashing damage plus 27 (6d8) radiant damage.

Slaying Longbow. *Ranged Weapon Attack:* +13 to hit, range 150/600 ft., one target. *Hit:* 15 (2d8 + 6) piercing damage plus 27 (6d8) radiant damage. If the target is a creature that has 100 hit points or fewer, it must succeed on a DC 15 Constitution saving throw or die.

Flying Sword. The solar releases its greatsword to hover magically in an unoccupied space within 5 feet of it. If the solar can see the sword, the solar can mentally command it as a bonus action to fly up to 50 feet and either make one attack against a target or return to the solar's hands. If the hovering sword is targeted by any effect, the solar is considered to be holding it. The hovering sword falls if the solar dies.

Healing Touch (4/Day). The solar touches another creature. The target magically regains 40 (8d8 + 4) hit points and is freed from any curse, disease, poison, blindness, or deafness.

Legendary Actions

The solar can take 3 legendary actions, choosing from the options below. Only one legendary action option can be used at a time and only at the end of another creature's turn. The solar regains spent legendary actions at the start of its turn.

Teleport. The solar magically teleports, along with any equipment it is wearing or carrying, up to 120 feet to an unoccupied space it can see.

Searing Burst (Costs 2 Actions). The solar emits magical, divine energy. Each creature of its choice in a 10-foot radius must make a DC 23 Dexterity saving throw, taking 14 (4d6) fire damage plus 14 (4d6) radiant damage on a failed save, or half as much damage on a successful one.

Blinding Gaze (Costs 3 Actions). The solar targets one creature it can see within 30 feet of it. If the target can see it, the target must succeed on a DC 15 Constitution saving throw or be blinded until magic such as the *lesser restoration* spell removes the blindness.

Animated Objects

Animated objects are crafted with potent magic to follow the commands of their creators. When not commanded, they follow the last order they received to the best of their ability, and can act independently to fulfill simple instructions. Some animated objects (including many of those created in the Feywild) might converse fluently or adopt a persona, but most are simple automatons.

Constructed Nature. An animated object doesn't require air, food, drink, or sleep.

The magic that animates an object is dispelled when the construct drops to 0 hit points. An animated object reduced to 0 hit points becomes inanimate and is too damaged to be of much use or value to anyone.

Animated Armor

This empty steel shell clamors as it moves, heavy plates banging and grinding against one another like the vengeful spirit of a fallen knight. Ponderous but persistent, this magical guardian is almost always a suit of plate armor.

To add to its menace, animated armor is frequently enchanted with scripted speech, so the armor can utter warnings, demand passwords, or deliver riddles. Rare suits of animated armor are able to carry on an actual conversation.

Flying Sword

A flying sword dances through the air, fighting with the confidence of a warrior that can't be injured. Swords are the most common weapons animated with magic. Axes, clubs, daggers, maces, spears, and even self-loading crossbows are also known to exist in animated object form.

Rug of Smothering

Would-be thieves and careless heroes arrive at the doorsteps of an enemy's abode, eyes and ears alert for traps, only to end their quest prematurely as the rugs beneath their feet animate and smother them to death.

A rug of smothering can be made in many different forms, from a finely woven carpet fit for a queen to a coarse mat in a peasant's hovel. Creatures with the ability to sense magic detect the rug's false magical aura.

In some cases, a rug of smothering is disguised as a *carpet of flying* or another beneficial magic item. However, a character who stands or sits on the rug, or who attempts to utter a word of command, is quickly trapped as the rug of smothering rolls itself tightly around its victim.

Animated Armor
Medium construct, unaligned

Armor Class 18 (natural armor)
Hit Points 33 (6d8 + 6)
Speed 25 ft.

STR	DEX	CON	INT	WIS	CHA
14 (+2)	11 (+0)	13 (+1)	1 (−5)	3 (−4)	1 (−5)

Damage Immunities poison, psychic
Condition Immunities blinded, charmed, deafened, exhaustion, frightened, paralyzed, petrified, poisoned
Senses blindsight 60 ft. (blind beyond this radius), passive Perception 6
Languages —
Challenge 1 (200 XP)

Antimagic Susceptibility. The armor is incapacitated while in the area of an *antimagic field*. If targeted by *dispel magic*, the armor must succeed on a Constitution saving throw against the caster's spell save DC or fall unconscious for 1 minute.

False Appearance. While the armor remains motionless, it is indistinguishable from a normal suit of armor.

Actions

Multiattack. The armor makes two melee attacks.

Slam. *Melee Weapon Attack:* +4 to hit, reach 5 ft., one target. *Hit:* 5 (1d6 + 2) bludgeoning damage.

> "LYIN' NEXT TO THE CHEST WERE THE
> BONES OF CAP'N SCORNBLADE HIMSELF,
> STILL CLUTCHIN' HIS RUSTY SWORD.
> IMAGINE MY SURPRISE WHEN THE BLADE
> FLEW FROM HIS BONY GRASP!
> STILL GOT THE SCAR."
> —LEVITY QUICKSTITCH, HALFLING ROGUE

RUG OF SMOTHERING

Large construct, unaligned

Armor Class 12
Hit Points 33 (6d10)
Speed 10 ft.

STR	DEX	CON	INT	WIS	CHA
17 (+3)	14 (+2)	10 (+0)	1 (−5)	3 (−4)	1 (−5)

Damage Immunities poison, psychic
Condition Immunities blinded, charmed, deafened, frightened,
  paralyzed, petrified, poisoned
Senses blindsight 60 ft. (blind beyond this radius),
  passive Perception 6
Languages —
Challenge 2 (450 XP)

Antimagic Susceptibility. The rug is incapacitated while in
the area of an *antimagic field*. If targeted by *dispel magic*, the
rug must succeed on a Constitution saving throw against the
caster's spell save DC or fall unconscious for 1 minute.

Damage Transfer. While it is grappling a creature, the rug takes
only half the damage dealt to it, and the creature grappled by
the rug takes the other half.

False Appearance. While the rug remains motionless, it is
indistinguishable from a normal rug.

ACTIONS

Smother. *Melee Weapon Attack:* +5 to hit, reach 5 ft., one
Medium or smaller creature. *Hit:* The creature is grappled
(escape DC 13). Until this grapple ends, the target is restrained,
blinded, and at risk of suffocating, and the rug can't smother
another target. In addition, at the start of each of the target's
turns, the target takes 10 (2d6 + 3) bludgeoning damage.

FLYING SWORD

Small construct, unaligned

Armor Class 17 (natural armor)
Hit Points 17 (5d6)
Speed 0 ft., fly 50 ft. (hover)

STR	DEX	CON	INT	WIS	CHA
12 (+1)	15 (+2)	11 (+0)	1 (−5)	5 (−3)	1 (−5)

Saving Throws Dex +4
Damage Immunities poison, psychic
Condition Immunities blinded, charmed, deafened, frightened,
  paralyzed, petrified, poisoned
Senses blindsight 60 ft. (blind beyond this radius),
  passive Perception 7
Languages —
Challenge 1/4 (50 XP)

Antimagic Susceptibility. The sword is incapacitated while in
the area of an *antimagic field*. If targeted by *dispel magic*, the
sword must succeed on a Constitution saving throw against
the caster's spell save DC or fall unconscious for 1 minute.

False Appearance. While the sword remains motionless and
isn't flying, it is indistinguishable from a normal sword.

ACTIONS

Longsword. *Melee Weapon Attack:* +3 to hit, reach 5 ft., one
target. *Hit:* 5 (1d8 + 1) slashing damage.

A

ANKHEG

An ankheg resembles an enormous many-legged insect, its long antennae twitching in response to any movement around it. Its legs end in sharp hooks adapted for burrowing and grasping its prey, and its powerful mandibles can snap a small tree in half.

Lurkers in the Earth. The ankheg uses its powerful mandibles to dig winding tunnels deep beneath the ground. When it hunts, an ankheg burrows upward, waiting below the surface until its antennae detect movement from above. Then it bursts from the earth and seizes prey in its mandibles, crushing and grinding while it secretes acidic digestive enzymes. These enzymes help dissolve a victim for easy swallowing, but the ankheg can also squirt acid to take down foes.

Bane of Field and Forest. Although ankhegs receive a certain portion of their nutrients from the soil through which they burrow, they must supplement their diet with fresh meat. Pastures teeming with grazing livestock and forests rife with game are an ankheg's prime hunting grounds. Ankhegs are thus the bane of farmers and rangers everywhere.

Earthen Tunnels. As it burrows through earth, the ankheg leaves a narrow, partially collapsed tunnel in its wake. In these tunnels, one might find the remnants of molted ankheg chitin, hatched ankheg eggs, or the grisly remains of ankheg victims, including coins or other treasures scattered during the creature's attack.

ANKHEG

Large monstrosity, unaligned

Armor Class 14 (natural armor), 11 while prone
Hit Points 39 (6d10 + 6)
Speed 30 ft., burrow 10 ft.

STR	DEX	CON	INT	WIS	CHA
17 (+3)	11 (+0)	13 (+1)	1 (−5)	13 (+1)	6 (−2)

Senses darkvision 60 ft., tremorsense 60 ft.,
  passive Perception 11
Languages —
Challenge 2 (450 XP)

ACTIONS

Bite. *Melee Weapon Attack:* +5 to hit, reach 5 ft., one target. *Hit:* 10 (2d6 + 3) slashing damage plus 3 (1d6) acid damage. If the target is a Large or smaller creature, it is grappled (escape DC 13). Until this grapple ends, the ankheg can bite only the grappled creature and has advantage on attack rolls to do so.

Acid Spray (Recharge 6). The ankheg spits acid in a line that is 30 feet long and 5 feet wide, provided that it has no creature grappled. Each creature in that line must make a DC 13 Dexterity saving throw, taking 10 (3d6) acid damage on a failed save, or half as much damage on a successful one.

AZER

Natives of the Elemental Plane of Fire, azers are master crafters, expert miners, and sworn foes of the efreet. In appearance and manner, an azer resembles a male dwarf, but this is a facade. Beneath its metallic-looking skin, an azer is a being of fire, which outwardly manifests in its fiery hair and beard.

Made, Not Born. Azers don't reproduce. They are each crafted from bronze by another azer and imbued with a portion of the crafter's inner flame. Each azer is sculpted with unique features. This crafting process limits the growth of the azer population and is the primary reason that these creatures remain rare.

Volcanic Dwellers. Azers dwell in a kingdom on the border between the Elemental Plane of Earth and the Elemental Plane of Fire—a range of mountains and volcanoes whose spires rise as a series of fortresses. Beneath mountain peaks, under volcanic calderas, and amid rivers of magma, azers extract gleaming metals and glittering gems from the earth. Squads of azer patrol the passes and tunnels of their realm, fending off the salamander raiders whose efreet masters order strikes against the azer kingdom.

Enemies of the Efreet. Long ago, the efreet and the azers were allies. Azers helped create the City of Brass, forging that home of the efreet into one of the most wondrous places in creation. When the azers had finished their work, the efreet betrayed them, making a failed attempt to enslave the azers so as to protect the secrets of the city. Despite occasional raids and skirmishes, however, the two sides have so far refrained from all-out conflict. The azers believe that only the threat of them revealing the hidden ways into the City of Brass keeps the efreet in check.

Masters of Metal and Gems. Azers are masterful artisans, and create beautiful works from the gems and precious metals found in their volcanic habitat. They rate the value of such treasures above all other things, sometimes dispatching parties across the planes to seek out rare metals and gemstones.

When azers are called by magic to the Material Plane, it is typically to help forge an elaborate magic item or work of art, for it is said that their skill in such craft knows no equal.

Living Fire. An azer doesn't require food, drink, or sleep.

AZER
Medium elemental, lawful neutral

Armor Class 17 (natural armor, shield)
Hit Points 39 (6d8 + 12)
Speed 30 ft.

STR	DEX	CON	INT	WIS	CHA
17 (+3)	12 (+1)	15 (+2)	12 (+1)	13 (+1)	10 (+0)

Saving Throws Con +4
Damage Immunities fire, poison
Condition Immunities poisoned
Senses passive Perception 11
Languages Ignan
Challenge 2 (450 XP)

Heated Body. A creature that touches the azer or hits it with a melee attack while within 5 feet of it takes 5 (1d10) fire damage.

Heated Weapons. When the azer hits with a metal melee weapon, it deals an extra 3 (1d6) fire damage (included in the attack).

Illumination. The azer sheds bright light in a 10-foot radius and dim light for an additional 10 feet.

ACTIONS

Warhammer. *Melee Weapon Attack:* +5 to hit, reach 5 ft., one target. *Hit:* 7 (1d8 + 3) bludgeoning damage, or 8 (1d10 + 3) bludgeoning damage if used with two hands to make a melee attack, plus 3 (1d6) fire damage.

"GIVE ME A HUNDRED AZER SLAVES, AND I CAN FORGE AN EMPIRE THAT WOULD MAKE THE GODS TREMBLE."
—ARAKSES AL-SAQAR, EFREETI PASHA

BANSHEE

When night falls, unlucky travelers hear the faint cries of the forlorn dead. This woeful spirit is a banshee, a spiteful creature formed from the spirit of a female elf.

Banshees appear as luminous, wispy forms that vaguely recall their mortal features. A banshee's face is wreathed in a wild tangle of hair, its body clad in wispy rags that flutter and stream around it.

Divine Wrath. Banshees are the undead remnants of elves who, blessed with great beauty, failed to use their gift to bring joy to the world. Instead, they used their beauty to corrupt and control others. Elves afflicted by the banshee's curse experience no gladness, feeling only distress in the presence of the living. As the curse takes its toll, their minds and bodies decay, until death completes their transformation into undead monsters.

Sorrow Bound. A banshee becomes forever bound to the place of its demise, unable to venture more than five miles from there. It is forced to relive every moment of its life with perfect recall, yet always refuses to accept responsibility for its doom.

Beauty Hoarders. The vanity that inspired the banshee's cursed creation persists in undeath. These creatures covet beautiful objects: fine jewelry, paintings, statues, and other objects of art. At the same time, a banshee abhors any mirrored surface, for it can't bear to see the horror of its own existence. A single glimpse of itself is enough to send a banshee into a rage.

Undead Nature. A banshee doesn't require air, food, drink, or sleep.

BANSHEE
Medium undead, chaotic evil

Armor Class 12
Hit Points 58 (13d8)
Speed 0 ft., fly 40 ft. (hover)

STR	DEX	CON	INT	WIS	CHA
1 (−5)	14 (+2)	10 (+0)	12 (+1)	11 (+0)	17 (+3)

Saving Throws Wis +2, Cha +5
Damage Resistances acid, fire, lightning, thunder; bludgeoning, piercing, and slashing from nonmagical attacks
Damage Immunities cold, necrotic, poison
Condition Immunities charmed, exhaustion, frightened, grappled, paralyzed, petrified, poisoned, prone, restrained
Senses darkvision 60 ft., passive Perception 10
Languages Common, Elvish
Challenge 4 (1,100 XP)

Detect Life. The banshee can magically sense the presence of creatures up to 5 miles away that aren't undead or constructs. She knows the direction they're in but not their exact locations.

Incorporeal Movement. The banshee can move through other creatures and objects as if they were difficult terrain. She takes 5 (1d10) force damage if she ends her turn inside an object.

ACTIONS

Corrupting Touch. *Melee Spell Attack:* +4 to hit, reach 5 ft., one target. *Hit:* 12 (3d6 + 2) necrotic damage.

Horrifying Visage. Each non-undead creature within 60 feet of the banshee that can see her must succeed on a DC 13 Wisdom saving throw or be frightened for 1 minute. A frightened target can repeat the saving throw at the end of each of its turns, with disadvantage if the banshee is within line of sight, ending the effect on itself on a success. If a target's saving throw is successful or the effect ends for it, the target is immune to the banshee's Horrifying Visage for the next 24 hours.

Wail (1/Day). The banshee releases a mournful wail, provided that she isn't in sunlight. This wail has no effect on constructs and undead. All other creatures within 30 feet of her that can hear her must make a DC 13 Constitution saving throw. On a failure, a creature drops to 0 hit points. On a success, a creature takes 10 (3d6) psychic damage.

BASILISK
Medium monstrosity, unaligned

Armor Class 15 (natural armor)
Hit Points 52 (8d8 + 16)
Speed 20 ft.

STR	DEX	CON	INT	WIS	CHA
16 (+3)	8 (–1)	15 (+2)	2 (–4)	8 (–1)	7 (–2)

Senses darkvision 60 ft., passive Perception 9
Languages —
Challenge 3 (700 XP)

Petrifying Gaze. If a creature starts its turn within 30 feet of the basilisk and the two of them can see each other, the basilisk can force the creature to make a DC 12 Constitution saving throw if the basilisk isn't incapacitated. On a failed save, the creature magically begins to turn to stone and is restrained. It must repeat the saving throw at the end of its next turn. On a success, the effect ends. On a failure, the creature is petrified until freed by the *greater restoration* spell or other magic.

A creature that isn't surprised can avert its eyes to avoid the saving throw at the start of its turn. If it does so, it can't see the basilisk until the start of its next turn, when it can avert its eyes again. If it looks at the basilisk in the meantime, it must immediately make the save.

If the basilisk sees its reflection within 30 feet of it in bright light, it mistakes itself for a rival and targets itself with its gaze.

ACTIONS

Bite. *Melee Weapon Attack:* +5 to hit, reach 5 ft., one target. *Hit:* 10 (2d6 + 3) piercing damage plus 7 (2d6) poison damage.

BASILISK

Travelers sometimes find objects that look like pieces of remarkably lifelike stone carvings of wildlife. Missing parts appear to have been bitten off. Seasoned explorers regard such relics as warnings, knowing that the basilisk that created them is likely to be nearby.

Adaptable Predators. Basilisks thrive in arid, temperate, or tropical climates. They lair in caves or other sheltered sites. Most often, basilisks are encountered underground.

A basilisk born and raised in captivity can be domesticated and trained. Such a trained basilisk knows how to avoid meeting the eyes of those its master wishes to protect from its gaze, but it makes a daunting guardian beast. Because of this use, basilisk eggs are highly prized.

Gaze of Stone. Basilisks are ponderous for hunting creatures, but they needn't chase prey. Meeting a basilisk's supernatural gaze can be enough to affect a rapid transformation, transforming a victim into porous stone. Basilisks, with their strong jaws, are able to consume the stone. The stone returns to organic form in the basilisk's gullet.

Some alchemists are said to know how to process the basilisk's gullet and the fluids contained within. Properly handled, the gullet produces an oil that can return petrified creatures to flesh and life. Unfortunately for such a victim, any parts lost in stone form remain absent if the creature revives. Revivification using the oil is impossible if a vital part of the petrified creature, such as its head, is detached.

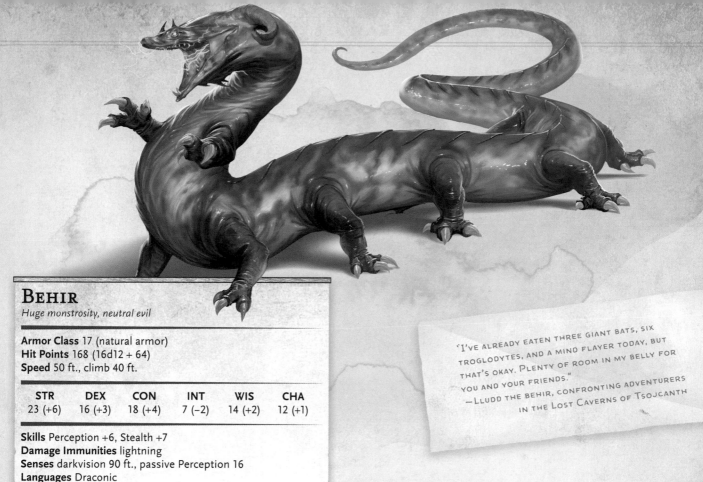

Behir

Huge monstrosity, neutral evil

Armor Class 17 (natural armor)
Hit Points 168 (16d12 + 64)
Speed 50 ft., climb 40 ft.

STR	DEX	CON	INT	WIS	CHA
23 (+6)	16 (+3)	18 (+4)	7 (−2)	14 (+2)	12 (+1)

Skills Perception +6, Stealth +7
Damage Immunities lightning
Senses darkvision 90 ft., passive Perception 16
Languages Draconic
Challenge 11 (7,200 XP)

Actions

Multiattack. The behir makes two attacks: one with its bite and one to constrict.

Bite. *Melee Weapon Attack:* +10 to hit, reach 10 ft., one target. *Hit:* 22 (3d10 + 6) piercing damage.

Constrict. *Melee Weapon Attack:* +10 to hit, reach 5 ft., one Large or smaller creature. *Hit:* 17 (2d10 + 6) bludgeoning damage plus 17 (2d10 + 6) slashing damage. The target is grappled (escape DC 16) if the behir isn't already constricting a creature, and the target is restrained until this grapple ends.

Lightning Breath (Recharge 5–6). The behir exhales a line of lightning that is 20 feet long and 5 feet wide. Each creature in that line must make a DC 16 Dexterity saving throw, taking 66 (12d10) lightning damage on a failed save, or half as much damage on a successful one.

Swallow. The behir makes one bite attack against a Medium or smaller target it is grappling. If the attack hits, the target is also swallowed, and the grapple ends. While swallowed, the target is blinded and restrained, it has total cover against attacks and other effects outside the behir, and it takes 21 (6d6) acid damage at the start of each of the behir's turns. A behir can have only one creature swallowed at a time.

If the behir takes 30 damage or more on a single turn from the swallowed creature, the behir must succeed on a DC 14 Constitution saving throw at the end of that turn or regurgitate the creature, which falls prone in a space within 10 feet of the behir. If the behir dies, a swallowed creature is no longer restrained by it and can escape from the corpse by using 15 feet of movement, exiting prone.

"I'VE ALREADY EATEN THREE GIANT BATS, SIX TROGLODYTES, AND A MIND FLAYER TODAY, BUT THAT'S OKAY. PLENTY OF ROOM IN MY BELLY FOR YOU AND YOUR FRIENDS."
—LLUDD THE BEHIR, CONFRONTING ADVENTURERS IN THE LOST CAVERNS OF TSOJCANTH

Behir

The serpentine behir crawls along floors and clambers up walls to reach its prey. Its lightning breath can incinerate most creatures, even as more powerful foes are constricted in its coils and eaten alive.

A behir's monstrous form resembles a combination of centipede and crocodile. Its scaled hide ranges from ultramarine to deep blue in color, fading to pale blue on its underside.

Cavern Predators. Behirs lair in places inaccessible to other creatures, favoring locations where would-be intruders must make a harrowing climb to reach them. Deep pits, high caves in cliff walls, and caverns reached only by narrow, twisting tunnels are prime sites for a behir ambush. A behir's dozen legs allow it to scramble through its lair site with ease. When not climbing, it moves even faster by folding its legs beside its body and slithering like a snake.

Behirs swallow their prey whole, after which they enter a period of dormancy while they digest. While dormant, a behir chooses a hiding place where intruders in its lair might overlook it.

Foes of the Dragons. In times long forgotten, giants and dragons engaged in seemingly endless war. Storm giants created the first behirs as weapons against the dragons, and behirs retain a natural hatred for dragonkind.

A behir never makes its lair in an area it knows to be inhabited by a dragon. If a dragon attempts to establish a lair within a few dozen miles of a behir's lair, the behir is compelled to kill the dragon or drive it off. Only if the dragon proves too powerful to fight does a behir back down, seeking out a new lair site a great distance away.

B

BEHOLDERS

One glance at a beholder is enough to assess its foul and otherworldly nature. Aggressive, hateful, and greedy, these aberrations dismiss all other creatures as lesser beings, toying with them or destroying them as they choose.

A beholder's spheroid body levitates at all times, and its great bulging eye sits above a wide, toothy maw, while the smaller eyestalks that crown its body twist and turn to keep its foes in sight. When a beholder sleeps, it closes its central eye but leaves its smaller eyes open and alert.

Xenophobic Isolationists. Enemies abound, or so every beholder believes. Beholders are convinced that other creatures resent them for their brilliance and magical power, even as they dismiss those lesser creatures as crude and disgusting. Beholders always suspect others of plotting against them, even when no other creatures are around.

The disdain a beholder has for other creatures extends to other beholders. Each beholder believes its form to be an ideal, and that any deviation from that form is a flaw in the racial purity of its kind. Beholders vary greatly in their physical forms, making conflict between them inevitable. Some beholders are protected by overlapping chitinous plates. Some have smooth hides. Some have eyestalks that writhe like tentacles, while others' stalks bear crustacean-like joints. Even slight differences of coloration in hide can turn two beholders into lifelong enemies.

Eye Tyrant. Some beholders manage to channel their xenophobic tendencies into a terrible despotism. Rather than live in isolation, the aptly named eye tyrants enslave those other creatures, founding and controlling vast empires. An eye tyrant sometimes carves out a domain within or under a major city, commanding networks of agents that operate on their master's behalf.

Alien Lairs. Because they refuse to share territory with others, most beholders withdraw to frigid hills, abandoned ruins, and deep caverns to scheme. A beholder's lair is carved out by its disintegration eye ray, emphasizing vertical passages connecting chambers stacked on top of each other. Such an environment allows a beholder to move freely, even as it prevents intruders from easily creeping about. When intruders do break in, the height of its open ceilings allows a beholder to float up and harry foes on the floor.

As alien as their creator, the rooms in a beholder's lair reflect the creature's arrogance. It festoons its chambers with trophies from the battles it has won, including petrified adventurers standing frozen in their horrified final moments, pieces of other beholders, and magic items wrested from powerful foes. A beholder judges its own worth by its acquisitions, and it never willingly parts with its treasures.

A BEHOLDER'S LAIR

A beholder's central lair is typically a large, spacious cavern with high ceilings, where it can attack without fear of closing to melee range. A beholder encountered in its lair has a challenge rating of 14 (11,500 XP).

Lair Actions

When fighting inside its lair, a beholder can invoke the ambient magic to take lair actions. On initiative count 20 (losing initiative ties), the beholder can take one lair action to cause one of the following effects:

- A 50-foot square area of ground within 120 feet of the beholder becomes slimy; that area is difficult terrain until initiative count 20 on the next round.
- Walls within 120 feet of the beholder sprout grasping appendages until initiative count 20 on the round after next. Each creature of the beholder's choice that starts its turn within 10 feet of such a wall must succeed on a DC 15 Dexterity saving throw or be grappled. Escaping requires a successful DC 15 Strength (Athletics) or Dexterity (Acrobatics) check.
- An eye opens on a solid surface within 60 feet of the beholder. One random eye ray of the beholder shoots from that eye at a target of the beholder's choice that it can see. The eye then closes and disappears.

The beholder can't repeat an effect until they have all been used, and it can't use the same effect two rounds in a row.

Regional Effects

A region containing a beholder's lair is warped by the creature's unnatural presence, which creates one or more of the following effects:

- Creatures within 1 mile of the beholder's lair sometimes feel as if they're being watched when they aren't.
- When the beholder sleeps, minor warps in reality occur within 1 mile of its lair and then vanish 24 hours later. Marks on cave walls might change subtly, an eerie trinket might appear where none existed before, harmless slime might coat a statue, and so on. These effects apply only to natural surfaces and to nonmagical objects that aren't on anyone's person.

If the beholder dies, these effects fade over the course of 1d10 days.

Death Tyrant

On rare occasions, a beholder's sleeping mind drifts to places beyond its normal madness, imagining a reality in which it exists beyond death. When such dreams take hold, a beholder can transform, its flesh sloughing away to leave a death tyrant behind. This monster possesses the cunning and much of the magic it had in life, but it is fueled by the power of undeath.

A death tyrant appears as a massive, naked skull, with a pinpoint of red light gleaming in its hollow eye socket. With its eyestalks rotted away, ten spectral eyes hover above the creature and glare in all directions.

Deathly Despot. As they did when they were beholders, death tyrants lord their power over other creatures. Moreover, a beholder's ability to quash magical energy with its central eye gives way to a more sinister power in a death tyrant, which can transform former slaves and enemies into undead servants.

Zombies created by a death tyrant are used and discarded as needed. They stand guard at the entrances to the death tyrant's lair or guard its treasure vaults.

Acting as bait for traps or as combat fodder, zombies keep powerful enemies distracted while the death tyrant moves into position and prepares to destroy them.

Armies of the Dead. A death tyrant that embraces undeath becomes an engine of destruction. Driven by a hunger for power and security, it advances against humanoid settlements, using its eye rays to destroy every creature it encounters, then building an army of undead. If left unchecked, a death tyrant might wipe out the population of a city in weeks, then set its undead eye on wider conquest. As each settlement falls, the death tyrant's zombie forces build to overwhelming numbers.

Undead Nature. A death tyrant doesn't require air, food, drink, or sleep.

A Death Tyrant's Lair

A death tyrant's lair is usually the same site it held as a beholder, but it contains more trappings of death and decay. A death tyrant encountered in its lair has a challenge rating of 15 (13,000 XP).

Lair Actions

When fighting inside its lair, a death tyrant can invoke the ambient magic to take lair actions. On initiative count 20 (losing initiative ties), the death tyrant can take one lair action to cause one of the following effects:

- An area that is a 50-foot cube within 120 feet of the tyrant is filled with spectral eyes and tentacles. To creatures other than the death tyrant, that area is lightly obscured and difficult terrain until initiative count 20 on the next round.
- Walls sprout spectral appendages until initiative count 20 on the round after next. Any creature, including one on the Ethereal Plane, that is hostile to the tyrant and starts its turn within 10 feet of a wall must succeed on a DC 17 Dexterity saving throw or be grappled. Escaping requires a successful DC 17 Strength (Athletics) or Dexterity (Acrobatics) check.
- A spectral eye opens in the air at a point within 50 feet of the tyrant. One random eye ray of the tyrant shoots from that eye, which is considered to be an ethereal source, at a target of the tyrant's choice. The eye then closes and disappears.

The death tyrant can't repeat an effect until all three have been used, and it can't use the same effect on consecutive rounds.

Regional Effects

A region containing a death tyrant's lair is warped by the creature's unnatural presence, which creates one or more of the following effects:

- Creatures within 1 mile of the tyrant's lair sometimes feel as if they're being watched even when they aren't.
- When a creature hostile to the tyrant and aware of its existence finishes a long rest within 1 mile of the tyrant's lair, roll a d20 for that creature. On a roll of 10 or lower, the creature is subjected to one random eye ray of the tyrant.

If the death tyrant dies, these effects fade over the course of 1d10 days.

"EVERY BEHOLDER THINKS IT IS THE EPITOME
OF BEHOLDERKIND, AND THE ONLY THING IT
FEARS IS THAT IT MIGHT BE WRONG."
—VALKARA IRONFELL, DWARF SAGE

BEHOLDER

Large aberration, lawful evil

Armor Class 18 (natural armor)
Hit Points 180 (19d10 + 76)
Speed 0 ft., fly 20 ft. (hover)

STR	DEX	CON	INT	WIS	CHA
10 (+0)	14 (+2)	18 (+4)	17 (+3)	15 (+2)	17 (+3)

Saving Throws Int +8, Wis +7, Cha +8
Skills Perception +12
Condition Immunities prone
Senses darkvision 120 ft., passive Perception 22
Languages Deep Speech, Undercommon
Challenge 13 (10,000 XP)

Antimagic Cone. The beholder's central eye creates an area of antimagic, as in the *antimagic field* spell, in a 150-foot cone. At the start of each of its turns, the beholder decides which way the cone faces and whether the cone is active. The area works against the beholder's own eye rays.

ACTIONS

Bite. *Melee Weapon Attack:* +5 to hit, reach 5 ft., one target. *Hit:* 14 (4d6) piercing damage.

Eye Rays. The beholder shoots three of the following magical eye rays at random (reroll duplicates), choosing one to three targets it can see within 120 feet of it:

1. *Charm Ray.* The targeted creature must succeed on a DC 16 Wisdom saving throw or be charmed by the beholder for 1 hour, or until the beholder harms the creature.
2. *Paralyzing Ray.* The targeted creature must succeed on a DC 16 Constitution saving throw or be paralyzed for 1 minute. The target can repeat the saving throw at the end of each of its turns, ending the effect on itself on a success.
3. *Fear Ray.* The targeted creature must succeed on a DC 16 Wisdom saving throw or be frightened for 1 minute. The target can repeat the saving throw at the end of each of its turns, ending the effect on itself on a success.
4. *Slowing Ray.* The targeted creature must succeed on a DC 16 Dexterity saving throw. On a failed save, the target's speed is halved for 1 minute. In addition, the creature can't take reactions, and it can take either an action or a bonus action on its turn, not both. The creature can repeat the saving throw at the end of each of its turns, ending the effect on itself on a success.
5. *Enervation Ray.* The targeted creature must make a DC 16 Constitution saving throw, taking 36 (8d8) necrotic damage on a failed save, or half as much damage on a successful one.
6. *Telekinetic Ray.* If the target is a creature, it must succeed on a DC 16 Strength saving throw or the beholder moves it up to 30 feet in any direction. It is restrained by the ray's telekinetic grip until the start of the beholder's next turn or until the beholder is incapacitated.
   If the target is an object weighing 300 pounds or less that isn't being worn or carried, it is moved up to 30 feet in any direction. The beholder can also exert fine control on objects with this ray, such as manipulating a simple tool or opening a door or a container.
7. *Sleep Ray.* The targeted creature must succeed on a DC 16 Wisdom saving throw or fall asleep and remain unconscious for 1 minute. The target awakens if it takes damage or another creature takes an action to wake it. This ray has no effect on constructs and undead.
8. *Petrification Ray.* The targeted creature must make a DC 16 Dexterity saving throw. On a failed save, the creature begins to turn to stone and is restrained. It must repeat the saving throw at the end of its next turn. On a success, the effect ends. On a failure, the creature is petrified until freed by the *greater restoration* spell or other magic.
9. *Disintegration Ray.* If the target is a creature, it must succeed on a DC 16 Dexterity saving throw or take 45 (10d8) force damage. If this damage reduces the creature to 0 hit points, its body becomes a pile of fine gray dust.
   If the target is a Large or smaller nonmagical object or creation of magical force, it is disintegrated without a saving throw. If the target is a Huge or larger object or creation of magical force, this ray disintegrates a 10-foot cube of it.
10. *Death Ray.* The targeted creature must succeed on a DC 16 Dexterity saving throw or take 55 (10d10) necrotic damage. The target dies if the ray reduces it to 0 hit points.

LEGENDARY ACTIONS

The beholder can take 3 legendary actions, using the Eye Ray option below. It can take only one legendary action at a time and only at the end of another creature's turn. The beholder regains spent legendary actions at the start of its turn.

Eye Ray. The beholder uses one random eye ray.

DEATH TYRANT

Large undead, lawful evil

Armor Class 19 (natural armor)
Hit Points 187 (25d10 + 50)
Speed 0 ft., fly 20 ft. (hover)

STR	DEX	CON	INT	WIS	CHA
10 (+0)	14 (+2)	14 (+2)	19 (+4)	15 (+2)	19 (+4)

Saving Throws Str +5, Con +7, Int +9, Wis +7, Cha +9
Skills Perception +12
Damage Immunities poison
Condition Immunities charmed, exhaustion, paralyzed, petrified, poisoned, prone
Senses darkvision 120 ft., passive Perception 22
Languages Deep Speech, Undercommon
Challenge 14 (11,500 XP)

Negative Energy Cone. The death tyrant's central eye emits an invisible, magical 150-foot cone of negative energy. At the start of each of its turns, the tyrant decides which way the cone faces and whether the cone is active.

Any creature in that area can't regain hit points. Any humanoid that dies there becomes a zombie under the tyrant's command. The dead humanoid retains its place in the initiative order and animates at the start of its next turn, provided that its body hasn't been completely destroyed.

ACTIONS

Bite. *Melee Weapon Attack:* +5 to hit, reach 5 ft., one target. *Hit:* 14 (4d6) piercing damage.

Eye Rays. The death tyrant shoots three of the following magical eye rays at random (reroll duplicates), choosing one to three targets it can see within 120 feet of it:

1. Charm Ray. The targeted creature must succeed on a DC 17 Wisdom saving throw or be charmed by the tyrant for 1 hour, or until the beholder harms the creature.

2. Paralyzing Ray. The targeted creature must succeed on a DC 17 Constitution saving throw or be paralyzed for 1 minute. The target can repeat the saving throw at the end of each of its turns, ending the effect on itself on a success.

3. Fear Ray. The targeted creature must succeed on a DC 17 Wisdom saving throw or be frightened for 1 minute. The target can repeat the saving throw at the end of each of its turns, ending the effect on itself on a success.

4. Slowing Ray. The targeted creature must succeed on a DC 17 Dexterity saving throw. On a failed save, the target's speed is halved for 1 minute. In addition, the creature can't take reactions, and it can take either an action or a bonus action on its turn, not both. The creature can repeat the saving throw at the end of each of its turns, ending the effect on itself on a success.

5. Enervation Ray. The targeted creature must make a DC 17 Constitution saving throw, taking 36 (8d8) necrotic damage on a failed save, or half as much damage on a successful one.

6. Telekinetic Ray. If the target is a creature, it must succeed on a DC 17 Strength saving throw or the tyrant moves it up to 30 feet in any direction. The target is restrained by the ray's telekinetic grip until the start of the tyrant's next turn or until the tyrant is incapacitated.

If the target is an object weighing 300 pounds or less that isn't being worn or carried, it is moved up to 30 feet in any direction. The tyrant can also exert fine control on objects with this ray, such as manipulating a simple tool or opening a door or a container.

7. Sleep Ray. The targeted creature must succeed on a DC 17 Wisdom saving throw or fall asleep and remain unconscious for 1 minute. The target awakens if it takes damage or another creature takes an action to wake it. This ray has no effect on constructs and undead.

8. Petrification Ray. The targeted creature must make a DC 17 Dexterity saving throw. On a failed save, the creature begins to turn to stone and is restrained. It must repeat the saving throw at the end of its next turn. On a success, the effect ends. On a failure, the creature is petrified until freed by the *greater restoration* spell or other magic.

9. Disintegration Ray. If the target is a creature, it must succeed on a DC 17 Dexterity saving throw or take 45 (10d8) force damage. If this damage reduces the creature to 0 hit points, its body becomes a pile of fine gray dust.

If the target is a Large or smaller nonmagical object or creation of magical force, it is disintegrated without a saving throw. If the target is a Huge or larger object or creation of magical force, this ray disintegrates a 10-foot cube of it.

10. Death Ray. The targeted creature must succeed on a DC 17 Dexterity saving throw or take 55 (10d10) necrotic damage. The target dies if the ray reduces it to 0 hit points.

LEGENDARY ACTIONS

The death tyrant can take 3 legendary actions, using the Eye Ray option below. It can take only one legendary action at a time and only at the end of another creature's turn. The tyrant regains spent legendary actions at the start of its turn.

Eye Ray. The death tyrant uses one random eye ray.

Spectator

A spectator is a lesser beholder that is summoned from another plane of existence by a magical ritual, the components of which include four beholder eyestalks that are consumed by the ritual's magic. Appropriately, a spectator has four eyestalks, two on each side of the wide eye at the center of its four-foot diameter body.

Magical Guardians. A summoned spectator guards a location or a treasure of its summoner's choice for 101 years, allowing no creature but its summoner to enter the area or access the item, unless the summoner instructed otherwise. If the item is stolen or destroyed before the years have all passed, a summoned spectator vanishes. It otherwise never abandons its post.

Glimmers of Madness. Though it can speak, a spectator communicates primarily by way of telepathy. It is civil while on guard, openly discussing its orders and its summoner. However, even a brief conversation with a spectator is enough to reveal quirks in its personality brought on by its years of isolation. It might invent imaginary enemies, refer to itself in the third person, or try to adopt the voice of its summoner.

Like any beholder, a spectator views itself as the epitome of its kind, and it has an intense hatred of other spectators. If two spectators encounter one another, they almost always fight to the death.

Freed from Service. When a spectator has fulfilled its service, it is free to do as it pleases. Many take up residence in the places they previously guarded, especially if their summoners have died. With the spectator's loss of purpose, the flickers of madness it displayed during its servitude flourish.

Spectator

Medium aberration, lawful neutral

Armor Class 14 (natural armor)
Hit Points 39 (6d8 + 12)
Speed 0 ft., fly 30 ft. (hover)

STR	DEX	CON	INT	WIS	CHA
8 (−1)	14 (+2)	14 (+2)	13 (+1)	14 (+2)	11 (+0)

Skills Perception +6
Condition Immunities prone
Senses darkvision 120 ft., passive Perception 16
Languages Deep Speech, Undercommon, telepathy 120 ft.
Challenge 3 (700 XP)

Actions

Bite. *Melee Weapon Attack:* +1 to hit, reach 5 ft., one target. *Hit:* 2 (1d6 − 1) piercing damage.

Eye Rays. The spectator shoots up to two of the following magical eye rays at one or two creatures it can see within 90 feet of it. It can use each ray only once on a turn.

  1. *Confusion Ray.* The target must succeed on a DC 13 Wisdom saving throw, or it can't take reactions until the end of its next turn. On its turn, the target can't move, and it uses its action to make a melee or ranged attack against a randomly determined creature within range. If the target can't attack, it does nothing on its turn.

  2. *Paralyzing Ray.* The target must succeed on a DC 13 Constitution saving throw or be paralyzed for 1 minute. The target can repeat the saving throw at the end of each of its turns, ending the effect on itself on a success.

  3. *Fear Ray.* The target must succeed on a DC 13 Wisdom saving throw or be frightened for 1 minute. The target can repeat the saving throw at the end of each of its turns, with disadvantage if the spectator is visible to the target, ending the effect on itself on a success.

  4. *Wounding Ray.* The target must make a DC 13 Constitution saving throw, taking 16 (3d10) necrotic damage on a failed save, or half as much damage on a successful one.

Create Food and Water. The spectator magically creates enough food and water to sustain itself for 24 hours.

Reactions

Spell Reflection. If the spectator makes a successful saving throw against a spell, or a spell attack misses it, the spectator can choose another creature (including the spellcaster) it can see within 30 feet of it. The spell targets the chosen creature instead of the spectator. If the spell forced a saving throw, the chosen creature makes its own save. If the spell was an attack, the attack roll is rerolled against the chosen creature.

BLIGHTS

Awakened plants gifted with the powers of intelligence and mobility, blights plague lands contaminated by darkness. Drinking that darkness from the soil, a blight carries out the will of ancient evil and attempts to spread that evil wherever it can.

Roots of the Gulthias Tree. Legends tell of a vampire named Gulthias who worked terrible magic and raised up an abominable tower called Nightfang Spire. Gulthias was undone when a hero plunged a wooden stake through his heart, but as the vampire was destroyed, his blood infused the stake with a dreadful power. In time, tendrils of new growth sprouted from the wood, growing into a sapling infused with the vampire's evil essence. It is said that a mad druid discovered the sapling, transplanting it to an underground grotto where it could grow. From this Gulthias tree came the seeds from which the first blights were sown.

Dark Conquest. Wherever a tree or plant is contaminated by a fragment of an evil mind or power, a Gulthias tree can rise to infest and corrupt the surrounding forest. Its evil spreads through root and soil to other plants, which perish or transform into blights. As those blights spread, they poison and uproot healthy plants, replacing them with brambles, toxic weeds, and others of their kind. In time, an infestation of blights can turn any land or forest into a place of corruption.

In forests infested with blights, trees and plants grow with supernatural speed. Vines and undergrowth rapidly spread through buildings and overrun trails and roads. After blights have killed or driven off their inhabitants, whole villages can disappear in the space of days.

Controlled by Evil. Blights are independent creatures, but most act under a Gulthias tree's control, often displaying the habits and traits of the life force or spirit that spawned them. By attacking their progenitor's old foes or seeking out treasures valuable to it, they carry on the legacy of long-lost evil.

NEEDLE BLIGHT

In the shadows of a forest, needle blights might be taken at a distance for shuffling, hunched humanoids. Up close, these creatures reveal themselves as horrid plants whose conifer-like needles grow across their bodies in quivering clumps. A needle blight lashes out with these needles or launches them as an aerial assault that can punch through armor and flesh.

When needle blights detect a threat, they loose a pollen that the wind carries to other needle blights throughout the forest. Alerted to their foes' location, needle blights converge from all sides to drench their roots in blood.

BEHOLD THE LEGACY OF
GULTHIAS THE VAMPIRE: PLANTS
WITH A TASTE FOR BLOOD.

TWIG BLIGHT

Twig blights can root in soil, which they do when living prey are scarce. While rooted, they resemble woody shrubs. When it pulls its roots free of the ground to move, a twig blight's branches twist together to form a humanoid-looking body with a head and limbs.

Twig blights seek out campsites and watering holes, rooting there to set up ambushes for potential victims coming to drink or rest. Huddled together in groups, twig blights blend in with an area's natural vegetation or with piles of debris or firewood.

Given how dry they are, twig blights are particularly susceptible to fire.

VINE BLIGHT

Appearing as masses of slithering creepers, vine blights hide in undergrowth and wait for prey to draw near. By animating the plants around them, vine blights entangle and hinder their foes before attacking.

Vine blights are the only blights capable of speech. Through its connection to the evil spirit of the Gulthias tree it serves, a vine blight speaks in a fractured version of its dead master's voice, taunting victims or bargaining with powerful foes.

NEEDLE BLIGHT
Medium plant, neutral evil

Armor Class 12 (natural armor)
Hit Points 11 (2d8 + 2)
Speed 30 ft.

STR	DEX	CON	INT	WIS	CHA
12 (+1)	12 (+1)	13 (+1)	4 (−3)	8 (−1)	3 (−4)

Condition Immunities blinded, deafened
Senses blindsight 60 ft. (blind beyond this radius), passive Perception 9
Languages understands Common but can't speak
Challenge 1/4 (50 XP)

ACTIONS

Claws. *Melee Weapon Attack:* +3 to hit, reach 5 ft., one target. *Hit:* 6 (2d4 + 1) piercing damage.

Needles. *Ranged Weapon Attack:* +3 to hit, range 30/60 ft., one target. *Hit:* 8 (2d6 + 1) piercing damage.

TWIG BLIGHT
Small plant, neutral evil

Armor Class 13 (natural armor)
Hit Points 4 (1d6 + 1)
Speed 20 ft.

STR	DEX	CON	INT	WIS	CHA
6 (−2)	13 (+1)	12 (+1)	4 (−3)	8 (−1)	3 (−4)

Skills Stealth +3
Damage Vulnerabilities fire
Condition Immunities blinded, deafened
Senses blindsight 60 ft. (blind beyond this radius), passive Perception 9
Languages understands Common but can't speak
Challenge 1/8 (25 XP)

False Appearance. While the blight remains motionless, it is indistinguishable from a dead shrub.

ACTIONS

Claws. *Melee Weapon Attack:* +3 to hit, reach 5 ft., one target. *Hit:* 3 (1d4 + 1) piercing damage.

VINE BLIGHT
Medium plant, neutral evil

Armor Class 12 (natural armor)
Hit Points 26 (4d8 + 8)
Speed 10 ft.

STR	DEX	CON	INT	WIS	CHA
15 (+2)	8 (−1)	14 (+2)	5 (−3)	10 (+0)	3 (−4)

Skills Stealth +1
Condition Immunities blinded, deafened
Senses blindsight 60 ft. (blind beyond this radius), passive Perception 10
Languages Common
Challenge 1/2 (100 XP)

False Appearance. While the blight remains motionless, it is indistinguishable from a tangle of vines.

ACTIONS

Constrict. *Melee Weapon Attack:* +4 to hit, reach 10 ft., one target. *Hit:* 9 (2d6 + 2) bludgeoning damage, and a Large or smaller target is grappled (escape DC 12). Until this grapple ends, the target is restrained, and the blight can't constrict another target.

Entangling Plants (Recharge 5–6). Grasping roots and vines sprout in a 15-foot radius centered on the blight, withering away after 1 minute. For the duration, that area is difficult terrain for nonplant creatures. In addition, each creature of the blight's choice in that area when the plants appear must succeed on a DC 12 Strength saving throw or become restrained. A creature can use its action to make a DC 12 Strength check, freeing itself or another entangled creature within reach on a success.

BUGBEARS

Bugbears are born for battle and mayhem. Surviving by raiding and hunting, they bully the weak and despise being bossed around, but their love of carnage means they will fight for powerful masters if bloodshed and treasure are assured.

Goblinoids. Bugbears are often found in the company of their cousins, hobgoblins and goblins. Bugbears usually enslave goblins they encounter, and they bully hobgoblins into giving them gold and food in return for serving as scouts and shock troops. Even when paid, bugbears are at best unreliable allies, yet goblins and hobgoblins understand that no matter how much bugbears might drain a tribe of resources, these creatures are a potent force.

Followers of Hruggek. Bugbears worship Hruggek, a lesser god who dwells on the plane of Acheron. In the absence of their goblinoid kin, bugbears form loose war bands, each one led by its fiercest member. Bugbears believe that when they die, their spirits have a chance to fight at Hruggek's side. They try to prove themselves worthy by defeating as many foes as possible.

Venal Ambushers. Despite their intimidating builds, bugbears move with surprising stealth. They are fond of setting ambushes and flee when outmatched. They are dependable mercenaries as long as they are supplied food, drink, and treasure, but a bugbear forgets any bond when its life is on the line. A wounded member of a bugbear band might be left behind to help the rest of the band escape. Afterward, that bugbear might help pursuers track down its former companions if doing so saves its life.

BUGBEAR
Medium humanoid (goblinoid), chaotic evil

Armor Class 16 (hide armor, shield)
Hit Points 27 (5d8 + 5)
Speed 30 ft.

STR	DEX	CON	INT	WIS	CHA
15 (+2)	14 (+2)	13 (+1)	8 (–1)	11 (+0)	9 (–1)

Skills Stealth +6, Survival +2
Senses darkvision 60 ft., passive Perception 10
Languages Common, Goblin
Challenge 1 (200 XP)

Brute. A melee weapon deals one extra die of its damage when the bugbear hits with it (included in the attack).

Surprise Attack. If the bugbear surprises a creature and hits it with an attack during the first round of combat, the target takes an extra 7 (2d6) damage from the attack.

ACTIONS

Morningstar. *Melee Weapon Attack:* +4 to hit, reach 5 ft., one target. *Hit:* 11 (2d8 + 2) piercing damage.

Javelin. *Melee or Ranged Weapon Attack:* +4 to hit, reach 5 ft. or range 30/120 ft., one target. *Hit:* 9 (2d6 + 2) piercing damage in melee or 5 (1d6 + 2) piercing damage at range.

BUGBEAR CHIEF
Medium humanoid (goblinoid), chaotic evil

Armor Class 17 (chain shirt, shield)
Hit Points 65 (10d8 + 20)
Speed 30 ft.

STR	DEX	CON	INT	WIS	CHA
17 (+3)	14 (+2)	14 (+2)	11 (+0)	12 (+1)	11 (+0)

Skills Intimidation +2, Stealth +6, Survival +3
Senses darkvision 60 ft., passive Perception 11
Languages Common, Goblin
Challenge 3 (700 XP)

Brute. A melee weapon deals one extra die of its damage when the bugbear hits with it (included in the attack).

Heart of Hruggek. The bugbear has advantage on saving throws against being charmed, frightened, paralyzed, poisoned, stunned, or put to sleep.

Surprise Attack. If the bugbear surprises a creature and hits it with an attack during the first round of combat, the target takes an extra 7 (2d6) damage from the attack.

ACTIONS

Multiattack. The bugbear makes two melee attacks.

Morningstar. *Melee Weapon Attack:* +5 to hit, reach 5 ft., one target. *Hit:* 12 (2d8 + 3) piercing damage.

Javelin. *Melee or Ranged Weapon Attack:* +5 to hit, reach 5 ft. or range 30/120 ft., one target. *Hit:* 10 (2d6 + 3) piercing damage in melee or 6 (1d6 + 3) piercing damage at range.

BULETTE

A bulette is a massive predator that terrorizes any lands it inhabits. Also called a "land shark," it lives only to feed. Irascible and rapacious, bulettes fear no other creature, and they attack with no regard for superior numbers or strength.

Underground Hunters. Bulettes use their powerful claws to tunnel through the earth when they hunt. Heedless of obstruction, they uproot trees, cause landslides in loose slopes, and leave sinkholes behind them. When vibrations in the soil and rock alert a bulette to movement, it shoots to the surface, its jaws spread wide as it attacks.

Wandering Monster. A bulette ranges across temperate lands, feeding on any animals and humanoids it comes across. These creatures dislike dwarf and elf flesh, although they often kill them before realizing what they are. A bulette loves halfling meat the most, and it is never happier than when chasing plump halflings across an open field.

A bulette has no lair, but roams a hunting territory up to thirty miles wide. Its sole criterion for territory is availability of food, and when it has eaten everything in an area, a bulette moves on. These creatures often home in on humanoid settlements, terrorizing them until their panicked residents have fled, or until the bulette is slain.

All creatures shun bulettes, which treat anything that moves as food—even other predators and bulettes. Bulettes come together only to mate, resulting in a bloody act of claws and teeth that usually ends with the male's death and consumption.

Arcane Creation. Some sages believe the bulette is the result of a mad wizard's experiments at crossbreeding snapping turtles and armadillos, with infusions of demon ichor. Bulettes have been thought to be extinct at different times, but after years without a sighting, the creatures inevitably reappear. Because their young are almost never seen, some sages suspect that bulettes maintain secret nesting grounds from which adults strike out into the world.

BULETTE
Large monstrosity, unaligned

Armor Class 17 (natural armor)
Hit Points 94 (9d10 + 45)
Speed 40 ft., burrow 40 ft.

STR	DEX	CON	INT	WIS	CHA
19 (+4)	11 (+0)	21 (+5)	2 (−4)	10 (+0)	5 (−3)

Skills Perception +6
Senses darkvision 60 ft., tremorsense 60 ft., passive Perception 16
Languages —
Challenge 5 (1,800 XP)

Standing Leap. The bulette's long jump is up to 30 feet and its high jump is up to 15 feet, with or without a running start.

ACTIONS

Bite. *Melee Weapon Attack:* +7 to hit, reach 5 ft., one target. *Hit:* 30 (4d12 + 4) piercing damage.

Deadly Leap. If the bulette jumps at least 15 feet as part of its movement, it can then use this action to land on its feet in a space that contains one or more other creatures. Each of those creatures must succeed on a DC 16 Strength or Dexterity saving throw (target's choice) or be knocked prone and take 14 (3d6 + 4) bludgeoning damage plus 14 (3d6 + 4) slashing damage. On a successful save, the creature takes only half the damage, isn't knocked prone, and is pushed 5 feet out of the bulette's space into an unoccupied space of the creature's choice. If no unoccupied space is within range, the creature instead falls prone in the bulette's space.

Bullywug

Life as a bullywug is nasty, brutish, and wet. These frog-headed amphibious humanoids must stay constantly moist, dwelling in rainy forests, marshes, and damp caves. Always hungry and thoroughly evil, bullywugs overwhelm opponents with superior numbers when they can, but they flee from serious threats to search for easier prey.

Bullywugs have green, gray, or mottled yellow skin that shifts through shades of gray, green, and brown, allowing them to blend in with their surroundings. They wear crude armor and wield simple weapons, and can deliver a powerful bite to foes that press too close.

Foul Aristocracy. Bullywugs consider themselves the right and proper rulers of the swamps. They follow an etiquette of sorts when dealing with outsiders and each other, subject to the whims and fancies of their leader—a self-styled lord of the muck. Bullywugs introduce themselves with grand-sounding titles, make great shows of bowing and debasing themselves before their superiors, and endlessly vie to win their superiors' favor.

A bullywug has two ways to advance among its kind. It can either murder its rivals, though it must take pains to keep its criminal deeds secret, or it can find a treasure or magic item and present it as tribute or a token of obeisance to its liege. A bullywug that murders its rivals without cunning is likely to be executed, so it's more common for bullywugs to stage raids against caravans and settlements, with the goal of securing precious baubles to impress their lords and win their good graces. Invariably, such fine goods are reduced to filthy tatters through abuse and neglect. Once a gift loses its sheen, a bullywug lord invariably demands that its subjects bring it more treasure as tribute.

Unruly Diplomacy. Bullywugs love nothing more than lording over those who trespass on their territories. Their warriors attempt to capture intruders rather than simply slaying them.

Captives are dragged before the king or queen—a bullywug of unusually large size—and forced to beg for mercy. Bribes, treasure, and flattery can trick the bullywug ruler into letting its captives go, but not before it tries to impress its "guests" with the majesty of its treasure and its realm. Struck with a deep inferiority complex, bullywug lords fancy themselves as kings and queens, but desperately crave the fear and respect of outsiders.

Amphibian Allies. Bullywugs speak a language that allows them to communicate over large areas by croaking like frogs. News of intruders or other events in the swamp spread within minutes across this crude communication system.

Simple concepts in the language are understandable to frogs and toads. Bullywugs use this capability to form strong bonds with giant frogs, which they train as guardians and hunters. Larger specimens are sometimes used as mounts as well. The frogs' ability to swallow creatures whole provides a bullywug hunting band an easy means of carrying prey back to their villages.

Bullywug
Medium humanoid (bullywug), neutral evil

Armor Class 15 (hide armor, shield)
Hit Points 11 (2d8 + 2)
Speed 20 ft., swim 40 ft.

STR	DEX	CON	INT	WIS	CHA
12 (+1)	12 (+1)	13 (+1)	7 (−2)	10 (+0)	7 (−2)

Skills Stealth +3
Senses passive Perception 10
Languages Bullywug
Challenge 1/4 (50 XP)

Amphibious. The bullywug can breathe air and water.

Speak with Frogs and Toads. The bullywug can communicate simple concepts to frogs and toads when it speaks in Bullywug.

Swamp Camouflage. The bullywug has advantage on Dexterity (Stealth) checks made to hide in swampy terrain.

Standing Leap. The bullywug's long jump is up to 20 feet and its high jump is up to 10 feet, with or without a running start.

Actions

Multiattack. The bullywug makes two melee attacks: one with its bite and one with its spear.

Bite. *Melee Weapon Attack:* +3 to hit, reach 5 ft., one target. *Hit:* 3 (1d4 + 1) bludgeoning damage.

Spear. *Melee or Ranged Weapon Attack:* +3 to hit, reach 5 ft. or range 20/60 ft., one target. *Hit:* 4 (1d6 + 1) piercing damage, or 5 (1d8 + 1) piercing damage if used with two hands to make a melee attack.

> "THEY CRAWL FROM THEIR MOTHERS'
> WOMBS TO SPREAD CORRUPTION
> THROUGHOUT THE MULTIVERSE.
> WHAT'S NOT TO LOVE?"
> —BABA YAGA

CAMBION

A cambion is the offspring of a fiend (usually a succubus or incubus) and a humanoid (usually a human). Cambions inherit aspects of both parents, but their horns, leathery wings, and sinewy tails are hallmarks of their otherworldly parentage.

Born to Be Bad. Cambions grow into ruthless adults whose wickedness and perversion horrifies even the most devoted mortal parent. Even as a youth, a cambion identifies its rightful place as an overlord of mortals. It might orchestrate uprisings in towns and cities, gathering gangs of humanoids and lesser devils to serve it.

Pawns of the Mighty. A cambion forced to serve its fiendish parent does so out of admiration and dread, but also with the expectation that it will one day rise to a place of prominence. Cambions raised in the Nine Hells serve as soldiers, envoys, and personal attendants to greater devils. In the Abyss, a cambion carries only as much authority as it can muster through sheer strength and force of will.

Spawn of Graz'zt. The demon lord Graz'zt is fond of procreating with humanoids who have made pacts with fiends, and he has sired many cambions who help him sow chaos across the multiverse. These cambions are characterized by charcoal-black skin, cloven hooves, six-fingered hands, and unearthly beauty.

CAMBION
Medium fiend, any evil alignment

Armor Class 19 (scale mail)
Hit Points 82 (11d8 + 33)
Speed 30 ft., fly 60 ft.

STR	DEX	CON	INT	WIS	CHA
18 (+4)	18 (+4)	16 (+3)	14 (+2)	12 (+1)	16 (+3)

Saving Throws Str +7, Con +6, Int +5, Cha +6
Skills Deception +6, Intimidation +6, Perception +4, Stealth +7
Damage Resistances cold, fire, lightning, poison; bludgeoning, piercing, and slashing from nonmagical attacks
Senses darkvision 60 ft., passive Perception 14
Languages Abyssal, Common, Infernal
Challenge 5 (1,800 XP)

Fiendish Blessing. The AC of the cambion includes its Charisma bonus.

Innate Spellcasting. The cambion's spellcasting ability is Charisma (spell save DC 14). The cambion can innately cast the following spells, requiring no material components:

3/day each: *alter self, command, detect magic*
1/day: *plane shift* (self only)

ACTIONS

Multiattack. The cambion makes two melee attacks or uses its Fire Ray twice.

Spear. *Melee or Ranged Weapon Attack:* +7 to hit, reach 5 ft. or range 20/60 ft., one target. *Hit:* 7 (1d6 + 4) piercing damage, or 8 (1d8 + 4) piercing damage if used with two hands to make a melee attack, plus 3 (1d6) fire damage.

Fire Ray. *Ranged Spell Attack:* +7 to hit, range 120 ft., one target. *Hit:* 10 (3d6) fire damage.

Fiendish Charm. One humanoid the cambion can see within 30 feet of it must succeed on a DC 14 Wisdom saving throw or be magically charmed for 1 day. The charmed target obeys the cambion's spoken commands. If the target suffers any harm from the cambion or another creature or receives a suicidal command from the cambion, the target can repeat the saving throw, ending the effect on itself on a success. If a target's saving throw is successful, or if the effect ends for it, the creature is immune to the cambion's Fiendish Charm for the next 24 hours.

Carrion Crawler

Carrion crawlers scour putrid flesh from carcasses and gobble the slimy bones that remain. They aggressively attack any creature that trespasses on their territory or disturbs their feasting.

Carrion Eaters. A carrion crawler follows the scent of death to its food, but it prefers not to compete with other scavengers. These foul creatures thus hunker down in territories where death is plentiful and other carrion eaters have limited mobility. Caves, sewers, dungeons, and forested marshes are their favored lairs, but carrion crawlers are also drawn to battlefields and cemeteries.

A carrion crawler roams on the hunt, its tentacles probing the air for the scent of blood or decay. In tunnels or ruins, carrion crawlers scurry across the ceiling as they move toward food. In this way, they avoid contact with oozes, otyughs, and other dangerous inhabitants of the darkness, even as they surprise potential meals that don't think to look up.

Patient Predators. Whether in subterranean darkness or while hunting at night, light signals a potential meal. A carrion crawler might follow a light source from a distance for hours, hoping to pick up the scent of blood. Despite their great size, carrion crawlers can also easily set up ambushes by waiting around blind corners for prey to come to them.

When facing potential prey or intruders, a carrion crawler lets its poison do the work. Once a victim goes rigid with paralysis, the carrion crawler wraps it with its tentacles and drags it away to a high ledge or isolated passageway, where it can be killed safely. The monster then resumes patrolling its territory while waiting for its meal to ripen.

Carrion Crawler
Large monstrosity, unaligned

Armor Class 13 (natural armor)
Hit Points 51 (6d10 + 18)
Speed 30 ft., climb 30 ft.

STR	DEX	CON	INT	WIS	CHA
14 (+2)	13 (+1)	16 (+3)	1 (−5)	12 (+1)	5 (−3)

Skills Perception +3
Senses darkvision 60 ft., passive Perception 13
Languages —
Challenge 2 (450 XP)

Keen Smell. The carrion crawler has advantage on Wisdom (Perception) checks that rely on smell.

Spider Climb. The carrion crawler can climb difficult surfaces, including upside down on ceilings, without needing to make an ability check.

Actions

Multiattack. The carrion crawler makes two attacks: one with its tentacles and one with its bite.

Tentacles. *Melee Weapon Attack:* +8 to hit, reach 10 ft., one creature. *Hit:* 4 (1d4 + 2) poison damage, and the target must succeed on a DC 13 Constitution saving throw or be poisoned for 1 minute. Until this poison ends, the target is paralyzed. The target can repeat the saving throw at the end of each of its turns, ending the poison on itself on a success.

Bite. *Melee Weapon Attack:* +4 to hit, reach 5 ft., one target. *Hit:* 7 (2d4 + 2) piercing damage.

"I hear centaurs make excellent mounts!"
—Batley Summerfoot, a halfling adventurer
who never read HOOVES OF FURY,
by Irvil Grayborn of Sundown

Centaur

Large monstrosity, neutral good

Armor Class 12
Hit Points 45 (6d10 + 12)
Speed 50 ft.

STR	DEX	CON	INT	WIS	CHA
18 (+4)	14 (+2)	14 (+2)	9 (–1)	13 (+1)	11 (+0)

Skills Athletics +6, Perception +3, Survival +3
Senses passive Perception 13
Languages Elvish, Sylvan
Challenge 2 (450 XP)

Charge. If the centaur moves at least 30 feet straight toward a target and then hits it with a pike attack on the same turn, the target takes an extra 10 (3d6) piercing damage.

Actions

Multiattack. The centaur makes two attacks: one with its pike and one with its hooves or two with its longbow.

Pike. *Melee Weapon Attack:* +6 to hit, reach 10 ft., one target. *Hit:* 9 (1d10 + 4) piercing damage.

Hooves. *Melee Weapon Attack:* +6 to hit, reach 5 ft., one target. *Hit:* 11 (2d6 + 4) bludgeoning damage.

Longbow. *Ranged Weapon Attack:* +4 to hit, range 150/600 ft., one target. *Hit:* 6 (1d8 + 2) piercing damage.

Centaur

Reclusive wanderers and omen-readers of the wild, centaurs avoid conflict but fight fiercely when pressed. They roam the vast wilderness, keeping far from borders, laws, and the company of other creatures.

Wilderness Nomads. Centaur tribes range across lands with mild to hot climates, where a centaur requires only light furs or oiled skins to deal with inclement weather. They are hunter-gatherers and rarely build shelters or even use tents.

Centaur migrations span continents and take decades to repeat, so that a centaur tribe might not retread the same path for generations. These long-ranging patterns can lead to conflict when centaurs encounter settlements of other creatures built along their traditional routes.

Reluctant Settlers. A centaur that can't keep pace with the rest of its tribe is left behind. Some such centaurs vanish into the wilderness and are never seen again. Those that can bear the loss of their tribe might take up residence among other races. Frontier settlements value the nature knowledge of their centaur residents. Many such communities owe their survival to the insight and acumen of a centaur.

Despite their reclusive nature, centaurs trade with elves and with the caravans of other benevolent humanoids they meet during their wanderings. A trader might save the life of a wounded or an elderly centaur unfit for long travel, escorting it to a settlement where it can peacefully live out the rest of its days.

CHIMERA
Large monstrosity, chaotic evil

Armor Class 14 (natural armor)
Hit Points 114 (12d10 + 48)
Speed 30 ft., fly 60 ft.

STR	DEX	CON	INT	WIS	CHA
19 (+4)	11 (+0)	19 (+4)	3 (−4)	14 (+2)	10 (+0)

Skills Perception +8
Senses darkvision 60 ft., passive Perception 18
Languages understands Draconic but can't speak
Challenge 6 (2,300 XP)

ACTIONS

Multiattack. The chimera makes three attacks: one with its bite, one with its horns, and one with its claws. When its fire breath is available, it can use the breath in place of its bite or horns.

Bite. *Melee Weapon Attack:* +7 to hit, reach 5 ft., one target. *Hit:* 11 (2d6 + 4) piercing damage.

Horns. *Melee Weapon Attack:* +7 to hit, reach 5 ft., one target. *Hit:* 10 (1d12 + 4) bludgeoning damage.

Claws. *Melee Weapon Attack:* +7 to hit, reach 5 ft., one target. *Hit:* 11 (2d6 + 4) slashing damage.

Fire Breath (Recharge 5–6). The dragon head exhales fire in a 15-foot cone. Each creature in that area must make a DC 15 Dexterity saving throw, taking 31 (7d8) fire damage on a failed save, or half as much damage on a successful one.

CHIMERA

Chimeras were created after mortals summoned Demogorgon to the world. The Prince of Demons, unimpressed with the creatures that surrounded it, transformed them into horrific, multi-headed monstrosities. This act gave rise to the first chimeras.

Gifted with demonic cruelty, a chimera serves as a grim reminder of what happens when demon princes find their way to the Material Plane. A typical specimen has the hindquarters of a large goat, the forequarters of a lion, and the leathery wings of a dragon, along with the heads of all three of those creatures. The monster likes to surprise its victims, swooping down from the sky and engulfing prey with its fiery breath before landing.

Conflicted Creature. A chimera combines the worst aspects of its three parts. Its dragon head drives it to raid, plunder, and accumulate a great hoard. Its leonine nature compels it to hunt and kill powerful creatures that threaten its territory. Its goat head grants it a vicious, stubborn streak that compels it to fight to the death.

These three aspects drive a chimera to stake out a territory that is as large as 10 miles wide. It preys on wild game, viewing more powerful creatures as rivals to be humiliated and defeated. Its greatest rivals are dragons, griffons, manticores, perytons, and wyverns.

When it hunts, the chimera looks for easy ways to amuse itself. It enjoys the fear and suffering of weaker creatures. The monster often toys with its prey, breaking off an attack prematurely and leaving a creature wounded and terrified before returning to finish it off.

Servant of Evil. Though chimeras are far from cunning, their draconic ego makes them susceptible to flattery and gifts. If offered food and treasure, a chimera might spare a traveler. A villain can lure a chimera into service by keeping it well fed and its treasure hoard well stocked.

C

CHUUL

Survivors of the ancient aboleth empire, chuuls are crustaceans the aboleths modified and endowed with sentience. They follow the ingrained directives of their creators, as they have done since the dawn of time.

Primeval Relics. In the primeval ages, aboleths ruled a vast empire that spanned the oceans of the world. In those days, the aboleths used mighty magic and bent the minds of the nascent creatures of the mortal realm. However, they were bound to the water and could not enforce their will beyond it without servants. Therefore, they created chuuls.

Perfectly obedient, the chuuls collected sentient creatures and magic at the aboleths' command. Chuuls were designed to endure the ages of the world, growing in size and strength as the eons passed. When the aboleths' empire crumbled with the rise of the gods, the chuuls were cast adrift. However, these creatures continue to do what they did for the aboleths, slowly collecting humanoids, gathering treasure, amassing magic, and consolidating power.

Tireless Guardians. Chuul still guard the ruins of the ancient aboleth empire. They linger in silent observance of eons-old commands. Rumors and ancient maps sometimes lure treasure seekers to these ruins, but the reward for their boldness is death.

CHUUL
Large aberration, chaotic evil

Armor Class 16 (natural armor)
Hit Points 93 (11d10 + 33)
Speed 30 ft., swim 30 ft.

STR	DEX	CON	INT	WIS	CHA
19 (+4)	10 (+0)	16 (+3)	5 (−3)	11 (+0)	5 (−3)

Skills Perception +4
Damage Immunities poison
Condition Immunities poisoned
Senses darkvision 60 ft., passive Perception 14
Languages understands Deep Speech but can't speak
Challenge 4 (1,100 XP)

Amphibious. The chuul can breathe air and water.

Sense Magic. The chuul senses magic within 120 feet of it at will. This trait otherwise works like the *detect magic* spell but isn't itself magical.

ACTIONS

Multiattack. The chuul makes two pincer attacks. If the chuul is grappling a creature, the chuul can also use its tentacles once.

Pincer. *Melee Weapon Attack:* +6 to hit, reach 10 ft., one target. *Hit:* 11 (2d6 + 4) bludgeoning damage. The target is grappled (escape DC 14) if it is a Large or smaller creature and the chuul doesn't have two other creatures grappled.

Tentacles. One creature grappled by the chuul must succeed on a DC 13 Constitution saving throw or be poisoned for 1 minute. Until this poison ends, the target is paralyzed. The target can repeat the saving throw at the end of each of its turns, ending the effect on itself on a success.

Whatever riches that the explorers bring with them adds to the hoard guarded by the chuuls. Chuuls can sense magic at a distance. This sense couples with an innate drive that leads them to slay explorers, take their gear, and bury it in secret locales aboleths dictated eons ago.

Waiting Servants. Although the aboleths' ancient empire fell long ago, the psychic bonds between them and their created servants remain intact. Chuuls that come into contact with aboleths immediately assume their old roles. Such chuuls redirect their compulsions to the service of the aboleths' sinister purposes.

CLOAKER

Large aberration, chaotic neutral

Armor Class 14 (natural armor)
Hit Points 78 (12d10 + 12)
Speed 10 ft., fly 40 ft.

STR	DEX	CON	INT	WIS	CHA
17 (+3)	15 (+2)	12 (+1)	13 (+1)	12 (+1)	14 (+2)

Skills Stealth +5
Senses darkvision 60 ft., passive Perception 11
Languages Deep Speech, Undercommon
Challenge 8 (3,900 XP)

Damage Transfer. While attached to a creature, the cloaker takes only half the damage dealt to it (rounded down), and that creature takes the other half.

False Appearance. While the cloaker remains motionless without its underside exposed, it is indistinguishable from a dark leather cloak.

Light Sensitivity. While in bright light, the cloaker has disadvantage on attack rolls and Wisdom (Perception) checks that rely on sight.

ACTIONS

Multiattack. The cloaker makes two attacks: one with its bite and one with its tail.

Bite. *Melee Weapon Attack:* +6 to hit, reach 5 ft., one creature. *Hit:* 10 (2d6 + 3) piercing damage, and if the target is Large or smaller, the cloaker attaches to it. If the cloaker has advantage against the target, the cloaker attaches to the target's head, and the target is blinded and unable to breathe while the cloaker is attached. While attached, the cloaker can make this attack only against the target and has advantage on the attack roll. The cloaker can detach itself by spending 5 feet of its movement. A creature, including the target, can take its action to detach the cloaker by succeeding on a DC 16 Strength check.

Tail. *Melee Weapon Attack:* +6 to hit, reach 10 ft., one creature. *Hit:* 7 (1d8 + 3) slashing damage.

Moan. Each creature within 60 feet of the cloaker that can hear its moan and that isn't an aberration must succeed on a DC 13 Wisdom saving throw or become frightened until the end of the cloaker's next turn. If a creature's saving throw is successful, the creature is immune to the cloaker's moan for the next 24 hours

Phantasms (Recharges after a Short or Long Rest). The cloaker magically creates three illusory duplicates of itself if it isn't in bright light. The duplicates move with it and mimic its actions, shifting position so as to make it impossible to track which cloaker is the real one. If the cloaker is ever in an area of bright light, the duplicates disappear.

Whenever any creature targets the cloaker with an attack or a harmful spell while a duplicate remains, that creature rolls randomly to determine whether it targets the cloaker or one of the duplicates. A creature is unaffected by this magical effect if it can't see or if it relies on senses other than sight.

A duplicate has the cloaker's AC and uses its saving throws. If an attack hits a duplicate, or if a duplicate fails a saving throw against an effect that deals damage, the duplicate disappears.

CLOAKER

Cloakers earned their names for the resemblance they bear to dark leathery cloaks. Lurking in remote dungeons and caves, these stealthy predators wait to slay lone or injured prey stumbling through the darkness.

Camouflaged Lurkers. Like a stingray, a cloaker's body is composed of cartilage and muscle. With its tail and fins unfurled, it flies through darkness and lurks among the shadows of caverns the same way a stingray glides through water and hides on the ocean floor. Parallel rows of round, black eyespots run along its back like buttons, and the ivory-colored claws on its cowl resemble bone clasps.

When a cloaker unfurls and moves to attack, it reveals its pale underside and makes its true nature evident. Red eyes glow above rows of sharp teeth, and a long pendulous tail whips behind it.

Opportunistic Predators. When hunting, cloakers glide through the shadows at a safe distance behind groups of other creatures traversing the Underdark. They follow parties of humanoids to prey on the wounded after a battle, or pursue herds of Underdark beasts, attacking the sick, the weak, or the straggling.

Cloakers strike quickly and consume their meals as swiftly as possible, enveloping and devouring their victims. While it feeds, a cloaker uses its swift, whiplike tail for defense, although it rarely takes a stand against dangerous foes or groups of creatures. As an added defense, cloakers can create illusory duplicates of themselves.

Haunting Moan. Cloakers' thoughts are alien to other life-forms, and they communicate with one another through subsonic moans inaudible to most creatures. At higher intensities, a cloaker's haunting moan becomes audible, evoking sensations of doom and dread in creatures that hear it.

Cloaker Conclaves. Cloakers prefer isolation, but they sometimes convene with other cloakers for defense or to exchange information about new dangers, suitable hunting grounds, or developments that might affect their habitats. When this convergence is complete, the cloakers separate again.

Cockatrice

Small monstrosity, unaligned

Armor Class 11
Hit Points 27 (6d6 + 6)
Speed 20 ft., fly 40 ft.

STR	DEX	CON	INT	WIS	CHA
6 (−2)	12 (+1)	12 (+1)	2 (−4)	13 (+1)	5 (−3)

Senses darkvision 60 ft., passive Perception 11
Languages —
Challenge 1/2 (100 XP)

Actions

Bite. *Melee Weapon Attack:* +3 to hit, reach 5 ft., one creature. *Hit:* 3 (1d4 + 1) piercing damage, and the target must succeed on a DC 11 Constitution saving throw against being magically petrified. On a failed save, the creature begins to turn to stone and is restrained. It must repeat the saving throw at the end of its next turn. On a success, the effect ends. On a failure, the creature is petrified for 24 hours.

Cockatrice

The cockatrice looks like a hideous hybrid of lizard, bird, and bat, and it is infamous for its ability to turn flesh to stone. These omnivores have a diet that consists of berries, nuts, flowers, and small animals such as insects, mice, and frogs—things they can swallow whole. They would be no threat to anything else if not for their fierce and frenzied response to even a hint of danger. A cockatrice flies into the face of any threat, squawking and madly beating its wings as its head darts out to peck. The smallest scratch from a cockatrice's beak can spell doom as its victim slowly turns to stone from the injury.

Couatl

Medium celestial, lawful good

Armor Class 19 (natural armor)
Hit Points 97 (13d8 + 39)
Speed 30 ft., fly 90 ft.

STR	DEX	CON	INT	WIS	CHA
16 (+3)	20 (+5)	17 (+3)	18 (+4)	20 (+5)	18 (+4)

Saving Throws Con +5, Wis +7, Cha +6
Damage Resistances radiant
Damage Immunities psychic; bludgeoning, piercing, and
    slashing from nonmagical attacks
Senses truesight 120 ft., passive Perception 15
Languages all, telepathy 120 ft.
Challenge 4 (1,100 XP)

Innate Spellcasting. The couatl's spellcasting ability is
Charisma (spell save DC 14). It can innately cast the following
spells, requiring only verbal components:

At will: *detect evil and good, detect magic, detect thoughts*
3/day each: *bless, create food and water, cure wounds, lesser
    restoration, protection from poison, sanctuary, shield*
1/day each: *dream, greater restoration, scrying*

Magic Weapons. The couatl's weapon attacks are magical.

Shielded Mind. The couatl is immune to scrying and to any
effect that would sense its emotions, read its thoughts, or
detect its location.

Actions

Bite. *Melee Weapon Attack:* +8 to hit, reach 5 ft., one creature.
Hit: 8 (1d6 + 5) piercing damage, and the target must succeed
on a DC 13 Constitution saving throw or be poisoned for
24 hours. Until this poison ends, the target is unconscious.
Another creature can use an action to shake the target awake.

Constrict. *Melee Weapon Attack:* +6 to hit, reach 10 ft., one
Medium or smaller creature. *Hit:* 10 (2d6 + 3) bludgeoning
damage, and the target is grappled (escape DC 15). Until this
grapple ends, the target is restrained, and the couatl can't
constrict another target.

Change Shape. The couatl magically polymorphs into a
humanoid or beast that has a challenge rating equal to or
less than its own, or back into its true form. It reverts to its
true form if it dies. Any equipment it is wearing or carrying is
absorbed or borne by the new form (the couatl's choice).

In a new form, the couatl retains its game statistics and
ability to speak, but its AC, movement modes, Strength,
Dexterity, and other actions are replaced by those of the new
form, and it gains any statistics and capabilities (except class
features, legendary actions, and lair actions) that the new
form has but that it lacks. If the new form has a bite attack, the
couatl can use its bite in that form.

Couatl

Couatls are benevolent serpentine beings of great
intellect and insight. Their brilliantly colored wings and
gentle manner speak to their celestial origins.

Divine Caretakers. Couatls were created as
guardians and caretakers by a benevolent god not
worshiped since the dawn of time, and which is
forgotten now by all but the couatls themselves. Most of
the divine mandates given to these beings are long since
fulfilled or failed. However, a number of couatls still
watch over ancient power, await fulfillment of prophecy,
or safeguard the heirs of creatures they once guided
and protected. Regardless of a couatl's task, it prefers to
remain hidden, revealing itself only as a last resort.

Truth Tellers. A couatl can't lie, but it can withhold
information, answer questions vaguely, or allow
others to jump to the wrong conclusions if doing so is
necessary to protect something, to keep promises, or to
hide the secret of its existence.

Ancient and Few. A couatl can live for ages without
sustenance, even surviving without air, but these
creatures can die of disease or the passage of time. A
couatl can sense its end up to a century beforehand, but
it has no insight into the manner of its demise.

If a couatl has already accomplished what it set out
to do, it accepts its fate. However, if its imminent death
endangers the completion of its goals, it actively seeks
out another couatl with which to produce offspring.

The mating ritual of couatls is a beautiful and
elaborate dance of magic and light, which results in
a gem-like egg from which a new couatl hatches. The
parent that sought out the mate raises the newborn
couatl and instructs it as to its duties, so that it can
complete whatever task the parent leaves unfinished.

CRAWLING CLAW

Crawling claws are the severed hands of murderers animated by dark magic so that they can go on killing. Wizards and warlocks of a dark bent use crawling claws as extra hands in their labors.

Magical Origins. Through dark necromantic rituals, the life force of a murderer is bound to its severed hand, haunting and animating it. If a dead murderer's spirit already manifests as another undead creature, if the murderer is raised from death, or if the spirit has long passed on to another plane, the ritual fails.

The ritual invoked to create a crawling claw works best with a hand recently severed from a murderer. To this end, ritualists and their servants frequent public executions to gain possession of suitable hands, or make bargains with assassins and torturers.

Creator's Control. A crawling claw can't be turned, nor can it be controlled by spells that control undead. These foul monsters are entirely bound to the will of their creator, which can concentrate on a claw in sight to mentally command its every action. If the crawling claw's creator doesn't command it, the claw follows its last command to the best of its ability.

Commands given to a crawling claw must be simple. A claw can't be tasked with finding and killing a particular person, because its limited senses and intelligence prevent it from tracking and picking out specific individuals. However, a command to kill all creatures in a particular locale works. A crawling claw can easily feel out the contours of keys and doorknobs, crawling from room to room on a blind killing spree.

Malign Intelligence. A crawling claw possesses little of the intellect and memories of the individual of which it was once a living part. The hate, jealousy, or greed that drove that person to murder lingers on, however, amplified by the claw's torturous fragmented state. Left to its own devices, a crawling claw imitates and recreates the same murderous acts it committed in life.

Living Claws. If a crawling claw is animated from the severed hand of a still-living murderer, the ritual binds the claw to the murderer's soul. The disembodied hand can then return to its former limb, its undead flesh knitting to the living arm from which it was severed.

Made whole again, the murderer acts as though the hand had never been severed and the ritual had never taken place. When the crawling claw separates again, the living body falls into a coma. Destroying the crawling claw while it is away from the body kills the murderer. However, killing the murderer has no effect on the crawling claw.

Undead Nature. A crawling claw doesn't require air, food, drink, or sleep.

> "Makes you wonder what can be done with all those other murderer parts, doesn't it?"
> —Evangeliza Lavain, necromancer

CRAWLING CLAW
Tiny undead, neutral evil

Armor Class 12
Hit Points 2 (1d4)
Speed 20 ft., climb 20 ft.

STR	DEX	CON	INT	WIS	CHA
13 (+1)	14 (+2)	11 (+0)	5 (−3)	10 (+0)	4 (−3)

Damage Immunities poison
Condition Immunities charmed, exhaustion, poisoned
Senses blindsight 30 ft. (blind beyond this radius), passive Perception 10
Languages understands Common but can't speak
Challenge 0 (10 XP)

Turn Immunity. The claw is immune to effects that turn undead.

ACTIONS

Claw. *Melee Weapon Attack:* +3 to hit, reach 5 ft., one target. *Hit:* 3 (1d4 + 1) bludgeoning or slashing damage (claw's choice).

Cyclops

Cyclopes are one-eyed giants that eke out a meager existence in wild lands. Isolationists by nature, they avoid contact with other races and try to drive away strangers in their territory.

Nonreligious. Legends claim that the cyclopes are the spawn of one of the gods of the giants, but these creatures pay little heed to any deities. They see little benefit in prayer and dislike ritual, which they perceive as complex and foreign. However, a cyclops that gains direct benefit from some site of divine power, or which is threatened by a supernatural force or creature, will pay homage as long as the benefit or threat remains.

Unsophisticated. Though they are reasonably intelligent, cyclopes live simple, reclusive lives, keeping herds of animals for food. They prefer to dwell alone or in small family groups, lairing in caves, ruins, or rough structures of dry stone construction they build themselves. A cyclops keeps its herd animals with it at night, sealing the entrance to its home with boulders to let it serve double duty as a barn.

A cyclops lairs within a day's journey of other cyclopes, so that they can meet to trade goods or seek mates. They craft weapons and tools of wood and stone, but will use metal when they can find it. Although cyclopes understand the Giant tongue, they write nothing and speak little, using grunts and gestures for their interactions with each other.

Cyclopes don't use money for trade, but they value gold, shells, and other glittering and colorful objects as jewelry. A cyclops might wear a necklace strung with feathers and silver coins, but also with pewter goblets, cutlery, and other bits of ruined metal.

Unwise. Cyclopes aren't great thinkers or strategists. Slow to learn and bound to their traditional ways, they find innovation difficult. Although they are a terrifying threat in combat due to their size and strength, they can often be tricked by clever foes.

Cyclopes can be cowed and awed by obvious displays of magic. Rustics with little exposure to magic, they can be deceived into mistaking a warlock, cleric, or other caster for a powerful divine figure. However, their sense of pride causes them to react with vengeful, bloodthirsty violence once they learn that the individual they assumed was a "god" is a mere mortal.

Cyclops

Huge giant, chaotic neutral

Armor Class 14 (natural armor)
Hit Points 138 (12d12 + 60)
Speed 30 ft.

STR	DEX	CON	INT	WIS	CHA
22 (+6)	11 (+0)	20 (+5)	8 (−1)	6 (−2)	10 (+0)

Senses passive Perception 8
Languages Giant
Challenge 6 (2,300 XP)

Poor Depth Perception. The cyclops has disadvantage on any attack roll against a target more than 30 feet away.

Actions

Multiattack. The cyclops makes two greatclub attacks.

Greatclub. *Melee Weapon Attack:* +9 to hit, reach 10 ft., one target. *Hit:* 19 (3d8 + 6) bludgeoning damage.

Rock. *Ranged Weapon Attack:* +9 to hit, range 30/120 ft., one target. *Hit:* 28 (4d10 + 6) bludgeoning damage.

DARKMANTLE

A darkmantle clings to cavern ceilings, remaining perfectly still as it waits for creatures to pass beneath it. From a distance, it can pass itself off as a stalactite or a lump of stone. Then it drops from the ceiling and unfurls, surrounding itself with magical darkness as it engulfs and crushes its prey.

Darkmantles are found throughout the Underdark, but they are equally common on the Shadowfell. Thriving in that dark realm, they fill an ecological niche similar to bats on the Material Plane. Intelligent creatures of the Shadowfell sometimes train darkmantles as guardians or companions.

> "REMIND ME AGAIN WHY WE'RE ON THIS QUEST?"
> —ETHELREDE THE FIGHTER, AFTER HIS FIRST
> DARKMANTLE ENCOUNTER

DARKMANTLE
Small monstrosity, unaligned

Armor Class 11
Hit Points 22 (5d6 + 5)
Speed 10 ft., fly 30 ft.

STR	DEX	CON	INT	WIS	CHA
16 (+3)	12 (+1)	13 (+1)	2 (−4)	10 (+0)	5 (−3)

Skills Stealth +3
Senses blindsight 60 ft., passive Perception 10
Languages —
Challenge 1/2 (100 XP)

Echolocation. The darkmantle can't use its blindsight while deafened.

False Appearance. While the darkmantle remains motionless, it is indistinguishable from a cave formation such as a stalactite or stalagmite.

ACTIONS

Crush. *Melee Weapon Attack:* +5 to hit, reach 5 ft., one creature. *Hit:* 6 (1d6 + 3) bludgeoning damage, and the darkmantle attaches to the target. If the target is Medium or smaller and the darkmantle has advantage on the attack roll, it attaches by engulfing the target's head, and the target is also blinded and unable to breathe while the darkmantle is attached in this way.

While attached to the target, the darkmantle can attack no other creature except the target but has advantage on its attack rolls. The darkmantle's speed also becomes 0, it can't benefit from any bonus to its speed, and it moves with the target.

A creature can detach the darkmantle by making a successful DC 13 Strength check as an action. On its turn, the darkmantle can detach itself from the target by using 5 feet of movement.

Darkness Aura (1/Day). A 15-foot radius of magical darkness extends out from the darkmantle, moves with it, and spreads around corners. The darkness lasts as long as the darkmantle maintains concentration, up to 10 minutes (as if concentrating on a spell). Darkvision can't penetrate this darkness, and no natural light can illuminate it. If any of the darkness overlaps with an area of light created by a spell of 2nd level or lower, the spell creating the light is dispelled.

DEATH KNIGHT

When a paladin that falls from grace dies without seeking atonement, dark powers can transform the once-mortal knight into a hateful undead creature. A death knight is a skeletal warrior clad in plate armor. Beneath its helmet, one can see the knight's skull with malevolent pinpoints of light burning in its eye sockets.

Eldritch Power. The death knight retains the ability to cast divine spells, but no death knight can use its magic to heal. It also attracts and commands lesser undead, although death knights that serve powerful fiends might have fiendish followers instead. Death knights often use warhorse skeletons and nightmares as mounts.

Immortal Until Redeemed. A death knight can arise anew even after it has been destroyed. Only when it atones for a life of wickedness or finds redemption can it finally escape its undead purgatory and truly perish.

Undead Nature. A death knight doesn't require air, food, drink, or sleep.

LORD SOTH

Lord Soth began his fall from grace with an act of heroism, saving an elf named Isolde from an ogre. Soth and Isolde fell in love, but Soth was already married. He had a servant dispose of his wife and was charged with murder, but fled with Isolde. When his castle fell under siege, he prayed for guidance and was told that he must atone for his misdeeds by completing a quest, but growing fears about Isolde's fidelity caused him to abandon his quest. Because his mission was not accomplished, a great cataclysm swept the land. When Isolde gave birth to a son, Soth refused to believe that the child was his and slew them both. All were incinerated in a fire that swept through the castle, yet Soth would find no rest in death, becoming a death knight.

DEATH KNIGHT

Medium undead, chaotic evil

Armor Class 20 (plate, shield)
Hit Points 180 (19d8 + 95)
Speed 30 ft.

STR	DEX	CON	INT	WIS	CHA
20 (+5)	11 (+0)	20 (+5)	12 (+1)	16 (+3)	18 (+4)

Saving Throws Dex +6, Wis +9, Cha +10
Damage Immunities necrotic, poison
Condition Immunities exhaustion, frightened, poisoned
Senses darkvision 120 ft., passive Perception 13
Languages Abyssal, Common
Challenge 17 (18,000 XP)

Magic Resistance. The death knight has advantage on saving throws against spells and other magical effects.

Marshal Undead. Unless the death knight is incapacitated, it and undead creatures of its choice within 60 feet of it have advantage on saving throws against features that turn undead.

Spellcasting. The death knight is a 19th-level spellcaster. Its spellcasting ability is Charisma (spell save DC 18, +10 to hit with spell attacks). It has the following paladin spells prepared:

1st level (4 slots): *command, compelled duel, searing smite*
2nd level (3 slots): *hold person, magic weapon*
3rd level (3 slots): *dispel magic, elemental weapon*
4th level (3 slots): *banishment, staggering smite*
5th level (2 slots): *destructive wave* (necrotic)

ACTIONS

Multiattack. The death knight makes three longsword attacks.

Longsword. *Melee Weapon Attack:* +11 to hit, reach 5 ft., one target. *Hit:* 9 (1d8 + 5) slashing damage, or 10 (1d10 + 5) slashing damage if used with two hands, plus 18 (4d8) necrotic damage.

Hellfire Orb (1/Day). The death knight hurls a magical ball of fire that explodes at a point it can see within 120 feet of it. Each creature in a 20-foot-radius sphere centered on that point must make a DC 18 Dexterity saving throw. The sphere spreads around corners. A creature takes 35 (10d6) fire damage and 35 (10d6) necrotic damage on a failed save, or half as much damage on a successful one.

REACTIONS

Parry. The death knight adds 6 to its AC against one melee attack that would hit it. To do so, the death knight must see the attacker and be wielding a melee weapon.

DEMILICH

Tiny undead, neutral evil

Armor Class 20 (natural armor)
Hit Points 80 (20d4)
Speed 0 ft., fly 30 ft. (hover)

STR	DEX	CON	INT	WIS	CHA
1 (−5)	20 (+5)	10 (+0)	20 (+5)	17 (+3)	20 (+5)

Saving Throws Con +6, Int +11, Wis +9, Cha +11
Damage Resistances bludgeoning, piercing, and slashing from magic weapons
Damage Immunities necrotic, poison, psychic; bludgeoning, piercing, and slashing from nonmagical attacks
Condition Immunities charmed, deafened, exhaustion, frightened, paralyzed, petrified, poisoned, prone, stunned
Senses truesight 120 ft., passive Perception 13
Languages —
Challenge 18 (20,000 XP)

Avoidance. If the demilich is subjected to an effect that allows it to make a saving throw to take only half damage, it instead takes no damage if it succeeds on the saving throw, and only half damage if it fails.

Legendary Resistance (3/Day). If the demilich fails a saving throw, it can choose to succeed instead.

Turn Immunity. The demilich is immune to effects that turn undead.

ACTIONS

Howl (Recharge 5–6). The demilich emits a bloodcurdling howl. Each creature within 30 feet of the demilich that can hear the howl must succeed on a DC 15 Constitution saving throw or drop to 0 hit points. On a successful save, the creature is frightened until the end of its next turn.

Life Drain. The demilich targets up to three creatures that it can see within 10 feet of it. Each target must succeed on a DC 19 Constitution saving throw or take 21 (6d6) necrotic damage, and the demilich regains hit points equal to the total damage dealt to all targets.

LEGENDARY ACTIONS

The demilich can take 3 legendary actions, choosing from the options below. Only one legendary action option can be used at a time and only at the end of another creature's turn. The demilich regains spent legendary actions at the start of its turn.

Flight. The demilich flies up to half its flying speed.
Cloud of Dust. The demilich magically swirls its dusty remains. Each creature within 10 feet of the demilich, including around a corner, must succeed on a DC 15 Constitution saving throw or be blinded until the end of the demilich's next turn. A creature that succeeds on the saving throw is immune to this effect until the end of the demilich's next turn.
Energy Drain (Costs 2 Actions). Each creature within 30 feet of the demilich must make a DC 15 Constitution saving throw. On a failed save, the creature's hit point maximum is magically reduced by 10 (3d6). If a creature's hit point maximum is reduced to 0 by this effect, the creature dies. A creature's hit point maximum can be restored with the *greater restoration* spell or similar magic.
Vile Curse (Costs 3 Actions). The demilich targets one creature it can see within 30 feet of it. The target must succeed on a DC 15 Wisdom saving throw or be magically cursed. Until the curse ends, the target has disadvantage on attack rolls and saving throws. The target can repeat the saving throw at the end of each of its turns, ending the curse on a success.

Demilich

The immortality granted to a lich lasts only as long as it feeds mortal souls to its phylactery. If it falters or fails in that task, its bones turn to dust until only its skull remains. This "demilich" contains only a fragment of the lich's malevolent life force—just enough so that if it is disturbed, these remains rise into the air and assume a wraithlike form. The skull then emits a terrifying howl that can slay the weak-hearted and leave others trembling with fear. Left alone, it sinks back down and returns to the empty peace of its existence.

Few liches seek to become demiliches, for it means an end to the existence they hoped to preserve by becoming undead. However, time can erode the lich's reason and memory, causing it to retreat into its ancient tomb and forget to feed on souls. The spells it once knew fade from its mind, and it no longer channels the arcane energy it wielded as a lich. However, even as a mere skull it remains a deadly and vexing enemy.

Enduring Existence. Even after a lich is reduced to a demilich state, its phylactery survives. As long as its phylactery is intact, the demilich can't be permanently destroyed. Its skull reforms after 1d10 days, restoring the creature to its wretched state. If it has the presence of mind to do so, a demilich can reclaim its former power by feeding just one soul to its phylactery. Doing so restores the demilich to lich form, reconstituting its undead body.

Undead Nature. A demilich doesn't require air, food, drink, or sleep. So great is a demilich's will to survive that it always has the maximum number of hit points for its Hit Dice, instead of average hit points.

A Demilich's Lair

A demilich hides its earthly remains and treasures in a labyrinthine tomb guarded by monsters and traps. At the heart of this labyrinth rests the demilich's skull and the dust from its other bones.

In its crypt, a demilich has access to lair actions and additional uses for its legendary actions. Its whole lair also has unique traits. A demilich in its lair has a challenge rating of 20 (24,500 XP).

Lair Actions

On initiative count 20 (losing initiative ties), the demilich rolls a d20. On a result of 11 or higher, the demilich takes a lair action to cause one of the following effects. It can't use the same effect two rounds in a row.

- The tomb trembles violently for a moment. Each creature on the floor of the tomb must succeed on a DC 19 Dexterity saving throw or be knocked prone.
- The demilich targets one creature it can see within 60 feet of it. An *antimagic field* fills the space of the target, moving with it until initiative count 20 on the next round.
- The demilich targets any number of creatures it can see within 30 feet of it. No target can regain hit points until initiative count 20 on the next round.

Lair Traits

A demilich's tomb might have any or all of the following effects in place:

- The first time a non-evil creature enters the tomb's area, the creature takes 16 (3d10) necrotic damage.
- Monsters in the tomb have advantage on saving throws against being charmed or frightened, and against features that turn undead.
- The tomb is warded against the magical travel of creatures the demilich hasn't authorized. Such creatures can't teleport into or out of the tomb's area or use planar travel to enter or leave it. Effects that allow teleportation or planar travel work within the tomb as long as they aren't used to leave or enter the tomb's area.

If the demilich is destroyed, these effects fade over the course of 10 days.

ACERERAK AND HIS DISCIPLES

The transformation into a demilich isn't a bitter end for all liches that experience it. Made as a conscious choice, the path of the demilich becomes the next step in a dark evolution. The lich Acererak—a powerful wizard and demonologist and the infamous master of the Tomb of Horrors—anticipated his own transformation, preparing for it by setting enchanted gemstones into his skull's eye sockets and teeth. Each of these soul gems possessed the power to capture the souls on which his phylactery would feed.

Acererak abandoned his physical body, accepting that it would molder and dissolve to dust while he traveled the planes as a disembodied consciousness. If the skull that was his last physical remains was ever disturbed, its gems would claim the souls of the insolent intruders to his tomb, magically transferring them to his phylactery.

Liches who follow Acererak's path believe that by becoming free of their bodies, they can continue their quest for power beyond the mortal world. As their patron did, they secure their remains within well-guarded vaults, using soul gems to maintain their phylacteries and destroy the adventurers who disturb their lairs.

Acererak or another demilich like him has a challenge rating of 21 (33,000 XP), or 23 (50,000 XP) in its lair, and gains the following additional action option.

Trap Soul. The demilich targets one creature that it can see within 30 feet of it. The target must make a DC 19 Charisma saving throw. On a failed save, the target's soul is magically trapped inside one of the demilich's gems. While the soul is trapped, the target's body and all the equipment it is carrying cease to exist. On a successful save, the target takes 24 (7d6) necrotic damage, and if this damage reduces the target to 0 hit points, its soul is trapped as if it failed the saving throw. A soul trapped in a gem for 24 hours is devoured and ceases to exist.

If the demilich drops to 0 hit points, it is destroyed and turns to powder, leaving behind its gems. Crushing a gem releases any soul trapped within, at which point the target's body re-forms in an unoccupied space nearest to the gem and in the same state as when it was trapped.

DEMONS

Spawned in the Infinite Layers of the Abyss, demons are the embodiment of chaos and evil—engines of destruction barely contained in monstrous form. Possessing no compassion, empathy, or mercy, they exist only to destroy.

Spawn of Chaos. The Abyss creates demons as extensions of itself, spontaneously forming fiends out of filth and carnage. Some are unique monstrosities, while others represent uniform strains virtually identical to each other. Other demons (such as manes) are created from mortal souls shunned or cursed by the gods, or which are otherwise trapped in the Abyss.

Capricious Elevation. Demons respect power and power alone. A greater demon commands shrieking mobs of lesser demons because it can destroy any lesser demon that dares to refuse its commands. A demon's status grows with the blood it spills; the more enemies that fall before it, the greater it becomes.

A demon might spawn as a manes, then become a dretch, and eventually transform to a vrock after untold time spent fighting and surviving in the Abyss. Such elevations are rare, however, for most demons are destroyed before they attain significant power. The greatest of those that do survive make up the ranks of the demon lords that threaten to tear the Abyss apart with their endless warring.

By expending considerable magical power, demon lords can raise lesser demons into greater forms, though such promotions never stem from a demon's deeds or accomplishments. Rather, a demon lord might warp a manes into a quasit when it needs an invisible spy, or turn an army of dretches into hezrous when marching against a rival lord. Demon lords only rarely elevate demons to the highest ranks, fearful of inadvertently creating rivals to their own power.

Abyssal Invasions. Wherever they wander across the Abyss, demons search for portals to the other planes. They crave the chance to slip free of their native realm and spread their dark influence across the multiverse, undoing the works of the gods, tearing down civilizations, and reducing the cosmos to despair and ruin.

Some of the darkest legends of the mortal realm are built around the destruction wrought by demons set loose in the world. As such, even nations embroiled in bitter conflict will set their differences aside to help contain an outbreak of demons, or to seal off abyssal breaches before these fiends can break free.

Signs of Corruption. Demons carry the stain of abyssal corruption with them, and their mere presence changes the world for the worse. Plants wither and die in areas where abyssal breaches and demons appear. Animals shun the sites where a demon has made a kill. The site of a demonic infestation might be fouled by a stench that never abates, by areas of bitter cold or burning heat, or by permanent shadows that mark the places where these fiends lingered.

Eternal Evil. Outside the Abyss, death is a minor nuisance that no demon fears. Mundane weapons can't stop these fiends, and many demons are resistant to the energy of the most potent spells. When a lucky hero manages to drop a demon in combat, the fiend dissolves into foul ichor. It then instantly reforms in the Abyss, its mind and essence intact even as its hatred is inflamed. The only way to truly destroy a demon is to seek it in the Abyss and kill it there.

Protected Essence. A powerful demon can take steps to safeguard its life essence, using secret methods and abyssal metals to create an amulet into which part of that essence is ceded. If the demon's abyssal form is ever destroyed, the amulet allows the fiend to reform at a time and place of its choosing.

Obtaining a demonic amulet is a dangerous enterprise, and simply seeking such a device risks drawing the attention of the demon that created it. A creature possessing a demonic amulet can exact favors from the demon whose life essence the amulet holds— or inflict great pain if the fiend resists. If an amulet is destroyed, the demon that created it is trapped in the Abyss for a year and a day.

Demonic Cults. Despite the dark risks involved in dealing with fiends, the mortal realm is filled with creatures that covet demonic power. Demon lords manipulate these mortal servants into performing ever greater acts of depravity, furthering the demon lord's ambitions in exchange for magic and other boons. However, a demon regards any mortals in its service as tools to use and then discard at its whim, consigning their mortal souls to the Abyss.

Demon Summoning. Few acts are as dangerous as summoning a demon, and even mages who bargain freely with devils fear the fiends of the Abyss. Though demons yearn to sow chaos on the Material Plane, they show no gratitude when brought there, raging against their prisons and demanding release.

Those who would risk summoning a demon might do so to wrest information from it, press it into service, or send it on a mission that only a creature of absolute evil can complete. Preparation is key, and experienced summoners know the specific spells and magic items that can force a demon to bend to another's will. If a single mistake is made, a demon that breaks free shows no mercy as it makes its summoner the first victim of its wrath.

Bound Demons. *The Book of Vile Darkness*, the *Black Scrolls of Ahm*, and the *Demonomicon of Iggwilv* are the foremost authorities on demonic matters. These ancient tomes describe techniques that can trap the essence of a demon on the Material Plane, placing it within a weapon, idol, or piece of jewelry and preventing the fiend's return to the Abyss.

An object that binds a demon must be specially prepared with unholy incantations and innocent blood. It radiates a palpable evil, chilling and fouling the air around it. A creature that handles such an object experiences unsettling dreams and wicked impulses, but is able to control the demon whose essence is trapped within the object. Destroying the object frees the demon, which immediately seeks revenge against its binder.

Demonic Possession. No matter how secure its bindings, a powerful demon often finds a way to escape an object that holds it. When a demonic essence emerges from its container, it can possess a mortal host. Sometimes a fiend employs stealth to hide a successful possession. Other times, it unleashes the full brunt of its fiendish drives through its new form.

As long as the demon remains in possession of its host, the soul of that host is in danger of being dragged to the Abyss with the demon if it is exorcised from the flesh, or if the host dies. If a demon possesses a creature and the object binding the demon is destroyed, the possession lasts until powerful magic is used to drive the demonic spirit out of its host.

Demon Lords

The chaotic power of the Abyss rewards demons of particular ruthlessness and ingenuity with a dark blessing, transforming them into unique fiends whose power can rival the gods. These demon lords rule through cunning or brute force, hoping to one day claim the prize of absolute control over all the Abyss.

Reward for Outsiders. Although most demon lords rise up from the vast and uncountable mobs of demons rampaging across the Abyss, the plane also rewards outsiders that conquer any of its infinite layers. The elven goddess Lolth became a demon lord after Corellon Larethian cast her into the Abyss for betraying elvenkind. Sages claim that the Dark Prince Graz'zt originated on some other plane before stealing his abyssal title from another long-forgotten demon lord.

Power and Control. The greatest sign of a demon lord's power is its ability to reshape an abyssal realm. A layer of the Abyss controlled by a demon lord becomes a twisted reflection of that fiend's vile personality, and demon lords seldom leave their realms for fear of allowing another creature to reshape and seize it.

As with other demons, a demon lord that dies on another plane has its essence return to the Abyss, where it reforms into a new body. Likewise, a demon lord that dies in the Abyss is permanently destroyed. Most demon lords keep a portion of their essence safely stored away to prevent such a fate.

Baphomet

The demon lord Baphomet, also known as the Horned King and the Prince of Beasts, rules over minotaurs and other savage creatures. If he had his way, civilization would crumble and all races would embrace their base animal savagery.

The Prince of Beasts appears as a huge, black-furred minotaur with iron horns, red eyes, and a blood-soaked mouth. His iron crown is topped with the rotting heads of his enemies, while his dark armor is set with spikes and skull-like serrations. He carries a huge glaive named Heartcleaver, but often hurls it into the fray so as to face his enemies with horns and hooves.

Demogorgon

The Sibilant Beast and the self-styled Prince of Demons, Demogorgon yearns for nothing less than undoing the order of the multiverse. An insane assemblage of features and drives, the Prince of Demons inspires fear and hatred among other demons and demon lords.

Demogorgon towers three times the height of a human, his body as sinuous as a snake's and as powerful as a great ape's. Suckered tentacles take the place of his arms. His saurian lower torso ends in webbed and clawed feet, and a forked tail whose whip-like tips are armed with cruel blades. The Prince of Demons has two baleful baboon heads, both of them mad. It is only the conflict between the two halves of his dual nature that keeps the demon lord's ambitions in check.

GRAZ'ZT

The demon lord Graz'zt appears as a darkly handsome figure nearly nine feet tall. Those who refer to the Dark Prince as the most humanoid of the demon lords vastly underestimate the capacity for evil in his scheming heart.

Graz'zt is a striking physical specimen, whose demonic nature shows in his ebon skin, pointed ears, yellow fangs, crown of horns, and six-fingered hands. He delights in finery, pageantry, and sating his decadent desires with subjects and consorts alike, among whom incubi and succubi are often his favorites.

JUIBLEX

The demon lord of slimes and oozes, Juiblex is a stew of noxious fluids that lurks in the abyssal depths. The wretched Faceless Lord cares nothing for cultists or mortal servants, and its sole desire is to turn all creatures into formless copies of its horrid self.

In its resting state, Juiblex spreads out in a noxious mass, bubbling and filling the air with a profound stench. On the rare occasions when creatures confront the demon lord, Juiblex draws itself up into a shuddering cone of slime striated with veins of black and green. Baleful red eyes swim within its gelatinous body, while dripping pseudopods of ooze lash out hungrily at any creature they can reach.

LOLTH

The Demon Queen of Spiders is the evil matron of the drow. Her every thought is touched by malice, and the depth of her viciousness can surprise even her most faithful priestesses. She directs her faithful while she weaves plots across the worlds of the Material Plane, looking forward to the time when her drow followers bring those worlds under her control.

Lolth appears as a lithe, imperious drow matriarch when she manifests to her followers in the mortal realm, which she does with unusual frequency. When battle breaks out—or if she has a reason to remind her followers to fear her—Lolth's lower body transforms into that of a huge demonic spider, whose spike-tipped legs and mandibles tear foes apart.

ORCUS

Known as the Demon Prince of Undeath and the Blood Lord, the demon lord Orcus is worshiped by the undead and by living creatures that channel the power of undeath. A brooding and nihilistic entity, Orcus yearns to make the multiverse a place of death and darkness, forever unchanging except by his will.

The Demon Prince of Undeath is a foul and corpulent creature, with a humanoid torso, powerful goat legs, and the desiccated head of a ram. His sore-ridden body stinks of disease, but his decaying head and glowing red eyes are as a creature already dead. Great black bat wings sprout from his back, stirring reeking air as he moves.

Orcus wields a malevolent artifact known as the *Wand of Orcus*, a mace-like rod of obsidian topped by a humanoid skull. He surrounds himself with undead, and living creatures not under his control are anathema to him.

YEENOGHU

Known as the Gnoll Lord and the Beast of Butchery, the demon lord Yeenoghu hungers for slaughter and senseless destruction. Gnolls are his mortal instruments, and he drives them to ever-greater atrocities in his name. Delighting in sorrow and hopelessness, the Gnoll Lord yearns to turn the world into a wasteland in which the last surviving gnolls tear each other apart for the right to feast upon the dead.

Yeenoghu appears as a huge, scarred gnoll with a spiky crest of black spines, and eyes that burn with emerald flame. His armor is a patchwork of shields and breastplates claimed from fallen foes, and decorated by those foes' flayed skins. Yeenoghu can summon a triple flail he calls the Butcher, which he wields to deadly effect or wills to fly independently into battle as he tears foes apart with teeth and claws.

OTHER DEMON LORDS

No one knows the full number of demon lords that rage in the Abyss. Given the infinite depths of that plane, powerful demons constantly rise to become demon lords, then fall almost as quickly. Among the demon lords whose power has endured long enough for demonologists to name them are Fraz-Urb'luu, the Prince of Deception; Kostchtchie, the Prince of Wrath; Pazuzu, Prince of the Lower Aerial Kingdoms; and Zuggtmoy, Lady of Fungi.

DEMON TYPES

Demonologists organize the chaotic distribution of demons into broad categories of power known as types. Most demons fit into one of six major types, with the weakest categorized as Type 1 and the strongest as Type 6. Demons outside the six main types are categorized as minor demons and demon lords.

DEMONS BY TYPE

Type	Examples
1	barlgura, shadow demon, vrock
2	chasme, hezrou
3	glabrezu, yochlol
4	nalfeshnee
5	marilith
6	balor, goristro

BALOR

Figures of ancient and terrible evil, balors rule as generals over demonic armies, yearning to seize power while destroying any creatures that oppose them.

Wielding a flaming whip and a longsword that channels the power of the storm, a balor's battle prowess is fueled by hatred and rage. It channels this demonic fury in its death throes, falling within a blast of fire that can destroy even the hardiest foes.

BARLGURA

The barlgura represents the savagery and brutality of the Abyss. Barlguras gather in packs to take down tougher foes, keep gruesome trophies from their victories, and decorate their territory with such objects.

A barlgura looks like a hulking orangutan with a gruesome, drooping visage and tusks jutting from its jaw. Standing just under 8 feet tall, it has broad shoulders and weighs 650 pounds. It moves apishly along the ground, but it climbs with great speed and agility.

CHASME

This loathsome demon resembles an unspeakable crossing of humanoid and fly. A chasme shuffles about on four spindly legs that can find purchase on walls and ceilings. A droning sound precedes the approach of a chasme, inflicting foes with a terrible lethargy that leaves them open to attack.

The lowly chasmes serve more powerful masters as interrogators or taskmasters. A chasme lives to dole out torture as punishment, and has a knack for spotting demons that have deserted their lords. Capturing and returning such traitors allows a chasme to torment the victim without fear of reprisal.

DRETCH

Dretches are among the weakest of demons—repulsive, self-loathing creatures doomed to spend eternity in a state of perpetual discontent. Their low intelligence makes dretches unsuitable for anything but the simplest tasks. However, what they lack in potential, they make up for in sheer malice. Dretches mill about in mobs, voicing their displeasure as an unsettling din of hoots, snarls, and grunts.

GLABREZU

A glabrezu takes great pleasure in destroying mortals through temptation, and these creatures are among the few demons to offer their service to creatures foolish enough to summon them.

Although glabrezus are devastating in combat, they prefer to tempt victims into ruin, using power or wealth as a lure. Engaging in guile, trickery, and evil bargains, a glabrezu hoards riches that it uses to fulfill promises to shortsighted summoners and weak-willed mortals. However, if its attempts to entice or deceive fail, a glabrezu has the strength to fight and win.

GORISTRO

The goristro resembles a fiendish minotaur towering more than twenty feet tall. When controlled by a demon lord, goristros make formidable living siege engines and prized pets. Goristros possess preternatural cunning when navigating labyrinthine passages and shifting corridors, pursuing foes in a terrifying hunt.

A hulking goristro sometimes bears a palanquin, carrying smaller demons on its broad shoulders, much like an elephant carries riders on its back.

HEZROU

Hezrous serve as foot soldiers in the demonic hordes of the Abyss. Although physically powerful, they are weak-minded and hezrous can easily be duped into sacrificing themselves by more powerful demons. As they press their attacks into the heart of an enemy's forces, their foul stench can sicken even the toughest foes.

MANES

Souls of evil creatures that descend to the Lower Planes are transformed into manes—the lowest form of demonkind. These wretched fiends attack any non-demon they see, and they are called to the Material Plane by those seeking to sow death and chaos.

Orcus, the Prince of Undeath, has the power to transform manes into undead monsters, most often ghouls and shadows. Other demon lords feed on manes, destroying them utterly. Otherwise, killing a manes causes it to dissipate into a cloud of reeking vapor that reforms into another manes after one day.

MARILITH

Terrible to behold, a marilith has the lower body of a great serpent and the upper torso of a humanoid female with six arms.

Wielding a wicked blade in each of its six hands, a marilith is a devastating foe that few can match in battle. These demons possess keen minds and a finely honed sense of tactics, and they are able to lead and unite other demons in common cause. Mariliths are often encountered as captains at the head of a demonic horde, where they embrace any opportunity to rush headlong into battle.

DEMON TRUE NAMES

Though demons all have common names, every demon lord and every demon of type 1 through 6 has a true name that it keeps secret. A demon can be forced to disclose its true name if charmed, and ancient scrolls and tomes are said to exist that list the true names of the most powerful demons.

A mortal who learns a demon's true name can use powerful summoning magic to call the demon from the Abyss and exercise some measure of control over it. However, most demons brought to the Material Plane in this manner do everything in their power to wreak havoc or sow discord and strife.

Nalfeshnee

The nalfeshnee is one of the most grotesque demons—a corpulent mockery of ape and boar standing twice the height of a human, with feathered wings that seem too small for its bloated body. These brutish features conceal a remarkable intelligence and cunning.

Nalfeshnees are devastating in combat, using their wings to soar above the front ranks and reach vulnerable adversaries that can be dispatched with little effort. From the thick of battle, they telepathically bellow commands to lesser demons, even as they inspire a sense of dread that forces their foes to scatter and run.

Nalfeshnees feed on hatred and despair, but they crave humanoid flesh above all else. They keep their larders filled with humanoids abducted from the Material Plane, then eat those creatures alive during elaborate feasts. Thinking of themselves as refined and cultured, nalfeshnees employ stained and rusted cutlery when they dine.

Quasit

Quasits infest the Lower Planes. Physically weak, they keep to the shadows to plot mischief and wickedness. More powerful demons use quasits as spies and messengers when they aren't devouring them or pulling them apart to pass the time.

A quasit can assume animal forms, but in its true form it looks like a 2-foot-tall green humanoid with a barbed tail and horns. The quasit has clawed fingers and toes, and these claws can deliver an irritating poison. It prefers to be invisible when it attacks.

Shadow Demon

When a demon's body is destroyed but the fiend is prevented from reforming in the Abyss, its essence sometimes takes on a vague physical form. These shadow demons exist outside the normal abyssal hierarchy, since their creation results most often from mortal magic, not from transformation or promotion.

Shadow demons all but disappear in the darkness, and they can creep about without making a sound. A shadow demon uses its insubstantial claws to feast on its victim's fears, to taste its memories, and drink in its doubts. Bright light harries this fiend and shows its distinct shape, resolving it from a blur of darkness to a winged humanoid creature whose lower body trails off into nothing, and whose claws rend a victim's mind.

Shadowy Nature. A shadow demon doesn't require air, food, drink, or sleep.

Vrock

Vrocks are dull-witted, capricious fiends that live only to create pain and carnage. A vrock resembles a giant hybrid of humanoid and vulture, its gnarled, bestial body and broad wings stinking of offal.

Vrocks gobble humanoid flesh whenever they can, stunning potential prey with an ear-splitting shriek, then swooping down to attack with beak and claw. Vrocks can shake their wings, releasing clouds of toxic spores.

Coveting pretty things, vrocks turn against each other for the chance to lay claim to cheap jewelry or ornamental stones. Despite their love of treasure, vrocks are difficult to bribe, seeing no reason to bargain when they can simply take what they want from a would-be bargainer's corpse.

Yochlol

The yochlols are the Handmaidens of Lolth—extensions of the Spider Queen's will dedicated to acting as her spies, taskmasters, and agents of villainy. They attend their goddess in the Demonweb Pits, but Lolth sometimes dispatches yochlols to the Material Plane to guard her temples and to aid her most devout priestesses. Yochlols don't form outside Lolth's realm of the Demonweb, and they serve no demon lords except their queen.

Outside the Abyss, a yochlol can assume the guise of a female drow or monstrous spider to conceal its demonic form. In its true form, the fiend appears as a pillar of yellow slime with a single malevolent eye. In its drow and true form, a yochlol's touch carries the same venomous touch as its spider form's bite.

Variant: Demon Summoning

Some demons can have an action option that allows them to summon other demons.

Summon Demon (1/Day). The demon chooses what to summon and attempts a magical summoning.

- A **balor** has a 50 percent chance of summoning 1d8 vrocks, 1d6 hezrous, 1d4 glabrezus, 1d3 nalfeshnees, 1d2 mariliths, or one goristro.
- A **barlgura** has a 30 percent chance of summoning one barlgura.
- A **chasme** has a 30 percent chance of summoning one chasme.
- A **glabrezu** has a 30 percent chance of summoning 1d3 vrocks, 1d2 hezrous, or one glabrezu.
- A **hezrou** has a 30 percent chance of summoning 2d6 dretches or one hezrou.
- A **marilith** has a 50 percent chance of summoning 1d6 vrocks, 1d4 hezrous, 1d3 glabrezus, 1d2 nalfeshnees, or one marilith.
- A **nalfeshnee** has a 50 percent chance of summoning 1d4 vrocks, 1d3 hezrous, 1d2 glabrezus, or one nalfeshnee.
- A **vrock** has a 30 percent chance of summoning 2d4 dretches or one vrock.
- A **yochlol** has a 50 percent chance of summoning one yochlol.

A summoned demon appears in an unoccupied space within 60 feet of its summoner, acts as an ally of its summoner, and can't summon other demons. It remains for 1 minute, until it or its summoner dies, or until its summoner dismisses it as an action.

Demons are painfully difficult to summon and control. It is not a burden for the weak of heart or the weak of spirit.

—From the DEMONOMICON OF IGGWILV

BALOR
Huge fiend (demon), chaotic evil

Armor Class 19 (natural armor)
Hit Points 262 (21d12 + 126)
Speed 40 ft., fly 80 ft.

STR	DEX	CON	INT	WIS	CHA
26 (+8)	15 (+2)	22 (+6)	20 (+5)	16 (+3)	22 (+6)

Saving Throws Str +14, Con +12, Wis +9, Cha +12
Damage Resistances cold, lightning; bludgeoning, piercing, and slashing from nonmagical attacks
Damage Immunities fire, poison
Condition Immunities poisoned
Senses truesight 120 ft., passive Perception 13
Languages Abyssal, telepathy 120 ft.
Challenge 19 (22,000 XP)

Death Throes. When the balor dies, it explodes, and each creature within 30 feet of it must make a DC 20 Dexterity saving throw, taking 70 (20d6) fire damage on a failed save, or half as much damage on a successful one. The explosion ignites flammable objects in that area that aren't being worn or carried, and it destroys the balor's weapons.

Fire Aura. At the start of each of the balor's turns, each creature within 5 feet of it takes 10 (3d6) fire damage, and flammable objects in the aura that aren't being worn or carried ignite. A creature that touches the balor or hits it with a melee attack while within 5 feet of it takes 10 (3d6) fire damage.

Magic Resistance. The balor has advantage on saving throws against spells and other magical effects.

Magic Weapons. The balor's weapon attacks are magical.

ACTIONS

Multiattack. The balor makes two attacks: one with its longsword and one with its whip.

Longsword. *Melee Weapon Attack:* +14 to hit, reach 10 ft., one target. *Hit:* 21 (3d8 + 8) slashing damage plus 13 (3d8) lightning damage. If the balor scores a critical hit, it rolls damage dice three times, instead of twice.

Whip. *Melee Weapon Attack:* +14 to hit, reach 30 ft., one target. *Hit:* 15 (2d6 + 8) slashing damage plus 10 (3d6) fire damage, and the target must succeed on a DC 20 Strength saving throw or be pulled up to 25 feet toward the balor.

Teleport. The balor magically teleports, along with any equipment it is wearing or carrying, up to 120 feet to an unoccupied space it can see.

Barlgura

Large fiend (demon), chaotic evil

Armor Class 15 (natural armor)
Hit Points 68 (8d10 + 24)
Speed 40 ft., climb 40 ft.

STR	DEX	CON	INT	WIS	CHA
18 (+4)	15 (+2)	16 (+3)	7 (−2)	14 (+2)	9 (−1)

Saving Throws Dex +5, Con +6
Skills Perception +5, Stealth +5
Damage Resistances cold, fire, lightning
Damage Immunities poison
Condition Immunities poisoned
Senses blindsight 30 ft., darkvision 120 ft., passive Perception 15
Languages Abyssal, telepathy 120 ft.
Challenge 5 (1,800 XP)

Innate Spellcasting. The barlgura's spellcasting ability is Wisdom (spell save DC 13). The barlgura can innately cast the following spells, requiring no material components:

1/day each: *entangle, phantasmal force*
2/day each: *disguise self, invisibility* (self only)

Reckless. At the start of its turn, the barlgura can gain advantage on all melee weapon attack rolls it makes during that turn, but attack rolls against it have advantage until the start of its next turn.

Running Leap. The barlgura's long jump is up to 40 feet and its high jump is up to 20 feet when it has a running start.

Actions

Multiattack. The barlgura makes three attacks: one with its bite and two with its fists.

Bite. *Melee Weapon Attack:* +7 to hit, reach 5 ft., one target. *Hit:* 11 (2d6 + 4) piercing damage.

Fist. *Melee Weapon Attack:* +7 to hit, reach 5 ft., one target. *Hit:* 9 (1d10 + 4) bludgeoning damage.

CHASME

Large fiend (demon), chaotic evil

Armor Class 15 (natural armor)
Hit Points 84 (13d10 + 13)
Speed 20 ft., fly 60 ft.

STR	DEX	CON	INT	WIS	CHA
15 (+2)	15 (+2)	12 (+1)	11 (+0)	14 (+2)	10 (+0)

Saving Throws Dex +5, Wis +5
Skills Perception +5
Damage Resistances cold, fire, lightning
Damage Immunities poison
Condition Immunities poisoned
Senses blindsight 10 ft., darkvision 120 ft., passive Perception 15
Languages Abyssal, telepathy 120 ft.
Challenge 6 (2,300 XP)

Drone. The chasme produces a horrid droning sound to which demons are immune. Any other creature that starts its turn within 30 feet of the chasme must succeed on a DC 12 Constitution saving throw or fall unconscious for 10 minutes. A creature that can't hear the drone automatically succeeds on the save. The effect on the creature ends if it takes damage or if another creature takes an action to splash it with holy water. If a creature's saving throw is successful or the effect ends for it, it is immune to the drone for the next 24 hours.

Magic Resistance. The chasme has advantage on saving throws against spells and other magical effects.

Spider Climb. The chasme can climb difficult surfaces, including upside down on ceilings, without needing to make an ability check.

ACTIONS

Proboscis. *Melee Weapon Attack:* +5 to hit, reach 5 ft., one creature. *Hit:* 16 (4d6 + 2) piercing damage plus 24 (7d6) necrotic damage, and the target's hit point maximum is reduced by an amount equal to the necrotic damage taken. If this effect reduces a creature's hit point maximum to 0, the creature dies. This reduction to a creature's hit point maximum lasts until the creature finishes a long rest or until it is affected by a spell like *greater restoration*.

DRETCH

Small fiend (demon), chaotic evil

Armor Class 11 (natural armor)
Hit Points 18 (4d6 + 4)
Speed 20 ft.

STR	DEX	CON	INT	WIS	CHA
11 (+0)	11 (+0)	12 (+1)	5 (−3)	8 (−1)	3 (−4)

Damage Resistances cold, fire, lightning
Damage Immunities poison
Condition Immunities poisoned
Senses darkvision 60 ft., passive Perception 9
Languages Abyssal, telepathy 60 ft. (works only with creatures that understand Abyssal)
Challenge 1/4 (50 XP)

ACTIONS

Multiattack. The dretch makes two attacks: one with its bite and one with its claws.

Bite. *Melee Weapon Attack:* +2 to hit, reach 5 ft., one target. *Hit:* 3 (1d6) piercing damage.

Claws. *Melee Weapon Attack:* +2 to hit, reach 5 ft., one target. *Hit:* 5 (2d4) slashing damage.

Fetid Cloud (1/Day). A 10-foot radius of disgusting green gas extends out from the dretch. The gas spreads around corners, and its area is lightly obscured. It lasts for 1 minute or until a strong wind disperses it. Any creature that starts its turn in that area must succeed on a DC 11 Constitution saving throw or be poisoned until the start of its next turn. While poisoned in this way, the target can take either an action or a bonus action on its turn, not both, and can't take reactions.

D

Glabrezu
Large fiend (demon), chaotic evil

Armor Class 17 (natural armor)
Hit Points 157 (15d10 + 75)
Speed 40 ft.

STR	DEX	CON	INT	WIS	CHA
20 (+5)	15 (+2)	21 (+5)	19 (+4)	17 (+3)	16 (+3)

Saving Throws Str +9, Con +9, Wis +7, Cha +7
Damage Resistances cold, fire, lightning; bludgeoning, piercing, and slashing from nonmagical attacks
Damage Immunities poison
Condition Immunities poisoned
Senses truesight 120 ft., passive Perception 13
Languages Abyssal, telepathy 120 ft.
Challenge 9 (5,000 XP)

Innate Spellcasting. The glabrezu's spellcasting ability is Intelligence (spell save DC 16). The glabrezu can innately cast the following spells, requiring no material components:

At will: *darkness, detect magic, dispel magic*
1/day each: *confusion, fly, power word stun*

Magic Resistance. The glabrezu has advantage on saving throws against spells and other magical effects.

Actions

Multiattack. The glabrezu makes four attacks: two with its pincers and two with its fists. Alternatively, it makes two attacks with its pincers and casts one spell.

Pincer. *Melee Weapon Attack:* +9 to hit, reach 10 ft., one target. *Hit:* 16 (2d10 + 5) bludgeoning damage. If the target is a Medium or smaller creature, it is grappled (escape DC 15). The glabrezu has two pincers, each of which can grapple only one target.

Fist. *Melee Weapon Attack:* +9 to hit, reach 5 ft., one target. *Hit:* 7 (2d4 + 2) bludgeoning damage.

Goristro
Huge fiend (demon), chaotic evil

Armor Class 19 (natural armor)
Hit Points 310 (23d12 + 161)
Speed 40 ft.

STR	DEX	CON	INT	WIS	CHA
25 (+7)	11 (+0)	25 (+7)	6 (−2)	13 (+1)	14 (+2)

Saving Throws Str +13, Dex +6, Con +13, Wis +7
Skills Perception +7
Damage Resistances cold, fire, lightning; bludgeoning, piercing, and slashing from nonmagical attacks
Damage Immunities poison
Condition Immunities poisoned
Senses darkvision 120 ft., passive Perception 17
Languages Abyssal
Challenge 17 (18,000 XP)

Charge. If the goristro moves at least 15 feet straight toward a target and then hits it with a gore attack on the same turn, the target takes an extra 38 (7d10) piercing damage. If the target is a creature, it must succeed on a DC 21 Strength saving throw or be pushed up to 20 feet away and knocked prone.

Labyrinthine Recall. The goristro can perfectly recall any path it has traveled.

Magic Resistance. The goristro has advantage on saving throws against spells and other magical effects.

Siege Monster. The goristro deals double damage to objects and structures.

Actions

Multiattack. The goristro makes three attacks: two with its fists and one with its hoof.

Fist. *Melee Weapon Attack:* +13 to hit, reach 10 ft., one target. *Hit:* 20 (3d8 + 7) bludgeoning damage.

Hoof. *Melee Weapon Attack:* +13 to hit, reach 5 ft., one target. *Hit:* 23 (3d10 + 7) bludgeoning damage. If the target is a creature, it must succeed on a DC 21 Strength saving throw or be knocked prone.

Gore. *Melee Weapon Attack:* +13 to hit, reach 10 ft., one target. *Hit:* 45 (7d10 + 7) piercing damage.

> "Have no pity for this damnable wretch. Bloody thing could grow up to be a demon lord one day."
> —Emirikol the Chaotic

Hezrou

Large fiend (demon), chaotic evil

Armor Class 16 (natural armor)
Hit Points 136 (13d10 + 65)
Speed 30 ft.

STR	DEX	CON	INT	WIS	CHA
19 (+4)	17 (+3)	20 (+5)	5 (−3)	12 (+1)	13 (+1)

Saving Throws Str +7, Con +8, Wis +4
Damage Resistances cold, fire, lightning; bludgeoning, piercing, and slashing from nonmagical attacks
Damage Immunities poison
Condition Immunities poisoned
Senses darkvision 120 ft., passive Perception 11
Languages Abyssal, telepathy 120 ft.
Challenge 8 (3,900 XP)

Magic Resistance. The hezrou has advantage on saving throws against spells and other magical effects.

Stench. Any creature that starts its turn within 10 feet of the hezrou must succeed on a DC 14 Constitution saving throw or be poisoned until the start of its next turn. On a successful saving throw, the creature is immune to the hezrou's stench for 24 hours.

Actions

Multiattack. The hezrou makes three attacks: one with its bite and two with its claws.

Bite. *Melee Weapon Attack:* +7 to hit, reach 5 ft., one target. *Hit:* 15 (2d10 + 4) piercing damage.

Claw. *Melee Weapon Attack:* +7 to hit, reach 5 ft., one target. *Hit:* 11 (2d6 + 4) slashing damage.

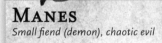

Manes

Small fiend (demon), chaotic evil

Armor Class 9
Hit Points 9 (2d6 + 2)
Speed 20 ft.

STR	DEX	CON	INT	WIS	CHA
10 (+0)	9 (−1)	13 (+1)	3 (−4)	8 (−1)	4 (−3)

Damage Resistances cold, fire, lightning
Damage Immunities poison
Condition Immunities charmed, frightened, poisoned
Senses darkvision 60 ft., passive Perception 9
Languages understands Abyssal but can't speak
Challenge 1/8 (25 XP)

Actions

Claws. *Melee Weapon Attack:* +2 to hit, reach 5 ft., one target. *Hit:* 5 (2d4) slashing damage.

"THE TEMPLE WAS STREWN WITH BODY PARTS. WE CONCLUDED THAT THE CULTISTS HAD SUMMONED A POWERFUL DEMON AND NOT LIVED TO REGRET IT. NOT WANTING TO GET HACKED TO PIECES OURSELVES, WE CUT SHORT OUR EXPEDITION AND RETURNED TO THE VILLAGE OF HOMMLET WITH OUR TAILS BETWEEN OUR LEGS. RUFUS AND BURNE HAD A GOOD LAUGH AT OUR EXPENSE, LET ME TELL YOU."
—NELUMÉ, A YOUNG HALF-ELF WIZARD, CHRONICLING HER ONE AND ONLY VISIT TO THE TEMPLE OF ELEMENTAL EVIL

MARILITH

Large fiend (demon), chaotic evil

Armor Class 18 (natural armor)
Hit Points 189 (18d10 + 90)
Speed 40 ft.

STR	DEX	CON	INT	WIS	CHA
18 (+4)	20 (+5)	20 (+5)	18 (+4)	16 (+3)	20 (+5)

Saving Throws Str +9, Con +10, Wis +8, Cha +10
Damage Resistances cold, fire, lightning; bludgeoning, piercing, and slashing from nonmagical attacks
Damage Immunities poison
Condition Immunities poisoned
Senses truesight 120 ft., passive Perception 13
Languages Abyssal, telepathy 120 ft.
Challenge 16 (15,000 XP)

Magic Resistance. The marilith has advantage on saving throws against spells and other magical effects.

Magic Weapons. The marilith's weapon attacks are magical.

Reactive. The marilith can take one reaction on every turn in a combat.

ACTIONS

Multiattack. The marilith makes seven attacks: six with its longswords and one with its tail.

Longsword. *Melee Weapon Attack:* +9 to hit, reach 5 ft., one target. *Hit:* 13 (2d8 + 4) slashing damage.

Tail. *Melee Weapon Attack:* +9 to hit, reach 10 ft., one creature. *Hit:* 15 (2d10 + 4) bludgeoning damage. If the target is Medium or smaller, it is grappled (escape DC 19). Until this grapple ends, the target is restrained, the marilith can automatically hit the target with its tail, and the marilith can't make tail attacks against other targets.

Teleport. The marilith magically teleports, along with any equipment it is wearing or carrying, up to 120 feet to an unoccupied space it can see.

REACTIONS

Parry. The marilith adds 5 to its AC against one melee attack that would hit it. To do so, the marilith must see the attacker and be wielding a melee weapon.

Nalfeshnee

Large fiend (demon), chaotic evil

Armor Class 18 (natural armor)
Hit Points 184 (16d10 + 96)
Speed 20 ft., fly 30 ft.

STR	DEX	CON	INT	WIS	CHA
21 (+5)	10 (+0)	22 (+6)	19 (+4)	12 (+1)	15 (+2)

Saving Throws Con +11, Int +9, Wis +6, Cha +7
Damage Resistances cold, fire, lightning; bludgeoning, piercing, and slashing from nonmagical attacks
Damage Immunities poison
Condition Immunities poisoned
Senses truesight 120 ft., passive Perception 11
Languages Abyssal, telepathy 120 ft.
Challenge 13 (10,000 XP)

Magic Resistance. The nalfeshnee has advantage on saving throws against spells and other magical effects.

Actions

Multiattack. The nalfeshnee uses Horror Nimbus if it can. It then makes three attacks: one with its bite and two with its claws.

Bite. *Melee Weapon Attack:* +10 to hit, reach 5 ft., one target. *Hit:* 32 (5d10 + 5) piercing damage.

Claw. *Melee Weapon Attack:* +10 to hit, reach 10 ft., one target. *Hit:* 15 (3d6 + 5) slashing damage.

Horror Nimbus (Recharge 5–6). The nalfeshnee magically emits scintillating, multicolored light. Each creature within 15 feet of the nalfeshnee that can see the light must succeed on a DC 15 Wisdom saving throw or be frightened for 1 minute. A creature can repeat the saving throw at the end of each of its turns, ending the effect on itself on a success. If a creature's saving throw is successful or the effect ends for it, the creature is immune to the nalfeshnee's Horror Nimbus for the next 24 hours.

Teleport. The nalfeshnee magically teleports, along with any equipment it is wearing or carrying, up to 120 feet to an unoccupied space it can see.

QUASIT

Tiny fiend (demon, shapechanger), chaotic evil

Armor Class 13
Hit Points 7 (3d4)
Speed 40 ft.

STR	DEX	CON	INT	WIS	CHA
5 (−3)	17 (+3)	10 (+0)	7 (−2)	10 (+0)	10 (+0)

Skills Stealth +5
Damage Resistances cold, fire, lightning; bludgeoning, piercing, and slashing from nonmagical attacks
Damage Immunities poison
Condition Immunities poisoned
Senses darkvision 120 ft., passive Perception 10
Languages Abyssal, Common
Challenge 1 (200 XP)

Shapechanger. The quasit can use its action to polymorph into a beast form that resembles a bat (speed 10 ft. fly 40 ft.), a centipede (40 ft., climb 40 ft.), or a toad (40 ft., swim 40 ft.), or back into its true form. Its statistics are the same in each form, except for the speed changes noted. Any equipment it is wearing or carrying isn't transformed. It reverts to its true form if it dies.

Magic Resistance. The quasit has advantage on saving throws against spells and other magical effects.

ACTIONS

Claws (Bite in Beast Form). Melee Weapon Attack: +4 to hit, reach 5 ft., one target. Hit: 5 (1d4 + 3) piercing damage, and the target must succeed on a DC 10 Constitution saving throw or take 5 (2d4) poison damage and become poisoned for 1 minute. The target can repeat the saving throw at the end of each of its turns, ending the effect on itself on a success.

Scare (1/Day). One creature of the quasit's choice within 20 feet of it must succeed on a DC 10 Wisdom saving throw or be frightened for 1 minute. The target can repeat the saving throw at the end of each of its turns, with disadvantage if the quasit is within line of sight, ending the effect on itself on a success.

Invisibility. The quasit magically turns invisible until it attacks or uses Scare, or until its concentration ends (as if concentrating on a spell). Any equipment the quasit wears or carries is invisible with it.

SHADOW DEMON
Medium fiend (demon), chaotic evil

Armor Class 13
Hit Points 66 (12d8 + 12)
Speed 30 ft., fly 30 ft.

STR	DEX	CON	INT	WIS	CHA
1 (−5)	17 (+3)	12 (+1)	14 (+2)	13 (+1)	14 (+2)

Saving Throws Dex +5, Cha +4
Skills Stealth +7
Damage Vulnerabilities radiant
Damage Resistances acid, fire, necrotic, thunder; bludgeoning, piercing, and slashing from nonmagical attacks
Damage Immunities cold, lightning, poison
Condition Immunities exhaustion, grappled, paralyzed, petrified, poisoned, prone, restrained
Senses darkvision 120 ft., passive Perception 11
Languages Abyssal, telepathy 120 ft.
Challenge 4 (1,100 XP)

Incorporeal Movement. The demon can move through other creatures and objects as if they were difficult terrain. It takes 5 (1d10) force damage if it ends its turn inside an object.

Light Sensitivity. While in bright light, the demon has disadvantage on attack rolls, as well as on Wisdom (Perception) checks that rely on sight.

Shadow Stealth. While in dim light or darkness, the demon can take the Hide action as a bonus action.

ACTIONS

Claws. *Melee Weapon Attack:* +5 to hit, reach 5 ft., one creature. *Hit:* 10 (2d6 + 3) psychic damage or, if the demon had advantage on the attack roll, 17 (4d6 + 3) psychic damage.

VROCK
Large fiend (demon), chaotic evil

Armor Class 15 (natural armor)
Hit Points 104 (11d10 + 44)
Speed 40 ft., fly 60 ft.

STR	DEX	CON	INT	WIS	CHA
17 (+3)	15 (+2)	18 (+4)	8 (−1)	13 (+1)	8 (−1)

Saving Throws Dex +5, Wis +4, Cha +2
Damage Resistances cold, fire, lightning; bludgeoning, piercing, and slashing from nonmagical attacks
Damage Immunities poison
Condition Immunities poisoned
Senses darkvision 120 ft., passive Perception 11
Languages Abyssal, telepathy 120 ft.
Challenge 6 (2,300 XP)

Magic Resistance. The vrock has advantage on saving throws against spells and other magical effects.

ACTIONS

Multiattack. The vrock makes two attacks: one with its beak and one with its talons.

Beak. *Melee Weapon Attack:* +6 to hit, reach 5 ft., one target. *Hit:* 10 (2d6 + 3) piercing damage.

Talons. *Melee Weapon Attack:* +6 to hit, reach 5 ft., one target. *Hit:* 14 (2d10 + 3) slashing damage.

Spores (Recharge 6). A 15-foot-radius cloud of toxic spores extends out from the vrock. The spores spread around corners. Each creature in that area must succeed on a DC 14 Constitution saving throw or become poisoned. While poisoned in this way, a target takes 5 (1d10) poison damage at the start of each of its turns. A target can repeat the saving throw at the end of each of its turns, ending the effect on itself on a success. Emptying a vial of holy water on the target also ends the effect on it.

Stunning Screech (1/Day). The vrock emits a horrific screech. Each creature within 20 feet of it that can hear it and that isn't a demon must succeed on a DC 14 Constitution saving throw or be stunned until the end of the vrock's next turn.

Yochlol
Medium fiend (demon, shapechanger), chaotic evil

Armor Class 15 (natural armor)
Hit Points 136 (16d8 + 64)
Speed 30 ft., climb 30 ft.

STR	DEX	CON	INT	WIS	CHA
15 (+2)	14 (+2)	18 (+4)	13 (+1)	15 (+2)	15 (+2)

Saving Throws Dex +6, Int +5, Wis +6, Cha +6
Skills Deception +10, Insight +6
Damage Resistances cold, fire, lightning; bludgeoning, piercing, and slashing from nonmagical attacks
Damage Immunities poison
Condition Immunities poisoned
Senses darkvision 120 ft., passive Perception 12
Languages Abyssal, Elvish, Undercommon
Challenge 10 (5,900 XP)

Shapechanger. The yochlol can use its action to polymorph into a form that resembles a female drow or giant spider, or back into its true form. Its statistics are the same in each form. Any equipment it is wearing or carrying isn't transformed. It reverts to its true form if it dies.

Magic Resistance. The yochlol has advantage on saving throws against spells and other magical effects.

Spider Climb. The yochlol can climb difficult surfaces, including upside down on ceilings, without needing to make an ability check.

Innate Spellcasting. The yochlol's spellcasting ability is Charisma (spell save DC 14). The yochlol can innately cast the following spells, requiring no material components:

At will: *detect thoughts*, *web*
1/day: *dominate person*

Web Walker. The yochlol ignores movement restrictions caused by webbing.

Actions

Multiattack. The yochlol makes two melee attacks.

Slam (Bite in Spider Form). *Melee Weapon Attack:* +6 to hit, reach 5 ft. (10 ft. in demon form), one target. *Hit:* 5 (1d6 + 2) bludgeoning (piercing in spider form) damage plus 21 (6d6) poison damage.

Mist Form. The yochlol transforms into toxic mist or reverts to its true form. Any equipment it is wearing or carrying is also transformed. It reverts to its true form if it dies.

While in mist form, the yochlol is incapacitated and can't speak. It has a flying speed of 30 feet, can hover, and can pass through any space that isn't airtight. It has advantage on Strength, Dexterity, and Constitution saving throws, and it is immune to nonmagical damage.

While in mist form, the yochlol can enter a creature's space and stop there. Each time that creature starts its turn with the yochlol in its space, the creature must succeed on a DC 14 Constitution saving throw or be poisoned until the start of its next turn. While poisoned in this way, the target is incapacitated.

DEVILS

Devils personify tyranny, with a totalitarian society dedicated to the domination of mortal life. The shadow of the Nine Hells of Baator extends far across the multiverse, and Asmodeus, the dark lord of Nessus, strives to subjugate the cosmos to satisfy his thirst for power. To do so, he must continually expand his infernal armies, sending his servants to the mortal realm to corrupt the souls from which new devils are spawned.

Lords of Tyranny. Devils live to conquer, enslave, and oppress. They take perverse delight in exercising authority over the weak, and any creature that defies the authority of a devil faces swift and cruel punishment. Every interaction is an opportunity for a devil to display its power, and all devils have a keen understanding of how to use and abuse their power.

Devils understand the failings that plague intelligent mortals, and they use that knowledge to lead mortals into temptation and darkness, turning creatures into slaves to their own corruption. Devils on the Material Plane use their influence to manipulate humanoid rulers, whispering evil thoughts, fomenting paranoia, and eventually driving them to tyrannical actions.

Obedience and Ambition. In accordance with their lawful alignment, devils obey even when they envy or dislike their superiors, knowing that their obedience will be rewarded. The hierarchy of the Nine Hells depends on this unswerving loyalty, without which that fiendish plane would become as anarchic as the Abyss.

At the same time, it is in the nature of devils to scheme, creating in some a desire to rule that eclipses their contentment to be ruled. This singular ambition is strongest among the archdevils whom Asmodeus appoints to rule the nine layers of the Nine Hells. These high-ranking fiends are the only devils to ever sample true power, which they crave like the sweetest ambrosia.

Dark Dealers and Soul Mongers. Devils are confined to the Lower Planes, but they can travel beyond those planes by way of portals or powerful summoning magic. They love to strike bargains with mortals seeking to gain some benefit or prize, but a mortal making such a bargain must be wary. Devils are crafty negotiators and positively ruthless at enforcing the terms of an agreement. Moreover, a contract with even the lowliest devil is enforced by Asmodeus's will. Any mortal creature that breaks such a contract instantly forfeits its soul, which is spirited away to the Nine Hells.

To own a creature's soul is to have absolute control over that creature, and most devils accept no other currency in exchange for the fiendish power and boons they can provide. A soul is usually forfeited when a mortal dies naturally, for devils are immortal and can wait years for a contract to play out. If a contract allows a devil to claim a mortal's soul before death, it can instantly return to the Nine Hells with the soul in its possession. Only divine intervention can release a soul after a devil has claimed it.

THE INFERNAL HIERARCHY

The Nine Hells has a rigid hierarchy that defines every aspect of its society. Asmodeus is the supreme ruler of all devils, and the only creature in the Nine Hells with the powers of a lesser god. Worshiped as such in the Material Plane, Asmodeus inspires the evil humanoid cults that take his name. In the Nine Hells, he commands scores of pit fiend generals, which in turn command legions of subordinates.

A supreme tyrant, a brilliant deceiver, and a master of subtlety, Asmodeus protects his throne by keeping his friends close and his enemies closer. He delegates most matters of rulership to the pit fiends and lesser archdevils that make up the infernal bureaucracy of the Nine Hells, even as he knows that those powerful devils conspire to usurp the Throne of Baator from which he rules. Asmodeus appoints archdevils, and he can strip any member of the infernal hierarchy of rank and status as he likes.

If it dies outside the Nine Hells, a devil disappears in a cloud of sulfurous smoke or dissolves into a pool of ichor, instantly returning to its home layer, where it reforms at full strength. Devils that die in the Nine Hells are destroyed forever—a fate that even Asmodeus fears.

Archdevils. The archdevils include all the current and deposed rulers of the Nine Hells (see the Layers and Lords of the Nine Hells table), as well as the dukes and duchesses that make up their courts, attend them as advisers, and hope to supplant them. Every archdevil is a unique being with an appearance that reflects its particular evil nature.

Greater Devils. The greater devils include the pit fiends, erinyes, horned devils, and ice devils that command lesser devils and attend the archdevils.

Lesser Devils. The lesser devils include numerous strains of fiends, including imps, chain devils, spined devils, bearded devils, barbed devils, and bone devils.

Lemures. The lowest form of devil, lemures are the twisted and tormented souls of evil and corrupted mortals. A lemure killed in the Nine Hells is only permanently destroyed if it is killed with a blessed weapon or if its shapeless corpse is splashed with holy water before it can return to life.

Promotion and Demotion. When the soul of an evil mortal sinks into the Nine Hells, it takes on the physical form of a wretched lemure. Archdevils and greater devils have the power to promote lemures to lesser devils. Archdevils can promote lesser devils to greater devils, and Asmodeus alone can promote a greater devil to archdevil status. This diabolic promotion invokes a brief, painful transformation, with the devil's memories passing intact from one form to the next.

Low-level promotions are typically based on need, such as when a pit fiend transforms lemures into imps to gain invisible spies under its command. High-level promotions are almost always based on merit, such as when a bone devil that distinguishes itself in battle is transformed into a horned devil by the archdevil it serves. A devil is seldom promoted more than one step at a time in the hierarchy of infernal forms.

INFERNAL HIERARCHY

1. lemure

Lesser devils
2. imp
3. spined devil
4. bearded devil
5. barbed devil
6. chain devil
7. bone devil

Greater devils
8. horned devil
9. erinyes
10. ice devil
11. pit fiend

Archdevils
12. duke or duchess
13. archduke or archduchess

Demotion is the customary punishment for failure or disobedience among the devils. Archdevils or greater devils can demote a lesser devil to a lemure, which loses all memory of its prior existence. An archdevil can demote a greater devil to lesser devil status, but the demoted devil retains its memories—and might seek vengeance if the severity of the demotion is excessive.

No devil can promote or demote another devil that has not sworn fealty to it, preventing rival archdevils from demoting each other's most powerful servants. Since all devils swear fealty to Asmodeus, he can freely demote any other devil, transforming it into whatever infernal form he desires.

THE NINE HELLS

The Nine Hells are a single plane comprising nine separate layers (see the Layers and Lords of the Nine Hells table). The first eight layers are each ruled by archdevils that answer to the greatest archdevil of all: Asmodeus, the Archduke of Nessus, the ninth layer. To reach the deepest layer of the Nine Hells, one must descend through all eight of the layers above it, in order. The most expeditious means of doing so is the River Styx, which plunges ever deeper as it flows from one layer to the next. Only the most courageous adventurers can withstand the torment and horror of that journey.

DEVIL TRUE NAMES AND TALISMANS

Though devils all have common names, every devil above a lemure in station also has a true name that it keeps secret. A devil can be forced to disclose its true name if charmed, and ancient scrolls and tomes are said to exist that list the true names of certain devils.

A mortal who learns a devil's true name can use powerful summoning magic to call the devil from the Nine Hells and bind it into service. Binding can also be accomplished with the help of a devil talisman. Each of these ancient relics is inscribed with the true name of a devil it controls, and was bathed in the blood of a worthy sacrifice—typically someone the creator loved—when crafted.

However it is summoned, a devil brought to the Material Plane typically resents being pressed into service. However, the devil seizes every opportunity to corrupt its summoner so that the summoner's soul ends up in the Nine Hells. Only imps are truly content to be summoned, and they easily commit to serving a summoner as a familiar, but they still do their utmost to corrupt those who summon them.

Some devils can have an action option that allows them to summon other devils.

Summon Devil (1/Day). The devil chooses what to summon and attempts a magical summoning.

- A **barbed devil** has a 30 percent chance of summoning one barbed devil.
- A **bearded devil** has a 30 percent chance of summoning one bearded devil.
- A **bone devil** has a 40 percent chance of summoning 2d6 spined devils or one bone devil.
- An **erinyes** has a 50 percent chance of summoning 3d6 spined devils, 1d6 bearded devils, or one erinyes.
- A **horned devil** has a 30 percent chance of summoning one horned devil.
- An **ice devil** has a 60 percent chance of summoning one ice devil.
- A **pit fiend** summons 2d4 bearded devils, 1d4 barbed devils, or one erinyes with no chance of failure.

A summoned devil appears in an unoccupied space within 60 feet of its summoner, acts as an ally of its summoner, and can't summon other devils. It remains for 1 minute, until it or its summoner dies, or until its summoner dismisses it as an action.

BARBED DEVIL (HAMATULA)

Creatures of unbridled greed and desire, barbed devils act as guards to the more powerful denizens of the Nine Hells and their vaults. Resembling a tall humanoid covered in sharp barbs, spines, and hooks, a barbed devil has gleaming eyes that are ever watchful for objects and creatures it might claim for itself. These fiends welcome any chance to fight when victory promises reward.

Barbed devils are known for an alertness that makes them difficult to surprise, and they attend to their duties without boredom or distraction. They use their sharp claws as weapons or hurl balls of flame at foes that try to flee them.

BEARDED DEVIL (BARBAZU)

Bearded devils serve archdevils as shock troops, fighting shoulder-to-shoulder and reveling in the glory of battle. They respond with violence to any slight, real or imagined, gorging themselves on violence as their infernal saw-toothed glaives carve a path through their foes.

A bearded devil is humanoid in form, with pointed ears, scaly skin, a long tail, and claws that clearly show its fiendish nature. These devils take their names from the snakelike growths that adorn their chins, which they use to lash and poison enemies, weakening them with their virulent venom.

BONE DEVIL (OSYLUTH)

Driven by hate, lust, and envy, bone devils act as the cruel taskmasters of the Nine Hells. They set weaker devils to work, taking special delight in seeing fiends that defy them demoted. At the same time, they long for promotion and are bitterly envious of their superiors, attempting to curry favor though it irks them to do so.

A bone devil appears as a humanoid husk, with dried skin stretched tight across its skeletal frame. It bears a fearsome skull-like head and the tail of a scorpion, and a foul odor of decay hangs in the air around it. Though they are devastating in combat with their claws, bone devils also wield hooked polearms made of bone, which they use to subdue enemies before striking with their venomous tails.

CHAIN DEVIL (KYTON)

This ominous fiend wears chains like a shroud. Driving lesser creatures before it with its fearsome gaze, a chain devil animates the chains that cover its body as well as inanimate chains nearby, which sprout hooks, blades, and spikes to eviscerate enemies.

Chain devils act as sadistic jailers and torturers in the infernal realms, relishing pain and living to inflict it on others. They are called on to torment mortal souls trapped in the Nine Hells, inflicting their sadistic fury on the horrid lemures in which those souls manifest.

ERINYES

The most beautiful and striking of all lesser and greater devils, the erinyes are fierce and disciplined warriors. Sweeping down from the skies, they bring swift death to creatures that have wronged their masters or defied the edicts of Asmodeus. The erinyes appear as male or female humanoids with statuesque builds and large feathery wings. Most wear stylized armor and horned helms, and carry exquisite swords and bows. A few also use *ropes of entanglement* to ensnare powerful foes.

LAYERS AND LORDS OF THE NINE HELLS

Layer	Layer Name	Archduke or Archduchess	Previous Rulers	Primary Inhabitants
1	Avernus	Zariel	Bel, Tiamat	Erinyes, imps, spined devils
2	Dis	Dispater	—	Bearded devils, erinyes, imps, spined devils
3	Minauros	Mammon	—	Bearded devils, chain devils, imps, spined devils
4	Phlegethos	Belial and Fierna	—	Barbed devils, bone devils, imps, spined devils
5	Stygia	Levistus	Geryon	Bone devils, erinyes, ice devils, imps
6	Malbolge	Glasya	Malagard, Moloch	Barbed devils, bone devils, horned devils, imps
7	Maladomini	Baalzebul	—	Barbed devils, bone devils, horned devils, imps
8	Cania	Mephistopheles	—	Horned devils, ice devils, imps, pit fiends
9	Nessus	Asmodeus	—	All devils

Legends tell that the first erinyes were angels that fell from the Upper Planes because of temptation or misdeed. Erinyes are always willing to take advantage of being mistaken for celestials in their missions of conquest and corruption.

HORNED DEVIL (MALEBRANCHE)

Horned devils are lazy to the point of belligerence and reluctant to put themselves in harm's way. Moreover, they hate and fear any creature stronger than themselves. When they are sufficiently provoked or antagonized, the fury of these fiends can be terrifying.

A malebranche stands as tall as an ogre and is sheathed in scales as tough as iron. The flying infantry of the hellish legions, horned devils follow orders to the letter. Their huge wings and sweeping horns create an intimidating presence as they drop from the sky and strike with deadly forks and lashing tails.

ICE DEVIL (GELUGON)

Found most commonly on the cold layers of Stygia and Cania, ice devils serve as commanders of the infernal armies of the Nine Hells, tormenting lesser devils as an outlet for their anger and resentment. Coveting the power of their pit fiend superiors, ice devils work ceaselessly toward promotion, slaughtering the enemies of the Nine Hells and claiming as many souls as they can for their archdevil masters.

Resembling a giant bipedal insect, an ice devil has clawed hands and feet, powerful mandibles, and a long tail covered in razor-sharp spikes. Some carry barbed spears whose icy touch can render a foe all but helpless in combat.

IMP

Imps are found throughout the Lower Planes, either running errands for their infernal masters, spying on rivals, or misleading and waylaying mortals. An imp will proudly serve an evil master of any kind, but it can't be relied on to carry out tasks with any speed or efficiency.

An imp can assume animal form at will, but in its natural state it resembles a diminutive red-skinned humanoid with a barbed tail, small horns, and leathery wings. It strikes while invisible, attacking with its poison stinger.

LEMURE

A lemure arises when a mortal soul is twisted by evil and banished to the Nine Hells for eternity. The lowest type of devil, lemures are repugnant, shapeless creatures doomed to suffer torment until they are promoted to a higher form of devil, most commonly an imp.

A lemure resembles a molten mass of flesh with a vaguely humanoid head and torso. A permanent expression of anguish twists across its face, its feeble mouth babbling even though it can't speak.

VARIANT: IMP FAMILIAR

Imps can be found in the service to mortal spellcasters, acting as advisors, spies, and familiars. An imp urges its master to acts of evil, knowing the mortal's soul is a prize the imp might ultimately claim. Imps display an unusual loyalty to their masters, and an imp can be quite dangerous if its master is threatened. Some such imps have the following trait.

Familiar. The imp can enter into a contract to serve another creature as a familiar, forming a telepathic bond with its willing master. While the two are bonded, the master can sense what the imp senses as long as they are within 1 mile of each other. While the imp is within 10 feet of its master, the master shares the imp's Magic Resistance trait. If its master violates the terms of the contract, the imp can end its service as a familiar, ending the telepathic bond.

PIT FIEND

The undisputed lords of most other devils, pit fiends attend the archdukes and archduchesses of the Nine Hells and carry out their wishes. These mighty devils are the generals of the Nine Hells, leading its infernal legions into battle.

With an inflated sense of superiority and entitlement, pit fiends form a grotesque aristocracy in the infernal realm. These domineering and manipulative tyrants conspire to eliminate anything that stands between them and their desires, even as they negotiate the convoluted and dangerous politics of the Nine Hells.

A pit fiend is a hulking monster with a whip-like tail and enormous wings that it wraps around itself like a cloak. Armored scales cover its body, and its fanged maw drips a venom that can lay the mightiest mortal creatures low. Fearless in battle, a pit fiend takes on the most powerful foes in single combat, demonstrating its supremacy and an arrogance that prevents it from acknowledging any chance of defeat.

SPINED DEVIL (SPINAGON)

Smaller than most other devils, spinagons act as messengers and spies for greater devils and archdevils. They are the eyes and ears of the Nine Hells, and even fiends that despise a spined devil's weakness treat it with a modicum of respect.

A spined devil's body and tail bristle with spines, and it can fling its tail spines as ranged weapons. The spines burst into flame on impact.

When not delivering messages or gathering intelligence, spined devils serve in the infernal legions as flying artillery, making up for their relative weakness by mobbing together to overwhelm their foes. Though they crave promotion and power, spined devils are craven by nature, and they will quickly scatter if a fight goes against them.

BARBED DEVIL

Medium fiend (devil), lawful evil

Armor Class 15 (natural armor)
Hit Points 110 (13d8 + 52)
Speed 30 ft.

STR	DEX	CON	INT	WIS	CHA
16 (+3)	17 (+3)	18 (+4)	12 (+1)	14 (+2)	14 (+2)

Saving Throws Str +6, Con +7, Wis +5, Cha +5
Skills Deception +5, Insight +5, Perception +8
Damage Resistances cold; bludgeoning, piercing, and slashing from nonmagical attacks not made with silvered weapons
Damage Immunities fire, poison
Condition Immunities poisoned
Senses darkvision 120 ft., passive Perception 18
Languages Infernal, telepathy 120 ft.
Challenge 5 (1,800 XP)

Barbed Hide. At the start of each of its turns, the barbed devil deals 5 (1d10) piercing damage to any creature grappling it.

Devil's Sight. Magical darkness doesn't impede the devil's darkvision.

Magic Resistance. The devil has advantage on saving throws against spells and other magical effects.

ACTIONS

Multiattack. The devil makes three melee attacks: one with its tail and two with its claws. Alternatively, it can use Hurl Flame twice.

Claw. *Melee Weapon Attack:* +6 to hit, reach 5 ft., one target. *Hit:* 6 (1d6 + 3) piercing damage.

Tail. *Melee Weapon Attack:* +6 to hit, reach 5 ft., one target. *Hit:* 10 (2d6 + 3) piercing damage.

Hurl Flame. *Ranged Spell Attack:* +5 to hit, range 150 ft., one target. *Hit:* 10 (3d6) fire damage. If the target is a flammable object that isn't being worn or carried, it also catches fire.

BEARDED DEVIL

Medium fiend (devil), lawful evil

Armor Class 13 (natural armor)
Hit Points 52 (8d8 + 16)
Speed 30 ft.

STR	DEX	CON	INT	WIS	CHA
16 (+3)	15 (+2)	15 (+2)	9 (−1)	11 (+0)	11 (+0)

Saving Throws Str +5, Con +4, Wis +2
Damage Resistances cold; bludgeoning, piercing, and slashing from nonmagical attacks not made with silvered weapons
Damage Immunities fire, poison
Condition Immunities poisoned
Senses darkvision 120 ft., passive Perception 10
Languages Infernal, telepathy 120 ft.
Challenge 3 (700 XP)

Devil's Sight. Magical darkness doesn't impede the devil's darkvision.

Magic Resistance. The devil has advantage on saving throws against spells and other magical effects.

Steadfast. The devil can't be frightened while it can see an allied creature within 30 feet of it.

ACTIONS

Multiattack. The devil makes two attacks: one with its beard and one with its glaive.

Beard. *Melee Weapon Attack:* +5 to hit, reach 5 ft., one creature. *Hit:* 6 (1d8 + 2) piercing damage, and the target must succeed on a DC 12 Constitution saving throw or be poisoned for 1 minute. While poisoned in this way, the target can't regain hit points. The target can repeat the saving throw at the end of each of its turns, ending the effect on itself on a success.

Glaive. *Melee Weapon Attack:* +5 to hit, reach 10 ft., one target. *Hit:* 8 (1d10 + 3) slashing damage. If the target is a creature other than an undead or a construct, it must succeed on a DC 12 Constitution saving throw or lose 5 (1d10) hit points at the start of each of its turns due to an infernal wound. Each time the devil hits the wounded target with this attack, the damage dealt by the wound increases by 5 (1d10). Any creature can take an action to stanch the wound with a successful DC 12 Wisdom (Medicine) check. The wound also closes if the target receives magical healing.

VARIANT: BONE DEVIL POLEARM

Some bone devils have the following action options.

Multiattack. The devil makes two attacks: one with its hooked polearm and one with its sting.

Hooked Polearm. *Melee Weapon Attack:* +8 to hit, reach 10 ft., one target. *Hit:* 17 (2d12 + 4) piercing damage. If the target is a Huge or smaller creature, it is grappled (escape DC 14). Until this grapple ends, the devil can't use its polearm on another target.

BONE DEVIL

Large fiend (devil), lawful evil

Armor Class 19 (natural armor)
Hit Points 142 (15d10 + 60)
Speed 40 ft., fly 40 ft.

STR	DEX	CON	INT	WIS	CHA
18 (+4)	16 (+3)	18 (+4)	13 (+1)	14 (+2)	16 (+3)

Saving Throws Int +5, Wis +6, Cha +7
Skills Deception +7, Insight +6
Damage Resistances cold; bludgeoning, piercing, and slashing from nonmagical attacks not made with silvered weapons
Damage Immunities fire, poison
Condition Immunities poisoned
Senses darkvision 120 ft., passive Perception 12
Languages Infernal, telepathy 120 ft.
Challenge 9 (5,000 XP)

Devil's Sight. Magical darkness doesn't impede the devil's darkvision.

Magic Resistance. The devil has advantage on saving throws against spells and other magical effects.

ACTIONS

Multiattack. The devil makes three attacks: two with its claws and one with its sting.

Claw. *Melee Weapon Attack:* +8 to hit, reach 10 ft., one target. *Hit:* 8 (1d8 + 4) slashing damage.

Sting. *Melee Weapon Attack:* +8 to hit, reach 10 ft., one target. *Hit:* 13 (2d8 + 4) piercing damage plus 17 (5d6) poison damage, and the target must succeed on a DC 14 Constitution saving throw or become poisoned for 1 minute. The target can repeat the saving throw at the end of each of its turns, ending the effect on itself on a success.

D

CHAIN DEVIL
Medium fiend (devil), lawful evil

Armor Class 16 (natural armor)
Hit Points 85 (10d8 + 40)
Speed 30 ft.

STR	DEX	CON	INT	WIS	CHA
18 (+4)	15 (+2)	18 (+4)	11 (+0)	12 (+1)	14 (+2)

Saving Throws Con +7, Wis +4, Cha +5
Damage Resistances cold; bludgeoning, piercing, and slashing from nonmagical attacks not made with silvered weapons
Damage Immunities fire, poison
Condition Immunities poisoned
Senses darkvision 120 ft., passive Perception 11
Languages Infernal, telepathy 120 ft.
Challenge 8 (3,900 XP)

Devil's Sight. Magical darkness doesn't impede the devil's darkvision.

Magic Resistance. The devil has advantage on saving throws against spells and other magical effects.

ACTIONS

Multiattack. The devil makes two attacks with its chains.

Chain. *Melee Weapon Attack:* +8 to hit, reach 10 ft., one target. *Hit:* 11 (2d6 + 4) slashing damage. The target is grappled (escape DC 14) if the devil isn't already grappling a creature. Until this grapple ends, the target is restrained and takes 7 (2d6) piercing damage at the start of each of its turns.

Animate Chains (Recharges after a Short or Long Rest). Up to four chains the devil can see within 60 feet of it magically sprout razor-edged barbs and animate under the devil's control, provided that the chains aren't being worn or carried.

Each animated chain is an object with AC 20, 20 hit points, resistance to piercing damage, and immunity to psychic and thunder damage. When the devil uses Multiattack on its turn, it can use each animated chain to make one additional chain attack. An animated chain can grapple one creature of its own but can't make attacks while grappling. An animated chain reverts to its inanimate state if reduced to 0 hit points or if the devil is incapacitated or dies.

REACTIONS

Unnerving Mask. When a creature the devil can see starts its turn within 30 feet of the devil, the devil can create the illusion that it looks like one of the creature's departed loved ones or bitter enemies. If the creature can see the devil, it must succeed on a DC 14 Wisdom saving throw or be frightened until the end of its turn.

> "They live by the sword and kill by the sword. Their beauty is nothing compared to their wrath."
> —FROM THE BOOK OF VILE DARKNESS

VARIANT: ROPE OF ENTANGLEMENT

Some erinyes carry a *rope of entanglement* (detailed in the *Dungeon Master's Guide*). When such an erinyes uses its Multiattack, the erinyes can use the rope in place of two of the attacks.

ERINYES

Medium fiend (devil), lawful evil

Armor Class 18 (plate)
Hit Points 153 (18d8 + 72)
Speed 30 ft., fly 60 ft.

STR	DEX	CON	INT	WIS	CHA
18 (+4)	16 (+3)	18 (+4)	14 (+2)	14 (+2)	18 (+4)

Saving Throws Dex +7, Con +8, Wis +6, Cha +8
Damage Resistances cold; bludgeoning, piercing, and slashing from nonmagical attacks not made with silvered weapons
Damage Immunities fire, poison
Condition Immunities poisoned
Senses truesight 120 ft., passive Perception 12
Languages Infernal, telepathy 120 ft.
Challenge 12 (8,400 XP)

Hellish Weapons. The erinyes's weapon attacks are magical and deal an extra 13 (3d8) poison damage on a hit (included in the attacks).

Magic Resistance. The erinyes has advantage on saving throws against spells and other magical effects.

ACTIONS

Multiattack. The erinyes makes three attacks.

Longsword. *Melee Weapon Attack:* +8 to hit, reach 5 ft., one target. *Hit:* 8 (1d8 + 4) slashing damage, or 9 (1d10 + 4) slashing damage if used with two hands, plus 13 (3d8) poison damage.

Longbow. *Ranged Weapon Attack:* +7 to hit, range 150/600 ft., one target. *Hit:* 7 (1d8 + 3) piercing damage plus 13 (3d8) poison damage, and the target must succeed on a DC 14 Constitution saving throw or be poisoned. The poison lasts until it is removed by the *lesser restoration* spell or similar magic.

REACTIONS

Parry. The erinyes adds 4 to its AC against one melee attack that would hit it. To do so, the erinyes must see the attacker and be wielding a melee weapon.

HORNED DEVIL
Large fiend (devil), lawful evil

Armor Class 18 (natural armor)
Hit Points 178 (17d10 + 85)
Speed 20 ft., fly 60 ft.

STR	DEX	CON	INT	WIS	CHA
22 (+6)	17 (+3)	21 (+5)	12 (+1)	16 (+3)	17 (+3)

Saving Throws Str +10, Dex +7, Wis +7, Cha +7
Damage Resistances cold; bludgeoning, piercing, and slashing from nonmagical attacks not made with silvered weapons
Damage Immunities fire, poison
Condition Immunities poisoned
Senses darkvision 120 ft., passive Perception 13
Languages Infernal, telepathy 120 ft.
Challenge 11 (7,200 XP)

Devil's Sight. Magical darkness doesn't impede the devil's darkvision.

Magic Resistance. The devil has advantage on saving throws against spells and other magical effects.

ACTIONS

Multiattack. The devil makes three melee attacks: two with its fork and one with its tail. It can use Hurl Flame in place of any melee attack.

Fork. *Melee Weapon Attack:* +10 to hit, reach 10 ft., one target. *Hit:* 15 (2d8 + 6) piercing damage.

Tail. *Melee Weapon Attack:* +10 to hit, reach 10 ft., one target. *Hit:* 10 (1d8 + 6) piercing damage. If the target is a creature other than an undead or a construct, it must succeed on a DC 17 Constitution saving throw or lose 10 (3d6) hit points at the start of each of its turns due to an infernal wound. Each time the devil hits the wounded target with this attack, the damage dealt by the wound increases by 10 (3d6). Any creature can take an action to stanch the wound with a successful DC 12 Wisdom (Medicine) check. The wound also closes if the target receives magical healing.

Hurl Flame. *Ranged Spell Attack:* +7 to hit, range 150 ft., one target. *Hit:* 14 (4d6) fire damage. If the target is a flammable object that isn't being worn or carried, it also catches fire.

VARIANT: ICE DEVIL SPEAR

Some ice devils have the following action options.

Multiattack. The devil makes two attacks: one with its spear and one with its tail.

Ice Spear. *Melee Weapon Attack:* +10 to hit, reach 10 ft., one target. *Hit:* 14 (2d8 + 5) piercing damage plus 10 (3d6) cold damage. If the target is a creature, it must succeed on a DC 15 Constitution saving throw, or for 1 minute, its speed is reduced by 10 feet; it can take either an action or a bonus action on each of its turns, not both; and it can't take reactions. The target can repeat the saving throw at the end of each of its turns, ending the effect on itself on a success.

ICE DEVIL

Large fiend (devil), lawful evil

Armor Class 18 (natural armor)
Hit Points 180 (19d10 + 76)
Speed 40 ft.

STR	DEX	CON	INT	WIS	CHA
21 (+5)	14 (+2)	18 (+4)	18 (+4)	15 (+2)	18 (+4)

Saving Throws Dex +7, Con +9, Wis +7, Cha +9
Damage Resistances bludgeoning, piercing, and slashing from nonmagical attacks not made with silvered weapons
Damage Immunities cold, fire, poison
Condition Immunities poisoned
Senses blindsight 60 ft., darkvision 120 ft., passive Perception 12
Languages Infernal, telepathy 120 ft.
Challenge 14 (11,500 XP)

Devil's Sight. Magical darkness doesn't impede the devil's darkvision.

Magic Resistance. The devil has advantage on saving throws against spells and other magical effects.

ACTIONS

Multiattack. The devil makes three attacks: one with its bite, one with its claws, and one with its tail.

Bite. *Melee Weapon Attack:* +10 to hit, reach 5 ft., one target. *Hit:* 12 (2d6 + 5) piercing damage plus 10 (3d6) cold damage.

Claws. *Melee Weapon Attack:* +10 to hit, reach 5 ft., one target. *Hit:* 10 (2d4 + 5) slashing damage plus 10 (3d6) cold damage.

Tail. *Melee Weapon Attack:* +10 to hit, reach 10 ft., one target. *Hit:* 12 (2d6 + 5) bludgeoning damage plus 10 (3d6) cold damage.

Wall of Ice (Recharge 6). The devil magically forms an opaque wall of ice on a solid surface it can see within 60 feet of it. The wall is 1 foot thick and up to 30 feet long and 10 feet high, or it's a hemispherical dome up to 20 feet in diameter.

When the wall appears, each creature in its space is pushed out of it by the shortest route. The creature chooses which side of the wall to end up on, unless the creature is incapacitated. The creature then makes a DC 17 Dexterity saving throw, taking 35 (10d6) cold damage on a failed save, or half as much damage on a successful one.

The wall lasts for 1 minute or until the devil is incapacitated or dies. The wall can be damaged and breached; each 10-foot section has AC 5, 30 hit points, vulnerability to fire damage, and immunity to acid, cold, necrotic, poison, and psychic damage. If a section is destroyed, it leaves behind a sheet of frigid air in the space the wall occupied. Whenever a creature finishes moving through the frigid air on a turn, willingly or otherwise, the creature must make a DC 17 Constitution saving throw, taking 17 (5d6) cold damage on a failed save, or half as much damage on a successful one. The frigid air dissipates when the rest of the wall vanishes.

IMP

Tiny fiend (devil, shapechanger), lawful evil

Armor Class 13
Hit Points 10 (3d4 + 3)
Speed 20 ft., fly 40 ft.

STR	DEX	CON	INT	WIS	CHA
6 (−2)	17 (+3)	13 (+1)	11 (+0)	12 (+1)	14 (+2)

Skills Deception +4, Insight +3, Persuasion +4, Stealth +5
Damage Resistances cold; bludgeoning, piercing, and slashing from nonmagical attacks not made with silvered weapons
Damage Immunities fire, poison
Condition Immunities poisoned
Senses darkvision 120 ft., passive Perception 11
Languages Infernal, Common
Challenge 1 (200 XP)

Shapechanger. The imp can use its action to polymorph into a beast form that resembles a rat (speed 20 ft.), a raven (20 ft., fly 60 ft.), or a spider (20 ft., climb 20 ft.), or back into its true form. Its statistics are the same in each form, except for the speed changes noted. Any equipment it is wearing or carrying isn't transformed. It reverts to its true form if it dies.

Devil's Sight. Magical darkness doesn't impede the imp's darkvision.

Magic Resistance. The imp has advantage on saving throws against spells and other magical effects.

ACTIONS

Sting (Bite in Beast Form). *Melee Weapon Attack:* +5 to hit, reach 5 ft., one target. *Hit:* 5 (1d4 + 3) piercing damage, and the target must make a DC 11 Constitution saving throw, taking 10 (3d6) poison damage on a failed save, or half as much damage on a successful one.

Invisibility. The imp magically turns invisible until it attacks or until its concentration ends (as if concentrating on a spell). Any equipment the imp wears or carries is invisible with it.

LEMURE

Medium fiend (devil), lawful evil

Armor Class 7
Hit Points 13 (3d8)
Speed 15 ft.

STR	DEX	CON	INT	WIS	CHA
10 (+0)	5 (−3)	11 (+0)	1 (−5)	11 (+0)	3 (−4)

Damage Resistances cold
Damage Immunities fire, poison
Condition Immunities charmed, frightened, poisoned
Senses darkvision 120 ft., passive Perception 10
Languages understands Infernal but can't speak
Challenge 0 (10 XP)

Devil's Sight. Magical darkness doesn't impede the lemure's darkvision.

Hellish Rejuvenation. A lemure that dies in the Nine Hells comes back to life with all its hit points in 1d10 days unless it is killed by a good-aligned creature with a *bless* spell cast on that creature or its remains are sprinkled with holy water.

ACTIONS

Fist. *Melee Weapon Attack:* +3 to hit, reach 5 ft., one target. *Hit:* 2 (1d4) bludgeoning damage.

"Your war-torn kingdom is rife with corruption, its people dying from starvation and strife. They cry out for new leadership—someone with the charisma and the courage to put an end to the turmoil and suffering. You could be that someone!"
—Herobaal the Pit Fiend

PIT FIEND

Large fiend (devil), lawful evil

Armor Class 19 (natural armor)
Hit Points 300 (24d10 + 168)
Speed 30 ft., fly 60 ft.

STR	DEX	CON	INT	WIS	CHA
26 (+8)	14 (+2)	24 (+7)	22 (+6)	18 (+4)	24 (+7)

Saving Throws Dex +8, Con +13, Wis +10
Damage Resistances cold; bludgeoning, piercing, and slashing from nonmagical attacks not made with silvered weapons
Damage Immunities fire, poison
Condition Immunities poisoned
Senses truesight 120 ft., passive Perception 14
Languages Infernal, telepathy 120 ft.
Challenge 20 (25,000 XP)

Fear Aura. Any creature hostile to the pit fiend that starts its turn within 20 feet of the pit fiend must make a DC 21 Wisdom saving throw, unless the pit fiend is incapacitated. On a failed save, the creature is frightened until the start of its next turn. If a creature's saving throw is successful, the creature is immune to the pit fiend's Fear Aura for the next 24 hours.

Magic Resistance. The pit fiend has advantage on saving throws against spells and other magical effects.

Magic Weapons. The pit fiend's weapon attacks are magical.

Innate Spellcasting. The pit fiend's spellcasting ability is Charisma (spell save DC 21). The pit fiend can innately cast the following spells, requiring no material components:

At will: *detect magic, fireball*
3/day each: *hold monster, wall of fire*

ACTIONS

Multiattack. The pit fiend makes four attacks: one with its bite, one with its claw, one with its mace, and one with its tail.

Bite. *Melee Weapon Attack:* +14 to hit, reach 5 ft., one target. *Hit:* 22 (4d6 + 8) piercing damage. The target must succeed on a DC 21 Constitution saving throw or become poisoned. While poisoned in this way, the target can't regain hit points, and it takes 21 (6d6) poison damage at the start of each of its turns. The poisoned target can repeat the saving throw at the end of each of its turns, ending the effect on itself on a success.

Claw. *Melee Weapon Attack:* +14 to hit, reach 10 ft., one target. *Hit:* 17 (2d8 + 8) slashing damage.

Mace. *Melee Weapon Attack:* +14 to hit, reach 10 ft., one target. *Hit:* 15 (2d6 + 8) bludgeoning damage plus 21 (6d6) fire damage.

Tail. *Melee Weapon Attack:* +14 to hit, reach 10 ft., one target. *Hit:* 24 (3d10 + 8) bludgeoning damage.

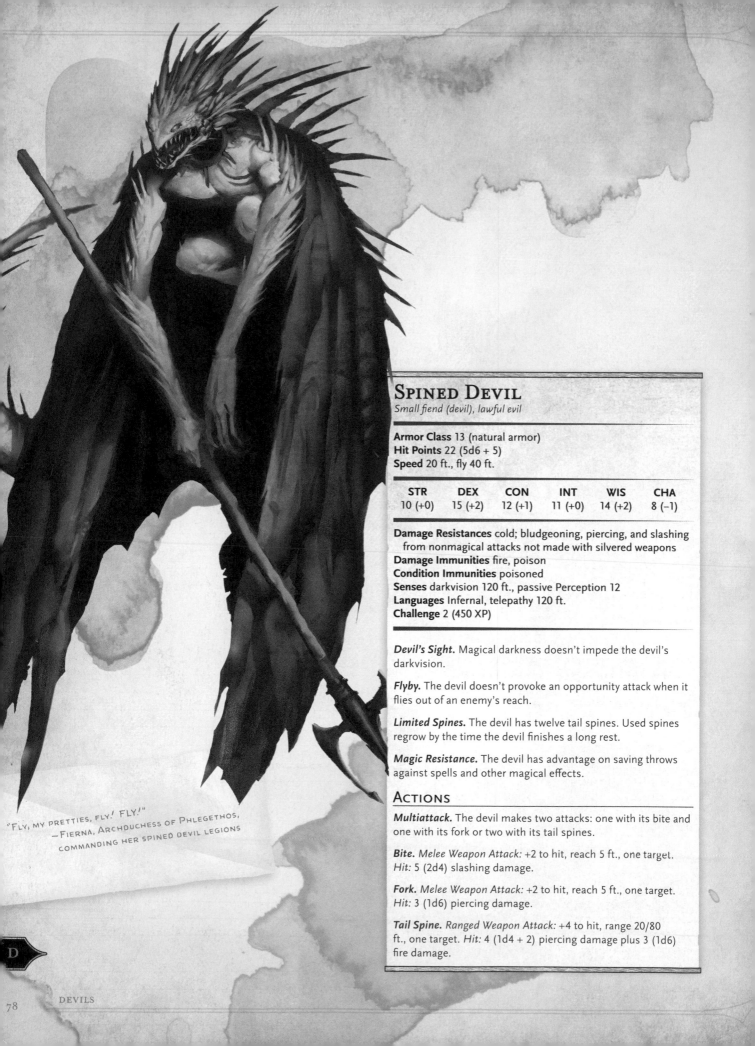

"FLY, MY PRETTIES, FLY! FLY!"
—FIERNA, ARCHDUCHESS OF PHLEGETHOS,
COMMANDING HER SPINED DEVIL LEGIONS

SPINED DEVIL

Small fiend (devil), lawful evil

Armor Class 13 (natural armor)
Hit Points 22 (5d6 + 5)
Speed 20 ft., fly 40 ft.

STR	DEX	CON	INT	WIS	CHA
10 (+0)	15 (+2)	12 (+1)	11 (+0)	14 (+2)	8 (−1)

Damage Resistances cold; bludgeoning, piercing, and slashing
  from nonmagical attacks not made with silvered weapons
Damage Immunities fire, poison
Condition Immunities poisoned
Senses darkvision 120 ft., passive Perception 12
Languages Infernal, telepathy 120 ft.
Challenge 2 (450 XP)

Devil's Sight. Magical darkness doesn't impede the devil's
darkvision.

Flyby. The devil doesn't provoke an opportunity attack when it
flies out of an enemy's reach.

Limited Spines. The devil has twelve tail spines. Used spines
regrow by the time the devil finishes a long rest.

Magic Resistance. The devil has advantage on saving throws
against spells and other magical effects.

ACTIONS

Multiattack. The devil makes two attacks: one with its bite and
one with its fork or two with its tail spines.

Bite. *Melee Weapon Attack:* +2 to hit, reach 5 ft., one target.
Hit: 5 (2d4) slashing damage.

Fork. *Melee Weapon Attack:* +2 to hit, reach 5 ft., one target.
Hit: 3 (1d6) piercing damage.

Tail Spine. *Ranged Weapon Attack:* +4 to hit, range 20/80
ft., one target. *Hit:* 4 (1d4 + 2) piercing damage plus 3 (1d6)
fire damage.

Dinosaurs

Dinosaurs, or behemoths, are among the oldest reptiles in the world. Predatory dinosaurs are savage, territorial hunters. Herbivorous dinosaurs are less aggressive, but they might attack to defend their young, or if startled or harassed.

Dinosaurs come in many sizes and shapes. Larger varieties often have drab coloration, while smaller dinosaurs have colorful markings akin to birds. Dinosaurs roam rugged and isolated areas that humanoids seldom visit, including remote mountain valleys, inaccessible plateaus, tropical islands, and deep fens.

Allosaurus

The allosaurus is a predator possessing great size, strength, and speed. It can run down almost any prey over open ground, pouncing to pull creatures down with its wicked claws.

Ankylosaurus

Thick armor plating covers the body of the plant-eating ankylosaurus, which defends itself against predators with a knobbed tail that delivers a devastating strike. Some varieties of ankylosaurus have spiked tails that deal piercing damage instead of bludgeoning damage.

Plesiosaurus

A plesiosaurus is a marine dinosaur whose compact body is driven by powerful flippers. Predatory and aggressive, it attacks any creature it encounters. Its flexible neck accounts for a third of its total length, letting it twist in any direction to deliver a powerful bite.

Pteranodon

These flying reptiles have wingspans of 15 to 20 feet and typically dive for small marine prey, though they are opportunists and will attack any creature that appears edible. A pteranodon has no teeth, instead using its sharp beak to stab prey too large to swallow with one gulp.

Triceratops

One of the most aggressive of the herbivorous dinosaurs, a triceratops has a skull that flares out to form a protective plate of bone. With its great horns and formidable speed, a triceratops gores and tramples would-be predators to death.

Tyrannosaurus Rex

This enormous predator terrorizes all other creatures in its territory. Despite its size and weight, a tyrannosaurus is a swift runner. It chases anything it thinks it can eat, and there are few creatures it won't try to devour whole. While prowling for substantial prey, a tyrannosaurus subsists on carrion, and on any smaller creatures that try to dart in to steal its meal.

Allosaurus

Large beast, unaligned

Armor Class 13 (natural armor)
Hit Points 51 (6d10 + 18)
Speed 60 ft.

STR	DEX	CON	INT	WIS	CHA
19 (+4)	13 (+1)	17 (+3)	2 (–4)	12 (+1)	5 (–3)

Skills Perception +5
Senses passive Perception 15
Languages —
Challenge 2 (450 XP)

Pounce. If the allosaurus moves at least 30 feet straight toward a creature and then hits it with a claw attack on the same turn, that target must succeed on a DC 13 Strength saving throw or be knocked prone. If the target is prone, the allosaurus can make one bite attack against it as a bonus action.

Actions

Bite. *Melee Weapon Attack:* +6 to hit, reach 5 ft., one target. *Hit:* 15 (2d10 + 4) piercing damage.

Claw. *Melee Weapon Attack:* +6 to hit, reach 5 ft., one target. *Hit:* 8 (1d8 + 4) slashing damage.

Ankylosaurus

Huge beast, unaligned

Armor Class 15 (natural armor)
Hit Points 68 (8d12 + 16)
Speed 30 ft.

STR	DEX	CON	INT	WIS	CHA
19 (+4)	11 (+0)	15 (+2)	2 (–4)	12 (+1)	5 (–3)

Senses passive Perception 11
Languages —
Challenge 3 (700 XP)

Actions

Tail. *Melee Weapon Attack:* +7 to hit, reach 10 ft., one target. *Hit:* 18 (4d6 + 4) bludgeoning damage. If the target is a creature, it must succeed on a DC 14 Strength saving throw or be knocked prone.

PLESIOSAURUS
Large beast, unaligned

Armor Class 13 (natural armor)
Hit Points 68 (8d10 + 24)
Speed 20 ft., swim 40 ft.

STR	DEX	CON	INT	WIS	CHA
18 (+4)	15 (+2)	16 (+3)	2 (–4)	12 (+1)	5 (–3)

Skills Perception +3, Stealth +4
Senses passive Perception 13
Languages —
Challenge 2 (450 XP)

Hold Breath. The plesiosaurus can hold its breath for 1 hour.

ACTIONS

Bite. *Melee Weapon Attack:* +6 to hit, reach 10 ft., one target. *Hit:* 14 (3d6 + 4) piercing damage.

TRICERATOPS
Huge beast, unaligned

Armor Class 13 (natural armor)
Hit Points 95 (10d12 + 30)
Speed 50 ft.

STR	DEX	CON	INT	WIS	CHA
22 (+6)	9 (–1)	17 (+3)	2 (–4)	11 (+0)	5 (–3)

Senses passive Perception 10
Languages —
Challenge 5 (1,800 XP)

Trampling Charge. If the triceratops moves at least 20 feet straight toward a creature and then hits it with a gore attack on the same turn, that target must succeed on a DC 13 Strength saving throw or be knocked prone. If the target is prone, the triceratops can make one stomp attack against it as a bonus action.

ACTIONS

Gore. *Melee Weapon Attack:* +9 to hit, reach 5 ft., one target. *Hit:* 24 (4d8 + 6) piercing damage.

Stomp. *Melee Weapon Attack:* +9 to hit, reach 5 ft., one prone creature. *Hit:* 22 (3d10 + 6) bludgeoning damage

PTERANODON
Medium beast, unaligned

Armor Class 13 (natural armor)
Hit Points 13 (3d8)
Speed 10 ft., fly 60 ft.

STR	DEX	CON	INT	WIS	CHA
12 (+1)	15 (+2)	10 (+0)	2 (–4)	9 (–1)	5 (–3)

Skills Perception +1
Senses passive Perception 11
Languages —
Challenge 1/4 (50 XP)

Flyby. The pteranodon doesn't provoke an opportunity attack when it flies out of an enemy's reach.

ACTIONS

Bite. *Melee Weapon Attack:* +3 to hit, reach 5 ft., one target. *Hit:* 6 (2d4 + 1) piercing damage.

TYRANNOSAURUS REX
Huge beast, unaligned

Armor Class 13 (natural armor)
Hit Points 136 (13d12 + 52)
Speed 50 ft.

STR	DEX	CON	INT	WIS	CHA
25 (+7)	10 (+0)	19 (+4)	2 (–4)	12 (+1)	9 (–1)

Skills Perception +4
Senses passive Perception 14
Languages —
Challenge 8 (3,900 XP)

ACTIONS

Multiattack. The tyrannosaurus makes two attacks: one with its bite and one with its tail. It can't make both attacks against the same target.

Bite. *Melee Weapon Attack:* +10 to hit, reach 10 ft., one target. *Hit:* 33 (4d12 + 7) piercing damage. If the target is a Medium or smaller creature, it is grappled (escape DC 17). Until this grapple ends, the target is restrained, and the tyrannosaurus can't bite another target.

Tail. *Melee Weapon Attack:* +10 to hit, reach 10 ft., one target. *Hit:* 20 (3d8 + 7) bludgeoning damage.

Displacer Beast

This monstrous predator takes its name from its ability to displace light so that it appears to be several feet away from its actual location. A displacer beast resembles a sleek great cat covered in blue-black fur. However, its otherworldly origins are clear in its six legs and the two tentacles sprouting from its shoulders, both ending in pads tipped with spiky protrusions. A displacer beast's eyes glow with an awful malevolence that persists even in death.

Unseelie Origins. Displacer beasts roamed the twilight lands of the Feywild for ages, until they were captured and trained by the Unseelie Court. The warriors of the court selectively bred the beasts to reinforce their ferocious and predatory nature, using them to hunt unicorns, pegasi, and other wondrous prey. However, it didn't take long for the displacer beasts to use their malevolent intelligence to escape their masters.

Running and breeding freely in the Feywild, the displacer beasts soon came to the attention of the Seelie Court. With blink dog companions at their side, fey hunters drove these predators to the fringes of the Feywild, where many crossed over to the Material Plane. To this day, displacer beasts and blink dogs attack each other on sight.

Love of the Kill. Displacer beasts kill not just for food but also for sport. They target prey even when not hungry, often toying with their victims to entertain themselves until they are ready to eat. After killing its prey using its tentacles, a displacer beast drags the corpse to a quiet place where it can feed without distraction.

Displacer beasts hunt alone or in small prides that demonstrate skill at setting ambushes. A single beast will strike and withdraw, luring prey into a densely wooded area where its packmates wait. Packs of displacer beasts hunting near trade roads recall the frequency and schedule of regular caravans, laying down ambushes to pick off those caravans.

Prized Guards and Pets. Intelligent evil creatures favor displacer beasts as pets, but a displacer beast enters such an alliance only if it appears beneficial. A displacer beast might guard a vault or act as a bodyguard for a prominent individual.

Displacer Beast

Large monstrosity, lawful evil

Armor Class 13 (natural armor)
Hit Points 85 (10d10 + 30)
Speed 40 ft.

STR	DEX	CON	INT	WIS	CHA
18 (+4)	15 (+2)	16 (+3)	6 (–2)	12 (+1)	8 (–1)

Senses darkvision 60 ft., passive Perception 11
Languages —
Challenge 3 (700 XP)

Avoidance. If the displacer beast is subjected to an effect that allows it to make a saving throw to take only half damage, it instead takes no damage if it succeeds on the saving throw, and only half damage if it fails.

Displacement. The displacer beast projects a magical illusion that makes it appear to be standing near its actual location, causing attack rolls against it to have disadvantage. If it is hit by an attack, this trait is disrupted until the end of its next turn. This trait is also disrupted while the displacer beast is incapacitated or has a speed of 0.

Actions

Multiattack. The displacer beast makes two attacks with its tentacles.

Tentacle. *Melee Weapon Attack:* +6 to hit, reach 10 ft., one target. *Hit:* 7 (1d6 + 4) bludgeoning damage plus 3 (1d6) piercing damage.

DOPPELGANGER

Doppelgangers are devious shapeshifters that take on the appearance of other humanoids, throwing off pursuit or luring victims to their doom with misdirection and disguise. Few creatures spread fear, suspicion, and deceit better than doppelgangers. Found in every land and culture, they can take on the guise of any individual of any race.

Stealing Secrets. A doppelganger's adopted form allows it to blend into almost any group or community, but its transformation doesn't impart languages, mannerisms, memory, or personality. Doppelgangers often follow or capture creatures they intend to impersonate, studying them and probing their minds for secrets. A doppelganger can read a creature's surface thoughts, allowing it to glean that creature's name, desires, and fears, along with a few scattered memories. A doppelganger impersonating a specific creature as part of a long-term plot might keep its double alive and close at hand for weeks, probing the victim's mind daily to learn how to behave and speak authentically.

Hedonistic Swindlers. Doppelgangers work alone or in small groups, with group roles shifting from con to con. While one doppelganger takes the place of a murdered merchant or noble, the others take on a number of identities as circumstances warrant, playing the parts of family or servants while they live off the victim's riches.

Changelings. Doppelgangers are too lazy or self-interested to raise their young. They assume attractive male forms and seduce women, leaving them to raise their progeny. A doppelganger child appears to be a normal member of its mother's species until it reaches adolescence, at which point it discovers its true nature and is driven to seek out its kind to join them.

DOPPELGANGER
Medium monstrosity (shapechanger), neutral

Armor Class 14
Hit Points 52 (8d8 + 16)
Speed 30 ft.

STR	DEX	CON	INT	WIS	CHA
11 (+0)	18 (+4)	14 (+2)	11 (+0)	12 (+1)	14 (+2)

Skills Deception +6, Insight +3
Condition Immunities charmed
Senses darkvision 60 ft., passive Perception 11
Languages Common
Challenge 3 (700 XP)

Shapechanger. The doppelganger can use its action to polymorph into a Small or Medium humanoid it has seen, or back into its true form. Its statistics, other than its size, are the same in each form. Any equipment it is wearing or carrying isn't transformed. It reverts to its true form if it dies.

Ambusher. In the first round of a combat, the doppelganger has advantage on attack rolls against any creature it surprised.

Surprise Attack. If the doppelganger surprises a creature and hits it with an attack during the first round of combat, the target takes an extra 10 (3d6) damage from the attack.

ACTIONS

Multiattack. The doppelganger makes two melee attacks.

Slam. *Melee Weapon Attack:* +6 to hit, reach 5 ft., one target. *Hit:* 7 (1d6 + 4) bludgeoning damage.

Read Thoughts. The doppelganger magically reads the surface thoughts of one creature within 60 feet of it. The effect can penetrate barriers, but 3 feet of wood or dirt, 2 feet of stone, 2 inches of metal, or a thin sheet of lead blocks it. While the target is in range, the doppelganger can continue reading its thoughts, as long as the doppelganger's concentration isn't broken (as if concentrating on a spell). While reading the target's mind, the doppelganger has advantage on Wisdom (Insight) and Charisma (Deception, Intimidation, and Persuasion) checks against the target.

Dracolich

Even as long-lived as they are, all dragons must eventually die. This thought doesn't sit well with many dragons, some of which allow themselves to be transformed by necromantic energy and ancient rituals into powerful undead dracoliches. Only the most narcissistic dragons choose this path, knowing that by doing so, they sever all ties to their kin and the dragon gods.

Beyond Death. A dracolich retains its shape and size upon transforming, its skin and scales drawing tight to its bones or sloughing away to leave a skeletal form behind. Its eyes appear as glowing points of light floating in shadowy sockets, hinting at the malevolence of its undead mind.

Though many dragons pursue vain goals of destruction and dominance, dracoliches are more nefarious than the most evil dragons, driven to rule over all. A dracolich is a fiendishly intelligent tyrant that crafts complex webs of foul schemes, attracting servants motivated by greed and a lust for power. Acting from the shadows and actively plotting to keep its existence a secret, a dracolich is a cunning and challenging foe.

Dracolich Phylacteries. Creating a dracolich requires the cooperation of the dragon and a group of mages or cultists that can perform the proper ritual. During the ritual, the dragon consumes a toxic brew that slays it instantly. The attendant spellcasters then ensnare its spirit and transfer it to a special gemstone that functions like a lich's phylactery. As the dragon's flesh rots away, the spirit inside the gem returns to animate the dragon's bones.

If a dracolich's physical form is ever destroyed, its spirit returns to the gem as long as the two are on the same plane. If the gem comes into contact with another dragon's corpse, the dracolich's spirit can take possession of that corpse to become a new dracolich. If the dracolich's spirit gem is taken to another plane, the dracolich's spirit has nowhere to go when its undead body is destroyed and simply passes into the afterlife.

Dracolich Template

Only an ancient or adult true dragon can be transformed into a dracolich. Younger dragons that attempt to undergo the transformation die, as do other creatures that aren't true dragons but possess the dragon type, such as pseudodragons and wyverns. A shadow dragon can't be transformed into a dracolich, for it has already lost too much of its physical form.

When a dragon becomes a dracolich, it retains its statistics except as described below. The dragon loses any trait, such as Amphibious, that assumes a living physiology. The dracolich might retain or lose any or all of its lair actions or inherit new ones, as the DM sees fit.

Type. The dracolich's type changes from dragon to undead, and it no longer requires air, food, drink, or sleep.

Damage Resistance. The dracolich has resistance to necrotic damage.

Damage Immunities. The dracolich has immunity to poison. It also retains any immunities it had prior to becoming a dracolich.

Condition Immunities. The dracolich can't be charmed, frightened, paralyzed, or poisoned. It also doesn't suffer from exhaustion.

Magic Resistance. The dracolich has advantage on saving throws against spells and other magical effects.

Adult Blue Dracolich

Huge undead, lawful evil

Armor Class 19 (natural armor)
Hit Points 225 (18d12 + 108)
Speed 40 ft., burrow 30 ft., fly 80 ft.

STR	DEX	CON	INT	WIS	CHA
25 (+7)	10 (+0)	23 (+6)	16 (+3)	15 (+2)	19 (+4)

Saving Throws Dex +5, Con +11, Wis +7, Cha +9
Skills Perception +12, Stealth +5
Damage Resistances necrotic
Damage Immunities lightning, poison
Condition Immunities charmed, exhaustion, frightened, paralyzed, poisoned
Senses blindsight 60 ft., darkvision 120 ft., passive Perception 22
Languages Common, Draconic
Challenge 17 (18,000 XP)

Legendary Resistance (3/Day). If the dracolich fails a saving throw, it can choose to succeed instead.

Magic Resistance. The dracolich has advantage on saving throws against spells and other magical effects.

Actions

Multiattack. The dracolich can use its Frightful Presence. It then makes three attacks: one with its bite and two with its claws.

Bite. *Melee Weapon Attack:* +12 to hit, reach 10 ft., one target. *Hit:* 18 (2d10 + 7) piercing damage plus 5 (1d10) lightning damage.

Claw. *Melee Weapon Attack:* +12 to hit, reach 5 ft., one target. *Hit:* 14 (2d6 + 7) slashing damage.

Tail. *Melee Weapon Attack:* +12 to hit, reach 15 ft., one target. *Hit:* 16 (2d8 + 7) bludgeoning damage.

Frightful Presence. Each creature of the dracolich's choice that is within 120 feet of the dracolich and aware of it must succeed on a DC 18 Wisdom saving throw or become frightened for 1 minute. A creature can repeat the saving throw at the end of each of its turns, ending the effect on itself on a success. If a creature's saving throw is successful or the effect ends for it, the creature is immune to the dracolich's Frightful Presence for the next 24 hours.

Lightning Breath (Recharge 5–6). The dracolich exhales lightning in a 90-foot line that is 5 feet wide. Each creature in that line must make a DC 20 Dexterity saving throw, taking 66 (12d10) lightning damage on a failed save, or half as much damage on a successful one.

Legendary Actions

The dracolich can take 3 legendary actions, choosing from the options below. Only one legendary action option can be used at a time and only at the end of another creature's turn. The dracolich regains spent legendary actions at the start of its turn.

Detect. The dracolich makes a Wisdom (Perception) check.
Tail Attack. The dracolich makes a tail attack.
Wing Attack (Costs 2 Actions). The dracolich beats its tattered wings. Each creature within 10 feet of the dracolich must succeed on a DC 21 Dexterity saving throw or take 14 (2d6 + 7) bludgeoning damage and be knocked prone. After beating its wings this way, the dracolich can fly up to half its flying speed.

Dragon, Shadow

Shadow dragons are true dragons that were either born in the Shadowfell or transformed by years spent within its dismal confines. Some shadow dragons embrace the Shadowfell for its bleak landscapes and desolation. Others seek to return to the Material Plane, hungry to spread the darkness and evil of the Plane of Shadow.

Dark Portals. Portals to the Shadowfell manifest in forlorn places and the deep gloom of subterranean caverns. The dragons that lair in such places often discover these portals and find themselves transported to a new realm. Ancient dragons that sleep in their lairs for months or years at a time might find themselves spirited away, never knowing that a portal has formed without their knowledge as they dream.

Recast in Shadow. The transformation to a shadow dragon happens over a period of years, during which time a dragon's scales lose their luster and fade to a charcoal hue. Its leathery wings become translucent, its eyes paling to pools of opalescent gray. Shadow dragons find sunlight abhorrent, and they are weaker in bright light than they are in darkness. Darkness makes the dragon fade to a spectral shadow of its former self.

The magical nature of dragons holds an attraction for the Shadowfell, which seems somehow to crave the might and majesty of these great reptiles. The Shadowfell also has a dispiriting effect on its denizens, such that the longer a creature remains on the plane, the more it accepts the plane's malaise. As months and years pass for a dragon on the Shadowfell, it becomes aware of the transformation being wrought upon it, and yet can do nothing to prevent it.

Back in the World. A shadow dragon is so suffused with the power of the Shadowfell that even a return to the Material Plane can't undo its transformation. Some shadow dragons attempt to lure other creatures from the mortal realm back to the Shadowfell to keep them company, at least until they tire of their guests and devour them. Others are happy to leave the Shadowfell behind forever, understanding that treasure and power are easier to come by in the Material Plane.

Shadow Dragon Template

Only a true dragon can transform into a shadow dragon, and only if it is born in the Shadowfell or remains there for several years. A dracolich can't be turned into a shadow dragon, since it loses its draconic nature when it becomes undead.

When a dragon becomes a shadow dragon, it retains its statistics except as described below. The shadow

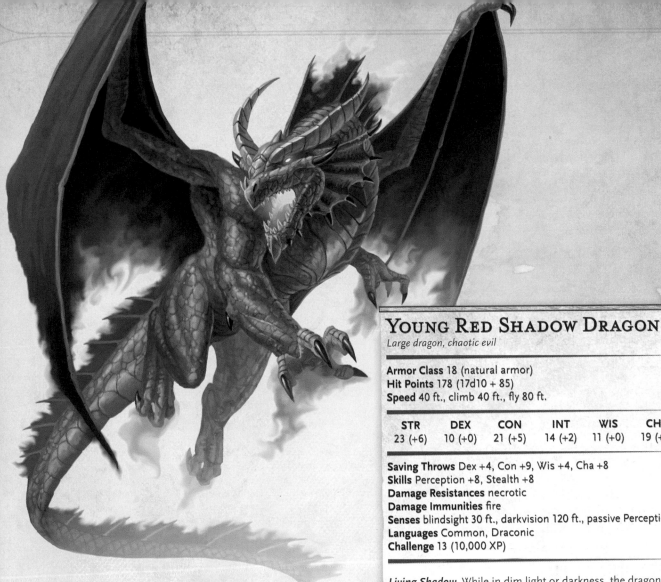

dragon might retain or lose any or all of its lair actions or inherit new ones, as the DM sees fit.

Damage Resistances. The dragon has resistance to necrotic damage.

Skill Proficiency: Stealth. The dragon's proficiency bonus is doubled for its Dexterity (Stealth) checks.

Living Shadow. While in dim light or darkness, the dragon has resistance to damage that isn't force, psychic, or radiant.

Shadow Stealth. While in dim light or darkness, the dragon can take the Hide action as a bonus action.

Sunlight Sensitivity. While in sunlight, the dragon has disadvantage on attack rolls, as well as on Wisdom (Perception) checks that rely on sight.

New Action: Bite. If the dragon deals acid, cold, fire, lightning, or poison damage with its bite, change that damage type to necrotic.

New Action: Shadow Breath. Any damage-dealing breath weapon possessed by the dragon deals necrotic damage instead of its original damage type. A humanoid reduced to 0 hit points by this damage dies, and an undead shadow rises from its corpse and acts immediately after the dragon in the initiative count. The shadow is under the dragon's control.

YOUNG RED SHADOW DRAGON

Large dragon, chaotic evil

Armor Class 18 (natural armor)
Hit Points 178 (17d10 + 85)
Speed 40 ft., climb 40 ft., fly 80 ft.

STR	DEX	CON	INT	WIS	CHA
23 (+6)	10 (+0)	21 (+5)	14 (+2)	11 (+0)	19 (+4)

Saving Throws Dex +4, Con +9, Wis +4, Cha +8
Skills Perception +8, Stealth +8
Damage Resistances necrotic
Damage Immunities fire
Senses blindsight 30 ft., darkvision 120 ft., passive Perception 18
Languages Common, Draconic
Challenge 13 (10,000 XP)

Living Shadow. While in dim light or darkness, the dragon has resistance to damage that isn't force, psychic, or radiant.

Shadow Stealth. While in dim light or darkness, the dragon can take the Hide action as a bonus action.

Sunlight Sensitivity. While in sunlight, the dragon has disadvantage on attack rolls, as well as on Wisdom (Perception) checks that rely on sight.

ACTIONS

Multiattack. The dragon makes three attacks: one with its bite and two with its claws.

Bite. *Melee Weapon Attack:* +10 to hit, reach 10 ft., one target. *Hit:* 17 (2d10 + 6) piercing damage plus 3 (1d6) necrotic damage.

Claw. *Melee Weapon Attack:* +10 to hit, reach 5 ft., one target. *Hit:* 13 (2d6 + 6) slashing damage.

Shadow Breath (Recharge 5–6). The dragon exhales shadowy fire in a 30-foot cone. Each creature in that area must make a DC 18 Dexterity saving throw, taking 56 (16d6) necrotic damage on a failed save, or half as much damage on a successful one. A humanoid reduced to 0 hit points by this damage dies, and an undead shadow rises from its corpse and acts immediately after the dragon in the initiative count. The shadow is under the dragon's control.

Dragons

True dragons are winged reptiles of ancient lineage and fearsome power. They are known and feared for their predatory cunning and greed, with the oldest dragons accounted as some of the most powerful creatures in the world. Dragons are also magical creatures whose innate power fuels their dreaded breath weapons and other preternatural abilities.

Many creatures, including wyverns and dragon turtles, have draconic blood. However, true dragons fall into the two broad categories of chromatic and metallic dragons. The black, blue, green, red, and white dragons are selfish, evil, and feared by all. The brass, bronze, copper, gold, and silver dragons are noble, good, and highly respected by the wise.

Though their goals and ideals vary tremendously, all true dragons covet wealth, hoarding mounds of coins and gathering gems, jewels, and magic items. Dragons with large hoards are loath to leave them for long, venturing out of their lairs only to patrol or feed.

True dragons pass through four distinct stages of life, from lowly wyrmlings to ancient dragons, which can live for over a thousand years. In that time, their might can become unrivaled and their hoards can grow beyond price.

Dragon Age Categories

Category	Size	Age Range
Wyrmling	Medium	5 years or less
Young	Large	6–100 years
Adult	Huge	101–800 years
Ancient	Gargantuan	801 years or more

Variant: Dragons as Innate Spellcasters

Dragons are innately magical creatures that can master a few spells as they age, using this variant.

A young or older dragon can innately cast a number of spells equal to its Charisma modifier. Each spell can be cast once per day, requiring no material components, and the spell's level can be no higher than one-third the dragon's challenge rating (rounded down). The dragon's bonus to hit with spell attacks is equal to its proficiency bonus + its Charisma bonus. The dragon's spell save DC equals 8 + its proficiency bonus + its Charisma modifier.

Chromatic Dragons

The black, blue, green, red, and white dragons represent the evil side of dragonkind. Aggressive, gluttonous, and vain, chromatic dragons are dark sages and powerful tyrants feared by all creatures—including each other.

Driven by Greed. Chromatic dragons lust after treasure, and this greed colors their every scheme and plot. They believe that the world's wealth belongs to them by right, and a chromatic dragon seizes that wealth without regard for the humanoids and other creatures that have "stolen" it. With its piles of coins, gleaming gems, and magic items, a dragon's hoard is the stuff of legend. However, chromatic dragons have no interest in commerce, amassing wealth for no other reason than to have it.

Creatures of Ego. Chromatic dragons are united by their sense of superiority, believing themselves the most powerful and worthy of all mortal creatures. When they interact with other creatures, it is only to further their own interests. They believe in their innate right to rule, and this belief is the cornerstone of every chromatic dragon's personality and worldview. Trying to humble a chromatic dragon is like trying to convince the wind to stop blowing. To these creatures, humanoids are animals, fit to serve as prey or beasts of burden, and wholly unworthy of respect.

Dangerous Lairs. A dragon's lair serves as the seat of its power and a vault for its treasure. With its innate toughness and tolerance for severe environmental effects, a dragon selects or builds a lair not for shelter but for defense, favoring multiple entrances and exits, and security for its hoard.

Most chromatic dragon lairs are hidden in dangerous and remote locations to prevent all but the most audacious mortals from reaching them. A black dragon might lair in the heart of a vast swamp, while a red dragon might claim the caldera of an active volcano. In addition to the natural defenses of their lairs, powerful chromatic dragons use magical guardians, traps, and subservient creatures to protect their treasures.

Queen of Evil Dragons. Tiamat the Dragon Queen is the chief deity of evil dragonkind. She dwells on Avernus, the first layer of the Nine Hells. As a lesser god, Tiamat has the power to grant spells to her worshipers, though she is loath to share her power. She epitomizes the avarice of evil dragons, believing that the multiverse and all its treasures will one day be hers and hers alone.

Tiamat is a gigantic dragon whose five heads reflect the forms of the chromatic dragons that worship her—black, blue, green, red, and white. She is a terror on the battlefield, capable of annihilating whole armies with her five breath weapons, her formidable spellcasting, and her fearsome claws.

Tiamat's most hated enemy is Bahamut the Platinum Dragon, with whom she shares control of the faith of dragonkind. She also holds a special enmity for Asmodeus, who long ago stripped her of the rule of Avernus and who continues to curb the Dragon Queen's power.

ANCIENT BLACK DRAGON
Gargantuan dragon, chaotic evil

Armor Class 22 (natural armor)
Hit Points 367 (21d20 + 147)
Speed 40 ft., fly 80 ft., swim 40 ft.

STR	DEX	CON	INT	WIS	CHA
27 (+8)	14 (+2)	25 (+7)	16 (+3)	15 (+2)	19 (+4)

Saving Throws Dex +9, Con +14, Wis +9, Cha +11
Skills Perception +16, Stealth +9
Damage Immunities acid
Senses blindsight 60 ft., darkvision 120 ft., passive Perception 26
Languages Common, Draconic
Challenge 21 (33,000 XP)

Amphibious. The dragon can breathe air and water.

Legendary Resistance (3/Day). If the dragon fails a saving throw, it can choose to succeed instead.

ACTIONS

Multiattack. The dragon can use its Frightful Presence. It then makes three attacks: one with its bite and two with its claws.

Bite. *Melee Weapon Attack:* +15 to hit, reach 15 ft., one target. *Hit:* 19 (2d10 + 8) piercing damage plus 9 (2d8) acid damage.

Claw. *Melee Weapon Attack:* +15 to hit, reach 10 ft., one target. *Hit:* 15 (2d6 + 8) slashing damage.

Tail. *Melee Weapon Attack:* +15 to hit, reach 20 ft., one target. *Hit:* 17 (2d8 + 8) bludgeoning damage.

Frightful Presence. Each creature of the dragon's choice that is within 120 feet of the dragon and aware of it must succeed on a DC 19 Wisdom saving throw or become frightened for 1 minute. A creature can repeat the saving throw at the end of each of its turns, ending the effect on itself on a success. If a creature's saving throw is successful or the effect ends for it, the creature is immune to the dragon's Frightful Presence for the next 24 hours.

Acid Breath (Recharge 5–6). The dragon exhales acid in a 90-foot line that is 10 feet wide. Each creature in that line must make a DC 22 Dexterity saving throw, taking 67 (15d8) acid damage on a failed save, or half as much damage on a successful one.

LEGENDARY ACTIONS

The dragon can take 3 legendary actions, choosing from the options below. Only one legendary action option can be used at a time and only at the end of another creature's turn. The dragon regains spent legendary actions at the start of its turn.

Detect. The dragon makes a Wisdom (Perception) check.
Tail Attack. The dragon makes a tail attack.
Wing Attack (Costs 2 Actions). The dragon beats its wings. Each creature within 15 feet of the dragon must succeed on a DC 23 Dexterity saving throw or take 15 (2d6 + 8) bludgeoning damage and be knocked prone. The dragon can then fly up to half its flying speed.

Adult Black Dragon
Huge dragon, chaotic evil

Armor Class 19 (natural armor)
Hit Points 195 (17d12 + 85)
Speed 40 ft., fly 80 ft., swim 40 ft.

STR	DEX	CON	INT	WIS	CHA
23 (+6)	14 (+2)	21 (+5)	14 (+2)	13 (+1)	17 (+3)

Saving Throws Dex +7, Con +10, Wis +6, Cha +8
Skills Perception +11, Stealth +7
Damage Immunities acid
Senses blindsight 60 ft., darkvision 120 ft., passive Perception 21
Languages Common, Draconic
Challenge 14 (11,500 XP)

Amphibious. The dragon can breathe air and water.

Legendary Resistance (3/Day). If the dragon fails a saving throw, it can choose to succeed instead.

Actions

Multiattack. The dragon can use its Frightful Presence. It then makes three attacks: one with its bite and two with its claws.

Bite. *Melee Weapon Attack:* +11 to hit, reach 10 ft., one target. *Hit:* 17 (2d10 + 6) piercing damage plus 4 (1d8) acid damage.

Claw. *Melee Weapon Attack:* +11 to hit, reach 5 ft., one target. *Hit:* 13 (2d6 + 6) slashing damage.

Tail. *Melee Weapon Attack:* +11 to hit, reach 15 ft., one target. *Hit:* 15 (2d8 + 6) bludgeoning damage.

Frightful Presence. Each creature of the dragon's choice that is within 120 feet of the dragon and aware of it must succeed on a DC 16 Wisdom saving throw or become frightened for 1 minute. A creature can repeat the saving throw at the end of each of its turns, ending the effect on itself on a success. If a creature's saving throw is successful or the effect ends for it, the creature is immune to the dragon's Frightful Presence for the next 24 hours.

Acid Breath (Recharge 5–6). The dragon exhales acid in a 60-foot line that is 5 feet wide. Each creature in that line must make a DC 18 Dexterity saving throw, taking 54 (12d8) acid damage on a failed save, or half as much damage on a successful one.

Legendary Actions

The dragon can take 3 legendary actions, choosing from the options below. Only one legendary action option can be used at a time and only at the end of another creature's turn. The dragon regains spent legendary actions at the start of its turn.

Detect. The dragon makes a Wisdom (Perception) check.
Tail Attack. The dragon makes a tail attack.
Wing Attack (Costs 2 Actions). The dragon beats its wings. Each creature within 10 feet of the dragon must succeed on a DC 19 Dexterity saving throw or take 13 (2d6 + 6) bludgeoning damage and be knocked prone. The dragon can then fly up to half its flying speed.

Young Black Dragon
Large dragon, chaotic evil

Armor Class 18 (natural armor)
Hit Points 127 (15d10 + 45)
Speed 40 ft., fly 80 ft., swim 40 ft.

STR	DEX	CON	INT	WIS	CHA
19 (+4)	14 (+2)	17 (+3)	12 (+1)	11 (+0)	15 (+2)

Saving Throws Dex +5, Con +6, Wis +3, Cha +5
Skills Perception +6, Stealth +5
Damage Immunities acid
Senses blindsight 30 ft., darkvision 120 ft., passive Perception 16
Languages Common, Draconic
Challenge 7 (2,900 XP)

Amphibious. The dragon can breathe air and water.

Actions

Multiattack. The dragon makes three attacks: one with its bite and two with its claws.

Bite. *Melee Weapon Attack:* +7 to hit, reach 10 ft., one target. *Hit:* 15 (2d10 + 4) piercing damage plus 4 (1d8) acid damage.

Claw. *Melee Weapon Attack:* +7 to hit, reach 5 ft., one target. *Hit:* 11 (2d6 + 4) slashing damage.

Acid Breath (Recharge 5–6). The dragon exhales acid in a 30-foot line that is 5 feet wide. Each creature in that line must make a DC 14 Dexterity saving throw, taking 49 (11d8) acid damage on a failed save, or half as much damage on a successful one.

Black Dragon Wyrmling
Medium dragon, chaotic evil

Armor Class 17 (natural armor)
Hit Points 33 (6d8 + 6)
Speed 30 ft., fly 60 ft., swim 30 ft.

STR	DEX	CON	INT	WIS	CHA
15 (+2)	14 (+2)	13 (+1)	10 (+0)	11 (+0)	13 (+1)

Saving Throws Dex +4, Con +3, Wis +2, Cha +3
Skills Perception +4, Stealth +4
Damage Immunities acid
Senses blindsight 10 ft., darkvision 60 ft., passive Perception 14
Languages Draconic
Challenge 2 (450 XP)

Amphibious. The dragon can breathe air and water.

Actions

Bite. *Melee Weapon Attack:* +4 to hit, reach 5 ft., one target. *Hit:* 7 (1d10 + 2) piercing damage plus 2 (1d4) acid damage.

Acid Breath (Recharge 5–6). The dragon exhales acid in a 15-foot line that is 5 feet wide. Each creature in that line must make a DC 11 Dexterity saving throw, taking 22 (5d8) acid damage on a failed save, or half as much damage on a successful one.

D

Black Dragon

The most evil-tempered and vile of the chromatic dragons, black dragons collect the wreckage and treasures of fallen peoples. These dragons loathe seeing the weak prosper and revel in the collapse of humanoid kingdoms. They make their homes in fetid swamps and crumbling ruins where kingdoms once stood.

With deep-socketed eyes and broad nasal openings, a black dragon's face resembles a skull. Its curving, segmented horns are bone-colored near the base and darken to dead black at the tips. As a black dragon ages, the flesh around its horns and cheekbones deteriorates as though eaten by acid, leaving thin layers of hide that enhance its skeletal appearance. A black dragon's head is marked by spikes and horns. Its tongue is flat with a forked tip, drooling slime whose acidic scent adds to the dragon's reek of rotting vegetation and foul water.

When it hatches, a black dragon has glossy black scale. As it ages, its scales become thicker and duller, helping it blend in to the marshes and blasted ruins that are its home.

Brutal and Cruel. All chromatic dragons are evil, but black dragons stand apart for their sadistic nature. A black dragon lives to watch its prey beg for mercy, and will often offer the illusion of respite or escape before finishing off its enemies.

A black dragon strikes at its weakest enemies first, ensuring a quick and brutal victory, which bolsters its ego as it terrifies its remaining foes. On the verge of defeat, a black dragon does anything it can to save itself, but it accepts death before allowing any other creature to claim mastery over it.

Foes and Servants. Black dragons hate and fear other dragons. They spy on draconic rivals from afar, looking for opportunities to slay weaker dragons and avoid stronger ones. If a stronger dragon threatens it, a black dragon abandons its lair and seeks out new territory.

Evil lizardfolk venerate and serve black dragons, raiding humanoid settlements for treasure and food to give as tribute and building crude draconic effigies along the borders of their dragon master's domain.

A black dragon's malevolent influence might also cause the spontaneous creation of evil shambling mounds that seek out and slay good creatures approaching the dragon's lair.

Kobolds infest the lairs of many black dragons like vermin. They become as cruel as their dark masters, often torturing and weakening captives with centipede bites and scorpion stings before delivering them to sate the dragon's hunger.

Wealth of the Ancients. Black dragons hoard the treasures and magic items of crumbled empires and conquered kingdoms to remind themselves of their greatness. The more civilizations a dragon outlasts, the more entitled it feels to claim the wealth of current civilizations for itself.

A Black Dragon's Lair

Black dragons dwell in swamps on the frayed edges of civilization. A black dragon's lair is a dismal cave, grotto, or ruin that is at least partially flooded, providing pools where the dragon rests, and where its victims can ferment. The lair is littered with the acid-pitted bones of previous victims and the fly-ridden carcasses of fresh kills, watched over by crumbling statues. Centipedes, scorpions, and snakes infest the lair, which is filled with the stench of death and decay.

Lair Actions

On initiative count 20 (losing initiative ties), the dragon takes a lair action to cause one of the following effects; the dragon can't use the same effect two rounds in a row:

- Pools of water that the dragon can see within 120 feet of it surge outward in a grasping tide. Any creature on the ground within 20 feet of such a pool must succeed on a DC 15 Strength saving throw or be pulled up to 20 feet into the water and knocked prone.
- A cloud of swarming insects fills a 20-foot-radius sphere centered on a point the dragon chooses within 120 feet of it. The cloud spreads around corners and remains until the dragon dismisses it as an action, uses this lair action again, or dies. The cloud is lightly obscured. Any creature in the cloud when it appears must make on a DC 15 Constitution saving throw, taking 10 (3d6) piercing damage on a failed save, or half as much damage on a successful one. A creature that ends its turn in the cloud takes 10 (3d6) piercing damage.
- Magical darkness spreads from a point the dragon chooses within 60 feet of it, filling a 15-foot-radius sphere until the dragon dismisses it as an action, uses this lair action again, or dies. The darkness spreads around corners. A creature with darkvision can't see through this darkness, and nonmagical light can't illuminate it. If any of the effect's area overlaps with an area of light created by a spell of 2nd level or lower, the spell that created the light is dispelled.

Regional Effects

The region containing a legendary black dragon's lair is warped by the dragon's magic, which creates one or more of the following effects:

- The land within 6 miles of the lair takes twice as long as normal to traverse, since the plants grow thick and twisted, and the swamps are thick with reeking mud.
- Water sources within 1 mile of the lair are supernaturally fouled. Enemies of the dragon that drink such water regurgitate it within minutes.
- Fog lightly obscures the land within 6 miles of the lair.

If the dragon dies, vegetation remains as it has grown, but other effects fade over 1d10 days.

ANCIENT BLUE DRAGON

Gargantuan dragon, lawful evil

Armor Class 22 (natural armor)
Hit Points 481 (26d20 + 208)
Speed 40 ft., burrow 40 ft., fly 80 ft.

STR	DEX	CON	INT	WIS	CHA
29 (+9)	10 (+0)	27 (+8)	18 (+4)	17 (+3)	21 (+5)

Saving Throws Dex +7, Con +15, Wis +10, Cha +12
Skills Perception +17, Stealth +7
Damage Immunities lightning
Senses blindsight 60 ft., darkvision 120 ft., passive Perception 27
Languages Common, Draconic
Challenge 23 (50,000 XP)

Legendary Resistance (3/Day). If the dragon fails a saving throw, it can choose to succeed instead.

ACTIONS

Multiattack. The dragon can use its Frightful Presence. It then makes three attacks: one with its bite and two with its claws.

Bite. *Melee Weapon Attack:* +16 to hit, reach 15 ft., one target. *Hit:* 20 (2d10 + 9) piercing damage plus 11 (2d10) lightning damage.

Claw. *Melee Weapon Attack:* +16 to hit, reach 10 ft., one target. *Hit:* 16 (2d6 + 9) slashing damage.

Tail. *Melee Weapon Attack:* +16 to hit, reach 20 ft., one target. *Hit:* 18 (2d8 + 9) bludgeoning damage.

Frightful Presence. Each creature of the dragon's choice that is within 120 feet of the dragon and aware of it must succeed on a DC 20 Wisdom saving throw or become frightened for 1 minute. A creature can repeat the saving throw at the end of each of its turns, ending the effect on itself on a success. If a creature's saving throw is successful or the effect ends for it, the creature is immune to the dragon's Frightful Presence for the next 24 hours.

Lightning Breath (Recharge 5–6). The dragon exhales lightning in a 120-foot line that is 10 feet wide. Each creature in that line must make a DC 23 Dexterity saving throw, taking 88 (16d10) lightning damage on a failed save, or half as much damage on a successful one.

LEGENDARY ACTIONS

The dragon can take 3 legendary actions, choosing from the options below. Only one legendary action option can be used at a time and only at the end of another creature's turn. The dragon regains spent legendary actions at the start of its turn.

Detect. The dragon makes a Wisdom (Perception) check.
Tail Attack. The dragon makes a tail attack.
Wing Attack (Costs 2 Actions). The dragon beats its wings. Each creature within 15 feet of the dragon must succeed on a DC 24 Dexterity saving throw or take 16 (2d6 + 9) bludgeoning damage and be knocked prone. The dragon can then fly up to half its flying speed.

D

ADULT BLUE DRAGON
Huge dragon, lawful evil

Armor Class 19 (natural armor)
Hit Points 225 (18d12 + 108)
Speed 40 ft., burrow 30 ft., fly 80 ft.

STR	DEX	CON	INT	WIS	CHA
25 (+7)	10 (+0)	23 (+6)	16 (+3)	15 (+2)	19 (+4)

Saving Throws Dex +5, Con +11, Wis +7, Cha +9
Skills Perception +12, Stealth +5
Damage Immunities lightning
Senses blindsight 60 ft., darkvision 120 ft., passive Perception 22
Languages Common, Draconic
Challenge 16 (15,000 XP)

Legendary Resistance (3/Day). If the dragon fails a saving throw, it can choose to succeed instead.

ACTIONS

Multiattack. The dragon can use its Frightful Presence. It then makes three attacks: one with its bite and two with its claws.

Bite. *Melee Weapon Attack:* +12 to hit, reach 10 ft., one target. *Hit:* 18 (2d10 + 7) piercing damage plus 5 (1d10) lightning damage.

Claw. *Melee Weapon Attack:* +12 to hit, reach 5 ft., one target. *Hit:* 14 (2d6 + 7) slashing damage.

Tail. *Melee Weapon Attack:* +12 to hit, reach 15 ft., one target. *Hit:* 16 (2d8 + 7) bludgeoning damage.

Frightful Presence. Each creature of the dragon's choice that is within 120 feet of the dragon and aware of it must succeed on a DC 17 Wisdom saving throw or become frightened for 1 minute. A creature can repeat the saving throw at the end of each of its turns, ending the effect on itself on a success. If a creature's saving throw is successful or the effect ends for it, the creature is immune to the dragon's Frightful Presence for the next 24 hours.

Lightning Breath (Recharge 5–6). The dragon exhales lightning in a 90-foot line that is 5 feet wide. Each creature in that line must make a DC 19 Dexterity saving throw, taking 66 (12d10) lightning damage on a failed save, or half as much damage on a successful one.

LEGENDARY ACTIONS

The dragon can take 3 legendary actions, choosing from the options below. Only one legendary action option can be used at a time and only at the end of another creature's turn. The dragon regains spent legendary actions at the start of its turn.

Detect. The dragon makes a Wisdom (Perception) check.
Tail Attack. The dragon makes a tail attack.
Wing Attack (Costs 2 Actions). The dragon beats its wings. Each creature within 10 feet of the dragon must succeed on a DC 20 Dexterity saving throw or take 14 (2d6 + 7) bludgeoning damage and be knocked prone. The dragon can then fly up to half its flying speed.

YOUNG BLUE DRAGON
Large dragon, lawful evil

Armor Class 18 (natural armor)
Hit Points 152 (16d10 + 64)
Speed 40 ft., burrow 20 ft., fly 80 ft.

STR	DEX	CON	INT	WIS	CHA
21 (+5)	10 (+0)	19 (+4)	14 (+2)	13 (+1)	17 (+3)

Saving Throws Dex +4, Con +8, Wis +5, Cha +7
Skills Perception +9, Stealth +4
Damage Immunities lightning
Senses blindsight 30 ft., darkvision 120 ft., passive Perception 19
Languages Common, Draconic
Challenge 9 (5,000 XP)

ACTIONS

Multiattack. The dragon makes three attacks: one with its bite and two with its claws.

Bite. *Melee Weapon Attack:* +9 to hit, reach 10 ft., one target. *Hit:* 16 (2d10 + 5) piercing damage plus 5 (1d10) lightning damage.

Claw. *Melee Weapon Attack:* +9 to hit, reach 5 ft., one target. *Hit:* 12 (2d6 + 5) slashing damage.

Lightning Breath (Recharge 5–6). The dragon exhales lightning in an 60-foot line that is 5 feet wide. Each creature in that line must make a DC 16 Dexterity saving throw, taking 55 (10d10) lightning damage on a failed save, or half as much damage on a successful one.

BLUE DRAGON WYRMLING
Medium dragon, lawful evil

Armor Class 17 (natural armor)
Hit Points 52 (8d8 + 16)
Speed 30 ft., burrow 15 ft., fly 60 ft.

STR	DEX	CON	INT	WIS	CHA
17 (+3)	10 (+0)	15 (+2)	12 (+1)	11 (+0)	15 (+2)

Saving Throws Dex +2, Con +4, Wis +2, Cha +4
Skills Perception +4, Stealth +2
Damage Immunities lightning
Senses blindsight 10 ft., darkvision 60 ft., passive Perception 14
Languages Draconic
Challenge 3 (700 XP)

ACTIONS

Bite. *Melee Weapon Attack:* +5 to hit, reach 5 ft., one target. *Hit:* 8 (1d10 + 3) piercing damage plus 3 (1d6) lightning damage.

Lightning Breath (Recharge 5–6). The dragon exhales lightning in a 30-foot line that is 5 feet wide. Each creature in that line must make a DC 12 Dexterity saving throw, taking 22 (4d10) lightning damage on a failed save, or half as much damage on a successful one.

Blue Dragon

Vain and territorial, blue dragons soar through the skies over deserts, preying on caravans and plundering herds and settlements in the verdant lands beyond the desert's reach. These dragons can also be found in dry steppes, searing badlands, and rocky coasts. They guard their territories against all potential competitors, especially brass dragons.

A blue dragon is recognized by its dramatic frilled ears and the massive ridged horn atop its blunt head. Rows of spikes extend back from its nostrils to line its brow, and cluster on its jutting lower jaw.

A blue dragon's scales vary in color from an iridescent azure to a deep indigo, polished to a glossy finish by the desert sands. As the dragon ages, its scales become thicker and harder, and its hide hums and crackles with static electricity. These effects intensify when the dragon is angry or about to attack, giving off an odor of ozone and dusty air.

Vain and Deadly. A blue dragon will not stand for any remark or insinuation that it is weak or inferior, taking great pleasure in lording its power over humanoids and other lesser creatures.

A blue dragon is a patient and methodical combatant. When fighting on its own terms, it turns combat into an extended affair of hours or even days, attacking from a distance with volleys of lightning, then flying well out of harm's reach as it waits to attack again.

Desert Predators. Though they sometimes eat cacti and other desert plants to sate their great hunger, blue dragons are carnivores. They prefer to dine on herd animals, cooking those creatures with their lightning breath before gorging themselves. Their dining habits make blue dragons an enormous threat to desert caravans and nomadic tribes, which become convenient collections of food and treasure to a dragon's eye.

When it hunts, a blue dragon buries itself in the desert sand so that only the horn on its nose pokes above the surface, appearing to be an outcropping of stone. When prey draws near, the dragon rises up, sand pouring from its wings like an avalanche as it attacks.

Overlords and Minions. Blue dragons covet valuable and talented creatures whose service reinforces their sense of superiority. Bards, sages, artists, wizards, and assassins can become valuable agents for a blue dragon, which rewards loyal service handsomely.

A blue dragon keeps its lair secret and well protected, and even its most trusted servants are rarely allowed within. It encourages ankhegs, giant scorpions, and other creatures of the desert to dwell near its lair for additional security. Older blue dragons sometimes attract air elementals and other creatures to serve them.

Hoarders of Gems. Though blue dragons collect anything that looks valuable, they are especially fond of gems. Considering blue to be the most noble and beautiful of colors, they covet sapphires, favoring jewelry and magic items adorned with those gems.

A blue dragon buries its most valuable treasures deep in the sand, while scattering a few less valuable trinkets in plainer sight over hidden sinkholes to punish and eliminate would-be thieves.

A Blue Dragon's Lair

Blue dragons make their lairs in barren places, using their lightning breath and their burrowing ability to carve out crystallized caverns and tunnels beneath the sands.

Thunderstorms rage around a legendary blue dragon's lair, and narrow tubes lined with glassy sand ventilate the lair, all the while avoiding the deadly sinkholes that are the dragon's first line of defense.

A blue dragon will collapse the caverns that make up its lair if that lair is invaded. The dragon then burrows out, leaving its attackers to be crushed and suffocated. When it returns later, it collects its possessions—along with the wealth of the dead intruders.

Lair Actions

On initiative count 20 (losing initiative ties), the dragon takes a lair action to cause one of the following effects; the dragon can't use the same effect two rounds in a row:

- Part of the ceiling collapses above one creature that the dragon can see within 120 feet of it. The creature must succeed on a DC 15 Dexterity saving throw or take 10 (3d6) bludgeoning damage and be knocked prone and buried. The buried target is restrained and unable to breathe or stand up. A creature can take an action to make a DC 10 Strength check, ending the buried state on a success.
- A cloud of sand swirls about in a 20-foot-radius sphere centered on a point the dragon can see within 120 feet of it. The cloud spreads around corners. Each creature in the cloud must succeed on a DC 15 Constitution saving throw or be blinded for 1 minute. A creature can repeat the saving throw at the end of each of its turns, ending the effect on itself on a success.
- Lightning arcs, forming a 5-foot-wide line between two of the lair's solid surfaces that the dragon can see. They must be within 120 feet of the dragon and 120 feet of each other. Each creature in that line must succeed on a DC 15 Dexterity saving throw or take 10 (3d6) lightning damage.

Regional Effects

The region containing a legendary blue dragon's lair is warped by the dragon's magic, which creates one or more of the following effects:

- Thunderstorms rage within 6 miles of the lair.
- Dust devils scour the land within 6 miles of the lair. A dust devil has the statistics of an air elemental, but it can't fly, has a speed of 50 feet, and has an Intelligence and Charisma of 1 (−5).
- Hidden sinkholes form in and around the dragon's lair. A sinkhole can be spotted from a safe distance with a successful DC 20 Wisdom (Perception) check. Otherwise, the first creature to step on the thin crust covering the sinkhole must succeed on a DC 15 Dexterity saving throw or fall 1d6 × 10 feet into the sinkhole.

If the dragon dies, the dust devils disappear immediately, and the thunderstorms abate within 1d10 days. Any sinkholes remain where they are.

ANCIENT GREEN DRAGON
Gargantuan dragon, lawful evil

Armor Class 21 (natural armor)
Hit Points 385 (22d20 + 154)
Speed 40 ft., fly 80 ft., swim 40 ft.

STR	DEX	CON	INT	WIS	CHA
27 (+8)	12 (+1)	25 (+7)	20 (+5)	17 (+3)	19 (+4)

Saving Throws Dex +8, Con +14, Wis +10, Cha +11
Skills Deception +11, Insight +10, Perception +17, Persuasion +11, Stealth +8
Damage Immunities poison
Condition Immunities poisoned
Senses blindsight 60 ft., darkvision 120 ft., passive Perception 27
Languages Common, Draconic
Challenge 22 (41,000 XP)

Amphibious. The dragon can breathe air and water.

Legendary Resistance (3/Day). If the dragon fails a saving throw, it can choose to succeed instead.

ACTIONS

Multiattack. The dragon can use its Frightful Presence. It then makes three attacks: one with its bite and two with its claws.

Bite. *Melee Weapon Attack:* +15 to hit, reach 15 ft., one target. *Hit:* 19 (2d10 + 8) piercing damage plus 10 (3d6) poison damage.

Claw. *Melee Weapon Attack:* +15 to hit, reach 10 ft., one target. *Hit:* 22 (4d6 + 8) slashing damage.

Tail. *Melee Weapon Attack:* +15 to hit, reach 20 ft., one target. *Hit:* 17 (2d8 + 8) bludgeoning damage.

Frightful Presence. Each creature of the dragon's choice that is within 120 feet of the dragon and aware of it must succeed on a DC 19 Wisdom saving throw or become frightened for 1 minute. A creature can repeat the saving throw at the end of each of its turns, ending the effect on itself on a success. If a creature's saving throw is successful or the effect ends for it, the creature is immune to the dragon's Frightful Presence for the next 24 hours.

Poison Breath (Recharge 5–6). The dragon exhales poisonous gas in a 90-foot cone. Each creature in that area must make a DC 22 Constitution saving throw, taking 77 (22d6) poison damage on a failed save, or half as much damage on a successful one.

LEGENDARY ACTIONS

The dragon can take 3 legendary actions, choosing from the options below. Only one legendary action option can be used at a time and only at the end of another creature's turn. The dragon regains spent legendary actions at the start of its turn.

Detect. The dragon makes a Wisdom (Perception) check.
Tail Attack. The dragon makes a tail attack.
Wing Attack (Costs 2 Actions). The dragon beats its wings. Each creature within 15 feet of the dragon must succeed on a DC 23 Dexterity saving throw or take 15 (2d6 + 8) bludgeoning damage and be knocked prone. The dragon can then fly up to half its flying speed.

ADULT GREEN DRAGON

Huge dragon, lawful evil

Armor Class 19 (natural armor)
Hit Points 207 (18d12 + 90)
Speed 40 ft., fly 80 ft., swim 40 ft.

STR	DEX	CON	INT	WIS	CHA
23 (+6)	12 (+1)	21 (+5)	18 (+4)	15 (+2)	17 (+3)

Saving Throws Dex +6, Con +10, Wis +7, Cha +8
Skills Deception +8, Insight +7, Perception +12, Persuasion +8, Stealth +6
Damage Immunities poison
Condition Immunities poisoned
Senses blindsight 60 ft., darkvision 120 ft., passive Perception 22
Languages Common, Draconic
Challenge 15 (13,000 XP)

Amphibious. The dragon can breathe air and water.

Legendary Resistance (3/Day). If the dragon fails a saving throw, it can choose to succeed instead.

ACTIONS

Multiattack. The dragon can use its Frightful Presence. It then makes three attacks: one with its bite and two with its claws.

Bite. *Melee Weapon Attack:* +11 to hit, reach 10 ft., one target. *Hit:* 17 (2d10 + 6) piercing damage plus 7 (2d6) poison damage.

Claw. *Melee Weapon Attack:* +11 to hit, reach 5 ft., one target. *Hit:* 13 (2d6 + 6) slashing damage.

Tail. *Melee Weapon Attack:* +11 to hit, reach 15 ft., one target. *Hit:* 15 (2d8 + 6) bludgeoning damage.

Frightful Presence. Each creature of the dragon's choice that is within 120 feet of the dragon and aware of it must succeed on a DC 16 Wisdom saving throw or become frightened for 1 minute. A creature can repeat the saving throw at the end of each of its turns, ending the effect on itself on a success. If a creature's saving throw is successful or the effect ends for it, the creature is immune to the dragon's Frightful Presence for the next 24 hours.

Poison Breath (Recharge 5–6). The dragon exhales poisonous gas in a 60-foot cone. Each creature in that area must make a DC 18 Constitution saving throw, taking 56 (16d6) poison damage on a failed save, or half as much damage on a successful one.

LEGENDARY ACTIONS

The dragon can take 3 legendary actions, choosing from the options below. Only one legendary action option can be used at a time and only at the end of another creature's turn. The dragon regains spent legendary actions at the start of its turn.

Detect. The dragon makes a Wisdom (Perception) check.
Tail Attack. The dragon makes a tail attack.
Wing Attack (Costs 2 Actions). The dragon beats its wings. Each creature within 10 feet of the dragon must succeed on a DC 19 Dexterity saving throw or take 13 (2d6 + 6) bludgeoning damage and be knocked prone. The dragon can then fly up to half its flying speed.

YOUNG GREEN DRAGON

Large dragon, lawful evil

Armor Class 18 (natural armor)
Hit Points 136 (16d10 + 48)
Speed 40 ft., fly 80 ft., swim 40 ft.

STR	DEX	CON	INT	WIS	CHA
19 (+4)	12 (+1)	17 (+3)	16 (+3)	13 (+1)	15 (+2)

Saving Throws Dex +4, Con +6, Wis +4, Cha +5
Skills Deception +5, Perception +7, Stealth +4
Damage Immunities poison
Condition Immunities poisoned
Senses blindsight 30 ft., darkvision 120 ft., passive Perception 17
Languages Common, Draconic
Challenge 8 (3,900 XP)

Amphibious. The dragon can breathe air and water.

ACTIONS

Multiattack. The dragon makes three attacks: one with its bite and two with its claws.

Bite. *Melee Weapon Attack:* +7 to hit, reach 10 ft., one target. *Hit:* 15 (2d10 + 4) piercing damage plus 7 (2d6) poison damage.

Claw. *Melee Weapon Attack:* +7 to hit, reach 5 ft., one target. *Hit:* 11 (2d6 + 4) slashing damage.

Poison Breath (Recharge 5–6). The dragon exhales poisonous gas in a 30-foot cone. Each creature in that area must make a DC 14 Constitution saving throw, taking 42 (12d6) poison damage on a failed save, or half as much damage on a successful one.

Green Dragon

The most cunning and treacherous of true dragons, green dragons use misdirection and trickery to get the upper hand against their enemies. Nasty tempered and thoroughly evil, they take special pleasure in subverting and corrupting the good-hearted. In the ancient forests they roam, green dragons demonstrate an aggression that is often less about territory than it is about gaining power and wealth with as little effort as possible.

A green dragon is recognized by its curved jawline and the crest that begins near its eyes and continues down its spine, reaching full height just behind the skull. A green dragon has no external ears, but bears leathery spiked plates that run down the sides of its neck.

A wyrmling green dragon's thin scales are a shade of green so dark as to appear nearly black. As a green dragon ages, its scales grow larger and lighter, turning shades of forest, emerald, and olive green to help it blend in with its wooded surroundings. Its wings have a dappled pattern, darker near the leading edges and lighter toward the trailing edges.

A green dragon's legs are longer in relation to its body than with any other dragon, enabling it to easily pass over underbrush and forest debris when it walks. With its equally long neck, an older green dragon can peer over the tops of trees without rearing up.

Capricious Hunters. A green dragon hunts by patrolling its forest territory from the air and the ground. It eats any creature it can see, and will consume shrubs and small trees when hungry enough, but its favorite prey is elves.

Green dragons are consummate liars and masters of double talk. They favor intimidation of lesser creatures, but employ more subtle manipulations when dealing with other dragons. A green dragon attacks animals and monsters with no provocation, especially when dealing with potential threats to its territory. When dealing with sentient creatures, a green dragon demonstrates a lust for power that rivals its draconic desire for treasure, and it is always on the lookout for creatures that can help it further its ambitions.

A green dragon stalks its victims as it plans its assault, sometimes shadowing creatures for days. If a target is weak, the dragon enjoys the terror its appearance evokes before it attacks. It never slays all its foes, preferring to use intimidation to establish control over survivors. It then learns what it can about other creatures' activities near its territory, and about any treasure to be found nearby. Green dragons occasionally release prisoners if they can be ransomed. Otherwise, a creature must prove its value to the dragon daily or die.

Manipulative Schemers. A wily and subtle creature, a green dragon bends other creatures to its will by assessing and playing off their deepest desires. Any creature foolish enough to attempt to subdue a green dragon eventually realizes that the creature is only pretending to serve while it assesses its would-be master.

When manipulating other creatures, green dragons are honey-tongued, smooth, and sophisticated. Among their own kind, they are loud, crass, and rude, especially when dealing with dragons of the same age and status.

Conflict and Corruption. Green dragons sometimes clash with other dragons over territory where forest crosses over into other terrain. A green dragon typically pretends to back down, only to wait and watch—sometimes for decades—for the chance to slay the other dragon, then claim its lair and hoard.

Green dragons accept the servitude of sentient creatures such as goblinoids, ettercaps, ettins, kobolds, orcs, and yuan-ti. They also delight in corrupting and bending elves to their will. A green dragon sometimes wracks its minions' minds with fear to the point of insanity, with the fog that spreads throughout its forest reflecting those minions' tortured dreams.

Living Treasures. A green dragon's favored treasures are the sentient creatures it bends to its will, including significant figures such as popular heroes, well-known sages, and renowned bards. Among material treasures, a green dragon favors emeralds, wood carvings, musical instruments, and sculptures of humanoid subjects.

A Green Dragon's Lair

The forest-loving green dragons sometimes compete for territory with black dragons in marshy woods and with white dragons in subarctic taiga. However, a forest controlled by a green dragon is easy to spot. A perpetual fog hangs in the air in a legendary green dragon's wood, carrying an acrid whiff of the creature's poison breath. The moss-covered trees grow close together except where winding pathways trace their way like a maze into the heart of the forest. The light that reaches the

---

Green Dragon Wyrmling

Medium dragon, lawful evil

Armor Class 17 (natural armor)
Hit Points 38 (7d8 + 7)
Speed 30 ft., fly 60 ft., swim 30 ft.

STR	DEX	CON	INT	WIS	CHA
15 (+2)	12 (+1)	13 (+1)	14 (+2)	11 (+0)	13 (+1)

Saving Throws Dex +3, Con +3, Wis +2, Cha +3
Skills Perception +4, Stealth +3
Damage Immunities poison
Condition Immunities poisoned
Senses blindsight 10 ft., darkvision 60 ft., passive Perception 14
Languages Draconic
Challenge 2 (450 XP)

Amphibious. The dragon can breathe air and water.

Actions

Bite. *Melee Weapon Attack:* +4 to hit, reach 5 ft., one target. *Hit:* 7 (1d10 + 2) piercing damage plus 3 (1d6) poison damage.

Poison Breath (Recharge 5–6). The dragon exhales poisonous gas in a 15-foot cone. Each creature in that area must make a DC 11 Constitution saving throw, taking 21 (6d6) poison damage on a failed save, or half as much damage on a successful one.

forest floor carries an emerald green cast, and every sound seems muffled.

At the center of its forest, a green dragon chooses a cave in a sheer cliff or hillside for its lair, preferring an entrance hidden from prying eyes. Some seek out cave mouths concealed behind waterfalls, or partly submerged caverns that can be accessed through lakes or streams. Others conceal the entrances to their lairs with vegetation.

Lair Actions

On initiative count 20 (losing initiative ties), the dragon takes a lair action to cause one of the following effects; the dragon can't use the same effect two rounds in a row:

- Grasping roots and vines erupt in a 20-foot radius centered on a point on the ground that the dragon can see within 120 feet of it. That area becomes difficult terrain, and each creature there must succeed on a DC 15 Strength saving throw or be restrained by the roots and vines. A creature can be freed if it or another creature takes an action to make a DC 15 Strength check and succeeds. The roots and vines wilt away when the dragon uses this lair action again or when the dragon dies.
- A wall of tangled brush bristling with thorns springs into existence on a solid surface within 120 feet of the dragon. The wall is up to 60 feet long, 10 feet high, and 5 feet thick, and it blocks line of sight. When the wall appears, each creature in its area must make a DC 15 Dexterity saving throw. A creature that fails the save takes 18 (4d8) piercing damage and is pushed 5 feet out of the wall's space, appearing on whichever side of the wall it wants. A creature can move through the wall, albeit slowly and painfully. For every 1 foot a creature travels through the wall, it must spend 4 feet of movement. Furthermore, a creature in the wall's space must make a DC 15 Dexterity saving throw once each round it's in contact with the wall, taking 18 (4d8) piercing damage on a failed save, or half as much damage on a successful one. Each 10-foot section of wall has AC 5, 15 hit points, vulnerability to fire damage, resistance to bludgeoning and piercing damage, and immunity to psychic damage. The wall sinks back into the ground when the dragon uses this lair action again or when the dragon dies.
- Magical fog billows around one creature the dragon can see within 120 feet of it. The creature must succeed on a DC 15 Wisdom saving throw or be charmed by the dragon until initiative count 20 on the next round.

Regional Effects

The region containing a legendary green dragon's lair is warped by the dragon's magic, which creates one or more of the following effects:

- Thickets form labyrinthine passages within 1 mile of the dragon's lair. The thickets act as 10-foot-high, 10-foot-thick walls that block line of sight. Creatures can move through the thickets, with every 1 foot a creature moves costing it 4 feet of movement. A creature in the thickets must make a DC 15 Dexterity saving throw once each round it's in contact with the thickets or take 3 (1d6) piercing damage from thorns.

  Each 10-foot-cube of thickets has AC 5, 30 hit points, resistance to bludgeoning and piercing damage, vulnerability to fire damage, and immunity to psychic and thunder damage.
- Within 1 mile of its lair, the dragon leaves no physical evidence of its passage unless it wishes to. Tracking it there is impossible except by magical means. In addition, it ignores movement impediments and damage from plants in this area that are neither magical nor creatures, including the thickets described above. The plants remove themselves from the dragon's path.
- Rodents and birds within 1 mile of the dragon's lair serve as the dragon's eyes and ears. Deer and other large game are strangely absent, hinting at the presence of an unnaturally hungry predator.

If the dragon dies, the rodents and birds lose their supernatural link to it. The thickets remain, but within 1d10 days, they become mundane plants and normal difficult terrain, losing their thorns.

"I see an ancient elf king, his majesty long since faded, slumped and half asleep in his throne. A green dragon whispers in the king's ear, corrupting and twisting the king's dreams. This dragon's name is Cyan Bloodbane, and he means the destruction of us all."
—Pelios of Ergoth, Silvanesti seer

ANCIENT RED DRAGON

Gargantuan dragon, chaotic evil

Armor Class 22 (natural armor)
Hit Points 546 (28d20 + 252)
Speed 40 ft., climb 40 ft., fly 80 ft.

STR	DEX	CON	INT	WIS	CHA
30 (+10)	10 (+0)	29 (+9)	18 (+4)	15 (+2)	23 (+6)

Saving Throws Dex +7, Con +16, Wis +9, Cha +13
Skills Perception +16, Stealth +7
Damage Immunities fire
Senses blindsight 60 ft., darkvision 120 ft., passive Perception 26
Languages Common, Draconic
Challenge 24 (62,000 XP)

Legendary Resistance (3/Day). If the dragon fails a saving throw, it can choose to succeed instead.

ACTIONS

Multiattack. The dragon can use its Frightful Presence. It then makes three attacks: one with its bite and two with its claws.

Bite. Melee Weapon Attack: +17 to hit, reach 15 ft., one target. *Hit:* 21 (2d10 + 10) piercing damage plus 14 (4d6) fire damage.

Claw. Melee Weapon Attack: +17 to hit, reach 10 ft., one target. *Hit:* 17 (2d6 + 10) slashing damage.

Tail. Melee Weapon Attack: +17 to hit, reach 20 ft., one target. *Hit:* 19 (2d8 + 10) bludgeoning damage.

Frightful Presence. Each creature of the dragon's choice that is within 120 feet of the dragon and aware of it must succeed on a DC 21 Wisdom saving throw or become frightened for 1 minute. A creature can repeat the saving throw at the end of each of its turns, ending the effect on itself on a success. If a creature's saving throw is successful or the effect ends for it, the creature is immune to the dragon's Frightful Presence for the next 24 hours.

Fire Breath (Recharge 5–6). The dragon exhales fire in a 90-foot cone. Each creature in that area must make a DC 24 Dexterity saving throw, taking 91 (26d6) fire damage on a failed save, or half as much damage on a successful one.

LEGENDARY ACTIONS

The dragon can take 3 legendary actions, choosing from the options below. Only one legendary action option can be used at a time and only at the end of another creature's turn. The dragon regains spent legendary actions at the start of its turn.

Detect. The dragon makes a Wisdom (Perception) check.
Tail Attack. The dragon makes a tail attack.
Wing Attack (Costs 2 Actions). The dragon beats its wings. Each creature within 15 feet of the dragon must succeed on a DC 25 Dexterity saving throw or take 17 (2d6 + 10) bludgeoning damage and be knocked prone. The dragon can then fly up to half its flying speed.

ADULT RED DRAGON
Huge dragon, chaotic evil

Armor Class 19 (natural armor)
Hit Points 256 (19d12 + 133)
Speed 40 ft., climb 40 ft., fly 80 ft.

STR	DEX	CON	INT	WIS	CHA
27 (+8)	10 (+0)	25 (+7)	16 (+3)	13 (+1)	21 (+5)

Saving Throws Dex +6, Con +13, Wis +7, Cha +11
Skills Perception +13, Stealth +6
Damage Immunities fire
Senses blindsight 60 ft., darkvision 120 ft., passive Perception 23
Languages Common, Draconic
Challenge 17 (18,000 XP)

Legendary Resistance (3/Day). If the dragon fails a saving throw, it can choose to succeed instead.

ACTIONS

Multiattack. The dragon can use its Frightful Presence. It then makes three attacks: one with its bite and two with its claws.

Bite. *Melee Weapon Attack:* +14 to hit, reach 10 ft., one target. *Hit:* 19 (2d10 + 8) piercing damage plus 7 (2d6) fire damage.

Claw. *Melee Weapon Attack:* +14 to hit, reach 5 ft., one target. *Hit:* 15 (2d6 + 8) slashing damage.

Tail. *Melee Weapon Attack:* +14 to hit, reach 15 ft., one target. *Hit:* 17 (2d8 + 8) bludgeoning damage.

Frightful Presence. Each creature of the dragon's choice that is within 120 feet of the dragon and aware of it must succeed on a DC 19 Wisdom saving throw or become frightened for 1 minute. A creature can repeat the saving throw at the end of each of its turns, ending the effect on itself on a success. If a creature's saving throw is successful or the effect ends for it, the creature is immune to the dragon's Frightful Presence for the next 24 hours.

Fire Breath (Recharge 5–6). The dragon exhales fire in a 60-foot cone. Each creature in that area must make a DC 21 Dexterity saving throw, taking 63 (18d6) fire damage on a failed save, or half as much damage on a successful one.

LEGENDARY ACTIONS

The dragon can take 3 legendary actions, choosing from the options below. Only one legendary action option can be used at a time and only at the end of another creature's turn. The dragon regains spent legendary actions at the start of its turn.

Detect. The dragon makes a Wisdom (Perception) check.
Tail Attack. The dragon makes a tail attack.
Wing Attack (Costs 2 Actions). The dragon beats its wings. Each creature within 10 feet of the dragon must succeed on a DC 22 Dexterity saving throw or take 15 (2d6 + 8) bludgeoning damage and be knocked prone. The dragon can then fly up to half its flying speed.

YOUNG RED DRAGON
Large dragon, chaotic evil

Armor Class 18 (natural armor)
Hit Points 178 (17d10 + 85)
Speed 40 ft., climb 40 ft., fly 80 ft.

STR	DEX	CON	INT	WIS	CHA
23 (+6)	10 (+0)	21 (+5)	14 (+2)	11 (+0)	19 (+4)

Saving Throws Dex +4, Con +9, Wis +4, Cha +8
Skills Perception +8, Stealth +4
Damage Immunities fire
Senses blindsight 30 ft., darkvision 120 ft., passive Perception 18
Languages Common, Draconic
Challenge 10 (5,900 XP)

ACTIONS

Multiattack. The dragon makes three attacks: one with its bite and two with its claws.

Bite. *Melee Weapon Attack:* +10 to hit, reach 10 ft., one target. *Hit:* 17 (2d10 + 6) piercing damage plus 3 (1d6) fire damage.

Claw. *Melee Weapon Attack:* +10 to hit, reach 5 ft., one target. *Hit:* 13 (2d6 + 6) slashing damage.

Fire Breath (Recharge 5–6). The dragon exhales fire in a 30-foot cone. Each creature in that area must make a DC 17 Dexterity saving throw, taking 56 (16d6) fire damage on a failed save, or half as much damage on a successful one.

RED DRAGON WYRMLING
Medium dragon, chaotic evil

Armor Class 17 (natural armor)
Hit Points 75 (10d8 + 30)
Speed 30 ft., climb 30 ft., fly 60 ft.

STR	DEX	CON	INT	WIS	CHA
19 (+4)	10 (+0)	17 (+3)	12 (+1)	11 (+0)	15 (+2)

Saving Throws Dex +2, Con +5, Wis +2, Cha +4
Skills Perception +4, Stealth +2
Damage Immunities fire
Senses blindsight 10 ft., darkvision 60 ft., passive Perception 14
Languages Draconic
Challenge 4 (1,100 XP)

ACTIONS

Bite. *Melee Weapon Attack:* +6 to hit, reach 5 ft., one target. *Hit:* 9 (1d10 + 4) piercing damage plus 3 (1d6) fire damage.

Fire Breath (Recharge 5–6). The dragon exhales fire in a 15-foot cone. Each creature in that area must make a DC 13 Dexterity saving throw, taking 24 (7d6) fire damage on a failed save, or half as much damage on a successful one.

RED DRAGON

The most covetous of the true dragons, red dragons tirelessly seek to increase their treasure hoards. They are exceptionally vain, even for dragons, and their conceit is reflected in their proud bearing and their disdain for other creatures.

The odor of sulfur and pumice surrounds a red dragon, whose swept-back horns and spinal frill define its silhouette. Its beaked snout vents smoke at all times, and its eyes dance with flame when it is angry. Its wings are the longest of any chromatic dragon, and have a blue-black tint along the trailing edge that resembles metal burned blue by fire.

The scales of a red dragon wyrmling are a bright glossy scarlet, turning a dull, deeper red and becoming as thick and strong as metal as the dragon ages. Its pupils also fade as it ages, and the oldest red dragons have eyes that resemble molten lava orbs.

Mountain Masters. Red dragons prefer mountainous terrain, badlands, and any other locale where they can perch high and survey their domain. Their preference for mountains brings them into conflict with the hill-dwelling copper dragons from time to time.

Arrogant Tyrants. Red dragons fly into destructive rages and act on impulse when angered. They are so ferocious and vengeful that they are regarded as the archetypical evil dragon by many cultures.

No other dragon comes close to the arrogance of the red dragon. These creatures see themselves as kings and emperors, and view the rest of dragonkind as inferior. Believing that they are chosen by Tiamat to rule in her name, red dragons consider the world and every creature in it as thcirs to command.

Status and Slaves. Red dragons are fiercely territorial and isolationist. However, they yearn to know about events in the wider world, and they make use of lesser creatures as informants, messengers, and spies. They are most interested in news about other red dragons, with which they compete constantly for status.

When it requires servants, a red dragon demands fealty from chaotic evil humanoids. If allegiance isn't forthcoming, it slaughters a tribe's leaders and claims lordship over the survivors. Creatures serving a red dragon live in constant terror of being roasted and eaten for displeasing it. They spend most of their time fawning over the creature in an attempt to stay alive.

Obsessive Collectors. Red dragons value wealth above all else, and their treasure hoards are legendary. They covet anything of monetary value, and can often judge the worth of a bauble to within a copper piece at a glance. A red dragon has a special affection for treasure claimed from powerful enemies it has slain, exhibiting that treasure to prove its superiority.

A red dragon knows the value and provenance of every item in its hoard, along with each item's exact location. It might notice the absence of a single coin, igniting its rage as it tracks down and slays the thief without mercy. If the thief can't be found, the dragon goes on a rampage, laying waste to towns and villages in an attempt to sate its wrath.

A RED DRAGON'S LAIR

Red dragons lair in high mountains or hills, dwelling in caverns under snow-capped peaks, or within the deep halls of abandoned mines and dwarven strongholds. Caves with volcanic or geothermal activity are the most highly prized red dragon lairs, creating hazards that hinder intruders and letting searing heat and volcanic gases wash over a dragon as it sleeps.

With its hoard well protected deep within the lair, a red dragon spends as much of its time outside the mountain as in it. For a red dragon, the great heights of the world are the throne from which it can look out to survey all it controls—and the wider world it seeks to control.

Throughout the lair complex, servants erect monuments to the dragon's power, telling the grim story of its life, the enemies it has slain, and the nations it has conquered.

LAIR ACTIONS

On initiative count 20 (losing initiative ties), the dragon takes a lair action to cause one of the following effects; the dragon can't use the same effect two rounds in a row:

- Magma erupts from a point on the ground the dragon can see within 120 feet of it, creating a 20-foot-high, 5-foot-radius geyser. Each creature in the geyser's area must make a DC 15 Dexterity saving throw, taking 21 (6d6) fire damage on a failed save, or half as much damage on a successful one.
- A tremor shakes the lair in a 60-foot radius around the dragon. Each creature other than the dragon on the ground in that area must succeed on a DC 15 Dexterity saving throw or be knocked prone.
- Volcanic gases form a cloud in a 20-foot-radius sphere centered on a point the dragon can see within 120 feet of it. The sphere spreads around corners, and its area is lightly obscured. It lasts until initiative count 20 on the next round. Each creature that starts its turn in the cloud must succeed on a DC 13 Constitution saving throw or be poisoned until the end of its turn. While poisoned in this way, a creature is incapacitated.

REGIONAL EFFECTS

The region containing a legendary red dragon's lair is warped by the dragon's magic, which creates one or more of the following effects:

- Small earthquakes are common within 6 miles of the dragon's lair.
- Water sources within 1 mile of the lair are supernaturally warm and tainted by sulfur.
- Rocky fissures within 1 mile of the dragon's lair form portals to the Elemental Plane of Fire, allowing creatures of elemental fire into the world to dwell nearby.

If the dragon dies, these effects fade over the course of 1d10 days.

Ancient White Dragon

Gargantuan dragon, chaotic evil

Armor Class 20 (natural armor)
Hit Points 333 (18d20 + 144)
Speed 40 ft., burrow 40 ft., fly 80 ft., swim 40 ft.

STR	DEX	CON	INT	WIS	CHA
26 (+8)	10 (+0)	26 (+8)	10 (+0)	13 (+1)	14 (+2)

Saving Throws Dex +6, Con +14, Wis +7, Cha +8
Skills Perception +13, Stealth +6
Damage Immunities cold
Senses blindsight 60 ft., darkvision 120 ft., passive Perception 23
Languages Common, Draconic
Challenge 20 (25,000 XP)

Ice Walk. The dragon can move across and climb icy surfaces without needing to make an ability check. Additionally, difficult terrain composed of ice or snow doesn't cost it extra moment.

Legendary Resistance (3/Day). If the dragon fails a saving throw, it can choose to succeed instead.

ACTIONS

Multiattack. The dragon can use its Frightful Presence. It then makes three attacks: one with its bite and two with its claws.

Bite. *Melee Weapon Attack:* +14 to hit, reach 15 ft., one target. *Hit:* 19 (2d10 + 8) piercing damage plus 9 (2d8) cold damage.

Claw. *Melee Weapon Attack:* +14 to hit, reach 10 ft., one target. *Hit:* 15 (2d6 + 8) slashing damage.

Tail. *Melee Weapon Attack:* +14 to hit, reach 20 ft., one target. *Hit:* 17 (2d8 + 8) bludgeoning damage.

Frightful Presence. Each creature of the dragon's choice that is within 120 feet of the dragon and aware of it must succeed on a DC 16 Wisdom saving throw or become frightened for 1 minute. A creature can repeat the saving throw at the end of each of its turns, ending the effect on itself on a success. If a creature's saving throw is successful or the effect ends for it, the creature is immune to the dragon's Frightful Presence for the next 24 hours.

Cold Breath (Recharge 5–6). The dragon exhales an icy blast in a 90-foot cone. Each creature in that area must make a DC 22 Constitution saving throw, taking 72 (16d8) cold damage on a failed save, or half as much damage on a successful one.

LEGENDARY ACTIONS

The dragon can take 3 legendary actions, choosing from the options below. Only one legendary action option can be used at a time and only at the end of another creature's turn. The dragon regains spent legendary actions at the start of its turn.

Detect. The dragon makes a Wisdom (Perception) check.
Tail Attack. The dragon makes a tail attack.
Wing Attack (Costs 2 Actions). The dragon beats its wings. Each creature within 15 feet of the dragon must succeed on a DC 22 Dexterity saving throw or take 15 (2d6 + 8) bludgeoning damage and be knocked prone. The dragon can then fly up to half its flying speed.

ADULT WHITE DRAGON
Huge dragon, chaotic evil

Armor Class 18 (natural armor)
Hit Points 200 (16d12 + 96)
Speed 40 ft., burrow 30 ft., fly 80 ft., swim 40 ft.

STR	DEX	CON	INT	WIS	CHA
22 (+6)	10 (+0)	22 (+6)	8 (−1)	12 (+1)	12 (+1)

Saving Throws Dex +5, Con +11, Wis +6, Cha +6
Skills Perception +11, Stealth +5
Damage Immunities cold
Senses blindsight 60 ft., darkvision 120 ft., passive Perception 21
Languages Common, Draconic
Challenge 13 (10,000 XP)

Ice Walk. The dragon can move across and climb icy surfaces without needing to make an ability check. Additionally, difficult terrain composed of ice or snow doesn't cost it extra moment.

Legendary Resistance (3/Day). If the dragon fails a saving throw, it can choose to succeed instead.

ACTIONS

Multiattack. The dragon can use its Frightful Presence. It then makes three attacks: one with its bite and two with its claws.

Bite. *Melee Weapon Attack:* +11 to hit, reach 10 ft., one target. *Hit:* 17 (2d10 + 6) piercing damage plus 4 (1d8) cold damage.

Claw. *Melee Weapon Attack:* +11 to hit, reach 5 ft., one target. *Hit:* 13 (2d6 + 6) slashing damage.

Tail. *Melee Weapon Attack:* +11 to hit, reach 15 ft., one target. *Hit:* 15 (2d8 + 6) bludgeoning damage.

Frightful Presence. Each creature of the dragon's choice that is within 120 feet of the dragon and aware of it must succeed on a DC 14 Wisdom saving throw or become frightened for 1 minute. A creature can repeat the saving throw at the end of each of its turns, ending the effect on itself on a success. If a creature's saving throw is successful or the effect ends for it, the creature is immune to the dragon's Frightful Presence for the next 24 hours.

Cold Breath (Recharge 5–6). The dragon exhales an icy blast in a 60-foot cone. Each creature in that area must make a DC 19 Constitution saving throw, taking 54 (12d8) cold damage on a failed save, or half as much damage on a successful one.

LEGENDARY ACTIONS

The dragon can take 3 legendary actions, choosing from the options below. Only one legendary action option can be used at a time and only at the end of another creature's turn. The dragon regains spent legendary actions at the start of its turn.

Detect. The dragon makes a Wisdom (Perception) check.
Tail Attack. The dragon makes a tail attack.
Wing Attack (Costs 2 Actions). The dragon beats its wings. Each creature within 10 feet of the dragon must succeed on a DC 19 Dexterity saving throw or take 13 (2d6 + 6) bludgeoning damage and be knocked prone. The dragon can then fly up to half its flying speed.

YOUNG WHITE DRAGON
Large dragon, chaotic evil

Armor Class 17 (natural armor)
Hit Points 133 (14d10 + 56)
Speed 40 ft., burrow 20 ft., fly 80 ft., swim 40 ft.

STR	DEX	CON	INT	WIS	CHA
18 (+4)	10 (+0)	18 (+4)	6 (−2)	11 (+0)	12 (+1)

Saving Throws Dex +3, Con +7, Wis +3, Cha +4
Skills Perception +6, Stealth +3
Damage Immunities cold
Senses blindsight 30 ft., darkvision 120 ft., passive Perception 16
Languages Common, Draconic
Challenge 6 (2,300 XP)

Ice Walk. The dragon can move across and climb icy surfaces without needing to make an ability check. Additionally, difficult terrain composed of ice or snow doesn't cost it extra moment.

ACTIONS

Multiattack. The dragon makes three attacks: one with its bite and two with its claws.

Bite. *Melee Weapon Attack:* +7 to hit, reach 10 ft., one target. *Hit:* 15 (2d10 + 4) piercing damage plus 4 (1d8) cold damage.

Claw. *Melee Weapon Attack:* +7 to hit, reach 5 ft., one target. *Hit:* 11 (2d6 + 4) slashing damage.

Cold Breath (Recharge 5–6). The dragon exhales an icy blast in a 30-foot cone. Each creature in that area must make a DC 15 Constitution saving throw, taking 45 (10d8) cold damage on a failed save, or half as much damage on a successful one.

White Dragon

The smallest, least intelligent, and most animalistic of the chromatic dragons, white dragons dwell in frigid climes, favoring arctic areas or icy mountains. They are vicious, cruel reptiles driven by hunger and greed.

A white dragon has feral eyes, a sleek profile, and a spined crest. The scales of a wyrmling white dragon glisten pure white. As the dragon ages, its sheen disappears and some of its scales begin to darken, so that by the time it is old, it is mottled by patches of pale blue and light gray. This patterning helps the dragon blend into the realms of ice and stone in which it hunts, and to fade from view when it soars across a cloud-filled sky.

Primal and Vengeful. White dragons lack the cunning and tactics of most other dragons. However, their bestial nature makes them the best hunters among all dragonkind, singularly focused on surviving and slaughtering their enemies. A white dragon consumes only food that has been frozen, devouring creatures killed by its breath weapon while they are still stiff and frigid. It encases other kills in ice or buries them in snow near its lair, and finding such a larder is a good indication that a white dragon dwells nearby.

A white dragon also keeps the bodies of its greatest enemies as trophies, freezing corpses where it can look upon them and gloat. The remains of giants, remorhazes, and other dragons are often positioned prominently within a white dragon's lair as warnings to intruders.

Though only moderately intelligent, white dragons have extraordinary memories. They recall every slight and defeat, and have been known to conduct malicious vendettas against creatures that have offended them. This often includes silver dragons, which lair in the same territories as whites. White dragons can speak as all dragons can, but they rarely talk unless moved to do so.

Lone Masters. White dragons avoid all other dragons except whites of the opposite sex. Even then, when white dragons seek each other out as mates, they stay together only long enough to conceive offspring before fleeing into isolation again.

White dragons can't abide rivals near their lairs. As a result, a white dragon attacks other creatures without provocation, viewing such creatures as either too weak or too powerful to live. The only creatures that typically serve a white dragon are intelligent humanoids that demonstrate enough strength to assuage the dragon's wrath, and can put up with sustaining regular losses as a result of its hunger. This includes dragon-worshiping kobolds, which are commonly found in their lairs.

Powerful creatures can sometimes gain a white dragon's obedience through a demonstration of physical or magical might. Frost giants challenge white dragons to prove their own strength and improve their status in their clans, and their cracked bones litter many a white dragon's lair. However, a white dragon defeated by a frost giant often becomes its servant, accepting the mastery of a superior creature in exchange for asserting its own domination over the other creatures that serve or oppose the giant.

Treasure Under Ice. White dragons love the cold sparkle of ice and favor treasure with similar qualities, particularly diamonds. However, in their remote arctic climes, the treasure hoards of white dragons more often contain walrus and mammoth tusk ivory, whale-bone sculptures, figureheads from ships, furs, and magic items seized from overly bold adventurers.

Loose coins and gems are spread across a white dragon's lair, glittering like stars when the light strikes them. Larger treasures and chests are encased in layers of rime created by the white dragon's breath, and held safe beneath layers of transparent ice. The dragon's great strength allows it to easily access its wealth, while lesser creatures must spend hours chipping away or melting the ice to reach the dragon's main hoard.

A white dragon's flawless memory means that it knows how it came to possess every coin, gem, and magic item in its hoard, and it associates each item with a specific victory. White dragons are notoriously difficult to bribe, since any offers of treasure are seen as an insult to their ability to simply slay the creature making the offer and seize the treasure on their own.

A White Dragon's Lair

White dragons lair in icy caves and deep subterranean chambers far from the sun. They favor high mountain vales accessible only by flying, caverns in cliff faces, and labyrinthine ice caves in glaciers. White dragons love vertical heights in their caverns, flying up to the ceiling to latch on like bats or slithering down icy crevasses.

A legendary white dragon's innate magic deepens the cold in the area around its lair. Mountain caverns are fast frozen by the white dragon's presence. A white dragon can often detect intruders by the way the keening wind in its lair changes tone.

White Dragon Wyrmling

Medium dragon, chaotic evil

Armor Class 16 (natural armor)
Hit Points 32 (5d8 + 10)
Speed 30 ft., burrow 15 ft., fly 60 ft., swim 30 ft.

STR	DEX	CON	INT	WIS	CHA
14 (+2)	10 (+0)	14 (+2)	5 (−3)	10 (+0)	11 (+0)

Saving Throws Dex +2, Con +4, Wis +2, Cha +2
Skills Perception +4, Stealth +2
Damage Immunities cold
Senses blindsight 10 ft., darkvision 60 ft., passive Perception 14
Languages Draconic
Challenge 2 (450 XP)

Actions

Bite. *Melee Weapon Attack:* +4 to hit, reach 5 ft., one target. *Hit:* 7 (1d10 + 2) piercing damage plus 2 (1d4) cold damage.

Cold Breath (Recharge 5–6). The dragon exhales an icy blast of hail in a 15-foot cone. Each creature in that area must make a DC 12 Constitution saving throw, taking 22 (5d8) cold damage on a failed save, or half as much damage on a successful one.

A white dragon rests on high ice shelves and cliffs in its lair, the floor around it a treacherous morass of broken ice and stone, hidden pits, and slippery slopes. As foes struggle to move toward it, the dragon flies from perch to perch and destroys them with its freezing breath.

Lair Actions

On initiative count 20 (losing initiative ties), the dragon takes a lair action to cause one of the following effects; the dragon can't use the same effect two rounds in a row:

- Freezing fog fills a 20-foot-radius sphere centered on a point the dragon can see within 120 feet of it. The fog spreads around corners, and its area is heavily obscured. Each creature in the fog when it appears must make a DC 10 Constitution saving throw, taking 10 (3d6) cold damage on a failed save, or half as much damage on a successful one. A creature that ends its turn in the fog takes 10 (3d6) cold damage. A wind of at least 20 miles per hour disperses the fog. The fog otherwise lasts until the dragon uses this lair action again or until the dragon dies.
- Jagged ice shards fall from the ceiling, striking up to three creatures underneath that the dragon can see within 120 feet of it. The dragon makes one ranged attack roll (+7 to hit) against each target. On a hit, the target takes 10 (3d6) piercing damage.
- The dragon creates an opaque wall of ice on a solid surface it can see within 120 feet of it. The wall can be up to 30 feet long, 30 feet high, and 1 foot thick. When the wall appears, each creature within its area is pushed 5 feet out of the wall's space, appearing on whichever side of the wall it wants. Each 10-foot section of the wall has AC 5, 30 hit points, vulnerability to fire damage, and immunity to acid, cold, necrotic, poison, and psychic damage. The wall disappears when the dragon uses this lair action again or when the dragon dies.

Regional Effects

The region containing a legendary white dragon's lair is warped by the dragon's magic, which creates one or more of the following effects:

- Chilly fog lightly obscures the land within 6 miles of the dragon's lair.
- Freezing precipitation falls within 6 miles of the dragon's lair, sometimes forming blizzard conditions when the dragon is at rest.
- Icy walls block off areas in the dragon's lair. Each wall is 6 inches thick, and a 10-foot section has AC 5, 15 hit points, vulnerability to fire damage, and immunity to acid, cold, necrotic, poison, and psychic damage.

    If the dragon wishes to move through a wall, it can do so without slowing down. The portion of the wall the dragon moves through is destroyed, however.

If the dragon dies, the fog and precipitation fade within 1 day. The ice walls melt over the course of 1d10 days.

Metallic Dragons

Metallic dragons seek to preserve and protect, viewing themselves as one powerful race among the many races that have a place in the world.

Noble Curiosity. Metallic dragons covet treasure as do their evil chromatic kin, but they aren't driven as much by greed in their pursuit of wealth. Rather, metallic dragons are driven to investigate and collect, taking unclaimed relics and storing them in their lairs. A metallic dragon's treasure hoard is filled with items that reflect its persona, tell its history, and preserve its memories. Metallic dragons also seek to protect other creatures from dangerous magic. As such, powerful magic items and even evil artifacts are sometimes secreted away in a metallic dragon's hoard.

A metallic dragon can be persuaded to part with an item in its hoard for the greater good. However, another creature's need for or right to the item is often unclear from the dragon's point of view. A metallic dragon must be bribed or otherwise convinced to part with the item.

Solitary Shapeshifters. At some point in their long lives, metallic dragons gain the magical ability to assume the forms of humanoids and beasts. When a dragon learns how to disguise itself, it might immerse itself in other cultures for a time. Some dragons are too shy or paranoid to stray far from their lairs and their treasure hoards, but bolder dragons love to wander city streets in humanoid form, taking in the local culture and cuisine, and amusing themselves by observing how the smaller races live.

Some metallic dragons prefer to stay as far away from civilization as possible so as to not attract enemies. However, this means that they are often far out of touch with current events.

The Persistence of Memory. Metallic dragons have long memories, and they form opinions of humanoids based on previous contact with related humanoids. Good dragons can recognize humanoid bloodlines by smell, sniffing out each person they meet and remembering any relatives they have come into contact with over the years. A gold dragon might never suspect duplicity from a cunning villain, assuming that the villain is of the same mind and heart as a good and virtuous grandmother. On the other hand, the dragon might resent a noble paladin whose ancestor stole a silver statue from the dragon's hoard three centuries before.

King of Good Dragons. The chief deity of the metallic dragons is Bahamut, the Platinum Dragon. He dwells in the Seven Heavens of Mount Celestia, but often wanders the Material Plane in the magical guise of a venerable human male in peasant robes. In this form, he is usually accompanied by seven golden canaries—actually seven ancient gold dragons in polymorphed form.

Bahamut seldom interferes in the affairs of mortal creatures, though he makes exceptions to help thwart the machinations of Tiamat the Dragon Queen and her evil brood. Good-aligned clerics and paladins sometimes worship Bahamut for his dedication to justice and protection. As a lesser god, he has the power to grant divine spells.

Ancient Brass Dragon
Gargantuan dragon, chaotic good

Armor Class 20 (natural armor)
Hit Points 297 (17d20 + 119)
Speed 40 ft., burrow 40 ft., fly 80 ft.

STR	DEX	CON	INT	WIS	CHA
27 (+8)	10 (+0)	25 (+7)	16 (+3)	15 (+2)	19 (+4)

Saving Throws Dex +6, Con +13, Wis +8, Cha +10
Skills History +9, Perception +14, Persuasion +10, Stealth +6
Damage Immunities fire
Senses blindsight 60 ft., darkvision 120 ft., passive Perception 24
Languages Common, Draconic
Challenge 20 (25,000 XP)

Legendary Resistance (3/Day). If the dragon fails a saving throw, it can choose to succeed instead.

Actions

Multiattack. The dragon can use its Frightful Presence. It then makes three attacks: one with its bite and two with its claws.

Bite. *Melee Weapon Attack:* +14 to hit, reach 15 ft., one target. *Hit:* 19 (2d10 + 8) piercing damage.

Claw. *Melee Weapon Attack:* +14 to hit, reach 10 ft., one target. *Hit:* 15 (2d6 + 8) slashing damage.

Tail. *Melee Weapon Attack:* +14 to hit, reach 20 ft., one target. *Hit:* 17 (2d8 + 8) bludgeoning damage.

Frightful Presence. Each creature of the dragon's choice that is within 120 feet of the dragon and aware of it must succeed on a DC 18 Wisdom saving throw or become frightened for 1 minute. A creature can repeat the saving throw at the end of each of its turns, ending the effect on itself on a success. If a creature's saving throw is successful or the effect ends for it, the creature is immune to the dragon's Frightful Presence for the next 24 hours.

Breath Weapons (Recharge 5–6). The dragon uses one of the following breath weapons:

Fire Breath. The dragon exhales fire in an 90-foot line that is 10 feet wide. Each creature in that line must make a DC 21 Dexterity saving throw, taking 56 (16d6) fire damage on a failed save, or half as much damage on a successful one.

Sleep Breath. The dragon exhales sleep gas in a 90-foot cone. Each creature in that area must succeed on a DC 21 Constitution saving throw or fall unconscious for 10 minutes. This effect ends for a creature if the creature takes damage or someone uses an action to wake it.

Change Shape. The dragon magically polymorphs into a humanoid or beast that has a challenge rating no higher than its own, or back into its true form. It reverts to its true form if it dies. Any equipment it is wearing or carrying is absorbed or borne by the new form (the dragon's choice).

In a new form, the dragon retains its alignment, hit points, Hit Dice, ability to speak, proficiencies, Legendary Resistance, lair actions, and Intelligence, Wisdom, and Charisma scores, as well as this action. Its statistics and capabilities are otherwise replaced by those of the new form, except any class features or legendary actions of that form.

Legendary Actions

The dragon can take 3 legendary actions, choosing from the options below. Only one legendary action option can be used at a time and only at the end of another creature's turn. The dragon regains spent legendary actions at the start of its turn.

Detect. The dragon makes a Wisdom (Perception) check.
Tail Attack. The dragon makes a tail attack.
Wing Attack (Costs 2 Actions). The dragon beats its wings. Each creature within 15 feet of the dragon must succeed on a DC 22 Dexterity saving throw or take 15 (2d6 + 8) bludgeoning damage and be knocked prone. The dragon can then fly up to half its flying speed.

ADULT BRASS DRAGON

Huge dragon, chaotic good

Armor Class 18 (natural armor)
Hit Points 172 (15d12 + 75)
Speed 40 ft., burrow 30 ft., fly 80 ft.

STR	DEX	CON	INT	WIS	CHA
23 (+6)	10 (+0)	21 (+5)	14 (+2)	13 (+1)	17 (+3)

Saving Throws Dex +5, Con +10, Wis +6, Cha +8
Skills History +7, Perception +11, Persuasion +8, Stealth +5
Damage Immunities fire
Senses blindsight 60 ft., darkvision 120 ft., passive Perception 21
Languages Common, Draconic
Challenge 13 (10,000 XP)

Legendary Resistance (3/Day). If the dragon fails a saving throw, it can choose to succeed instead.

ACTIONS

Multiattack. The dragon can use its Frightful Presence. It then makes three attacks: one with its bite and two with its claws.

Bite. *Melee Weapon Attack:* +11 to hit, reach 10 ft., one target. *Hit:* 17 (2d10 + 6) piercing damage.

Claw. *Melee Weapon Attack:* +11 to hit, reach 5 ft., one target. *Hit:* 13 (2d6 + 6) slashing damage.

Tail. *Melee Weapon Attack:* +11 to hit, reach 15 ft., one target. *Hit:* 15 (2d8 + 6) bludgeoning damage.

Frightful Presence. Each creature of the dragon's choice that is within 120 feet of the dragon and aware of it must succeed on a DC 16 Wisdom saving throw or become frightened for 1 minute. A creature can repeat the saving throw at the end of each of its turns, ending the effect on itself on a success. If a creature's saving throw is successful or the effect ends for it, the creature is immune to the dragon's Frightful Presence for the next 24 hours.

Breath Weapons (Recharge 5–6). The dragon uses one of the following breath weapons.

Fire Breath. The dragon exhales fire in an 60-foot line that is 5 feet wide. Each creature in that line must make a DC 18 Dexterity saving throw, taking 45 (13d6) fire damage on a failed save, or half as much damage on a successful one.

Sleep Breath. The dragon exhales sleep gas in a 60-foot cone. Each creature in that area must succeed on a DC 18 Constitution saving throw or fall unconscious for 10 minutes. This effect ends for a creature if the creature takes damage or someone uses an action to wake it.

LEGENDARY ACTIONS

The dragon can take 3 legendary actions, choosing from the options below. Only one legendary action option can be used at a time and only at the end of another creature's turn. The dragon regains spent legendary actions at the start of its turn.

Detect. The dragon makes a Wisdom (Perception) check.
Tail Attack. The dragon makes a tail attack.
Wing Attack (Costs 2 Actions). The dragon beats its wings. Each creature within 10 feet of the dragon must succeed on a DC 19 Dexterity saving throw or take 13 (2d6 + 6) bludgeoning damage and be knocked prone. The dragon can then fly up to half its flying speed.

YOUNG BRASS DRAGON

Large dragon, chaotic good

Armor Class 17 (natural armor)
Hit Points 110 (13d10 + 39)
Speed 40 ft., burrow 20 ft., fly 80 ft.

STR	DEX	CON	INT	WIS	CHA
19 (+4)	10 (+0)	17 (+3)	12 (+1)	11 (+0)	15 (+2)

Saving Throws Dex +3, Con +6, Wis +3, Cha +5
Skills Perception +6, Persuasion +5, Stealth +3
Damage Immunities fire
Senses blindsight 30 ft., darkvision 120 ft., passive Perception 16
Languages Common, Draconic
Challenge 6 (2,300 XP)

ACTIONS

Multiattack. The dragon makes three attacks: one with its bite and two with its claws.

Bite. *Melee Weapon Attack:* +7 to hit, reach 10 ft., one target. *Hit:* 15 (2d10 + 4) piercing damage.

Claw. *Melee Weapon Attack:* +7 to hit, reach 5 ft., one target. *Hit:* 11 (2d6 + 4) slashing damage.

Breath Weapons (Recharge 5–6). The dragon uses one of the following breath weapons.

Fire Breath. The dragon exhales fire in a 40-foot line that is 5 feet wide. Each creature in that line must make a DC 14 Dexterity saving throw, taking 42 (12d6) fire damage on a failed save, or half as much damage on a successful one.

Sleep Breath. The dragon exhales sleep gas in a 30-foot cone. Each creature in that area must succeed on a DC 14 Constitution saving throw or fall unconscious for 5 minutes. This effect ends for a creature if the creature takes damage or someone uses an action to wake it.

Brass Dragon

The most gregarious of the true dragons, brass dragons crave conversation, sunlight, and hot, dry climates.

A brass dragon's head is defined by the broad protective plate that expands from its forehead and the spikes protruding from its chin. A frill runs the length of its neck, and its tapering wings extend down the length of its tail. A brass dragon wyrmling's scales are a dull, mottled brown. As it ages, the dragon's scales begin to shine, eventually taking on a warm, burnished luster. Its wings and frills are mottled green toward the edges, darkening with age. As a brass dragon grows older, its pupils fade until its eyes resemble molten metal orbs.

Boldly Talkative. A brass dragon engages in conversations with thousands of creatures throughout its long life, accumulating useful information which it will gladly share for gifts of treasure. If an intelligent creature tries to leave a brass dragon's presence without engaging in conversation, the dragon follows it. If the creature attempts to escape by magic or force, the dragon might respond with a fit of pique, using its sleep gas to incapacitate the creature. When it wakes, the creature finds itself pinned to the ground by giant claws or buried up to its neck in the sand while the dragon's thirst for small talk is slaked.

A brass dragon is trusting of creatures that appear to enjoy conversation as much as it does, but is smart enough to know when it is being manipulated. When that happens, the dragon often responds in kind, treating a bout of mutual trickery as a game.

Prized Treasures. Brass dragons covet magic items that allow them to converse with interesting personalities. An intelligent telepathic weapon or a magic lamp with a djinni bound inside it are among the greatest treasures a brass dragon can possess.

Brass dragons conceal their hoards under mounds of sand or in secret places far from their primary lairs. They have no trouble remembering where their treasure is buried, and therefore have no need for maps. Adventurers and wanderers should be wary if they happen across a chest hidden in an oasis or a treasure cache tucked away in a half-buried desert ruin, for these might be parts of a brass dragon's hoard.

A Brass Dragon's Lair

A brass dragon's desert lair is typically a ruin, canyon, or cave network with ceiling holes to allow for sunlight.

Lair Actions

On initiative count 20 (losing initiative ties), the dragon takes a lair action to cause one of the following effects:

- A strong wind blows around the dragon. Each creature within 60 feet of the dragon must succeed on a DC 15 Strength saving throw or be pushed 15 feet away from the dragon and knocked prone. Gases and vapors are dispersed by the wind, and unprotected flames are extinguished. Protected flames, such as lanterns, have a 50 percent chance of being extinguished.
- A cloud of sand swirls about in a 20-foot-radius sphere centered on a point the dragon can see within 120 feet of it. The cloud spreads around corners. Each creature in it must succeed on a DC 15 Constitution saving throw or be blinded for 1 minute. A creature can repeat the saving throw at the end of each of its turns, ending the effect on itself on a success.

Regional Effects

The region containing a legendary brass dragon's lair is warped by the dragon's magic, which creates one or more of the following effects:

- Tracks appear in the sand within 6 miles of the dragon's lair. The tracks lead to safe shelters and hidden water sources, while also leading away from areas that the dragon prefers to remain undisturbed.
- Images of Large or smaller monsters haunt the desert sands within 1 mile of the dragon's lair. These illusions move and appear real, although they can do no harm. A creature that examines an image from a distance can tell it's an illusion with a successful DC 20 Intelligence (Investigation) check. Any physical interaction with an image reveals it to be an illusion, because objects pass through it.
- Whenever a creature with an Intelligence of 3 or higher comes within 30 feet of a water source within 1 mile of the dragon's lair, the dragon becomes aware of the creature's presence and location.

If the dragon dies, the tracks fade in 1d10 days, but the other effects fade immediately.

Brass Dragon Wyrmling

Medium dragon, chaotic good

Armor Class 16 (natural armor)
Hit Points 16 (3d8 + 3)
Speed 30 ft., burrow 15 ft., fly 60 ft.

STR	DEX	CON	INT	WIS	CHA
15 (+2)	10 (+0)	13 (+1)	10 (+0)	11 (+0)	13 (+1)

Saving Throws Dex +2, Con +3, Wis +2, Cha +3
Skills Perception +4, Stealth +2
Damage Immunities fire
Senses blindsight 10 ft., darkvision 60 ft., passive Perception 14
Languages Draconic
Challenge 1 (200 XP)

Actions

Bite. *Melee Weapon Attack:* +4 to hit, reach 5 ft., one target. *Hit:* 7 (1d10 + 2) piercing damage.

Breath Weapons (Recharge 5–6). The dragon uses one of the following breath weapons.

Fire Breath. The dragon exhales fire in an 20-foot line that is 5 feet wide. Each creature in that line must make a DC 11 Dexterity saving throw, taking 14 (4d6) fire damage on a failed save, or half as much damage on a successful one.

Sleep Breath. The dragon exhales sleep gas in a 15-foot cone. Each creature in that area must succeed on a DC 11 Constitution saving throw or fall unconscious for 1 minute. This effect ends for a creature if the creature takes damage or someone uses an action to wake it.

Ancient Bronze Dragon
Gargantuan dragon, lawful good

Armor Class 22 (natural armor)
Hit Points 444 (24d20 + 192)
Speed 40 ft., fly 80 ft., swim 40 ft.

STR	DEX	CON	INT	WIS	CHA
29 (+9)	10 (+0)	27 (+8)	18 (+4)	17 (+3)	21 (+5)

Saving Throws Dex +7, Con +15, Wis +10, Cha +12
Skills Insight +10, Perception +17, Stealth +7
Damage Immunities lightning
Senses blindsight 60 ft., darkvision 120 ft., passive Perception 27
Languages Common, Draconic
Challenge 22 (41,000 XP)

Amphibious. The dragon can breathe air and water.

Legendary Resistance (3/Day). If the dragon fails a saving throw, it can choose to succeed instead.

Actions

Multiattack. The dragon can use its Frightful Presence. It then makes three attacks: one with its bite and two with its claws.

Bite. *Melee Weapon Attack:* +16 to hit, reach 15 ft., one target. *Hit:* 20 (2d10 + 9) piercing damage.

Claw. *Melee Weapon Attack:* +16 to hit, reach 10 ft., one target. *Hit:* 16 (2d6 + 9) slashing damage.

Tail. *Melee Weapon Attack:* +16 to hit, reach 20 ft., one target. *Hit:* 18 (2d8 + 9) bludgeoning damage.

Frightful Presence. Each creature of the dragon's choice that is within 120 feet of the dragon and aware of it must succeed on a DC 20 Wisdom saving throw or become frightened for 1 minute. A creature can repeat the saving throw at the end of each of its turns, ending the effect on itself on a success. If a creature's saving throw is successful or the effect ends for it, the creature is immune to the dragon's Frightful Presence for the next 24 hours.

Breath Weapons (Recharge 5–6). The dragon uses one of the following breath weapons.

Lightning Breath. The dragon exhales lightning in a 120-foot line that is 10 feet wide. Each creature in that line must make a DC 23 Dexterity saving throw, taking 88 (16d10) lightning damage on a failed save, or half as much damage on a successful one.

Repulsion Breath. The dragon exhales repulsion energy in a 30-foot cone. Each creature in that area must succeed on a DC 23 Strength saving throw. On a failed save, the creature is pushed 60 feet away from the dragon.

Change Shape. The dragon magically polymorphs into a humanoid or beast that has a challenge rating no higher than its own, or back into its true form. It reverts to its true form if it dies. Any equipment it is wearing or carrying is absorbed or borne by the new form (the dragon's choice).

In a new form, the dragon retains its alignment, hit points, Hit Dice, ability to speak, proficiencies, Legendary Resistance, lair actions, and Intelligence, Wisdom, and Charisma scores, as well as this action. Its statistics and capabilities are otherwise replaced by those of the new form, except any class features or legendary actions of that form.

Legendary Actions

The dragon can take 3 legendary actions, choosing from the options below. Only one legendary action option can be used at a time and only at the end of another creature's turn. The dragon regains spent legendary actions at the start of its turn.

Detect. The dragon makes a Wisdom (Perception) check.
Tail Attack. The dragon makes a tail attack.
Wing Attack (Costs 2 Actions). The dragon beats its wings. Each creature within 15 feet of the dragon must succeed on a DC 24 Dexterity saving throw or take 16 (2d6 + 9) bludgeoning damage and be knocked prone. The dragon can then fly up to half its flying speed.

Adult Bronze Dragon

Huge dragon, lawful good

Armor Class 19 (natural armor)
Hit Points 212 (17d12 + 102)
Speed 40 ft., fly 80 ft., swim 40 ft.

STR	DEX	CON	INT	WIS	CHA
25 (+7)	10 (+0)	23 (+6)	16 (+3)	15 (+2)	19 (+4)

Saving Throws Dex +5, Con +11, Wis +7, Cha +9
Skills Insight +7, Perception +12, Stealth +5
Damage Immunities lightning
Senses blindsight 60 ft., darkvision 120 ft., passive Perception 22
Languages Common, Draconic
Challenge 15 (13,000 XP)

Amphibious. The dragon can breathe air and water.

Legendary Resistance (3/Day). If the dragon fails a saving throw, it can choose to succeed instead.

Actions

Multiattack. The dragon can use its Frightful Presence. It then makes three attacks: one with its bite and two with its claws.

Bite. *Melee Weapon Attack:* +12 to hit, reach 10 ft., one target. *Hit:* 18 (2d10 + 7) piercing damage.

Claw. *Melee Weapon Attack:* +12 to hit, reach 5 ft., one target. *Hit:* 14 (2d6 + 7) slashing damage.

Tail. *Melee Weapon Attack:* +12 to hit, reach 15 ft., one target. *Hit:* 16 (2d8 + 7) bludgeoning damage.

Frightful Presence. Each creature of the dragon's choice that is within 120 feet of the dragon and aware of it must succeed on a DC 17 Wisdom saving throw or become frightened for 1 minute. A creature can repeat the saving throw at the end of each of its turns, ending the effect on itself on a success. If a creature's saving throw is successful or the effect ends for it, the creature is immune to the dragon's Frightful Presence for the next 24 hours.

Breath Weapons (Recharge 5–6). The dragon uses one of the following breath weapons.

Lightning Breath. The dragon exhales lightning in a 90-foot line that is 5 feet wide. Each creature in that line must make a DC 19 Dexterity saving throw, taking 66 (12d10) lightning damage on a failed save, or half as much damage on a successful one.

Repulsion Breath. The dragon exhales repulsion energy in a 30-foot cone. Each creature in that area must succeed on a DC 19 Strength saving throw. On a failed save, the creature is pushed 60 feet away from the dragon.

Change Shape. The dragon magically polymorphs into a humanoid or beast that has a challenge rating no higher than its own, or back into its true form. It reverts to its true form if it dies. Any equipment it is wearing or carrying is absorbed or borne by the new form (the dragon's choice).

In a new form, the dragon retains its alignment, hit points, Hit Dice, ability to speak, proficiencies, Legendary Resistance, lair actions, and Intelligence, Wisdom, and Charisma scores, as well as this action. Its statistics and capabilities are otherwise replaced by those of the new form, except any class features or legendary actions of that form.

Legendary Actions

The dragon can take 3 legendary actions, choosing from the options below. Only one legendary action option can be used at a time and only at the end of another creature's turn. The dragon regains spent legendary actions at the start of its turn.

Detect. The dragon makes a Wisdom (Perception) check.
Tail Attack. The dragon makes a tail attack.
Wing Attack (Costs 2 Actions). The dragon beats its wings. Each creature within 10 feet of the dragon must succeed on a DC 20 Dexterity saving throw or take 14 (2d6 + 7) bludgeoning damage and be knocked prone. The dragon can then fly up to half its flying speed.

Young Bronze Dragon

Large dragon, lawful good

Armor Class 18 (natural armor)
Hit Points 142 (15d10 + 60)
Speed 40 ft., fly 80 ft., swim 40 ft.

STR	DEX	CON	INT	WIS	CHA
21 (+5)	10 (+0)	19 (+4)	14 (+2)	13 (+1)	17 (+3)

Saving Throws Dex +3, Con +7, Wis +4, Cha +6
Skills Insight +4, Perception +7, Stealth +3
Damage Immunities lightning
Senses blindsight 30 ft., darkvision 120 ft., passive Perception 17
Languages Common, Draconic
Challenge 8 (3,900 XP)

Amphibious. The dragon can breathe air and water.

Actions

Multiattack. The dragon makes three attacks: one with its bite and two with its claws.

Bite. *Melee Weapon Attack:* +8 to hit, reach 10 ft., one target. *Hit:* 16 (2d10 + 5) piercing damage.

Claw. *Melee Weapon Attack:* +8 to hit, reach 5 ft., one target. *Hit:* 12 (2d6 + 5) slashing damage.

Breath Weapons (Recharge 5–6). The dragon uses one of the following breath weapons.

Lightning Breath. The dragon exhales lightning in a 60-foot line that is 5 feet wide. Each creature in that line must make a DC 15 Dexterity saving throw, taking 55 (10d10) lightning damage on a failed save, or half as much damage on a successful one.

Repulsion Breath. The dragon exhales repulsion energy in a 30-foot cone. Each creature in that area must succeed on a DC 15 Strength saving throw. On a failed save, the creature is pushed 40 feet away from the dragon.

Bronze Dragon

Bronze dragons are coastal dwellers that feed primarily on aquatic plants and fish. They take the forms of friendly animals to observe other creatures of interest. They are also fascinated by warfare and eagerly join armies fighting for a just cause.

A ribbed and fluted crest defines the shape of a bronze dragon's head. Curving horns extend out from the crest, echoed by spines on its lower jaw and chin. To help them swim, bronze dragons have webbed feet and smooth scales. A bronze wyrmling's scales are yellow tinged with green; only as the dragon approaches adulthood does its color deepen to a darker, rich bronze tone. The pupils of a bronze dragon's eyes fade as the dragon ages, until they resemble glowing green orbs.

Dragons of the Coast. Bronze dragons love to watch ships traveling up and down the coastlines near their lairs, sometimes taking the forms of dolphins or seagulls to inspect those ships and their crews more closely. A daring bronze dragon might slip aboard a ship in the guise of a bird or rat, inspecting the hold for treasure. If the dragon finds a worthy addition to its hoard, it barters with the ship's captain for the item.

War Machines. Bronze dragons actively oppose tyranny, and many bronze dragons yearn to test their mettle by putting their size and strength to good use.

When a conflict unfolds near its lair, a bronze dragon ascertains the underlying cause, then offers its services to any side that fights for good. Once a bronze dragon commits to a cause, it remains a staunch ally.

Well-Organized Wealth. Bronze dragons loot sunken ships and also collect colorful coral and pearls from the reefs and seabeds near their lairs. When a bronze dragon pledges to help an army wage war against tyranny, it asks for nominal payment. If such a request is beyond its allies' means, it might settle for a collection of old books on military history or a ceremonial item commemorating the alliance. A bronze dragon might also lay claim to a treasure held by the enemy that it feels would be safer under its protection.

A Bronze Dragon's Lair

A bronze dragon lairs in coastal caves. It might salvage a wrecked ship, reconstruct it within the confines of its lair, and use it as a treasure vault or nest for its eggs.

Lair Actions

On initiative count 20 (losing initiative ties), the dragon takes a lair action to cause one of the following effects:

- The dragon creates fog as though it had cast the *fog cloud* spell. The fog lasts until initiative count 20 on the next round.
- A thunderclap originates at a point the dragon can see within 120 feet of it. Each creature within a 20-foot radius centered on that point must make a DC 15 Constitution saving throw or take 5 (1d10) thunder damage and be deafened until the end of its next turn.

Regional Effects

The region containing a legendary bronze dragon's lair is warped by the dragon's magic.

Bronze Dragon Wyrmling

Medium dragon, lawful good

Armor Class 17 (natural armor)
Hit Points 32 (5d8 + 10)
Speed 30 ft., fly 60 ft., swim 30 ft.

STR	DEX	CON	INT	WIS	CHA
17 (+3)	10 (+0)	15 (+2)	12 (+1)	11 (+0)	15 (+2)

Saving Throws Dex +2, Con +4, Wis +2, Cha +4
Skills Perception +4, Stealth +2
Damage Immunities lightning
Senses blindsight 10 ft., darkvision 60 ft., passive Perception 14
Languages Draconic
Challenge 2 (450 XP)

Amphibious. The dragon can breathe air and water.

Actions

Bite. *Melee Weapon Attack:* +5 to hit, reach 5 ft., one target. *Hit:* 8 (1d10 + 3) piercing damage.

Breath Weapons (Recharge 5–6). The dragon uses one of the following breath weapons.

Lightning Breath. The dragon exhales lightning in a 40-foot line that is 5 feet wide. Each creature in that line must make a DC 12 Dexterity saving throw, taking 16 (3d10) lightning damage on a failed save, or half as much damage on a successful one.

Repulsion Breath. The dragon exhales repulsion energy in a 30-foot cone. Each creature in that area must succeed on a DC 12 Strength saving throw. On a failed save, the creature is pushed 30 feet away from the dragon.

- Once per day, the dragon can alter the weather in a 6-mile radius centered on its lair. The dragon doesn't need to be outdoors; otherwise the effect is identical to the *control weather* spell.
- Underwater plants within 6 miles of the dragon's lair take on dazzlingly brilliant hues.
- Within its lair, the dragon can set illusory sounds, such as soft music and strange echoes, so that they can be heard in various parts of the lair.

If the dragon dies, changed weather reverts to normal, as described in the spell, and the other effects fade in 1d10 days.

ACTIONS

Multiattack. The dragon can use its Frightful Presence. It then makes three attacks: one with its bite and two with its claws.

Bite. *Melee Weapon Attack:* +15 to hit, reach 15 ft., one target. *Hit:* 19 (2d10 + 8) piercing damage.

Claw. *Melee Weapon Attack:* +15 to hit, reach 10 ft., one target. *Hit:* 15 (2d6 + 8) slashing damage.

Tail. *Melee Weapon Attack:* +15 to hit, reach 20 ft., one target. *Hit:* 17 (2d8 + 8) bludgeoning damage.

Frightful Presence. Each creature of the dragon's choice that is within 120 feet of the dragon and aware of it must succeed on a DC 19 Wisdom saving throw or become frightened for 1 minute. A creature can repeat the saving throw at the end of each of its turns, ending the effect on itself on a success. If a creature's saving throw is successful or the effect ends for it, the creature is immune to the dragon's Frightful Presence for the next 24 hours.

Breath Weapons (Recharge 5–6). The dragon uses one of the following breath weapons.

Acid Breath. The dragon exhales acid in an 90-foot line that is 10 feet wide. Each creature in that line must make a DC 22 Dexterity saving throw, taking 63 (14d8) acid damage on a failed save, or half as much damage on a successful one.

Slowing Breath. The dragon exhales gas in a 90-foot cone. Each creature in that area must succeed on a DC 22 Constitution saving throw. On a failed save, the creature can't use reactions, its speed is halved, and it can't make more than one attack on its turn. In addition, the creature can use either an action or a bonus action on its turn, but not both. These effects last for 1 minute. The creature can repeat the saving throw at the end of each of its turns, ending the effect on itself with a successful save.

Change Shape. The dragon magically polymorphs into a humanoid or beast that has a challenge rating no higher than its own, or back into its true form. It reverts to its true form if it dies. Any equipment it is wearing or carrying is absorbed or borne by the new form (the dragon's choice).

In a new form, the dragon retains its alignment, hit points, Hit Dice, ability to speak, proficiencies, Legendary Resistance, lair actions, and Intelligence, Wisdom, and Charisma scores, as well as this action. Its statistics and capabilities are otherwise replaced by those of the new form, except any class features or legendary actions of that form.

LEGENDARY ACTIONS

The dragon can take 3 legendary actions, choosing from the options below. Only one legendary action option can be used at a time and only at the end of another creature's turn. The dragon regains spent legendary actions at the start of its turn.

Detect. The dragon makes a Wisdom (Perception) check.

Tail Attack. The dragon makes a tail attack.

Wing Attack (Costs 2 Actions). The dragon beats its wings. Each creature within 15 feet of the dragon must succeed on a DC 23 Dexterity saving throw or take 15 (2d6 + 8) bludgeoning damage and be knocked prone. The dragon can then fly up to half its flying speed.

ANCIENT COPPER DRAGON
Gargantuan dragon, chaotic good

Armor Class 21 (natural armor)
Hit Points 350 (20d20 + 140)
Speed 40 ft., climb 40 ft., fly 80 ft.

STR	DEX	CON	INT	WIS	CHA
27 (+8)	12 (+1)	25 (+7)	20 (+5)	17 (+3)	19 (+4)

Saving Throws Dex +8, Con +14, Wis +10, Cha +11
Skills Deception +11, Perception +17, Stealth +8
Damage Immunities acid
Senses blindsight 60 ft., darkvision 120 ft., passive Perception 27
Languages Common, Draconic
Challenge 21 (33,000 XP)

Legendary Resistance (3/Day). If the dragon fails a saving throw, it can choose to succeed instead.

ADULT COPPER DRAGON

Huge dragon, chaotic good

Armor Class 18 (natural armor)
Hit Points 184 (16d12 + 80)
Speed 40 ft., climb 40 ft., fly 80 ft.

STR	DEX	CON	INT	WIS	CHA
23 (+6)	12 (+1)	21 (+5)	18 (+4)	15 (+2)	17 (+3)

Saving Throws Dex +6, Con +10, Wis +7, Cha +8
Skills Deception +8, Perception +12, Stealth +6
Damage Immunities acid
Senses blindsight 60 ft., darkvision 120 ft., passive Perception 22
Languages Common, Draconic
Challenge 14 (11,500 XP)

Legendary Resistance (3/Day). If the dragon fails a saving throw, it can choose to succeed instead.

ACTIONS

Multiattack. The dragon can use its Frightful Presence. It then makes three attacks: one with its bite and two with its claws.

Bite. Melee Weapon Attack: +11 to hit, reach 10 ft., one target. *Hit:* 17 (2d10 + 6) piercing damage.

Claw. Melee Weapon Attack: +11 to hit, reach 5 ft., one target. *Hit:* 13 (2d6 + 6) slashing damage.

Tail. Melee Weapon Attack: +11 to hit, reach 15 ft., one target. *Hit:* 15 (2d8 + 6) bludgeoning damage.

Frightful Presence. Each creature of the dragon's choice that is within 120 feet of the dragon and aware of it must succeed on a DC 16 Wisdom saving throw or become frightened for 1 minute. A creature can repeat the saving throw at the end of each of its turns, ending the effect on itself on a success. If a creature's saving throw is successful or the effect ends for it, the creature is immune to the dragon's Frightful Presence for the next 24 hours.

Breath Weapons (Recharge 5–6). The dragon uses one of the following breath weapons.

Acid Breath. The dragon exhales acid in an 60-foot line that is 5 feet wide. Each creature in that line must make a DC 18 Dexterity saving throw, taking 54 (12d8) acid damage on a failed save, or half as much damage on a successful one.

Slowing Breath. The dragon exhales gas in a 60-foot cone. Each creature in that area must succeed on a DC 18 Constitution saving throw. On a failed save, the creature can't use reactions, its speed is halved, and it can't make more than one attack on its turn. In addition, the creature can use either an action or a bonus action on its turn, but not both. These effects last for 1 minute. The creature can repeat the saving throw at the end of each of its turns, ending the effect on itself with a successful save.

LEGENDARY ACTIONS

The dragon can take 3 legendary actions, choosing from the options below. Only one legendary action option can be used at a time and only at the end of another creature's turn. The dragon regains spent legendary actions at the start of its turn.

Detect. The dragon makes a Wisdom (Perception) check.
Tail Attack. The dragon makes a tail attack.
Wing Attack (Costs 2 Actions). The dragon beats its wings. Each creature within 10 feet of the dragon must succeed on a DC 19 Dexterity saving throw or take 13 (2d6 + 6) bludgeoning damage and be knocked prone. The dragon can then fly up to half its flying speed.

YOUNG COPPER DRAGON

Large dragon, chaotic good

Armor Class 17 (natural armor)
Hit Points 119 (14d10 + 42)
Speed 40 ft., climb 40 ft., fly 80 ft.

STR	DEX	CON	INT	WIS	CHA
19 (+4)	12 (+1)	17 (+3)	16 (+3)	13 (+1)	15 (+2)

Saving Throws Dex +4, Con +6, Wis +4, Cha +5
Skills Deception +5, Perception +7, Stealth +4
Damage Immunities acid
Senses blindsight 30 ft., darkvision 120 ft., passive Perception 17
Languages Common, Draconic
Challenge 7 (2,900 XP)

ACTIONS

Multiattack. The dragon makes three attacks: one with its bite and two with its claws.

Bite. Melee Weapon Attack: +7 to hit, reach 10 ft., one target. *Hit:* 15 (2d10 + 4) piercing damage.

Claw. Melee Weapon Attack: +7 to hit, reach 5 ft., one target. *Hit:* 11 (2d6 + 4) slashing damage.

Breath Weapons (Recharge 5–6). The dragon uses one of the following breath weapons.

Acid Breath. The dragon exhales acid in an 40-foot line that is 5 feet wide. Each creature in that line must make a DC 14 Dexterity saving throw, taking 40 (9d8) acid damage on a failed save, or half as much damage on a successful one.

Slowing Breath. The dragon exhales gas in a 30-foot cone. Each creature in that area must succeed on a DC 14 Constitution saving throw. On a failed save, the creature can't use reactions, its speed is halved, and it can't make more than one attack on its turn. In addition, the creature can use either an action or a bonus action on its turn, but not both. These effects last for 1 minute. The creature can repeat the saving throw at the end of each of its turns, ending the effect on itself with a successful save.

Copper Dragon

Copper dragons are incorrigible pranksters, joke tellers, and riddlers that live in hills and rocky uplands. Despite their gregarious and even-tempered natures, they possess a covetous, miserly streak, and can become dangerous when their hoards are threatened.

A copper dragon has brow plates jutting over its eyes, extending back to long horns that grow as a series of overlapping segments. Its backswept cheek ridges and jaw frills give it a pensive look. At birth, a copper dragon's scales are a ruddy brown with a metallic tint. As the dragon ages, its scales become more coppery in color, later taking on a green tint as it ages. A copper dragon's pupils fade with age, and the eyes of the oldest copper dragons resemble glowing turquoise orbs.

Good Hosts. A copper dragon appreciates wit, a good joke, humorous story, or riddle. A copper dragon becomes annoyed with any creature that doesn't laugh at its jokes or accept its tricks with good humor.

Copper dragons are particularly fond of bards. A dragon might carve out part of its lair as a temporary abode for a bard willing to regale it with stories, riddles, and music. To a copper dragon, such companionship is a treasure to be coveted.

Cautious and Crafty. When building its hoard, a copper dragon prefers treasures from the earth. Metals and precious stones are favorites of these creatures.

A copper dragon is wary when it comes to showing off its possessions. If it knows that other creatures seek a specific item in its hoard, a copper dragon will not admit to possessing the item. Instead, it might send curious treasure hunters on a wild goose chase to search for the object while it watches from afar for its own pleasure.

A Copper Dragon's Lair

Copper dragons dwell in dry uplands and on hilltops, where they make their lairs in narrow caves. False walls in the lair hide secret antechambers where the dragon stores valuable ores, art objects, and other oddities it has collected over its lifetime. Worthless items are put on display in open caves to tantalize treasure seekers and distract them from where the real treasure is hidden.

Lair Actions

On initiative count 20 (losing initiative ties), the dragon takes a lair action to cause one of the following effects:

- The dragon chooses a point on the ground that it can see within 120 feet of it. Stone spikes sprout from the ground in a 20-foot radius centered on that point. The effect is otherwise identical to the *spike growth* spell and lasts until the dragon uses this lair action again or until the dragon dies.
- The dragon chooses a 10-foot-square area on the ground that it can see within 120 feet of it. The ground in that area turns into 3-foot-deep mud. Each creature on the ground in that area when the mud appears must succeed on a DC 15 Dexterity saving throw or sink into the mud and become restrained. A creature can take an action to attempt a DC 15 Strength check, freeing itself or another creature within its reach and ending the restrained condition on a success. Moving 1 foot in the mud costs 2 feet of movement. On initiative count 20 on the next round, the mud hardens, and the Strength DC to work free increases to 20.

Regional Effects

The region containing a legendary copper dragon's lair is warped by the dragon's magic, which creates one or more of the following effects:

- Magic carvings of the dragon's smiling visage can be seen worked into stone terrain and objects within 6 miles of the dragon's lair.
- Tiny beasts such as rodents and birds that are normally unable to speak gain the magical ability to speak and understand Draconic while within 1 mile of the dragon's lair. These creatures speak well of the dragon, but can't divulge its whereabouts.
- Intelligent creatures within 1 mile of the dragon's lair are prone to fits of giggling. Even serious matters suddenly seem amusing.

If the dragon dies, the magic carvings fade over the course of 1d10 days. The other effects end immediately.

Copper Dragon Wyrmling

Medium dragon, chaotic good

Armor Class 16 (natural armor)
Hit Points 22 (4d8 + 4)
Speed 30 ft., climb 30 ft., fly 60 ft.

STR	DEX	CON	INT	WIS	CHA
15 (+2)	12 (+1)	13 (+1)	14 (+2)	11 (+0)	13 (+1)

Saving Throws Dex +3, Con +3, Wis +2, Cha +3
Skills Perception +4, Stealth +3
Damage Immunities acid
Senses blindsight 10 ft., darkvision 60 ft., passive Perception 14
Languages Draconic
Challenge 1 (200 XP)

Actions

Bite. *Melee Weapon Attack:* +4 to hit, reach 5 ft., one target. *Hit:* 7 (1d10 + 2) piercing damage.

Breath Weapons (Recharge 5–6). The dragon uses one of the following breath weapons.

Acid Breath. The dragon exhales acid in an 20-foot line that is 5 feet wide. Each creature in that line must make a DC 11 Dexterity saving throw, taking 18 (4d8) acid damage on a failed save, or half as much damage on a successful one.

Slowing Breath. The dragon exhales gas in a 15-foot cone. Each creature in that area must succeed on a DC 11 Constitution saving throw. On a failed save, the creature can't use reactions, its speed is halved, and it can't make more than one attack on its turn. In addition, the creature can use either an action or a bonus action on its turn, but not both. These effects last for 1 minute. The creature can repeat the saving throw at the end of each of its turns, ending the effect on itself with a successful save.

ANCIENT GOLD DRAGON
Gargantuan dragon, lawful good

Armor Class 22 (natural armor)
Hit Points 546 (28d20 + 252)
Speed 40 ft., fly 80 ft., swim 40 ft.

STR	DEX	CON	INT	WIS	CHA
30 (+10)	14 (+2)	29 (+9)	18 (+4)	17 (+3)	28 (+9)

Saving Throws Dex +9, Con +16, Wis +10, Cha +16
Skills Insight +10, Perception +17, Persuasion +16, Stealth +9
Damage Immunities fire
Senses blindsight 60 ft., darkvision 120 ft., passive Perception 27
Languages Common, Draconic
Challenge 24 (62,000 XP)

Amphibious. The dragon can breathe air and water.

Legendary Resistance (3/Day). If the dragon fails a saving throw, it can choose to succeed instead.

ACTIONS

Multiattack. The dragon can use its Frightful Presence. It then makes three attacks: one with its bite and two with its claws.

Bite. *Melee Weapon Attack:* +17 to hit, reach 15 ft., one target. *Hit:* 21 (2d10 + 10) piercing damage.

Claw. *Melee Weapon Attack:* +17 to hit, reach 10 ft., one target. *Hit:* 17 (2d6 + 10) slashing damage.

Tail. *Melee Weapon Attack:* +17 to hit, reach 20 ft., one target. *Hit:* 19 (2d8 + 10) bludgeoning damage.

Frightful Presence. Each creature of the dragon's choice that is within 120 feet of the dragon and aware of it must succeed on a DC 24 Wisdom saving throw or become frightened for 1 minute. A creature can repeat the saving throw at the end of each of its turns, ending the effect on itself on a success. If a creature's saving throw is successful or the effect ends for it, the creature is immune to the dragon's Frightful Presence for the next 24 hours.

Breath Weapons (Recharge 5–6). The dragon uses one of the following breath weapons.

   Fire Breath. The dragon exhales fire in a 90-foot cone. Each creature in that area must make a DC 24 Dexterity saving throw, taking 71 (13d10) fire damage on a failed save, or half as much damage on a successful one.

   Weakening Breath. The dragon exhales gas in a 90-foot cone. Each creature in that area must succeed on a DC 24 Strength saving throw or have disadvantage on Strength-based attack rolls, Strength checks, and Strength saving throws for 1 minute. A creature can repeat the saving throw at the end of each of its turns, ending the effect on itself on a success.

Change Shape. The dragon magically polymorphs into a humanoid or beast that has a challenge rating no higher than its own, or back into its true form. It reverts to its true form if it dies. Any equipment it is wearing or carrying is absorbed or borne by the new form (the dragon's choice).

   In a new form, the dragon retains its alignment, hit points, Hit Dice, ability to speak, proficiencies, Legendary Resistance, lair actions, and Intelligence, Wisdom, and Charisma scores, as

well as this action. Its statistics and capabilities are otherwise replaced by those of the new form, except any class features or legendary actions of that form.

LEGENDARY ACTIONS

The dragon can take 3 legendary actions, choosing from the options below. Only one legendary action option can be used at a time and only at the end of another creature's turn. The dragon regains spent legendary actions at the start of its turn.

Detect. The dragon makes a Wisdom (Perception) check.
Tail Attack. The dragon makes a tail attack.
Wing Attack (Costs 2 Actions). The dragon beats its wings. Each creature within 15 feet of the dragon must succeed on a DC 25 Dexterity saving throw or take 17 (2d6 + 10) bludgeoning damage and be knocked prone. The dragon can then fly up to half its flying speed.

Gold Dragon

The most powerful and majestic of the metallic dragons, gold dragons are dedicated foes of evil.

A gold dragon has a sagacious face anointed with flexible spines that resemble whiskers. Its horns sweep back from its nose and brow, echoing twin frills that adorn its long neck. A gold dragon's sail-like wings start at its shoulders and trace down to the tip of its tail, letting it fly with a distinctive rippling motion as if swimming through the air. A gold dragon wyrmling has scales of dark yellow with metallic flecks. Those flecks grow larger as the dragon matures. As a gold dragon ages, its pupils fade until its eyes resemble pools of molten gold.

Devourer of Wealth. Gold dragons can eat just about anything, but their preferred diet consists of pearls and gems. Thankfully, a gold dragon doesn't need to gorge itself on such wealth to feel satisfied. Gifts of treasure that it can consume are well received by a gold dragon, as long as they aren't bribes.

Reserved Shapeshifters. Gold dragons are respected by the other metallic dragons for their wisdom and fairness, but they are the most aloof and grim of the good-aligned dragons. They value their privacy to the extent that they rarely fraternize with other dragons except their own mates and offspring.

Older gold dragons can assume animal and humanoid forms. Rarely does a gold dragon in disguise reveal its true form. In the guise of a peddler, it might regularly visit a town to catch up on local gossip, patronize honest businesses, and lend a helping hand in unseen ways. In the guise of an animal, the dragon might befriend a lost child, a wandering minstrel, or an innkeeper, serving as a companion for days or weeks on end.

Master Hoarders. A gold dragon keeps its hoard in a well-guarded vault deep within its lair. Magical wards placed on the vault make it all but impossible to remove any treasures without the dragon knowing about it.

A Gold Dragon's Lair

Gold dragons make their homes in out-of-the-way places, where they can do as they please without arousing suspicion or fear. Most dwell near idyllic lakes

Adult Gold Dragon

Huge dragon, lawful good

Armor Class 19 (natural armor)
Hit Points 256 (19d12 + 133)
Speed 40 ft., fly 80 ft., swim 40 ft.

STR	DEX	CON	INT	WIS	CHA
27 (+8)	14 (+2)	25 (+7)	16 (+3)	15 (+2)	24 (+7)

Saving Throws Dex +8, Con +13, Wis +8, Cha +13
Skills Insight +8, Perception +14, Persuasion +13, Stealth +8
Damage Immunities fire
Senses blindsight 60 ft., darkvision 120 ft., passive Perception 24
Languages Common, Draconic
Challenge 17 (18,000 XP)

Amphibious. The dragon can breathe air and water.

Legendary Resistance (3/Day). If the dragon fails a saving throw, it can choose to succeed instead.

Actions

Multiattack. The dragon can use its Frightful Presence. It then makes three attacks: one with its bite and two with its claws.

Bite. *Melee Weapon Attack:* +14 to hit, reach 10 ft., one target. *Hit:* 19 (2d10 + 8) piercing damage.

Claw. *Melee Weapon Attack:* +14 to hit, reach 5 ft., one target. *Hit:* 15 (2d6 + 8) slashing damage.

Tail. *Melee Weapon Attack:* +14 to hit, reach 15 ft., one target. *Hit:* 17 (2d8 + 8) bludgeoning damage.

Frightful Presence. Each creature of the dragon's choice that is within 120 feet of the dragon and aware of it must succeed on a DC 21 Wisdom saving throw or become frightened for 1 minute. A creature can repeat the saving throw at the end of each of its turns, ending the effect on itself on a success. If a creature's saving throw is successful or the effect ends for it, the creature is immune to the dragon's Frightful Presence for the next 24 hours.

Breath Weapons (Recharge 5–6). The dragon uses one of the following breath weapons.

Fire Breath. The dragon exhales fire in a 60-foot cone. Each creature in that area must make a DC 21 Dexterity saving throw, taking 66 (12d10) fire damage on a failed save, or half as much damage on a successful one.

Weakening Breath. The dragon exhales gas in a 60-foot cone. Each creature in that area must succeed on a DC 21 Strength saving throw or have disadvantage on Strength-based attack rolls, Strength checks, and Strength saving throws for 1 minute. A creature can repeat the saving throw at the end of each of its turns, ending the effect on itself on a success.

Change Shape. The dragon magically polymorphs into a humanoid or beast that has a challenge rating no higher than its own, or back into its true form. It reverts to its true form if it dies. Any equipment it is wearing or carrying is absorbed or borne by the new form (the dragon's choice).

In a new form, the dragon retains its alignment, hit points, Hit Dice, ability to speak, proficiencies, Legendary Resistance, lair actions, and Intelligence, Wisdom, and Charisma scores, as well as this action. Its statistics and capabilities are otherwise replaced by those of the new form, except any class features or legendary actions of that form.

Legendary Actions

The dragon can take 3 legendary actions, choosing from the options below. Only one legendary action option can be used at a time and only at the end of another creature's turn. The dragon regains spent legendary actions at the start of its turn.

Detect. The dragon makes a Wisdom (Perception) check.
Tail Attack. The dragon makes a tail attack.
Wing Attack (Costs 2 Actions). The dragon beats its wings. Each creature within 10 feet of the dragon must succeed on a DC 22 Dexterity saving throw or take 15 (2d6 + 8) bludgeoning damage and be knocked prone. The dragon can then fly up to half its flying speed.

and rivers, mist-shrouded islands, cave complexes hidden behind sparkling waterfalls, or ancient ruins.

Lair Actions

On initiative count 20 (losing initiative ties), the dragon takes a lair action to cause one of the following effects; the dragon can't use the same effect two rounds in a row:

- The dragon glimpses the future, so it has advantage on attack rolls, ability checks, and saving throws until initiative count 20 on the next round.
- One creature the dragon can see within 120 feet of it must succeed on a DC 15 Charisma saving throw or be banished to a dream plane, a different plane of existence the dragon has imagined into being. To escape, the creature must use its action to make a Charisma check contested by the dragon's. If the creature wins, it escapes the dream plane. Otherwise, the effect ends on initiative count 20 on the next round. When the effect ends, the creature reappears in the space it left or in the nearest unoccupied space if that one is occupied.

Regional Effects

The region containing a legendary gold dragon's lair is warped by the dragon's magic, which creates one or more of the following effects:

- Whenever a creature that can understand a language sleeps or enters a state of trance or reverie within 6 miles of the dragon's lair, the dragon can establish telepathic contact with that creature and converse with it in its dreams. The creature remembers its conversation with the dragon upon waking.
- Banks of beautiful, opalescent mist manifest within 6 miles of the dragon's lair. The mist doesn't obscure anything. It assumes haunting forms when evil creatures are near the dragon or other non-evil creatures in the mist, warning such creatures of the danger.
- Gems and pearls within 1 mile of the dragon's lair sparkle and gleam, shedding dim light in a 5-foot radius.

If the dragon dies, these effects end immediately.

Young Gold Dragon

Large dragon, lawful good

Armor Class 18 (natural armor)
Hit Points 178 (17d10 + 85)
Speed 40 ft., fly 80 ft., swim 40 ft.

STR	DEX	CON	INT	WIS	CHA
23 (+6)	14 (+2)	21 (+5)	16 (+3)	13 (+1)	20 (+5)

Saving Throws Dex +6, Con +9, Wis +5, Cha +9
Skills Insight +5, Perception +9, Persuasion +9, Stealth +6
Damage Immunities fire
Senses blindsight 30 ft., darkvision 120 ft., passive Perception 19
Languages Common, Draconic
Challenge 10 (5,900 XP)

Amphibious. The dragon can breathe air and water.

Actions

Multiattack. The dragon makes three attacks: one with its bite and two with its claws.

Bite. *Melee Weapon Attack:* +10 to hit, reach 10 ft., one target. *Hit:* 17 (2d10 + 6) piercing damage.

Claw. *Melee Weapon Attack:* +10 to hit, reach 5 ft., one target. *Hit:* 13 (2d6 + 6) slashing damage.

Breath Weapons (Recharge 5–6). The dragon uses one of the following breath weapons.

Fire Breath. The dragon exhales fire in a 30-foot cone. Each creature in that area must make a DC 17 Dexterity saving throw, taking 55 (10d10) fire damage on a failed save, or half as much damage on a successful one.

Weakening Breath. The dragon exhales gas in a 30-foot cone. Each creature in that area must succeed on a DC 17 Strength saving throw or have disadvantage on Strength-based attack rolls, Strength checks, and Strength saving throws for 1 minute. A creature can repeat the saving throw at the end of each of its turns, ending the effect on itself on a success.

Gold Dragon Wyrmling

Medium dragon, lawful good

Armor Class 17 (natural armor)
Hit Points 60 (8d8 + 24)
Speed 30 ft., fly 60 ft., swim 30 ft.

STR	DEX	CON	INT	WIS	CHA
19 (+4)	14 (+2)	17 (+3)	14 (+2)	11 (+0)	16 (+3)

Saving Throws Dex +4, Con +5, Wis +2, Cha +5
Skills Perception +4, Stealth +4
Damage Immunities fire
Senses blindsight 10 ft., darkvision 60 ft., passive Perception 14
Languages Draconic
Challenge 3 (700 XP)

Amphibious. The dragon can breathe air and water.

Actions

Bite. *Melee Weapon Attack:* +6 to hit, reach 5 ft., one target. *Hit:* 9 (1d10 + 4) piercing damage.

Breath Weapons (Recharge 5–6). The dragon uses one of the following breath weapons.

Fire Breath. The dragon exhales fire in a 15-foot cone. Each creature in that area must make a DC 13 Dexterity saving throw, taking 22 (4d10) fire damage on a failed save, or half as much damage on a successful one.

Weakening Breath. The dragon exhales gas in a 15-foot cone. Each creature in that area must succeed on a DC 13 Strength saving throw or have disadvantage on Strength-based attack rolls, Strength checks, and Strength saving throws for 1 minute. A creature can repeat the saving throw at the end of each of its turns, ending the effect on itself on a success.

D

Actions

Multiattack. The dragon can use its Frightful Presence. It then makes three attacks: one with its bite and two with its claws.

Bite. *Melee Weapon Attack:* +17 to hit, reach 15 ft., one target. *Hit:* 21 (2d10 + 10) piercing damage.

Claw. *Melee Weapon Attack:* +17 to hit, reach 10 ft., one target. *Hit:* 17 (2d6 + 10) slashing damage.

Tail. *Melee Weapon Attack:* +17 to hit, reach 20 ft., one target. *Hit:* 19 (2d8 + 10) bludgeoning damage.

Frightful Presence. Each creature of the dragon's choice that is within 120 feet of the dragon and aware of it must succeed on a DC 21 Wisdom saving throw or become frightened for 1 minute. A creature can repeat the saving throw at the end of each of its turns, ending the effect on itself on a success. If a creature's saving throw is successful or the effect ends for it, the creature is immune to the dragon's Frightful Presence for the next 24 hours.

Breath Weapons (Recharge 5–6). The dragon uses one of the following breath weapons.

Cold Breath. The dragon exhales an icy blast in a 90-foot cone. Each creature in that area must make a DC 24 Constitution saving throw, taking 67 (15d8) cold damage on a failed save, or half as much damage on a successful one.

Paralyzing Breath. The dragon exhales paralyzing gas in a 90-foot cone. Each creature in that area must succeed on a DC 24 Constitution saving throw or be paralyzed for 1 minute. A creature can repeat the saving throw at the end of each of its turns, ending the effect on itself on a success.

Change Shape. The dragon magically polymorphs into a humanoid or beast that has a challenge rating no higher than its own, or back into its true form. It reverts to its true form if it dies. Any equipment it is wearing or carrying is absorbed or borne by the new form (the dragon's choice).

In a new form, the dragon retains its alignment, hit points, Hit Dice, ability to speak, proficiencies, Legendary Resistance, lair actions, and Intelligence, Wisdom, and Charisma scores, as well as this action. Its statistics and capabilities are otherwise replaced by those of the new form, except any class features or legendary actions of that form.

Legendary Actions

The dragon can take 3 legendary actions, choosing from the options below. Only one legendary action option can be used at a time and only at the end of another creature's turn. The dragon regains spent legendary actions at the start of its turn.

Detect. The dragon makes a Wisdom (Perception) check.

Tail Attack. The dragon makes a tail attack.

Wing Attack (Costs 2 Actions). The dragon beats its wings. Each creature within 15 feet of the dragon must succeed on a DC 25 Dexterity saving throw or take 17 (2d6 + 10) bludgeoning damage and be knocked prone. The dragon can then fly up to half its flying speed.

Ancient Silver Dragon
Gargantuan dragon, lawful good

Armor Class 22 (natural armor)
Hit Points 487 (25d20 + 225)
Speed 40 ft., fly 80 ft.

STR	DEX	CON	INT	WIS	CHA
30 (+10)	10 (+0)	29 (+9)	18 (+4)	15 (+2)	23 (+6)

Saving Throws Dex +7, Con +16, Wis +9, Cha +13
Skills Arcana +11, History +11, Perception +16, Stealth +7
Damage Immunities cold
Senses blindsight 60 ft., darkvision 120 ft., passive Perception 26
Languages Common, Draconic
Challenge 23 (50,000 XP)

Legendary Resistance (3/Day). If the dragon fails a saving throw, it can choose to succeed instead.

SILVER DRAGON

The friendliest and most social of the metallic dragons, silver dragons cheerfully assist good creatures in need.

A silver dragon shimmers as if sculpted from pure metal, its face given a noble cast by its high eyes and sweeping beard-like chin spikes. A spiny frill rises high over its head, tracing down its neck to the tip of its tail. A silver wyrmling's scales are blue-gray with silver highlights. As the dragon approaches adulthood, its color gradually brightens until its individual scales are barely visible. As a silver dragon grows older, its pupils fade until its eyes resemble orbs of mercury.

Dragons of Virtue. Silver dragons believe that living a moral life involves doing good deeds and ensuring that one's actions cause no undeserved harm to other sentient beings. They don't take it upon themselves to root out evil, as gold and bronze dragons do, but they will gladly oppose creatures that dare to commit evil acts or harm the innocent.

Friends of the Small Races. Silver dragons enjoy the company of other silver dragons. Their only true friendships outside their own kin arise in the company of humanoids, and many silver dragons spend as much time in humanoid form as they do in draconic form. A silver dragon adopts a benign humanoid persona such as a kindly old sage or a young wanderer, and it often has mortal companions with whom it develops strong friendships.

Silver dragons must step away from their humanoid lives on a regular basis, returning to their true forms to mate and rear offspring, or to tend to their hoards and personal affairs. Because many lose track of time while away, they sometimes return to find that their companions have grown old or died. Silver dragons often end up befriending several generations of humanoids within a single family as a result.

Respect for Humanity. Silver dragons befriend humanoids of all races, but shorter-lived races such as humans spark their curiosity in a way the longer-lived elves and dwarves don't. Humans have a drive and zest for life that silver dragons find fascinating.

Hoarding History. Silver dragons love to possess relics of humanoid history. This includes the great

ADULT SILVER DRAGON

Huge dragon, lawful good

Armor Class 19 (natural armor)
Hit Points 243 (18d12 + 126)
Speed 40 ft., fly 80 ft.

STR	DEX	CON	INT	WIS	CHA
27 (+8)	10 (+0)	25 (+7)	16 (+3)	13 (+1)	21 (+5)

Saving Throws Dex +5, Con +12, Wis +6, Cha +10
Skills Arcana +8, History +8, Perception +11, Stealth +5
Damage Immunities cold
Senses blindsight 60 ft., darkvision 120 ft., passive Perception 21
Languages Common, Draconic
Challenge 16 (15,000 XP)

Legendary Resistance (3/Day). If the dragon fails a saving throw, it can choose to succeed instead.

ACTIONS

Multiattack. The dragon can use its Frightful Presence. It then makes three attacks: one with its bite and two with its claws.

Bite. *Melee Weapon Attack:* +13 to hit, reach 10 ft., one target. *Hit:* 19 (2d10 + 8) piercing damage.

Claw. *Melee Weapon Attack:* +13 to hit, reach 5 ft., one target. *Hit:* 15 (2d6 + 8) slashing damage.

Tail. *Melee Weapon Attack:* +13 to hit, reach 15 ft., one target. *Hit:* 17 (2d8 + 8) bludgeoning damage.

Frightful Presence. Each creature of the dragon's choice that is within 120 feet of the dragon and aware of it must succeed on a DC 18 Wisdom saving throw or become frightened for 1 minute. A creature can repeat the saving throw at the end of each of its turns, ending the effect on itself on a success. If a creature's saving throw is successful or the effect ends for it, the creature is immune to the dragon's Frightful Presence for the next 24 hours.

Breath Weapons (Recharge 5–6). The dragon uses one of the following breath weapons.

Cold Breath. The dragon exhales an icy blast in a 60-foot cone. Each creature in that area must make a DC 20 Constitution saving throw, taking 58 (13d8) cold damage on a failed save, or half as much damage on a successful one.

Paralyzing Breath. The dragon exhales paralyzing gas in a 60-foot cone. Each creature in that area must succeed on a DC 20 Constitution saving throw or be paralyzed for 1 minute. A creature can repeat the saving throw at the end of each of its turns, ending the effect on itself on a success.

Change Shape. The dragon magically polymorphs into a humanoid or beast that has a challenge rating no higher than its own, or back into its true form. It reverts to its true form if it dies. Any equipment it is wearing or carrying is absorbed or borne by the new form (the dragon's choice).

In a new form, the dragon retains its alignment, hit points, Hit Dice, ability to speak, proficiencies, Legendary Resistance, lair actions, and Intelligence, Wisdom, and Charisma scores, as well as this action. Its statistics and capabilities are otherwise replaced by those of the new form, except any class features or legendary actions of that form.

LEGENDARY ACTIONS

The dragon can take 3 legendary actions, choosing from the options below. Only one legendary action option can be used at a time and only at the end of another creature's turn. The dragon regains spent legendary actions at the start of its turn.

Detect. The dragon makes a Wisdom (Perception) check.
Tail Attack. The dragon makes a tail attack.
Wing Attack (Costs 2 Actions). The dragon beats its wings. Each creature within 10 feet of the dragon must succeed on a DC 21 Dexterity saving throw or take 15 (2d6 + 8) bludgeoning damage and be knocked prone. The dragon can then fly up to half its flying speed.

piles of coins they covet, minted by current and fallen humanoid empires, as well as art objects and fine jewelry crafted by numerous races. Other treasures that make up their hoards can include intact ships, the remains of kings and queens, thrones, the crown jewels of ancient empires, inventions and contraptions, and monoliths carried from the ruins of fallen cities.

A Silver Dragon's Lair

Silver dragons dwell among the clouds, making their lairs on secluded cold mountain peaks. Though many are comfortable in natural cavern complexes or abandoned mines, silver dragons covet the lost outposts of humanoid civilization. An abandoned mountaintop citadel or a remote tower raised by a long-dead wizard is the sort of lair that every silver dragon dreams of.

Lair Actions

On initiative count 20 (losing initiative ties), the dragon takes a lair action to cause one of the following effects:

- The dragon creates fog as if it had cast the *fog cloud* spell. The fog lasts until initiative count 20 on the next round.

- A blisteringly cold wind blows through the lair near the dragon. Each creature within 120 feet of the dragon must succeed on a DC 15 Constitution saving throw or take 5 (1d10) cold damage. Gases and vapors are dispersed by the wind, and unprotected flames are extinguished. Protected flames, such as lanterns, have a 50 percent chance of being extinguished.

Regional Effects

The region containing a legendary silver dragon's lair is warped by the dragon's magic, which creates one or more of the following effects.

- Once per day, the dragon can alter the weather in a 6-mile radius centered on its lair. The dragon doesn't need to be outdoors; otherwise the effect is identical to the *control weather* spell.
- Within 1 mile of the lair, winds buoy non-evil creatures that fall due to no act of the dragon's or its allies. Such creatures descend at a rate of 60 feet per round and take no falling damage.
- Given days or longer to work, the dragon can make clouds and fog within its lair as solid as stone, forming structures and other objects as it wishes.

If the dragon dies, changed weather reverts to normal, as described in the spell, and the other effects fade in 1d10 days.

YOUNG SILVER DRAGON
Large dragon, lawful good

Armor Class 18 (natural armor)
Hit Points 168 (16d10 + 80)
Speed 40 ft., fly 80 ft.

STR	DEX	CON	INT	WIS	CHA
23 (+6)	10 (+0)	21 (+5)	14 (+2)	11 (+0)	19 (+4)

Saving Throws Dex +4, Con +9, Wis +4, Cha +8
Skills Arcana +6, History +6, Perception +8, Stealth +4
Damage Immunities cold
Senses blindsight 30 ft., darkvision 120 ft., passive Perception 18
Languages Common, Draconic
Challenge 9 (5,000 XP)

Actions

Multiattack. The dragon makes three attacks: one with its bite and two with its claws.

Bite. Melee Weapon Attack: +10 to hit, reach 10 ft., one target. *Hit:* 17 (2d10 + 6) piercing damage.

Claw. Melee Weapon Attack: +10 to hit, reach 5 ft., one target. *Hit:* 13 (2d6 + 6) slashing damage.

Breath Weapons (Recharge 5–6). The dragon uses one of the following breath weapons.

Cold Breath. The dragon exhales an icy blast in a 30-foot cone. Each creature in that area must make a DC 17 Constitution saving throw, taking 54 (12d8) cold damage on a failed save, or half as much damage on a successful one.
Paralyzing Breath. The dragon exhales paralyzing gas in a 30-foot cone. Each creature in that area must succeed on a DC 17 Constitution saving throw or be paralyzed for 1 minute. A creature can repeat the saving throw at the end of each of its turns, ending the effect on itself on a success.

SILVER DRAGON WYRMLING
Medium dragon, lawful good

Armor Class 17 (natural armor)
Hit Points 45 (6d8 + 18)
Speed 30 ft., fly 60 ft.

STR	DEX	CON	INT	WIS	CHA
19 (+4)	10 (+0)	17 (+3)	12 (+1)	11 (+0)	15 (+2)

Saving Throws Dex +2, Con +5, Wis +2, Cha +4
Skills Perception +4, Stealth +2
Damage Immunities cold
Senses blindsight 10 ft., darkvision 60 ft., passive Perception 14
Languages Draconic
Challenge 2 (450 XP)

Actions

Bite. Melee Weapon Attack: +6 to hit, reach 5 ft., one target. *Hit:* 9 (1d10 + 4) piercing damage.

Breath Weapons (Recharge 5–6). The dragon uses one of the following breath weapons.

Cold Breath. The dragon exhales an icy blast in a 15-foot cone. Each creature in that area must make a DC 13 Constitution saving throw, taking 18 (4d8) cold damage on a failed save, or half as much damage on a successful one.
Paralyzing Breath. The dragon exhales paralyzing gas in a 15-foot cone. Each creature in that area must succeed on a DC 13 Constitution saving throw or be paralyzed for 1 minute. A creature can repeat the saving throw at the end of each of its turns, ending the effect on itself on a success.

D

DRAGON TURTLE
Gargantuan dragon, neutral

Armor Class 20 (natural armor)
Hit Points 341 (22d20 + 110)
Speed 20 ft., swim 40 ft.

STR	DEX	CON	INT	WIS	CHA
25 (+7)	10 (+0)	20 (+5)	10 (+0)	12 (+1)	12 (+1)

Saving Throws Dex +6, Con +11, Wis +7
Damage Resistances fire
Senses darkvision 120 ft., passive Perception 11
Languages Aquan, Draconic
Challenge 17 (18,000 XP)

Amphibious. The dragon turtle can breathe air and water.

ACTIONS

Multiattack. The dragon turtle makes three attacks: one with its bite and two with its claws. It can make one tail attack in place of its two claw attacks.

Bite. Melee Weapon Attack: +13 to hit, reach 15 ft., one target. *Hit:* 26 (3d12 + 7) piercing damage.

Claw. Melee Weapon Attack: +13 to hit, reach 10 ft., one target. *Hit:* 16 (2d8 + 7) slashing damage.

Tail. Melee Weapon Attack: +13 to hit, reach 15 ft., one target. *Hit:* 26 (3d12 + 7) bludgeoning damage. If the target is a creature, it must succeed on a DC 20 Strength saving throw or be pushed up to 10 feet away from the dragon turtle and knocked prone.

Steam Breath (Recharge 5–6). The dragon turtle exhales scalding steam in a 60-foot cone. Each creature in that area must make a DC 18 Constitution saving throw, taking 52 (15d6) fire damage on a failed save, or half as much damage on a successful one. Being underwater doesn't grant resistance against this damage.

DRAGON TURTLE

Dragon turtles are among the most fearsome creatures of the oceans. As large and voracious as the oldest of its land-based dragon kin, a dragon turtle strikes with its deadly jaws, steaming breath, and crushing tail.

A dragon turtle's rough shell is the same dark green color as the deep water where this monster dwells. Silver highlights lining the shell resemble light dancing on open water, and a surfacing dragon turtle is sometimes mistaken for the reflection of the sun or moon on the waves.

Dragons of the Deep. Like true dragons, dragon turtles collect treasure, first by sinking ships and then by sifting through the wreckage for coins and other precious items. A dragon turtle swallows treasure for transport, then regurgitates it when it reaches its lair.

Dragon turtles dwell in caves hidden in coral reefs or beneath the seafloor, or along rugged stretches of coastline. If a choice cave is already inhabited, a dragon turtle attacks its current residents in an attempt to take over.

Mercenary Monsters. A dragon turtle is smart enough to be bribed, and pirates sailing seas patrolled by these creatures quickly learn to offer them treasure in exchange for safe passage. Clever sahuagin sometimes ally with dragon turtles, enticing them with treasure to use their blistering breath weapons in sahuagin raids against ships and coastal settlements.

Elemental Might. Dragon turtles sometimes find their way through sunken planar rifts to the Elemental Plane of Water. Those monstrous specimens can often be found in the service of marids, which strap magnificent coral thrones to the backs of dragon turtles and ride them as mounts.

"I failed the Spider Queen once. Never again."
—Pellanistra the drider

Drider

Large monstrosity, chaotic evil

Armor Class 19 (natural armor)
Hit Points 123 (13d10 + 52)
Speed 30 ft., climb 30 ft.

STR	DEX	CON	INT	WIS	CHA
16 (+3)	16 (+3)	18 (+4)	13 (+1)	14 (+2)	12 (+1)

Skills Perception +5, Stealth +9
Senses darkvision 120 ft., passive Perception 15
Languages Elvish, Undercommon
Challenge 6 (2,300 XP)

Fey Ancestry. The drider has advantage on saving throws against being charmed, and magic can't put the drider to sleep.

Innate Spellcasting. The drider's innate spellcasting ability is Wisdom (spell save DC 13). The drider can innately cast the following spells, requiring no material components:

At will: *dancing lights*
1/day each: *darkness, faerie fire*

Spider Climb. The drider can climb difficult surfaces, including upside down on ceilings, without needing to make an ability check.

Sunlight Sensitivity. While in sunlight, the drider has disadvantage on attack rolls, as well as on Wisdom (Perception) checks that rely on sight.

Web Walker. The drider ignores movement restrictions caused by webbing.

Actions

Multiattack. The drider makes three attacks, either with its longsword or its longbow. It can replace one of those attacks with a bite attack.

Bite. *Melee Weapon Attack:* +6 to hit, reach 5 ft., one creature. *Hit:* 2 (1d4) piercing damage plus 9 (2d8) poison damage.

Longsword. *Melee Weapon Attack:* +6 to hit, reach 5 ft., one target. *Hit:* 7 (1d8 + 3) slashing damage, or 8 (1d10 + 3) slashing damage if used with two hands.

Longbow. *Ranged Weapon Attack:* +6 to hit, range 150/600 ft., one target. *Hit:* 7 (1d8 + 3) piercing damage plus 4 (1d8) poison damage.

Drider

When a drow shows great promise, Lolth summons it to the Demonweb Pits for a test of faith and strength. Those that pass the test rise higher in the Spider Queen's favor. Those that fail are transformed into driders—a horrid hybrid of a drow and a giant spider that serves as a living reminder of Lolth's power. Only drow can be turned into driders, and the power to create these creatures resides with Lolth alone.

Scarred for Life. Drow transformed into driders return to the Material Plane as twisted and debased creatures. Driven by madness, they disappear into the Underdark to become hermits and hunters, either wandering alone or leading packs of giant spiders.

On rare occasion, a drider returns to the fringes of drow society despite its curse, most often to fulfill some longstanding vow or vendetta from its former life. Drow fear and shun the driders, holding them in lower esteem than slaves. However, they tolerate the presence of these creatures as living representatives of Lolth's will, and a reminder of the fate that awaits all who fail the Spider Queen.

Variant: Drider Spellcasting

Driders that were once drow spellcasters might retain their ability to cast spells. Such driders typically have a higher spellcasting ability (15 or 16) than other driders. Further, the drider gains the Spellcasting trait. A drider that was a drow divine spellcaster, therefore, could have a Wisdom of 16 (+3) and a Spellcasting trait as follows.

Spellcasting. The drider is a 7th-level spellcaster. Its spellcasting ability is Wisdom (spell save DC 14, +6 to hit with spell attacks). The drider has the following spells prepared from the cleric spell list:

Cantrips (at will): *poison spray, thaumaturgy*
1st level (4 slots): *bane, detect magic, sanctuary*
2nd level (3 slots): *hold person, silence*
3rd level (3 slots): *clairvoyance, dispel magic*
4th level (2 slots): *divination, freedom of movement*

Dryad

Travelers entering a forest might catch a glimpse of a feminine form flitting through the trees. Warm laughter hangs on the air, drawing those who hear it deeper into the emerald shadows.

Treebound. Powerful fey will sometimes bind lesser fey spirits to trees, transforming them into dryads. This is sometimes done as a punishment when the fey spirit falls in love with a mortal and that love is forbidden.

A dryad can emerge from the tree and travel the lands around it, but the tree remains her home and roots her to the world. As long as the tree remains healthy and unharmed, the dryad stays forever youthful and alluring. If the tree is harmed, she suffers. If the tree is ever destroyed, the dryad descends into madness.

Reclusive Fey. Dryads act as guardians of their woodland demesnes. Shy and reclusive, they watch interlopers from the trees. A dryad struck by the beauty of a stranger might investigate more closely, perhaps even try to lure the individual away to be charmed.

Dryads work with other sylvan creatures to defend their forests. Unicorns, treants, and satyrs live alongside them, in addition to druids that share the dryads' devotion to the woods they call home.

Woodland Magic. Dryads can speak with plants and animals. They can teleport from one tree to another, luring interlopers away from their groves. If pressed, a dryad can beguile humanoids with her enchantments, turning enemies into friends. They also know a handful of useful spells.

Dryad
Medium fey, neutral

Armor Class 11 (16 with *barkskin*)
Hit Points 22 (5d8)
Speed 30 ft.

STR	DEX	CON	INT	WIS	CHA
10 (+0)	12 (+1)	11 (+0)	14 (+2)	15 (+2)	18 (+4)

Skills Perception +4, Stealth +5
Senses darkvision 60 ft., passive Perception 14
Languages Elvish, Sylvan
Challenge 1 (200 XP)

Innate Spellcasting. The dryad's innate spellcasting ability is Charisma (spell save DC 14). The dryad can innately cast the following spells, requiring no material components:

At will: *druidcraft*
3/day each: *entangle*, *goodberry*
1/day each: *barkskin*, *pass without trace*, *shillelagh*

Magic Resistance. The dryad has advantage on saving throws against spells and other magical effects.

Speak with Beasts and Plants. The dryad can communicate with beasts and plants as if they shared a language.

Tree Stride. Once on her turn, the dryad can use 10 feet of her movement to step magically into one living tree within her reach and emerge from a second living tree within 60 feet of the first tree, appearing in an unoccupied space within 5 feet of the second tree. Both trees must be Large or bigger.

Actions

Club. *Melee Weapon Attack:* +2 to hit (+6 to hit with *shillelagh*), reach 5 ft., one target. *Hit:* 2 (1d4) bludgeoning damage, or 8 (1d8 + 4) bludgeoning damage with *shillelagh*.

Fey Charm. The dryad targets one humanoid or beast that she can see within 30 feet of her. If the target can see the dryad, it must succeed on a DC 14 Wisdom saving throw or be magically charmed. The charmed creature regards the dryad as a trusted friend to be heeded and protected. Although the target isn't under the dryad's control, it takes the dryad's requests or actions in the most favorable way it can.

Each time the dryad or its allies do anything harmful to the target, it can repeat the saving throw, ending the effect on itself on a success. Otherwise, the effect lasts 24 hours or until the dryad dies, is on a different plane of existence from the target, or ends the effect as a bonus action. If a target's saving throw is successful, the target is immune to the dryad's Fey Charm for the next 24 hours.

The dryad can have no more than one humanoid and up to three beasts charmed at a time.

DUERGAR

The tyrannical duergar, also known as gray dwarves, dwell in fantastic cities deep in the Underdark. Using ancient dwarven knowledge and myriad slaves, they work tirelessly to expand their subterranean kingdoms.

Most duergar (including females) are bald and have ashen gray skin. They wear drab clothing designed to blend in with stone, along with simple jewelry that reflects their severe and utilitarian demeanor.

Slaves to Slavers. The duergar were once dwarves, before their greed and endless delving beneath the earth brought them into contact with the mind flayers. Held in captivity for generations by the illithids, the dwarves eventually won their independence with the aid of the evil god Laduguer. Slavery had forever changed them, however, darkening their spirits to make the duergar as evil as the tyrants they had escaped. Despite winning their freedom, duergar are dour, pessimistic, untrusting creatures, always toiling and complaining, with no memory of what it means to be happy or proud. Their craftsmanship and accomplishments endure, yet they are bereft of warmth or artistry.

Duergar make war against their dwarven kin and all other subterranean races. They forge alliances when it is convenient, then break those alliances when they have nothing more to gain. They take and hold slaves to toil in the Underdark, regarding them as free labor and crude currency.

Tough as Stone. Like dwarves, duergar have strong constitutions. Adding to their physical stamina is an incredible mental fortitude resulting from their time as slaves of the illithids. A duergar's mind is a fortress, able to shrug off charms, illusions, and other spells.

Born of Darkness. The Underdark is saturated with strange magical power, which the duergar absorbed over generations of imprisonment. A duergar can

DUERGAR
Medium humanoid (dwarf), lawful evil

Armor Class 16 (scale mail, shield)
Hit Points 26 (4d8 + 8)
Speed 25 ft.

STR	DEX	CON	INT	WIS	CHA
14 (+2)	11 (+0)	14 (+2)	11 (+0)	10 (+0)	9 (−1)

Damage Resistances poison
Senses darkvision 120 ft., passive Perception 10
Languages Dwarvish, Undercommon
Challenge 1 (200 XP)

Duergar Resilience. The duergar has advantage on saving throws against poison, spells, and illusions, as well as to resist being charmed or paralyzed.

Sunlight Sensitivity. While in sunlight, the duergar has disadvantage on attack rolls, as well as on Wisdom (Perception) checks that rely on sight.

ACTIONS

Enlarge (Recharges after a Short or Long Rest). For 1 minute, the duergar magically increases in size, along with anything it is wearing or carrying. While enlarged, the duergar is Large, doubles its damage dice on Strength-based weapon attacks (included in the attacks), and makes Strength checks and Strength saving throws with advantage. If the duergar lacks the room to become Large, it attains the maximum size possible in the space available.

War Pick. Melee Weapon Attack: +4 to hit, reach 5 ft., one target. Hit: 6 (1d8 + 2) piercing damage, or 11 (2d8 + 2) piercing damage while enlarged.

Javelin. Melee or Ranged Weapon Attack: +4 to hit, reach 5 ft. or range 30/120 ft., one target. Hit: 5 (1d6 + 2) piercing damage, or 9 (2d6 + 2) piercing damage while enlarged.

Invisibility (Recharges after a Short or Long Rest). The duergar magically turns invisible until it attacks, casts a spell, or uses its Enlarge, or until its concentration is broken, up to 1 hour (as if concentrating on a spell). Any equipment the duergar wears or carries is invisible with it.

increase its size and strength for a short time, becoming a powerful ogre-sized warrior. If it faces a foe it can't fight, or when spying on creatures approaching its territory, it can just as easily become invisible to slip away into the darkness.

Eons spent in the Underdark also sharpened their darkvision, allowing them to see twice as far as other dwarves. This keen eyesight comes at a cost, however, as a duergar's vision is compromised by sunlight.

Infernal Master. Asmodeus, Lord of the Nine Hells, has been known to impersonate duergar gods in order to cultivate the evil brimming in the hearts of the gray dwarves. He offers them divine guidance and vengeance against their enemies while urging them on toward greater acts of tyranny, all the while concealing his true identity.

Elementals

Elementals are incarnations of the elements that make up the universe: air, earth, fire, and water. Though little more than animated energy on their own planes of existence, they can be called on by spellcasters and powerful beings to take shape and perform tasks.

Living Elements. On its home plane, an elemental is a bodiless life force. Its dim consciousness manifests as a physical shape only when focused by the power of magic. A wild spirit of elemental force has no desire except to course through the element of its native plane. Like beasts of the Material Plane, these elemental spirits have no society or culture, and little sense of being.

Conjured by Magic. Certain spells and magic items can conjure an elemental, summoning it from the Inner Planes to the Material Plane. Elementals instinctively resent being pulled from their native planes and bound into service. A creature that summons an elemental must assert force of will to control it.

Bound and Shaped. Powerful magic can bind an elemental spirit into a material template that defines a specific use and function. Invisible stalkers are air elementals bound to a specific form, in the same way that water elementals can be shaped into water weirds.

The strength of the magic and materials that bind an elemental determines how well the elemental functions in a bound form. Golems are elemental spirits bound to physical forms, but weaker materials such as flesh and clay can't bind elemental power sufficiently. Durable materials such as stone and iron require stronger magic, which consequently binds an elemental more securely.

Elemental Nature. An elemental doesn't require air, food, drink, or sleep.

Air Elemental

An air elemental is a funneling cloud of whirling air with a vague semblance of a face. Although it likes to race across the ground, picking up dust and debris as it goes, it can also fly and attack from above.

An air elemental can turn itself into a screaming cyclone, creating a whirlwind that batters creatures even as it flings them away.

Earth Elemental

An earth elemental plods forward like a walking hill, club-like arms of jagged stone swinging at its sides. Its head and body consist of dirt and stone, occasionally set with chunks of metal, gems, and bright minerals.

Earth elementals glide through rock and earth as though they were liquid. Earthbound creatures have much to fear from an earth elemental, since the elemental can pinpoint the precise location of any foe that stands on solid ground in its vicinity.

Fire Elemental

A faint humanoid shape threads through the core of this wild, moving flame. A fire elemental is a force of capricious devastation. Wherever it moves, it sets its surroundings ablaze, turning the world to ash, smoke, and cinders. Water can halt its destructive progress, causing the fire elemental to shrink back, hissing and smoking in pain and rage.

Water Elemental

A water elemental is a cresting wave that rolls across the ground, becoming nearly invisible at it courses through a larger body of water. It engulfs creatures that stand against it, filling their mouths and lungs as easily as it smothers flame.

AIR ELEMENTAL
Large elemental, neutral

Armor Class 15
Hit Points 90 (12d10 + 24)
Speed 0 ft., fly 90 ft. (hover)

STR	DEX	CON	INT	WIS	CHA
14 (+2)	20 (+5)	14 (+2)	6 (–2)	10 (+0)	6 (–2)

Damage Resistances lightning, thunder; bludgeoning, piercing, and slashing from nonmagical attacks
Damage Immunities poison
Condition Immunities exhaustion, grappled, paralyzed, petrified, poisoned, prone, restrained, unconscious
Senses darkvision 60 ft., passive Perception 10
Languages Auran
Challenge 5 (1,800 XP)

Air Form. The elemental can enter a hostile creature's space and stop there. It can move through a space as narrow as 1 inch wide without squeezing.

ACTIONS

Multiattack. The elemental makes two slam attacks.

Slam. *Melee Weapon Attack:* +8 to hit, reach 5 ft., one target. *Hit:* 14 (2d8 + 5) bludgeoning damage.

Whirlwind (Recharge 4–6). Each creature in the elemental's space must make a DC 13 Strength saving throw. On a failure, a target takes 15 (3d8 + 2) bludgeoning damage and is flung up 20 feet away from the elemental in a random direction and knocked prone. If a thrown target strikes an object, such as a wall or floor, the target takes 3 (1d6) bludgeoning damage for every 10 feet it was thrown. If the target is thrown at another creature, that creature must succeed on a DC 13 Dexterity saving throw or take the same damage and be knocked prone.
If the saving throw is successful, the target takes half the bludgeoning damage and isn't flung away or knocked prone.

EARTH ELEMENTAL
Large elemental, neutral

Armor Class 17 (natural armor)
Hit Points 126 (12d10 + 60)
Speed 30 ft., burrow 30 ft.

STR	DEX	CON	INT	WIS	CHA
20 (+5)	8 (–1)	20 (+5)	5 (–3)	10 (+0)	5 (–3)

Damage Vulnerabilities thunder
Damage Resistances bludgeoning, piercing, and slashing from nonmagical attacks
Damage Immunities poison
Condition Immunities exhaustion, paralyzed, petrified, poisoned, unconscious
Senses darkvision 60 ft., tremorsense 60 ft., passive Perception 10
Languages Terran
Challenge 5 (1,800 XP)

Earth Glide. The elemental can burrow through nonmagical, unworked earth and stone. While doing so, the elemental doesn't disturb the material it moves through.

Siege Monster. The elemental deals double damage to objects and structures.

ACTIONS

Multiattack. The elemental makes two slam attacks.

Slam. *Melee Weapon Attack:* +8 to hit, reach 10 ft., one target. *Hit:* 14 (2d8 + 5) bludgeoning damage.

E

Fire Elemental

Large elemental, neutral

Armor Class 13
Hit Points 102 (12d10 + 36)
Speed 50 ft.

STR	DEX	CON	INT	WIS	CHA
10 (+0)	17 (+3)	16 (+3)	6 (–2)	10 (+0)	7 (–2)

Damage Resistances bludgeoning, piercing, and slashing from nonmagical attacks
Damage Immunities fire, poison
Condition Immunities exhaustion, grappled, paralyzed, petrified, poisoned, prone, restrained, unconscious
Senses darkvision 60 ft., passive Perception 10
Languages Ignan
Challenge 5 (1,800 XP)

Fire Form. The elemental can move through a space as narrow as 1 inch wide without squeezing. A creature that touches the elemental or hits it with a melee attack while within 5 feet of it takes 5 (1d10) fire damage. In addition, the elemental can enter a hostile creature's space and stop there. The first time it enters a creature's space on a turn, that creature takes 5 (1d10) fire damage and catches fire; until someone takes an action to douse the fire, the creature takes 5 (1d10) fire damage at the start of each of its turns.

Illumination. The elemental sheds bright light in a 30-foot radius and dim light in an additional 30 feet.

Water Susceptibility. For every 5 feet the elemental moves in water, or for every gallon of water splashed on it, it takes 1 cold damage.

Actions

Multiattack. The elemental makes two touch attacks.

Touch. *Melee Weapon Attack:* +6 to hit, reach 5 ft., one target. *Hit:* 10 (2d6 + 3) fire damage. If the target is a creature or a flammable object, it ignites. Until a creature takes an action to douse the fire, the target takes 5 (1d10) fire damage at the start of each of its turns.

Water Elemental

Large elemental, neutral

Armor Class 14 (natural armor)
Hit Points 114 (12d10 + 48)
Speed 30 ft., swim 90 ft.

STR	DEX	CON	INT	WIS	CHA
18 (+4)	14 (+2)	18 (+4)	5 (–3)	10 (+0)	8 (–1)

Damage Resistances acid; bludgeoning, piercing, and slashing from nonmagical attacks
Damage Immunities poison
Condition Immunities exhaustion, grappled, paralyzed, petrified, poisoned, prone, restrained, unconscious
Senses darkvision 60 ft., passive Perception 10
Languages Aquan
Challenge 5 (1,800 XP)

Water Form. The elemental can enter a hostile creature's space and stop there. It can move through a space as narrow as 1 inch wide without squeezing.

Freeze. If the elemental takes cold damage, it partially freezes; its speed is reduced by 20 feet until the end of its next turn.

Actions

Multiattack. The elemental makes two slam attacks.

Slam. Melee *Weapon Attack:* +7 to hit, reach 5 ft., one target. *Hit:* 13 (2d8 + 4) bludgeoning damage.

Whelm (Recharge 4–6). Each creature in the elemental's space must make a DC 15 Strength saving throw. On a failure, a target takes 13 (2d8 + 4) bludgeoning damage. If it is Large or smaller, it is also grappled (escape DC 14). Until this grapple ends, the target is restrained and unable to breathe unless it can breathe water. If the saving throw is successful, the target is pushed out of the elemental's space.

The elemental can grapple one Large creature or up to two Medium or smaller creatures at one time with this ability. At the start of each of the elemental's turns, each grappled target takes 13 (2d8 + 4) bludgeoning damage. As an action, a creature within 5 feet of the elemental can pull a creature or an object out of it by succeeding on a DC 14 Strength check.

E

ELVES: DROW

Tens of thousands of years ago, the elves were divided, with those of benevolent disposition battling those that were selfish and cruel. The war among elvenkind ended when the good elves banished their malevolent kin to the subterranean depths. Here, in the lightless caverns and endless warrens of twisting passages, the dark elves—the drow—found refuge. They also found leadership in the only elven deity who had not forsaken them. At her command, the dark elves built an empire in the underworld.

Children of Lolth. The drow worship Lolth, a deity who resides in the Abyss. Known as the Spider Queen or the Demon Queen of Spiders, she is the figure around which the dark elves have built their subterranean civilization. Whatever she demands, the drow do.

The wickedest of elves, drow are seldom seen by the surface world. Though they plot to destroy the elves that banished them, they no longer see themselves as exiles. They are the destined rulers of the darkness, and when Lolth commands them to rise up and destroy their surface-dwelling kin, they will.

Creatures of Darkness. The drow have lived underground for so long that they have evolved to their surroundings and can see in the dark. However, they can no longer stand sunlight. When slaves are in short supply in the Underdark, the drow send raiding parties to the surface to capture humanoids under cover of darkness, bringing them back to their cities to be tortured into submission. Beyond those occasional excursions, the drow are content to remain in their subterranean realm, where they feel secure and in control.

Underdark Cities. The dark elves build fantastic cities in enormous caverns where food and water are abundant. Their ability to sculpt stone rivals that of the greatest dwarf artisans, yet their structures retain a decidedly elven aesthetic. Though appearing delicate, drow settlements are structurally sound and remarkably resilient. The drow like to hollow out enormous stalagmites and stalactites, creating populated spires that rise from the floors and ceilings.

A drow city is a sprawling metropolis enclosed by high walls. Non-drow visitors must conduct their business outside the walls under watchful eyes. The drow raise and keep giant spiders to help protect their cities against

---

VARIANT: DROW MAGIC ARMOR AND WEAPONS

Drow often wear magic armor and carry magic weapons that lose their enhancement bonuses permanently if they are exposed to sunlight for 1 hour or longer.

A **drow** wearing a +1 *chain shirt* and carrying a +1 *shortsword* has AC 19 and a +1 bonus on attack and damage rolls with shortsword attacks.

A **drow elite warrior** wearing +2 *studded leather* and carrying a +2 *shortsword* has AC 20 and a +2 bonus on attack and damage rolls with shortsword attacks.

A **drow priestess of Lolth** wearing +3 *scale mail* has AC 19.

intruders, even as they drape those cities in beautiful webbing, creating a gossamer snare to catch flying enemies that would otherwise soar over the walls.

Drow Magic. Just as the drow have adapted to underground life, so too has their magic. In addition to using that magic to carve their cities from stone, they empower their weapons, create dangerous new magic items, and summon demons from the Abyss. Drow spellcasters are supremely arrogant and never hesitate to use their magic in the most abhorrent ways.

Arms and Armor. Drow craft weapons made of adamantine, a dark and supernaturally hard metal. Drow artisans adorn their weapons and armor with web-like filigree and spider motifs, and mages sometimes imbue items with magic to enhance their effectiveness. However, such magic fades when exposed to sunlight, so that magical drow weapons and armor rarely retain their enhancement bonuses and magical properties when brought to the surface.

Cutthroat Politics. Drow politics are cutthroat and rife with intrigue. When drow work together, it is typically to destroy a common foe and ensure their own survival, and such alliances are short lived and fraught with peril.

Drow society is divided into noble houses, each ruled by a matron who seeks to raise the prestige and power of her house above all others. Other high-ranking members of the house are blood relatives, while the middling ranks are flush with drow from weaker families that have sworn fealty to the greater house. Clinging precariously to the bottom rung of a house's social ladder are the house slaves, made up of drow of low birth and the occasional non-drow captive.

Matriarchal Rule. Lolth, through her faithful priestesses, dictates the rules of drow society, ensuring that her orders and plots are carried out. Since Lolth is prone to manifesting on the Material Plane and directly punishing those that disobey her, the drow have learned to heed what she says and do as her priestesses command.

In drow society, males are subservient to females. A male drow might lead an Underdark patrol or a raiding party to the surface, but he reports to a female drow—either the matron of his house or one of her hand-picked female subordinates. Although male drow can fill almost any function in drow society, they can't be priests, nor can they rule a house.

Poison Predilection. Distilled from spider venom and the flora of the Underdark, poison can be found in abundance among the drow, and it plays an important part in their culture and politics. Drow mages concoct a viscid toxin that leaves enemies unconscious. Drow warriors coat their blades and crossbow bolts with this venom, looking forward to the interrogation and torture that follows combat.

DROW ELITE WARRIOR

Drow elite warriors defend their houses and their superiors against all enemies, although they specialize in fighting dwarves, gnomes, and elves (including other drow). They frequently raid surface settlements under cover of night, returning to the Underdark with prisoners and spoils in tow before dawn.

Elite warriors can be male or female.

DROW MAGE

Privileged drow males who lack the strength and fighting prowess to train as warriors have no recourse but to pursue the study of magic. For them, it is a matter of survival. Female drow with a natural affinity for the arcane arts may also become drow mages, although they are much less common.

DROW PRIESTESS OF LOLTH

Female drow with blood ties to a noble house are molded and trained from birth to become priestesses of Lolth. The Spider Queen doesn't allow male drow to hold such positions.

Such priestesses execute the will of the Spider Queen, and as a result, they wield tremendous power and influence in drow society. The matron mothers who rule the drow houses are the most powerful of Lolth's priestesses, but they must constantly balance their devotion to the Spider Queen with their devotion to their families.

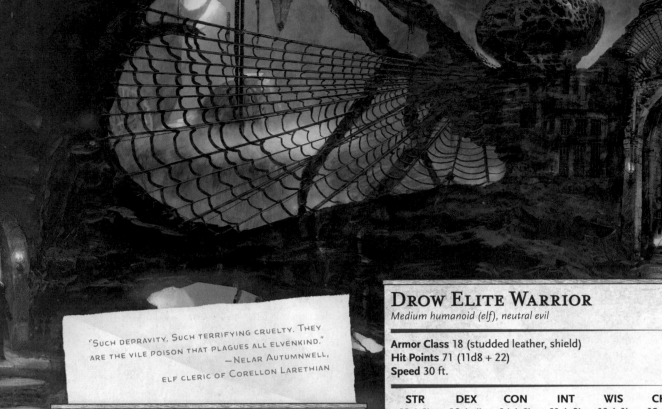

DROW

Medium humanoid (elf), neutral evil

Armor Class 15 (chain shirt)
Hit Points 13 (3d8)
Speed 30 ft.

STR	DEX	CON	INT	WIS	CHA
10 (+0)	14 (+2)	10 (+0)	11 (+0)	11 (+0)	12 (+1)

Skills Perception +2, Stealth +4
Senses darkvision 120 ft., passive Perception 12
Languages Elvish, Undercommon
Challenge 1/4 (50 XP)

Fey Ancestry. The drow has advantage on saving throws against being charmed, and magic can't put the drow to sleep.

Innate Spellcasting. The drow's spellcasting ability is Charisma (spell save DC 11). It can innately cast the following spells, requiring no material components:

At will: *dancing lights*
1/day each: *darkness, faerie fire*

Sunlight Sensitivity. While in sunlight, the drow has disadvantage on attack rolls, as well as on Wisdom (Perception) checks that rely on sight.

ACTIONS

Shortsword. *Melee Weapon Attack:* +4 to hit, reach 5 ft., one target. *Hit:* 5 (1d6 + 2) piercing damage.

Hand Crossbow. *Ranged Weapon Attack:* +4 to hit, range 30/120 ft., one target. *Hit:* 5 (1d6 + 2) piercing damage, and the target must succeed on a DC 13 Constitution saving throw or be poisoned for 1 hour. If the saving throw fails by 5 or more, the target is also unconscious while poisoned in this way. The target wakes up if it takes damage or if another creature takes an action to shake it awake.

DROW ELITE WARRIOR

Medium humanoid (elf), neutral evil

Armor Class 18 (studded leather, shield)
Hit Points 71 (11d8 + 22)
Speed 30 ft.

STR	DEX	CON	INT	WIS	CHA
13 (+1)	18 (+4)	14 (+2)	11 (+0)	13 (+1)	12 (+1)

Saving Throws Dex +7, Con +5, Wis +4
Skills Perception +4, Stealth +10
Senses darkvision 120 ft., passive Perception 14
Languages Elvish, Undercommon
Challenge 5 (1,800 XP)

Fey Ancestry. The drow has advantage on saving throws against being charmed, and magic can't put the drow to sleep.

Innate Spellcasting. The drow's spellcasting ability is Charisma (spell save DC 12). It can innately cast the following spells, requiring no material components:

At will: *dancing lights*
1/day each: *darkness, faerie fire, levitate* (self only)

Sunlight Sensitivity. While in sunlight, the drow has disadvantage on attack rolls, as well as on Wisdom (Perception) checks that rely on sight.

ACTIONS

Multiattack. The drow makes two shortsword attacks.

Shortsword. *Melee Weapon Attack:* +7 to hit, reach 5 ft., one target. *Hit:* 7 (1d6 + 4) piercing damage plus 10 (3d6) poison damage.

Hand Crossbow. *Ranged Weapon Attack:* +7 to hit, range 30/120 ft., one target. *Hit:* 7 (1d6 + 4) piercing damage, and the target must succeed on a DC 13 Constitution saving throw or be poisoned for 1 hour. If the saving throw fails by 5 or more, the target is also unconscious while poisoned in this way. The target wakes up if it takes damage or if another creature takes an action to shake it awake.

REACTIONS

Parry. The drow adds 3 to its AC against one melee attack that would hit it. To do so, the drow must see the attacker and be wielding a melee weapon.

Drow Mage

Medium humanoid (elf), neutral evil

Armor Class 12 (15 with *mage armor*)
Hit Points 45 (10d8)
Speed 30 ft.

STR	DEX	CON	INT	WIS	CHA
9 (−1)	14 (+2)	10 (+0)	17 (+3)	13 (+1)	12 (+1)

Skills Arcana +6, Deception +5, Perception +4, Stealth +5
Senses darkvision 120 ft., passive Perception 14
Languages Elvish, Undercommon
Challenge 7 (2,900 XP)

Fey Ancestry. The drow has advantage on saving throws against being charmed, and magic can't put the drow to sleep.

Innate Spellcasting. The drow's innate spellcasting ability is Charisma (spell save DC 12). It can innately cast the following spells, requiring no material components:

At will: *dancing lights*
1/day each: *darkness, faerie fire, levitate* (self only)

Spellcasting. The drow is a 10th-level spellcaster. Its spellcasting ability is Intelligence (spell save DC 14, +6 to hit with spell attacks). The drow has the following wizard spells prepared:

Cantrips (at will): *mage hand, minor illusion, poison spray, ray of frost*
1st level (4 slots): *mage armor, magic missile, shield, witch bolt*
2nd level (3 slots): *alter self, misty step, web*
3rd level (3 slots): *fly, lightning bolt*
4th level (3 slots): *Evard's black tentacles, greater invisibility*
5th level (2 slots): *cloudkill*

Sunlight Sensitivity. While in sunlight, the drow has disadvantage on attack rolls, as well as on Wisdom (Perception) checks that rely on sight.

Actions

Staff. *Melee Weapon Attack:* +2 to hit, reach 5 ft., one target. *Hit:* 2 (1d6 − 1) bludgeoning damage, or 3 (1d8 − 1) bludgeoning damage if used with two hands, plus 3 (1d6) poison damage.

Summon Demon (1/Day). The drow magically summons a quasit, or attempts to summon a shadow demon with a 50 percent chance of success. The summoned demon appears in an unoccupied space within 60 feet of its summoner, acts as an ally of its summoner, and can't summon other demons. It remains for 10 minutes, until it or its summoner dies, or until its summoner dismisses it as an action.

Drow Priestess of Lolth

Medium humanoid (elf), neutral evil

Armor Class 16 (scale mail)
Hit Points 71 (13d8 + 13)
Speed 30 ft.

STR	DEX	CON	INT	WIS	CHA
10 (+0)	14 (+2)	12 (+1)	13 (+1)	17 (+3)	18 (+4)

Saving Throws Con +4, Wis +6, Cha +7
Skills Insight +6, Perception +6, Religion +4, Stealth +5
Senses darkvision 120 ft., passive Perception 16
Languages Elvish, Undercommon
Challenge 8 (3,900 XP)

Fey Ancestry. The drow has advantage on saving throws against being charmed, and magic can't put the drow to sleep.

Innate Spellcasting. The drow's innate spellcasting ability is Charisma (spell save DC 15). She can innately cast the following spells, requiring no material components:

At will: *dancing lights*
1/day each: *darkness, faerie fire, levitate* (self only)

Spellcasting. The drow is a 10th-level spellcaster. Her spellcasting ability is Wisdom (save DC 14, +6 to hit with spell attacks). The drow has the following cleric spells prepared:

Cantrips (at will): *guidance, poison spray, resistance, spare the dying, thaumaturgy*
1st level (4 slots): *animal friendship, cure wounds, detect poison and disease, ray of sickness*
2nd level (3 slots): *lesser restoration, protection from poison, web*
3rd level (3 slots): *conjure animals* (2 giant spiders), *dispel magic*
4th level (3 slots): *divination, freedom of movement*
5th level (2 slots): *insect plague, mass cure wounds*

Sunlight Sensitivity. While in sunlight, the drow has disadvantage on attack rolls, as well as on Wisdom (Perception) checks that rely on sight.

Actions

Multiattack. The drow makes two scourge attacks.

Scourge. *Melee Weapon Attack:* +5 to hit, reach 5 ft., one target. *Hit:* 5 (1d6 + 2) piercing damage plus 17 (5d6) poison damage.

Summon Demon (1/Day). The drow attempts to magically summon a yochlol with a 30 percent chance of success. If the attempt fails, the drow takes 5 (1d10) psychic damage. Otherwise, the summoned demon appears in an unoccupied space within 60 feet of its summoner, acts as an ally of its summoner, and can't summon other demons. It remains for 10 minutes, until it or its summoner dies, or until its summoner dismisses it as an action.

EMPYREAN

Empyreans are the celestial children of the gods of the Upper Planes. They are universally beautiful, statuesque, and self-assured.

Manifest Emotion. An empyrean can experience deity-like fits of serenity or rage. It can affect the environment around it by its mood. When an empyrean is unhappy, the clouds might cry tears of salt water, the wildflowers in surrounding meadows might wilt, dead fish might wash ashore in lakes or rivers, or a nearby forest might lose the leaves from its trees. When an empyrean is jubilant, sunlight follows it everywhere, small animals frolic in its footsteps, and birds fill the sky with their pleasing songs.

Evil Empyreans. A few empyreans have turned to evil after venturing to the Lower Planes and becoming corrupted, or as the result of being cursed by evil gods. An evil empyrean can't survive long on the Upper Planes and usually retreats to the Material Plane, where it can rule over a kingdom of mortals as an indomitable tyrant.

Immortal Titans. Empyreans don't age but can be slain. Because few empyreans can imagine their own demise, they fight fearlessly when drawn into battle, refusing to believe that the end is upon them even when standing at death's door. When an empyrean dies, its spirit returns to its home plane. There, one of the fallen empyrean's parents resurrects the empyrean unless he or she has a good reason not to.

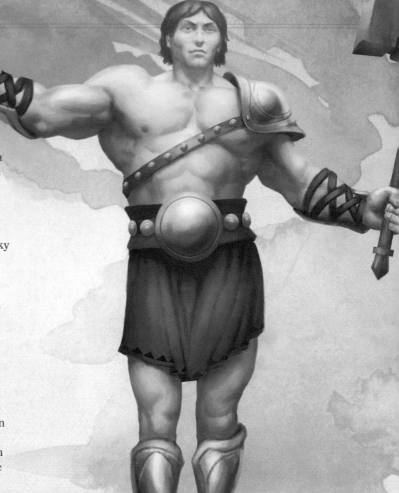

EMPYREAN

Huge celestial (titan), chaotic good (75%) or neutral evil (25%)

Armor Class 22 (natural armor)
Hit Points 313 (19d12 + 190)
Speed 50 ft., fly 50 ft., swim 50 ft.

STR	DEX	CON	INT	WIS	CHA
30 (+10)	21 (+5)	30 (+10)	21 (+5)	22 (+6)	27 (+8)

Saving Throws Str +17, Int +12, Wis +13, Cha +15
Skills Insight +13, Persuasion +15
Damage Immunities bludgeoning, piercing, and slashing from nonmagical attacks
Senses truesight 120 ft., passive Perception 16
Languages all
Challenge 23 (50,000 XP)

Innate Spellcasting. The empyrean's innate spellcasting ability is Charisma (spell save DC 23, +15 to hit with spell attacks). It can innately cast the following spells, requiring no material components:

At will: *greater restoration, pass without trace, water breathing, water walk*
1/day each: *commune, dispel evil and good, earthquake, fire storm, plane shift* (self only)

Legendary Resistance (3/Day). If the empyrean fails a saving throw, it can choose to succeed instead.

Magic Resistance. The empyrean has advantage on saving throws against spells and other magical effects.

Magic Weapons. The empyrean's weapon attacks are magical.

ACTIONS

Maul. *Melee Weapon Attack:* +17 to hit, reach 10 ft., one target. *Hit:* 31 (6d6 + 10) bludgeoning damage. If the target is a creature, it must succeed on a DC 15 Constitution saving throw or be stunned until the end of the empyrean's next turn.

Bolt. *Ranged Spell Attack:* +15 to hit, range 600 ft., one target. *Hit:* 24 (7d6) damage of one of the following types (empyrean's choice): acid, cold, fire, force, lightning, radiant, or thunder.

LEGENDARY ACTIONS

The empyrean can take 3 legendary actions, choosing from the options below. Only one legendary action option can be used at a time and only at the end of another creature's turn. The empyrean regains spent legendary actions at the start of its turn.

Attack. The empyrean makes one attack.
Bolster. The empyrean bolsters all nonhostile creatures within 120 feet of it until the end of its next turn. Bolstered creatures can't be charmed or frightened, and they gain advantage on ability checks and saving throws until the end of the empyrean's next turn.
Trembling Strike (Costs 2 Actions). The empyrean strikes the ground with its maul, triggering an earth tremor. All other creatures on the ground within 60 feet of the empyrean must succeed on a DC 25 Strength saving throw or be knocked prone.

ETTERCAP

Ettercaps are humanoid spiders that tend, feed, and watch over spiders the way a shepherd oversees a flock of sheep. They lair deep in remote forests.

Fine strands of silk stream from glands in an ettercap's abdomen, letting it shoot sticky strands of webbing to bind, entrap, or strangle its victims. It can also use its webbing to fashion elaborate snares and nets, which often festoon its lair.

Quiet Killers. When travelers and explorers venture into an ettercap's territory, the ettercap stalks them. Some meet their end wandering blindly into traps or sections of forest enclosed by webs. Others, the ettercap garrotes with strands of web or envenoms with its poisonous bite.

Sylvan Despoilers. Though they dwell in the wilds, ettercaps have no desire to live in harmony with nature. A forest infested with ettercaps transforms into a gloomy place, choked with webs and infested with giant spiders, giant insects, and other sinister predators. Creatures that wander too far into such a wood are soon lost in a maze of webs that dangle with the bones and lost treasures of the ettercaps' victims.

Enemies of the Fey. Ettercaps are natural enemies of fey creatures. The foul creatures set web snares to catch sprites and pixies, which they hungrily devour, and will encase a dryad's tree in webbing in a vain attempt to trap the dryad. Otherwise timid fey will sometimes approach outsiders for help in dealing with an ettercap infestation, being ill-equipped to deal with the malevolent creatures themselves.

ETTERCAP

Medium monstrosity, neutral evil

Armor Class 13 (natural armor)
Hit Points 44 (8d8 + 8)
Speed 30 ft., climb 30 ft.

STR	DEX	CON	INT	WIS	CHA
14 (+2)	15 (+2)	13 (+1)	7 (–2)	12 (+1)	8 (–1)

Skills Perception +3, Stealth +4, Survival +3
Senses darkvision 60 ft., passive Perception 13
Languages —
Challenge 2 (450 XP)

Spider Climb. The ettercap can climb difficult surfaces, including upside down on ceilings, without needing to make an ability check.

Web Sense. While in contact with a web, the ettercap knows the exact location of any other creature in contact with the same web.

Web Walker. The ettercap ignores movement restrictions caused by webbing.

ACTIONS

Multiattack. The ettercap makes two attacks: one with its bite and one with its claws.

Bite. *Melee Weapon Attack:* +4 to hit, reach 5 ft., one creature. *Hit:* 6 (1d8 + 2) piercing damage plus 4 (1d8) poison damage. The target must succeed on a DC 11 Constitution saving throw or be poisoned for 1 minute. The creature can repeat the saving throw at the end of each of its turns, ending the effect on itself on a success.

Claws. *Melee Weapon Attack:* +4 to hit, reach 5 ft., one target. *Hit:* 7 (2d4 + 2) slashing damage.

Web (Recharge 5–6). *Ranged Weapon Attack:* +4 to hit, range 30/60 ft., one Large or smaller creature. *Hit:* The creature is restrained by webbing. As an action, the restrained creature can make a DC 11 Strength check, escaping from the webbing on a success. The effect also ends if the webbing is destroyed. The webbing has AC 10, 5 hit points, vulnerability to fire damage, and immunity to bludgeoning, poison, and psychic damage.

ETTIN

An ettin is a foul, two-headed giant with the crude characteristics of an orc. It never bathes if it can help it, and its thick skin is usually encrusted with a thick layer of dirt and grime beneath the stinking hides it wears. Its long stringy hair hangs in an unkempt mess about its faces, and its breath reeks from mouths filled with crooked teeth and tusks.

Dual Personality. The twin heads of an ettin are two individuals trapped in the same brutish body. Each head has its own mind, personality, and name, and possesses unique preferences and quirks. Bound from birth, both minds only rarely experience privacy or solitude. This familiarity breeds contempt, and an ettin bullies and argues with itself constantly, its two heads each taking constant offense at the other's slights.

When other creatures refer to an ettin, they combine its double names to form a single compound name that applies to the creature as a whole. If an ettin has one head named Hargle and another named Vargle, other creatures call the ettin Harglevargle.

Solitary Lives. As much as an ettin argues with itself, it is even less tolerant of other ettins, since a conversation between two ettins almost always amounts to a shouting match between a crowd of four belligerent heads. Most ettins are solitary creatures as a result, tolerating one another only to reproduce.

An ettin's twin heads are always the same gender, with a body to match. Females are the dominant gender among ettins, and they initiate the ettins' mating rituals. After finding a suitable den, a female ettin hunts and conquers a male, which cares for and feeds her during her six-month pregnancy. Once the child is born, the male ettin is released from servitude. When the child is old enough to hunt for itself, the mother sends it away and abandons the den.

Two Heads are Better than One. When focused on a mutually beneficial purpose or united by a common threat, an ettin can resolve its personality differences and dedicate itself fully to a task. An ettin fights with a weapon in each hand, making twin attacks directed by its respective heads. When an ettin sleeps, one of its heads remains ever alert, gaining its only moments of privacy and keeping two eyes open for any creature that disturbs its precious solitude.

Orcish Ties. In ancient dialects of Common, the word "ettin" translates as "ugly giant." Legends tell of orcs that once stumbled upon a temple to Demogorgon, the magic of which transformed them into giant mockeries of the twin-headed Prince of Demons. Driven to near madness, these creatures scattered into the wilderness to become the first ettins.

Whatever the truth of the ettins' origin, orcs treat them as distant cousins, and orc tribes often entice ettins to serve as guards, scouts, and marauders. An ettin isn't particularly loyal to its orc handlers, but the orcs can win it over with the promise of food and loot.

ETTIN
Large giant, chaotic evil

Armor Class 12 (natural armor)
Hit Points 85 (10d10 + 30)
Speed 40 ft.

STR	DEX	CON	INT	WIS	CHA
21 (+5)	8 (−1)	17 (+3)	6 (−2)	10 (+0)	8 (−1)

Skills Perception +4
Senses darkvision 60 ft., passive Perception 14
Languages Giant, Orc
Challenge 4 (1,100 XP)

Two Heads. The ettin has advantage on Wisdom (Perception) checks and on saving throws against being blinded, charmed, deafened, frightened, stunned, and knocked unconscious.

Wakeful. When one of the ettin's heads is asleep, its other head is awake.

ACTIONS

Multiattack. The ettin makes two attacks: one with its battleaxe and one with its morningstar.

Battleaxe. *Melee Weapon Attack:* +7 to hit, reach 5 ft., one target. *Hit:* 14 (2d8 + 5) slashing damage.

Morningstar. *Melee Weapon Attack:* +7 to hit, reach 5 ft., one target. *Hit:* 14 (2d8 + 5) piercing damage.

FAERIE DRAGON

A faerie dragon is a cat-sized dragon with butterfly wings. It wears a sharp-toothed grin and expresses its delight by the twitching of its tail, its merriment fading only if it is attacked.

Invisible Tricksters. The only warning of a faerie dragon's presence is a stifled giggle. The dragon stays out of sight, watching invisibly as its victims contend with its pranks. When its fun is done, the dragon might reveal itself, depending on the disposition of its "prey."

Friendly and Bright. A faerie dragon has a sharp mind, a fondness for treasure and good company, and a puckish sense of humor. Travelers can play to a faerie dragon's draconic nature by offering it "treasure" in the form of sweets, baked goods, and baubles in exchange for information or safe passage through its territory.

The Colors of Age. A faerie dragon's scales change hue as it ages, moving through all the colors of the rainbow. All faerie dragons have innate spellcasting ability, gaining new spells as they mature.

Dragon Color	Age Range
Red	5 years or less
Orange	6–10 years
Yellow	11–20 years
Green	21–30 years
Blue	31–40 years
Indigo	41–50 years
Violet	51 years or more

FAERIE DRAGON

Tiny dragon, chaotic good

Armor Class 15
Hit Points 14 (4d4 + 4)
Speed 10 ft., fly 60 ft.

STR	DEX	CON	INT	WIS	CHA
3 (−4)	20 (+5)	13 (+1)	14 (+2)	12 (+1)	16 (+3)

Skills Arcana +4, Perception +3, Stealth +7
Senses darkvision 60 ft., passive Perception 13
Languages Draconic, Sylvan
Challenge 1 (200 XP) for a red, orange, or yellow faerie dragon; 2 (450 XP) for a green, blue, indigo, or violet faerie dragon

Superior Invisibility. As a bonus action, the dragon can magically turn invisible until its concentration ends (as if concentrating on a spell). Any equipment the dragon wears or carries is invisible with it.

Limited Telepathy. Using telepathy, the dragon can magically communicate with any other faerie dragon within 60 feet of it.

Magic Resistance. The dragon has advantage on saving throws against spells and other magical effects.

Innate Spellcasting. The dragon's innate spellcasting ability is Charisma (spell save DC 13). It can innately cast a number of spells, requiring no material components. As the dragon ages and changes color, it gains additional spells as shown below.

Red, 1/day each: *dancing lights, mage hand, minor illusion*
Orange, 1/day: *color spray*
Yellow, 1/day: *mirror image*
Green, 1/day: *suggestion*
Blue, 1/day: *major image*
Indigo, 1/day: *hallucinatory terrain*
Violet, 1/day: *polymorph*

ACTIONS

Bite. *Melee Weapon Attack:* +7 to hit, reach 5 ft., one creature. *Hit:* 1 piercing damage.

Euphoria Breath (Recharge 5–6). The dragon exhales a puff of euphoria gas at one creature within 5 feet of it. The target must succeed on a DC 11 Wisdom saving throw, or for 1 minute, the target can't take reactions and must roll a d6 at the start of each of its turns to determine its behavior during the turn:

1–4. The target takes no action or bonus action and uses all of its movement to move in a random direction.

5–6. The target doesn't move, and the only thing it can do on its turn is make a DC 11 Wisdom saving throw, ending the effect on itself on a success.

FLAMESKULL

Blazing green flames and mad, echoing laughter follow a disembodied skull as it patrols its demesne. When the undead flameskull discovers trespassers, it blasts the intruders with fiery rays from its eyes and dreadful spells called up from the dark recesses of its memory.

Dark spellcasters fashion flameskulls from the remains of dead wizards. When the ritual is complete, green flames erupt from the skull to complete its ghastly transformation.

Legacy of Life. A flameskull only dimly recalls its former life. Though it might speak in its old voice and recount key events from its past, it is but an echo of its former self. However, its undead transformation grants it full access to the magic it wielded in life, letting it cast spells while ignoring the material and somatic components it can no longer employ.

Eternally Bound. Intelligent and vigilant, a flameskull serves its creator by protecting a hidden treasure hoard, a secret chamber, or a specific individual. A flameskull carries out the directives given to it when it was created, and it interprets those commands to the letter. A flameskull's master must craft its instructions with care to ensure that the creature carries out its tasks properly.

Wreathed in Flame. The fire wreathing a flameskull burns continually, giving off bright light that the creature controls. It uses those flames as a weapon, focusing them to loose them as fiery rays from its eye sockets.

Eldritch Rejuvenation. A flameskull's shattered fragments reform unless they are splashed with holy water or subjected to a *dispel magic* or *remove curse* spell. If it can no longer fulfill its intended purpose, the re-formed flameskull is beholden to no one and becomes autonomous.

Undead Nature. A flameskull doesn't require air, food, drink, or sleep.

FLAMESKULL
Tiny undead, neutral evil

Armor Class 13
Hit Points 40 (9d4 + 18)
Speed 0 ft., fly 40 ft. (hover)

STR	DEX	CON	INT	WIS	CHA
1 (−5)	17 (+3)	14 (+2)	16 (+3)	10 (+0)	11 (+0)

Skills Arcana +5, Perception +2
Damage Resistances lightning, necrotic, piercing
Damage Immunities cold, fire, poison
Condition Immunities charmed, frightened, paralyzed, poisoned, prone
Senses darkvision 60 ft., passive Perception 12
Languages Common
Challenge 4 (1,100 XP)

Illumination. The flameskull sheds either dim light in a 15-foot radius, or bright light in a 15-foot radius and dim light for an additional 15 feet. It can switch between the options as an action.

Magic Resistance. The flameskull has advantage on saving throws against spells and other magical effects.

Rejuvenation. If the flameskull is destroyed, it regains all its hit points in 1 hour unless holy water is sprinkled on its remains or a *dispel magic* or *remove curse* spell is cast on them.

Spellcasting. The flameskull is a 5th-level spellcaster. Its spellcasting ability is Intelligence (spell save DC 13, +5 to hit with spell attacks). It requires no somatic or material components to cast its spells. The flameskull has the following wizard spells prepared:

Cantrip (at will): *mage hand*
1st level (3 slots): *magic missile, shield*
2nd level (2 slots): *blur, flaming sphere*
3rd level (1 slot): *fireball*

ACTIONS

Multiattack. The flameskull uses Fire Ray twice.

Fire Ray. *Ranged Spell Attack:* +5 to hit, range 30 ft., one target. *Hit:* 10 (3d6) fire damage.

FLUMPH

The mysterious flumphs drift through the Underdark, propelled through the air by the jets whose sound gives them their name. A flumph glows faintly, reflecting its moods in its color. Soft pink means it is amused, deep blue is sadness, green expresses curiosity, and crimson is anger.

Intelligent and Wise. Flumphs communicate telepathically. Though they resemble jellyfish, flumphs are sentient beings of great intelligence and wisdom, possessing advanced knowledge of religion, philosophy, mathematics, and countless other subjects.

Flumphs are sensitive to the emotional states of nearby creatures. If a creature's thoughts suggest goodness, a flumph seeks that creature out. When facing creatures that exude evil, a flumph flees.

Psionic Siphons. Flumphs feed by siphoning mental energy from psionic creatures, and they can be found lurking near communities of mind flayers, aboleths, githyanki, and githzerai. As passive parasites, they take only the mental energy they need, and most creatures feel no loss or discomfort from such feeding.

Consuming psionic energy reveals the thoughts and emotions of the creatures on which the flumphs feed. Since so many of those creatures are evil, flumphs are often subjected to thoughts, emotions, and hungers that sicken their pure nature. When flumphs encounter good-hearted adventurers, they eagerly share the dark secrets they have learned in the hopes of casting down their evil sources of energy, even if doing so means they must seek out new sources of nourishment.

Flumph Society. Flumphs live in complex and organized groups called cloisters, within which each flumph has a place and purpose. These harmonious groupings have no need for leaders, since all flumphs contribute in their own way.

"TRUST A FLUMPH."
—X THE MYSTIC'S 1ST RULE OF DUNGEON SURVIVAL

FLUMPH
Small aberration, lawful good

Armor Class 12
Hit Points 7 (2d6)
Speed 5 ft., fly 30 ft.

STR	DEX	CON	INT	WIS	CHA
6 (−2)	15 (+2)	10 (+0)	14 (+2)	14 (+2)	11 (+0)

Skills Arcana +4, History +4, Religion +4
Damage Vulnerabilities psychic
Senses darkvision 60 ft., passive Perception 12
Languages understands Undercommon but can't speak, telepathy 60 ft.
Challenge 1/8 (25 XP)

Advanced Telepathy. The flumph can perceive the content of any telepathic communication used within 60 feet of it, and it can't be surprised by creatures with any form of telepathy.

Prone Deficiency. If the flumph is knocked prone, roll a die. On an odd result, the flumph lands upside-down and is incapacitated. At the end of each of its turns, the flumph can make a DC 10 Dexterity saving throw, righting itself and ending the incapacitated condition if it succeeds.

Telepathic Shroud. The flumph is immune to any effect that would sense its emotions or read its thoughts, as well as all divination spells.

ACTIONS

Tendrils. *Melee Weapon Attack:* +4 to hit, reach 5 ft., one creature. *Hit:* 4 (1d4 + 2) piercing damage plus 2 (1d4) acid damage. At the end of each of its turns, the target must make a DC 10 Constitution saving throw, taking 2 (1d4) acid damage on a failure or ending the recurring acid damage on a success. A *lesser restoration* spell cast on the target also ends the recurring acid damage.

Stench Spray (1/Day). Each creature in a 15-foot cone originating from the flumph must succeed on a DC 10 Dexterity saving throw or be coated in a foul-smelling liquid. A coated creature exudes a horrible stench for 1d4 hours. The coated creature is poisoned as long as the stench lasts, and other creatures are poisoned while within 5 feet of the coated creature. A creature can remove the stench on itself by using a short rest to bathe in water, alcohol, or vinegar.

FOMORIAN

The most hideous and wicked of all giantkind are the godless fomorians, whose deformed bodies reflect their vile demeanors. Some have facial features randomly distributed around their misshapen, warty heads. Others have limbs of grossly different sizes and shapes, or emit terrible howls each time they draw breath through misshapen mouths. Their wretched appearance rarely evokes sympathy, however, for the fomorians brought their doom upon themselves with the evil that rules their hearts and minds.

Fey Curse. The elves remember when the fomorians were among the most handsome of races, possessed of brilliant minds and unrivaled magical ability. That physical perfection did not extend to their hearts, however, as a lust for magic and power consumed them.

The fomorians sought to conquer the Feywild and enslave its inhabitants, claiming those creatures' magic for themselves. When the fey united to defend their realm, the fomorians fought them and were subjected to a terrible curse.

One by one, the giants fell as their bodies were warped to reflect the evil in their hearts. Stripped of their grace and magical power, the wretched horrors fled from the light, delving deep beneath the world to nurse their hatred. Cursing their fate, they have ever after plotted vengeance against the fey that wronged them.

Giants of the Underdark. The fomorians dwell in eerily beautiful caverns in the Underdark, rarely venturing to the surface. Their lairs feature abundant access to water, fish, and mushroom forests, as well as to the creatures whose slave labor keeps the fomorians fed. When those slaves can no longer toil, they are slain and devoured. Wickedness and depravity are the cornerstones of fomorian society, in which the strongest and cruelest giants rule. Fomorians mark their territories with the corpses of their enemies, painting their cavern walls with blood or stitching together limbs and body parts to make mockeries of the creatures they have killed.

Ruined Flesh, Evil Minds. The deformities visited on the fomorians prevent them from hurling rocks like their giant kin, or wearing anything more than scraps of cloth. However, the grotesque positioning of their eyes, noses, and ears gives fomorians keen perceptive abilities, making it hard to surprise or ambush them.

The greed and evil of the fomorians lies at the heart of their degeneration and fall, and continues to plague them. Fomorians make alliances with other creatures when it suits them, but they are disloyal by nature and betray their allies on a whim.

Curse of the Evil Eye. Fomorians can pass their curse onto others using a power called the evil eye—a last vestige of the giants' once-remarkable spellcasting ability. A creature cursed by a fomorian's evil eye is magically twisted and deformed, gaining a glimpse into the pain and malice that has consumed this evil race.

FOMORIAN
Huge giant, chaotic evil

Armor Class 14 (natural armor)
Hit Points 149 (13d12 + 65)
Speed 30 ft.

STR	DEX	CON	INT	WIS	CHA
23 (+6)	10 (+0)	20 (+5)	9 (−1)	14 (+2)	6 (−2)

Skills Perception +8, Stealth +3
Senses darkvision 120 ft., passive Perception 18
Languages Giant, Undercommon
Challenge 8 (3,900 XP)

ACTIONS

Multiattack. The fomorian attacks twice with its greatclub or makes one greatclub attack and uses Evil Eye once.

Greatclub. *Melee Weapon Attack:* +9 to hit, reach 15 ft., one target. *Hit:* 19 (3d8 + 6) bludgeoning damage.

Evil Eye. The fomorian magically forces a creature it can see within 60 feet of it to make a DC 14 Charisma saving throw. The creature takes 27 (6d8) psychic damage on a failed save, or half as much damage on a successful one.

Curse of the Evil Eye (Recharges after a Short or Long Rest). With a stare, the fomorian uses Evil Eye, but on a failed save, the creature is also cursed with magical deformities. While deformed, the creature has its speed halved and has disadvantage on ability checks, saving throws, and attacks based on Strength or Dexterity.

The transformed creature can repeat the saving throw whenever it finishes a long rest, ending the effect on a success.

FUNGI

With its sky of jagged stone and perpetual night, the Underdark is home to all manner of fungi. Taking the place of plants in the subterranean realm, fungi are vital to the survival of many underground species, providing nourishment and shelter in the unforgiving darkness.

Fungi spawn in organic matter, then break that matter down to consume it, feeding on filth and corpses. As they mature, fungi eject spores that drift on the lightest breeze to spawn new fungi.

Not needing sunlight or warmth to grow, fungi thrive in every corner and crevice of the Underdark. Transformed by the magic that permeates that underground realm, Underdark fungi often develop potent defensive mechanisms or abilities of mimicry and attack. The largest specimens can spread to create vast subterranean forests in which countless creatures live and feed.

Gas Spore

The first gas spores are thought to have been spawned from dead beholders, whose moldering corpses fed a parasitic fungus with aberrant magic. Having long since adapted into a unique plant creature, a gas spore grows quickly and purposefully out of any corpse, creating a malevolent-looking mockery of the most feared denizen of the Underdark.

Eye Tyrant's Form. A gas spore is a spherical, balloon-like fungus that resembles a beholder from a distance, though its true nature becomes increasingly obvious as one approaches it. The monster possesses a blind central "eye" and rhizome growths sprouting from its upper surface, superficially resembling a beholder's eyestalks.

Death Burst. A gas spore is a hollow shell filled with a lighter-than-air gas that enables it to float as a beholder does. Piercing the shell with even the weakest attack causes the creature to burst apart, releasing a cloud of deadly spores. A creature that inhales the spores becomes host to them, and is often dead within a day. Its corpse then becomes the spawning ground from which new gas spores arise.

Beholder Memories. A gas spore that sprouts from a beholder's corpse sometimes carries within it memories of its deceased parent. When the gas spore explodes, its deadly spores cast those memories adrift. Any creature that inhales the spores and survives inherits one or more of the beholder's fragmented memories, and might gain useful information about the beholder's former lair and other nearby places and creatures of interest.

Shrieker

A shrieker is a human-sized mushroom that emits a piercing screech to drive off creatures that disturb it. Other creatures use the fungi as an alarm to signal the approach of prey, and various intelligent races of the Underdark cultivate shriekers on the outskirts of their communities to discourage trespassers.

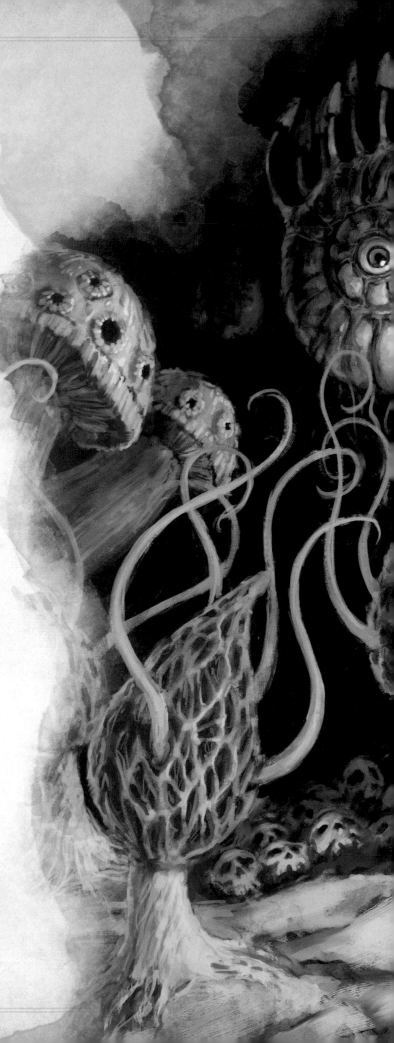

Gas Spore

Large plant, unaligned

Armor Class 5
Hit Points 1 (1d10 – 4)
Speed 0 ft., fly 10 ft. (hover)

STR	DEX	CON	INT	WIS	CHA
5 (–3)	1 (–5)	3 (–4)	1 (–5)	1 (–5)	1 (–5)

Damage Immunities poison
Condition Immunities blinded, deafened, frightened, paralyzed, poisoned, prone
Senses blindsight 30 ft. (blind beyond this radius), passive Perception 5
Languages —
Challenge 1/2 (100 XP)

Death Burst. The gas spore explodes when it drops to 0 hit points. Each creature within 20 feet of it must succeed on a DC 15 Constitution saving throw or take 10 (3d6) poison damage and become infected with a disease on a failed save. Creatures immune to the poisoned condition are immune to this disease.

Spores invade an infected creature's system, killing the creature in a number of hours equal to 1d12 + the creature's Constitution score, unless the disease is removed. In half that time, the creature becomes poisoned for the rest of the duration. After the creature dies, it sprouts 2d4 Tiny gas spores that grow to full size in 7 days.

Eerie Resemblance. The gas spore resembles a beholder. A creature that can see the gas spore can discern its true nature with a successful DC 15 Intelligence (Nature) check.

Actions

Touch. *Melee Weapon Attack:* +0 to hit, reach 5 ft., one creature. *Hit:* 1 poison damage, and the creature must succeed on a DC 10 Constitution saving throw or become infected with the disease described in the Death Burst trait.

Shrieker

Medium plant, unaligned

Armor Class 5
Hit Points 13 (3d8)
Speed 0 ft.

STR	DEX	CON	INT	WIS	CHA
1 (–5)	1 (–5)	10 (+0)	1 (–5)	3 (–4)	1 (–5)

Condition Immunities blinded, deafened, frightened
Senses blindsight 30 ft. (blind beyond this radius), passive Perception 6
Languages —
Challenge 0 (10 XP)

False Appearance. While the shrieker remains motionless, it is indistinguishable from an ordinary fungus.

Reactions

Shriek. When bright light or a creature is within 30 feet of the shrieker, it emits a shriek audible within 300 feet of it. The shrieker continues to shriek until the disturbance moves out of range and for 1d4 of the shrieker's turns afterward.

Violet Fungus

This purplish mushroom uses root-like feelers growing from its base to creep across cavern floors. The four stalks protruding from a violet fungi's central mass are used to lash out at prey, rotting flesh with the slightest touch. Any creature killed by a violet fungus decomposes rapidly. A new violet fungus sprouts from the moldering corpse, growing to full size in 2d6 days.

Violet Fungus

Medium plant, unaligned

Armor Class 5
Hit Points 18 (4d8)
Speed 5 ft.

STR	DEX	CON	INT	WIS	CHA
3 (–4)	1 (–5)	10 (+0)	1 (–5)	3 (–4)	1 (–5)

Condition Immunities blinded, deafened, frightened
Senses blindsight 30 ft. (blind beyond this radius), passive Perception 6
Languages —
Challenge 1/4 (50 XP)

False Appearance. While the violet fungus remains motionless, it is indistinguishable from an ordinary fungus.

Actions

Multiattack. The fungus makes 1d4 Rotting Touch attacks.

Rotting Touch. *Melee Weapon Attack:* +2 to hit, reach 10 ft., one creature. *Hit:* 4 (1d8) necrotic damage.

Galeb Duhr

The galeb duhr is a boulder-like creature with stumpy appendages that act as arms and legs. It has the ability to animate the rocks and boulders around it, and is thus usually encountered in rocky terrain.

Powerful magic allows a spellcaster to summon a galeb duhr from the Plane of Earth. Some galeb duhr also form naturally in places touched by that plane. The galeb duhr is imbued with greater intelligence than most elementals, allowing it to better assess threats and to communicate with creatures entering its guarded area.

Stone Guardian. A galeb duhr doesn't age or require sustenance, making it an excellent sentinel. A powerful druid might charge a galeb duhr with protecting a stone circle or sacred hilltop. Another galeb duhr might be created to guard an underground tomb or a wizard's tower. When it chooses to, the galeb duhr can make itself look like an ordinary boulder, remaining perfectly still for years at a time.

Galeb Duhr

Medium elemental, neutral

Armor Class 16 (natural armor)
Hit Points 85 (9d8 + 45)
Speed 15 ft. (30 ft. when rolling, 60 ft. rolling downhill)

STR	DEX	CON	INT	WIS	CHA
20 (+5)	14 (+2)	20 (+5)	11 (+0)	12 (+1)	11 (+0)

Damage Resistances bludgeoning, piercing, and slashing from nonmagical attacks
Damage Immunities poison
Condition Immunities exhaustion, paralyzed, poisoned, petrified
Senses darkvision 60 ft., tremorsense 60 ft., passive Perception 11
Languages Terran
Challenge 6 (2,300 XP)

False Appearance. While the galeb duhr remains motionless, it is indistinguishable from a normal boulder.

Rolling Charge. If the galeb duhr rolls at least 20 feet straight toward a target and then hits it with a slam attack on the same turn, the target takes an extra 7 (2d6) bludgeoning damage. If the target is a creature, it must succeed on a DC 16 Strength saving throw or be knocked prone.

Actions

Slam. *Melee Weapon Attack:* +8 to hit, reach 5 ft., one target. *Hit:* 12 (2d6 + 5) bludgeoning damage.

Animate Boulders (1/Day). The galeb duhr magically animates up to two boulders it can see within 60 feet of it. A boulder has statistics like those of a galeb duhr, except it has Intelligence 1 and Charisma 1, it can't be charmed or frightened, and it lacks this action option. A boulder remains animated as long as the galeb duhr maintains concentration, up to 1 minute (as if concentrating on a spell).

A galeb duhr is permanently bound to the Material Plane, so that when it dies, it doesn't return to the Plane of Earth. It has an excellent memory and is more than happy to share information regarding its environment with creatures it doesn't regard as threats.

Stone Connection. A galeb duhr can become one with the earth around it, allowing it to imbue nearby rocks and boulders with a semblance of life. The galeb duhr uses its animated boulders to frighten away interlopers and defend whatever it has been charged to protect. When it needs to move close to those intruders, it presses its limbs tight to its body and rolls forward at a furious pace.

Gargoyle

The inanimate gargoyles that perch atop great buildings are inspired by these malevolent creatures of elemental earth that resemble grotesque, fiendish statues. A gargoyle lurks among masonry and ruins, as still as any stone sculpture, and delights in the terror it creates when it breaks from its suspended pose, as well as the pain it inflicts on its victims.

Animate Stone. Gargoyles cling to rocky cliffs and mountains, or roost on ledges in underground caves. They haunt city rooftops, perching vulture-like among the high stone arches and buttresses of castles and cathedrals, and they can hold themselves so still that they appear inanimate. Able to maintain this state for years, a gargoyle makes an ideal sentry.

Deadly Reputation. Gargoyles have a reputation for cruelty. Statues carved into the likenesses of gargoyles appear in the architecture of countless cultures to frighten away trespassers. Although such sculptures are only decorative, real gargoyles can hide among them to ambush unsuspecting victims. A gargoyle might alleviate the tedium of its watch by catching and tormenting birds or rodents, but its long wait only increases its craving for harming sentient creatures.

Cruel Servants. Gargoyles are easily inspired by the cunning of an intelligent master. They enjoy simple tasks such as guarding a master's home, torturing and killing interlopers, and anything else that involves minimum effort and maximum pain and carnage.

Gargoyles sometimes serve demons for their propensity for wanton chaos and destruction. Powerful spellcasters can also easily enlist gargoyle guardians to keep watch over their gates and walls. Gargoyles have the patience and fortitude of stone, and will serve even the cruelest master for years without complaint.

Elemental Nature. A gargoyle doesn't require air, food, drink, or sleep.

Gargoyle

Medium elemental, chaotic evil

Armor Class 15 (natural armor)
Hit Points 52 (7d8 + 21)
Speed 30 ft., fly 60 ft.

STR	DEX	CON	INT	WIS	CHA
15 (+2)	11 (+0)	16 (+3)	6 (−2)	11 (+0)	7 (−2)

Damage Resistances bludgeoning, piercing, and slashing from nonmagical attacks not made with adamantine weapons
Damage Immunities poison
Condition Immunities exhaustion, petrified, poisoned
Senses darkvision 60 ft., passive Perception 10
Languages Terran
Challenge 2 (450 XP)

False Appearance. While the gargoyle remains motionless, it is indistinguishable from an inanimate statue.

Actions

Multiattack. The gargoyle makes two attacks: one with its bite and one with its claws.

Bite. *Melee Weapon Attack:* +4 to hit, reach 5 ft., one target. *Hit:* 5 (1d6 + 2) piercing damage.

Claws. *Melee Weapon Attack:* +4 to hit, reach 5 ft., one target. *Hit:* 5 (1d6 + 2) slashing damage.

Shards of Elemental Evil

As Ogrémoch, the evil Prince of Elemental Earth, treads his stony realm, it leaves shards of broken rock in his wake. Imbued with slivers of sentience, these shards thrum with the essence of the elemental prince, growing over long years into vaguely humanoid rock formations that resolve at last into the hard, cruel shapes of gargoyles.

Ogrémoch doesn't create gargoyles deliberately, but they are a physical manifestation of his evil. Gargoyles are mockeries of the elemental air that Ogrémoch despises. They are heavy creatures of living stone, yet capable of flight. Like their creator, they possess a fundamental hatred for beings of elemental air, aarakocra in particular, and relish every opportunity to destroy such creatures.

On their home plane, gargoyles carve out earth motes that Ogrémoch hurtles into Aaqa, the domain of the aarakocra and the benevolent Wind Dukes the bird folk serve in the Elemental Plane of Air.

Genies

Genies are rare elemental creatures out of story and legend. Only a few can be found on the Material Plane. The rest reside on the Elemental Planes, where they rule from lavish palaces and are attended by worshipful slaves.

Genies are as brilliant as they are mighty, as proud as they are majestic. Haughty and decadent, they have a profound sense of entitlement that stems from the knowledge that few creatures except the gods and other genies can challenge their power.

Creatures of the Elements. A genie is born when the soul of a sentient living creature melds with the primordial matter of an elemental plane. Only under rare circumstances does such an elemental-infused soul coalesce into a manifest form and create a genie.

A genie usually retains no connection to the soul that gave it form. That life force is a building block that determines the genie's form and apparent gender, as well as one or two key personality traits. Although they resemble humanoid beings, genies are elemental spirits given physical form. They don't mate with other genies or produce genie offspring, as all new genies are born out of the same mysterious fusion of spirit energy and elemental power. A genie with a stronger connection to its mortal soul might choose to sire a child with a mortal, although such offspring are rare.

When a genie perishes, it leaves nothing behind except what it was wearing or carrying, along with a small trace of its native element: a pile of dust, a gust of wind, a flash of fire and smoke, or a burst of water and foam.

Rule or Be Ruled. Mortal slaves serve to validate a genie's power and high self-opinion. A hundred flattering voices are music to a genie's ears, while two hundred mortal slaves prostrated at its feet are proof that it is lord and master. Genies view slaves as living property, and a genie without property amounts to nothing among its own kind. As a result, many genies treasure their slaves, treating them as honored members of their households. Evil genies freely threaten and abuse their slaves, but never to the extent that the slaves are no longer of use.

In contrast to their love of slaves, most genies loathe being bound to service themselves. A genie obeys the will of another only when bribed or compelled by magic. All genies command the power of their native element, but a rare few also possess the power to grant wishes. For both these reasons, mortal mages often seek to bind genies into service.

Decadent Nobility. Noble genies are the rarest of their kind. They are used to getting what they want, and have learned to trade their ability to grant wishes to attain the objects of their desire. This constant indulgence has made them decadent, while their supreme power over reality makes them haughty and arrogant. Their vast palaces overflow with wonders and sensory delights beyond imagination.

Noble genies cultivate the jealousy and envy of other genies, asserting their superiority at every opportunity. Other genies respect the influence of the noble genies, knowing how unwise it is to defy a creature that can alter reality at a whim. A genie isn't beholden to any noble genie, however, and will sometimes choose to defy a noble genie's will and risk the consequences.

The Power of Worship. Genies acknowledge the gods as powerful entities but have no desire to court or worship them. They find the endless fawning and mewling of religious devotees tiresome—except as it is directed toward them by their worshipful slaves.

Their miraculous powers, the grandeur of their abodes, and the numbers of their slaves allow some genies to deceive themselves into believing they are as powerful as the gods. Some go so far as to demand that mortals of other realms—even whole continents or worlds—bow down before them.

Dao

Dao are greedy, malicious genies from the Elemental Plane of Earth. They adorn themselves with jewelry crafted from precious gems and rare metals, and when they fly, their lower bodies become columns of swirling sand. A dao isn't happy unless it is the envy of other dao.

All That Glitters. The dao dwell in complexes of twisting tunnels and glittering ore-veined caverns on the Elemental Plane of Earth. These mazeworks are continually expanding as the dao delve into and reshape the rock around them. Dao care nothing for the poverty or misfortune of others. A dao might grind powdered gems and gold dust over its food to heighten the experience of eating, devouring its wealth as mortals consume a precious spice.

Lords of the Earth. A dao never assists a mortal unless the genie has something to gain, preferably treasure. Among the genies, dao are on speaking and trading terms with the efreet, but they have nothing but scorn for djinn and marids. Other races native to the Elemental Plane of Earth avoid the dao, which are always seeking new slaves to mine the mazeworks of their floating earth islands.

Proud Slavers. The dao trade for the finest slaves that money can buy, forcing them to work in dangerous subterranean realms that rumble with earthquakes.

As much as they enjoy enslaving others, the dao hate being enslaved. Powerful wizards have been known to lure dao to the Material Plane and trap them in the confines of magic gemstones or iron flasks. Unfortunately for the dao, their greed makes it relatively easy for mages to cozen them into service.

Djinni

Proud, sensuous genies from the Elemental Plane of Air, the djinn are attractive, tall, well-muscled humanoids with blue skin and dark eyes. They dress in airy, shimmering silks, designed as much for comfort as to flaunt their musculature.

Airy Aesthetes. Djinn rule floating islands of cloudstuff covered with enormous pavilions, or topped with wondrous buildings, courtyards, fountains, and gardens. Creatures of comfort and ease, djinn enjoy succulent fruits, pungent wines, fine perfumes, and beautiful music.

Djinn are known for their sense of mischief and their favorable attitude toward mortals. Among genies, djinn deal coolly with efreet and marids, whom they view as haughty. They openly despise dao and strike against them with little provocation.

Masters of the Wind. Masters of the air, the djinn ride powerful whirlwinds that they create and direct on a whim, and which can even carry passengers. Creatures that stand against a djinni are assaulted by wind and thunder, even as the djinni spins away on that wind if outmatched in combat. When a djinni flies, its lower body transforms into a column of swirling air.

Accepting Servitors. The djinn believe that servitude is a matter of fate, and that no being can contest the hand of fate. As a result, of all the genies, djinn are the ones most amenable to servitude, though they never enjoy it. Djinn treat their slaves more like servants deserving of kindness and protection, and they part with them reluctantly.

A mortal who desires the brief service of a djinni can entreat it with fine gifts, or use flattery to bribe it into compliance. Powerful wizards are able to forgo such niceties, however, if they can summon, bind into service, or imprison a djinni using magic. Long-term service displeases a djinni, and imprisonment is inexcusable. Djinn resent the cruel wizards that have imprisoned their kind in bottles, iron flasks, and wind instruments throughout the ages. Betrayal, particularly by a mortal whom a djinni trusted, is a vile deed that only deadly vengeance can amend.

Efreeti

Hulking genies of the Elemental Plane of Fire, the efreet are masters of flame, immune to fire and able to create it on a whim. Fine silk caftans and damask robes drape their magma-red or coal-black skin, and they bedeck themselves in brass and gold torcs, chains, and rings, all glittering with jewels. When an efreeti flies, its lower body transforms into a column of smoke and embers.

Haughty and Cruel. The efreet are deceptive, cunning, and cruel to the point of ruthlessness. They despise being forced into servitude and are relentless in pursuit of vengeance against creatures that have wronged them. Efreet don't see themselves in this light, naturally, and regard their race as fair and orderly, even as they admit to an enlightened sense of self-interest.

Spiteful Slavers. Efreet view all other creatures as enemies or potential serfs. They raid the Material Plane and the elemental planes for slaves, which they capture and bring back to their homes on the Elemental Plane of Fire. The efreet rule as oppressive tyrants, promoting only the cruelest among their slaves. Those overseers are given whips to help keep the rank-and-file slaves in line.

Planar Raiders. Most efreet reside on the Elemental Plane of Fire, either in great domed fortresses of black glass and basalt surrounded by churning lakes of fire, or in the fabled City of Brass. Additionally, efreet military outposts thronging with their minions and slaves can be found scattered throughout the planes.

On the Material Plane, efreet dwell in fiery regions such as volcanoes and the burning expanses of the world's deserts. Their love of the desert brings them into conflict with the djinn that ride the desert whirlwinds, and with the earthbound dao. Efreet utterly despise marids, with whom they have maintained a passionate conflict throughout the history of both races.

Marid

Hailing from the Elemental Plane of Water, the marids are the most wondrous of genie-kind. Although all genies wield great power, even the lowliest marid sees itself as clearly superior to the flighty djinn, the ground-hugging dao, and the fuming efreet.

Large and piscine, marids are a strange sight to behold, particularly when clad in the finely stitched vests and colorful pantaloons they favor. They speak in voices as soft as the sea breeze or as sonorous as storm waves breaking against a rocky cliff. In flight, their lower bodies transform into columns of foamy water.

Water Lords. Water is a marid's native element, and the genie can manipulate water in virtually any way it desires. A marid can walk on water and breathe naturally beneath its surface. It can create water or shape clouds of fog and mist from the vapor in the air. It can even transform itself into mist, or use water as a weapon to bludgeon its foes.

Marid Homes. Marids are rare on the Material Plane. They inhabit mighty and majestic coral fortresses located in the Elemental Plane of Water. These citadels float in the depths of the plane and contain opulent, air-filled chambers where slaves and guests reside.

A marid doesn't expect much from its slaves, simply wanting to have them for the status of ownership. Marids go out of their way to obtain skilled slaves, and aren't above kidnapping mortal artists, entertainers, or storytellers for use in their courts.

Egotistical Hierarchs. All marids claim a title of nobility, and the race is awash in shahs, sultans, muftis, and khedives. Most of these titles are mere pretense on the part of the self-important marids.

Marids treat all others—including other genies—as inferiors of various grades, ranging from poor cousins to petty annoyances. They tolerate djinn, dislike dao, and despise efreet.

Humanoids are among the lowest of the creatures that marids must tolerate, although they sometimes deal with powerful wizards and exceptional leaders on an almost-equal footing. Doing so has sometimes proven to be a mistake, since wizards have managed to imprison marids in conch shells, flasks, and decanters over the ages. Bribery and flattery are the best means of dealing with marids, to which an obsequious mortal is a creature that knows its place.

Whimsical Storytellers. Marids are champion tale-tellers, whose favorite legends emphasize the prowess of marids in general and of the speaker in particular. Fanciful genies, they lie often and creatively. They aren't always malicious in their deception, but embellishments suit their fancy. Marids consider it a crime for a lesser being to interrupt one of their tales, and offending a marid is a sure way to invoke its wrath.

Dao

Large elemental, neutral evil

Armor Class 18 (natural armor)
Hit Points 187 (15d10 + 105)
Speed 30 ft., burrow 30 ft., fly 30 ft.

STR	DEX	CON	INT	WIS	CHA
23 (+6)	12 (+1)	24 (+7)	12 (+1)	13 (+1)	14 (+2)

Saving Throws Int +5, Wis +5, Cha +6
Condition Immunities petrified
Senses darkvision 120 ft., passive Perception 11
Languages Terran
Challenge 11 (7,200 XP)

Earth Glide. The dao can burrow through nonmagical, unworked earth and stone. While doing so, the dao doesn't disturb the material it moves through.

Elemental Demise. If the dao dies, its body disintegrates into crystalline powder, leaving behind only equipment the dao was wearing or carrying.

Innate Spellcasting. The dao's innate spellcasting ability is Charisma (spell save DC 14, +6 to hit with spell attacks). It can innately cast the following spells, requiring no material components:

At will: *detect evil and good*, *detect magic*, *stone shape*
3/day each: *passwall*, *move earth*, *tongues*
1/day each: *conjure elemental* (earth elemental only), *gaseous form*, *invisibility*, *phantasmal killer*, *plane shift*, *wall of stone*

Sure-Footed. The dao has advantage on Strength and Dexterity saving throws made against effects that would knock it prone.

Actions

Multiattack. The dao makes two fist attacks or two maul attacks.

Fist. *Melee Weapon Attack:* +10 to hit, reach 5 ft., one target. *Hit:* 15 (2d8 + 6) bludgeoning damage.

Maul. *Melee Weapon Attack:* +10 to hit, reach 5 ft., one target. *Hit:* 20 (4d6 + 6) bludgeoning damage. If the target is a Huge or smaller creature, it must succeed on a DC 18 Strength check or be knocked prone.

G

DJINNI

Large elemental, chaotic good

Armor Class 17 (natural armor)
Hit Points 161 (14d10 + 84)
Speed 30 ft., fly 90 ft.

STR	DEX	CON	INT	WIS	CHA
21 (+5)	15 (+2)	22 (+6)	15 (+2)	16 (+3)	20 (+5)

Saving Throws Dex +6, Wis +7, Cha +9
Damage Immunities lightning, thunder
Senses darkvision 120 ft., passive Perception 13
Languages Auran
Challenge 11 (7,200 XP)

Elemental Demise. If the djinni dies, its body disintegrates into a warm breeze, leaving behind only equipment the djinni was wearing or carrying.

Innate Spellcasting. The djinni's innate spellcasting ability is Charisma (spell save DC 17, +9 to hit with spell attacks). It can innately cast the following spells, requiring no material components:

At will: *detect evil and good, detect magic, thunderwave*

3/day each: *create food and water* (can create wine instead of water), *tongues, wind walk*
1/day each: *conjure elemental* (air elemental only), *creation, gaseous form, invisibility, major image, plane shift*

ACTIONS

Multiattack. The djinni makes three scimitar attacks.

Scimitar. *Melee Weapon Attack:* +9 to hit, reach 5 ft., one target. *Hit:* 12 (2d6 + 5) slashing damage plus 3 (1d6) lightning or thunder damage (djinni's choice).

Create Whirlwind. A 5-foot-radius, 30-foot-tall cylinder of swirling air magically forms on a point the djinni can see within 120 feet of it. The whirlwind lasts as long as the djinni maintains concentration (as if concentrating on a spell). Any creature but the djinni that enters the whirlwind must succeed on a DC 18 Strength saving throw or be restrained by it. The djinni can move the whirlwind up to 60 feet as an action, and creatures restrained by the whirlwind move with it. The whirlwind ends if the djinni loses sight of it.

A creature can use its action to free a creature restrained by the whirlwind, including itself, by succeeding on a DC 18 Strength check. If the check succeeds, the creature is no longer restrained and moves to the nearest space outside the whirlwind.

"The armies of the Grand Sultan are bolstered by legions of devils, his palace warded by the spells of a thousand archmagi, his treasures guarded by red dragons and fire elementals. No one has plundered the efreeti's fabled vaults and lived to tell the tale. By the grace of a thousand winds, you could be the first."
—A djinni enticing adventurers to free her caliph from a magic lamp in the Charcoal Palace of the City of Brass

EFREETI
Large elemental, lawful evil

Armor Class 17 (natural armor)
Hit Points 200 (16d10 + 112)
Speed 40 ft., fly 60 ft.

STR	DEX	CON	INT	WIS	CHA
22 (+6)	12 (+1)	24 (+7)	16 (+3)	15 (+2)	16 (+3)

Saving Throws Int +7, Wis +6, Cha +7
Damage Immunities fire
Senses darkvision 120 ft., passive Perception 12
Languages Ignan
Challenge 11 (7,200 XP)

Elemental Demise. If the efreeti dies, its body disintegrates in a flash of fire and puff of smoke, leaving behind only equipment the efreeti was wearing or carrying.

Innate Spellcasting. The efreeti's innate spellcasting ability is Charisma (spell save DC 15, +7 to hit with spell attacks). It can innately cast the following spells, requiring no material components:

At will: *detect magic*
3/day: *enlarge/reduce, tongues*
1/day each: *conjure elemental* (fire elemental only), *gaseous form, invisibility, major image, plane shift, wall of fire*

ACTIONS

Multiattack. The efreeti makes two scimitar attacks or uses its Hurl Flame twice.

Scimitar. *Melee Weapon Attack:* +10 to hit, reach 5 ft., one target. *Hit:* 13 (2d6 + 6) slashing damage plus 7 (2d6) fire damage.

Hurl Flame. *Ranged Spell Attack:* +7 to hit, range 120 ft., one target. *Hit:* 17 (5d6) fire damage.

MARID

Large elemental, chaotic neutral

Armor Class 17 (natural armor)
Hit Points 229 (17d10 + 136)
Speed 30 ft., fly 60 ft., swim 90 ft.

STR	DEX	CON	INT	WIS	CHA
22 (+6)	12 (+1)	26 (+8)	18 (+4)	17 (+3)	18 (+4)

Saving Throws Dex +5, Wis +7, Cha +8
Damage Resistances acid, cold, lightning
Senses blindsight 30 ft., darkvision 120 ft., passive Perception 13
Languages Aquan
Challenge 11 (7,200 XP)

Amphibious. The marid can breathe air and water.

Elemental Demise. If the marid dies, its body disintegrates into a burst of water and foam, leaving behind only equipment the marid was wearing or carrying.

Innate Spellcasting. The marid's innate spellcasting ability is Charisma (spell save DC 16, +8 to hit with spell attacks). It can innately cast the following spells, requiring no material components:

At will: *create or destroy water, detect evil and good, detect magic, fog cloud, purify food and drink*
3/day each: *tongues, water breathing, water walk*
1/day each: *conjure elemental* (water elemental only), *control water, gaseous form, invisibility, plane shift*

ACTIONS

Multiattack. The marid makes two trident attacks.

Trident. *Melee or Ranged Weapon Attack:* +10 to hit, reach 5 ft. or range 20/60 ft., one target. *Hit:* 13 (2d6 + 6) piercing damage, or 15 (2d8 + 6) piercing damage if used with two hands to make a melee attack.

Water Jet. The marid magically shoots water in a 60-foot line that is 5 feet wide. Each creature in that line must make a DC 16 Dexterity saving throw. On a failure, a target takes 21 (6d6) bludgeoning damage and, if it is Huge or smaller, is pushed up to 20 feet away from the marid and knocked prone. On a success, a target takes half the bludgeoning damage, but is neither pushed nor knocked prone.

GHOST

A ghost is the soul of a once-living creature, bound to haunt a specific location, creature, or object that held significance to it in its life.

Unfinished Business. A ghost yearns to complete some unresolved task from its life. It might seek to avenge its own death, fulfill an oath, or relay a message to a loved one. A ghost might not realize that it has died and continue the everyday routine of its life. Others are driven by wickedness or spite, as with a ghost that refuses to rest until every member of a certain family or organization is dead.

The surest way to rid an area of a ghost is to resolve its unfinished business. A ghost can be destroyed more easily by invoking a weakness tied to its former life. The ghost of a person tortured to death might be killed again by the implements of that torture. The ghost of a gardener might become more vulnerable when exposed to a potent floral fragrance.

Ghostly Manifestations. Sensations of profound sadness, loneliness, and unfulfilled yearning emanate from places where ghostly hauntings occur. Strange sounds or unnatural silences create an unsettling atmosphere. Cold spots settle in rooms that have roaring fires. A choking stench might seep into the area, inanimate objects might move of their own accord, and corpses might rise from the grave. The ghost has no control over these manifestations; they simply occur.

Undead Nature. A ghost doesn't require air, food, drink, or sleep.

GHOST

Medium undead, any alignment

Armor Class 11
Hit Points 45 (10d8)
Speed 0 ft., fly 40 ft. (hover)

STR	DEX	CON	INT	WIS	CHA
7 (−2)	13 (+1)	10 (+0)	10 (+0)	12 (+1)	17 (+3)

Damage Resistances acid, fire, lightning, thunder; bludgeoning, piercing, and slashing from nonmagical attacks
Damage Immunities cold, necrotic, poison
Condition Immunities charmed, exhaustion, frightened, grappled, paralyzed, petrified, poisoned, prone, restrained
Senses darkvision 60 ft., passive Perception 11
Languages any languages it knew in life
Challenge 4 (1,100 XP)

Ethereal Sight. The ghost can see 60 feet into the Ethereal Plane when it is on the Material Plane, and vice versa.

Incorporeal Movement. The ghost can move through other creatures and objects as if they were difficult terrain. It takes 5 (1d10) force damage if it ends its turn inside an object.

ACTIONS

Withering Touch. *Melee Weapon Attack:* +5 to hit, reach 5 ft., one target. *Hit:* 17 (4d6 + 3) necrotic damage.

Etherealness. The ghost enters the Ethereal Plane from the Material Plane, or vice versa. It is visible on the Material Plane while it is in the Border Ethereal, and vice versa, yet it can't affect or be affected by anything on the other plane.

Horrifying Visage. Each non-undead creature within 60 feet of the ghost that can see it must succeed on a DC 13 Wisdom saving throw or be frightened for 1 minute. If the save fails by 5 or more, the target also ages 1d4 × 10 years. A frightened target can repeat the saving throw at the end of each of its turns, ending the frightened condition on itself on a success. If a target's saving throw is successful or the effect ends for it, the target is immune to this ghost's Horrifying Visage for the next 24 hours. The aging effect can be reversed with a *greater restoration* spell, but only within 24 hours of it occurring.

Possession (Recharge 6). One humanoid that the ghost can see within 5 feet of it must succeed on a DC 13 Charisma saving throw or be possessed by the ghost; the ghost then disappears, and the target is incapacitated and loses control of its body. The ghost now controls the body but doesn't deprive the target of awareness. The ghost can't be targeted by any attack, spell, or other effect, except ones that turn undead, and it retains its alignment, Intelligence, Wisdom, Charisma, and immunity to being charmed and frightened. It otherwise uses the possessed target's statistics, but doesn't gain access to the target's knowledge, class features, or proficiencies.

The possession lasts until the body drops to 0 hit points, the ghost ends it as a bonus action, or the ghost is turned or forced out by an effect like the *dispel evil and good* spell. When the possession ends, the ghost reappears in an unoccupied space within 5 feet of the body. The target is immune to this ghost's Possession for 24 hours after succeeding on the saving throw or after the possession ends.

GHOULS

Ghouls roam the night in packs, driven by an insatiable hunger for humanoid flesh.

Devourers of Flesh. Like maggots or carrion beetles, ghouls thrive in places rank with decay and death. A ghoul haunts a place where it can gorge on dead flesh and decomposing organs. When it can't feed on the dead, it pursues living creatures and attempts to make corpses of them. Though they gain no nourishment from the corpses they devour, ghouls are driven by an unending hunger that compels them to consume. A ghoul's undead flesh never rots, and this monster can persist in a crypt or tomb for untold ages without feeding.

Abyssal Origins. Ghouls trace their origins to the Abyss. Doresain, the first of their kind, was an elf worshiper of Orcus. Turning against his own people, he feasted on humanoid flesh to honor the Demon Prince of Undeath. As a reward for his service, Orcus transformed Doresain into the first ghoul. Doresain served Orcus faithfully in the Abyss, creating ghouls from the demon lord's other servants until an incursion by Yeenoghu, the demonic Gnoll Lord, robbed Doresain of his abyssal domain. When Orcus would not intervene on his behalf, Doresain turned to the elf gods for salvation, and they took pity on him and helped him escape certain destruction. Since then, elves have been immune to the ghouls' paralytic touch.

Ghasts. Orcus sometimes infuses a ghoul with a stronger dose of abyssal energy, making a ghast. Whereas ghouls are little more than savage beasts, a ghast is cunning and can inspire a pack of ghouls to follow its commands.

GHAST
Medium undead, chaotic evil

Armor Class 13
Hit Points 36 (8d8)
Speed 30 ft.

STR	DEX	CON	INT	WIS	CHA
16 (+3)	17 (+3)	10 (+0)	11 (+0)	10 (+0)	8 (−1)

Damage Resistances necrotic
Damage Immunities poison
Condition Immunities charmed, exhaustion, poisoned
Senses darkvision 60 ft., passive Perception 10
Languages Common
Challenge 2 (450 XP)

Stench. Any creature that starts its turn within 5 feet of the ghast must succeed on a DC 10 Constitution saving throw or be poisoned until the start of its next turn. On a successful saving throw, the creature is immune to the ghast's Stench for 24 hours.

Turning Defiance. The ghast and any ghouls within 30 feet of it have advantage on saving throws against effects that turn undead.

ACTIONS

Bite. *Melee Weapon Attack:* +3 to hit, reach 5 ft., one creature. *Hit:* 12 (2d8 + 3) piercing damage.

Claws. *Melee Weapon Attack:* +5 to hit, reach 5 ft., one target. *Hit:* 10 (2d6 + 3) slashing damage. If the target is a creature other than an undead, it must succeed on a DC 10 Constitution saving throw or be paralyzed for 1 minute. The target can repeat the saving throw at the end of each of its turns, ending the effect on itself on a success.

GHOUL
Medium undead, chaotic evil

Armor Class 12
Hit Points 22 (5d8)
Speed 30 ft.

STR	DEX	CON	INT	WIS	CHA
13 (+1)	15 (+2)	10 (+0)	7 (−2)	10 (+0)	6 (−2)

Damage Immunities poison
Condition Immunities charmed, exhaustion, poisoned
Senses darkvision 60 ft., passive Perception 10
Languages Common
Challenge 1 (200 XP)

ACTIONS

Bite. *Melee Weapon Attack:* +2 to hit, reach 5 ft., one creature. *Hit:* 9 (2d6 + 2) piercing damage.

Claws. *Melee Weapon Attack:* +4 to hit, reach 5 ft., one target. *Hit:* 7 (2d4 + 2) slashing damage. If the target is a creature other than an elf or undead, it must succeed on a DC 10 Constitution saving throw or be paralyzed for 1 minute. The target can repeat the saving throw at the end of each of its turns, ending the effect on itself on a success.

GIANTS

Ancient empires once cast long shadows over a world that quaked beneath the giants' feet. In those lost days, these towering figures were dragon slayers, dreamers, crafters, and kings, but their kind fell from glory long ago. However, even divided among secluded clans scattered throughout the world, the giants maintain the customs and traditions of old.

Old as Legend. In remote regions of the world, the last remaining plinths, monoliths, and statues of the great giant empires bow their heads in desolate obscurity. Where once those empires sprawled across all lands, now the giants dwell in isolated tribes and clans.

Giants are almost as old as dragons, which were still young when the giants' heavy feet first shook the foundations of the world. As they spread across new lands, giants and dragons fought bitter generational wars that nearly brought both sides low. No living giant remembers what started the conflict, but myths and tales of their race's glorious dawn are still sung in their steadings and holdfasts, vilifying the primeval wyrms. Giants and dragons continue to harbor grudges against one another, and it is seldom that they will meet or occupy the same area without a fight.

THE ORDNING

Each of the main giant races—the cloud, fire, frost, hill, stone, and storm giants—are related by common elements of history, religion, and culture. They view one another as kindred, keeping any inherent animosity over territory and ambition to a minimum.

Giants belong to a caste structure called the ordning. Based on social class and highly organized, the ordning assigns a social rank to each giant. By understanding its place in the ordning, a giant knows which other giants are inferior or superior to it, since no two giants are equal. Each of the giant races analyzes a different combination of skills or qualities to determine the ordning. Giants make excelling in these qualities the purpose of their lives.

At the highest level of the ordning, the races of the giants are also ranked according to status. Storm giants are the highest in the ordning, followed by cloud giants, fire giants, frost giants, stone giants, hill giants, and finally giant kin such as fomorians, ettins, and ogres.

Regardless of a giant's rank among its own race, the chief of a hill giant tribe is inferior to the most common of stone giants. The lowest ranked giant of any type is superior to the highest ranked giant of an inferior type. It isn't considered evil to disrespect or even betray a giant of another type, merely rude.

"BOULDERS ASSAILED OUR WALLS AND CAST THEM DOWN, LEAVIN' GAPS THROUGH WHICH THE GIANTS STRODE, WEAPONS IN HAND."
—CAPTAIN DWERN ADDLESTONE'S PARTIAL ACCOUNT OF THE SIEGE OF STERNGATE

Cloud Giant

Cloud giants live extravagant lives high above the world, showing little concern for the plights of other races except as amusement. They are muscular with light skin and have hair of silver or blue.

High and Mighty. Cloud giants are spread to the winds, encompassing vast areas of the world. In times of need, scattered cloud giant families band together as a unified clan. However, they can seldom do so quickly.

Attuned to the magic of their airy domains, cloud giants are able to turn into mist and create clouds of billowing fog. They dwell in castles on high mountain peaks, or on the solid clouds that once held their fiefs. Still gracing the skies on occasion, these magic clouds are a lasting remnant of the giants' lost empires.

Better spellcasters than most other giants, some cloud giants can control weather, bring storms, and steer the wind almost as well as their cousins, the storm giants.

Affluent Princes. Although cloud giants are lower in the ordning than storm giants, the reclusive storm giants rarely engage with the rest of giantkind. As a result, many cloud giants see themselves as having the highest status and power among the giant races. They order lesser giants to seek out wealth and art on their behalf, employing fire giants as smiths and crafters, and using frost giants as reavers, raiders, and plunderers. Dimwitted hill giants serve them as brutes and combat fodder—sometimes fighting for the cloud giants' amusement. A cloud giant might order hill or frost giants to steal from nearby humanoid lands, which it considers to be a fair tax for its continued beneficence.

On their mountain summits and solid clouds, cloud giants keep extraordinary gardens. Grapes as big as apples grow there, along with apples the size of pumpkins, and pumpkins the size of wagons. From the errant seeds of these gardens, tales of cottage-sized produce and magic beans are spread in the mortal realm.

As humanoid nobles keep an aerie for hunting hawks, so do cloud giants keep griffons, perytons, and wyverns as their own flying beasts of prey. Such creatures also patrol the cloud giants' gardens by night, along with trained predators such as owlbears and lions.

Children of the Trickster. The patron god and father of the cloud giants is Memnor the Trickster, the cleverest and slyest of the giant deities. Cloud giants align themselves according to the aspects and exploits of Memnor that they most admire, with evil cloud giants emulating his deceitfulness and self-interest and good cloud giants emulating his intellect and silver-tongued speech. Family members usually align in the same direction.

Wealth and Power. A cloud giant earns its place in the ordning by the treasure it accumulates, the wealth it wears, and the gifts it bestows on other cloud giants. However, value is only one part of the assessment. The extravagances a cloud giant wears or places about its home must also be beautiful or wondrous. Sacks of gold or gems are worth less to a cloud giant than the jewelry that might be crafted from those materials, creating treasures that bring esteem to a cloud giant's household.

Rather than steal from one another or fight over treasures, cloud giants are inveterate gamblers with a hunger for high risks and high rewards. They frequently bet on the outcome of events nominally outside their control, such as the lives of lesser creatures. Ordning ranks and kings' ransoms can be won and lost in bets over the military triumphs of humanoid nations. Fixing wagers by interfering in the conflict causes the loss of the bet, but such deceit is considered to be cheating only if it is discovered. Otherwise, it is cleverness honoring Memnor.

Fire Giant

Master crafters and organized warriors, fire giants dwell among volcanoes, lava floes, and rocky mountains. They are ruthless militaristic brutes whose mastery of metalwork is legendary.

Fire Forged. Fire giant fortresses are built around and inside volcanoes or near magma-filled caverns. The blistering heat of their homes fuels the fire giants' forges, and causes the iron of their fortress walls to glow a comforting orange. In lands far removed from volcanic heat, fire giants mine coal to burn. Traditional smithies occupy places of honor in their demesnes, and the giants' stony fortresses constantly belch plumes of sooty smoke. In more remote outposts, fire giants burn wood to keep their forge fires lit, deforesting leagues of land in all directions.

CLOUD GIANT BOULDER

FROST GIANT BOULDER

FIRE GIANT BOULDER

HILL GIANT BOULDER

STONE GIANT BOULDER

STORM GIANT BOULDER

Fire giants shun cold as much as their cousins the frost giants hate heat. They can adapt to cold environments with effort, though, keeping their hearth fires burning bright and wearing heavy woolen clothing and furs to stay warm.

Martial Experts. From birth, a fire giant is taught to embrace a legacy of war. At the cradle, its parents chant songs of battle. As children, fire giants play at war, hurling igneous rocks at one another across the banks of magma rivers. In later years, formal martial training becomes an integral part of life in the giants' fortresses and underground realms of smoke and ash. The fire giants' songs are odes of battles lost and won, while their dances are martial formations of pounding feet that resound like smiths' hammers throughout their smoky halls.

Just as fire giants pass down their knowledge of crafting from generation to generation, their renowned fighting prowess comes not from wild fury but from endless discipline and training. Enemies make the mistake of underestimating fire giants based on their brutish manner, learning too late that these giants live for combat and can be shrewd tacticians.

Feudal Lords. Humanoids conquered in war become serfs to the fire giants. The serfs work the farms and fields on the outskirts of fire giant halls and fortresses, raising livestock and harvesting fields whose bounty is almost entirely tithed to the fire giant kings.

Fire giant crafters work through insight and experience rather than writing or arithmetic. Though most fire giants place little worth on such frivolousness, they sometimes keep slaves at court who are versed in such skills. Serfs not destined for court or the fields (especially dwarves) are taken to the fire giants' mountainous realms to mine ore and gemstones from deep within the earth.

Fire giants low in the ordning manage the mine tunnels and the slaves that toil there, few of which survive the difficult and dangerous work for long. Though fire giants are skilled in the engineering of mine tunnels and the gathering of ore, they place less importance on the safety of their slaves than on smelting and working the bounty those slaves produce.

Skilled Artisans. Fire giants have a fearsome reputation as soldiers and conquerors, and for their ability to burn, plunder, and destroy. Yet among the giants, fire giants produce the greatest crafters and artists. They excel at smelting and smith work, as they do at the engineering of metal and stone, and the quality of their artistry shows even in their implements of destruction and their weapons of war.

Fire giants strive to build the strongest fortresses and most potent siege weapons. They experiment with alloys to create the hardest armor, then forge the swords that can pierce it. Such work requires brawn and brains in equal measure, and fire giants high in the ordning tend to be the smartest and strongest of their kind.

"And here is where Angerroth the barbarian fell against the giant horde. His bones are under that boulder over there."
—Elder Zelane of Istivin, recounting the Giant Wars

Frost Giant

Gigantic reavers from the freezing lands beyond civilization, frost giants are fierce, hardy warriors that survive on the spoils of their raids and pillaging. They respect only brute strength and skill in battle, demonstrating both with their scars and the grisly trophies they take from their enemies.

Hearts of Ice. Frost giants are creatures of ice and snow. Their hair and beards are pale white or light blue, matted with frost and clattering with icicles. Their flesh is as blue as glacial ice.

Frost giants dwell in high peaks and glacial rifts where the sun hides its golden head by winter. Crops don't grow in their frozen homelands, and they keep little livestock beyond what they capture in their raids against civilized lands. They hunt the wild game of the tundra and mountains but don't cook it, since meat from a fresh kill tastes sufficiently hot to their palate.

Reavers of the Storm. The war horns of the frost giants howl as they march from their ice fortresses and glacial rifts amid the howling blizzard. When that storm clears, villages and steadings lay in ruins, ravens descending to feed on the corpses of any creatures foolish or unlucky enough to stand in the giants' path.

Inns and taverns suffer the brunt of the damage, their cellars gutted and their casks of ale and mead gone. Smithies are likewise toppled, their iron and steel claimed. Curiously undisturbed are the houses of moneylenders and wealthy citizens, for the reavers have little use for coins or baubles. Frost giants prize gems and jewelry large enough to be worn and noticed. However, even those treasures are most often saved for trading opportunities with other giants more adept at crafting metal weapons and armor.

Rulers by Might. Frost giants respect brute strength above all else, and a frost giant's place in the ordning depends on evidence of physical might, such as superior musculature, scars from battles of renown, or trophies fashioned from the bodies of slain enemies. Tasks such as hunting, childrearing, and crafting are given to giants based on their physical strength and hardiness.

When frost giants of different clans meet and their status is unclear, they wrestle for dominance. Such meetings might resemble festivals where giants cheer on their champions, making bold boasts and challenges. At other times, the informal ceremony can become a chaotic free-for-all where both clans rush into a melee that fells trees, shatters the ice on frozen lakes, and causes avalanches on the snowy mountainsides.

Make War, Not Goods. Though frost giants consider the menial crafting of goods beneath them, carving and leatherwork are valued skills. They make their clothing from the skins and bones of beasts, and carve bone or ivory into jewelry and the handles of weapons and tools. They reuse the weapons and armor of their smaller foes, stringing shields into scale armor and lashing sword blades to wooden hafts to make giant-sized spears. The greatest battle trophies come from conquered dragons, and the greatest frost giant jarls wear armor of dragon scales or wield picks and mauls made of a dragon's teeth or claws.

Hill Giant

Hill giants are selfish, dimwitted brutes that hunt, forage, and raid in constant search of food. They blunder through hills and forests devouring what they can, bullying smaller creatures into feeding them. Their laziness and dullness would long ago have spelled their end if not for their formidable size and strength.

Primitive. Hill giants dwell in hills and mountain valleys across the world, congregating in steadings built of rough timber or in clusters of well-defended mud-and-wattle huts. Their skins are tan from lives spent lumbering up and down the hilly slopes and dozing beneath the sun. Their weapons are uprooted trees and rocks pulled from the earth. The sweat of their bodies adds to the reek of the crude animal skins they wear, poorly stitched together with hair and leather thongs.

Bigger Means Better. In a hill giant's world, humanoids and animals are easy prey that can be hunted with impunity. Creatures such as dragons and other giants are tough adversaries. Hill giants equate size with power.

Hill giants don't realize they follow an ordning. They know only that other giants are larger and stronger than they are, which means they are to be obeyed. A hill giant tribe's chief is usually the tallest and fattest giant that can still move about. Only on rare occasion does a hill giant with more brains than bulk use its cunning to gain the favor of giants of higher status, cleverly subverting the social order.

Voracious Eaters. With nothing else to occupy them, hill giants eat as often as possible. A hill giant hunts and forages alone or with a dire wolf companion, so as to not have to share with other tribe members. The giant eats anything that isn't obviously deadly, such as creatures known to be poisonous. Rotten meat is fair game, though, as are decaying plants and even mud.

Farmers fear and loathe hill giants. Where a predator such as an ankheg might burrow through fields and consume a cow or two before being driven off, a hill giant will consume a whole herd of cattle before moving on to sheep, goats, and chickens, then tearing into fruits, vegetables, and grain. If a farm family is at hand, the giant might snack on them too.

Stupid and Deadly. The hill giants' ability to digest nearly anything has allowed them to survive for eons as savages, eating and breeding in the hills like animals. They have never needed to adapt and change, so their minds and emotions remain simple and undeveloped.

With no culture of their own, hill giants ape the traditions of creatures they manage to observe for a time before eating them. They don't think about their own size and strength, however. Tribes of hill giants attempting to imitate elves have been known to topple entire forests by trying to live in trees. Others attempting to take over humanoid towns or villages get only as far as the doors and windows of a building, taking out its walls and roof as they attempt to enter.

In conversation, hill giants are blunt and direct, and they have little concept of deception. A hill giant might be fooled into running from another giant if a number of villagers cover themselves in blankets and stand on one another's shoulders holding a giant-painted pumpkin head. Reasoning with a hill giant is futile, although clever creatures can sometimes encourage a giant to take actions that benefit them.

Raging Bullies. A hill giant that feels as though it has been deceived, insulted, or made into a fool vents its terrible wrath on anything it encounters. Even after smashing those who offended it into pulp, the giant rampages until its rage abates, it notices something more interesting, or it grows hungry.

If a hill giant proclaims itself king over a territory where other humanoids live, it rules strictly by terror and tyranny. Its decisions shift with its mood, and if it forgets the title it bestowed upon itself, it might eat its subjects on a whim.

Stone Giant

Stone giants are reclusive, quiet, and peaceful as long as they are left alone. Their granite-gray skin, gaunt features, and black, sunken eyes endow stone giants with a stern countenance. They are private creatures, hiding their lives and art away from the world.

Inhabitants of a Stone World. Secluded caves are the homes of the stone giants. Cavern networks are their towns, rocky tunnels their roads, and underground streams their waterways. Isolated mountain ranges are their continents, with the vast spans of land between seen as oceans that the stone giants only rarely cross.

In their dark, quiet caves, stone giants wordlessly chip away at elaborate carvings, measuring time in the echoing drip of water into cavern pools. In the deepest chambers of a stone giant settlement, far from the chittering of bats or the patrols paced out by the giants' cave bear companions, are holy places where silence and darkness are complete. Stone takes on its most sacred quality in these cavern cathedrals, their buttresses and columns carved with a beauty that shames the legendary stonecraft of the dwarves.

Carvers and Seers. Among stone giants, artistry ranks as the greatest virtue. They create intricate murals, paint sprawling murals across cavern walls, and indulge in a wide variety of other artistic disciplines. They esteem stone carving as the greatest of skills.

Stone giants strive to draw shapes out of raw stone, which they believe reveal meaning inspired by their god, Skoraeus Stonebones. The giants appoint the tribe's best carvers as their leaders, shamans, and prophets. The holy hands of such giants become the hands of the god as they work.

Graceful Athletes. Despite their great size and musculature, stone giants are lithe and graceful. Skilled rock throwers are granted positions of high rank in the giants' ordning, testing and demonstrating their ability to hurl and catch enormous boulders. Such giants take the front ranks when a tribe has cause to defend its home or attack its enemies. However, even in combat, artistry is key. A stone giant hurling a rock performs not just a feat of brute strength but also one of stunning athleticism and poise.

Dreamers under Sky. Stone giants view the world outside their underground homes as a realm of dreams where nothing is entirely true or real. They behave in the surface world the way humanoids might behave in their own dreams, making little account for their actions and never fully trusting what they see or hear. A promise made above ground need not be kept. Insults can be made without apology. Killing prey or sentient beings is no cause for guilt in the dreaming world beneath the sky.

Stone giants lacking in athletic grace or artistic skill dwell at the fringes of their society, serving as the tribe's outlying guardians and far-wandering hunters. When trespassers stray too far into the mountain territory of a stone giant clan, those guardians greet them with hurled rocks and showers of splintered stone. Survivors of such encounters spread tales of stone giant violence, never realizing how little those brutes dwelling in the unreal dreaming world resemble their quiet and artistic kin.

STORM GIANT

Storm giants are contemplative seers that live in places far removed from mortal civilization. Most have pale purple-gray skin and hair, and glittering emerald eyes. Some rare storm giants are violet-skinned, with deep violet or blue-black hair and silvery gray or purple

GIANT GODS

When the giants' ancient empires fell, Annam, father of all giants, forsook his children and the world. He swore never to look upon either again until the giants had returned to their glory and reclaimed their birthright as rulers of the world. As a result, giants pray not to Annam but to his divine children, along with a host of hero-deities and godly villains that make up the giants' pantheon.

Chief among these gods are the children of Annam, whose sons represent each type of giant: Stronmaus for storm giants, Memnor for cloud giants, Skoraeus Stonebones for stone giants, Thrym for frost giants, Surtur for fire giants, and Grolantor for hill giants. Not all giants automatically revere their kind's primary deity, however. Many good cloud giants refuse to worship the deceitful Memnor, and a storm giant dwelling in the icy mountains of the north might pay more homage to Thrym than Stronmaus. Other giants feel a stronger connection to Annam's daughters, who include Hiatea, the huntress and home warden; Iallanis, goddess of love and peace; and Diancastra, an impetuous and arrogant trickster.

Some giants abandon their own gods and fall prey to demon cults, paying homage to Baphomet or Kostchtchie. To worship them or any other non-giant deity is a great sin against the ordning, and almost certain to make a giant an outcast.

eyes. They are benevolent and wise unless angered, in response to which the fury of a storm giant can affect the fate of thousands.

Distant Prophet-Kings. Storm giants live in isolated refuges so far above the surface of the world or below the sea that they are beyond the reach of most other creatures. Some make their abodes in cloud-top castles so high that flying dragons appear as specks below. Others live atop mountain peaks that pierce the clouds. Some occupy palaces covered with algae and coral at the bottom of the ocean, or grim fortresses in undersea rifts.

Detached Oracles. Storm giants recall the glory of ancient giant empires forged by the god Annam. They seek to restore what was lost when those empires fell. They don't compete for status in the ordning but live out the centuries of their existence in contemplative seclusion, watching the starry heavens and the ocean's depths for signs, symbols, and omens of Annam's favor.

Storm giants see the events of the world in a wide perspective. They can foretell the rise and fall of kings and empires, see the beginnings and ends of fortune and disaster, and find the patterns within seemingly unrelated events. By reading omens and prophesying, storm giants learn of vast secrets previously unknown and troves of lore utterly forgotten.

Kings will rise and fall, wars will be won and lost, and good and evil will wrestle in conflict. Storm giants have watched these events in the manner of mortal gods over many lifetimes, and they know it is pointless to intervene. Even so, a storm giant might willingly disclose certain secrets to benevolent beings that visit its remote domain with specific purpose. Such creatures must speak and act respectfully, however, for a storm giant roused to anger is a force of utter destruction.

Solitary Lives. Storm giants communicate infrequently with others of their kind. They do so usually to compare signs and omens or engage in a rare courtship. Storm giant parents stay together to raise a child to maturity, then return to the solitary isolation they cherish.

Some humanoid cultures worship storm giants as they would worship lesser gods, creating myths and stories around the giants' exploits and vast knowledge. A storm giant is governed by the dictates of its conscience, however, and not by any culture's laws or codes of honor. As such, a storm giant that bends its mind toward greed or gains a taste for petty power can easily become a terrible threat.

| HILL GIANT | FIRE GIANT | STONE GIANT | FROST GIANT | CLOUD GIANT | STORM GIANT |
| 16' TALL | 18' TALL | 18' TALL | 21' TALL | 24' TALL | 26' TALL |

CLOUD GIANT
Huge giant, neutral good (50%) or neutral evil (50%)

Armor Class 14 (natural armor)
Hit Points 200 (16d12 + 96)
Speed 40 ft.

STR	DEX	CON	INT	WIS	CHA
27 (+8)	10 (+0)	22 (+6)	12 (+1)	16 (+3)	16 (+3)

Saving Throws Con +10, Wis +7, Cha +7
Skills Insight +7, Perception +7
Senses passive Perception 17
Languages Common, Giant
Challenge 9 (5,000 XP)

Keen Smell. The giant has advantage on Wisdom (Perception) checks that rely on smell.

Innate Spellcasting. The giant's innate spellcasting ability is Charisma. It can innately cast the following spells, requiring no material components:

At will: *detect magic, fog cloud, light*
3/day each: *feather fall, fly, misty step, telekinesis*
1/day each: *control weather, gaseous form*

ACTIONS

Multiattack. The giant makes two morningstar attacks.

Morningstar. *Melee Weapon Attack:* +12 to hit, reach 10 ft., one target. *Hit:* 21 (3d8 + 8) piercing damage.

Rock. *Ranged Weapon Attack:* +12 to hit, range 60/240 ft., one target. *Hit:* 30 (4d10 + 8) bludgeoning damage.

FIRE GIANT
Huge giant, lawful evil

Armor Class 18 (plate)
Hit Points 162 (13d12 + 78)
Speed 30 ft.

STR	DEX	CON	INT	WIS	CHA
25 (+7)	9 (−1)	23 (+6)	10 (+0)	14 (+2)	13 (+1)

Saving Throws Dex +3, Con +10, Cha +5
Skills Athletics +11, Perception +6
Damage Immunities fire
Senses passive Perception 16
Languages Giant
Challenge 9 (5,000 XP)

ACTIONS

Multiattack. The giant makes two greatsword attacks.

Greatsword. *Melee Weapon Attack:* +11 to hit, reach 10 ft., one target. *Hit:* 28 (6d6 + 7) slashing damage.

Rock. *Ranged Weapon Attack:* +11 to hit, range 60/240 ft., one target. *Hit:* 29 (4d10 + 7) bludgeoning damage.

FROST GIANT
Huge giant, neutral evil

Armor Class 15 (patchwork armor)
Hit Points 138 (12d12 + 60)
Speed 40 ft.

STR	DEX	CON	INT	WIS	CHA
23 (+6)	9 (−1)	21 (+5)	9 (−1)	10 (+0)	12 (+1)

Saving Throws Con +8, Wis +3, Cha +4
Skills Athletics +9, Perception +3
Damage Immunities cold
Senses passive Perception 13
Languages Giant
Challenge 8 (3,900 XP)

ACTIONS

Multiattack. The giant makes two greataxe attacks.

Greataxe. *Melee Weapon Attack:* +9 to hit, reach 10 ft., one target. *Hit:* 25 (3d12 + 6) slashing damage.

Rock. *Ranged Weapon Attack:* +9 to hit, range 60/240 ft., one target. *Hit:* 28 (4d10 + 6) bludgeoning damage.

HILL GIANT
Huge giant, chaotic evil

Armor Class 13 (natural armor)
Hit Points 105 (10d12 + 40)
Speed 40 ft.

STR	DEX	CON	INT	WIS	CHA
21 (+5)	8 (−1)	19 (+4)	5 (−3)	9 (−1)	6 (−2)

Skills Perception +2
Senses passive Perception 12
Languages Giant
Challenge 5 (1,800 XP)

ACTIONS

Multiattack. The giant makes two greatclub attacks.

Greatclub. *Melee Weapon Attack:* +8 to hit, reach 10 ft., one target. *Hit:* 18 (3d8 + 5) bludgeoning damage.

Rock. *Ranged Weapon Attack:* +8 to hit, range 60/240 ft., one target. *Hit:* 21 (3d10 + 5) bludgeoning damage.

Stone Giant

Huge giant, neutral

Armor Class 17 (natural armor)
Hit Points 126 (11d12 + 55)
Speed 40 ft.

STR	DEX	CON	INT	WIS	CHA
23 (+6)	15 (+2)	20 (+5)	10 (+0)	12 (+1)	9 (−1)

Saving Throws Dex +5, Con +8, Wis +4
Skills Athletics +12, Perception +4
Senses darkvision 60 ft., passive Perception 14
Languages Giant
Challenge 7 (2,900 XP)

Stone Camouflage. The giant has advantage on Dexterity (Stealth) checks made to hide in rocky terrain.

Actions

Multiattack. The giant makes two greatclub attacks.

Greatclub. *Melee Weapon Attack:* +9 to hit, reach 15 ft., one target. *Hit:* 19 (3d8 + 6) bludgeoning damage.

Rock. *Ranged Weapon Attack:* +9 to hit, range 60/240 ft., one target. *Hit:* 28 (4d10 + 6) bludgeoning damage. If the target is a creature, it must succeed on a DC 17 Strength saving throw or be knocked prone.

Reactions

Rock Catching. If a rock or similar object is hurled at the giant, the giant can, with a successful DC 10 Dexterity saving throw, catch the missile and take no bludgeoning damage from it.

Storm Giant

Huge giant, chaotic good

Armor Class 16 (scale mail)
Hit Points 230 (20d12 + 100)
Speed 50 ft., swim 50 ft.

STR	DEX	CON	INT	WIS	CHA
29 (+9)	14 (+2)	20 (+5)	16 (+3)	18 (+4)	18 (+4)

Saving Throws Str +14, Con +10, Wis +9, Cha +9
Skills Arcana +8, Athletics +14, History +8, Perception +9
Damage Resistances cold
Damage Immunities lightning, thunder
Senses passive Perception 19
Languages Common, Giant
Challenge 13 (10,000 XP)

Amphibious. The giant can breathe air and water.

Innate Spellcasting. The giant's innate spellcasting ability is Charisma (spell save DC 17). It can innately cast the following spells, requiring no material components:

At will: *detect magic, feather fall, levitate, light*
3/day each: *control weather, water breathing*

Actions

Multiattack. The giant makes two greatsword attacks.

Greatsword. *Melee Weapon Attack:* +14 to hit, reach 10 ft., one target. *Hit:* 30 (6d6 + 9) slashing damage.

Rock. *Ranged Weapon Attack:* +14 to hit, range 60/240 ft., one target. *Hit:* 35 (4d12 + 9) bludgeoning damage.

Lightning Strike (Recharge 5–6). The giant hurls a magical lightning bolt at a point it can see within 500 feet of it. Each creature within 10 feet of that point must make a DC 17 Dexterity saving throw, taking 54 (12d8) lightning damage on a failed save, or half as much damage on a successful one.

GIBBERING MOUTHER

Of all the terrors created by foul sorcery, gibbering mouthers are among the most wicked and depraved. This creature is the composite eyes, mouths, and liquefied matter of its former victims. Driven to insanity by the destruction of their bodies and absorption into the mouther, those victims gibber incoherent madness, forced to consume everything in reach.

Amoeboid Form. The gibbering mouther's body is an amorphous mass of mouths and eyes that propels itself by oozing forward, fastening several mouths to the ground and pulling its bulk behind. Though it moves slowly, it swims through water, mud, and quicksand with ease.

Mouths of Madness. When a gibbering mouther senses prey, its mouths begin to murmur and chatter, each with a different voice: deep or shrill, wailing or ululating, crying out in agony or ecstasy. This cacophonous gibbering overcomes the senses of any creature that hears it, causing most to flee in terror. Others are overcome with madness or stand paralyzed, fixated on the horrific creature as it oozes forward to consume them.

All-Consuming. Driven to devour any creature it can reach, a gibbering mouther flows over victims transfixed by its mad ranting, its multitudinous voices temporarily silenced as it gnaws and swallows living flesh. The monster liquefies stone with which it comes into contact, hindering creatures that overcome its gibbering and attempt to flee.

A gibbering mouther leaves nothing of its prey behind. However, even as the last of a victim's body is consumed, its eyes and mouth boil to the surface, ready to join the chorus of tormented gibbering that welcomes the monster's next meal.

GIBBERING MOUTHER

Medium aberration, neutral

Armor Class 9
Hit Points 67 (9d8 + 27)
Speed 10 ft., swim 10 ft.

STR	DEX	CON	INT	WIS	CHA
10 (+0)	8 (−1)	16 (+3)	3 (−4)	10 (+0)	6 (−2)

Condition Immunities prone
Senses darkvision 60 ft., passive Perception 10
Languages —
Challenge 2 (450 XP)

Aberrant Ground. The ground in a 10-foot radius around the mouther is doughlike difficult terrain. Each creature that starts its turn in that area must succeed on a DC 10 Strength saving throw or have its speed reduced to 0 until the start of its next turn.

Gibbering. The mouther babbles incoherently while it can see any creature and isn't incapacitated. Each creature that starts its turn within 20 feet of the mouther and can hear the gibbering must succeed on a DC 10 Wisdom saving throw. On a failure, the creature can't take reactions until the start of its next turn and rolls a d8 to determine what it does during its turn. On a 1 to 4, the creature does nothing. On a 5 or 6, the creature takes no action or bonus action and uses all its movement to move in a randomly determined direction. On a 7 or 8, the creature makes a melee attack against a randomly determined creature within its reach or does nothing if it can't make such an attack.

ACTIONS

Multiattack. The gibbering mouther makes one bite attack and, if it can, uses its Blinding Spittle.

Bites. *Melee Weapon Attack:* +2 to hit, reach 5 ft., one creature. *Hit:* 17 (5d6) piercing damage. If the target is Medium or smaller, it must succeed on a DC 10 Strength saving throw or be knocked prone. If the target is killed by this damage, it is absorbed into the mouther.

Blinding Spittle (Recharge 5–6). The mouther spits a chemical glob at a point it can see within 15 feet of it. The glob explodes in a blinding flash of light on impact. Each creature within 5 feet of the flash must succeed on a DC 13 Dexterity saving throw or be blinded until the end of the mouther's next turn.

GITH

The warlike githyanki and the contemplative githzerai are a sundered people—two cultures that utterly despise one another. Before there were githyanki or githzerai, these creatures were a single race enslaved by the mind flayers. Although they attempted to overthrow their masters many times, their rebellions were repeatedly crushed until a great leader named Gith arose.

After much bloodshed, Gith and her followers threw off the yoke of their illithid masters, but another leader named Zerthimon emerged in the aftermath of battle. Zerthimon challenged Gith's motives, claiming that her strict martial leadership and desire for vengeance amounted to little more than another form of slavery for her people. A rift erupted between followers of each leader, and they eventually became the two races whose enmity endures to this day.

Whether these tall, gaunt creatures were peaceful or savage, cultured or primitive before the mind flayers enslaved and changed them, none can say. Not even the original name of their race remains from that distant time.

GITHYANKI

The githyanki plunder countless worlds from the decks of their astral vessels and the backs of red dragons. Feathers, beads, gems, and precious metals decorate their armor and weapons—the legendary silver swords with which they cut through their foes. Since winning their freedom from the mind flayers, the githyanki have become ruthless conquerors under the rulership of their dread lich-queen, Vlaakith.

Astral Raiders. The githyanki despise all other races, undertaking devastating raids that take them from their strongholds in the Astral Plane to the farflung corners of the multiverse. War is the ultimate expression of githyanki culture, and their pitiless black eyes know no mercy. After a raid, they leave shattered survivors enough food and resources to weakly endure. Later, the githyanki return to their conquered foes, plundering them again and again.

Followers of Gith. In their own language, githyanki means "followers of Gith." Under the guidance of Gith, the githyanki stratified into a militaristic society, with a strict caste system, dedicated to the ongoing fight against the victims and sworn enemies of their race. When their leader Gith perished, she was replaced by her undead adviser, Vlaakith. The lich-queen forbade worship of all beings except herself.

Of all their enemies, the githyanki most hate their former masters, the mind flayers. Their close kin, the githzerai, are second in their enmity. All other creatures are treated with simple contempt by the githyanki, whose xenophobic pride defines their view of inferior races.

Silver Swords. In ancient times, gith knights created special weapons to combat their mind flayer masters. These silver swords channel the force of the wielder's will, dealing psychic as well as physical damage. A githyanki can't become a knight until it masters the singular discipline needed to will such a blade into existence. A silver sword is equivalent to a greatsword, and takes on the properties of a *+3 greatsword* in the hands of its creator.

In the eyes of the githyanki, each *silver sword* is a priceless relic and a work of art. Githyanki knights will hunt down and destroy any non-githyanki that dares to carry or wield a silver sword, reclaiming it for their people.

Red Dragon Riders. In the uprising against the illithids, Gith sought allies. Her adviser Vlaakith appealed to Tiamat, the goddess of evil dragonkind, and Gith ventured into the Nine Hells to meet with her. Only Tiamat now knows what passed between them, but Gith returned to the Astral Plane with the Dragon Queen's red dragon consort Ephelomon, who proclaimed that his kind would forever act as allies to the githyanki. Not all red dragons honor the alliance kindled so long ago, but most at least don't consider the githyanki their enemies.

Outposts in the Mortal Realm. Since creatures that dwell on the Astral Plane don't age, the githyanki establish creches in remote areas of the Material Plane to raise their young. Doubling as military academies, these creches train young githyanki to harness their psychic and combat abilities. When a githyanki grows to adulthood and slays a mind flayer as part of a sacred rite of passage, it is permitted to rejoin its people on the Astral Planc.

GITHZERAI

Focused philosophers and austere ascetics, the githzerai pursue lives of rigid order. Lean and muscular, they wear unadorned clothing free of ornamentation, keeping their own counsel and trusting few creatures outside of their own kind. Having turned their backs on their warlike githyanki kin, the githzerai maintain a strict monastic lifestyle, dwelling on islands of order in the vast sea of chaos that is the plane of Limbo.

Psionic Adepts. The progenitors of the githzerai adapted to—and were transformed by—the psychic environment imposed on them by their illithid overlords. Under the teachings of Zerthimon, who called on his people to abandon the warlike ambitions of Gith, the githzerai focused their mental energy on creating physical and psychic barriers to protect them from attack, psychic or otherwise. Fighting is personal to a githzerai, which uses its mind to daze and incapacitate opponents, leaving them vulnerable to physical punishment.

Order amid Chaos. The githzerai willingly dwell in the heart of utter chaos in Limbo—a twisting, mercurial plane prone to manipulation and subjugation by githzerai minds strong enough to master it. Limbo is a maelstrom of primal matter and energy, its terrain a storm of rock and earth swept up in torrents of murky liquid, buffeted by strong winds, blasted by fire, and chilled by crushing walls of ice.

The forces of Limbo react to sentience, however. Using the power of their minds, the githzerai tame the plane's chaotic elements, causing them to settle into fixed and survivable forms and creating oases and sanctuaries within the maelstrom.

Githzerai fortress-monasteries stand resolute against the chaos that surrounds them, virtually impervious to the turmoil of their surroundings, because the githzerai will it. Each monastery is overseen by monks that impose a strict schedule of chants, meals, martial arts training, and devotions according to their own philosophy. Behind their psionically fortified walls, the githzerai embrace thought, learning, psionic power, order, and discipline above all other things.

The social hierarchy of the githzerai is based on merit, and those githzerai who are the wisest teachers and the most skilled at physical and mental combat become leaders. The githzerai revere great heroes and teachers of the past, emulating those figures' virtues in their everyday lives.

Disciples of Zerthimon. Githzerai revere Zerthimon, the founder of their race. Although Gith won their people's freedom, Zerthimon saw her as unfit to lead. He believed that her warmongering would soon make her a tyrant no better than the mind flayers.

Skilled githzerai monks that best exemplify the teachings and principles of Zerthimon are called zerths. These powerful and disciplined monks can shift their bodies from one plane to another using only the power of their minds.

Beyond Limbo. Though githzerai rarely deal with thc rcalms bcyond Limbo, advanccd monks of othcr races sometimes seek out a githzerai monastery and attempt to gain admittance as students. More rarely, a githzerai master establishes a hidden monastery on the Material Plane to train young githzerai or to spread the philosophy and teachings of Zerthimon.

As disciplined as they are, the githzerai have never forgotten their long imprisonment by the mind flayers. As a special devotion, they organize a *rrakkma*—an illithid hunting party—to other planes, not returning to their monasteries until they slay at least as many illithids as there are hunters in the party.

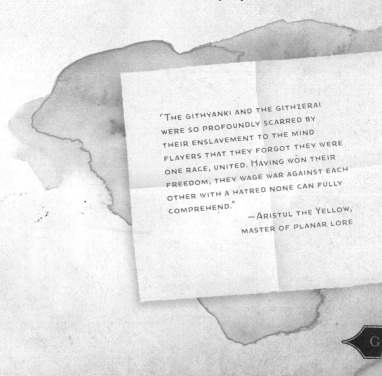

"The githyanki and the githzerai were so profoundly scarred by their enslavement to the mind flayers that they forgot they were one race, united. Having won their freedom, they wage war against each other with a hatred none can fully comprehend."

—Aristul the Yellow,
Master of Planar Lore

GITHYANKI WARRIOR

Medium humanoid (gith), lawful evil

Armor Class 17 (half plate)
Hit Points 49 (9d8 + 9)
Speed 30 ft.

STR	DEX	CON	INT	WIS	CHA
15 (+2)	14 (+2)	12 (+1)	13 (+1)	13 (+1)	10 (+0)

Saving Throws Con +3, Int +3, Wis +3
Senses passive Perception 11
Languages Gith
Challenge 3 (700 XP)

Innate Spellcasting (Psionics). The githyanki's innate spellcasting ability is Intelligence. It can innately cast the following spells, requiring no components:

At will: *mage hand* (the hand is invisible)
3/day each: *jump, misty step, nondetection* (self only)

ACTIONS

Multiattack. The githyanki makes two greatsword attacks.

Greatsword. *Melee Weapon Attack:* +4 to hit, reach 5 ft., one target. *Hit:* 9 (2d6 + 2) slashing damage plus 7 (2d6) psychic damage.

GITHYANKI KNIGHT

Medium humanoid (gith), lawful evil

Armor Class 18 (plate)
Hit Points 91 (14d8 + 28)
Speed 30 ft.

STR	DEX	CON	INT	WIS	CHA
16 (+3)	14 (+2)	15 (+2)	14 (+2)	14 (+2)	15 (+2)

Saving Throws Con +5, Int +5, Wis +5
Senses passive Perception 12
Languages Gith
Challenge 8 (3,900 XP)

Innate Spellcasting (Psionics). The githyanki's innate spellcasting ability is Intelligence (spell save DC 13, +5 to hit with spell attacks). It can innately cast the following spells, requiring no components:

At will: *mage hand* (the hand is invisible)
3/day each: *jump, misty step, nondetection* (self only), *tongues*
1/day each: *plane shift, telekinesis*

ACTIONS

Multiattack. The githyanki makes two silver greatsword attacks.

Silver Greatsword. *Melee Weapon Attack:* +9 to hit, reach 5 ft., one target. *Hit:* 13 (2d6 + 6) slashing damage plus 10 (3d6) psychic damage. This is a magic weapon attack. On a critical hit against a target in an astral body (as with the *astral projection* spell), the githyanki can cut the silvery cord that tethers the target to its material body, instead of dealing damage.

Githzerai Monk

Medium humanoid (gith), lawful neutral

Armor Class 14
Hit Points 38 (7d8 + 7)
Speed 30 ft.

STR	DEX	CON	INT	WIS	CHA
12 (+1)	15 (+2)	12 (+1)	13 (+1)	14 (+2)	10 (+0)

Saving Throws Str +3, Dex +4, Int +3, Wis +4
Skills Insight +4, Perception +4
Senses passive Perception 14
Languages Gith
Challenge 2 (450 XP)

Innate Spellcasting (Psionics). The githzerai's innate spellcasting ability is Wisdom. It can innately cast the following spells, requiring no components:

At will: *mage hand* (the hand is invisible)
3/day each: *feather fall, jump, see invisibility, shield*

Psychic Defense. While the githzerai is wearing no armor and wielding no shield, its AC includes its Wisdom modifier.

Actions

Multiattack. The githzerai makes two unarmed strikes.

Unarmed Strike. *Melee Weapon Attack:* +4 to hit, reach 5 ft., one target. *Hit:* 6 (1d8 + 2) bludgeoning damage plus 9 (2d8) psychic damage. This is a magic weapon attack.

Githzerai Zerth

Medium humanoid (gith), lawful neutral

Armor Class 17
Hit Points 84 (13d8 + 26)
Speed 30 ft.

STR	DEX	CON	INT	WIS	CHA
13 (+1)	18 (+4)	15 (+2)	16 (+3)	17 (+3)	12 (+1)

Saving Throws Str +4, Dex +7, Int +6, Wis +6
Skills Arcana +6, Insight +6, Perception +6
Senses passive Perception 16
Languages Gith
Challenge 6 (2,300 XP)

Innate Spellcasting (Psionics). The githzerai's spellcasting ability is Wisdom (spell save DC 14, +6 to hit with spell attacks). It can innately cast the following spells, requiring no components:

At will: *mage hand* (the hand is invisible)
3/day each: *feather fall, jump, see invisibility, shield*
1/day each: *phantasmal killer, plane shift*

Psychic Defense. While the githzerai is wearing no armor and wielding no shield, its AC includes its Wisdom modifier.

Actions

Multiattack. The githzerai makes two unarmed strikes.

Unarmed Strike. *Melee Weapon Attack:* +7 to hit, reach 5 ft., one target. *Hit:* 11 (2d6 + 4) bludgeoning damage plus 13 (3d8) psychic damage. This is a magic weapon attack.

GNOLLS

Gnolls are feral humanoids that attack settlements along the frontiers and borderlands of civilization without warning, slaughtering their victims and devouring their flesh.

Demonic Origin. The origin of the gnolls traces back to a time when the demon lord Yeenoghu found his way to the Material Plane and ran amok. Packs of ordinary hyenas followed in his wake, scavenging the demon lord's kills. Those hyenas were transformed into the first gnolls, parading after Yeenoghu until he was banished back to the Abyss. The gnolls then scattered across the face of the world, a dire reminder of demonic power.

Nomadic Destroyers. Gnolls are dangerous because they strike at random. They emerge from the wilderness, plunder and slaughter, then move elsewhere. They attack like a plague of locusts, pillaging settlements and leaving little behind but razed buildings, gnawed corpses, and befouled land. Gnolls choose easy targets for their raids. Armored warriors holed up in a fortified castle will survive a rampaging gnoll horde unscathed, even as the towns, villages, and farms that surround the castle are ablaze, their people slaughtered and devoured.

Gnolls rarely build permanent structures or craft anything of lasting value. They don't make weapons or armor, but scavenge such items from the corpses of their fallen victims, stringing ears, teeth, scalps, and other trophies from their foes onto their patchwork armor.

Thirst for Blood. No goodness or compassion resides in the heart of a gnoll. Like a demon, it lacks anything resembling a conscience, and can't be taught or coerced to put aside its destructive tendencies. The gnolls' frenzied bloodlust makes them an enemy to all, and when they lack a common foe, they fight among themselves. Even the most savage orcs avoid allying with gnolls.

GNOLL PACK LORD

The alpha of a gnoll pack is the pack lord, ruling by might and cunning. A pack lord earns the best of a gnoll pack's spoils, food, valuable trinkets, and magic items. It ornaments its body with brutal piercings and grotesque trophies, dyeing its fur with demonic sigils, hoping Yeenoghu will make it invulnerable.

GNOLL FANG OF YEENOGHU

Gnolls celebrate their victories by performing demonic rituals and making blood offerings to Yeenoghu. Sometimes the demon lord rewards his worshipers by allowing one of them to be possessed by a demonic spirit. Marked as Yeenoghu's favorite, the lucky recipient becomes a fang of Yeenoghu, the chosen of the Gnoll Lord. In much the same way Yeenoghu created the first gnolls, a hyena that feasts on a fang's slain foe undergoes a horrible transformation, becoming a full-grown adult gnoll. Depending on the number of hyenas in a region, a fang of Yeenoghu can lead to a startling increase in the gnoll population. Finding and killing the fang is the only way to keep that population in check.

GNOLL
Medium humanoid (gnoll), chaotic evil

Armor Class 15 (hide armor, shield)
Hit Points 22 (5d8)
Speed 30 ft.

STR	DEX	CON	INT	WIS	CHA
14 (+2)	12 (+1)	11 (+0)	6 (−2)	10 (+0)	7 (−2)

Senses darkvision 60 ft., passive Perception 10
Languages Gnoll
Challenge 1/2 (100 XP)

Rampage. When the gnoll reduces a creature to 0 hit points with a melee attack on its turn, the gnoll can take a bonus action to move up to half its speed and make a bite attack.

ACTIONS

Bite. *Melee Weapon Attack:* +4 to hit, reach 5 ft., one creature. *Hit:* 4 (1d4 + 2) piercing damage.

Spear. *Melee or Ranged Weapon Attack:* +4 to hit, reach 5 ft. or range 20/60 ft., one target. *Hit:* 5 (1d6 + 2) piercing damage, or 6 (1d8 + 2) piercing damage if used with two hands to make a melee attack.

Longbow. *Ranged Weapon Attack:* +3 to hit, range 150/600 ft., one target. *Hit:* 5 (1d8 + 1) piercing damage.

GNOLL PACK LORD
Medium humanoid (gnoll), chaotic evil

Armor Class 15 (chain shirt)
Hit Points 49 (9d8 + 9)
Speed 30 ft.

STR	DEX	CON	INT	WIS	CHA
16 (+3)	14 (+2)	13 (+1)	8 (−1)	11 (+0)	9 (−1)

Senses darkvision 60 ft., passive Perception 10
Languages Gnoll
Challenge 2 (450 XP)

Rampage. When the gnoll reduces a creature to 0 hit points with a melee attack on its turn, the gnoll can take a bonus action to move up to half its speed and make a bite attack.

ACTIONS

Multiattack. The gnoll makes two attacks, either with its glaive or its longbow, and uses its Incite Rampage if it can.

Bite. *Melee Weapon Attack:* +5 to hit, reach 5 ft., one creature. *Hit:* 5 (1d4 + 3) piercing damage.

Glaive. *Melee Weapon Attack:* +5 to hit, reach 10 ft., one target. *Hit:* 8 (1d10 + 3) slashing damage.

Longbow. *Ranged Weapon Attack:* +4 to hit, range 150/600 ft., one target. *Hit:* 6 (1d8 + 2) piercing damage.

Incite Rampage (Recharge 5–6). One creature the gnoll can see within 30 feet of it can use its reaction to make a melee attack if it can hear the gnoll and has the Rampage trait.

GNOLL FANG OF YEENOGHU
Medium fiend (gnoll), chaotic evil

Armor Class 14 (hide armor)
Hit Points 65 (10d8 + 20)
Speed 30 ft.

STR	DEX	CON	INT	WIS	CHA
17 (+3)	15 (+2)	15 (+2)	10 (+0)	11 (+0)	13 (+1)

Saving Throws Con +4, Wis +2, Cha +3
Senses darkvision 60 ft., passive Perception 10
Languages Abyssal, Gnoll
Challenge 4 (1,100 XP)

Rampage. When the gnoll reduces a creature to 0 hit points with a melee attack on its turn, the gnoll can take a bonus action to move up to half its speed and make a bite attack.

ACTIONS

Multiattack. The gnoll makes three attacks: one with its bite and two with its claws.

Bite. *Melee Weapon Attack:* +5 to hit, reach 5 ft., one creature. *Hit:* 6 (1d6 + 3) piercing damage, and the target must succeed on a DC 12 Constitution saving throw or take 7 (2d6) poison damage.

Claw. *Melee Weapon Attack:* +5 to hit, reach 5 ft., one target. *Hit:* 7 (1d8 + 3) slashing damage.

GNOME, DEEP (SVIRFNEBLIN)

Deep gnomes, or svirfneblin, live far below the world's surface in twisting warrens and sculpted caverns. They survive by virtue of their stealth, cleverness, and tenacity. Their gray skin allows them to blend in with surrounding stonework. They are also surprisingly heavy and strong for their size. An average adult weighs 100 to 120 pounds and stands 3 feet tall.

A typical svirfneblin enclave contains several hundred deep gnomes and is strongly fortified. Secret tunnels lead to and from the settlement, and the deep gnomes use these as evacuation routes when the enclave comes under attack.

Established Gender Roles. Male svirfneblin are bald, while females have stringy gray hair. Traditionally, females run the enclaves while males scour the outskirts in search of enemies and deposits of precious gemstones.

Gemstone Harvesters. Svirfneblin cherish fine gemstones, especially rubies, which they harvest from mines deep in the Underdark. The hunt for gems often brings them into conflict with beholders, drow, kuo-toa, duergar, and mind flayers. Of all their natural enemies, deep gnomes fear and despise the murderous, demon-worshiping drow the most.

Earth Friends. Deep gnomes are often encountered in the company of creatures from the Elemental Plane of Earth. Some svirfneblin can summon such creatures. Earth creatures guard svirfneblin settlements, especially xorn enticed to service with the promise of gems to feed on.

DEEP GNOME (SVIRFNEBLIN)
Small humanoid (gnome), neutral good

Armor Class 15 (chain shirt)
Hit Points 16 (3d6 + 6)
Speed 20 ft.

STR	DEX	CON	INT	WIS	CHA
15 (+2)	14 (+2)	14 (+2)	12 (+1)	10 (+0)	9 (−1)

Skills Investigation +3, Perception +2, Stealth +4
Senses darkvision 120 ft., passive Perception 12
Languages Gnomish, Terran, Undercommon
Challenge 1/2 (100 XP)

Stone Camouflage. The gnome has advantage on Dexterity (Stealth) checks made to hide in rocky terrain.

Gnome Cunning. The gnome has advantage on Intelligence, Wisdom, and Charisma saving throws against magic.

Innate Spellcasting. The gnome's innate spellcasting ability is Intelligence (spell save DC 11). It can innately cast the following spells, requiring no material components:

At will: *nondetection* (self only)
1/day each: *blindness/deafness, blur, disguise self*

ACTIONS

War Pick. *Melee Weapon Attack:* +4 to hit, reach 5 ft., one target. *Hit:* 6 (1d8 + 2) piercing damage.

Poisoned Dart. *Ranged Weapon Attack:* +4 to hit, range 30/120 ft., one creature. *Hit:* 4 (1d4 + 2) piercing damage, and the target must succeed on a DC 12 Constitution saving throw or be poisoned for 1 minute. The target can repeat the saving throw at the end of each of its turns, ending the effect on itself on a success.

G

GOBLINS

Goblins are small, black-hearted, selfish humanoids that lair in caves, abandoned mines, despoiled dungeons, and other dismal settings. Individually weak, goblins gather in large—sometimes overwhelming—numbers. They crave power and regularly abuse whatever authority they obtain.

Goblinoids. Goblins belong to a family of creatures called goblinoids. Their larger cousins, hobgoblins and bugbears, like to bully goblins into submission. Goblins are lazy and undisciplined, making them poor servants, laborers, and guards.

Malicious Glee. Motivated by greed and malice, goblins can't help but celebrate the few times they have the upper hand. They dance, caper with sheer joy when victory is theirs. Once their revels have ended, goblins delight in the torment of other creatures and embrace all manner of wickedness.

Leaders and Followers. Goblins are ruled by the strongest or smartest among them. A goblin boss might command a single lair, while a goblin king or queen (who is nothing more than a glorified goblin boss) rules hundreds of goblins, spread out among multiple lairs to ensure the tribe's survival. Goblin bosses are easily ousted, and many goblin tribes are taken over by hobgoblin warlords or bugbear chiefs.

Challenging Lairs. Goblins festoon their lairs with alarms designed to signal the arrival of intruders. Those lairs are also riddled with narrow tunnels and bolt-holes that human-sized creatures can't navigate, but which goblins can crawl through with ease, allowing them to flee or to circle around and surprise their enemies.

Rat Keepers and Wolf Riders. Goblins have an affinity for rats and wolves, raising them to serve as companions and mounts, respectively. Like rats, goblins shun sunlight and sleep underground during the day. Like wolves, they are pack hunters, made bolder by their numbers. When they hunt from the backs of wolves, goblins use hit-and-run attacks.

Worshipers of Maglubiyet. Maglubiyet the Mighty One, the Lord of Depths and Darkness, is the greater god of goblinoids. Envisioned by most goblins as an eleven-foot-tall battle-scarred goblin with black skin and fire erupting from his eyes, he is worshiped not out of adoration but fear. Goblins believe that when they die in battle, their spirits join the ranks of Maglubiyet's army on the plane of Acheron. This is a "privilege" that most goblins dread, fearing the Mighty One's eternal tyranny even more than death.

"If you want soldiers or thugs, hire hobgoblins. If you want someone clubbed to death in their sleep, hire bugbears. If you want mean little fools, hire goblins."
—Stalman Klim, Slave Lord

GOBLIN BOSS

Small humanoid (goblinoid), neutral evil

Armor Class 17 (chain shirt, shield)
Hit Points 21 (6d6)
Speed 30 ft.

STR	DEX	CON	INT	WIS	CHA
10 (+0)	14 (+2)	10 (+0)	10 (+0)	8 (–1)	10 (+0)

Skills Stealth +6
Senses darkvision 60 ft., passive Perception 9
Languages Common, Goblin
Challenge 1 (200 XP)

Nimble Escape. The goblin can take the Disengage or Hide action as a bonus action on each of its turns.

ACTIONS

Multiattack. The goblin makes two attacks with its scimitar. The second attack has disadvantage.

Scimitar. *Melee Weapon Attack:* +4 to hit, reach 5 ft., one target. *Hit:* 5 (1d6 + 2) slashing damage.

Javelin. *Melee or Ranged Weapon Attack:* +2 to hit, reach 5 ft. or range 30/120 ft., one target. *Hit:* 3 (1d6) piercing damage.

REACTIONS

Redirect Attack. When a creature the goblin can see targets it with an attack, the goblin chooses another goblin within 5 feet of it. The two goblins swap places, and the chosen goblin becomes the target instead.

GOBLIN

Small humanoid (goblinoid), neutral evil

Armor Class 15 (leather armor, shield)
Hit Points 7 (2d6)
Speed 30 ft.

STR	DEX	CON	INT	WIS	CHA
8 (–1)	14 (+2)	10 (+0)	10 (+0)	8 (–1)	8 (–1)

Skills Stealth +6
Senses darkvision 60 ft., passive Perception 9
Languages Common, Goblin
Challenge 1/4 (50 XP)

Nimble Escape. The goblin can take the Disengage or Hide action as a bonus action on each of its turns.

ACTIONS

Scimitar. *Melee Weapon Attack:* +4 to hit, reach 5 ft., one target. *Hit:* 5 (1d6 + 2) slashing damage.

Shortbow. *Ranged Weapon Attack:* +4 to hit, range 80/320 ft., one target. *Hit:* 5 (1d6 + 2) piercing damage.

Golems

Golems are made from humble materials—clay, flesh and bones, iron, or stone—but they possess astonishing power and durability. A golem has no ambitions, needs no sustenance, feels no pain, and knows no remorse. An unstoppable juggernaut, it exists to follow its creator's orders, and it protects or attacks as that creator demands.

To create a golem, one requires a *manual of golems* (see the *Dungeon Master's Guide*). The comprehensive illustrations and instructions in a manual detail the process for creating a golem of a particular type.

Elemental Spirit in Material Form. The construction of a golem begins with the building of its body, requiring great command of the craft of sculpting, stonecutting, ironworking, or surgery. Sometimes a golem's creator is the master of the art, but often the individual who desires a golem must enlist master artisans to do the work.

After constructing the body from clay, flesh, iron, or stone, the golem's creator infuses it with a spirit from the Elemental Plane of Earth. This tiny spark of life has no memory, personality, or history. It is simply the impetus to move and obey. This process binds the spirit to the artificial body and subjects it to the will of the golem's creator.

Ageless Guardians. Golems can guard sacred sites, tombs, and treasure vaults long after the deaths of their creators, carrying out their appointed tasks for all eternity while brushing off physical damage and ignoring all but the most potent spells.

A golems can be created with a special amulet or other item that allows the possessor of the item to control the golem. Golems whose creators are long dead can thus be harnessed to serve a new master.

Blind Obedience. When its creator or possessor is on hand to command it, a golem performs flawlessly. If the golem is left without instructions or is incapacitated, it continues to follow its last orders to the best of its ability. When it can't fulfill its orders, a golem might react violently—or stand and do nothing. A golem that has been given conflicting orders sometimes alternates between them.

A golem can't think or act for itself. Though it understands its commands perfectly, it has no grasp of language beyond that understanding, and can't be reasoned with or tricked with words.

Constructed Nature. A golem doesn't require air, food, drink, or sleep.

> "Beyond the unopenable doors lay a grand hall ending before a towering stone throne, upon which sat an iron statue taller and wider than two men. In one hand it clutched an iron sword, in the other, a feather whip. We should have turned back then."
> —Mordenkainen the Archmage, chronicling his party's harrowing exploits in the dungeons below Maure Castle

Clay Golem

Sculpted from clay, this bulky golem stands head and shoulders taller than most human-sized creatures. It is human shaped, but its proportions are off.

Clay golems are often divinely endowed with purpose by priests of great faith. However, clay is a weak vessel for life force. If the golem is damaged, the elemental spirit bound into it can break free. Such a golem runs amok, smashing everything around it until it is destroyed or completely repaired.

Flesh Golem

A flesh golem is a grisly assortment of humanoid body parts stitched and bolted together into a muscled brute imbued with formidable strength. Its brain is capable of simple reason, though its thoughts are no more sophisticated than those of a young child. The golem's muscle tissue responds to the power of lightning, invigorating the creature with vitality and strength. Powerful enchantments protect the golem's skin, deflecting spells and all but the most potent weapons.

A flesh golem lurches with a stiff-jointed gait, as if not in complete control of its body. Its dead flesh isn't an ideal container for an elemental spirit, which sometimes howls incoherently to vent its outrage. If the spirit breaks free of its creator's will, the golem goes berserk until calmed, or until its shell of flesh is destroyed or completely healed.

Iron Golem

The mightiest of the golems, the iron golem is a massive, towering giant wrought of heavy metal. An iron golem's shape can be worked into any form, though most are fashioned to look like giant suits of armor. Its fist can destroy creatures with a single blow, and its clanging steps shake the earth beneath its feet. Iron golems wield enormous blades to extend their reach, and all can belch clouds of deadly poison.

An iron golem's body is smelted with rare tinctures and admixtures. Though other golems bear weaknesses inherent in their materials or the power of the elemental spirit bound within them, iron golems were designed to be nearly invulnerable. Their iron bodies imprison the spirits that drive them, and are susceptible only to weapons imbued with magic or the strength of adamantine.

Stone Golem

Stone golems display great variety in shape and form, cut and chiseled from stone to appear as tall, impressive statues. Though most bear humanoid features, stone golems can be carved in any form the sculptor can imagine. Ancient stone golems found in sealed tombs or flanking the gates of lost cities sometimes take the forms of giant beasts.

Like other golems, stone golems are nearly impervious to spells and ordinary weapons. Creatures that fight a stone golem can feel the ebb and flow of time slow down around them, almost as though they were made of stone themselves.

G

"THE MORE RIGID ITS PHYSICAL FORM, THE LESS LIKELY THE GOLEM IS TO LOSE ITS SENSE OF PURPOSE. THE CLAY ONES CAN BE A BIT TWITCHY."
—WORDS OF WARNING IN THE MANUAL OF CLAY GOLEMS

CLAY GOLEM
Large construct, unaligned

Armor Class 14 (natural armor)
Hit Points 133 (14d10 + 56)
Speed 20 ft.

STR	DEX	CON	INT	WIS	CHA
20 (+5)	9 (−1)	18 (+4)	3 (−4)	8 (−1)	1 (−5)

Damage Immunities acid, poison, psychic; bludgeoning, piercing, and slashing from nonmagical attacks not made with adamantine weapons
Condition Immunities charmed, exhaustion, frightened, paralyzed, petrified, poisoned
Senses darkvision 60 ft., passive Perception 9
Languages understands the languages of its creator but can't speak
Challenge 9 (5,000 XP)

Acid Absorption. Whenever the golem is subjected to acid damage, it takes no damage and instead regains a number of hit points equal to the acid damage dealt.

Berserk. Whenever the golem starts its turn with 60 hit points or fewer, roll a d6. On a 6, the golem goes berserk. On each of its turns while berserk, the golem attacks the nearest creature it can see. If no creature is near enough to move to and attack, the golem attacks an object, with preference for an object smaller than itself. Once the golem goes berserk, it continues to do so until it is destroyed or regains all its hit points.

Immutable Form. The golem is immune to any spell or effect that would alter its form.

Magic Resistance. The golem has advantage on saving throws against spells and other magical effects.

Magic Weapons. The golem's weapon attacks are magical.

ACTIONS

Multiattack. The golem makes two slam attacks.

Slam. *Melee Weapon Attack:* +8 to hit, reach 5 ft., one target. *Hit:* 16 (2d10 + 5) bludgeoning damage. If the target is a creature, it must succeed on a DC 15 Constitution saving throw or have its hit point maximum reduced by an amount equal to the damage taken. The target dies if this attack reduces its hit point maximum to 0. The reduction lasts until removed by the *greater restoration* spell or other magic.

Haste (Recharge 5–6). Until the end of its next turn, the golem magically gains a +2 bonus to its AC, has advantage on Dexterity saving throws, and can use its slam attack as a bonus action.

FLESH GOLEM
Medium construct, neutral

Armor Class 9
Hit Points 93 (11d8 + 44)
Speed 30 ft.

STR	DEX	CON	INT	WIS	CHA
19 (+4)	9 (−1)	18 (+4)	6 (−2)	10 (+0)	5 (−3)

Damage Immunities lightning, poison; bludgeoning, piercing, and slashing from nonmagical attacks not made with adamantine weapons
Condition Immunities charmed, exhaustion, frightened, paralyzed, petrified, poisoned
Senses darkvision 60 ft., passive Perception 10
Languages understands the languages of its creator but can't speak
Challenge 5 (1,800 XP)

Berserk. Whenever the golem starts its turn with 40 hit points or fewer, roll a d6. On a 6, the golem goes berserk. On each of its turns while berserk, the golem attacks the nearest creature it can see. If no creature is near enough to move to and attack, the golem attacks an object, with preference for an object smaller than itself. Once the golem goes berserk, it continues to do so until it is destroyed or regains all its hit points.

The golem's creator, if within 60 feet of the berserk golem, can try to calm it by speaking firmly and persuasively. The golem must be able to hear its creator, who must take an action to make a DC 15 Charisma (Persuasion) check. If the check succeeds, the golem ceases being berserk. If it takes damage while still at 40 hit points or fewer, the golem might go berserk again.

Aversion of Fire. If the golem takes fire damage, it has disadvantage on attack rolls and ability checks until the end of its next turn.

Immutable Form. The golem is immune to any spell or effect that would alter its form.

Lightning Absorption. Whenever the golem is subjected to lightning damage, it takes no damage and instead regains a number of hit points equal to the lightning damage dealt.

Magic Resistance. The golem has advantage on saving throws against spells and other magical effects.

Magic Weapons. The golem's weapon attacks are magical.

ACTIONS

Multiattack. The golem makes two slam attacks.

Slam. *Melee Weapon Attack:* +7 to hit, reach 5 ft., one target. *Hit:* 13 (2d8 + 4) bludgeoning damage.

Iron Golem
Large construct, unaligned

Armor Class 20 (natural armor)
Hit Points 210 (20d10 + 100)
Speed 30 ft.

STR	DEX	CON	INT	WIS	CHA
24 (+7)	9 (−1)	20 (+5)	3 (−4)	11 (+0)	1 (−5)

Damage Immunities fire, poison, psychic; bludgeoning, piercing, and slashing from nonmagical attacks not made with adamantine weapons
Condition Immunities charmed, exhaustion, frightened, paralyzed, petrified, poisoned
Senses darkvision 120 ft., passive Perception 10
Languages understands the languages of its creator but can't speak
Challenge 16 (15,000 XP)

Fire Absorption. Whenever the golem is subjected to fire damage, it takes no damage and instead regains a number of hit points equal to the fire damage dealt.

Immutable Form. The golem is immune to any spell or effect that would alter its form.

Magic Resistance. The golem has advantage on saving throws against spells and other magical effects.

Magic Weapons. The golem's weapon attacks are magical.

Actions

Multiattack. The golem makes two melee attacks.

Slam. *Melee Weapon Attack:* +13 to hit, reach 5 ft., one target. *Hit:* 20 (3d8 + 7) bludgeoning damage.

Sword. *Melee Weapon Attack:* +13 to hit, reach 10 ft., one target. *Hit:* 23 (3d10 + 7) slashing damage.

Poison Breath (Recharge 6). The golem exhales poisonous gas in a 15-foot cone. Each creature in that area must make a DC 19 Constitution saving throw, taking 45 (10d8) poison damage on a failed save, or half as much damage on a successful one.

Stone Golem
Large construct, unaligned

Armor Class 17 (natural armor)
Hit Points 178 (17d10 + 85)
Speed 30 ft.

STR	DEX	CON	INT	WIS	CHA
22 (+6)	9 (−1)	20 (+5)	3 (−4)	11 (+0)	1 (−5)

Damage Immunities poison, psychic; bludgeoning, piercing, and slashing from nonmagical attacks not made with adamantine weapons
Condition Immunities charmed, exhaustion, frightened, paralyzed, petrified, poisoned
Senses darkvision 120 ft., passive Perception 10
Languages understands the languages of its creator but can't speak
Challenge 10 (5,900 XP)

Immutable Form. The golem is immune to any spell or effect that would alter its form.

Magic Resistance. The golem has advantage on saving throws against spells and other magical effects.

Magic Weapons. The golem's weapon attacks are magical.

Actions

Multiattack. The golem makes two slam attacks.

Slam. *Melee Weapon Attack:* +10 to hit, reach 5 ft., one target. *Hit:* 19 (3d8 + 6) bludgeoning damage.

Slow (Recharge 5–6). The golem targets one or more creatures it can see within 10 feet of it. Each target must make a DC 17 Wisdom saving throw against this magic. On a failed save, a target can't use reactions, its speed is halved, and it can't make more than one attack on its turn. In addition, the target can take either an action or a bonus action on its turn, not both. These effects last for 1 minute. A target can repeat the saving throw at the end of each of its turns, ending the effect on itself on a success.

Gorgon
Large monstrosity, unaligned

Armor Class 19 (natural armor)
Hit Points 114 (12d10 + 48)
Speed 40 ft.

STR	DEX	CON	INT	WIS	CHA
20 (+5)	11 (+0)	18 (+4)	2 (−4)	12 (+1)	7 (−2)

Skills Perception +4
Condition Immunities petrified
Senses darkvision 60 ft., passive Perception 14
Languages —
Challenge 5 (1,800 XP)

Trampling Charge. If the gorgon moves at least 20 feet straight toward a creature and then hits it with a gore attack on the same turn, that target must succeed on a DC 16 Strength saving throw or be knocked prone. If the target is prone, the gorgon can make one attack with its hooves against it as a bonus action.

Actions

Gore. *Melee Weapon Attack:* +8 to hit, reach 5 ft., one target. *Hit:* 18 (2d12 + 5) piercing damage.

Hooves. *Melee Weapon Attack:* +8 to hit, reach 5 ft., one target. *Hit:* 16 (2d10 + 5) bludgeoning damage.

Petrifying Breath (Recharge 5–6). The gorgon exhales petrifying gas in a 30-foot cone. Each creature in that area must succeed on a DC 13 Constitution saving throw. On a failed save, a target begins to turn to stone and is restrained. The restrained target must repeat the saving throw at the end of its next turn. On a success, the effect ends on the target. On a failure, the target is petrified until freed by the *greater restoration* spell or other magic.

Gorgon

Few creatures that encounter a gorgon live to tell about it. Its body is covered in iron plates, and its nostrils fume with green vapor.

Horrific Structure. A gorgon's iron plates range from steely black to gleaming silver, but this natural armor in no way hinders its movement or mobility. The oils of its body lubricate the armor. A sick or inactive gorgon gathers rust like fungus or mange. When a rusty gorgon moves, its plates squeal as they rub together.

Monstrous Predator. When a gorgon spots potential prey, it charges with a hideous clamor of metal on metal. When the gorgon hits, it pulverizes the foe and sends its sprawling, then tramples it to death with its cruel hooves. Faced with multiple foes, the gorgon exhales its deadly vapor to overcome the creatures it touches by turning them to stone. When it grows hungry, it smashes its petrified prey to rubble and uses its strong teeth to grind the stone into a powder that provides nourishment. The crisscrossing network of trampled trails and splintered trees that surrounds a gorgon lair is strewn with the uneaten fragments of its shattered foes.

allowing them to detect the presence of creatures and objects in their immediate vicinity. The creature's ability to manipulate electricity to sense and move also allow it to absorb lightning without harm.

Although solitary by nature, grells sometimes gather in small groups called covens.

Floating Ambushers. A grell prefers to ambush lone creatures or stragglers, hovering silently near the ceiling of a passage or cavern until a suitable target passes below, whereupon it descends quickly and wraps its tentacles around its prey. It then floats away to its lair with the paralyzed creature in its clutches.

Alien Devourers. Grell are alien predators that group other creatures into three categories: edibles, inedibles, and Great Eaters (those rare creatures that might prey on a grell). Grells have no compunction about attacking creatures they classify as edible, including humanoids. They tend to avoid bigger creatures that they have little hope of carrying away.

A grell will sometimes allow adventurers to wage war on the other monstrous inhabitants of the dungeon complex it calls home, staying out of the adventurers' way as they dispose of larger threats while waiting for the right time to strike.

"OUR INTREPID ROGUE CLIMBED UP THE SHAFT TO SECURE A ROPE. THERE WAS A GASP, AND THE ROPE FELL. WE NEVER SAW HER AGAIN."
—AN ADVENTURER'S ACCOUNT OF A GRELL ATTACK IN KHYBER, PUBLISHED IN THE KORRANBERG CHRONICLE

GRELL

A grell resembles a bulbous floating brain with a wide, sharp beak. Its ten long tentacles are made of hundreds of ring-shaped muscles sheathed in tough fibrous hide. Sharp barbs line the tip each tentacle and inject paralytic venom. The grell can partially retract its barbs into its tentacles to handle or manipulate objects it doesn't want to pierce or tear.

Grells have no eyes and floats by means of a sort of levitation. They have keen hearing, however, and their skin is sensitive to vibrations and electrical fields,

GRELL

Medium aberration, neutral evil

Armor Class 12
Hit Points 55 (10d8 + 10)
Speed 10 ft., fly 30 ft. (hover)

STR	DEX	CON	INT	WIS	CHA
15 (+2)	14 (+2)	13 (+1)	12 (+1)	11 (+0)	9 (−1)

Skills Perception +4, Stealth +6
Damage Immunities lightning
Condition Immunities blinded, prone
Senses blindsight 60 ft. (blind beyond this radius), passive Perception 14
Languages Grell
Challenge 3 (700 XP)

ACTIONS

Multiattack. The grell makes two attacks: one with its tentacles and one with its beak.

Tentacles. *Melee Weapon Attack:* +4 to hit, reach 10 ft., one creature. *Hit:* 7 (1d10 + 2) piercing damage, and the target must succeed on a DC 11 Constitution saving throw or be poisoned for 1 minute. The poisoned target is paralyzed, and it can repeat the saving throw at the end of each of its turns, ending the effect on a success.

The target is also grappled (escape DC 15). If the target is Medium or smaller, it is also restrained until this grapple ends. While grappling the target, the grell has advantage on attack rolls against it and can't use this attack against other targets. When the grell moves, any Medium or smaller target it is grappling moves with it.

Beak. *Melee Weapon Attack:* +4 to hit, reach 5 ft., one creature. *Hit:* 7 (2d4 + 2) piercing damage.

GRICK

Medium monstrosity, neutral

Armor Class 14 (natural armor)
Hit Points 27 (6d8)
Speed 30 ft., climb 30 ft.

STR	DEX	CON	INT	WIS	CHA
14 (+2)	14 (+2)	11 (+0)	3 (−4)	14 (+2)	5 (−3)

Damage Resistances bludgeoning, piercing, and slashing from nonmagical attacks
Senses darkvision 60 ft., passive Perception 12
Languages —
Challenge 2 (450 XP)

Stone Camouflage. The grick has advantage on Dexterity (Stealth) checks made to hide in rocky terrain.

ACTIONS

Multiattack. The grick makes one attack with its tentacles. If that attack hits, the grick can make one beak attack against the same target.

Tentacles. *Melee Weapon Attack:* +4 to hit, reach 5 ft., one target. *Hit:* 9 (2d6 + 2) slashing damage.

Beak. *Melee Weapon Attack:* +4 to hit, reach 5 ft., one target. *Hit:* 5 (1d6 + 2) piercing damage.

GRICK ALPHA

Large monstrosity, neutral

Armor Class 18 (natural armor)
Hit Points 75 (10d10 + 20)
Speed 30 ft., climb 30 ft.

STR	DEX	CON	INT	WIS	CHA
18 (+4)	16 (+3)	15 (+2)	4 (−3)	14 (+2)	9 (−1)

Damage Resistances bludgeoning, piercing, and slashing from nonmagical attacks
Senses darkvision 60 ft., passive Perception 12
Languages —
Challenge 7 (2,900 XP)

Stone Camouflage. The grick has advantage on Dexterity (Stealth) checks made to hide in rocky terrain.

ACTIONS

Multiattack. The grick makes two attacks: one with its tail and one with its tentacles. If it hits with its tentacles, the grick can make one beak attack against the same target.

Tail. *Melee Weapon Attack:* +7 to hit, reach 10 ft., one target. *Hit:* 11 (2d6 + 4) bludgeoning damage.

Tentacles. *Melee Weapon Attack:* +7 to hit, reach 10 ft., one target. *Hit:* 22 (4d8 + 4) slashing damage.

Beak. *Melee Weapon Attack:* +7 to hit, reach 10 ft., one target. *Hit:* 13 (2d8 + 4) piercing damage.

GRICK

The wormlike grick waits unseen, blending in with the rock of the caves and caverns it haunts. Only when prey comes near does it rear up, its four barbed tentacles unfurling to reveal its hungry, snapping beak.

Passive Predators. Gricks rarely hunt. Instead, they drag their rubbery bodies to places where creatures regularly pass, lurking out of sight amid rocky rubble and debris, squeezing into burrows, holes, or crevices, climbing up to ledges, or coiling around stalactites to drop on unwary prey. A grick consumes virtually anything that moves except for other gricks. It targets the nearest prey, grabbing a fallen creature with its tentacles and dragging it off to eat alone.

Roving Ambushers. Gricks remain in an area until the food supply dwindles, often because sentient creatures become aware of their presence and plot alternate routes around their lairs. When prey is scarce in the Underdark, gricks venture aboveground to hunt in the wilderness, lurking in trees or on cliff-side ledges. A grick pack is often led by a single well-fed, oversized alpha around which the others congregate.

Spoils of Slaughter. Over time, grick lairs accumulate the cast-off possessions of intelligent prey, and expert guides know to look out for these telltale signs. Underdark explorers sometimes seal off the routes leading to and from a grick lair to starve them, then claim the wealth of the foul creatures' victims.

Griffon

Griffons are ferocious avian carnivores with the muscular bodies of lions and the head, forelegs, and wings of eagles. When they attack, griffons are as swift and deadly as eagles, even as they strike with a lion's savage might and grace.

Horse Eaters. Griffons hunt in small prides, flying high over plains and forests near their rocky cliff-side aeries. Herd animals and horses are the prey they crave above all others, though they also hunt and kill hippogriffs. When it spots horses, a griffon screeches to alert its pride mates, which descend quickly toward their prey.

Those riding or herding horses dread the griffon's piercing cry, preparing themselves for the bloody fight that inevitably follows. A griffon ignores a horse's rider when possible, and a rider that abandons its mount, or a herder that releases one or two horses, can escape unharmed while the griffon targets its chosen prey. Riders who attempt to protect their horses attract the full fury of an attacking griffon.

Sky Dwellers. Griffons lair in high rocky clifftop aeries, building their nests from sticks, leaves, and the bones of their prey. Once griffons establish a territory, they remain in that area until the food supply has been exhausted.

Aggressive and territorial, griffons engage in brutal aerial combat to defend their aeries, tearing and shredding the wings of flying intruders to send them spiraling to the ground. Creatures that climb to a griffon's lair are plucked from the cliffs and eaten, or are knocked from the heights to go tumbling to their deaths.

Trained Mounts. A griffon raised from an egg can be trained to serve as a mount. However, such training is time consuming, expensive (mostly for the ample food the creature requires), and dangerous. Expert trainers well versed in the griffon's legendary ferocity are typically the only ones able to raise these creatures safely.

Once trained, a griffon is a fierce and loyal steed. It bonds with one master for life, fighting to the death to protect that rider. A griffon mount retains its ravenous appetite for horseflesh, and a wise master ensures that a griffon remains satiated with other prey when passing through civilized lands.

Griffon
Large monstrosity, unaligned

Armor Class 12
Hit Points 59 (7d10 + 21)
Speed 30 ft., fly 80 ft.

STR	DEX	CON	INT	WIS	CHA
18 (+4)	15 (+2)	16 (+3)	2 (−4)	13 (+1)	8 (−1)

Skills Perception +5
Senses darkvision 60 ft., passive Perception 15
Languages —
Challenge 2 (450 XP)

Keen Sight. The griffon has advantage on Wisdom (Perception) checks that rely on sight.

Actions

Multiattack. The griffon makes two attacks: one with its beak and one with its claws.

Beak. *Melee Weapon Attack:* +6 to hit, reach 5 ft., one target. *Hit:* 8 (1d8 + 4) piercing damage.

Claws. *Melee Weapon Attack:* +6 to hit, reach 5 ft., one target. *Hit:* 11 (2d6 + 4) slashing damage.

G

Grimlock

The degenerate subterranean grimlocks were once human, but their worship of the mind flayers over generations of prowling the Underdark transformed them into blind, monstrous cannibals long ago.

Debased Cultists. The empire of the mind flayers once spread across many worlds, enslaving countless races. Among those were human cultures whose high priests the mind flayers subverted using their insidious powers of thought control. Those leaders gradually turned the faiths of their followers toward the illithids, which they worshiped as blasphemous deities.

Over time, the rituals of these enslaved humans created fervent cannibal cults that regarded the brain eating of the mind flayers as a holy sacrament. The illithids commanded their worshipers to abduct other sentient creatures to be sacrificed. After the victims' brains had been consumed, the mind flayers gave the lifeless bodies to the cultists.

Blind Hunters. When the rule of the mind flayers crumbled, their cults faced constant warfare from their enemies, the same creatures that had once been their victims. The cults fled into the Underdark domains of their illithid gods. Over generations in that lightless realm, the cultists learned to rely on their other senses for survival. In time, their eyes withered away and eyelids sealed, leaving only covered eye sockets behind.

A grimlock's ears prick up at the faintest footfall or whisper echoing down stone passageways. It can speak in tones too low for most other humanoids to hear. The odors of sweat, flesh, and blood awaken its hunger, and it can track by such scents like a bloodhound. To enhance their senses, grimlocks leave trails of blood, piles of dung, or the viscera of slain prey in places far from their lairs. When intruders pass through those areas, they carry the foul scents with them, warning the grimlocks of their approach.

For most creatures, blindness is an enormous hindrance. For a grimlock with its other heightened senses, sightlessness is a boon. A grimlock isn't fooled by visual illusions or misperceptions. It is fearless as it stalks prey.

Endless War. Grimlocks still venerate the mind flayers, serving them whenever possible. Grimlocks also recall the war in which they were driven underground. To them, it has never ended. They continue to return to the surface world to abduct captives for their illithid masters.

Grimlock

Medium humanoid (grimlock), neutral evil

Armor Class 11
Hit Points 11 (2d8 + 2)
Speed 30 ft.

STR	DEX	CON	INT	WIS	CHA
16 (+3)	12 (+1)	12 (+1)	9 (−1)	8 (−1)	6 (−2)

Skills Athletics +5, Perception +3, Stealth +3
Condition Immunities blinded
Senses blindsight 30 ft. or 10 ft. while deafened (blind beyond this radius), passive Perception 13
Languages Undercommon
Challenge 1/4 (50 XP)

Blind Senses. The grimlock can't use its blindsight while deafened and unable to smell.

Keen Hearing and Smell. The grimlock has advantage on Wisdom (Perception) checks that rely on hearing or smell.

Stone Camouflage. The grimlock has advantage on Dexterity (Stealth) checks made to hide in rocky terrain.

Actions

Spiked Bone Club. *Melee Weapon Attack:* +5 to hit, reach 5 ft., one target. *Hit:* 5 (1d4 + 3) bludgeoning damage plus 2 (1d4) piercing damage.

Hags

Hags represent all that is evil and cruel. Though they resemble withered crones, there is nothing mortal about these monstrous creatures, whose forms reflect only the wickedness in their hearts.

Faces of Evil. Ancient beings with origins in the Feywild, hags are cankers on the mortal world. Their withered faces are framed by long, frayed hair, horrid moles and warts dot their blotchy skin, and their long, skinny fingers are tipped by claws that can slice open flesh with a touch. Their simple clothes are always tattered and filthy.

All hags possess magical powers, and some have an affinity for spellcasting. They can alter their forms or curse their foes, and their arrogance inspires them to view their magic as a challenge to the magic of the gods, whom they blaspheme at every opportunity.

Hag Covens

When hags must work together, they form covens, in spite of their selfish natures. A coven is made up of hags of any type, all of whom are equals within the group. However, each of the hags continues to desire more personal power.

A coven consists of three hags so that any arguments between two hags can be settled by the third. If more than three hags ever come together, as might happen if two covens come into conflict, the result is usually chaos.

Shared Spellcasting. While all three members of a hag coven are within 30 feet of one another, they can each cast the following spells from the wizard's spell list but must share the spell slots among themselves:

1st level (4 slots): *identify, ray of sickness*
2nd level (3 slots): *hold person, locate object*
3rd level (3 slots): *bestow curse, counterspell, lightning bolt*
4th level (3 slots): *phantasmal killer, polymorph*
5th level (2 slots): *contact other plane, scrying*
6th level (1 slot): *eyebite*

For casting these spells, each hag is a 12th-level spellcaster that uses Intelligence as her spellcasting ability. The spell save DC is 12 + the hag's Intelligence modifier, and the spell attack bonus is 4 + the hag's Intelligence modifier.

Hag Eye. A hag coven can craft a magic item called a *hag eye*, which is made from a real eye coated in varnish and often fitted to a pendant or other wearable item. The *hag eye* is usually entrusted to a minion for safekeeping and transport. A hag in the coven can take an action to see what the *hag eye* sees if the *hag eye* is on the same plane of existence. A *hag eye* has AC 10, 1 hit point, and darkvision with a radius of 60 feet. If it is destroyed, each coven member takes 3d10 psychic damage and is blinded for 24 hours.

A hag coven can have only one *hag eye* at a time, and creating a new one requires all three members of the coven to perform a ritual. The ritual takes 1 hour, and the hags can't perform it while blinded. During the ritual, if the hags take any action other than performing the ritual, they must start over.

Hags name themselves in darkly whimsical ways, claiming monikers such as Black Morwen, Peggy Pigknuckle, Grandmother Titchwillow, Nanna Shug, Rotten Ethel, or Auntie Wormtooth.

Monstrous Motherhood. Hags propagate by snatching and devouring human infants. After stealing a baby from its cradle or its mother's womb, the hag consumes the poor child. A week later, the hag gives birth to a daughter who looks human until her thirteenth birthday, whereupon the child transforms into the spitting image of her hag mother.

Hags sometimes raise the daughters they spawn, creating covens. A hag might also return the child to its grieving parents, only to watch from the shadows as the child grows up to become a horror.

Dark Bargains. Arrogant to a fault, hags believe themselves to be the most cunning of creatures, and they treat all others as inferior. Even so, a hag is open to dealing with mortals as long as those mortals show the proper respect and deference. Over their long lives, hags accumulate much knowledge of local lore, dark creatures, and magic, which they are pleased to sell.

Hags enjoy watching mortals bring about their own downfall, and a bargain with a hag is always dangerous. The terms of such bargains typically involve demands to compromise principles or give up something dear—especially if the thing lost diminishes or negates the knowledge gained through the bargain.

A Foul Nature. Hags love the macabre and festoon their garb with dead things and accentuate their appearance with bones, bits of flesh, and filth. They nurture blemishes and pick at wounds to produce weeping, suppurating flesh. Attractive creatures evoke disgust in a hag, which might "help" such creatures by disfiguring or transforming them.

This embrace of the disturbing and unpleasant extends to all aspects of a hag's life. A hag might fly in a magical giant's skull, landing it on a tree shaped to resemble an enormous headless body. Another might travel with a menagerie of monsters and slaves kept in cages, and disguised by illusions to lure unwary creatures close. Hags sharpen their teeth on millstones and spin cloth from the intestines of their victims, reacting with glee to the horror their actions invoke.

Dark Sorority. Hags maintain contact with each other and share knowledge. Through such contacts, it is likely that any given hag knows of every other hag in existence. Hags don't like each other, but they abide by an ageless code of conduct. Hags announce their presence before crossing into another hag's territory, bring gifts when entering another hag's dwelling, and break no oaths given to other hags—as long as the oath isn't given with the fingers crossed.

Some humanoids make the mistake of thinking that the hags' rules of conduct apply to all creatures. When confronted by such an individual, a hag might find it amusing to string the fool along for a while before teaching it a permanent lesson.

Dark Lairs. Hags dwell in dark and twisted woods, bleak moors, storm-lashed seacoasts, and gloomy swamps. In time, the landscape around a hag's lair reflects the creature's noxiousness, such that the land itself can attack and kill trespassers. Trees twisted by darkness attack passersby, while vines snake through the undergrowth to snare and drag off creatures one at a time. Foul stinking fogs turn the air to poison, and conceal pools of quicksand and sinkholes that consume unwary wanderers.

Green Hag

The wretched and hateful green hags dwell in dying forests, lonely swamps, and misty moors, making their homes in caves. Green hags love to manipulate other creatures into doing their bidding, masking their intentions behind layers of deception. They lure victims to them by mimicking voices calling out for help, or drive unwanted visitors away by imitating the cries of fierce beasts.

Obsession with Tragedy. Green hags revel in the failings and tragedies of other creatures. They derive joy from bringing people low and seeing hope turn into despair, not just for individuals but also for whole nations.

Covens. A green hag that is part of a coven (see the "Hag Covens" sidebar) has a challenge rating of 5 (1,800 XP).

Green Hag
Medium fey, neutral evil

Armor Class 17 (natural armor)
Hit Points 82 (11d8 + 33)
Speed 30 ft.

STR	DEX	CON	INT	WIS	CHA
18 (+4)	12 (+1)	16 (+3)	13 (+1)	14 (+2)	14 (+2)

Skills Arcana +3, Deception +4, Perception +4, Stealth +3
Senses darkvision 60 ft., passive Perception 14
Languages Common, Draconic, Sylvan
Challenge 3 (700 XP)

Amphibious. The hag can breathe air and water.

Innate Spellcasting. The hag's innate spellcasting ability is Charisma (spell save DC 12). She can innately cast the following spells, requiring no material components:

At will: *dancing lights, minor illusion, vicious mockery*

Mimicry. The hag can mimic animal sounds and humanoid voices. A creature that hears the sounds can tell they are imitations with a successful DC 14 Wisdom (Insight) check.

Actions

Claws. *Melee Weapon Attack:* +6 to hit, reach 5 ft., one target. *Hit:* 13 (2d8 + 4) slashing damage.

Illusory Appearance. The hag covers herself and anything she is wearing or carrying with a magical illusion that makes her look like another creature of her general size and humanoid shape. The illusion ends if the hag takes a bonus action to end it or if she dies.

The changes wrought by this effect fail to hold up to physical inspection. For example, the hag could appear to have smooth skin, but someone touching her would feel her rough flesh. Otherwise, a creature must take an action to visually inspect the illusion and succeed on a DC 20 Intelligence (Investigation) check to discern that the hag is disguised.

Invisible Passage. The hag magically turns invisible until she attacks or casts a spell, or until her concentration ends (as if concentrating on a spell). While invisible, she leaves no physical evidence of her passage, so she can be tracked only by magic. Any equipment she wears or carries is invisible with her.

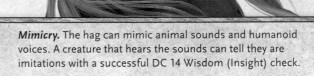

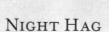

Night Hag

Sly and subversive, night hags want to see the virtuous turn to villainy: love turned into obsession, kindness turned to hate, devotion to disregard, and generosity to selfishness. Night hags take perverse joy in corrupting mortals.

Night hags were once creatures of the Feywild, but their foulness saw them exiled to Hades long ago, where they degenerated into fiends. The night hags have long since spread across the Lower Planes.

Soulmongers. While a humanoid sleeps, a night hag can straddle the person ethereally and intrude upon its dreams. Any creature with truesight can see the hag's spectral form straddling its prey. The ethereal hag fills her victim's head with doubts and fears, in the hope of tricking it into performing evil acts in the waking world. The hag continues her nightly visitations until the victim finally expires in its sleep. If the hag has driven her victim to commit evil deeds, she traps its corrupted soul in her *soul bag* (see the "Night Hag Items" sidebar) for transport to Hades.

Covens. A night hag that is part of a coven (see the "Hag Covens" sidebar) has a challenge rating of 7 (2,900 XP).

Night Hag

Medium fiend, neutral evil

Armor Class 17 (natural armor)
Hit Points 112 (15d8 + 45)
Speed 30 ft.

STR	DEX	CON	INT	WIS	CHA
18 (+4)	15 (+2)	16 (+3)	16 (+3)	14 (+2)	16 (+3)

Skills Deception +7, Insight +6, Perception +6, Stealth +6
Damage Resistances cold, fire; bludgeoning, piercing, and slashing from nonmagical attacks not made with silvered weapons
Condition Immunities charmed
Senses darkvision 120 ft., passive Perception 16
Languages Abyssal, Common, Infernal, Primordial
Challenge 5 (1,800 XP)

Innate Spellcasting. The hag's innate spellcasting ability is Charisma (spell save DC 14, +6 to hit with spell attacks). She can innately cast the following spells, requiring no material components:

At will: *detect magic, magic missile*
2/day each: *plane shift* (self only), *ray of enfeeblement, sleep*

Magic Resistance. The hag has advantage on saving throws against spells and other magical effects.

Actions

Claws (Hag Form Only). *Melee Weapon Attack:* +7 to hit, reach 5 ft., one target. *Hit:* 13 (2d8 + 4) slashing damage.

Change Shape. The hag magically polymorphs into a Small or Medium female humanoid, or back into her true form. Her statistics are the same in each form. Any equipment she is wearing or carrying isn't transformed. She reverts to her true form if she dies.

Etherealness. The hag magically enters the Ethereal Plane from the Material Plane, or vice versa. To do so, the hag must have a *heartstone* in her possession.

Nightmare Haunting (1/Day). While on the Ethereal Plane, the hag magically touches a sleeping humanoid on the Material Plane. A *protection from evil and good* spell cast on the target prevents this contact, as does a *magic circle*. As long as the contact persists, the target has dreadful visions. If these visions last for at least 1 hour, the target gains no benefit from its rest, and its hit point maximum is reduced by 5 (1d10). If this effect reduces the target's hit point maximum to 0, the target dies, and if the target was evil, its soul is trapped in the hag's *soul bag*. The reduction to the target's hit point maximum lasts until removed by the *greater restoration* spell or similar magic.

NIGHT HAG ITEMS

A night hag carries two very rare magic items that she must craft for herself. If either object is lost, the night hag will go to great lengths to retrieve it, as creating a new tool takes time and effort.

Heartstone. This lustrous black gem allows a night hag to become ethereal while it is in her possession. The touch of a *heartstone* also cures any disease. Crafting a *heartstone* takes 30 days.

Soul Bag. When an evil humanoid dies as a result of a night hag's Nightmare Haunting, the hag catches the soul in this black sack made of stitched flesh. A *soul bag* can hold only one evil soul at a time, and only the night hag who crafted the bag can catch a soul with it. Crafting a *soul bag* takes 7 days and a humanoid sacrifice (whose flesh is used to make the bag).

SEA HAG

Sea hags live in dismal and polluted underwater lairs, surrounded by merrow and other aquatic monsters.

Beauty drives a sea hag to fits of anger. When confronted with something beautiful, the hag might simply attack it or deface it. If something beautiful gives hope, a sea hag wants it to cause despair. If it inspires courage, the sea hag wants it to cause fear.

Ugly Inside and Out. Sea hags are by far the ugliest of all hags, with slimy scales covering their pallid skin. A sea hag's hair resembles seaweed and covers her emaciated body, and her glassy eyes seem as lifeless as a doll's. Although a sea hag can hide her true form under a veil of illusion, the hag is cursed to forever appear ugly. Her illusory form appears haggard at best.

Covens. A sea hag that is part of a coven (see the "Hag Covens" sidebar) has a challenge rating of 4 (1,100 XP).

SEA HAG

Medium fey, chaotic evil

Armor Class 14 (natural armor)
Hit Points 52 (7d8 + 21)
Speed 30 ft., swim 40 ft.

STR	DEX	CON	INT	WIS	CHA
16 (+3)	13 (+1)	16 (+3)	12 (+1)	12 (+1)	13 (+1)

Senses darkvision 60 ft., passive Perception 11
Languages Aquan, Common, Giant
Challenge 2 (450 XP)

Amphibious. The hag can breathe air and water.

Horrific Appearance. Any humanoid that starts its turn within 30 feet of the hag and can see the hag's true form must make a DC 11 Wisdom saving throw. On a failed save, the creature is frightened for 1 minute. A creature can repeat the saving throw at the end of each of its turns, with disadvantage if the hag is within line of sight, ending the effect on itself on a success. If a creature's saving throw is successful or the effect ends for it, the creature is immune to the hag's Horrific Appearance for the next 24 hours.

Unless the target is surprised or the revelation of the hag's true form is sudden, the target can avert its eyes and avoid making the initial saving throw. Until the start of its next turn, a creature that averts its eyes has disadvantage on attack rolls against the hag.

ACTIONS

Claws. *Melee Weapon Attack:* +5 to hit, reach 5 ft., one target. *Hit:* 10 (2d6 + 3) slashing damage.

Death Glare. The hag targets one frightened creature she can see within 30 feet of her. If the target can see the hag, it must succeed on a DC 11 Wisdom saving throw against this magic or drop to 0 hit points.

Illusory Appearance. The hag covers herself and anything she is wearing or carrying with a magical illusion that makes her look like an ugly creature of her general size and humanoid shape. The effect ends if the hag takes a bonus action to end it or if she dies.

The changes wrought by this effect fail to hold up to physical inspection. For example, the hag could appear to have no claws, but someone touching her hand might feel the claws. Otherwise, a creature must take an action to visually inspect the illusion and succeed on a DC 16 Intelligence (Investigation) check to discern that the hag is disguised.

HALF-DRAGON

When a dragon in polymorphed form mates with another creature, the union sometimes produces half-dragon offspring. A creature might also transform into a half-dragon as a result of a mad wizard's spell or a ritual bath in dragon's blood. In all these cases, the result is a creature that combines the essence of a dragon with the form of its original race. Regardless of origin, all half-dragons have similar appearances and special abilities.

Draconic Nature. Half-dragons can't procreate. Those that wish to do so must almost always resort to magic. By way of compensation, half-dragons are blessed with long life. A typical half-dragon's life span is twice that of its nondraconic line, so that a half-dragon human might live more than a century and a half.

Half-dragons inherit personality traits common to their draconic heritage. For example, half-gold dragons are often shy and secretive, while half-copper dragons are impish and playful. Half-green dragons are deceitful, while half-white dragons are often dim-witted brutes. These traits are tempered by a half-dragon's other lineage, but greed, arrogance, and paranoia are qualities that even good-aligned half-dragons often possess.

HALF-DRAGON TEMPLATE

A beast, humanoid, giant, or monstrosity can become a half-dragon. It keeps its statistics, except as follows.

Challenge. To avoid recalculating the creature's challenge rating, apply the template only to a creature that meets the optional prerequisite in the Breath Weapon table below. Otherwise, use the guidelines in the *Dungeon Master's Guide* to recalculate the rating after you apply the template.

Senses. The half-dragon gains blindsight with a radius of 10 feet and darkvision with a radius of 60 feet.

Resistances. The half-dragon gains resistance to a type of damage based on its color.

Color	Damage Resistance
Black or copper	Acid
Blue or bronze	Lightning
Brass, gold, or red	Fire
Green	Poison
Silver or white	Cold

Languages. The half-dragon speaks Draconic, in addition to any other languages it knows.

New Action: Breath Weapon. The half-dragon has the breath weapon of its dragon half. The half-dragon's size determines how this action functions.

Size	Breath Weapon	Optional Prerequisite
Large or smaller	As a wyrmling	Challenge 2 or higher
Huge	As a young dragon	Challenge 7 or higher
Gargantuan	As an adult dragon	Challenge 8 or higher

SAMPLE HALF-DRAGON

Here the half-dragon template has been applied to a human veteran who wears plate armor.

HALF-RED DRAGON VETERAN

Medium humanoid (human), any alignment

Armor Class 18 (plate)
Hit Points 65 (10d8 + 20)
Speed 30 ft.

STR	DEX	CON	INT	WIS	CHA
16 (+3)	13 (+1)	14 (+2)	10 (+0)	11 (+0)	10 (+0)

Skills Athletics +5, Perception +2
Damage Resistances fire
Senses blindsight 10 ft., darkvision 60 ft., passive Perception 12
Languages Common, Draconic
Challenge 5 (1,800 XP)

ACTIONS

Multiattack. The veteran makes two longsword attacks. If it has a shortsword drawn, it can also make a shortsword attack.

Longsword. *Melee Weapon Attack:* +5 to hit, reach 5 ft., one target. *Hit:* 7 (1d8 + 3) slashing damage, or 8 (1d10 + 3) slashing damage if used with two hands.

Shortsword. *Melee Weapon Attack:* +5 to hit, reach 5 ft., one target. *Hit:* 6 (1d6 + 3) piercing damage.

Heavy Crossbow. *Ranged Weapon Attack:* +3 to hit, range 100/400 ft., one target. *Hit:* 6 (1d10 + 1) piercing damage.

Fire Breath (Recharge 5–6). The veteran exhales fire in a 15-foot cone. Each creature in that area must make a DC 15 Dexterity saving throw, taking 24 (7d6) fire damage on a failed save, or half as much damage on a successful one.

H

Harpy

Taking glee in suffering and death, the sadistic harpy is always on the hunt for prey. Its sweet song has lured countless adventurers to their deaths, drawing them in close for the harpy to kill and then consume.

A harpy combines the body, legs, and wings of a vulture with the torso, arms, and head of a human. Its wicked talons and bone club make it a formidable threat in combat, and its eyes reflect the absolute evil of its soul.

Divine Curse. Long ago, an elf wandering a forest heard birdsong so pure and wholesome that she was moved to tears. Following the music, she came upon a clearing where stood a handsome elf youth who had also paused to hear the bird's song. This was Fenmarel Mestarine, a reclusive elf god. His divine presence stole her heart as he fled, vanishing into the woods as if he was never there.

Though the elf searched the woods and called for her stranger, she found no sign of his passage. Driven to despair by her longing, she begged the gods to help her. Aerdrie Faenya, elf goddess of the sky, heard the elf's cries and was moved to her aid. She appeared as the bird whose song had entranced the outcast god, then taught that song of beauty and seduction to the elf.

When her singing failed to draw Fenmarel Mestarine to her side, the elf cursed the gods, invoking a dreadful power and transforming her into the first harpy. The curse worked its magic on the elf's spirit as well as her body, turning her desire for love into a hunger for flesh, even as her beautiful song continued to draw creatures to her deadly embrace.

Harpy Song. To hear a harpy's song is to hear music more beautiful than anything else in the world. A traveler that succumbs to the entrancing effect of that singing is compelled to blunder toward its source. A harpy sometimes charms victims before it attacks, but a more effective use of its song is to lure prey over cliffs, into bogs and quicksand, or into deadly pits. Creatures trapped or incapacitated then become easy targets for the harpy's wrath.

Sadistic Cowards. Harpies haunt bleak coastal cliffs and other places hazardous to non-flying creatures. Harpies have no interest in a fair fight, and they never attack unless they have a clear advantage. If a fight turns against a harpy, it lacks the cunning to adapt and will flee and go hungry rather than risk straight-up combat.

When they attack, harpies play with their food, delighting in the "music" their victims make as they scream. A harpy takes its time dismembering a helpless foe and can spend days torturing a victim before the merciful end.

Gruesome Collectors. Harpies take shiny baubles, valuable objects, and other trophies from their victims, sometimes fighting with each other for the right to claim the choicest prizes. When no valuable objects can be found, a harpy takes hair, bones, or body parts to line its nest. A harpy's lair is usually hidden in remote ruins, where adventurers can discover valuable treasure and magic hidden beneath foul piles of offal.

Harpy

Medium monstrosity, chaotic evil

Armor Class 11
Hit Points 38 (7d8 + 7)
Speed 20 ft., fly 40 ft.

STR	DEX	CON	INT	WIS	CHA
12 (+1)	13 (+1)	12 (+1)	7 (−2)	10 (+0)	13 (+1)

Senses passive Perception 10
Languages Common
Challenge 1 (200 XP)

Actions

Multiattack. The harpy makes two attacks: one with its claws and one with its club.

Claws. *Melee Weapon Attack:* +3 to hit, reach 5 ft., one target. *Hit:* 6 (2d4 + 1) slashing damage.

Club. *Melee Weapon Attack:* +3 to hit, reach 5 ft., one target. *Hit:* 3 (1d4 + 1) bludgeoning damage.

Luring Song. The harpy sings a magical melody. Every humanoid and giant within 300 feet of the harpy that can hear the song must succeed on a DC 11 Wisdom saving throw or be charmed until the song ends. The harpy must take a bonus action on its subsequent turns to continue singing. It can stop singing at any time. The song ends if the harpy is incapacitated.

While charmed by the harpy, a target is incapacitated and ignores the songs of other harpies. If the charmed target is more than 5 feet away from the harpy, the target must move on its turn toward the harpy by the most direct route, trying to get within 5 feet. It doesn't avoid opportunity attacks, but before moving into damaging terrain, such as lava or a pit, and whenever it takes damage from a source other than the harpy, the target can repeat the saving throw. A charmed target can also repeat the saving throw at the end of each of its turns. If the saving throw is successful, the effect ends on it.

A target that successfully saves is immune to this harpy's song for the next 24 hours.

Hell Hound

Monstrous, fire-breathing fiends that take the form of powerful dogs, hell hounds are found on the battlefields of Acheron and throughout the Lower Planes. On the Material Plane, hell hounds are most commonly seen in service to devils, fire giants, and other evil creatures that use them as guard animals and companions.

Burning Hunger. Hell hounds hunt in packs, feeding on any creature that appears edible. They avoid potentially dangerous foes in favor of targeting the weakest prey with their savage bite and fiery breath, demonstrating a relentless determination as they pursue that prey to the bitter end.

When hell hounds feed, the flesh they consume stokes the infernal fires that burn within them. When a hell hound dies, that fire consumes the creature's remains in a billowing eruption of smoke and blazing embers, leaving nothing behind but scorched tufts of black fur.

Evil to the Core. Hell hounds are smarter than mundane beasts, and their lawful nature makes them good at following orders. However, a hell hound's evil disposition means that the creature can't be trained to be anything other than a ruthless killer. If a hell hound isn't allowed to indulge its malevolent hunger, it quickly abandons or turns against its master.

Hell Hound
Medium fiend, lawful evil

Armor Class 15 (natural armor)
Hit Points 45 (7d8 + 14)
Speed 50 ft.

STR	DEX	CON	INT	WIS	CHA
17 (+3)	12 (+1)	14 (+2)	6 (−2)	13 (+1)	6 (−2)

Skills Perception +5
Damage Immunities fire
Senses darkvision 60 ft., passive Perception 15
Languages understands Infernal but can't speak it
Challenge 3 (700 XP)

Keen Hearing and Smell. The hound has advantage on Wisdom (Perception) checks that rely on hearing or smell.

Pack Tactics. The hound has advantage on an attack roll against a creature if at least one of the hound's allies is within 5 feet of the creature and the ally isn't incapacitated.

Actions

Bite. *Melee Weapon Attack:* +5 to hit, reach 5 ft., one target. *Hit:* 7 (1d8 + 3) piercing damage plus 7 (2d6) fire damage.

Fire Breath (Recharge 5–6). The hound exhales fire in a 15-foot cone. Each creature in that area must make a DC 12 Dexterity saving throw, taking 21 (6d6) fire damage on a failed save, or half as much damage on a successful one.

Helmed Horror

This construct possesses intelligence, the ability to reason and adjust its tactics, and an unswerving devotion to its maker that persists even after its maker's demise. Resembling an animated suit of empty plate armor, a helmed horror serves without ambition or emotion.

Magical Purpose. Though it takes more magical resources to create a helmed horror than a lesser suit of animated armor, the helmed horror requires less direction and maintenance as it carries out its appointed tasks. A helmed horror follows its orders with complete loyalty, and is intelligent enough to understand the difference between an order's intent and its exact wording. Unlike many constructs, it seeks to fulfill the former rather than slavishly follow the latter.

Tactical Cunning. A helmed horror fights with the cunning of a skilled warrior, taking to the air as it attacks weaker characters and spellcasters first. However, a helmed horror lacks the insight to change its environment, fortify it, or otherwise take active measures to improve its defensive position.

Constructed Nature. A helmed horror doesn't require air, food, drink, or sleep.

Helmed Horror
Medium construct, neutral

Armor Class 20 (plate, shield)
Hit Points 60 (8d8 + 24)
Speed 30 ft., fly 30 ft.

STR	DEX	CON	INT	WIS	CHA
18 (+4)	13 (+1)	16 (+3)	10 (+0)	10 (+0)	10 (+0)

Skills Perception +4
Damage Resistances bludgeoning, piercing, and slashing from nonmagical attacks not made with adamantine weapons
Damage Immunities force, necrotic, poison
Condition Immunities blinded, charmed, deafened, frightened, paralyzed, petrified, poisoned, stunned
Senses blindsight 60 ft. (blind beyond this radius), passive Perception 14
Languages understands the languages of its creator but can't speak
Challenge 4 (1,100 XP)

Magic Resistance. The helmed horror has advantage on saving throws against spells and other magical effects.

Spell Immunity. The helmed horror is immune to three spells chosen by its creator. Typical immunities include *fireball*, *heat metal*, and *lightning bolt*.

Actions

Multiattack. The helmed horror makes two longsword attacks.

Longsword. *Melee Weapon Attack:* +6 to hit, reach 5 ft., one target. *Hit:* 8 (1d8 + 4) slashing damage, or 9 (1d10 + 4) slashing damage if used with two hands.

Hippogriff

A beast whose magical origins are lost to history, a hippogriff possesses the wings and forelimbs of an eagle, the hindquarters of a horse, and a head that combines the features of both animals.

Reclusive and omnivorous, hippogriffs mate for life and seldom venture more than a few miles from their nest. When defending its mate or its young, a hippogriff fights to the death. Hippogriffs don't lay eggs but give birth to live young.

Dragons, griffons, and wyverns have a taste for hippogriff meat and frequently prey on these creatures.

Flying Mounts. A hippogriff raised in captivity can be trained to be a faithful companion and mount. Of all the creatures that can serve as flying mounts, hippogriffs are among the easiest to train and the most loyal once trained properly.

HIPPOGRIFF
Large monstrosity, unaligned

Armor Class 11
Hit Points 19 (3d10 + 3)
Speed 40 ft., fly 60 ft.

STR	DEX	CON	INT	WIS	CHA
17 (+3)	13 (+1)	13 (+1)	2 (−4)	12 (+1)	8 (−1)

Skills Perception +5
Senses passive Perception 15
Languages —
Challenge 1 (200 XP)

Keen Sight. The hippogriff has advantage on Wisdom (Perception) checks that rely on sight.

ACTIONS

Multiattack. The hippogriff makes two attacks: one with its beak and one with its claws.

Beak. *Melee Weapon Attack:* +5 to hit, reach 5 ft., one target. *Hit:* 8 (1d10 + 3) piercing damage.

Claws. *Melee Weapon Attack:* +5 to hit, reach 5 ft., one target. *Hit:* 10 (2d6 + 3) slashing damage.

HOBGOBLINS

War horns sound, stones fly from catapults, and the thunder of a thousand booted feet echoes across the land as hobgoblins march to battle. Across the borderlands of civilization, settlements and settlers must contend with these aggressive humanoids, whose thirst for conquest is never satisfied.

Hobgoblins have dark orange or red-orange skin, and hair ranging from dark red-brown to dark gray. Yellow or dark brown eyes peer out beneath their beetling brows, and their wide mouths sport sharp and yellowed teeth. A male hobgoblin might have a large blue or red nose, which symbolizes virility and power among goblinkin. Hobgoblins can live as long as humans, though their love of warfare and battle means that few do.

Goblinoids. Hobgoblins belong to a family of creatures called goblinoids. They are often found lording over their cousins, the smaller goblins and the ferocious bugbears.

Martial Might. A hobgoblin measures virtue by physical strength and martial prowess, caring about nothing except the opportunity to demonstrate skill and cunning in battle. Hobgoblins of high military rank attain their positions by force, then hold those positions by imposing their authority through draconian measures.

Hobgoblins train to fight with a variety of weapons, and have great skill at crafting arms, armor, siege engines, and other military devices. Organized and disciplined, they take exceptional care of their weapons, armor, and personal possessions. They favor the bold colors associated with their tribes, and trim their often-elaborate uniforms with blood-red piping and leather dyed black.

Military Legions. Hobgoblins organize themselves into tribal bands known as legions. In their martial society, every hobgoblin has a rank, from the powerful leaders and champions, to the rank-and-file foot soldiers, to the goblins that find themselves driven into the front lines at spear point. A legion is headed by a warlord with several captains serving under its command. A hobgoblin warlord is a ruthless tyrant more interested in strategy, victory, glory, reputation, and dominion than leading troops into battle.

As loyal and disciplined as hobgoblins are in their own legion, rival legions compete constantly for reputation and status. Meetings between legions erupt in violence if troops aren't restrained, and only exceptionally powerful leaders can force legions to cooperate on the battlefield.

Strategic Thinkers. Hobgoblins have a strong grasp of tactics and discipline, and can carry out sophisticated battle plans under the direction of a strategically minded leader. However, they hate elves and attack them first in battle over any other opponents, even if doing so would be a tactical error.

Legions often supplement their ranks with less reliable and more expendable troops, including goblins, bugbears, orcs, evil humans, ogres, and giants.

Beast Trainers. Hobgoblins have a long history of training animals to service. Like the more civilized races, they use oxen and horses to transport goods and weaponry over long distances. They communicate with each other using trained ravens, and keep vicious wolves to guard prisoners and protect hobgoblin camps. Hobgoblin cavalry use trained worgs as steeds, in the same way that goblins ride wolves. Some tribes even keep carnivorous apes as fighting beasts.

Conquer and Control. Hobgoblins claim lands with abundant resources, and they can be found in forests and mountains, near mines and humanoid settlements, and anywhere else that wood, metal, and potential slaves can be found. They build and conquer strongholds in strategically advantageous locations, which they then use as staging areas to expand their territory.

Hobgoblin warlords never tire of combat, but they don't take up arms lightly. Before they attack, hobgoblins conduct thorough reconnaissance to gauge the strengths and weaknesses of their foes. When assaulting a stronghold, they surround it first to cut off escape routes and supply lines, then slowly starve their enemies out.

Hobgoblins fortify their own holdings, bolstering existing defenses with innovations of their own. Whether they lair in cavern complexes, dungeons, ruins, or forests, they protect their strongholds with ditches, fences, gates, guard towers, pit traps, and crude catapults or ballistas.

Legion of Maglubiyet. Hobgoblins worship Maglubiyet the Mighty One, the greater god of goblinoids. As terrifying as this figure is, hobgoblins don't fear death, believing that when they die in battle, their spirits join the honored ranks of Maglubiyet's army on the plane of Acheron.

> They break before our shields,
> They fall beneath our blades;
> Their home is ours to conquer,
> Their children our slaves.
> Acheron! Acheron!
> Victory is ours!
>
> —Translation of a
> Hobgoblin War Chant

HOBGOBLIN

Medium humanoid (goblinoid), lawful evil

Armor Class 18 (chain mail, shield)
Hit Points 11 (2d8 + 2)
Speed 30 ft.

STR	DEX	CON	INT	WIS	CHA
13 (+1)	12 (+1)	12 (+1)	10 (+0)	10 (+0)	9 (−1)

Senses darkvision 60 ft., passive Perception 10
Languages Common, Goblin
Challenge 1/2 (100 XP)

Martial Advantage. Once per turn, the hobgoblin can deal an extra 7 (2d6) damage to a creature it hits with a weapon attack if that creature is within 5 feet of an ally of the hobgoblin that isn't incapacitated.

ACTIONS

Longsword. *Melee Weapon Attack:* +3 to hit, reach 5 ft., one target. *Hit:* 5 (1d8 + 1) slashing damage, or 6 (1d10 + 1) slashing damage if used with two hands.

Longbow. *Ranged Weapon Attack:* +3 to hit, range 150/600 ft., one target. *Hit:* 5 (1d8 + 1) piercing damage.

HOBGOBLIN CAPTAIN

Medium humanoid (goblinoid), lawful evil

Armor Class 17 (half plate)
Hit Points 39 (6d8 + 12)
Speed 30 ft.

STR	DEX	CON	INT	WIS	CHA
15 (+2)	14 (+2)	14 (+2)	12 (+1)	10 (+0)	13 (+1)

Senses darkvision 60 ft., passive Perception 10
Languages Common, Goblin
Challenge 3 (700 XP)

Martial Advantage. Once per turn, the hobgoblin can deal an extra 10 (3d6) damage to a creature it hits with a weapon attack if that creature is within 5 feet of an ally of the hobgoblin that isn't incapacitated.

ACTIONS

Multiattack. The hobgoblin makes two greatsword attacks.

Greatsword. *Melee Weapon Attack:* +4 to hit, reach 5 ft., one target. *Hit:* 9 (2d6 + 2) piercing damage.

Javelin. *Melee or Ranged Weapon Attack:* +4 to hit, reach 5 ft. or range 30/120 ft., one target. *Hit:* 5 (1d6 + 2) piercing damage.

Leadership (Recharges after a Short or Long Rest). For 1 minute, the hobgoblin can utter a special command or warning whenever a nonhostile creature that it can see within 30 feet of it makes an attack roll or a saving throw. The creature can add a d4 to its roll provided it can hear and understand the hobgoblin. A creature can benefit from only one Leadership die at a time. This effect ends if the hobgoblin is incapacitated.

HOBGOBLIN WARLORD
Medium humanoid (goblinoid), lawful evil

Armor Class 20 (plate, shield)
Hit Points 97 (13d8 + 39)
Speed 30 ft.

STR	DEX	CON	INT	WIS	CHA
16 (+3)	14 (+2)	16 (+3)	14 (+2)	11 (+0)	15 (+2)

Saving Throws Int +5, Wis +3, Cha +5
Senses darkvision 60 ft., passive Perception 10
Languages Common, Goblin
Challenge 6 (2,300 XP)

Martial Advantage. Once per turn, the hobgoblin can deal an extra 14 (4d6) damage to a creature it hits with a weapon attack if that creature is within 5 feet of an ally of the hobgoblin that isn't incapacitated.

ACTIONS

Multiattack. The hobgoblin makes three melee attacks. Alternatively, it can make two ranged attacks with its javelins.

Longsword. *Melee Weapon Attack:* +9 to hit, reach 5 ft., one target. *Hit:* 7 (1d8 + 3) slashing damage, or 8 (1d10 + 3) slashing damage if used with two hands.

Shield Bash. *Melee Weapon Attack:* +9 to hit, reach 5 ft., one creature. *Hit:* 5 (1d4 + 3) bludgeoning damage. If the target is Large or smaller, it must succeed on a DC 14 Strength saving throw or be knocked prone.

Javelin. *Melee or Ranged Weapon Attack:* +9 to hit, reach 5 ft. or range 30/120 ft., one target. *Hit:* 6 (1d6 + 3) piercing damage.

Leadership (Recharges after a Short or Long Rest). For 1 minute, the hobgoblin can utter a special command or warning whenever a nonhostile creature that it can see within 30 feet of it makes an attack roll or a saving throw. The creature can add a d4 to its roll provided it can hear and understand the hobgoblin. A creature can benefit from only one Leadership die at a time. This effect ends if the hobgoblin is incapacitated.

REACTIONS

Parry. The hobgoblin adds 3 to its AC against one melee attack that would hit it. To do so, the hobgoblin must see the attacker and be wielding a melee weapon.

H

HOMUNCULUS

Shaping a mixture of clay, ash, mandrake root, and blood, one can channel rare ritual magic to create a faithful, squirrel-sized companion.

A homunculus is a construct that acts as an extension of its creator, with the two sharing thoughts, senses, and language through a mystical bond. A master can have only one homunculus at a time (attempts to create another one always fail), and when its master dies, the homunculus also dies.

Shared Mind. A homunculus knows everything its creator knows, including all the languages the creator can speak and read. Likewise, everything the construct senses is known to its master, even over great distances, provided both are on the same plane. Functioning as a spy, a scout, an emissary, or a messenger, a homunculus is an invaluable servant for a spellcaster engaged in secret experimentation or adventuring.

HOMUNCULUS
Tiny construct, neutral

Armor Class 13 (natural armor)
Hit Points 5 (2d4)
Speed 20 ft., fly 40 ft.

STR	DEX	CON	INT	WIS	CHA
4 (−3)	15 (+2)	11 (+0)	10 (+0)	10 (+0)	7 (−2)

Damage Immunities poison
Condition Immunities charmed, poisoned
Senses darkvision 60 ft., passive Perception 10
Languages understands the languages of its creator but can't speak
Challenge 0 (10 XP)

Telepathic Bond. While the homunculus is on the same plane of existence as its master, it can magically convey what it senses to its master, and the two can communicate telepathically.

ACTIONS

Bite. *Melee Weapon Attack:* +4 to hit, reach 5 ft., one creature. *Hit:* 1 piercing damage, and the target must succeed on a DC 10 Constitution saving throw or be poisoned for 1 minute. If the saving throw fails by 5 or more, the target is instead poisoned for 5 (1d10) minutes and unconscious while poisoned in this way.

Hook Horror

Hook Horror
Large monstrosity, neutral

Armor Class 15 (natural armor)
Hit Points 75 (10d10 + 20)
Speed 30 ft., climb 30 ft.

STR	DEX	CON	INT	WIS	CHA
18 (+4)	10 (+0)	15 (+2)	6 (−2)	12 (+1)	7 (−2)

Skills Perception +3
Senses blindsight 60 ft., darkvision 10 ft., passive Perception 13
Languages Hook Horror
Challenge 3 (700 XP)

Echolocation. The hook horror can't use its blindsight while deafened.

Keen Hearing. The hook horror has advantage on Wisdom (Perception) checks that rely on hearing.

Actions

Multiattack. The hook horror makes two hook attacks.

Hook. *Melee Weapon Attack:* +6 to hit, reach 10 ft., one target. *Hit:* 11 (2d6 + 4) piercing damage.

A fierce predator of the Underdark, the hook horror aggressively defends its hunting grounds. The subterranean caverns where these creatures dwell echo with the constant clacking and scraping of their hooks as they wend their way up cliffs and along cavern walls.

The monstrous hook horror has a head resembling a vulture's and the torso of an enormous beetle, with an exoskeleton studded by sharp, bony protuberances. It gains its name from its long, powerfully built arms and legs, which end in wickedly curved hooked claws.

Echoes in the Dark. Hook horrors communicate by striking their hooks against their exoskeletons or the stone surfaces around them. What sounds to others like random clacking noise is actually a complex language that only hook horrors understand, and which carries for miles through the echoing Underdark.

Pack Predators. The omnivorous hook horrors eat lichens, fungi, plants, and any creature they can catch. A hook horror's hooked limbs give it excellent purchase on rock surfaces, and these creatures use their climbing skills to ambush prey from above. They hunt in packs, working together against the largest and most dangerous opponents. If a battle goes poorly, a hook horror quickly climbs a cavern wall to flee.

Dedicated Clans. Hook horrors live in extended family groups or clans. Each clan is ruled by the eldest female, who typically places her mate in charge of the clan's hunters. Hook horrors lay eggs, which are clustered in a central, well-defended area of a clan's home caverns.

Hydra

The hydra is a reptilian horror with a crocodilian body and multiple heads on long, serpentine necks. Although its heads can be severed, the hydra magically regrows them in short order. A typical specimen has five heads.

At the dawn of time, Tiamat, the Queen of Evil Dragons, slew a rival dragon god named Lernaea and cast her blood across the multiverse. Each drop that fell upon a world spawned a multi-headed hydra consumed by a hunger as great as the fallen god's hatred. Great champions are known to test their mettle against these fearsome creatures.

Everlasting Hunger. A rapacious and gluttonous monster, a hydra snatches and tears apart its prey in a frenzy of feeding. When a hydra has cleared a territory of food and driven off any creatures smart enough to avoid it, it moves on to seek its meals elsewhere. A hydra's hunger is so great that if it can't feed, it might turn against itself, its heads attacking each other as the creature eats itself alive.

Hardy Water Dwellers. Hydras are natural swimmers, dwelling in rivers, along lakeshores, in ocean shallows, and in wetland bogs. A hydra rarely requires shelter from the elements, so it doesn't normally have a lair. Only in colder climes are hydras drawn to the protection of sheltered caverns and ruins.

When a hydra sleeps, at least one of its heads remains awake and alert, making the creature difficult to catch by surprise.

Hydra
Huge monstrosity, unaligned

Armor Class 15 (natural armor)
Hit Points 172 (15d12 + 75)
Speed 30 ft., swim 30 ft.

STR	DEX	CON	INT	WIS	CHA
20 (+5)	12 (+1)	20 (+5)	2 (–4)	10 (+0)	7 (–2)

Skills Perception +6
Senses darkvision 60 ft., passive Perception 16
Languages —
Challenge 8 (3,900 XP)

Hold Breath. The hydra can hold its breath for 1 hour.

Multiple Heads. The hydra has five heads. While it has more than one head, the hydra has advantage on saving throws against being blinded, charmed, deafened, frightened, stunned, and knocked unconscious.

Whenever the hydra takes 25 or more damage in a single turn, one of its heads dies. If all its heads die, the hydra dies.

At the end of its turn, it grows two heads for each of its heads that died since its last turn, unless it has taken fire damage since its last turn. The hydra regains 10 hit points for each head regrown in this way.

Reactive Heads. For each head the hydra has beyond one, it gets an extra reaction that can be used only for opportunity attacks.

Wakeful. While the hydra sleeps, at least one of its heads is awake.

Actions

Multiattack. The hydra makes as many bite attacks as it has heads.

Bite. *Melee Weapon Attack:* +8 to hit, reach 10 ft., one target. *Hit:* 10 (1d10 + 5) piercing damage.

Intellect Devourer

An intellect devourer resembles a walking brain protected by a crusty covering and set on bestial clawed legs. This foul aberration feeds on the intelligence of sentient creatures, taking over a victim's body on behalf of its mind flayer masters.

Illithid Creations. Mind flayers breed intellect devourers to serve as roaming hunters of the Underdark, creating an intellect devourer by taking the brain of a thrall and subjecting it to a horrible ritual. As it sprouts legs, the brain becomes an intelligent predator as twisted and evil as its masters.

Deadly Puppet Masters. An intellect devourer consumes a creature's mind and memories, then turns the host body into a puppet under its control. An intellect devourer typically uses its puppet host to lure others into the domain of the mind flayers to be enthralled or consumed.

Intellect Devourer

Tiny aberration, lawful evil

Armor Class 12
Hit Points 21 (6d4 + 6)
Speed 40 ft.

STR	DEX	CON	INT	WIS	CHA
6 (−2)	14 (+2)	13 (+1)	12 (+1)	11 (+0)	10 (+0)

Skills Perception +2, Stealth +4
Damage Resistances bludgeoning, piercing, and slashing from nonmagical attacks
Condition Immunities blinded
Senses blindsight 60 ft. (blind beyond this radius), passive Perception 12
Languages understands Deep Speech but can't speak, telepathy 60 ft.
Challenge 2 (450 XP)

Detect Sentience. The intellect devourer can sense the presence and location of any creature within 300 feet of it that has an Intelligence of 3 or higher, regardless of interposing barriers, unless the creature is protected by a *mind blank* spell.

Actions

Multiattack. The intellect devourer makes one attack with its claws and uses Devour Intellect.

Claws. *Melee Weapon Attack:* +4 to hit, reach 5 ft., one target. *Hit:* 7 (2d4 + 2) slashing damage.

Devour Intellect. The intellect devourer targets one creature it can see within 10 feet of it that has a brain. The target must succeed on a DC 12 Intelligence saving throw against this magic or take 11 (2d10) psychic damage. Also on a failure, roll 3d6: If the total equals or exceeds the target's Intelligence score, that score is reduced to 0. The target is stunned until it regains at least one point of Intelligence.

Body Thief. The intellect devourer initiates an Intelligence contest with an incapacitated humanoid within 5 feet of it that isn't protected by *protection from evil and good*. If it wins the contest, the intellect devourer magically consumes the target's brain, teleports into the skull, and takes control of the body. While there, the intellect devourer has total cover against attacks and other effects originating outside its host. The intellect devourer retains its Intelligence, Wisdom, and Charisma scores, as well as its understanding of Deep Speech, its telepathy, and its traits. It otherwise adopts the target's statistics. It knows everything the creature knew, including spells and languages.

If the host body dies, the intellect devourer must leave it. A *protection from evil and good* spell cast on the body drives the intellect devourer out. The intellect devourer is also forced out if the target regains its devoured brain by means of a *wish*. By spending 5 feet of its movement, the intellect devourer can voluntarily leave the body, teleporting to the nearest unoccupied space within 5 feet of it. The body then dies, unless its brain is restored within 1 round.

Invisible Stalker

Medium elemental, neutral

Armor Class 14
Hit Points 104 (16d8 + 32)
Speed 50 ft., fly 50 ft. (hover)

STR	DEX	CON	INT	WIS	CHA
16 (+3)	19 (+4)	14 (+2)	10 (+0)	15 (+2)	11 (+0)

Skills Perception +8, Stealth +10
Damage Resistances bludgeoning, piercing, and slashing from nonmagical attacks
Damage Immunities poison
Condition Immunities exhaustion, grappled, paralyzed, petrified, poisoned, prone, restrained, unconscious
Senses darkvision 60 ft., passive Perception 18
Languages Auran, understands Common but doesn't speak it
Challenge 6 (2,300 XP)

Invisibility. The stalker is invisible.

Faultless Tracker. The stalker is given a quarry by its summoner. The stalker knows the direction and distance to its quarry as long as the two of them are on the same plane of existence. The stalker also knows the location of its summoner.

Actions

Multiattack. The stalker makes two slam attacks.

Slam. *Melee Weapon Attack:* +6 to hit, reach 5 ft., one target. *Hit:* 10 (2d6 + 3) bludgeoning damage.

Invisible Stalker

An invisible stalker is an air elemental that has been summoned from its native plane and transformed by powerful magic. Its sole purpose is to hunt down creatures and retrieve objects for its summoner. When it is defeated or the magic that binds it expires, an invisible stalker vanishes in a gust of wind.

Directed Hunter. When an invisible stalker is created, it stays at its summoner's side until it is given a task to perform. If an assignment doesn't involve hunting down and slaying a specific creature or recovering an object, the magic that created the invisible stalker ends and the elemental is released. Otherwise, it completes the task, then returns to its summoner for more commands, forced to serve until the magic that binds it expires. If its summoner dies in the interim, the invisible stalker vanishes after completing its task.

An invisible stalker is an unwilling servant at best. It resents any undertaking assigned to it. A mission that requires significant time might drive the invisible stalker to pervert the intent of a command unless it is worded carefully.

Unseen Threat. Invisible stalkers are composed of air and are naturally invisible. A creature might hear and feel an invisible stalker in passing, but the elemental remains invisible even when it attacks. A spell that allows someone to see the invisible reveals only the invisible stalker's vague outline.

Elemental Nature. An invisible stalker requires no air, food, drink, or sleep.

J

JACKALWERE

Ordinary jackals tainted by demonic power, jackalweres haunt roads and trails, waylaying and murdering those they meet.

A jackalwere has three physical forms that it shifts between. In its true form, it is indistinguishable from a normal jackal. It can take human form, often appearing gaunt and affecting a wretched demeanor to beg goodwill from strangers. When travelers welcome a jackalwere into their midst, the monster adopts its human-sized hybrid form, with the fur and head of a jackal but standing on two legs as it attacks.

Beguilers and Cowards. The demon lord Graz'zt created jackalweres to serve his devoted servants, the lamias. Reaching out from the Abyss, he bestowed jackals with the gift of speech and the ability to assume humanoid forms. A jackalwere is born to lie, and perceptive creatures might notice it wincing in pain when it speaks the truth.

A jackalwere prefers to fight alongside jackals and others of its kind. Under the direction of jackalweres, jackals are fierce and loyal companions.

Supernatural Servants. Jackalweres kidnap humanoids for their lamia masters, condemning victims to a lifetime of slavery or an agonizing death. A jackalwere's magical gaze renders a foe unconscious, allowing the monster to bind a creature or drag it away. A jackalwere might also use its gaze to incapacitate a deadly enemy long enough to make good its escape.

JACKALWERE

Medium humanoid (shapechanger), chaotic evil

Armor Class 12
Hit Points 18 (4d8)
Speed 40 ft.

STR	DEX	CON	INT	WIS	CHA
11 (+0)	15 (+2)	11 (+0)	13 (+1)	11 (+0)	10 (+0)

Skills Deception +4, Perception +2, Stealth +4
Damage Immunities bludgeoning, piercing, and slashing from nonmagical attacks not made with silvered weapons
Senses passive Perception 12
Languages Common (can't speak in jackal form)
Challenge 1/2 (100 XP)

Shapechanger. The jackalwere can use its action to polymorph into a specific Medium human or a jackal-humanoid hybrid, or back into its true form (that of a Small jackal). Other than its size, its statistics are the same in each form. Any equipment it is wearing or carrying isn't transformed. It reverts to its true form if it dies.

Keen Hearing and Smell. The jackalwere has advantage on Wisdom (Perception) checks that rely on hearing or smell.

Pack Tactics. The jackalwere has advantage on an attack roll against a creature if at least one of the jackalwere's allies is within 5 feet of the creature and the ally isn't incapacitated.

ACTIONS

Bite (Jackal or Hybrid Form Only). *Melee Weapon Attack:* +4 to hit, reach 5 ft., one target. *Hit:* 4 (1d4 + 2) piercing damage.

Scimitar (Human or Hybrid Form Only). *Melee Weapon Attack:* +4 to hit, reach 5 ft., one target. *Hit:* 5 (1d6 + 2) slashing damage.

Sleep Gaze. The jackalwere gazes at one creature it can see within 30 feet of it. The target must make a DC 10 Wisdom saving throw. On a failed save, the target succumbs to a magical slumber, falling unconscious for 10 minutes or until someone uses an action to shake the target awake. A creature that successfully saves against the effect is immune to this jackalwere's gaze for the next 24 hours. Undead and creatures immune to being charmed aren't affected by it.

Kenku

Kenku are feathered humanoids that wander the world as vagabonds, driven by greed. They can perfectly imitate any sound they hear.

Fallen Flocks. Kenku wear ill-fitting cloaks, robes, and rags. These garments cover the soft, sleek feathers of their bodies, shrouding their bare arms and legs. They tread lightly when they walk, on talons made for grasping the branches of trees and seizing prey from the lofty skies. Soft as the wind they move, so as not to draw attention to their shameful forms.

Once, the kenku held the wind in their wings, embracing the gusty sky and singing the sweet language of birdsong. Serving a master whose identity is now lost to their memory, the kenku coveted the glittering baubles of his household, and longed to speak so that they could cajole and swindle others out of such treasures. Stealing the secret of speech from a volume in their master's library, they disguised themselves in rags to beg for pretty things. When their master learned of their greed, he stripped away their wings as punishment, forcing them to beg forever.

Speech in Pantomime. Kenku can mimic the sound of anything they hear. A kenku asking for money might make the sound of coins clinking together, and a kenku referring to a busy marketplace can reproduce the cacophony of hawking vendors, barking dogs, bleating sheep, and the cries of street urchins. When mimicking voices, they can only repeat words and phrases they have heard, not create new sentences. To converse with a kenku is to witness a performance of imitated sounds and almost nonsensical verse.

Kenku speak to one another in much the same way. Because they are adept at interpreting one another's glances and gestures, the sounds they make to communicate complex ideas or emotions can be succinct. Groups of kenku also develop secret codes. For example, a cat's meow might be the secret code for "Prepare to attack!" or "Flee for your lives!"

Their talent for mimicry extends to handwriting, and criminal organizations often employ kenku to forge documents. When a kenku commits a crime, it might forge evidence to implicate another creature.

The Wistful Wingless. All kenku pine for the ability to fly, and thus the punishments they mete out to one another often involve false wings, such as heavy wings of wood borne as a mark of shame. As a final, tragic reminder of the wings they once had, kenku carry out executions by hurling their condemned from tall buildings or cliffs.

Kenku

Medium humanoid (kenku), chaotic neutral

Armor Class 13
Hit Points 13 (3d8)
Speed 30 ft.

STR	DEX	CON	INT	WIS	CHA
10 (+0)	16 (+3)	10 (+0)	11 (+0)	10 (+0)	10 (+0)

Skills Deception +4, Perception +2, Stealth +5
Senses passive Perception 12
Languages understands Auran and Common but speaks only through the use of its Mimicry trait
Challenge 1/4 (50 XP)

Ambusher. In the first round of a combat, the kenku has advantage on attack rolls against any creature it surprised.

Mimicry. The kenku can mimic any sounds it has heard, including voices. A creature that hears the sounds can tell they are imitations with a successful DC 14 Wisdom (Insight) check.

Actions

Shortsword. Melee Weapon Attack: +5 to hit, reach 5 ft., one target. Hit: 6 (1d6 + 3) piercing damage.

Shortbow. Ranged Weapon Attack: +5 to hit, range 80/320 ft., one target. Hit: 6 (1d6 + 3) piercing damage.

"IF YOU HEAR A BABY CRYING IN AN ALLEY, WALK THE OTHER WAY. THAT'S MY ADVICE TO YOU."
—ENDROTH KNAG, CITY WATCH CORPORAL IN WATERDEEP

Kobolds

Kobolds are craven reptilian humanoids that worship evil dragons as demigods and serve them as minions and toadies. Kobolds inhabit dragons' lairs when they can but more commonly infest dungeons, gathering treasures and trinkets to add to their own tiny hoards.

Strength in Numbers. Kobolds are egg-laying creatures. They mature quickly and can live to be "great wyrms" more than a century old. However, many kobolds perish before they reach the end of their first decade. Physically weak, they are easy prey for predators. This vulnerability forces them to band together. Their superior numbers can win battles against powerful adversaries, but often with massive casualties on the kobold side.

Tunnelers and Builders. Kobolds make up for their physical ineptitude with a cleverness for trap making and tunneling. Their lairs consist of low tunnels through which they move easily but which hinder larger humanoids. Kobolds also riddle their lairs with traps. The most insidious kobold traps make use of natural hazards and other creatures. A trip wire might connect to a spring-loaded trap that hurls clay pots of flesh-eating green slime or flings crates of venomous giant centipedes at intruders.

The Lost God. In addition to the dragons they revere, kobolds worship a lesser god named Kurtulmak. Legends speak of how Kurtulmak served as Tiamat's vassal in the Nine Hells until Garl Glittergold, the god of gnomes, stole a trinket from the Dragon Queen's hoard. Tiamat sent Kurtulmak to retrieve the trinket, but Garl Glittergold played a trick on him, collapsing the earth and trapping the kobold god in an underground maze for eternity. For this reason, kobolds hate gnomes and pranks of any kind. Kurtulmak's most devoted worshipers dedicate themselves to finding and releasing their lost god from his prison-maze.

Winged Kobolds. A few kobolds are born with leathery wings and can fly. Known as *urds,* they like to lurk on high ledges and drop rocks on passersby. Although the urds' wings are seen as gifts from Tiamat, the Dragon Queen, wingless kobolds are envious of those gifts and don't get along with the urds.

Winged Kobold

Small humanoid (kobold), lawful evil

Armor Class 13
Hit Points 7 (3d6 − 3)
Speed 30 ft., fly 30 ft.

STR	DEX	CON	INT	WIS	CHA
7 (−2)	16 (+3)	9 (−1)	8 (−1)	7 (−2)	8 (−1)

Senses darkvision 60 ft., passive Perception 8
Languages Common, Draconic
Challenge 1/4 (50 XP)

Sunlight Sensitivity. While in sunlight, the kobold has disadvantage on attack rolls, as well as on Wisdom (Perception) checks that rely on sight.

Pack Tactics. The kobold has advantage on an attack roll against a creature if at least one of the kobold's allies is within 5 feet of the creature and the ally isn't incapacitated.

Actions

Dagger. *Melee Weapon Attack:* +5 to hit, reach 5 ft., one target. *Hit:* 5 (1d4 + 3) piercing damage.

Dropped Rock. *Ranged Weapon Attack:* +5 to hit, one target directly below the kobold. *Hit:* 6 (1d6 + 3) bludgeoning damage.

Kobold

Small humanoid (kobold), lawful evil

Armor Class 12
Hit Points 5 (2d6 − 2)
Speed 30 ft.

STR	DEX	CON	INT	WIS	CHA
7 (−2)	15 (+2)	9 (−1)	8 (−1)	7 (−2)	8 (−1)

Senses darkvision 60 ft., passive Perception 8
Languages Common, Draconic
Challenge 1/8 (25 XP)

Sunlight Sensitivity. While in sunlight, the kobold has disadvantage on attack rolls, as well as on Wisdom (Perception) checks that rely on sight.

Pack Tactics. The kobold has advantage on an attack roll against a creature if at least one of the kobold's allies is within 5 feet of the creature and the ally isn't incapacitated.

Actions

Dagger. *Melee Weapon Attack:* +4 to hit, reach 5 ft., one target. *Hit:* 4 (1d4 + 2) piercing damage.

Sling. *Ranged Weapon Attack:* +4 to hit, range 30/120 ft., one target. *Hit:* 4 (1d4 + 2) bludgeoning damage.

Kraken

Beneath the waves, the kraken sleeps for untold ages, awaiting some fell sign or calling. Land-born mortals who sail the open sea forget the reasons their ancestors dreaded the ocean, even as the races of the deep ignore strange gaps in their histories when their civilizations nearly vanished after the appearance of the tentacled horror.

Leviathans of Legend. At the beginning of time, krakens served as fierce warriors of the gods. When the gods' wars ended, the krakens shrugged free of their servitude, never again to be bound by other beings.

Whole nations quake in fear when the kraken emerges from its dark demesne, and even in the middle of the deepest oceans, storms rise or abate according to its will. The kraken is a primeval force that obliterates the greatest achievements of civilization as if they were castles in the sand. Its devastating attacks can destroy ocean trade and halt communication between coastal cities.

An ominous darkness presages a kraken's attack, and a cloud of inky poison colors the water around it. Galleons and warships vanish when its tentacles uncoil from the deep, the kraken breaking their masts like kindling before drawing down ships and crew.

Not even landlocked surface dwellers are safe from a kraken's wrath. Krakens can breathe air as easily as water, and some crawl up rivers to nest in freshwater lakes, destroying cities and towns along the way. Adventurers tell of these monsters lairing in the ruins of lakeside citadels, their tentacles twined around leaning towers of disintegrating stone.

Mortal Foes. Some krakens are virtual gods, with cults and minions spread across sea and land. Others are allied with Olhydra, the evil Princess of Elemental Water, and use her cultists to enforce their will on land and sea. A kraken pleased with its worshipers can becalm rough seas and bring a bounteous harvest of fish to the faithful. However, the devious mind of a kraken is ancient beyond reckoning, and is ultimately bent to the ruination of all things.

A Kraken's Lair

A kraken lives in dark depths, usually a sunken rift or a cavern filled with detritus, treasure, and wrecked ships.

Lair Actions
On initiative count 20 (losing initiative ties), the kraken takes a lair action to cause one of the following magical effects:

- A strong current moves through the kraken's lair. Each creature within 60 feet of the kraken must succeed on a DC 23 Strength saving throw or be pushed up to 60 feet away from the kraken. On a success, the creature is pushed 10 feet away from the kraken.
- Creatures in the water within 60 feet of the kraken have vulnerability to lightning damage until initiative count 20 on the next round.
- The water in the kraken's lair becomes electrically charged. All creatures within 120 feet of the kraken must succeed on a DC 23 Constitution saving throw,

taking 10 (3d6) lightning damage on a failed save, or half as much damage on a successful one.

REGIONAL EFFECTS

The region containing a kraken's lair is warped by the creature's blasphemous presence, creating the following magical effects:

- The kraken can alter the weather at will in a 6-mile radius centered on its lair. The effect is identical to the *control weather* spell.
- Water elementals coalesce within 6 miles of the lair. These elementals can't leave the water and have Intelligence and Charisma scores of 1 (−5).
- Aquatic creatures within 6 miles of the lair that have an Intelligence score of 2 or lower are charmed by the kraken and aggressive toward intruders in the area.

When the kraken dies, all of these regional effects fade immediately.

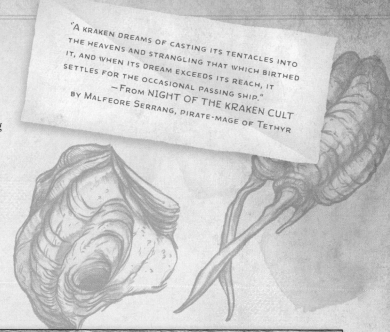

"A kraken dreams of casting its tentacles into the heavens and strangling that which birthed it, and when its dream exceeds its reach, it settles for the occasional passing ship."
—From NIGHT OF THE KRAKEN CULT *by* MALFEORE SERRANG, *pirate-mage of Tethyr*

KRAKEN

Gargantuan monstrosity (titan), chaotic evil

Armor Class 18 (natural armor)
Hit Points 472 (27d20 + 189)
Speed 20 ft., swim 60 ft.

STR	DEX	CON	INT	WIS	CHA
30 (+10)	11 (+0)	25 (+7)	22 (+6)	18 (+4)	20 (+5)

Saving Throws Str +17, Dex +7, Con +14, Int +13, Wis +11
Damage Immunities lightning; bludgeoning, piercing, and slashing from nonmagical attacks
Condition Immunities frightened, paralyzed
Senses truesight 120 ft., passive Perception 14
Languages understands Abyssal, Celestial, Infernal, and Primordial but can't speak, telepathy 120 ft.
Challenge 23 (50,000 XP)

Amphibious. The kraken can breathe air and water.

Freedom of Movement. The kraken ignores difficult terrain, and magical effects can't reduce its speed or cause it to be restrained. It can spend 5 feet of movement to escape from nonmagical restraints or being grappled.

Siege Monster. The kraken deals double damage to objects and structures.

ACTIONS

Multiattack. The kraken makes three tentacle attacks, each of which it can replace with one use of Fling.

Bite. *Melee Weapon Attack:* +17 to hit, reach 5 ft., one target. *Hit:* 23 (3d8 + 10) piercing damage. If the target is a Large or smaller creature grappled by the kraken, that creature is swallowed, and the grapple ends. While swallowed, the creature is blinded and restrained, it has total cover against attacks and other effects outside the kraken, and it takes 42 (12d6) acid damage at the start of each of the kraken's turns.

If the kraken takes 50 damage or more on a single turn from a creature inside it, the kraken must succeed on a DC 25 Constitution saving throw at the end of that turn or regurgitate all swallowed creatures, which fall prone in a space within 10 feet of the kraken. If the kraken dies, a swallowed creature is no longer restrained by it and can escape from the corpse using 15 feet of movement, exiting prone.

Tentacle. *Melee Weapon Attack:* +17 to hit, reach 30 ft., one target. *Hit:* 20 (3d6 + 10) bludgeoning damage, and the target is grappled (escape DC 18). Until this grapple ends, the target is restrained. The kraken has ten tentacles, each of which can grapple one target.

Fling. One Large or smaller object held or creature grappled by the kraken is thrown up to 60 feet in a random direction and knocked prone. If a thrown target strikes a solid surface, the target takes 3 (1d6) bludgeoning damage for every 10 feet it was thrown. If the target is thrown at another creature, that creature must succeed on a DC 18 Dexterity saving throw or take the same damage and be knocked prone.

Lightning Storm. The kraken magically creates three bolts of lightning, each of which can strike a target the kraken can see within 120 feet of it. A target must make a DC 23 Dexterity saving throw, taking 22 (4d10) lightning damage on a failed save, or half as much damage on a successful one.

LEGENDARY ACTIONS

The kraken can take 3 legendary actions, choosing from the options below. Only one legendary action option can be used at a time and only at the end of another creature's turn. The kraken regains spent legendary actions at the start of its turn.

Tentacle Attack or Fling. The kraken makes one tentacle attack or uses its Fling.
Lightning Storm (Costs 2 Actions). The kraken uses Lightning Storm.
Ink Cloud (Costs 3 Actions). While underwater, the kraken expels an ink cloud in a 60-foot radius. The cloud spreads around corners, and that area is heavily obscured to creatures other than the kraken. Each creature other than the kraken that ends its turn there must succeed on a DC 23 Constitution saving throw, taking 16 (3d10) poison damage on a failed save, or half as much damage on a successful one. A strong current disperses the cloud, which otherwise disappears at the end of the kraken's next turn.

Kuo-toa

Kuo-toa are degenerate fishlike humanoids that once inhabited the shores and islands of the surface world. Long ago humans and their ilk drove the kuo-toa underground, where they dwell in madness and everlasting night. Kuo-toa can no longer abide daylight.

Mad Slaves. At the height of the illithid empire, the mind flayers captured kuo-toa by the thousands and forced them into bondage. The kuo-toa were simple creatures, never meant to endure the oppressive mental force the illithids unleashed against them. By the time the mind flayers abandoned them, the prolonged psychic subjugation endured by the kuo-toa had driven them mad.

Their minds shattered beyond repair, the kuo-toa adopted a religious fervor, inventing gods to protect them against threats. Most notable of these threats are the drow, which have slain the kuo-toa on sight since the days when the two races first met.

God Makers. Kuo-toa worship gods of their own insane creation, but if enough kuo-toa believe that a god is real, the energy of their collective subconscious can cause that god to manifest as a physical entity. The form a kuo-toa god takes depends on the inspiration for its divine image, and is usually random or nonsensical.

One of the most revered gods of the kuo-toa is Blibdoolpoolp the Sea Mother, who takes the form of a female human with a crayfish head, a crayfish's claws, and an articulated shell covering her shoulders. Blibdoolpoolp was likely invented by a kuo-toa that improved on a broken human statue by adding the limbs and head of a crustacean. In sudden awe of its handiwork, it then named the resulting form a god.

Kuo-toa that cross paths with an aboleth often find themselves worshiping it as a god, their madness blinding them to the fact that the aboleth is merely using them for its own nefarious ends.

Theocratic Rulers. Kuo-toa archpriests are surrounded by fanatical devotees of their faith. The archpriest of a kuo-toa domain demands that all its subjects worship a specific god. An archpriest's mad belief in its god is so fervent that it manifests the powers of a high cleric. The archpriest can also bestow spells to devout underlings called whips. One or more of

---

Variant: Kuo-toa Monitor

A kuo-toa monitor has a challenge rating of 3 (700 XP). It has the same statistics as a kuo-toa whip except that it adds its Wisdom modifier to its Armor Class (AC 13), loses the Spellcaster trait, and replaces the whip's action options with the following action options.

Multiattack. The kuo-toa makes one bite attack and two unarmed strikes.

Bite. *Melee Weapon Attack:* +6 to hit, reach 5 ft., one target. *Hit:* 4 (1d4 + 2) piercing damage.

Unarmed Strike. *Melee Weapon Attack:* +6 to hit, reach 5 ft., one target. *Hit:* 5 (1d6 + 2) bludgeoning damage plus 3 (1d6) lightning damage, and the target can't take reactions until the end of the kuo-toa's next turn.

these whips are also the archpriest's children, and their primary role in kuo-toan society is to fight to the death to claim the throne when the archpriest dies. If a whip displeases the archpriest, the archpriest can strip it of its spellcasting ability, if not its life.

The archpriest's decrees are enforced by monitors, devout kuo-toa that act as the archpriest's eyes and ears. Monitors are deadly hand-to-hand combatants, and lesser kuo-toa live in fear of them.

Kuo-toa Gear. Many weapons of the kuo-toa are designed to capture rather than kill. Nets are common, though some carry pincer staffs (also called mancatchers) designed to trap and immobilize foes. Kuo-toa warriors also treat their shields with a sticky goo that catches incoming weapons.

In general, kuo-toa don't like the weight of armor on their slippery bodies and rely on their natural rubbery hides for protection. However, they like to wear jewelry made from scavenged bones, shells, pearls, gems, and carapace fragments.

"THEY INVENT THEIR OWN GODS ... THE VERY DEFINITION OF INSANITY."
—SABAL MIZZRYM OF MENZOBERRANZAN

KUO-TOA

Medium humanoid (kuo-toa), neutral evil

Armor Class 13 (natural armor, shield)
Hit Points 18 (4d8)
Speed 30 ft., swim 30 ft.

STR	DEX	CON	INT	WIS	CHA
13 (+1)	10 (+0)	11 (+0)	11 (+0)	10 (+0)	8 (−1)

Skills Perception +4
Senses darkvision 120 ft., passive Perception 14
Languages Undercommon
Challenge 1/4 (50 XP)

Amphibious. The kuo-toa can breathe air and water.

Otherworldly Perception. The kuo-toa can sense the presence of any creature within 30 feet of it that is invisible or on the Ethereal Plane. It can pinpoint such a creature that is moving.

Slippery. The kuo-toa has advantage on ability checks and saving throws made to escape a grapple.

Sunlight Sensitivity. While in sunlight, the kuo-toa has disadvantage on attack rolls, as well as on Wisdom (Perception) checks that rely on sight.

ACTIONS

Bite. *Melee Weapon Attack:* +3 to hit, reach 5 ft., one target. *Hit:* 3 (1d4 + 1) piercing damage.

Spear. *Melee or Ranged Weapon Attack:* +3 to hit, reach 5 ft. or range 20/60 ft., one target. *Hit:* 4 (1d6 + 1) piercing damage, or 5 (1d8 + 1) piercing damage if used with two hands to make a melee attack.

Net. *Ranged Weapon Attack:* +3 to hit, range 5/15 ft., one Large or smaller creature. *Hit:* The target is restrained. A creature can use its action to make a DC 10 Strength check to free itself or another creature in a net, ending the effect on a success. Dealing 5 slashing damage to the net (AC 10) frees the target without harming it and destroys the net.

REACTIONS

Sticky Shield. When a creature misses the kuo-toa with a melee weapon attack, the kuo-toa uses its sticky shield to catch the weapon. The attacker must succeed on a DC 11 Strength saving throw, or the weapon becomes stuck to the kuo-toa's shield. If the weapon's wielder can't or won't let go of the weapon, the wielder is grappled while the weapon is stuck. While stuck, the weapon can't be used. A creature can pull the weapon free by taking an action to make a DC 11 Strength check and succeeding.

K

Kuo-toa Archpriest

Medium humanoid (kuo-toa), neutral evil

Armor Class 13 (natural armor)
Hit Points 97 (13d8 + 39)
Speed 30 ft., swim 30 ft.

STR	DEX	CON	INT	WIS	CHA
16 (+3)	14 (+2)	16 (+3)	13 (+1)	16 (+3)	14 (+2)

Skills Perception +9, Religion +6
Senses darkvision 120 ft., passive Perception 19
Languages Undercommon
Challenge 6 (2,300 XP)

Amphibious. The kuo-toa can breathe air and water.

Otherworldly Perception. The kuo-toa can sense the presence of any creature within 30 feet of it that is invisible or on the Ethereal Plane. It can pinpoint such a creature that is moving.

Slippery. The kuo-toa has advantage on ability checks and saving throws made to escape a grapple.

Sunlight Sensitivity. While in sunlight, the kuo-toa has disadvantage on attack rolls, as well as on Wisdom (Perception) checks that rely on sight.

Spellcasting. The kuo-toa is a 10th-level spellcaster. Its spellcasting ability is Wisdom (spell save DC 14, +6 to hit with spell attacks). The kuo-toa has the following cleric spells prepared:

Cantrips (at will): *guidance, sacred flame, thaumaturgy*
1st level (4 slots): *detect magic, sanctuary, shield of faith*
2nd level (3 slots): *hold person, spiritual weapon*
3rd level (3 slots): *spirit guardians, tongues*
4th level (3 slots): *control water, divination*
5th level (2 slots): *mass cure wounds, scrying*

Actions

Multiattack. The kuo-toa makes two melee attacks.

Scepter. *Melee Weapon Attack:* +6 to hit, reach 5 ft., one target. *Hit:* 6 (1d6 + 3) bludgeoning damage plus 14 (4d6) lightning damage.

Unarmed Strike. *Melee Weapon Attack:* +6 to hit, reach 5 ft., one target. *Hit:* 5 (1d4 + 3) bludgeoning damage.

Kuo-toa Whip

Medium humanoid (kuo-toa), neutral evil

Armor Class 11 (natural armor)
Hit Points 65 (10d8 + 20)
Speed 30 ft., swim 30 ft.

STR	DEX	CON	INT	WIS	CHA
14 (+2)	10 (+0)	14 (+2)	12 (+1)	14 (+2)	11 (+0)

Skills Perception +6, Religion +4
Senses darkvision 120 ft., passive Perception 16
Languages Undercommon
Challenge 1 (200 XP)

Amphibious. The kuo-toa can breathe air and water.

Otherworldly Perception. The kuo-toa can sense the presence of any creature within 30 feet of it that is invisible or on the Ethereal Plane. It can pinpoint such a creature that is moving.

Slippery. The kuo-toa has advantage on ability checks and saving throws made to escape a grapple.

Sunlight Sensitivity. While in sunlight, the kuo-toa has disadvantage on attack rolls, as well as on Wisdom (Perception) checks that rely on sight.

Spellcasting. The kuo-toa is a 2nd-level spellcaster. Its spellcasting ability is Wisdom (spell save DC 12, +4 to hit with spell attacks). The kuo-toa has the following cleric spells prepared:

Cantrips (at will): *sacred flame, thaumaturgy*
1st level (3 slots): *bane, shield of faith*

Actions

Multiattack. The kuo-toa makes two attacks: one with its bite and one with its pincer staff.

Bite. *Melee Weapon Attack:* +4 to hit, reach 5 ft., one target. *Hit:* 4 (1d4 + 2) piercing damage.

Pincer Staff. *Melee Weapon Attack:* +4 to hit, reach 10 ft., one target. *Hit:* 5 (1d6 + 2) piercing damage. If the target is a Medium or smaller creature, it is grappled (escape DC 14). Until this grapple ends, the kuo-toa can't use its pincer staff on another target.

LAMIA

Ruined desert cities and the tombs of forgotten monarchs make perfect lairs for the wicked lamias. These decadent monsters take what has been forgotten and make it the seat of their hedonistic rule, surrounding themselves with sycophants. Lamias rely on jackalweres to perform various tasks, sending them across the wastes to capture slaves or steal treasures from caravans, encampments, or villages, concealed by the lamia's magic as they attack.

A lamia has a beautiful humanoid upper body that merges into a powerful four-legged leonine form. Its vicious black claws speak to its predatory nature, as does its hunger for torture and humanoid flesh.

Tyrants of Pleasure. Lamias adorn their crumbling havens with finery stolen from passing caravans, then use magic to further accentuate their lairs, masking decay with illusion. A lair's breathtaking gardens, finely decorated apartments, and numerous slaves seem at odds with its remoteness and state of ruin.

Using its intoxicating touch, a lamia weakens the minds of its enemies, making them more susceptible to its enchantment spells and turning them into its slaves. Those it beguiles with *geas* spells are pitted against each other in elaborate contests for the lamia's amusement.

Vain Predators. Always anxious to gain more wealth and slaves, a lamia uses a pool of water or a mirror in conjunction with a *scrying* spell to view its domain. A lamia uses this power to watch over trade routes and nearby settlements, or to seek out objects and creatures it fancies.

Lamias are particularly fond of seeking out adventurers with pure hearts to seduce and corrupt to evil, savoring the destruction of their virtue. They use their magic to lure potential victims to their lairs, relying on illusion and their thralls to capture hapless foes. Lamias prize beauty and strength above all else, however. Any prisoner that falls short of their esteem becomes the main course in a horrible feast, or is set free to die while wandering the wastes.

As long as they have slaves to face their enemies, lamias fight from the fringes, beguiling foes with magic if they can. A lamia pressed into melee never stays there for long, shredding flesh with claw and dagger before springing away to safety.

Minions of Graz'zt. The demon lord Graz'zt creates lamias from his mortal servants, granting them immortality in return for monstrous power and an oath of fealty. Graz'zt sometimes tasks lamias with guarding locations important to him, but lamias in his service remain free to spread their evil as they see fit.

LAMIA
Large monstrosity, chaotic evil

Armor Class 13 (natural armor)
Hit Points 97 (13d10 + 26)
Speed 30 ft.

STR	DEX	CON	INT	WIS	CHA
16 (+3)	13 (+1)	15 (+2)	14 (+2)	15 (+2)	16 (+3)

Skills Deception +7, Insight +4, Stealth +3
Senses darkvision 60 ft., passive Perception 12
Languages Abyssal, Common
Challenge 4 (1,100 XP)

Innate Spellcasting. The lamia's innate spellcasting ability is Charisma (spell save DC 13). It can innately cast the following spells, requiring no material components.

At will: *disguise self* (any humanoid form), *major image*
3/day each: *charm person, mirror image, scrying, suggestion*
1/day: *geas*

ACTIONS

Multiattack. The lamia makes two attacks: one with its claws and one with its dagger or Intoxicating Touch.

Claws. *Melee Weapon Attack:* +5 to hit, reach 5 ft., one target. *Hit:* 14 (2d10 + 3) slashing damage.

Dagger. *Melee Weapon Attack:* +5 to hit, reach 5 ft., one target. *Hit:* 5 (1d4 + 3) piercing damage.

Intoxicating Touch. *Melee Spell Attack:* +5 to hit, reach 5 ft., one creature. *Hit:* The target is magically cursed for 1 hour. Until the curse ends, the target has disadvantage on Wisdom saving throws and all ability checks.

Spellcasting. The lich is an 18th-level spellcaster. Its spellcasting ability is Intelligence (spell save DC 20, +12 to hit with spell attacks). The lich has the following wizard spells prepared:

Cantrips (at will): *mage hand, prestidigitation, ray of frost*
1st level (4 slots): *detect magic, magic missile, shield, thunderwave*
2nd level (3 slots): *detect thoughts, invisibility, Melf's acid arrow, mirror image*
3rd level (3 slots): *animate dead, counterspell, dispel magic, fireball*
4th level (3 slots): *blight, dimension door*
5th level (3 slots): *cloudkill, scrying*
6th level (1 slot): *disintegrate, globe of invulnerability*
7th level (1 slot): *finger of death, plane shift*
8th level (1 slot): *dominate monster, power word stun*
9th level (1 slot): *power word kill*

Turn Resistance. The lich has advantage on saving throws against any effect that turns undead.

ACTIONS

Paralyzing Touch. *Melee Spell Attack:* +12 to hit, reach 5 ft., one creature. *Hit:* 10 (3d6) cold damage. The target must succeed on a DC 18 Constitution saving throw or be paralyzed for 1 minute. The target can repeat the saving throw at the end of each of its turns, ending the effect on itself on a success.

LEGENDARY ACTIONS

The lich can take 3 legendary actions, choosing from the options below. Only one legendary action option can be used at a time and only at the end of another creature's turn. The lich regains spent legendary actions at the start of its turn.

Cantrip. The lich casts a cantrip.
Paralyzing Touch (Costs 2 Actions). The lich uses its Paralyzing Touch.
Frightening Gaze (Costs 2 Actions). The lich fixes its gaze on one creature it can see within 10 feet of it. The target must succeed on a DC 18 Wisdom saving throw against this magic or become frightened for 1 minute. The frightened target can repeat the saving throw at the end of each of its turns, ending the effect on itself on a success. If a target's saving throw is successful or the effect ends for it, the target is immune to the lich's gaze for the next 24 hours.
Disrupt Life (Costs 3 Actions). Each non-undead creature within 20 feet of the lich must make a DC 18 Constitution saving throw against this magic, taking 21 (6d6) necrotic damage on a failed save, or half as much damage on a successful one.

LICH
Medium undead, any evil alignment

Armor Class 17 (natural armor)
Hit Points 135 (18d8 + 54)
Speed 30 ft.

STR	DEX	CON	INT	WIS	CHA
11 (+0)	16 (+3)	16 (+3)	20 (+5)	14 (+2)	16 (+3)

Saving Throws Con +10, Int +12, Wis +9
Skills Arcana +18, History +12, Insight +9, Perception +9
Damage Resistances cold, lightning, necrotic
Damage Immunities poison; bludgeoning, piercing, and slashing from nonmagical attacks
Condition Immunities charmed, exhaustion, frightened, paralyzed, poisoned
Senses truesight 120 ft., passive Perception 19
Languages Common plus up to five other languages
Challenge 21 (33,000 XP)

Legendary Resistance (3/Day). If the lich fails a saving throw, it can choose to succeed instead.

Rejuvenation. If it has a phylactery, a destroyed lich gains a new body in 1d10 days, regaining all its hit points and becoming active again. The new body appears within 5 feet of the phylactery.

Lich

Liches are the remains of great wizards who embrace undeath as a means of preserving themselves. They further their own power at any cost, having no interest in the affairs of the living except where those affairs interfere with their own. Scheming and insane, they hunger for long-forgotten knowledge and the most terrible secrets. Because the shadow of death doesn't hang over them, they can conceive plans that take years, decades, or centuries to come to fruition.

A lich is a gaunt and skeletal humanoid with withered flesh stretched tight across its bones. Its eyes succumbed to decay long ago, but points of light burn in its empty sockets. It is often garbed in the moldering remains of fine clothing and jewelry worn and dulled by the passage of time.

Secrets of Undeath. No wizard takes up the path to lichdom on a whim, and the process of becoming a lich is a well-guarded secret. Wizards that seek lichdom must make bargains with fiends, evil gods, or other foul entities. Many turn to Orcus, Demon Prince of Undeath, whose power has created countless liches. However, those that control the power of lichdom always demand fealty and service for their knowledge.

A lich is created by an arcane ritual that traps the wizard's soul within a phylactery. Doing so binds the soul to the mortal world, preventing it from traveling to the Outer Planes after death. A phylactery is traditionally an amulet in the shape of a small box, but it can take the form of any item possessing an interior space into which arcane sigils of naming, binding, immortality, and dark magic are scribed in silver.

With its phylactery prepared, the future lich drinks a potion of transformation—a vile concoction of poison mixed with the blood of a sentient creature whose soul is sacrificed to the phylactery. The wizard falls dead, then rises as a lich as its soul is drawn into the phylactery, where it forever remains.

Soul Sacrifices. A lich must periodically feed souls to its phylactery to sustain the magic preserving its body and consciousness. It does this using the *imprisonment* spell. Instead of choosing one of the normal options of the spell, the lich uses the spell to magically trap the target's body and soul inside its phylactery. The phylactery must be on the same plane as the lich for the spell to work. A lich's phylactery can hold only one creature at a time, and a *dispel magic* cast as a 9th-level spell upon the phylactery releases any creature imprisoned within it. A creature imprisoned in the phylactery for 24 hours is consumed and destroyed utterly, whereupon nothing short of divine intervention can restore it to life.

A lich that fails or forgets to maintain its body with sacrificed souls begins to physically fall apart, and might eventually become a demilich.

Death and Restoration. When a lich's body is broken by accident or assault, the will and mind of the lich drains from it, leaving only a lifeless corpse behind. Within days, a new body reforms next to the lich's phylactery, coalescing out of glowing smoke that issues from the device. Because the destruction of its phylactery means the possibility of eternal death, a lich usually keeps its phylactery in a hidden, well-guarded location.

Destroying a lich's phylactery is no easy task and often requires a special ritual, item, or weapon. Every phylactery is unique, and discovering the key to its destruction can be a quest in and of itself.

Lonely Existence. From time to time, a lich might be stirred from its single-minded pursuit of power to take an interest in the world around it, most often when some great event reminds it of the life it once led. It otherwise lives in isolation, engaging only with those creatures whose service helps secure its lair.

Few liches call themselves by their former names, instead adopting monikers such as the Black Hand or the Forgotten King.

Magic Collectors. Liches collect spells and magic items. In addition to its spell repertoire, a lich has ready access to potions, scrolls, libraries of spellbooks, one or more wands, and perhaps a staff or two. It has no qualms about putting these treasures to use whenever its lair comes under attack.

Undead Nature. A lich doesn't require air, food, drink, or sleep.

A Lich's Lair

A lich often haunts the abode it favored in life, such as a lonely tower, a haunted ruin, or an academy of black magic. Alternatively, some liches construct secret tombs filled with powerful guardians and traps.

Everything about a lich's lair reflects its keen mind and wicked cunning, including the magic and mundane traps that secure it. Undead, constructs, and bound demons lurk in shadowy recesses, emerging to destroy those who dare to disturb the lich's work.

A lich encountered in its lair has a challenge rating of 22 (41,000 XP).

Lair Actions

On initiative count 20 (losing initiative ties), the lich can take a lair action to cause one of the following magical effects; the lich can't use the same effect two rounds in a row:

- The lich rolls a d8 and regains a spell slot of that level or lower. If it has no spent spell slots of that level or lower, nothing happens.
- The lich targets one creature it can see within 30 feet of it. A crackling cord of negative energy tethers the lich to the target. Whenever the lich takes damage, the target must make a DC 18 Constitution saving throw. On a failed save, the lich takes half the damage (rounded down), and the target takes the remaining damage. This tether lasts until initiative count 20 on the next round or until the lich or the target is no longer in the lich's lair.
- The lich calls forth the spirits of creatures that died in its lair. These apparitions materialize and attack one creature that the lich can see within 60 feet of it. The target must succeed on a DC 18 Constitution saving throw, taking 52 (15d6) necrotic damage on a failed save, or half as much damage on a success. The apparitions then disappear.

LIZARDFOLK

Lizardfolk are primitive reptilian humanoids that lurk in the swamps and jungles of the world. Their hut villages thrive in forbidding grottos, half-sunken ruins, and watery caverns.

Territorial Xenophobes. Lizardfolk deal and trade with other races only rarely. Fiercely territorial, they use camouflaged scouts to guard the perimeter of their domain. When unwelcome visitors are detected, a tribe sends a hunting band to harass or drive the trespassers off, or tricks them into blundering into the lairs of crocodiles and other dangerous creatures.

Lizardfolk have no notion of traditional morality, and they find the concepts of good and evil utterly alien. Truly neutral creatures, they kill when it is expedient and do whatever it takes to survive.

Lizardfolk rarely stray beyond their claimed hunting grounds. Any creature that enters their territory is fair game to be stalked, killed, and devoured. They make no distinction between humanoids, beasts, and monsters. Similarly, lizardfolk don't like reaching too far beyond their borders, where they could easily become the hunted instead of the hunters.

Occasions might arise when lizardfolk will form alliances with their neighbors. These lizardfolk usually learn firsthand that humans, dwarves, halflings, and elves can sometimes prove helpful or trustworthy. Once lizardfolk forge ties with outsiders, they are steadfast and fierce allies.

Great Feasts and Sacrifices. Lizardfolk are omnivorous, but they have a taste for humanoid flesh. Prisoners are often taken back to their camps to become the centerpieces of great feasts and rites involving dancing, storytelling, and ritual combat. Victims are either cooked and eaten by the tribe, or are sacrificed to Semuanya, the lizardfolk god.

Canny Crafters. Though they aren't skilled artisans, lizardfolk craft tools and ornamental jewelry out of the bones of their kills, and they use the hides and shells of dead monsters to create shields.

Lizardfolk Leaders. Lizardfolk respect and fear magic with a religious awe. Lizardfolk shamans lead their tribes, overseeing rites and ceremonies performed to honor Semuanya. From time to time, however, a lizardfolk tribe produces a powerful figure touched not by Semuanya but by Sess'inek—a reptilian demon lord who seeks to corrupt and control the lizardfolk.

Lizardfolk born in Sess'inek's image are larger and more cunning than other lizardfolk, and are thoroughly evil. These lizard kings and queens dominate lizardfolk tribes, usurping a shaman's authority and inspiring uncharacteristic aggression among their subjects.

Dragon Worshipers. Lizardfolk speak Draconic, which they are thought to have learned from dragons in ancient times. A tribe that wanders into the territory of a dragon will offer it tribute to win its favor. An evil dragon might exploit lizardfolk for its own vile ends, turning them into raiders and plunderers.

LIZARDFOLK
Medium humanoid (lizardfolk), neutral

Armor Class 15 (natural armor, shield)
Hit Points 22 (4d8 + 4)
Speed 30 ft., swim 30 ft.

STR	DEX	CON	INT	WIS	CHA
15 (+2)	10 (+0)	13 (+1)	7 (−2)	12 (+1)	7 (−2)

Skills Perception +3, Stealth +4, Survival +5
Senses passive Perception 13
Languages Draconic
Challenge 1/2 (100 XP)

Hold Breath. The lizardfolk can hold its breath for 15 minutes.

ACTIONS

Multiattack. The lizardfolk makes two melee attacks, each one with a different weapon.

Bite. *Melee Weapon Attack:* +4 to hit, reach 5 ft., one target. *Hit:* 5 (1d6 + 2) piercing damage.

Heavy Club. *Melee Weapon Attack:* +4 to hit, reach 5 ft., one target. *Hit:* 5 (1d6 + 2) bludgeoning damage.

Javelin. *Melee or Ranged Weapon Attack:* +4 to hit, reach 5 ft. or range 30/120 ft., one target. *Hit:* 5 (1d6 + 2) piercing damage.

Spiked Shield. *Melee Weapon Attack:* +4 to hit, reach 5 ft., one target. *Hit:* 5 (1d6 + 2) piercing damage.

LIZARDFOLK SHAMAN

Medium humanoid (lizardfolk), neutral

Armor Class 13 (natural armor)
Hit Points 27 (5d8 + 5)
Speed 30 ft., swim 30 ft.

STR	DEX	CON	INT	WIS	CHA
15 (+2)	10 (+0)	13 (+1)	10 (+0)	15 (+2)	8 (−1)

Skills Perception +4, Stealth +4, Survival +6
Senses passive Perception 14
Languages Draconic
Challenge 2 (450 XP)

Hold Breath. The lizardfolk can hold its breath for 15 minutes.

Spellcasting (Lizardfolk Form Only). The lizardfolk is a 5th-level spellcaster. Its spellcasting ability is Wisdom (spell save DC 12, +4 to hit with spell attacks). The lizardfolk has the following druid spells prepared:

Cantrips (at will): *druidcraft, produce flame, thorn whip*
1st level (4 slots): *entangle, fog cloud*
2nd level (3 slots): *heat metal, spike growth*
3rd level (2 slots): *conjure animals* (reptiles only), *plant growth*

ACTIONS

Multiattack (Lizardfolk Form Only). The lizardfolk makes two attacks: one with its bite and one with its claws.

Bite. *Melee Weapon Attack:* +4 to hit, reach 5 ft., one target. *Hit:* 5 (1d6 + 2) piercing damage, or 7 (1d10 + 2) piercing damage in crocodile form. If the lizardfolk is in crocodile form and the target is a Large or smaller creature, the target is grappled (escape DC 12). Until this grapple ends, the target is restrained, and the lizardfolk can't bite another target. If the lizardfolk reverts to its true form, the grapple ends.

Claws (Lizardfolk Form Only). *Melee Weapon Attack:* +4 to hit, reach 5 ft., one target. *Hit:* 4 (1d4 + 2) slashing damage.

Change Shape (Recharges after a Short or Long Rest). The lizardfolk magically polymorphs into a crocodile, remaining in that form for up to 1 hour. It can revert to its true form as a bonus action. Its statistics, other than its size, are the same in each form. Any equipment it is wearing or carrying isn't transformed. It reverts to its true form if it dies.

> "IN ALL MY DEALINGS WITH THE LIZARDFOLK, I WAS NEVER ABLE TO TELL WHAT THEY WERE THINKING. THEIR REPTILIAN EYES BELIED NO HINT OF THEIR INTENTIONS. I GAVE THEM SUPPLIES. THEY GAVE ME THE WILLIES."
> —A MERCHANT'S ACCOUNT OF HIS EXPERIENCE WITH THE LIZARDFOLK TRIBES OF THE LIZARD MARSH

LIZARD KING/QUEEN

Medium humanoid (lizardfolk), chaotic evil

Armor Class 15 (natural armor)
Hit Points 78 (12d8 + 24)
Speed 30 ft., swim 30 ft.

STR	DEX	CON	INT	WIS	CHA
17 (+3)	12 (+1)	15 (+2)	11 (+0)	11 (+0)	15 (+2)

Saving Throws Con +4, Wis +2
Skills Perception +4, Stealth +5, Survival +4
Condition Immunities frightened
Senses darkvision 60 ft., passive Perception 14
Languages Abyssal, Draconic
Challenge 4 (1,100 XP)

Hold Breath. The lizardfolk can hold its breath for 15 minutes.

Skewer. Once per turn, when the lizardfolk makes a melee attack with its trident and hits, the target takes an extra 10 (3d6) damage, and the lizardfolk gains temporary hit points equal to the extra damage dealt.

ACTIONS

Multiattack. The lizardfolk makes two attacks: one with its bite and one with its claws or trident or two melee attacks with its trident.

Bite. *Melee Weapon Attack:* +5 to hit, reach 5 ft., one target. *Hit:* 6 (1d6 + 3) piercing damage.

Claws. *Melee Weapon Attack:* +5 to hit, reach 5 ft., one target. *Hit:* 5 (1d4 + 3) slashing damage.

Trident. *Melee or Ranged Weapon Attack:* +5 to hit, reach 5 ft. or range 20/60 ft., one target. *Hit:* 6 (1d6 + 3) piercing damage, or 7 (1d8 + 3) piercing damage if used with two hands to make a melee attack.

LYCANTHROPES

One of the most ancient and feared of all curses, lycanthropy can transform the most civilized humanoid into a ravening beast. In its natural humanoid form, a creature cursed by lycanthropy appears as its normal self. Over time, however, many lycanthropes acquire features suggestive of their animal form. In that animal form, a lycanthrope resembles a powerful version of a normal animal. On close inspection, its eyes show a faint spark of unnatural intelligence and might glow red in the dark.

Evil lycanthropes hide among normal folk, emerging in animal form at night to spread terror and bloodshed, especially under a full moon. Good lycanthropes are reclusive and uncomfortable around other civilized creatures, often living alone in wilderness areas far from villages and towns.

Curse of Lycanthropy. A humanoid creature can be afflicted with the curse of lycanthropy after being wounded by a lycanthrope, or if one or both of its parents are lycanthropes. A *remove curse* spell can rid an afflicted lycanthrope of the curse, but a natural born lycanthrope can be freed of the curse only with a *wish*.

A lycanthrope can either resist its curse or embrace it. By resisting the curse, a lycanthrope retains its normal alignment and personality while in humanoid form. It lives its life as it always has, burying deep the bestial urges raging inside it. However, when the full moon rises, the curse becomes too strong to resist, transforming the individual into its beast form—or into a horrible hybrid form that combines animal and humanoid traits. When the moon wanes, the beast within can be controlled once again. Especially if the cursed creature is unaware of its condition, it might not remember the events of its transformation, though those memories often haunt a lycanthrope as bloody dreams.

Some individuals see little point in fighting the curse and accept what they are. With time and experience, they learn to master their shapechanging ability and can assume beast form or hybrid form at will. Most lycanthropes that embrace their bestial natures succumb to bloodlust, becoming evil, opportunistic creatures that prey on the weak.

WEREBEAR

Werebears are powerful lycanthropes with the ability to temper their monstrous natures and reject their violent impulses. In humanoid form, they are large, muscular, and covered in hair matching the color of their ursine form's fur. A werebear is a loner by nature, fearing what might happen to innocent creatures around it when its bestial nature takes over.

> ### VARIANT: NONHUMAN LYCANTHROPES
>
> The statistics presented in this section assume a base creature of human. However, you can also use the statistics to represent nonhuman lycanthropes, adding verisimilitude by allowing a nonhuman lycanthrope to retain one or more of its humanoid racial traits. For example, an elf werewolf might have the Fey Ancestry trait.

When a werebear transforms, it grows to enormous size, lashing out with weapons or claws. It fights with the ferocity of a bear, though even in its bestial forms, it avoids biting so as to not pass on its curse. Typically, a werebear passes on its lycanthropy only to chosen companions or apprentices, spending the time that follows helping the new lycanthrope accept the curse in order to control it.

Solitary creatures, werebears act as wardens over their territory, protecting flora and fauna alike from humanoid or monstrous intrusion. Though most werebears are of good alignment, some are every bit as evil as other lycanthropes.

WEREBOAR

Wereboars are ill-tempered and vulgar brutes. As humanoids, they are stocky and muscular, with short, stiff hair. In their humanoid and hybrid forms, they use heavy weapons, while in hybrid or animal form, they gain a devastating goring attack through which their curse is spread. A wereboar infects other creatures indiscriminately, relishing the fact that the more its victims resist the curse, the more savage and bestial they become.

Wereboars live in small family groups in remote forest areas, building ramshackle huts or dwelling in caves. They are suspicious of strangers but sometimes ally themselves with orcs.

WERERAT

Wererats are cunning lycanthropes with sly, avaricious personalities. They are wiry and twitchy in humanoid form, with thin hair and darting eyes. In their humanoid and hybrid forms, wererats prefer light weapons and use ambush tactics rather than fighting as a pack. Although a wererat can deliver a nasty bite in its rat form, it favors that form for stealthy infiltration and escape rather than combat.

A wererat clan operates much like a thieves' guild, with wererats transmitting their curse only to creatures they want to induct into the clan. Wererats that are accidentally cursed or break loose from the clan's control are quickly hunted down and killed.

Wererat clans are found throughout urban civilization, often dwelling in cellars and catacombs. These creatures are common in the sewers beneath major cities, viewing those subterranean areas as their hunting grounds. Rats and giant rats are commonly found living among wererats.

WERETIGER

Weretigers are ferocious hunters and warriors with a haughty and fastidious nature. Lithe and sleekly muscular in humanoid form, they are taller than average and meticulously groomed. Weretigers grow to enormous size in animal and hybrid form, but they fight in their more refined humanoid form when they can. They don't like to pass on their curse, because every new weretiger means competition for territory and prey.

Weretigers live in jungles on the fringes of humanoid civilization, traveling to isolated settlements to trade or revel. They live and hunt alone or in small family groups.

WEREWOLF

A werewolf is a savage predator. In its humanoid form, a werewolf has heightened senses, a fiery temper, and a tendency to eat rare meat. Its wolf form is a fearsome predator, but its hybrid form is more terrifying by far—a furred and well-muscled humanoid body topped by a ravening wolf's head. A werewolf can wield weapons in hybrid form, though it prefers to tear foes apart with its powerful claws and bite.

Most werewolves flee civilized lands not long after becoming afflicted. Those that reject the curse fear what will happen if they remain among their friends and family. Those that embrace the curse fear discovery and the consequences of their murderous acts. In the wild, werewolves form packs that also include wolves and dire wolves.

> ### PLAYER CHARACTERS AS LYCANTHROPES
>
> A character who becomes a lycanthrope retains his or her statistics except as specified by lycanthrope type. The character gains the lycanthrope's speeds in nonhumanoid form, damage immunities, traits, and actions that don't involve equipment. The character is proficient with the lycanthrope's natural attacks, such as its bite or claws, which deal damage as shown in the lycanthrope's statistics. The character can't speak while in animal form.
>
> A humanoid hit by an attack that carries the curse of lycanthropy must succeed on a Constitution saving throw (DC 8 + the lycanthrope's proficiency bonus + the lycanthrope's Constitution modifier) or be cursed. If the character embraces the curse, his or her alignment becomes the one defined for the lycanthrope. The DM is free to decide that a change in alignment places the character under DM control until the curse of lycanthropy is removed.
>
> The following information applies to specific lycanthropes.
>
> *Werebear.* The character gains a Strength of 19 if his or her score isn't already higher, and a +1 bonus to AC while in bear or hybrid form (from natural armor). Attack and damage rolls for the natural weapons are based on Strength.
>
> *Wereboar.* The character gains a Strength of 17 if his or her score isn't already higher, and a +1 bonus to AC while in boar or hybrid form (from natural armor). Attack and damage rolls for the tusks are based on Strength. For the Charge trait, the DC is 8 + the character's proficiency bonus + Strength modifier.
>
> *Wererat.* The character gains a Dexterity of 15 if his or her score isn't already higher. Attack and damage rolls for the bite are based on whichever is higher of the character's Strength and Dexterity.
>
> *Weretiger.* The character gains a Strength of 17 if his or her score isn't already higher. Attack and damage rolls for the natural weapons are based on Strength. For the Pounce trait, the DC is 8 + the character's proficiency bonus + Strength modifier.
>
> *Werewolf.* The character gains a Strength of 15 if his or her score isn't already higher, and a +1 bonus to AC while in wolf or hybrid form (from natural armor). Attack and damage rolls for the natural weapons are based on Strength.

Werebear

Medium humanoid (human, shapechanger), neutral good

Armor Class 10 in humanoid form, 11 (natural armor) in bear
and hybrid form
Hit Points 135 (18d8 + 54)
Speed 30 ft. (40 ft., climb 30 ft. in bear or hybrid form)

STR	DEX	CON	INT	WIS	CHA
19 (+4)	10 (+0)	17 (+3)	11 (+0)	12 (+1)	12 (+1)

Skills Perception +7
Damage Immunities bludgeoning, piercing, and slashing from
nonmagical attacks not made with silvered weapons
Senses passive Perception 17
Languages Common (can't speak in bear form)
Challenge 5 (1,800 XP)

Shapechanger. The werebear can use its action to polymorph
into a Large bear-humanoid hybrid or into a Large bear, or back
into its true form, which is humanoid. Its statistics, other than
its size and AC, are the same in each form. Any equipment it is
wearing or carrying isn't transformed. It reverts to its true form
if it dies.

Keen Smell. The werebear has advantage on Wisdom
(Perception) checks that rely on smell.

Actions

Multiattack. In bear form, the werebear makes two claw
attacks. In humanoid form, it makes two greataxe attacks. In
hybrid form, it can attack like a bear or a humanoid.

Bite (Bear or Hybrid Form Only). *Melee Weapon Attack:* +7
to hit, reach 5 ft., one target. *Hit:* 15 (2d10 + 4) piercing
damage. If the target is a humanoid, it must succeed on a
DC 14 Constitution saving throw or be cursed with werebear
lycanthropy.

Claw (Bear or Hybrid Form Only). *Melee Weapon Attack:* +7 to
hit, reach 5 ft., one target. *Hit:* 13 (2d8 + 4) slashing damage.

Greataxe (Humanoid or Hybrid Form Only). *Melee Weapon
Attack:* +7 to hit, reach 5 ft., one target. *Hit:* 10 (1d12 + 4)
slashing damage.

L

WEREBOAR

Medium humanoid (human, shapechanger), neutral evil

Armor Class 10 in humanoid form, 11 (natural armor) in boar or hybrid form
Hit Points 78 (12d8 + 24)
Speed 30 ft. (40 ft. in boar form)

STR	DEX	CON	INT	WIS	CHA
17 (+3)	10 (+0)	15 (+2)	10 (+0)	11 (+0)	8 (−1)

Skills Perception +2
Damage Immunities bludgeoning, piercing, and slashing from nonmagical attacks not made with silvered weapons
Senses passive Perception 12
Languages Common (can't speak in boar form)
Challenge 4 (1,100 XP)

Shapechanger. The wereboar can use its action to polymorph into a boar-humanoid hybrid or into a boar, or back into its true form, which is humanoid. Its statistics, other than its AC, are the same in each form. Any equipment it is wearing or carrying isn't transformed. It reverts to its true form if it dies.

Charge (Boar or Hybrid Form Only). If the wereboar moves at least 15 feet straight toward a target and then hits it with its tusks on the same turn, the target takes an extra 7 (2d6) slashing damage. If the target is a creature, it must succeed on a DC 13 Strength saving throw or be knocked prone.

Relentless (Recharges after a Short or Long Rest). If the wereboar takes 14 damage or less that would reduce it to 0 hit points, it is reduced to 1 hit point instead.

ACTIONS

Multiattack (Humanoid or Hybrid Form Only). The wereboar makes two attacks, only one of which can be with its tusks.

Maul (Humanoid or Hybrid Form Only). *Melee Weapon Attack:* +5 to hit, reach 5 ft., one target. *Hit:* 10 (2d6 + 3) bludgeoning damage.

Tusks (Boar or Hybrid Form Only). *Melee Weapon Attack:* +5 to hit, reach 5 ft., one target. *Hit:* 10 (2d6 + 3) slashing damage. If the target is a humanoid, it must succeed on a DC 12 Constitution saving throw or be cursed with wereboar lycanthropy.

WERERAT

Medium humanoid (human, shapechanger), lawful evil

Armor Class 12
Hit Points 33 (6d8 + 6)
Speed 30 ft.

STR	DEX	CON	INT	WIS	CHA
10 (+0)	15 (+2)	12 (+1)	11 (+0)	10 (+0)	8 (−1)

Skills Perception +2, Stealth +4
Damage Immunities bludgeoning, piercing, and slashing from nonmagical attacks not made with silvered weapons
Senses darkvision 60 ft. (rat form only), passive Perception 12
Languages Common (can't speak in rat form)
Challenge 2 (450 XP)

Shapechanger. The wererat can use its action to polymorph into a rat-humanoid hybrid or into a giant rat, or back into its true form, which is humanoid. Its statistics, other than its size, are the same in each form. Any equipment it is wearing or carrying isn't transformed. It reverts to its true form if it dies.

Keen Smell. The wererat has advantage on Wisdom (Perception) checks that rely on smell.

ACTIONS

Multiattack (Humanoid or Hybrid Form Only). The wererat makes two attacks, only one of which can be a bite.

Bite (Rat or Hybrid Form Only). *Melee Weapon Attack:* +4 to hit, reach 5 ft., one target. *Hit:* 4 (1d4 + 2) piercing damage. If the target is a humanoid, it must succeed on a DC 11 Constitution saving throw or be cursed with wererat lycanthropy.

Shortsword (Humanoid or Hybrid Form Only). *Melee Weapon Attack:* +4 to hit, reach 5 ft., one target. *Hit:* 5 (1d6 + 2) piercing damage.

Hand Crossbow (Humanoid or Hybrid Form Only). *Ranged Weapon Attack:* +4 to hit, range 30/120 ft., one target. *Hit:* 5 (1d6 + 2) piercing damage.

Weretiger

Medium humanoid (human, shapechanger), neutral

Armor Class 12
Hit Points 120 (16d8 + 48)
Speed 30 ft. (40 ft. in tiger form)

STR	DEX	CON	INT	WIS	CHA
17 (+3)	15 (+2)	16 (+3)	10 (+0)	13 (+1)	11 (+0)

Skills Perception +5, Stealth +4
Damage Immunities bludgeoning, piercing, and slashing from nonmagical attacks not made with silvered weapons
Senses darkvision 60 ft., passive Perception 15
Languages Common (can't speak in tiger form)
Challenge 4 (1,100 XP)

Shapechanger. The weretiger can use its action to polymorph into a tiger-humanoid hybrid or into a tiger, or back into its true form, which is humanoid. Its statistics, other than its size, are the same in each form. Any equipment it is wearing or carrying isn't transformed. It reverts to its true form if it dies.

Keen Hearing and Smell. The weretiger has advantage on Wisdom (Perception) checks that rely on hearing or smell.

Pounce (Tiger or Hybrid Form Only). If the weretiger moves at least 15 feet straight toward a creature and then hits it with a claw attack on the same turn, that target must succeed on a DC 14 Strength saving throw or be knocked prone. If the target is prone, the weretiger can make one bite attack against it as a bonus action.

Actions

Multiattack (Humanoid or Hybrid Form Only). In humanoid form, the weretiger makes two scimitar attacks or two longbow attacks. In hybrid form, it can attack like a humanoid or make two claw attacks.

Bite (Tiger or Hybrid Form Only). *Melee Weapon Attack:* +5 to hit, reach 5 ft., one target. *Hit:* 8 (1d10 + 3) piercing damage. If the target is a humanoid, it must succeed on a DC 13 Constitution saving throw or be cursed with weretiger lycanthropy.

Claw (Tiger or Hybrid Form Only). *Melee Weapon Attack:* +5 to hit, reach 5 ft., one target. *Hit:* 7 (1d8 + 3) slashing damage.

Scimitar (Humanoid or Hybrid Form Only). *Melee Weapon Attack:* +5 to hit, reach 5 ft., one target. *Hit:* 6 (1d6 + 3) slashing damage.

Longbow (Humanoid or Hybrid Form Only). *Ranged Weapon Attack:* +4 to hit, range 150/600 ft., one target. *Hit:* 6 (1d8 + 2) piercing damage.

"The Company of the Black Moon—they used to be adventurers loyal to the realm. Now they roam the woods as a pack of werewolves. The king has promised estates, titles, and gold to anyone who can undo the curse afflicting them. I, for one, have no interest in such rewards."

—Thornstaff, elf druid

Werewolf

Medium humanoid (human, shapechanger), chaotic evil

Armor Class 11 in humanoid form, 12 (natural armor) in wolf or hybrid form
Hit Points 58 (9d8 + 18)
Speed 30 ft. (40 ft. in wolf form)

STR	DEX	CON	INT	WIS	CHA
15 (+2)	13 (+1)	14 (+2)	10 (+0)	11 (+0)	10 (+0)

Skills Perception +4, Stealth +3
Damage Immunities bludgeoning, piercing, and slashing from nonmagical attacks not made with silvered weapons
Senses passive Perception 14
Languages Common (can't speak in wolf form)
Challenge 3 (700 XP)

Shapechanger. The werewolf can use its action to polymorph into a wolf-humanoid hybrid or into a wolf, or back into its true form, which is humanoid. Its statistics, other than its AC, are the same in each form. Any equipment it is wearing or carrying isn't transformed. It reverts to its true form if it dies.

Keen Hearing and Smell. The werewolf has advantage on Wisdom (Perception) checks that rely on hearing or smell.

Actions

Multiattack (Humanoid or Hybrid Form Only). The werewolf makes two attacks: one with its bite and one with its claws or spear.

Bite (Wolf or Hybrid Form Only). *Melee Weapon Attack:* +4 to hit, reach 5 ft., one target. *Hit:* 6 (1d8 + 2) piercing damage. If the target is a humanoid, it must succeed on a DC 12 Constitution saving throw or be cursed with werewolf lycanthropy.

Claws (Hybrid Form Only). *Melee Weapon Attack:* +4 to hit, reach 5 ft., one creature. *Hit:* 7 (2d4 + 2) slashing damage.

Spear (Humanoid Form Only). *Melee or Ranged Weapon Attack:* +4 to hit, reach 5 ft. or range 20/60 ft., one creature. *Hit:* 5 (1d6 + 2) piercing damage, or 6 (1d8 + 2) piercing damage if used with two hands to make a melee attack.

Magmin

A grinning, mischievous magmin resembles a stumpy humanoid sculpted from a black shell of magma. Even when it isn't ablaze and radiating heat like a bonfire, small jets of flame erupt from its porous skin.

Summoned Pyromaniacs. Magmins are fire elemental spirits bound into physical forms by magic, and they appear in the Material Plane only when summoned. They view flammable objects as kindling for a grand conflagration, and only the magical control exerted by their summoners keeps them from setting everything they touch ablaze. Their propensity for fire and havoc makes them ideal for spreading chaos and destruction. A mob of magmins summoned inside a castle can reduce it to a burning shell within minutes.

Fiery Destruction. Although its flame is potent, the magmin's hard magma shell prevents it from instantly igniting everything it comes into contact with. However, like the fires inside them, magmins are capricious and unpredictable. Moreover, as simple elemental creations, they are oblivious to the harm their native element causes creatures of the Material Plane.

If it has the opportunity while in service to its master, a magmin seeks out areas of great heat, such as forest fires or the bubbling magma of an active volcano. At other times, a magmin compulsively looses fire from its fingertips, delighting in setting objects ablaze.

Magmin
Small elemental, chaotic neutral

Armor Class 14 (natural armor)
Hit Points 9 (2d6 + 2)
Speed 30 ft.

STR	DEX	CON	INT	WIS	CHA
7 (−2)	15 (+2)	12 (+1)	8 (−1)	11 (+0)	10 (+0)

Damage Resistances bludgeoning, piercing, and slashing from nonmagical attacks
Damage Immunities fire
Senses darkvision 60 ft., passive Perception 10
Languages Ignan
Challenge 1/2 (100 XP)

Death Burst. When the magmin dies, it explodes in a burst of fire and magma. Each creature within 10 feet of it must make a DC 11 Dexterity saving throw, taking 7 (2d6) fire damage on a failed save, or half as much damage on a successful one. Flammable objects that aren't being worn or carried in that area are ignited.

Ignited Illumination. As a bonus action, the magmin can set itself ablaze or extinguish its flames. While ablaze, the magmin sheds bright light in a 10-foot radius and dim light for an additional 10 feet.

Actions

Touch. *Melee Weapon Attack:* +4 to hit, reach 5 ft., one target. *Hit:* 7 (2d6) fire damage. If the target is a creature or a flammable object, it ignites. Until a creature takes an action to douse the fire, the target takes 3 (1d6) fire damage at the end of each of its turns.

"Manticores love the taste of human flesh. That's why, on trips through the mountains, I always travel with human guards."
—Marthok Uldarr, dwarf copper merchant

Manticore

A monster in every sense of the word, a manticore has a vaguely humanoid head, the body of a lion, and the wings of a dragon. A bristling mane stretches down the creature's back, and its long tail ends in a cluster of deadly spikes that can impale prey at impressive range.

Evil Predators. Manticores are fierce killers that hunt far and wide for prey. They work together to take down particularly large or dangerous creatures, sharing the meal once a kill is made. A manticore begins its attack with a volley of tail spikes, then lands and uses its claws and bite. When outdoors and outnumbered, it uses its wings to stay aloft, attacking from a distance until its spikes are depleted.

A manticore isn't particularly bright, but it possesses a malevolent nature and the ability to converse. In the course of attacking, it denigrates its foes and offers to kill them swiftly if they beg for their lives. If a manticore sees an advantage to be gained by sparing a creature's life, it does so, asking for a tribute or sacrifice equal to its loss of food.

Monstrous Relationships. Manticores serve wicked masters that treat them well and provide regular prey. A manticore might provide aerial support for an orc horde or a hobgoblin army. Another could serve as a hunting companion for a hill giant chief, or guard the entrance to a lamia's lair.

The manticores' greatest territorial rivals include chimeras, griffons, perytons, and wyverns. Manticores hunting as a pack often have the advantage of greater numbers. In addition to these creatures, manticores fear dragons and avoid them.

Manticore

Large monstrosity, lawful evil

Armor Class 14 (natural armor)
Hit Points 68 (8d10 + 24)
Speed 30 ft., fly 50 ft.

STR	DEX	CON	INT	WIS	CHA
17 (+3)	16 (+3)	17 (+3)	7 (−2)	12 (+1)	8 (−1)

Senses darkvision 60 ft., passive Perception 11
Languages Common
Challenge 3 (700 XP)

Tail Spike Regrowth. The manticore has twenty-four tail spikes. Used spikes regrow when the manticore finishes a long rest.

Actions

Multiattack. The manticore makes three attacks: one with its bite and two with its claws or three with its tail spikes.

Bite. *Melee Weapon Attack:* +5 to hit, reach 5 ft., one target. *Hit:* 7 (1d8 + 3) piercing damage.

Claw. *Melee Weapon Attack:* +5 to hit, reach 5 ft., one target. *Hit:* 6 (1d6 + 3) slashing damage.

Tail Spike. *Ranged Weapon Attack:* +5 to hit, range 100/200 ft., one target. *Hit:* 7 (1d8 + 3) piercing damage.

Medusa Lairs. Medusas live forever in seclusion, alienated from the world around them by their monstrous form and caprice. Their homes gradually fall into disrepair until they are little more than shadowy ruins covered with thorns and creepers, riddled with obstructions and hiding places. Foolhardy looters and adventurers who enter are often unaware of the medusa's presence until the creature is among them.

A medusa is subject to its own curse. By looking vainly on its reflection, it turns to stone as surely as any living mortal. As a result, a medusa destroys or removes any mirrors or reflective surfaces in its lair.

Medusa

As deadly as they are ravishing, the serpent-haired medusas suffer an immortal curse brought on by their vanity. They lurk in quiet exile among the tumbled ruins of their former lives, surrounded by the petrified remains of past admirers and would-be heroes.

Immortal Splendor. Men and women who desire eternal youth, beauty, and adoration might pray to malicious gods, beg dragons for ancient magic, or seek out powerful archmages to fulfill their wishes. Others make sacrifices to demon lords or archdevils, offering all in exchange for this gift, oblivious to the curse that accompanies it. Those who strike such bargains gain physical beauty, restored youth, immortality, and the adoration of all who behold them, granting them the influence and power they so desire. However, after years of the living like a demigod among mortals, the price for their vanity and hubris is exacted, and they are forever transformed into medusas. A medusa's hair turns into a nest of venomous serpents, and all who gaze upon the medusa are petrified, becoming stone monuments to its corruption.

MEDUSA
Medium monstrosity, lawful evil

Armor Class 15 (natural armor)
Hit Points 127 (17d8 + 51)
Speed 30 ft.

STR	DEX	CON	INT	WIS	CHA
10 (+0)	15 (+2)	16 (+3)	12 (+1)	13 (+1)	15 (+2)

Skills Deception +5, Insight +4, Perception +4, Stealth +5
Senses darkvision 60 ft., passive Perception 14
Languages Common
Challenge 6 (2,300 XP)

Petrifying Gaze. When a creature that can see the medusa's eyes starts its turn within 30 feet of the medusa, the medusa can force it to make a DC 14 Constitution saving throw if the medusa isn't incapacitated and can see the creature. If the saving throw fails by 5 or more, the creature is instantly petrified. Otherwise, a creature that fails the save begins to turn to stone and is restrained. The restrained creature must repeat the saving throw at the end of its next turn, becoming petrified on a failure or ending the effect on a success. The petrification lasts until the creature is freed by the *greater restoration* spell or other magic.

Unless surprised, a creature can avert its eyes to avoid the saving throw at the start of its turn. If the creature does so, it can't see the medusa until the start of its next turn, when it can avert its eyes again. If the creature looks at the medusa in the meantime, it must immediately make the save.

If the medusa sees itself reflected on a polished surface within 30 feet of it and in an area of bright light, the medusa is, due to its curse, affected by its own gaze.

ACTIONS

Multiattack. The medusa makes either three melee attacks—one with its snake hair and two with its shortsword—or two ranged attacks with its longbow.

Snake Hair. *Melee Weapon Attack:* +5 to hit, reach 5 ft., one creature. *Hit:* 4 (1d4 + 2) piercing damage plus 14 (4d6) poison damage.

Shortsword. *Melee Weapon Attack:* +5 to hit, reach 5 ft., one target. *Hit:* 5 (1d6 + 2) piercing damage.

Longbow. *Ranged Weapon Attack:* +5 to hit, range 150/600 ft., one target. *Hit:* 6 (1d8 + 2) piercing damage plus 7 (2d6) poison damage.

ICE MEPHIT

Mephits

Mephits are capricious, imp-like creatures native to the elemental planes. They come in six varieties, each one representing the mixture of two elements.

Ageless tricksters, mephits gather in large numbers on the Elemental Planes and in the Elemental Chaos. They also find their way to the Material Plane, where they prefer to dwell in places where their base elements are abundant. For example, a magma mephit is composed of earth and fire, and it favors volcanic lairs, while an ice mephit, which is composed of air and water, favors frigid locales.

Elemental Nature. A mephit doesn't require food, drink, or sleep.

Dust Mephit

Composed of earth and air, dust mephits are drawn to catacombs and find death morbidly fascinating.

Ice Mephit

Comprising frigid air and water, ice mephits are aloof and cold, surpassing all other mephits in pitiless cruelty.

Dust Mephit
Small elemental, neutral evil

Armor Class 12
Hit Points 17 (5d6)
Speed 30 ft., fly 30 ft.

STR	DEX	CON	INT	WIS	CHA
5 (−3)	14 (+2)	10 (+0)	9 (−1)	11 (+0)	10 (+0)

Skills Perception +2, Stealth +4
Damage Vulnerabilities fire
Damage Immunities poison
Condition Immunities poisoned
Senses darkvision 60 ft., passive Perception 12
Languages Auran, Terran
Challenge 1/2 (100 XP)

Death Burst. When the mephit dies, it explodes in a burst of dust. Each creature within 5 feet of it must then succeed on a DC 10 Constitution saving throw or be blinded for 1 minute. A blinded creature can repeat the saving throw on each of its turns, ending the effect on itself on a success.

Innate Spellcasting (1/Day). The mephit can innately cast *sleep*, requiring no material components. Its innate spellcasting ability is Charisma.

Actions

Claws. Melee Weapon Attack: +4 to hit, reach 5 ft., one creature. *Hit:* 4 (1d4 + 2) slashing damage.

Blinding Breath (Recharge 6). The mephit exhales a 15-foot cone of blinding dust. Each creature in that area must succeed on a DC 10 Dexterity saving throw or be blinded for 1 minute. A creature can repeat the saving throw at the end of each of its turns, ending the effect on itself on a success.

Ice Mephit
Small elemental, neutral evil

Armor Class 11
Hit Points 21 (6d6)
Speed 30 ft., fly 30 ft.

STR	DEX	CON	INT	WIS	CHA
7 (−2)	13 (+1)	10 (+0)	9 (−1)	11 (+0)	12 (+1)

Skills Perception +2, Stealth +3
Damage Vulnerabilities bludgeoning, fire
Damage Immunities cold, poison
Condition Immunities poisoned
Senses darkvision 60 ft., passive Perception 12
Languages Aquan, Auran
Challenge 1/2 (100 XP)

Death Burst. When the mephit dies, it explodes in a burst of jagged ice. Each creature within 5 feet of it must make a DC 10 Dexterity saving throw, taking 4 (1d8) slashing damage on a failed save, or half as much damage on a successful one.

False Appearance. While the mephit remains motionless, it is indistinguishable from an ordinary shard of ice.

Innate Spellcasting (1/Day). The mephit can innately cast *fog cloud*, requiring no material components. Its innate spellcasting ability is Charisma.

Actions

Claws. Melee Weapon Attack: +3 to hit, reach 5 ft., one creature. *Hit:* 3 (1d4 + 1) slashing damage plus 2 (1d4) cold damage.

Frost Breath (Recharge 6). The mephit exhales a 15-foot cone of cold air. Each creature in that area must succeed on a DC 10 Dexterity saving throw, taking 5 (2d4) cold damage on a failed save, or half as much damage on a successful one.

MAGMA MEPHIT

MUD MEPHIT

MAGMA MEPHIT

Composed of earth and fire, magma mephits glow a dull red color as they perspire beads of molten lava. They are slow to comprehend the meaning of others' words and actions.

MUD MEPHIT

Mud mephits are slow, unctuous creatures of earth and water. They drone their complaints to all who will listen, and beg incessantly for attention and treasure.

MAGMA MEPHIT
Small elemental, neutral evil

Armor Class 11
Hit Points 22 (5d6 + 5)
Speed 30 ft., fly 30 ft.

STR	DEX	CON	INT	WIS	CHA
8 (–1)	12 (+1)	12 (+1)	7 (–2)	10 (+0)	10 (+0)

Skills Stealth +3
Damage Vulnerabilities cold
Damage Immunities fire, poison
Condition Immunities poisoned
Senses darkvision 60 ft., passive Perception 10
Languages Ignan, Terran
Challenge 1/2 (100 XP)

Death Burst. When the mephit dies, it explodes in a burst of lava. Each creature within 5 feet of it must make a DC 11 Dexterity saving throw, taking 7 (2d6) fire damage on a failed save, or half as much damage on a successful one.

False Appearance. While the mephit remains motionless, it is indistinguishable from an ordinary mound of magma.

Innate Spellcasting (1/Day). The mephit can innately cast *heat metal* (spell save DC 10), requiring no material components. Its innate spellcasting ability is Charisma.

ACTIONS

Claws. *Melee Weapon Attack:* +3 to hit, reach 5 ft., one creature. *Hit:* 3 (1d4 + 1) slashing damage plus 2 (1d4) fire damage.

Fire Breath (Recharge 6). The mephit exhales a 15-foot cone of fire. Each creature in that area must make a DC 11 Dexterity saving throw, taking 7 (2d6) fire damage on a failed save, or half as much damage on a successful one.

MUD MEPHIT
Small elemental, neutral evil

Armor Class 11
Hit Points 27 (6d6 + 6)
Speed 20 ft., fly 20 ft., swim 20 ft.

STR	DEX	CON	INT	WIS	CHA
8 (–1)	12 (+1)	12 (+1)	9 (–1)	11 (+0)	7 (–2)

Skills Stealth +3
Damage Immunities poison
Condition Immunities poisoned
Senses darkvision 60 ft., passive Perception 10
Languages Aquan, Terran
Challenge 1/4 (50 XP)

Death Burst. When the mephit dies, it explodes in a burst of sticky mud. Each Medium or smaller creature within 5 feet of it must succeed on a DC 11 Dexterity saving throw or be restrained until the end of the creature's next turn.

False Appearance. While the mephit remains motionless, it is indistinguishable from an ordinary mound of mud.

ACTIONS

Fists. *Melee Weapon Attack:* +3 to hit, reach 5 ft., one creature. *Hit:* 4 (1d6 + 1) bludgeoning damage.

Mud Breath (Recharge 6). The mephit belches viscid mud onto one creature within 5 feet of it. If the target is Medium or smaller, it must succeed on a DC 11 Dexterity saving throw or be restrained for 1 minute. A creature can repeat the saving throw at the end of each of its turns, ending the effect on itself on a success.

Smoke Mephit

Smoke mephits are crude, lazy creatures of air and fire that billow smoke constantly. They rarely speak the truth and love to mock and mislead other creatures.

Steam Mephit

Composed of fire and water, steam mephits leave trails of hot water wherever they go, and they hiss with tendrils of steam. Bossy and hypersensitive, they are the self-appointed overlords of all mephits.

> ### Variant: Mephit Summoning
>
> Some mephits can have an action option that allows them to summon other mephits.
>
> **Summon Mephits (1/Day).** The mephit has a 25 percent chance of summoning 1d4 mephits of its kind. A summoned mephit appears in an unoccupied space within 60 feet of its summoner, acts as an ally of its summoner, and can't summon other mephits. It remains for 1 minute, until it or its summoner dies, or until its summoner dismisses it as an action.

Smoke Mephit

Small elemental, neutral evil

Armor Class 12
Hit Points 22 (5d6 + 5)
Speed 30 ft., fly 30 ft.

STR	DEX	CON	INT	WIS	CHA
6 (−2)	14 (+2)	12 (+1)	10 (+0)	10 (+0)	11 (+0)

Skills Perception +2, Stealth +4
Damage Immunities fire, poison
Condition Immunities poisoned
Senses darkvision 60 ft., passive Perception 12
Languages Auran, Ignan
Challenge 1/4 (50 XP)

Death Burst. When the mephit dies, it leaves behind a cloud of smoke that fills a 5-foot-radius sphere centered on its space. The sphere is heavily obscured. Wind disperses the cloud, which otherwise lasts for 1 minute.

Innate Spellcasting (1/Day). The mephit can innately cast *dancing lights*, requiring no material components. Its innate spellcasting ability is Charisma.

Actions

Claws. *Melee Weapon Attack:* +4 to hit, reach 5 ft., one creature. *Hit:* 4 (1d4 + 2) slashing damage.

Cinder Breath (Recharge 6). The mephit exhales a 15-foot cone of smoldering ash. Each creature in that area must succeed on a DC 10 Dexterity saving throw or be blinded until the end of the mephit's next turn.

Steam Mephit

Small elemental, neutral evil

Armor Class 10
Hit Points 21 (6d6)
Speed 30 ft., fly 30 ft.

STR	DEX	CON	INT	WIS	CHA
5 (−3)	11 (+0)	10 (+0)	11 (+0)	10 (+0)	12 (+1)

Damage Immunities fire, poison
Condition Immunities poisoned
Senses darkvision 60 ft., passive Perception 10
Languages Aquan, Ignan
Challenge 1/4 (50 XP)

Death Burst. When the mephit dies, it explodes in a cloud of steam. Each creature within 5 feet of the mephit must succeed on a DC 10 Dexterity saving throw or take 4 (1d8) fire damage.

Innate Spellcasting (1/Day). The mephit can innately cast *blur*, requiring no material components. Its innate spellcasting ability is Charisma.

Actions

Claws. *Melee Weapon Attack:* +2 to hit, reach 5 ft., one creature. *Hit:* 2 (1d4) slashing damage plus 2 (1d4) fire damage.

Steam Breath (Recharge 6). The mephit exhales a 15-foot cone of scalding steam. Each creature in that area must succeed on a DC 10 Dexterity saving throw, taking 4 (1d8) fire damage on a failed save, or half as much damage on a successful one.

Merfolk

Aquatic humanoids with the upper body of a human and the lower body of a fish, merfolk adorn their skin and scales with shell decorations.

Merfolk tribes and kingdoms span the world, and their people are as varied in color, culture, and outlook as the human races of the surface. Land folk and merfolk rarely meet except by chance, though starry-eyed mariners tell tales of romance with these creatures along the shoals of faraway islands.

Merfolk lack the materials and practical means to forge weapons beneath the waves, to write books and keep lore, or to shape stone to raise buildings and cities. As a result, most live in small hunter-gatherer tribes, each of which holds unique values and creeds. Only occasionally do merfolk unite under the rule of a single leader. They do so to face a common threat or to complete a conquest. Such unifications can be the beginning of undersea kingdoms with dynasties lasting hundreds of years.

Merfolk Settlements. Merfolk build their settlements in vast undersea caverns, mazes of coral, the ruins of sunken cities, or structures they carve from the rocky seabed. They live in water shallow enough that the passage of time can be marked by the gleam and fade of sunlight through the water. In the reefs and trenches near their settlements, merfolk harvest coral and farm the seabed, shepherding schools of fish as land-based farmers tend sheep. Only rarely do merfolk venture into the darkest depths of the ocean. In such depths and in their undersea caverns, merfolk rely on the light of bioluminescent flora and fauna, such as jellyfish, whose slow pulsing movements lend merfolk settlements an otherworldly aesthetic.

Merfolk defend their communities with spears crafted from whatever materials they can salvage from shipwrecks, beaches, and dead undersea creatures.

Merfolk

Medium humanoid (merfolk), neutral

Armor Class 11
Hit Points 11 (2d8 + 2)
Speed 10 ft., swim 40 ft.

STR	DEX	CON	INT	WIS	CHA
10 (+0)	13 (+1)	12 (+1)	11 (+0)	11 (+0)	12 (+1)

Skills Perception +2
Senses passive Perception 12
Languages Aquan, Common
Challenge 1/8 (25 XP)

Amphibious. The merfolk can breathe air and water.

Actions

Spear. *Melee or Ranged Weapon Attack:* +2 to hit, reach 5 ft. or range 20/60 ft., one target. *Hit:* 3 (1d6) piercing damage, or 4 (1d8) piercing damage if used with two hands to make a melee attack.

Merrow

Merrow haunt coastal waters, preying on fisherfolk, merfolk, and any other edible creature that crosses their path. These savage monsters snatch and devour unwary prey, hauling drowned corpses back to their underwater grottoes to feed.

Transformed Merfolk. Long ago, a tribe of merfolk found an idol of Demogorgon at the bottom of the sea. Not knowing what it was, they brought the artifact to their king. Everyone who touched the idol became afflicted with madness, including the king, who decreed that a sacrificial ritual be performed to open a gateway to the Abyss. The ocean turned red with the blood of slaughtered merfolk, but the ritual worked, and the king led the survivors through the underwater gate to Demogorgon's layer of the Abyss. The merfolk remained there for generations, fighting for their lives as the Abyss warped them completely, transforming them into hulking, evil monstrosities. Thus, the first merrow were born.

Coastal Bullies. Whenever an opportunity presents itself, the Prince of Demons sends merrow back to the Material Plane to wreak havoc in the oceans. The merrow are bullies, attacking all creatures smaller and weaker than themselves.

Merrow dwell in undersea caves filled with treasures and trophies, taken from their victims and sunken ships. They tie the rotting corpses of dead enemies and drowned sailors to strands of kelp to mark the borders of their territory.

Merrow

Large monstrosity, chaotic evil

Armor Class 13 (natural armor)
Hit Points 45 (6d10 + 12)
Speed 10 ft., swim 40 ft.

STR	DEX	CON	INT	WIS	CHA
18 (+4)	10 (+0)	15 (+2)	8 (−1)	10 (+0)	9 (−1)

Senses darkvision 60 ft., passive Perception 10
Languages Abyssal, Aquan
Challenge 2 (450 XP)

Amphibious. The merrow can breathe air and water.

Actions

Multiattack. The merrow makes two attacks: one with its bite and one with its claws or harpoon.

Bite. *Melee Weapon Attack:* +6 to hit, reach 5 ft., one target. *Hit:* 8 (1d8 + 4) piercing damage.

Claws. *Melee Weapon Attack:* +6 to hit, reach 5 ft., one target. *Hit:* 9 (2d4 + 4) slashing damage.

Harpoon. *Melee or Ranged Weapon Attack:* +6 to hit, reach 5 ft. or range 20/60 ft., one target. *Hit:* 11 (2d6 + 4) piercing damage. If the target is a Huge or smaller creature, it must succeed on a Strength contest against the merrow or be pulled up to 20 feet toward the merrow.

Mimic

Medium monstrosity (shapechanger), neutral

Armor Class 12 (natural armor)
Hit Points 58 (9d8 + 18)
Speed 15 ft.

STR	DEX	CON	INT	WIS	CHA
17 (+3)	12 (+1)	15 (+2)	5 (−3)	13 (+1)	8 (−1)

Skills Stealth +5
Damage Immunities acid
Condition Immunities prone
Senses darkvision 60 ft., passive Perception 11
Languages —
Challenge 2 (450 XP)

Shapechanger. The mimic can use its action to polymorph into an object or back into its true, amorphous form. Its statistics are the same in each form. Any equipment it is wearing or carrying isn't transformed. It reverts to its true form if it dies.

Adhesive (Object Form Only). The mimic adheres to anything that touches it. A Huge or smaller creature adhered to the mimic is also grappled by it (escape DC 13). Ability checks made to escape this grapple have disadvantage.

False Appearance (Object Form Only). While the mimic remains motionless, it is indistinguishable from an ordinary object.

Grappler. The mimic has advantage on attack rolls against any creature grappled by it.

Actions

Pseudopod. *Melee Weapon Attack:* +5 to hit, reach 5 ft., one target. *Hit:* 7 (1d8 + 3) bludgeoning damage. If the mimic is in object form, the target is subjected to its Adhesive trait.

Bite. *Melee Weapon Attack:* +5 to hit, reach 5 ft., one target. *Hit:* 7 (1d8 + 3) piercing damage plus 4 (1d8) acid damage.

Mimic

Mimics are shapeshifting predators able to take on the form of inanimate objects to lure creatures to their doom. In dungeons, these cunning creatures most often take the form of doors and chests, having learned that such forms attract a steady stream of prey.

Imitative Predators. Mimics can alter their outward texture to resemble wood, stone, and other basic materials, and they have evolved to assume the appearance of objects that other creatures are likely to come into contact with. A mimic in its altered form is nearly unrecognizable until potential prey blunders into its reach, whereupon the monster sprouts pseudopods and attacks.

When it changes shape, a mimic excretes an adhesive that helps it seize prey and weapons that touch it. The adhesive is absorbed when the mimic assumes its amorphous form and on parts the mimic uses to move itself.

Cunning Hunters. Mimics live and hunt alone, though they occasionally share their feeding grounds with other creatures. Although most mimics have only predatory intelligence, a rare few evolve greater cunning and the ability to carry on simple conversations in Common or Undercommon. Such mimics might allow safe passage through their domains or provide useful information in exchange for food.

"SOMETIMES A CHEST IS JUST A CHEST, BUT DON'T BET ON IT."
—X THE MYSTIC'S 3RD RULE OF DUNGEON SURVIVAL

MIND FLAYER

Mind flayers, also called illithids, are the scourge of sentient creatures across countless worlds. Psionic tyrants, slavers, and interdimensional voyagers, they are insidious masterminds that harvest entire races for their own twisted ends. Four tentacles snake from their octopus-like heads, flexing in hungry anticipation when sentient creatures come near.

In eons past, illithids controlled empires that spanned many worlds. They subjugated and consequently warped whole races of humanoid slaves, including the githyanki and githzerai, the grimlocks, and the kuo-toa. Conjoined by a collective consciousness, the illithids hatch plots as far-reaching and evil as their fathomless minds can conceive.

Since the fall of their empires, illithid collectives on the Material Plane have resided in the Underdark.

Psionic Commanders. Mind flayers possess psionic powers that enable them to control the minds of creatures such as troglodytes, grimlocks, quaggoths, and ogres. Illithids prefer to communicate via telepathy and use their telepathy when issuing commands to their thralls.

When an illithid meets strong resistance, it avoids initial combat as it orders its thralls to attack. Like physical extensions of the illithid's thoughts, these thralls interpose themselves between the mind flayer and its foes, sacrificing their lives so that their master can escape.

Hive Mind Colonies. Solitary mind flayers are likely rogues and outcasts. Most illithids belong to a colony of sibling mind flayers devoted to an elder brain—a massive brain-like being that resides in a briny pool near the center of a mind flayer community. From its pool, an elder brain telepathically dictates its desires to each individual mind flayer within 5 miles of it, for it is able to hold multiple mental conversations at once.

Hunger of the Mind. Illithids subsist on the brains of humanoids. The brains provide enzymes, hormones, and psychic energy necessary for their survival. An illithid healthy from a brain-rich diet secretes a thin glaze of mucus that coats its mauve skin.

An illithid experiences euphoria as it devours the brain of a humanoid, along with its memories, personality, and innermost fears. Mind flayers will sometimes harvest a brain rather than devour it, using it as part of some alien experiment or transforming it into an intellect devourer.

QUALITH

On the rare occasion that mind flayers need to write something down, they do so in Qualith. This system of tactile writing (similar to braille) is read by an illithid's tentacles. Qualith is written in four-line stanzas and is so alien in construction that non-illithids must resort to magic to discern its meaning. Though Qualith can be used to keep records, illithids most often use it to mark portals or other surfaces with warnings or instructions.

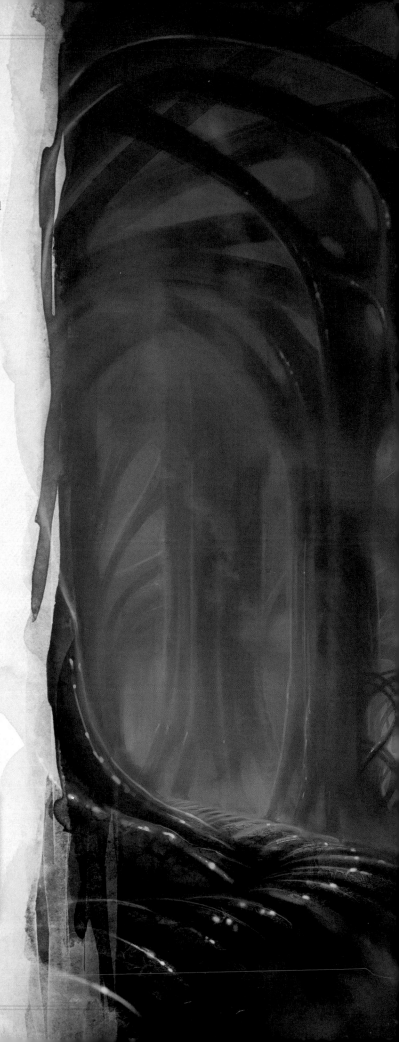

MIND FLAYER

Medium aberration, lawful evil

Armor Class 15 (breastplate)
Hit Points 71 (13d8 + 13)
Speed 30 ft.

STR	DEX	CON	INT	WIS	CHA
11 (+0)	12 (+1)	12 (+1)	19 (+4)	17 (+3)	17 (+3)

Saving Throws Int +7, Wis +6, Cha +6
Skills Arcana +7, Deception +6, Insight +6, Perception +6, Persuasion +6, Stealth +4
Senses darkvision 120 ft., passive Perception 16
Languages Deep Speech, Undercommon, telepathy 120 ft.
Challenge 7 (2,900 XP)

Magic Resistance. The mind flayer has advantage on saving throws against spells and other magical effects.

Innate Spellcasting (Psionics). The mind flayer's innate spellcasting ability is Intelligence (spell save DC 15). It can innately cast the following spells, requiring no components:

At will: *detect thoughts, levitate*
1/day each: *dominate monster, plane shift* (self only)

ACTIONS

Tentacles. *Melee Weapon Attack:* +7 to hit, reach 5 ft., one creature. *Hit:* 15 (2d10 + 4) psychic damage. If the target is Medium or smaller, it is grappled (escape DC 15) and must succeed on a DC 15 Intelligence saving throw or be stunned until this grapple ends.

Extract Brain. *Melee Weapon Attack:* +7 to hit, reach 5 ft., one incapacitated humanoid grappled by the mind flayer. *Hit:* 55 (10d10) piercing damage. If this damage reduces the target to 0 hit points, the mind flayer kills the target by extracting and devouring its brain.

Mind Blast (Recharge 5–6). The mind flayer magically emits psychic energy in a 60-foot cone. Each creature in that area must succeed on a DC 15 Intelligence saving throw or take 22 (4d8 + 4) psychic damage and be stunned for 1 minute. A creature can repeat the saving throw at the end of each of its turns, ending the effect on itself on a success.

VARIANT: MIND FLAYER ARCANIST

A few mind flayers supplement their psionic power with arcane spells. However, they are regarded as deviants by their illithid peers and usually shunned. A mind flayer arcanist has a challenge rating of 8 (3,900 XP) and the following trait.

Spellcasting. The mind flayer is a 10th-level spellcaster. Its spellcasting ability is Intelligence (spell save DC 15, +7 to hit with spell attacks). The mind flayer has the following wizard spells prepared:

Cantrips (at will): *blade ward, dancing lights, mage hand, shocking grasp*
1st level (4 slots): *detect magic, disguise self, shield, sleep*
2nd level (3 slots): *blur, invisibility, ray of enfeeblement*
3rd level (3 slots): *clairvoyance, lightning bolt, sending*
4th level (3 slots): *confusion, hallucinatory terrain*
5th level (2 slots): *telekinesis, wall of force*

MINOTAUR

A minotaur's roar is a savage battle cry that most civilized creatures fear. Born into the mortal realm by demonic rites, minotaurs are savage conquerors and carnivores that live for the hunt. Their brown or black fur is stained with the blood of fallen foes, and they carry the stench of death.

The Beast Within. Most minotaurs are solitary carnivores that roam labyrinthine dungeons, twisting caves, primeval woods, and the maze-like streets and passages of desolate ruins. A minotaur can visualize every route it might take to close the distance to its prey.

The scent of blood, the tearing of flesh, and the cracking of bones spur a minotaur's lust for carnage, overwhelming all thought and reason. In a blood rage, a minotaur charges anything it sees, butting and goring like a battering ram, then chopping the fallen in twain.

Apart from ambushing creatures that wander into its labyrinth, a minotaur cares little for strategy or tactics. Minotaurs seldom organize, they don't respect authority or hierarchy, and they are notoriously difficult to enslave, let alone control.

Cults of the Horned King. Minotaurs are the dark descendants of humanoids transformed by the rituals of cults that reject the oppression of authority by returning to nature. Inductees often mistake these cults for druidic circles or totemic religions whose ceremonies involve entering a labyrinth while wearing a ceremonial animal mask.

Within these bounded environments, cultists hunt, kill, and eat wild beasts, indulging their basest primal urges. In the end, however, sacrificial animals are exchanged for humanoid sacrifice—sometimes an inductee that tried to escape the cult after learning its secrets. These labyrinths become blood-soaked halls of slaughter, echoing to the cultists' savagery.

Unknown to all but their highest-ranking leaders, these mystery cults are creations of the demon lord Baphomet, the Horned King, whose layer of the Abyss is a gigantic labyrinth. Some of his followers are fervent supplicants that plead for strength and power. Others come to the cult seeking a life free from authority's chains—and are liberated of their humanity instead as Baphomet transforms them into the minotaurs that echo his own savage form.

Although they begin as creations of the Horned King, minotaurs can breed true with one another, giving rise to an independent race of Baphomet's savage children in the world.

MINOTAUR
Large monstrosity, chaotic evil

Armor Class 14 (natural armor)
Hit Points 76 (9d10 + 27)
Speed 40 ft.

STR	DEX	CON	INT	WIS	CHA
18 (+4)	11 (+0)	16 (+3)	6 (−2)	16 (+3)	9 (−1)

Skills Perception +7
Senses darkvision 60 ft., passive Perception 17
Languages Abyssal
Challenge 3 (700 XP)

Charge. If the minotaur moves at least 10 feet straight toward a target and then hits it with a gore attack on the same turn, the target takes an extra 9 (2d8) piercing damage. If the target is a creature, it must succeed on a DC 14 Strength saving throw or be pushed up to 10 feet away and knocked prone.

Labyrinthine Recall. The minotaur can perfectly recall any path it has traveled.

Reckless. At the start of its turn, the minotaur can gain advantage on all melee weapon attack rolls it makes during that turn, but attack rolls against it have advantage until the start of its next turn.

ACTIONS

Greataxe. *Melee Weapon Attack:* +6 to hit, reach 5 ft., one target. *Hit:* 17 (2d12 + 4) slashing damage.

Gore. *Melee Weapon Attack:* +6 to hit, reach 5 ft., one target. *Hit:* 13 (2d8 + 4) piercing damage.

Modrons

Modrons are beings of absolute law that adhere to a hive-like hierarchy. They inhabit the plane of Mechanus and tend its eternally revolving gears, their existence a clockwork routine of perfect order.

Absolute Law and Order. Under the direction of their leader, Primus, modrons increase order in the multiverse in accordance with laws beyond the comprehension of mortal minds. Their own minds are networked in a hierarchal pyramid, in which each modron receives commands from superiors and delegates orders to underlings. A modron carries out commands with total obedience, utmost efficiency, and an absence of morality or ego.

Modrons have no sense of self beyond what is necessary to fulfill their duties. They exist as a unified collective, divided by ranks, yet they always refer to themselves collectively. To a modron, there is no "I," but only "we" or "us."

Absolute Hierarchy. Modrons communicate only with their own rank and the ranks immediately above and below them. Modrons more than one rank away are either too advanced or too simple to understand.

Cogs of the Great Machine. If a modron is destroyed, its remains disintegrate. A replacement from the next lowest rank then transforms in a flash of light, gaining the physical form of its new rank. The promoted modron is replaced by one of its underlings in the same manner, all the way to the lowest levels of the hierarchy. There, a new modron is created by Primus, with a steady stream of monodrones leaving the Great Modron Cathedral on Mechanus as a result.

The Great Modron March. When the gears of Mechanus complete seventeen cycles once every 289 years, Primus sends a vast army of modrons across the Outer Planes, ostensibly on a reconnaissance mission. The march is long and dangerous, and only a small number of modrons returns to Mechanus.

Monodrone

A monodrone can perform one simple task at a time and can relay a single message of up to forty-eight words.

Duodrone

The blocky duodrones supervise units of monodrones and can perform up to two tasks at a time.

Tridrone

Tridrones are shaped like inverted pyramids. They lead lesser modrons in battle.

Quadrone

Astute combatants, quadrones serve as artillery and field officers in the regiments of modron armies.

Pentadrone

Pentadrones oversee Mechanus's worker populace and can improvise in response to new situations.

Variant: Rogue Modrons

A modron unit sometimes becomes defective, either through natural decay or exposure to chaotic forces. Rogue modrons don't act in accordance with Primus's wishes and directives, breaking laws, disobeying orders, and even engaging in violence. Other modrons hunt down such rogues.

A rogue modron loses the Axiomatic Mind trait and can have any alignment other than lawful neutral. Otherwise, it has the same statistics as a regular modron of its rank.

MONODRONE
Medium construct, lawful neutral

Armor Class 15 (natural armor)
Hit Points 5 (1d8 + 1)
Speed 30 ft., fly 30 ft.

STR	DEX	CON	INT	WIS	CHA
10 (+0)	13 (+1)	12 (+1)	4 (−3)	10 (+0)	5 (−3)

Senses truesight 120 ft., passive Perception 10
Languages Modron
Challenge 1/8 (25 XP)

Axiomatic Mind. The monodrone can't be compelled to act in a manner contrary to its nature or its instructions.

Disintegration. If the monodrone dies, its body disintegrates into dust, leaving behind its weapons and anything else it was carrying.

Actions

Dagger. *Melee Weapon Attack:* +3 to hit, reach 5 ft., one target. *Hit:* 3 (1d4 + 1) piercing damage.

Javelin. *Melee or Ranged Weapon Attack:* +2 to hit, reach 5 ft. or range 30/120 ft., one target. *Hit:* 3 (1d6) piercing damage.

DUODRONE

Medium construct, lawful neutral

Armor Class 15 (natural armor)
Hit Points 11 (2d8 + 2)
Speed 30 ft.

STR	DEX	CON	INT	WIS	CHA
11 (+0)	13 (+1)	12 (+1)	6 (−2)	10 (+0)	7 (−2)

Senses truesight 120 ft., passive Perception 10
Languages Modron
Challenge 1/4 (50 XP)

Axiomatic Mind. The duodrone can't be compelled to act in a manner contrary to its nature or its instructions.

Disintegration. If the duodrone dies, its body disintegrates into dust, leaving behind its weapons and anything else it was carrying.

ACTIONS

Multiattack. The duodrone makes two fist attacks or two javelin attacks.

Fist. *Melee Weapon Attack:* +2 to hit, reach 5 ft., one target. *Hit:* 2 (1d4) bludgeoning damage.

Javelin. *Melee or Ranged Weapon Attack:* +3 to hit, reach 5 ft. or range 30/120 ft., one target. *Hit:* 4 (1d6 + 1) piercing damage.

TRIDRONE

Medium construct, lawful neutral

Armor Class 15 (natural armor)
Hit Points 16 (3d8 + 3)
Speed 30 ft.

STR	DEX	CON	INT	WIS	CHA
12 (+1)	13 (+1)	12 (+1)	9 (−1)	10 (+0)	9 (−1)

Senses truesight 120 ft., passive Perception 10
Languages Modron
Challenge 1/2 (100 XP)

Axiomatic Mind. The tridrone can't be compelled to act in a manner contrary to its nature or its instructions.

Disintegration. If the tridrone dies, its body disintegrates into dust, leaving behind its weapons and anything else it was carrying.

ACTIONS

Multiattack. The tridrone makes three fist attacks or three javelin attacks.

Fist. *Melee Weapon Attack:* +3 to hit, reach 5 ft., one target. *Hit:* 3 (1d4 + 1) bludgeoning damage.

Javelin. *Melee or Ranged Weapon Attack:* +3 to hit, reach 5 ft. or range 30/120 ft., one target. *Hit:* 4 (1d6 + 1) piercing damage.

M

QUADRONE
Medium construct, lawful neutral

Armor Class 16 (natural armor)
Hit Points 22 (4d8 + 4)
Speed 30 ft., fly 30 ft.

STR	DEX	CON	INT	WIS	CHA
12 (+1)	14 (+2)	12 (+1)	10 (+0)	10 (+0)	11 (+0)

Skills Perception +2
Senses truesight 120 ft., passive Perception 12
Languages Modron
Challenge 1 (200 XP)

Axiomatic Mind. The quadrone can't be compelled to act in a manner contrary to its nature or its instructions.

Disintegration. If the quadrone dies, its body disintegrates into dust, leaving behind its weapons and anything else it was carrying.

ACTIONS

Multiattack. The quadrone makes two fist attacks or four shortbow attacks.

Fist. *Melee Weapon Attack:* +3 to hit, reach 5 ft., one target. *Hit:* 3 (1d4 + 1) bludgeoning damage.

Shortbow. *Ranged Weapon Attack:* +4 to hit, range 80/320 ft., one target. *Hit:* 5 (1d6 + 2) piercing damage.

PENTADRONE
Large construct, lawful neutral

Armor Class 16 (natural armor)
Hit Points 32 (5d10 + 5)
Speed 40 ft.

STR	DEX	CON	INT	WIS	CHA
15 (+2)	14 (+2)	12 (+1)	10 (+0)	10 (+0)	13 (+1)

Skills Perception +4
Senses truesight 120 ft., passive Perception 14
Languages Modron
Challenge 2 (450 XP)

Axiomatic Mind. The pentadrone can't be compelled to act in a manner contrary to its nature or its instructions.

Disintegration. If the pentadrone dies, its body disintegrates into dust, leaving behind its weapons and anything else it was carrying.

ACTIONS

Multiattack. The pentadrone makes five arm attacks.

Arm. *Melee Weapon Attack:* +4 to hit, reach 5 ft., one target. *Hit:* 5 (1d6 + 2) bludgeoning damage.

Paralysis Gas (Recharge 5–6). The pentadrone exhales a 30-foot cone of gas. Each creature in that area must succeed on a DC 11 Constitution saving throw or be paralyzed for 1 minute. A creature can repeat the saving throw at the end of each of its turns, ending the effect on itself on a success.

Mummies

Raised by dark funerary rituals, a mummy shambles from the shrouded stillness of a time-lost temple or tomb. Having been awoken from its rest, it punishes transgressors with the power of its unholy curse.

Preserved Wrath. The long burial rituals that accompany a mummy's entombment help protect its body from rot. In the embalming process, the newly dead creature's organs are removed and placed in special jars, and its corpse is treated with preserving oils, herbs, and wrappings. After the body has been prepared, the corpse is typically wrapped in linen bandages.

The Will of Dark Gods. An undead mummy is created when the priest of a death god or other dark deity ritually imbues a prepared corpse with necromantic magic. The mummy's linen wrappings are inscribed with necromantic markings before the burial ritual concludes with an invocation to darkness. As a mummy endures in undeath, it animates in response to conditions specified by the ritual. Most commonly, a transgression against its tomb, treasures, lands, or former loved ones will cause a mummy to rise.

The Punished. Once deceased, an individual has no say in whether or not its body is made into a mummy. Some mummies were powerful individuals who displeased a high priest or pharaoh, or who committed crimes of treason, adultery, or murder. As punishment, they were cursed with eternal undeath, embalmed, mummified, and sealed away. Other times, mummies acting as tomb guardians are created from slaves put to death specifically to serve a greater purpose.

Creature of Ritual. A mummy obeys the conditions and parameters laid down by the rituals that created it, driven only to punish transgressors. The overwhelming terror that foreshadows a mummy's attack can leave the intended victim paralyzed with fright. In the days following a mummy's touch, a victim's body rots from the outside in, until nothing but dust remains.

Ending a Mummy's Curse. Rare magic can undo or dispel the ritual that gave rise to a mummy, allowing it to truly die. More commonly, a mummy can be sent back to its endless rest by undoing the transgression that caused it to rise. A sacred idol might be replaced in its niche, a stolen treasure could be returned to its tomb, or a temple might be purified of despoiling bloodshed.

More ephemeral or permanent offenses, such as revealing a secret the mummy wished kept or killing an individual the mummy loved, can't be so easily remedied. In such cases, a mummy might slaughter all the creatures responsible and still not sate its wrath.

Undead Archives. Though they seldom bother to do so, mummies can speak. As a result, some serve as undead repositories of lost lore, and can be consulted by the descendants of those who created them. Powerful individuals sometimes intentionally sequester mummies away for occasional consultation.

Undead Nature. A mummy doesn't require air, food, drink, or sleep.

Mummy Lord

In the tombs of the ancients, tyrannical monarchs and the high priests of dark gods lie in dreamless rest, waiting for the time when they might reclaim their thrones and reforge their ancient empires. The regalia of their terrible rule still adorns their linen-wrapped bodies, their moldering robes stitched with evil symbols and bronze armor etched with devices of dynasties that fell a thousand years before.

Under the direction of the most powerful priests, the ritual that creates a mummy can be increased in potency. The mummy lord that rises from such a ritual retains the memories and personality of its former life, and is gifted with supernatural resilience. Dead emperors wield the same infamous rune-marked blades that they did in legend. Sorcerer lords work the forbidden magic that once controlled a terrified populace, and the dark gods reward dead priest-kings' prayers by imparting divine spells.

Heart of the Mummy Lord. As part of the ritual that creates a mummy lord, the creature's heart and viscera are removed from the corpse and placed in canopic jars. These jars are usually carved from limestone or made of pottery, etched or painted with religious hieroglyphs.

As long as its shriveled heart remains intact, a mummy lord can't be permanently destroyed. When it drops to 0 hit points, the mummy lord turns to dust and re-forms at full strength 24 hours later, rising out of dust in close proximity to the canopic jar containing its heart. A mummy lord can be destroyed or prevented from re-forming by burning its heart to ashes. For this reason, a mummy lord usually keeps its heart and viscera in a hidden tomb or vault.

The mummy lord's heart has AC 5, 25 hit points, and immunity to all damage except fire.

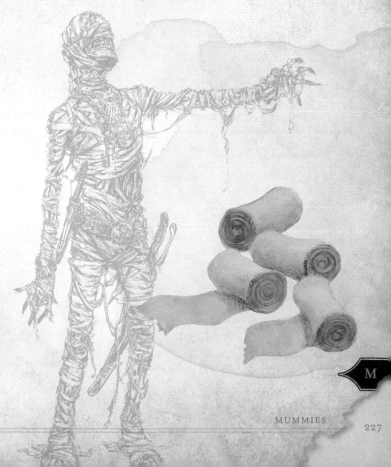

A Mummy Lord's Lair

A mummy lord watches over an ancient temple or tomb that is protected by lesser undead and rigged with traps. Hidden in this temple is the sarcophagus where a mummy lord keeps its greatest treasures.

A mummy lord encountered in its lair has a challenge rating of 16 (15,000 XP).

Lair Actions

On initiative count 20 (losing initiative ties), the mummy lord takes a lair action to cause one of the following effects; the mummy lord can't use the same effect two rounds in a row.

- Each undead creature in the lair can pinpoint the location of each living creature within 120 feet of it until initiative count 20 on the next round.

MUMMY

Medium undead, lawful evil

Armor Class 11 (natural armor)
Hit Points 58 (9d8 + 18)
Speed 20 ft.

STR	DEX	CON	INT	WIS	CHA
16 (+3)	8 (−1)	15 (+2)	6 (−2)	10 (+0)	12 (+1)

Saving Throws Wis +2
Damage Vulnerabilities fire
Damage Resistances bludgeoning, piercing, and slashing from nonmagical attacks
Damage Immunities necrotic, poison
Condition Immunities charmed, exhaustion, frightened, paralyzed, poisoned
Senses darkvision 60 ft., passive Perception 10
Languages the languages it knew in life
Challenge 3 (700 XP)

ACTIONS

Multiattack. The mummy can use its Dreadful Glare and makes one attack with its rotting fist.

Rotting Fist. *Melee Weapon Attack:* +5 to hit, reach 5 ft., one target. *Hit:* 10 (2d6 + 3) bludgeoning damage plus 10 (3d6) necrotic damage. If the target is a creature, it must succeed on a DC 12 Constitution saving throw or be cursed with mummy rot. The cursed target can't regain hit points, and its hit point maximum decreases by 10 (3d6) for every 24 hours that elapse. If the curse reduces the target's hit point maximum to 0, the target dies, and its body turns to dust. The curse lasts until removed by the *remove curse* spell or other magic.

Dreadful Glare. The mummy targets one creature it can see within 60 feet of it. If the target can see the mummy, it must succeed on a DC 11 Wisdom saving throw against this magic or become frightened until the end of the mummy's next turn. If the target fails the saving throw by 5 or more, it is also paralyzed for the same duration. A target that succeeds on the saving throw is immune to the Dreadful Glare of all mummies (but not mummy lords) for the next 24 hours.

"Before opening a sarcophagus, light a torch."
—X the Mystic's 7th rule of dungeon survival

- Each undead in the lair has advantage on saving throws against effects that turn undead until initiative count 20 on the next round.
- Until initiative count 20 on the next round, any non-undead creature that tries to cast a spell of 4th level or lower in the mummy lord's lair is wracked with pain. The creature can choose another action, but if it tries to cast the spell, it must make a DC 16 Constitution saving throw. On a failed save, it takes 1d6 necrotic damage per level of the spell, and the spell has no effect and is wasted.

REGIONAL EFFECTS

A mummy lord's temple or tomb is warped in any of the following ways by the creature's dark presence:

- Food instantly molders and water instantly evaporates when brought into the lair. Other nonmagical drinks are spoiled—wine turning to vinegar, for instance.
- Divination spells cast within the lair by creatures other than the mummy lord have a 25 percent chance to provide misleading results, as determined by the DM. If a divination spell already has a chance to fail or become unreliable when cast multiple times, that chance increases by 25 percent.
- A creature that takes treasure from the lair is cursed until the treasure is returned. The cursed target has disadvantage on all saving throws. The curse lasts until removed by a *remove curse* spell or other magic.

If the mummy lord is destroyed, these regional effects end immediately.

MUMMY LORD
Medium undead, lawful evil

Armor Class 17 (natural armor)
Hit Points 97 (13d8 + 39)
Speed 20 ft.

STR	DEX	CON	INT	WIS	CHA
18 (+4)	10 (+0)	17 (+3)	11 (+0)	18 (+4)	16 (+3)

Saving Throws Con +8, Int +5, Wis +9, Cha +8
Skills History +5, Religion +5
Damage Vulnerabilities fire
Damage Immunities necrotic, poison; bludgeoning, piercing, and slashing from nonmagical attacks
Condition Immunities charmed, exhaustion, frightened, paralyzed, poisoned
Senses darkvision 60 ft., passive Perception 14
Languages the languages it knew in life
Challenge 15 (13,000 XP)

Magic Resistance. The mummy lord has advantage on saving throws against spells and other magical effects.

Rejuvenation. A destroyed mummy lord gains a new body in 24 hours if its heart is intact, regaining all its hit points and becoming active again. The new body appears within 5 feet of the mummy lord's heart.

Spellcasting. The mummy lord is a 10th-level spellcaster. Its spellcasting ability is Wisdom (spell save DC 17, +9 to hit with spell attacks). The mummy lord has the following cleric spells prepared:

Cantrips (at will): *sacred flame, thaumaturgy*
1st level (4 slots): *command, guiding bolt, shield of faith*
2nd level (3 slots): *hold person, silence, spiritual weapon*
3rd level (3 slots): *animate dead, dispel magic*
4th level (3 slots): *divination, guardian of faith*
5th level (2 slots): *contagion, insect plague*
6th level (1 slot): *harm*

ACTIONS

Multiattack. The mummy can use its Dreadful Glare and makes one attack with its rotting fist.

Rotting Fist. Melee Weapon Attack: +9 to hit, reach 5 ft., one target. *Hit:* 14 (3d6 + 4) bludgeoning damage plus 21 (6d6) necrotic damage. If the target is a creature, it must succeed on a DC 16 Constitution saving throw or be cursed with mummy rot. The cursed target can't regain hit points, and its hit point maximum decreases by 10 (3d6) for every 24 hours that elapse. If the curse reduces the target's hit point maximum to 0, the target dies, and its body turns to dust. The curse lasts until removed by the *remove curse* spell or other magic.

Dreadful Glare. The mummy lord targets one creature it can see within 60 feet of it. If the target can see the mummy lord, it must succeed on a DC 16 Wisdom saving throw against this magic or become frightened until the end of the mummy's next turn. If the target fails the saving throw by 5 or more, it is also paralyzed for the same duration. A target that succeeds on the saving throw is immune to the Dreadful Glare of all mummies and mummy lords for the next 24 hours.

LEGENDARY ACTIONS

The mummy lord can take 3 legendary actions, choosing from the options below. Only one legendary action option can be used at a time and only at the end of another creature's turn. The mummy lord regains spent legendary actions at the start of its turn.

Attack. The mummy lord makes one attack with its rotting fist or uses its Dreadful Glare.
Blinding Dust. Blinding dust and sand swirls magically around the mummy lord. Each creature within 5 feet of the mummy lord must succeed on a DC 16 Constitution saving throw or be blinded until the end of the creature's next turn.
Blasphemous Word (Costs 2 Actions). The mummy lord utters a blasphemous word. Each non-undead creature within 10 feet of the mummy lord that can hear the magical utterance must succeed on a DC 16 Constitution saving throw or be stunned until the end of the mummy lord's next turn.
Channel Negative Energy (Costs 2 Actions). The mummy lord magically unleashes negative energy. Creatures within 60 feet of the mummy lord, including ones behind barriers and around corners, can't regain hit points until the end of the mummy lord's next turn.
Whirlwind of Sand (Costs 2 Actions). The mummy lord magically transforms into a whirlwind of sand, moves up to 60 feet, and reverts to its normal form. While in whirlwind form, the mummy lord is immune to all damage, and it can't be grappled, petrified, knocked prone, restrained, or stunned. Equipment worn or carried by the mummy lord remain in its possession.

M

MYCONIDS

Myconids are intelligent, ambulatory fungi that live in the Underdark, seek enlightenment, and deplore violence. If approached peacefully, myconids gladly provide shelter or allow safe passage through their colonies.

Circles and Melds. The largest myconid in a colony is its sovereign, which presides over one or more social groups called circles. A circle consists of twenty or more myconids that work, live, and meld together.

A meld is a form of communal meditation that allows myconids to transcend their dull subterranean existence. The myconids' rapport spores bind the participants into a group consciousness. Hallucination spores then induce a shared dream that provides entertainment and social interaction. Myconids consider melding to be the purpose of their existence. They use it in the pursuit of higher consciousness, collective union, and spiritual apotheosis. Myconids also use their rapport spores to communicate telepathically with other sentient creatures.

Myconid Reproduction. Like other fungi, myconids reproduce by mundane sporing. They carefully control their spores' release to avoid overpopulation.

SPORE SERVANT TEMPLATE

A spore servant is any Large or smaller creature brought back to life by the animating spores of a myconid sovereign. A creature that was never flesh and blood to begin with (such as a construct, elemental, ooze, plant, or undead) can't be turned into a spore servant. The following characteristics change or are added to a creature that becomes a spore servant.

Retained Characteristics. The servant retains its Armor Class, hit points, Hit Dice, Strength, Dexterity, Constitution, vulnerabilities, resistances, and immunities.

Lost Characteristics. The servant loses its original saving throw and skill bonuses, special senses, and special traits. It loses any action that isn't Multiattack or a melee weapon attack that deals bludgeoning, piercing, or slashing damage. If it has an action or a melee weapon attack that deals some other type of damage, it loses the ability to deal damage of that type, unless the damage comes from a piece of equipment, such as a magic item.

Type. The servant's type is plant, and it loses any tags.

Alignment. The servant is unaligned.

Speed. Reduce all the servant's speeds by 10 feet, to a minimum of 5 feet.

Ability Scores. The servant's ability scores change as follows: Int 2 (−4), Wis 6 (−2), Cha 1 (−5).

Senses. The servant has blindsight with a radius of 30 feet, and it is blind beyond this radius.

Condition Immunities. The servant can't be blinded, charmed, frightened, or paralyzed.

Languages. The servant loses all known languages, but it responds to orders given to it by myconids using rapport spores. The servant gives highest priority to orders received from the most powerful myconid.

Attacks. If the servant has no other means of dealing damage, it can use its fists or limbs to make unarmed strikes. On a hit, an unarmed strike deals bludgeoning damage equal to 1d4 + the servant's Strength modifier, or, if the servant is Large, 2d4 + its Strength modifier.

SAMPLE SPORE SERVANT

This spore servant statistics presented here use a quaggoth as the base creature.

MYCONID SPROUT
Small plant, lawful neutral

Armor Class 10
Hit Points 7 (2d6)
Speed 10 ft.

STR	DEX	CON	INT	WIS	CHA
8 (−1)	10 (+0)	10 (+0)	8 (−1)	11 (+0)	5 (−3)

Senses darkvision 120 ft., passive Perception 10
Languages —
Challenge 0 (10 XP)

Distress Spores. When the myconid takes damage, all other myconids within 240 feet of it can sense its pain.

Sun Sickness. While in sunlight, the myconid has disadvantage on ability checks, attack rolls, and saving throws. The myconid dies if it spends more than 1 hour in direct sunlight.

ACTIONS

Fist. *Melee Weapon Attack:* +1 to hit, reach 5 ft., one target. *Hit:* 1 (1d4 − 1) bludgeoning damage plus 2 (1d4) poison damage.

Rapport Spores (3/Day). A 10-foot radius of spores extends from the myconid. These spores can go around corners and affect only creatures with an Intelligence of 2 or higher that aren't undead, constructs, or elementals. Affected creatures can communicate telepathically with one another while they are within 30 feet of each other. The effect lasts for 1 hour.

QUAGGOTH SPORE SERVANT
Medium plant, unaligned

Armor Class 13 (natural armor)
Hit Points 45 (6d8 + 18)
Speed 20 ft., climb 20 ft.

STR	DEX	CON	INT	WIS	CHA
17 (+3)	12 (+1)	16 (+3)	2 (−4)	6 (−2)	1 (−5)

Damage Immunities poison
Condition Immunities blinded, charmed, frightened, paralyzed, poisoned
Senses blindsight 30 ft. (blind beyond this radius), passive Perception 8
Languages —
Challenge 1 (200 XP)

ACTIONS

Multiattack. The spore servant makes two claw attacks.

Claw. *Melee Weapon Attack:* +5 to hit, reach 5 ft., one target. *Hit:* 6 (1d6 + 3) slashing damage.

Myconid Sovereign

Large plant, lawful neutral

Armor Class 13 (natural armor)
Hit Points 60 (8d10 + 16)
Speed 30 ft.

STR	DEX	CON	INT	WIS	CHA
12 (+1)	10 (+0)	14 (+2)	13 (+1)	15 (+2)	10 (+0)

Senses darkvision 120 ft., passive Perception 12
Languages —
Challenge 2 (450 XP)

Distress Spores. When the myconid takes damage, all other myconids within 240 feet of it can sense its pain.

Sun Sickness. While in sunlight, the myconid has disadvantage on ability checks, attack rolls, and saving throws. The myconid dies if it spends more than 1 hour in direct sunlight.

Actions

Multiattack. The myconid uses either its Hallucination Spores or its Pacifying Spores, then makes a fist attack.

Fist. *Melee Weapon Attack:* +3 to hit, reach 5 ft., one target. *Hit:* 8 (3d4 + 1) bludgeoning damage plus 7 (3d4) poison damage.

Animating Spores (3/Day). The myconid targets one corpse of a humanoid or a Large or smaller beast within 5 feet of it and releases spores at the corpse. In 24 hours, the corpse rises as a spore servant. The corpse stays animated for 1d4 + 1 weeks or until destroyed, and it can't be animated again in this way.

Hallucination Spores. The myconid ejects spores at one creature it can see within 5 feet of it. The target must succeed on a DC 12 Constitution saving throw or be poisoned for 1 minute. The poisoned target is incapacitated while it hallucinates. The target can repeat the saving throw at the end of each of its turns, ending the effect on itself on a success.

Pacifying Spores. The myconid ejects spores at one creature it can see within 5 feet of it. The target must succeed on a DC 12 Constitution saving throw or be stunned for 1 minute. The target can repeat the saving throw at the end of each of its turns, ending the condition on itself on a success.

Rapport Spores. A 30-foot radius of spores extends from the myconid. These spores can go around corners and affect only creatures with an Intelligence of 2 or higher that aren't undead, constructs, or elementals. Affected creatures can communicate telepathically with one another while they are within 30 feet of each other. The effect lasts for 1 hour.

Myconid Adult

Medium plant, lawful neutral

Armor Class 12 (natural armor)
Hit Points 22 (4d8 + 4)
Speed 20 ft.

STR	DEX	CON	INT	WIS	CHA
10 (+0)	10 (+0)	12 (+1)	10 (+0)	13 (+1)	7 (−2)

Senses darkvision 120 ft., passive Perception 11
Languages —
Challenge 1/2 (100 XP)

Distress Spores. When the myconid takes damage, all other myconids within 240 feet of it can sense its pain.

Sun Sickness. While in sunlight, the myconid has disadvantage on ability checks, attack rolls, and saving throws. The myconid dies if it spends more than 1 hour in direct sunlight.

Actions

Fist. *Melee Weapon Attack:* +2 to hit, reach 5 ft., one target. *Hit:* 5 (2d4) bludgeoning damage plus 5 (2d4) poison damage.

Pacifying Spores (3/Day). The myconid ejects spores at one creature it can see within 5 feet of it. The target must succeed on a DC 11 Constitution saving throw or be stunned for 1 minute. The target can repeat the saving throw at the end of each of its turns, ending the effect on itself on a success.

Rapport Spores. A 20-foot radius of spores extends from the myconid. These spores can go around corners and affect only creatures with an Intelligence of 2 or higher that aren't undead, constructs, or elementals. Affected creatures can communicate telepathically with one another while they are within 30 feet of each other. The effect lasts for 1 hour.

M

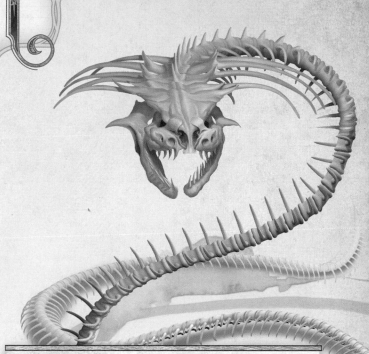

Nagas

Nagas are intelligent serpents that inhabit the ruins of the past, amassing arcane treasures and knowledge.

The first nagas were created as immortal guardians by a humanoid race long lost to history. When this race died out, the nagas deemed themselves the rightful inheritors of their masters' treasures and magical lore. Industrious and driven, nagas occasionally venture out from their lairs to track down magic items or rare spellbooks.

Nagas never feel the ravages of time or succumb to sickness. Even if it is struck down, a naga's immortal spirit reforms in a new body in a matter of days, ready to continue its eternal work.

Benevolent Dictators and Brutal Tyrants. A naga rules its domain with absolute authority. Whether it rules with compassion or by terrorizing its subjects, the naga believes itself the master of all other creatures that inhabit its domain.

Rivalry. Nagas have a long-standing enmity with the yuan-ti, with each race seeing itself as the epitome of serpentine evolution. Though cooperation between them is rare, nagas and yuan-ti sometimes set aside their differences to work toward common objectives. However, yuan-ti always chafe under a naga's authority.

Immortal Nature. A naga doesn't require air, food, drink, or sleep.

Bone Naga

In response to the long history of conflict between the yuan-ti and the nagas, yuan-ti created a necromantic ritual that could halt a naga's resurrection by transforming the living naga into a skeletal undead servitor. A bone naga retains only a few of the spells it knew in life.

Guardian Naga

Wise and good, the beautiful guardian nagas protect sacred places and items of magical power from falling into evil hands. In their hidden redoubts, they research spells and hatch convoluted plots to thwart the evil designs of their enemies.

A guardian naga doesn't seek out violence, warning off intruders rather than attacking. Only if its foes persist does the naga attack, accosting enemies with its spells and poisonous spittle.

Spirit Naga

Spirit nagas live in gloom and spitefulness, constantly plotting vengeance against creatures that have wronged them—or that they believe have wronged them. Lairing in dismal caverns and ruins, they devote their time to developing new spells and enslaving the mortals with which they surround themselves. A spirit naga likes to charm its foes, drawing them close so that it can sink its poisonous fangs into their flesh.

Bone Naga
Large undead, lawful evil

Armor Class 15 (natural armor)
Hit Points 58 (9d10 + 9)
Speed 30 ft.

STR	DEX	CON	INT	WIS	CHA
15 (+2)	16 (+3)	12 (+1)	15 (+2)	15 (+2)	16 (+3)

Damage Immunities poison
Condition Immunities charmed, exhaustion, paralyzed, poisoned
Senses darkvision 60 ft., passive Perception 12
Languages Common plus one other language
Challenge 4 (1,100 XP)

Spellcasting. The naga is a 5th-level spellcaster (spell save DC 12, +4 to hit with spell attacks) that needs only verbal components to cast its spells.

If the naga was a guardian naga in life, its spellcasting ability is Wisdom, and it has the following cleric spells prepared:

Cantrips (at will): *mending, sacred flame, thaumaturgy*
1st level (4 slots): *command, shield of faith*
2nd level (3 slots): *calm emotions, hold person*
3rd level (2 slots): *bestow curse*

If the naga was a spirit naga in life, its spellcasting ability is Intelligence, and it has the following wizard spells prepared:

Cantrips (at will): *mage hand, minor illusion, ray of frost*
1st level (4 slots): *charm person, sleep*
2nd level (3 slots): *detect thoughts, hold person*
3rd level (2 slots): *lightning bolt*

Actions

Bite. *Melee Weapon Attack:* +5 to hit, reach 10 ft., one creature. *Hit:* 10 (2d6 + 3) piercing damage plus 10 (3d6) poison damage.

"If you destroy me, I will return, and everyone you care about will suffer for it."
—Explictica Defilus, spirit naga

Guardian Naga

Large monstrosity, lawful good

Armor Class 18 (natural armor)
Hit Points 127 (15d10 + 45)
Speed 40 ft.

STR	DEX	CON	INT	WIS	CHA
19 (+4)	18 (+4)	16 (+3)	16 (+3)	19 (+4)	18 (+4)

Saving Throws Dex +8, Con +7, Int +7, Wis +8, Cha +8
Damage Immunities poison
Condition Immunities charmed, poisoned
Senses darkvision 60 ft., passive Perception 14
Languages Celestial, Common
Challenge 10 (5,900 XP)

Rejuvenation. If it dies, the naga returns to life in 1d6 days and regains all its hit points. Only a *wish* spell can prevent this trait from functioning.

Spellcasting. The naga is an 11th-level spellcaster. Its spellcasting ability is Wisdom (spell save DC 16, +8 to hit with spell attacks), and it needs only verbal components to cast its spells. It has the following cleric spells prepared:

Cantrips (at will): *mending, sacred flame, thaumaturgy*
1st level (4 slots): *command, cure wounds, shield of faith*
2nd level (3 slots): *calm emotions, hold person*
3rd level (3 slots): *bestow curse, clairvoyance*
4th level (3 slots): *banishment, freedom of movement*
5th level (2 slots): *flame strike, geas*
6th level (1 slot): *true seeing*

Actions

Bite. *Melee Weapon Attack:* +8 to hit, reach 10 ft., one creature. *Hit:* 8 (1d8 + 4) piercing damage, and the target must make a DC 15 Constitution saving throw, taking 45 (10d8) poison damage on a failed save, or half as much damage on a successful one.

Spit Poison. *Ranged Weapon Attack:* +8 to hit, range 15/30 ft., one creature. *Hit:* The target must make a DC 15 Constitution saving throw, taking 45 (10d8) poison damage on a failed save, or half as much damage on a successful one.

Spirit Naga

Large monstrosity, chaotic evil

Armor Class 15 (natural armor)
Hit Points 75 (10d10 + 20)
Speed 40 ft.

STR	DEX	CON	INT	WIS	CHA
18 (+4)	17 (+3)	14 (+2)	16 (+3)	15 (+2)	16 (+3)

Saving Throws Dex +6, Con +5, Wis +5, Cha +6
Damage Immunities poison
Condition Immunities charmed, poisoned
Senses darkvision 60 ft., passive Perception 12
Languages Abyssal, Common
Challenge 8 (3,900 XP)

Rejuvenation. If it dies, the naga returns to life in 1d6 days and regains all its hit points. Only a *wish* spell can prevent this trait from functioning.

Spellcasting. The naga is a 10th-level spellcaster. Its spellcasting ability is Intelligence (spell save DC 14, +6 to hit with spell attacks), and it needs only verbal components to cast its spells. It has the following wizard spells prepared:

Cantrips (at will): *mage hand, minor illusion, ray of frost*
1st level (4 slots): *charm person, detect magic, sleep*
2nd level (3 slots): *detect thoughts, hold person*
3rd level (3 slots): *lightning bolt, water breathing*
4th level (3 slots): *blight, dimension door*
5th level (2 slots): *dominate person*

Actions

Bite. *Melee Weapon Attack:* +7 to hit, reach 10 ft., one creature. *Hit:* 7 (1d6 + 4) piercing damage, and the target must make a DC 13 Constitution saving throw, taking 31 (7d8) poison damage on a failed save, or half as much damage on a successful one.

Nightmare
Large fiend, neutral evil

Armor Class 13 (natural armor)
Hit Points 68 (8d10 + 24)
Speed 60 ft., fly 90 ft.

STR	DEX	CON	INT	WIS	CHA
18 (+4)	15 (+2)	16 (+3)	10 (+0)	13 (+1)	15 (+2)

Damage Immunities fire
Senses passive Perception 11
Languages understands Abyssal, Common, and Infernal but can't speak
Challenge 3 (700 XP)

Confer Fire Resistance. The nightmare can grant resistance to fire damage to anyone riding it.

Illumination. The nightmare sheds bright light in a 10-foot radius and dim light for an additional 10 feet.

Actions

Hooves. *Melee Weapon Attack:* +6 to hit, reach 5 ft., one target. *Hit:* 13 (2d8 + 4) bludgeoning damage plus 7 (2d6) fire damage.

Ethereal Stride. The nightmare and up to three willing creatures within 5 feet of it magically enter the Ethereal Plane from the Material Plane, or vice versa.

Nightmare

A nightmare appears in a cloud of roiling smoke, its mane, tail, and hooves wreathed in flame. The creature's unearthly black form moves with supernatural speed, vanishing in a cloud of brimstone as quickly as it appeared.

Dread Steed. Also called a "demon horse" or "hell horse," the nightmare serves as a steed for creatures of exceptional evil, carrying demons, devils, death knights, liches, night hags, and other vile monsters. It resembles a fiendish horse, and a nightmare's fiery red eyes betray its malevolent intelligence.

A nightmare can be summoned from the Lower Planes, but unless a worthy sacrifice is offered to it as food upon its arrival, the nightmare displays no special loyalty to the creature it serves.

Creating a Nightmare. Nightmares don't appear naturally in the multiverse. They must be created from pegasi. The ritual that creates a nightmare requires the torturous removal of a pegasus's wings, driving that noble creature to evil as it is transformed by dark magic.

NOTHIC

Medium aberration, neutral evil

Armor Class 15 (natural armor)
Hit Points 45 (6d8 + 18)
Speed 30 ft.

STR	DEX	CON	INT	WIS	CHA
14 (+2)	16 (+3)	16 (+3)	13 (+1)	10 (+0)	8 (−1)

Skills Arcana +3, Insight +4, Perception +2, Stealth +5
Senses truesight 120 ft., passive Perception 12
Languages Undercommon
Challenge 2 (450 XP)

Keen Sight. The nothic has advantage on Wisdom (Perception) checks that rely on sight.

ACTIONS

Multiattack. The nothic makes two claw attacks.

Claw. *Melee Weapon Attack:* +4 to hit, reach 5 ft., one target. *Hit:* 6 (1d6 + 3) slashing damage.

Rotting Gaze. The nothic targets one creature it can see within 30 feet of it. The target must succeed on a DC 12 Constitution saving throw against this magic or take 10 (3d6) necrotic damage.

Weird Insight. The nothic targets one creature it can see within 30 feet of it. The target must contest its Charisma (Deception) check against the nothic's Wisdom (Insight) check. If the nothic wins, it magically learns one fact or secret about the target. The target automatically wins if it is immune to being charmed.

NOTHIC

A baleful eye peers out from the darkness, its gleam hinting at a weird intelligence and unnerving malevolence. Most times, a nothic is content to watch, weighing and assessing the creatures it encounters. When driven to violence, it uses its horrific gaze to rot the flesh from its enemies' bones.

Cursed Arcanists. Rather than gaining the godlike supremacy they crave, some wizards who devote their lives to unearthing arcane secrets are reduced to creeping, tormented monsters by a dark curse left behind by Vecna, a powerful lich who, in some worlds, has transcended his undead existence to become a god of secrets. Nothics retain no awareness of their former selves, skulking amid the shadows and haunting places rich in magical knowledge, drawn by memories and impulses they can't quite understand.

Dark Oracles. Nothics possess a strange magical insight that allows them to extract knowledge from other creatures. This grants them unique understanding of secret and forbidden lore, which they share for a price. A nothic covets magic items, greedily accepting such gifts from creatures that seek out its knowledge.

Lurkers in Magical Places. Nothics are notorious for infiltrating arcane academies and other places rich in magical learning. They are driven by the vague knowledge that there exists a method to reverse their condition. This isn't a clear sense of purpose, but rather an obsessive tug at the end of the mind. Some nothics are clever enough to realize that this is merely part of the strange lesson for their folly, a false hope to drive them to seek out more arcane secrets.

OGRES

Ogres are as lazy of mind as they are strong of body. They live by raiding, scavenging, and killing for food and pleasure. The average adult specimen stands between 9 and 10 feet tall and weighs close to a thousand pounds.

Furious Tempers. Ogres are notorious for their quick tempers, which flare at the smallest perceived offense. Insults and name-calling can rouse an ogre's wrath in an instant—as can stealing from it, bumping, jabbing, or prodding it, laughing, making faces, or simply looking at it the wrong way. When its rage is incited, an ogre lashes out in a frustrated tantrum until it runs out of objects or creatures to smash.

Gruesome Gluttons. Ogres eat almost anything, but they especially enjoy the taste of dwarves, halflings, and elves. When they can, they combine dinner with pleasure, chasing scurrying victims around before eating them raw. If enough of its victim remains after the ogre has gorged itself, it might make a loincloth from its quarry's skin and a necklace from its leftover bones. This macabre crafting is the height of ogre culture.

Greedy Collectors. An ogre's eyes glitter with avarice when it sees the possessions of others. Ogres carry rough sacks on their raids, which they fill with fabulous "treasure" taken from their victims. This might include a collection of battered helmets, a moldy wheel of cheese, a rough patch of animal fur fastened like a cloak, or a squealing, mud-spattered pig. Ogres also delight in the gleam of gold and silver, and they will fight one another over small handfuls of coins. Smarter creatures can earn an ogre's trust by offering it gold or a weapon forged for a creature of its size.

Legendary Stupidity. Few ogres can count to ten, even with their fingers in front of them. Most speak only a rudimentary form of Giant and know a smattering of Common words. Ogres believe what they are told and are easy to fool or confuse, but they break things they don't understand. Silver-tongued tricksters who test their talents on these savages typically end up eating their eloquent words—and then being eaten in turn.

Primitive Wanderers. Ogres clothe themselves in animal pelts and uproot trees for use as crude tools and weapons. They create stone-tipped javelins for hunting. When they establish lairs, they settle near the rural edges of civilized lands, taking advantage of poorly protected livestock, undefended larders, and unwary farmers.

An ogre sleeps in caves, animal dens, or under trees until it finds a cabin or isolated farmhouse, whereupon it kills the inhabitants and lairs there. Whenever it is bored or hungry, an ogre ventures out from its lair, attacking anything that crosses its path. Only after an ogre has depleted an area of food does it move on.

OGRE

Large giant, chaotic evil

Armor Class 11 (hide armor)
Hit Points 59 (7d10 + 21)
Speed 40 ft.

STR	DEX	CON	INT	WIS	CHA
19 (+4)	8 (−1)	16 (+3)	5 (−3)	7 (−2)	7 (−2)

Senses darkvision 60 ft., passive Perception 8
Languages Common, Giant
Challenge 2 (450 XP)

ACTIONS

Greatclub. *Melee Weapon Attack:* +6 to hit, reach 5 ft., one target. *Hit:* 13 (2d8 + 4) bludgeoning damage.

Javelin. *Melee or Ranged Weapon Attack:* +6 to hit, reach 5 ft. or range 30/120 ft., one target. *Hit:* 11 (2d6 + 4) piercing damage.

"WORST. DANCERS. EVER."
— RIDDLEFIDDLE THE SATYR, ON OGRES

Ogre Gangs. Ogres sometimes band together in small, nomadic groups, but they lack a true sense of tribalism. When bands of ogres meet, one might attempt to capture the members of the other group to increase its numbers. However, ogre bands are just as likely to trade members freely, especially if the welcoming band is temporarily flush with food and weapons.

Whenever possible, ogres gang up with other monsters to bully or prey on creatures weaker than themselves. They associate freely with goblinoids, orcs, and trolls, and practically worship giants. In the giants' complex social structure (known as the ordning), ogres rank beneath the lowest giants in status. As a result, an ogre will do nearly anything a giant asks.

HALF-OGRE (OGRILLON)

When an ogre mates with a human, hobgoblin, bugbear, or orc, the result is always a half-ogre. (Ogres don't mate with dwarves, halflings, or elves. They eat them.) Human mothers rarely survive the birth of a half-ogre offspring.

The half-ogre offspring of an ogre and an orc is also called an ogrillon. An adult half-ogre or ogrillon stands 8 feet tall and weighs 450 pounds on average.

HALF-OGRE
Large giant, any chaotic alignment

Armor Class 12 (hide armor)
Hit Points 30 (4d10 + 8)
Speed 30 ft.

STR	DEX	CON	INT	WIS	CHA
17 (+3)	10 (+0)	14 (+2)	7 (−2)	9 (−1)	10 (+0)

Senses darkvision 60 ft., passive Perception 9
Languages Common, Giant
Challenge 1 (200 XP)

ACTIONS

Battleaxe. *Melee Weapon Attack:* +5 to hit, reach 5 ft., one target. *Hit:* 12 (2d8 + 3) slashing damage, or 14 (2d10 + 3) slashing damage if used with two hands.

Javelin. *Melee or Ranged Weapon Attack:* +5 to hit, reach 5 ft. or range 30/120 ft., one target. *Hit:* 10 (2d6 + 3) piercing damage.

ONI

In nursery rhymes, oni are fearsome bogeymen that haunt the nightmares of children and adults alike, yet they are very real and always hungry. They find human babies especially delicious. Oni look like demonic ogres with blue or green skin, dark hair, and a pair of short ivory horns protruding from their foreheads. Their eyes are dark with strikingly white pupils, and their teeth and claws are jet black.

Night Haunters. By the light of day, an oni hides its true form with magic, gaining the trust of those it intends to betray when darkness descends. These creatures can change their size as well as their shape, appearing as humanoids as they pass through towns, pretending to be travelers, woodcutters, or frontier folk. In such a form, an oni takes stock of the selection of humanoids in a settlement and devises ways to abduct and devour some of them.

Magical Ogres. Oni are sometimes called ogre mages because of their innate magical ability. Though they are only distantly related to true ogres, they share the ogres' habit of joining forces with other evil creatures. An oni serves a master if doing so proves lucrative or provides it with a luxurious, well-defended home. Oni covet magic, and they work for evil wizards and hags in exchange for useful magic items.

Lock the door, blow out the light;
The hungry oni haunts the night.
Hide and tremble, little one;
The oni wants to have some fun.

Hear it scratching on the door;
See its shadow cross the floor.
The sun won't rise for quite a while;
Till then, beware the oni's smile.
—Children's rhyme

ONI

Large giant, lawful evil

Armor Class 16 (chain mail)
Hit Points 110 (13d10 + 39)
Speed 30 ft., fly 30 ft.

STR	DEX	CON	INT	WIS	CHA
19 (+4)	11 (+0)	16 (+3)	14 (+2)	12 (+1)	15 (+2)

Saving Throws Dex +3, Con +6, Wis +4, Cha +5
Skills Arcana +5, Deception +8, Perception +4
Senses darkvision 60 ft., passive Perception 14
Languages Common, Giant
Challenge 7 (2,900 XP)

Innate Spellcasting. The oni's innate spellcasting ability is Charisma (spell save DC 13). The oni can innately cast the following spells, requiring no material components:

At will: *darkness, invisibility*
1/day each: *charm person, cone of cold, gaseous form, sleep*

Magic Weapons. The oni's weapon attacks are magical.

Regeneration. The oni regains 10 hit points at the start of its turn if it has at least 1 hit point.

ACTIONS

Multiattack. The oni makes two attacks, either with its claws or its glaive.

Claw (Oni Form Only). *Melee Weapon Attack:* +7 to hit, reach 5 ft., one target. *Hit:* 8 (1d8 + 4) slashing damage.

Glaive. *Melee Weapon Attack:* +7 to hit, reach 10 ft., one target. *Hit:* 15 (2d10 + 4) slashing damage, or 9 (1d10 + 4) slashing damage in Small or Medium form.

Change Shape. The oni magically polymorphs into a Small or Medium humanoid, into a Large giant, or back into its true form. Other than its size, its statistics are the same in each form. The only equipment that is transformed is its glaive, which shrinks so that it can be wielded in humanoid form. If the oni dies, it reverts to its true form, and its glaive reverts to its normal size.

Oozes

Oozes thrive in the dark, shunning areas of bright light and extreme temperatures. They flow through the damp underground, feeding on any creature or object that can be dissolved, slinking along the ground, dripping from walls and ceilings, spreading across the edges of underground pools, and squeezing through cracks. The first warning an adventurer receives of an ooze's presence is often the searing pain of its acidic touch.

Oozes are drawn to movement and warmth. Organic material nourishes them, and when prey is scarce they feed on grime, fungus, and offal. Veteran explorers know that an immaculately clean passageway is a likely sign that an ooze lairs nearby.

Slow Death. An ooze kills its prey slowly. Some varieties, such as black puddings and gelatinous cubes, engulf creatures to prevent escape. The only upside of this torturous death is that a victim's comrades can come to the rescue before it is too late.

Since not every ooze digests every type of substance, some have coins, metal gear, bones, and other debris suspended within their quivering bodies. A slain ooze can be a rich source of treasure for its killers.

Unwitting Servants. Although an ooze lacks the intelligence to ally itself with other creatures, others that understand an ooze's need to feed might lure it into a location where it can be of use to them. Clever monsters keep oozes around to defend passageways or consume refuse. Likewise, an ooze can be enticed into a pit trap, where its captors feed it often enough to prevent it from coming after them. Crafty creatures place torches and flaming braziers in strategic areas to dissuade an ooze from leaving a particular tunnel or room.

Spawn of Juiblex. According to the *Demonomicon of Iggwilv* and other sources, oozes are scattered fragments or offspring of the demon lord Juiblex. Whether this is true or not, the Faceless Lord is one of the few beings that can control oozes and imbue them with a modicum of intelligence. Most of the time, oozes have no sense of tactics or self-preservation. They are direct and predictable, attacking and eating without cunning. Under the control of Juiblex, they exhibit glimmers of sentience and malevolent intent.

Ooze Nature. An ooze doesn't require sleep.

VARIANT: PSYCHIC GRAY OOZE

A gray ooze that lives a long time can evolve to become more intelligent and develop limited psionic ability. Such occurrences are more common in gray oozes that live near psionic creatures such as mind flayers, suggesting that the ooze can sense and mimic psionic ability.

A psionic gray ooze has an Intelligence score of 6 (−2), as well as the following additional action.

Psychic Crush (Recharge 5–6). The ooze targets one creature that it can sense within 60 feet of it. The target must make a DC 10 Intelligence saving throw, taking 10 (3d6) psychic damage on a failed save, or half as much damage on a successful one.

Black Pudding

A black pudding resembles a heaving mound of sticky black sludge. In dim passageways, the pudding appears to be little more than a blot of shadow.

Flesh, wood, metal, and bone dissolve when the pudding ebbs over them. Stone remains behind, wiped clean.

Gelatinous Cube

Gelatinous cubes scour dungeon passages in silent, predictable patterns, leaving perfectly clean paths in their wake. They consume living tissue while leaving bones and other materials undissolved.

A gelatinous cube is all but transparent, making it hard to spot until it attacks. A cube that is well fed can be easier to spot, since its victims' bones, coins, and other objects can be seen suspended inside the creature.

Gray Ooze

A gray ooze is stone turned to liquid by chaos. When it moves, it slithers like a liquid snake, rising to strike.

Ochre Jelly

Ochre jellies are yellowish blobs that can slide under doors and through narrow cracks in pursuit of creatures to devour. They have enough bestial cunning to avoid large groups of enemies.

An ochre jelly follows at a safe distance as it pursues its meal. Its digestive enzymes dissolve flesh quickly but have no effect on other substances such as bone, wood, and metal.

Black Pudding

Large ooze, unaligned

Armor Class 7
Hit Points 85 (10d10 + 30)
Speed 20 ft., climb 20 ft.

STR	DEX	CON	INT	WIS	CHA
16 (+3)	5 (–3)	16 (+3)	1 (–5)	6 (–2)	1 (–5)

Damage Immunities acid, cold, lightning, slashing
Condition Immunities blinded, charmed, deafened, exhaustion, frightened, prone
Senses blindsight 60 ft. (blind beyond this radius), passive Perception 8
Languages —
Challenge 4 (1,100 XP)

Amorphous. The pudding can move through a space as narrow as 1 inch wide without squeezing.

Corrosive Form. A creature that touches the pudding or hits it with a melee attack while within 5 feet of it takes 4 (1d8) acid damage. Any nonmagical weapon made of metal or wood that hits the pudding corrodes. After dealing damage, the weapon takes a permanent and cumulative –1 penalty to damage rolls. If its penalty drops to –5, the weapon is destroyed. Nonmagical ammunition made of metal or wood that hits the pudding is destroyed after dealing damage.

The pudding can eat through 2-inch-thick, nonmagical wood or metal in 1 round.

Spider Climb. The pudding can climb difficult surfaces, including upside down on ceilings, without needing to make an ability check.

Actions

Pseudopod. *Melee Weapon Attack:* +5 to hit, reach 5 ft., one target. *Hit:* 6 (1d6 + 3) bludgeoning damage plus 18 (4d8) acid damage. In addition, nonmagical armor worn by the target is partly dissolved and takes a permanent and cumulative –1 penalty to the AC it offers. The armor is destroyed if the penalty reduces its AC to 10.

Reactions

Split. When a pudding that is Medium or larger is subjected to lightning or slashing damage, it splits into two new puddings if it has at least 10 hit points. Each new pudding has hit points equal to half the original pudding's, rounded down. New puddings are one size smaller than the original pudding.

GELATINOUS CUBE
Large ooze, unaligned

Armor Class 6
Hit Points 84 (8d10 + 40)
Speed 15 ft.

STR	DEX	CON	INT	WIS	CHA
14 (+2)	3 (−4)	20 (+5)	1 (−5)	6 (−2)	1 (−5)

Condition Immunities blinded, charmed, deafened, exhaustion, frightened, prone
Senses blindsight 60 ft. (blind beyond this radius), passive Perception 8
Languages —
Challenge 2 (450 XP)

Ooze Cube. The cube takes up its entire space. Other creatures can enter the space, but a creature that does so is subjected to the cube's Engulf and has disadvantage on the saving throw.

Creatures inside the cube can be seen but have total cover.

A creature within 5 feet of the cube can take an action to pull a creature or object out of the cube. Doing so requires a successful DC 12 Strength check, and the creature making the attempt takes 10 (3d6) acid damage.

The cube can hold only one Large creature or up to four Medium or smaller creatures inside it at a time.

Transparent. Even when the cube is in plain sight, it takes a successful DC 15 Wisdom (Perception) check to spot a cube that has neither moved nor attacked. A creature that tries to enter the cube's space while unaware of the cube is surprised by the cube.

ACTIONS

Pseudopod. Melee Weapon Attack: +4 to hit, reach 5 ft., one creature. *Hit:* 10 (3d6) acid damage.

Engulf. The cube moves up to its speed. While doing so, it can enter Large or smaller creatures' spaces. Whenever the cube enters a creature's space, the creature must make a DC 12 Dexterity saving throw.

On a successful save, the creature can choose to be pushed 5 feet back or to the side of the cube. A creature that chooses not to be pushed suffers the consequences of a failed saving throw.

On a failed save, the cube enters the creature's space, and the creature takes 10 (3d6) acid damage and is engulfed. The engulfed creature can't breathe, is restrained, and takes 21 (6d6) acid damage at the start of each of the cube's turns. When the cube moves, the engulfed creature moves with it.

An engulfed creature can try to escape by taking an action to make a DC 12 Strength check. On a success, the creature escapes and enters a space of its choice within 5 feet of the cube.

Gray Ooze
Medium ooze, unaligned

Armor Class 8
Hit Points 22 (3d8 + 9)
Speed 10 ft., climb 10 ft.

STR	DEX	CON	INT	WIS	CHA
12 (+1)	6 (−2)	16 (+3)	1 (−5)	6 (−2)	2 (−4)

Skills Stealth +2
Damage Resistances acid, cold, fire
Condition Immunities blinded, charmed, deafened, exhaustion, frightened, prone
Senses blindsight 60 ft. (blind beyond this radius), passive Perception 8
Languages —
Challenge 1/2 (100 XP)

Amorphous. The ooze can move through a space as narrow as 1 inch wide without squeezing.

Corrode Metal. Any nonmagical weapon made of metal that hits the ooze corrodes. After dealing damage, the weapon takes a permanent and cumulative −1 penalty to damage rolls. If its penalty drops to −5, the weapon is destroyed. Nonmagical ammunition made of metal that hits the ooze is destroyed after dealing damage.

    The ooze can eat through 2-inch-thick, nonmagical metal in 1 round.

False Appearance. While the ooze remains motionless, it is indistinguishable from an oily pool or wet rock.

Actions

Pseudopod. *Melee Weapon Attack:* +3 to hit, reach 5 ft., one target. *Hit:* 4 (1d6 + 1) bludgeoning damage plus 7 (2d6) acid damage, and if the target is wearing nonmagical metal armor, its armor is partly corroded and takes a permanent and cumulative −1 penalty to the AC it offers. The armor is destroyed if the penalty reduces its AC to 10.

Ochre Jelly
Large ooze, unaligned

Armor Class 8
Hit Points 45 (6d10 + 12)
Speed 10 ft., climb 10 ft.

STR	DEX	CON	INT	WIS	CHA
15 (+2)	6 (−2)	14 (+2)	2 (−4)	6 (−2)	1 (−5)

Damage Resistances acid
Damage Immunities lightning, slashing
Condition Immunities blinded, charmed, deafened, exhaustion, frightened, prone
Senses blindsight 60 ft. (blind beyond this radius), passive Perception 8
Languages —
Challenge 2 (450 XP)

Amorphous. The jelly can move through a space as narrow as 1 inch wide without squeezing.

Spider Climb. The jelly can climb difficult surfaces, including upside down on ceilings, without needing to make an ability check.

Actions

Pseudopod. *Melee Weapon Attack:* +4 to hit, reach 5 ft., one target. *Hit:* 9 (2d6 + 2) bludgeoning damage plus 3 (1d6) acid damage.

Reactions

Split. When a jelly that is Medium or larger is subjected to lightning or slashing damage, it splits into two new jellies if it has at least 10 hit points. Each new jelly has hit points equal to half the original jelly's, rounded down. New jellies are one size smaller than the original jelly.

Orcs

Orcs are savage raiders and pillagers with stooped postures, low foreheads, and piggish faces with prominent lower canines that resemble tusks.

Gruumsh One-Eye. Orcs worship Gruumsh, the mightiest of the orc deities and their creator. The orcs believe that in ancient days, the gods gathered to divide the world among their followers. When Gruumsh claimed the mountains, he learned they had been taken by the dwarves. He laid claim to the forests, but those had been settled by the elves. Each place that Gruumsh wanted had already been claimed. The other gods laughed at Gruumsh, but he responded with a furious bellow. Grasping his mighty spear, he laid waste to the mountains, set the forests aflame, and carved great furrows in the fields. Such was the role of the orcs, he proclaimed, to take and destroy all that the other races would deny them. To this day, the orcs wage an endless war on humans, elves, dwarves, and other folk.

Orcs hold a particular hatred for elves. The elven god Corellon Larethian half-blinded Gruumsh with a well-placed arrow to the orc god's eye. Since then, the orcs have taken particular joy in slaughtering elves. Turning his injury into a baleful gift, Gruumsh grants divine might to any champion who willingly plucks out one of its eyes in his honor.

Tribes like Plagues. Orcs gather in tribes that exert their dominance and satisfy their bloodlust by plundering villages, devouring or driving off roaming herds, and slaying any humanoids that stand against them. After savaging a settlement, orcs pick it clean of wealth and items usable in their own lands. They set the remains of villages and camps ablaze, then retreat whence they came, their bloodlust satisfied.

Ranging Scavengers. Their lust for slaughter demands that orcs dwell always within striking distance of new targets. As such, they seldom settle permanently, instead converting ruins, cavern complexes, and defeated foes' villages into fortified camps and strongholds. Orcs build only for defense, making no innovation or improvement to their lairs beyond mounting the severed body parts of their victims on spiked stockade walls or pikes jutting up from moats and trenches.

When an existing territory is depleted of food, an orc tribe divides into roving bands that scout for choice hunting grounds. When each party returns, it brings back trophies and news of targets ripe for attack, the richest of which is chosen. The tribe then sets out en masse to carve a bloody path to its new territory.

On rare occasions, a tribe's leader chooses to hold onto a particularly defensible lair for decades. The orcs of such a tribe must range far across the countryside to sate their appetites.

Leadership and Might. Orc tribes are mostly patriarchal, flaunting such vivid or grotesque titles as Many-Arrows, Screaming Eye, and Elf Ripper. Occasionally, a powerful war chief unites scattered orc tribes into a single rampaging horde, which runs roughshod over other orc tribes and humanoid settlements from a position of overwhelming strength.

Strength and power are the greatest of orcish virtues, and orcs embrace all manner of mighty creatures in their tribes. Rejecting notions of racial purity, they proudly welcome ogres, trolls, half-orcs, and orogs into their ranks. As well, orcs respect and fear the size and power of evil giants, and often serve them as guards and soldiers.

Orc Crossbreeds. Luthic, the orc goddess of fertility and wife of Gruumsh, demands that orcs procreate often and indiscriminately so that orc hordes swell generation after generation. The orcs' drive to reproduce runs stronger than any other humanoid race, and they readily crossbreed with other races. When an orc procreates with a non-orc humanoid of similar size and stature (such as a human or a dwarf), the resulting child is either an orc or a half-orc. When an orc produces young with an ogre, the child is a half-ogre of intimidating strength and brutish features called an ogrillon.

ORC WAR CHIEF

The war chief of an orc tribe is its strongest and most cunning member. The reign of a war chief lasts only as long as it commands the fear and respect of other tribe members, whose bloodlust must be regularly satisfied lest the chief appear weak.

Scions of Slaughter. Gruumsh bestows special blessings upon war chiefs who prove themselves in battle time and again, imbuing them with slivers of his savagery. A war chief so blessed finds that his weapons cut deeper into his enemies, allowing him to inflict more carnage.

KING OBOULD MANY-ARROWS

King Obould of the Many-Arrows tribe is a legend among the orc war chiefs of the Forgotten Realms, and he is the most famous orc chief in the history of the D&D game.

Smarter and more intuitive than most of his kind, Obould slew his chieftain to take control of his tribe. Skilled in the arts of war and renowned for his violent temper, Obould proved himself a fierce opponent in battle time and again. Over the years, he subsumed other orc tribes into his own, until he commanded a horde of thousands.

Obould leveraged his strength and influence to carve out a kingdom for himself in the Spine of the World, a mountain range overlooking numerous dwarven, human, and elven strongholds.

After years of bloody conflict with his more civilized neighbors, Obould did the unthinkable and brokered a peace treaty with his enemies. This treaty confused many of the orcs under Obould's command. It was either a clever ploy by Obould to buy time while he strengthened his army for a final, decisive sweep across the Savage Frontier, or it was a troubling sign that Obould had forsaken the ways of Gruumsh and needed to be destroyed.

ORC EYE OF GRUUMSH

When an orc slays an elf in Gruumsh's name and offers the corpse of its foe as a sacrifice to the god of slaughter, an aspect of the god might appear. This aspect demands an additional sacrifice: one of the orc's eyes, symbolizing the loss Gruumsh suffered at the hands of his greatest enemy, Corellon Larethian.

If the orc plucks out one of its eyes, Gruumsh might grant the orc spellcasting ability and special favor, along with the right to call itself an Eye of Gruumsh. When not using their auguries to advise their war chiefs, these savage devotees of the god of slaughter hurl themselves into battle, their weapons stained with blood.

OROG

Orogs are orcs blessed with a surprisingly keen intellect that ordinary orcs believe is a gift from the orc goddess Luthic. Like Luthic, orogs prefer to live underground, although the scarcity of food often brings them to the surface to hunt. Orcs respect an orog's strength and cunning, and a lone orog might command an orc war band.

Stronger and Smarter. An orog uses its strength to bully other orcs and its intelligence to surprise enemies on the battlefield. Many an overconfident elf, human, or dwarf commander has watched a "simple" orc warlord execute a clever maneuver to outflank and destroy an opposing force, not realizing the orc is an orog.

When encountered in great numbers, orogs form their own detachments within much larger orc hordes, and they are always at the forefront of any attack, relying on their superior strength and tactical insight to overcome anything that stands in their way.

Few orc tribes actively seek out orogs to bolster their ranks. The orogs' superiority makes them ideal leaders, and thus deadly rivals to orc war chiefs, who must be wary of orog treachery.

Detached Killers. Wanting nothing more than to hack their enemies to pieces, orogs are a terrifying presence on the battlefield. They form no attachments, even to their parents and siblings, and have no concept of love or dedication. They worship the orc pantheon of gods—Gruumsh and Luthic foremost—because they believe that the gods have strength beyond reason, and physical might is all they respect.

Servants of Darkness. Mistrusted by orcs, some orogs form independent mercenary war bands that sell themselves to the highest bidder. As long as they are rewarded, orog mercenaries gladly serve as elite warriors and shock troops for evil wizards, depraved giants, and other villains.

He worked his serrated long knife savagely, tearing out the king's throat to the howls of approval from his legions. The ferocious orc didn't stop there, digging and ripping the blade back and forth unrelentingly until he took the head off the dwarf king's shoulders.

—An account of War Chief Hartusk's brutality in the aftermath of the Battle of the Cold Vale

TYPICAL ORC

ORC

Medium humanoid (orc), chaotic evil

Armor Class 13 (hide armor)
Hit Points 15 (2d8 + 6)
Speed 30 ft.

STR	DEX	CON	INT	WIS	CHA
16 (+3)	12 (+1)	16 (+3)	7 (–2)	11 (+0)	10 (+0)

Skills Intimidation +2
Senses darkvision 60 ft., passive Perception 10
Languages Common, Orc
Challenge 1/2 (100 XP)

Aggressive. As a bonus action, the orc can move up to its speed toward a hostile creature that it can see.

ACTIONS

Greataxe. *Melee Weapon Attack:* +5 to hit, reach 5 ft., one target. *Hit:* 9 (1d12 + 3) slashing damage.

Javelin. *Melee or Ranged Weapon Attack:* +5 to hit, reach 5 ft. or range 30/120 ft., one target. *Hit:* 6 (1d6 + 3) piercing damage.

ORC WAR CHIEF

Medium humanoid (orc), chaotic evil

Armor Class 16 (chain mail)
Hit Points 93 (11d8 + 44)
Speed 30 ft.

STR	DEX	CON	INT	WIS	CHA
18 (+4)	12 (+1)	18 (+4)	11 (+0)	11 (+0)	16 (+3)

Saving Throws Str +6, Con +6, Wis +2
Skills Intimidation +5
Senses darkvision 60 ft., passive Perception 10
Languages Common, Orc
Challenge 4 (1,100 XP)

Aggressive. As a bonus action, the orc can move up to its speed toward a hostile creature that it can see.

Gruumsh's Fury. The orc deals an extra 4 (1d8) damage when it hits with a weapon attack (included in the attacks).

ACTIONS

Multiattack. The orc makes two attacks with its greataxe or its spear.

Greataxe. *Melee Weapon Attack:* +6 to hit, reach 5 ft., one target. *Hit:* 15 (1d12 + 4 plus 1d8) slashing damage.

Spear. *Melee or Ranged Weapon Attack:* +6 to hit, reach 5 ft. or range 20/60 ft., one target. *Hit:* 12 (1d6 + 4 plus 1d8) piercing damage, or 13 (2d8 + 4) piercing damage if used with two hands to make a melee attack.

Battle Cry (1/Day). Each creature of the war chief's choice that is within 30 feet of it, can hear it, and not already affected by Battle Cry gain advantage on attack rolls until the start of the war chief's next turn. The war chief can then make one attack as a bonus action.

TYPICAL OROG

ORC EYE OF GRUUMSH
Medium humanoid (orc), chaotic evil

Armor Class 16 (ring mail, shield)
Hit Points 45 (6d8 + 18)
Speed 30 ft.

STR	DEX	CON	INT	WIS	CHA
16 (+3)	12 (+1)	16 (+3)	9 (−1)	13 (+1)	12 (+1)

Skills Intimidation +3, Religion +1
Senses darkvision 60 ft., passive Perception 11
Languages Common, Orc
Challenge 2 (450 XP)

Aggressive. As a bonus action, the orc can move up to its speed toward a hostile creature that it can see.

Gruumsh's Fury. The orc deals an extra 4 (1d8) damage when it hits with a weapon attack (included in the attack).

Spellcasting. The orc is a 3rd-level spellcaster. Its spellcasting ability is Wisdom (spell save DC 11, +3 to hit with spell attacks). The orc has the following cleric spells prepared:

Cantrips (at will): *guidance, resistance, thaumaturgy*
1st level (4 slots): *bless, command*
2nd level (2 slots): *augury, spiritual weapon* (spear)

ACTIONS

Spear. *Melee or Ranged Weapon Attack:* +5 to hit, reach 5 ft. or range 20/60 ft., one target. *Hit:* 11 (1d6 + 3 plus 1d8) piercing damage, or 12 (2d8 + 3) piercing damage if used with two hands to make a melee attack.

OROG
Medium humanoid (orc), chaotic evil

Armor Class 18 (plate)
Hit Points 42 (5d8 + 20)
Speed 30 ft.

STR	DEX	CON	INT	WIS	CHA
18 (+4)	12 (+1)	18 (+4)	12 (+1)	11 (+0)	12 (+1)

Skills Intimidation +5, Survival +2
Senses darkvision 60 ft., passive Perception 10
Languages Common, Orc
Challenge 2 (450 XP)

Aggressive. As a bonus action, the orog can move up to its speed toward a hostile creature that it can see.

ACTIONS

Multiattack. The orog makes two greataxe attacks.

Greataxe. *Melee Weapon Attack:* +6 to hit, reach 5 ft., one target. *Hit:* 10 (1d12 + 4) slashing damage.

Javelin. *Melee or Ranged Weapon Attack:* +6 to hit, reach 5 ft. or range 30/120 ft., one target. *Hit:* 7 (1d6 + 4) piercing damage.

OTYUGH

An otyugh is a grotesque, bulbous creature borne along on three sturdy legs, its eyes and nose set along a vine-like stalk that snakes from the top of its bloated body. Two rubbery tentacles end in spiky, leaf-like appendages that the otyugh uses to shovel food into its gaping maw.

An otyugh buries itself under mounds of offal and carrion, leaving only its sensory stalk exposed. When an edible creature happens by, the otyugh's tentacles erupt from the filth and grab hold of it.

Otyughs make the most of any opportunity to ambush and devour prey. They use a limited form of telepathy to urge sentient creatures toward their lairs, sometimes by pretending to be something else.

Dwellers in Darkness. Otyughs tolerate bright light only when considerable stores of carrion or garbage lie within reach. In the wilderness, they dwell in stagnant swamps, scum-filled ponds, and damp forest dells. The scent of graveyards, city sewers, village middens, and manure-filled animal pens attracts them to civilized areas.

Since otyughs lack concern for anything but food, their nests sometimes accumulate a variety of treasures shed from their victims and mixed among the junk.

Symbiotic Guardians. Sentient subterranean beings can coexist with otyughs, employing them as garbage disposals. With such plentiful sustenance, otyughs grow fat in their wallows, unmoved by any other drive or desire. This sedentary gluttony makes them reliable guardians. As long as it is fed, an otyugh refrains from attacking other creatures. However, would-be otyugh masters can easily underestimate the quantity of waste, carrion, and meat necessary to keep an otyugh from wandering off in search of food. More than one "trained" otyugh has eaten its keeper after devouring all the waste in its wallow.

OTYUGH
Large aberration, neutral

Armor Class 14 (natural armor)
Hit Points 114 (12d10 + 48)
Speed 30 ft.

STR	DEX	CON	INT	WIS	CHA
16 (+3)	11 (+0)	19 (+4)	6 (−2)	13 (+1)	6 (−2)

Saving Throws Con +7
Senses darkvision 120 ft., passive Perception 11
Languages Otyugh
Challenge 5 (1,800 XP)

Limited Telepathy. The otyugh can magically transmit simple messages and images to any creature within 120 feet of it that can understand a language. This form of telepathy doesn't allow the receiving creature to telepathically respond.

ACTIONS

Multiattack. The otyugh makes three attacks: one with its bite and two with its tentacles.

Bite. *Melee Weapon Attack:* +6 to hit, reach 5 ft., one target. *Hit:* 12 (2d8 + 3) piercing damage. If the target is a creature, it must succeed on a DC 15 Constitution saving throw against disease or become poisoned until the disease is cured. Every 24 hours that elapse, the target must repeat the saving throw, reducing its hit point maximum by 5 (1d10) on a failure. The disease is cured on a success. The target dies if the disease reduces its hit point maximum to 0. This reduction to the target's hit point maximum lasts until the disease is cured.

Tentacle. *Melee Weapon Attack:* +6 to hit, reach 10 ft., one target. *Hit:* 7 (1d8 + 3) bludgeoning damage plus 4 (1d8) piercing damage. If the target is Medium or smaller, it is grappled (escape DC 13) and restrained until the grapple ends. The otyugh has two tentacles, each of which can grapple one target.

Tentacle Slam. The otyugh slams creatures grappled by it into each other or a solid surface. Each creature must succeed on a DC 14 Constitution saving throw or take 10 (2d6 + 3) bludgeoning damage and be stunned until the end of the otyugh's next turn. On a successful save, the target takes half the bludgeoning damage and isn't stunned.

Owlbear

An owlbear's screech echoes through dark valleys and benighted forests, piercing the quiet night to announce the death of its prey. Feathers cover the thick, shaggy coat of its bearlike body, and the limpid pupils of its great round eyes stare furiously from its owlish head.

Deadly Ferocity. The owlbear's reputation for ferocity, aggression, stubbornness, and sheer ill temper makes it one of the most feared predators of the wild. There is little, if anything, that a hungry owlbear fears. Even monsters that outmatch an owlbear in size and strength avoid tangling with it, for this creature cares nothing about a foe's superior strength as it attacks without provocation.

Consummate Predators. An owlbear emerges from its den around sunset and hunts into the darkest hours of the night, hooting or screeching to declare its territory, to search for a mate, or to flush prey into its hunting grounds. These are typically forests familiar to the owlbear, and dense enough to limit its quarry's escape routes.

An owlbear makes its den in a cave or ruin littered with the bones of its prey. It drags partially devoured kills back to its den, storing portions of the carcass among the surrounding rocks, bushes, and trees. The scent of blood and rotting flesh hangs heavy near an owlbear's lair, attracting scavengers and thus luring more prey.

Owlbears hunt alone or in mated pairs. If quarry is plentiful, a family of owlbears might remain together for longer than is required to rear offspring. Otherwise, they part ways as soon as the young are ready to hunt.

Savage Companions. Although they are more intelligent than most animals, owlbears are difficult to tame. However, with enough time, food, and luck, an intelligent creature can train an owlbear to recognize it as a master, making it an unflinching guard or a fast and hardy mount. People of remote frontier settlements have even succeeded at racing owlbears, but spectators bet as often on which owlbear will attack its handler as they do on which will reach the finish line first.

Elven communities encourage owlbears to den beneath their treetop villages, using the beasts as a natural defense during the night. Hobgoblins favor owlbears as war beasts, and hill giants and frost giants sometimes keep owlbears as pets. A starved owlbear might show up in a gladiatorial arena, ruthlessly eviscerating and devouring its foes before a bloodthirsty audience.

Owlbear Origins. Scholars have long debated the origins of the owlbear. The most common theory is that a demented wizard created the first specimen by crossing a giant owl with a bear. However, venerable elves claim to have known these creatures for thousands of years, and some fey insist that owlbears have always existed in the Feywild.

"THE ONLY GOOD THING ABOUT OWLBEARS IS THAT THE WIZARD WHO CREATED THEM IS PROBABLY DEAD."

—XARSHEL RAVENSHADOW, GNOME PROFESSOR OF TRANSMUTATIVE SCIENCE AT MORGRAVE UNIVERSITY

Owlbear
Large monstrosity, unaligned

Armor Class 13 (natural armor)
Hit Points 59 (7d10 + 21)
Speed 40 ft.

STR	DEX	CON	INT	WIS	CHA
20 (+5)	12 (+1)	17 (+3)	3 (−4)	12 (+1)	7 (−2)

Skills Perception +3
Senses darkvision 60 ft., passive Perception 13
Languages —
Challenge 3 (700 XP)

Keen Sight and Smell. The owlbear has advantage on Wisdom (Perception) checks that rely on sight or smell.

Actions

Multiattack. The owlbear makes two attacks: one with its beak and one with its claws.

Beak. *Melee Weapon Attack:* +7 to hit, reach 5 ft., one creature. *Hit:* 10 (1d10 + 5) piercing damage.

Claws. *Melee Weapon Attack:* +7 to hit, reach 5 ft., one target. *Hit:* 14 (2d8 + 5) slashing damage.

P

"Behold, the pegasus. It can outrace a dragon in the open sky, and only the best among us can ever hope to ride one. A fitting emblem for our great house, don't you think?"

—Tyllenvane d'Orien, dragonmarked scion arguing to change the symbol of House Orien from the unicorn to the pegasus

PEGASUS

Large celestial, chaotic good

Armor Class 12
Hit Points 59 (7d10 + 21)
Speed 60 ft., fly 90 ft.

STR	DEX	CON	INT	WIS	CHA
18 (+4)	15 (+2)	16 (+3)	10 (+0)	15 (+2)	13 (+1)

Saving Throws Dex +4, Wis +4, Cha +3
Skills Perception +6
Senses passive Perception 16
Languages understands Celestial, Common, Elvish, and Sylvan but can't speak
Challenge 2 (450 XP)

ACTIONS

Hooves. *Melee Weapon Attack:* +6 to hit, reach 5 ft., one target. *Hit:* 11 (2d6 + 4) bludgeoning damage.

PEGASUS

The white winged horses known as pegasi soar through the skies, a vision of grace and majesty. When they touch down on solid ground, they linger only for a moment, drinking from mountain springs and pristine lakes. Any sound or sign of another creature startles them, sending them off to fly once more among the clouds.

Noble Mounts. Pegasi are highly prized as swift and reliable steeds, being faster and less temperamental than griffons, hippogriffs, and wyverns. However, these wild and shy creatures are as intelligent as humanoids, and so can't be traditionally broken and tamed. A pegasus must be persuaded to serve a good-aligned creature as a mount, but when it does so, it forges a lifelong bond with its new companion.

Born of the Planes. Pegasi trace their origins to the Olympian Glades of Arborea, where they soar through the skies of that plane and serve as faithful mounts to the Seldarine, the pantheon of elven gods. These gods have been known to send pegasi to the Material Plane to aid those in need.

Pegasi Nests. Pegasi mate for life, build their nests in hard-to-reach locations, and give birth to live young.

PERYTON

Although this monstrous carnivore feeds on any creature, it prefers humanoids, especially elves, half-elves, and humans. When it kills a humanoid, a peryton rips out its prey's heart and takes it back to its nest to be devoured.

The peryton is a bizarre creature that blends the body and wings of a bird of prey with the head of a stag. Its strangest feature is its shadow, which appears humanoid rather than reflecting the creature's physical form. Sages postulate that the first perytons were humans transformed by a hideous curse or magical experiment, but bards tell a different tale of a man whose infidelity caused his scorned wife to cut out the heart of her younger, more beautiful rival and consume it in a ritual intended to forever win her husband's heart. The ritual succeeded until the woman's villainy was exposed. She was hanged for her crime, but the lingering magic of her foul ritual caused the carrion birds that feasted on her corpse to transform into the first perytons.

Unnatural Hunger. A peryton's reproductive cycle depends on the heart of a freshly killed humanoid. The organ must be consumed by a female peryton before she can reproduce. When a peryton consumes a heart, its shadow changes for a brief time to reflect its true monstrous form.

When attacking a humanoid, a peryton is single-minded and relentless, fighting until it or its prey dies. If a peryton is somehow driven away, it stalks lost prey from afar, attacking again when the opportunity arises.

Bane of the Mountains. Perytons roost atop mountain ridges and lair in high caves. They prey on creatures living or wandering in the vales below, and travelers on lonely mountain roads learn to keep a wary eye on the sky. Because normal weapons are less effective against perytons, the folk of the mountains know to avoid confrontations with these monsters at all costs.

Established settlements are attractive to perytons as a renewable food source. As such, village councils and local nobles often hire adventurers to eliminate peryton nests.

PERYTON
Medium monstrosity, chaotic evil

Armor Class 13 (natural armor)
Hit Points 33 (6d8 + 6)
Speed 20 ft., fly 60 ft.

STR	DEX	CON	INT	WIS	CHA
16 (+3)	12 (+1)	13 (+1)	9 (−1)	12 (+1)	10 (+0)

Skills Perception +5
Damage Resistances bludgeoning, piercing, and slashing from nonmagical attacks
Senses passive Perception 15
Languages understands Common and Elvish but can't speak
Challenge 2 (450 XP)

Dive Attack. If the peryton is flying and dives at least 30 feet straight toward a target and then hits it with a melee weapon attack, the attack deals an extra 9 (2d8) damage to the target.

Flyby. The peryton doesn't provoke an opportunity attack when it flies out of an enemy's reach.

Keen Sight and Smell. The peryton has advantage on Wisdom (Perception) checks that rely on sight or smell.

ACTIONS

Multiattack. The peryton makes one gore attack and one talon attack.

Gore. *Melee Weapon Attack:* +5 to hit, reach 5 ft., one target. *Hit:* 7 (1d8 + 3) piercing damage.

Talons. *Melee Weapon Attack:* +5 to hit, reach 5 ft., one target. *Hit:* 8 (2d4 + 3) piercing damage.

Piercer

Medium monstrosity, unaligned

Armor Class 15 (natural armor)
Hit Points 22 (3d8 + 9)
Speed 5 ft., climb 5 ft.

STR	DEX	CON	INT	WIS	CHA
10 (+0)	13 (+1)	16 (+3)	1 (−5)	7 (−2)	3 (−4)

Skills Stealth +5
Senses blindsight 30 ft., darkvision 60 ft., passive Perception 8
Languages —
Challenge 1/2 (100 XP)

False Appearance. While the piercer remains motionless on the ceiling, it is indistinguishable from a normal stalactite.

Spider Climb. The piercer can climb difficult surfaces, including upside down on ceilings, without needing to make an ability check.

Actions

Drop. _Melee Weapon Attack:_ +3 to hit, one creature directly underneath the piercer. _Hit:_ 3 (1d6) piercing damage per 10 feet fallen, up to 21 (6d6). _Miss:_ The piercer takes half the normal falling damage for the distance fallen.

Piercer

Clinging to the ceilings of caverns and large subterranean passages, piercers blend in perfectly with natural rock, dropping in silence to impale unsuspecting foes on the ground below.

A piercer is the larval form of a roper, and the two creatures often attack in tandem. A rock-like shell encases a piercer's body, giving it the look and texture of a stalactite. That shell protects a soft, slug-like upper body that lets the piercer move across cavern walls and ceilings to position itself for prey. With its eye and mouth closed, the piercer is difficult to distinguish from ordinary rock formations.

Patient Hunters. Piercers can see, but they can also respond to noise and heat, waiting for living creatures to pass beneath them, then falling to attack. A piercer that misses its chance to kill must make its slow way back to the ceiling. A fallen piercer excretes a foul-smelling slime when attacked, making most predators think twice about eating it.

Piercers gather in colonies to maximize the effectiveness of their attacks, dropping simultaneously to increase the odds of striking prey. After a piercer successfully slays a creature, the others slowly creep toward the corpse to join in the feast.

PIXIE

Standing barely a foot tall, pixies resemble diminutive elves with gossamer wings like those of dragonflies or butterflies, bright as the clear dawn and as luminous as the full moonrise. Curious as cats and shy as deer, pixies go where they please. They like to spy on other creatures and can barely contain their excitement around them. The urge to introduce themselves and strike up a friendship is almost overwhelming; only a pixie's fear of being captured or attacked stays its hand. Those who wander through a pixie's glade might never see the creatures, yet hear the occasional giggle, gasp, or sigh.

Pixies array themselves like princes and princesses of the fey, wearing flowing gowns and doublets of silk that sparkle like moonlight on a pond. Some dress in acorns, leaves, bark, and the pelts of tiny woodland beasts. They take great pride in their regalia and beam with joy when they are complimented on their ensembles.

Magical Faerie Folk. With their innate power of invisibility, pixies rarely appear unless they wish to be seen. In the Feywild and on the Material Plane, pixies etch patterns of frost on winter ponds and rouse the buds in springtime. They cause flowers to sparkle with summer dew, and color the leaves with the blazing hues of autumn.

Pixie Dust. When pixies fly visibly, a shower of sparkling dust follows in their wake like the glittering tail of a shooting star. A mere sprinkle of pixie dust is said to be able to grant the power of flight, confuse a creature hopelessly, or send foes into a magical slumber. Only pixies can use their dust to its full potential, but these fey are constantly sought out by mages and monsters seeking to study or master their power.

Tiny Tricksters. While the arrival of visitors piques their curiosity, pixies are too shy to reveal themselves at first. They study the visitors from afar to gauge their temperament or play harmless tricks on them to measure their reactions. For example, pixies might tie a dwarf's boots together, create illusions of strange creatures or treasures, or use dancing lights to lead interlopers astray. If the visitors respond with hostility, the pixies give them a wide berth. If the visitors are good natured, the pixies are likely to be emboldened and more friendly. The fey might even emerge and offer to guide their "guests" along a safe route or invite them to a tiny yet satisfying feast prepared in their honor.

Opposed to Violence. Unlike their fey cousins, the sprites, pixies abhor weapons and would sooner flee than get into a physical altercation with any enemy.

PIXIE

Tiny fey, neutral good

Armor Class 15
Hit Points 1 (1d4 − 1)
Speed 10 ft., fly 30 ft.

STR	DEX	CON	INT	WIS	CHA
2 (−4)	20 (+5)	8 (−1)	10 (+0)	14 (+2)	15 (+2)

Skills Perception +4, Stealth +7
Senses passive Perception 14
Languages Sylvan
Challenge 1/4 (50 XP)

Magic Resistance. The pixie has advantage on saving throws against spells and other magical effects.

Innate Spellcasting. The pixie's innate spellcasting ability is Charisma (spell save DC 12). It can innately cast the following spells, requiring only its pixie dust as a component:

At will: *druidcraft*
1/day each: *confusion, dancing lights, detect evil and good, detect thoughts, dispel magic, entangle, fly, phantasmal force, polymorph, sleep*

ACTIONS

Superior Invisibility. The pixie magically turns invisible until its concentration ends (as if concentrating on a spell). Any equipment the pixie wears or carries is invisible with it.

Language of Emotion. Pseudodragons can't speak, but they communicate using a limited form of telepathy that allows them to share basic ideas such as hunger, curiosity, or affection. When it bonds with a companion, a pseudodragon can communicate what it sees and hears even over long distances.

A pseudodragon often vocalizes animal noises. A rasping purr indicates pleasure, while a hiss means unpleasant surprise. A bird-like chirping represents desire, and a growl always means anger or discontent.

VARIANT: PSEUDODRAGON FAMILIAR

Some pseudodragons are willing to serve spellcasters as a familiar. Such pseudodragons have the following trait.

Familiar. The pseudodragon can serve another creature as a familiar, forming a magic, telepathic bond with that willing companion. While the two are bonded, the companion can sense what the pseudodragon senses as long as they are within 1 mile of each other. While the pseudodragon is within 10 feet of its companion, the companion shares the pseudodragon's Magic Resistance trait. At any time and for any reason, the pseudodragon can end its service as a familiar, ending the telepathic bond.

PSEUDODRAGON
Tiny dragon, neutral good

Armor Class 13 (natural armor)
Hit Points 7 (2d4 + 2)
Speed 15 ft., fly 60 ft.

STR	DEX	CON	INT	WIS	CHA
6 (−2)	15 (+2)	13 (+1)	10 (+0)	12 (+1)	10 (+0)

Skills Perception +3, Stealth +4
Senses blindsight 10 ft., darkvision 60 ft., passive Perception 13
Languages understands Common and Draconic but can't speak
Challenge 1/4 (50 XP)

Keen Senses. The pseudodragon has advantage on Wisdom (Perception) checks that rely on sight, hearing, or smell.

Magic Resistance. The pseudodragon has advantage on saving throws against spells and other magical effects.

Limited Telepathy. The pseudodragon can magically communicate simple ideas, emotions, and images telepathically with any creature within 100 feet of it that can understand a language.

ACTIONS

Bite. Melee Weapon Attack: +4 to hit, reach 5 ft., one target. *Hit:* 4 (1d4 + 2) piercing damage.

Sting. Melee Weapon Attack: +4 to hit, reach 5 ft., one creature. *Hit:* 4 (1d4 + 2) piercing damage, and the target must succeed on a DC 11 Constitution saving throw or become poisoned for 1 hour. If the saving throw fails by 5 or more, the target falls unconscious for the same duration, or until it takes damage or another creature uses an action to shake it awake.

PSEUDODRAGON

The elusive pseudodragon dwells in the quiet places of the world, making its home in the hollows of trees and small caves. With its red-brown scales, horns, and a maw filled with sharp teeth, a pseudodragon resembles a tiny red dragon but its disposition is playful.

Quiet and Defensive. Pseudodragons have little interest in other creatures, and they avoid them whenever possible. If it is attacked, a pseudodragon fights back using the poisonous stinger at the tip of its tail, one jab of which can put a creature into a catatonic state that can last for hours.

Draconic Familiars. Mages often seek out pseudodragons, whose agreeable disposition, telepathic ability, and resistance to magic make them superior familiars. Pseudodragons are selective when it comes to choosing companions, but they can sometimes be won over with gifts of food or treasure. When a pseudodragon finds an agreeable companion, it bonds with that person as long as it is treated fairly. A pseudodragon puts up with no ill treatment, and it abandons a manipulative or abusive companion without warning.

PURPLE WORM

The massive burrowing monster known as the purple worm terrorizes the creatures of the Underdark as it chews through solid rock in pursuit of prey. A dim-witted, ravenous force of nature, this creature regards anything it encounters as food.

Ravenous Hunters. Loud noise attracts purple worms, which have been known to interrupt underground battles and tear through subterranean cities seeking prey. The underground civilizations of the drow, the duergar, and the mind flayers maintain special wards around their settlements to deter these monsters.

Though most common in the Underdark, purple worms are frequently seen on the surface world in rocky and mountainous lands. The maw of a purple worm is large enough to swallow a horse whole, and no creature is safe from its hunger. It lunges forward by rhythmically compressing and expanding its body, catching other Underdark dwellers by surprise with the speed of its advance.

Boons of the Worm. When a purple worm burrows through the ground, it consumes earth and rock, which it breaks down and constantly excretes. Precious metals and gems can thus be found within the bodies of purple worms, which are targeted by particularly brave and foolhardy treasure hunters.

A burrowing purple worm constantly creates new tunnels throughout the Underdark, which are quickly made use of by other creatures as corridors and highways. Because a purple worm rarely returns to its own tunnels, such passageways are a good place to avoid these monsters. Areas rich in prey quickly become interlaced with complex tunnel systems resulting from several worms hunting together.

PURPLE WORM
Gargantuan monstrosity, unaligned

Armor Class 18 (natural armor)
Hit Points 247 (15d20 + 90)
Speed 50 ft., burrow 30 ft.

STR	DEX	CON	INT	WIS	CHA
28 (+9)	7 (−2)	22 (+6)	1 (−5)	8 (−1)	4 (−3)

Saving Throws Con +11, Wis +4
Senses blindsight 30 ft., tremorsense 60 ft., passive Perception 9
Languages —
Challenge 15 (13,000 XP)

Tunneler. The worm can burrow through solid rock at half its burrow speed and leaves a 10-foot-diameter tunnel in its wake.

ACTIONS

Multiattack. The worm makes two attacks: one with its bite and one with its stinger.

Bite. *Melee Weapon Attack:* +9 to hit, reach 10 ft., one target. *Hit:* 22 (3d8 + 9) piercing damage. If the target is a Large or smaller creature, it must succeed on a DC 19 Dexterity saving throw or be swallowed by the worm. A swallowed creature is blinded and restrained, it has total cover against attacks and other effects outside the worm, and it takes 21 (6d6) acid damage at the start of each of the worm's turns.

If the worm takes 30 damage or more on a single turn from a creature inside it, the worm must succeed on a DC 21 Constitution saving throw at the end of that turn or regurgitate all swallowed creatures, which fall prone in a space within 10 feet of the worm. If the worm dies, a swallowed creature is no longer restrained by it and can escape from the corpse by using 20 feet of movement, exiting prone.

Tail Stinger. *Melee Weapon Attack:* +9 to hit, reach 10 ft., one creature. *Hit:* 19 (3d6 + 9) piercing damage, and the target must make a DC 19 Constitution saving throw, taking 42 (12d6) poison damage on a failed save, or half as much damage on a successful one.

Quaggoth

Savage and territorial, quaggoths climb the chasms of the Underdark. They maul their foes in a frenzy, becoming even more murderous in the face of death.

Quaggoth Origins. Quaggoths were never an enlightened species, but they were not always the brutal Underdark denizens they are today. In a distant age, quaggoth tribes dwelled upon the surface as nocturnal arboreal hunters, possessing their own language and culture. When elves appeared in the mortal realm, they clashed with the quaggoths, eventually driving them to near extinction. Only by fleeing deep into the Underdark did the quaggoths survive.

As they passed the ages deep beneath the world, the quaggoths' fur lost its color and their vision adapted to the darkness, even as the constant danger and weird magic of their new realm transformed them. Turning increasingly brutal and savage, they ate whatever food they could find—and when they could not find it, they preyed on each other. As cannibalism became part of their culture, their past was abandoned.

Servants of the Drow. The ancient enmity between quaggoths and surface elves makes them easy converts to the dark elf cause. In recent years, the drow have taken an interest in breeding quaggoths, encouraging their ferocity while strengthening their obedience. Wealthy drow houses have legions of quaggoths at their command. Even worse, the drow cultivate the quaggoths' hatred of the elves by leading them on surface raids against known elven enclaves.

Thonots. Some quaggoths absorb psionic energy that suffuses certain parts of the Underdark. When a tribe discovers that one of its own has inherited such powers, they press it into the role of tribal shaman, or thonot. A thonot keep a tribe's lore and ensures its superiority against enemies. A thonot that fails the tribe is slain and devoured in a cannibalistic ritual, in the hope that its power passes to another more worthy quaggoth.

Poison Immunity. Generations of hunting venomous subterranean creatures and perpetual exposure to the molds and fungi that grow in the depths have forced quaggoths to adapt immunities to poisons of all kinds.

Quaggoth

Medium humanoid (quaggoth), chaotic neutral

Armor Class 13 (natural armor)
Hit Points 45 (6d8 + 18)
Speed 30 ft., climb 30 ft.

STR	DEX	CON	INT	WIS	CHA
17 (+3)	12 (+1)	16 (+3)	6 (−2)	12 (+1)	7 (−2)

Skills Athletics +5
Damage Immunities poison
Condition Immunities poisoned
Senses darkvision 120 ft., passive Perception 11
Languages Undercommon
Challenge 2 (450 XP)

Wounded Fury. While it has 10 hit points or fewer, the quaggoth has advantage on attack rolls. In addition, it deals an extra 7 (2d6) damage to any target it hits with a melee attack.

Actions

Multiattack. The quaggoth makes two claw attacks.

Claw. *Melee Weapon Attack:* +5 to hit, reach 5 ft., one target. *Hit:* 6 (1d6 + 3) slashing damage.

Variant: Quaggoth Thonot

A quaggoth thonot is a normal quaggoth with a challenge rating of 3 (700 XP) and the following additional trait.

Innate Spellcasting (Psionics). The quaggoth's innate spellcasting ability is Wisdom (spell save DC 11). The quaggoth can innately cast the following spells, requiring no components:

At will: *feather fall, mage hand* (the hand is invisible)
1/day each: *cure wounds, enlarge/reduce, heat metal, mirror image*

Rakshasa

The rakshasa employs delicacy and misdirection in its pursuit of dominion over others. Few creatures ever see the fiend in its true form, for it can take on any guise it wants, although it prefers to masquerade as someone powerful or influential: a noble, cardinal, or rich merchant, for example. A rakshasa's true form combines the features of a human and a tiger, with one noteworthy deformity: its palms are where the backs of the hands would be on a human.

Evil Spirits in Mortal Flesh. Rakshasas originated long ago in the Nine Hells, when powerful devils created a dark ritual to free their essence from their fiendish bodies in order to escape the Lower Planes. A rakshasa enters the Material Plane to feed its appetite for humanoid flesh and evil schemes. It selects its prey with care, taking pains to keep its presence in the world a secret.

Evil Reborn. For a rakshasa, death on the Material Plane means an agonizing and torturous return to the Nine Hells, where its essence remains trapped until its body reforms—a process that can take months or years. When the rakshasa is reborn, it has all the memories and knowledge of its former life, and it seeks retribution against the one who slew it. If the target has somehow slipped through its grasp, the rakshasa might punish its killer's family, friends, or descendants.

Like devils, rakshasas killed in the Nine Hells are forever destroyed.

Rakshasa
Medium fiend, lawful evil

Armor Class 16 (natural armor)
Hit Points 110 (13d8 + 52)
Speed 40 ft.

STR	DEX	CON	INT	WIS	CHA
14 (+2)	17 (+3)	18 (+4)	13 (+1)	16 (+3)	20 (+5)

Skills Deception +10, Insight +8
Damage Vulnerabilities piercing from magic weapons wielded by good creatures
Damage Immunities bludgeoning, piercing, and slashing from nonmagical attacks
Senses darkvision 60 ft., passive Perception 13
Languages Common, Infernal
Challenge 13 (10,000 XP)

Limited Magic Immunity. The rakshasa can't be affected or detected by spells of 6th level or lower unless it wishes to be. It has advantage on saving throws against all other spells and magical effects.

Innate Spellcasting. The rakshasa's innate spellcasting ability is Charisma (spell save DC 18, +10 to hit with spell attacks). The rakshasa can innately cast the following spells, requiring no material components:

At will: *detect thoughts, disguise self, mage hand, minor illusion*
3/day each: *charm person, detect magic, invisibility, major image, suggestion*
1/day each: *dominate person, fly, plane shift, true seeing*

Actions

Multiattack. The rakshasa makes two claw attacks.

Claw. *Melee Weapon Attack:* +7 to hit, reach 5 ft., one target. *Hit:* 9 (2d6 + 2) slashing damage, and the target is cursed if it is a creature. The magical curse takes effect whenever the target takes a short or long rest, filling the target's thoughts with horrible images and dreams. The cursed target gains no benefit from finishing a short or long rest. The curse lasts until it is lifted by a *remove curse* spell or similar magic.

R

REMORHAZES

From beneath the snow and ice bursts a remorhaz in a cloud of steam, its body pulsing with internal fire. Winglike fins flare from the back of the creature's head, and its wide mouth brims with jagged teeth.

Arctic Predators. Remorhazes live in arctic climes, preying on elk, polar bears, and other creatures sharing their territory. They can't tolerate warm weather, having adapted to the cold by generating a furnace-like heat within their bodies. When hunting, a remorhaz burrows deep below the snow and ice and lies in wait for the faint vibrations created by a creature moving above it. While hidden under the ice and snow, it can lower its body temperature so that it doesn't melt its cover.

Young Ones. Frost giant hunters scour the icy wastes for remorhaz nests and eggs. The giants prize young remorhazes, which can be trained from hatching to obey commands and guard the giants' icy citadels. Unlike fully grown specimens, young remorhazes gnaw on their victims instead of swallowing them whole.

REMORHAZ
Huge monstrosity, unaligned

Armor Class 17 (natural armor)
Hit Points 195 (17d12 + 85)
Speed 30 ft., burrow 20 ft.

STR	DEX	CON	INT	WIS	CHA
24 (+7)	13 (+1)	21 (+5)	4 (–3)	10 (+0)	5 (–3)

Damage Immunities cold, fire
Senses darkvision 60 ft., tremorsense 60 ft., passive Perception 10
Languages —
Challenge 11 (7,200 XP)

Heated Body. A creature that touches the remorhaz or hits it with a melee attack while within 5 feet of it takes 10 (3d6) fire damage.

ACTIONS

Bite. *Melee Weapon Attack:* +11 to hit, reach 10 ft., one target. *Hit:* 40 (6d10 + 7) piercing damage plus 10 (3d6) fire damage. If the target is a creature, it is grappled (escape DC 17). Until this grapple ends, the target is restrained, and the remorhaz can't bite another target.

Swallow. The remorhaz makes one bite attack against a Medium or smaller creature it is grappling. If the attack hits, that creature takes the bite's damage and is swallowed, and the grapple ends. While swallowed, the creature is blinded and restrained, it has total cover against attacks and other effects outside the remorhaz, and it takes 21 (6d6) acid damage at the start of each of the remorhaz's turns.

If the remorhaz takes 30 damage or more on a single turn from a creature inside it, the remorhaz must succeed on a DC 15 Constitution saving throw at the end of that turn or regurgitate all swallowed creatures, which fall prone in a space within 10 feet of the remorhaz. If the remorhaz dies, a swallowed creature is no longer restrained by it and can escape from the corpse using 15 feet of movement, exiting prone.

YOUNG REMORHAZ
Large monstrosity, unaligned

Armor Class 14 (natural armor)
Hit Points 93 (11d10 + 33)
Speed 30 ft., burrow 20 ft.

STR	DEX	CON	INT	WIS	CHA
18 (+4)	13 (+1)	17 (+3)	3 (–4)	10 (+0)	4 (–3)

Damage Immunities cold, fire
Senses darkvision 60 ft., tremorsense 60 ft., passive Perception 10
Languages —
Challenge 5 (1,800 XP)

Heated Body. A creature that touches the remorhaz or hits it with a melee attack while within 5 feet of it takes 7 (2d6) fire damage.

ACTIONS

Bite. *Melee Weapon Attack:* +6 to hit, reach 5 ft., one target. *Hit:* 20 (3d10 + 4) piercing damage plus 7 (2d6) fire damage.

R

REVENANT

A revenant forms from the soul of a mortal who met a cruel and undeserving fate. It claws its way back into the world to seek revenge against the one who wronged it. The revenant reclaims its mortal body and superficially resembles a zombie. However, instead of lifeless eyes, a revenant's eyes burn with resolve and flare in the presence of its adversary. If the revenant's original body was destroyed or is otherwise unavailable, the spirit of the revenant enters another humanoid corpse. Regardless of the body the revenant uses as a vessel, its adversary always recognizes the revenant for what it truly is.

Hunger for Revenge. A revenant has only one year to exact revenge. When its adversary dies, or if the revenant fails to kill its adversary before its time runs out, it crumbles to dust and its soul fades into the afterlife. If its foe is too powerful for the revenant to destroy on its own, it seeks worthy allies to help it fulfill its quest.

Divine Justice. No magic can hide a creature pursued by a revenant, which always knows the direction and distance between it and the target of its vengeance. In cases where the revenant seeks revenge against more than one adversary, it pursues them one at a time, starting with the creature that dealt it the killing blow. If the revenant's body is destroyed, its soul flies forth to seek out a new corpse in which to resume its hunt.

Undead Nature. A revenant doesn't require air, food, drink, or sleep.

VARIANT: REVENANTS WITH SPELLS AND WEAPONS

Revenants that were spellcasters before they died might retain some or all of their spellcasting capabilities. Similarly, revenants that wore armor and wielded weapons in life might continue to do so.

REVENANT
Medium undead, neutral

Armor Class 13 (leather armor)
Hit Points 136 (16d8 + 64)
Speed 30 ft.

STR	DEX	CON	INT	WIS	CHA
18 (+4)	14 (+2)	18 (+4)	13 (+1)	16 (+3)	18 (+4)

Saving Throws Str +7, Con +7, Wis +6, Cha +7
Damage Resistances necrotic, psychic
Damage Immunities poison
Condition Immunities charmed, exhaustion, frightened, paralyzed, poisoned, stunned
Senses darkvision 60 ft., passive Perception 13
Languages the languages it knew in life
Challenge 5 (1,800 XP)

Regeneration. The revenant regains 10 hit points at the start of its turn. If the revenant takes fire or radiant damage, this trait doesn't function at the start of the revenant's next turn. The revenant's body is destroyed only if it starts its turn with 0 hit points and doesn't regenerate.

Rejuvenation. When the revenant's body is destroyed, its soul lingers. After 24 hours, the soul inhabits and animates another corpse on the same plane of existence and regains all its hit points. While the soul is bodiless, a *wish* spell can be used to force the soul to go to the afterlife and not return.

Turn Immunity. The revenant is immune to effects that turn undead.

Vengeful Tracker. The revenant knows the distance to and direction of any creature against which it seeks revenge, even if the creature and the revenant are on different planes of existence. If the creature being tracked by the revenant dies, the revenant knows.

ACTIONS

Multiattack. The revenant makes two fist attacks.

Fist. *Melee Weapon Attack:* +7 to hit, reach 5 ft., one target. *Hit:* 11 (2d6 + 4) bludgeoning damage. If the target is a creature against which the revenant has sworn vengeance, the target takes an extra 14 (4d6) bludgeoning damage. Instead of dealing damage, the revenant can grapple the target (escape DC 14) provided the target is Large or smaller.

Vengeful Glare. The revenant targets one creature it can see within 30 feet of it and against which it has sworn vengeance. The target must make a DC 15 Wisdom saving throw. On a failure, the target is paralyzed until the revenant deals damage to it, or until the end of the revenant's next turn. When the paralysis ends, the target is frightened of the revenant for 1 minute. The frightened target can repeat the saving throw at the end of each of its turns, with disadvantage if it can see the revenant, ending the frightened condition on itself on a success.

Roc

At first sight, a roc's silhouette looks much like any other bird of prey. As it descends, however, its unearthly size becomes terrifyingly clear. In flight, a roc's wingspan spreads two hundred feet or more. At rest, perched upon the mountain peaks that are its home, this monstrous bird rivals the oldest dragons in size.

Sky Titans. In the ancient days when giants battled dragons for control of the world, Annam, the father of the giant gods, created the rocs so that his worshipers might challenge the dragons' dominance of the air. When the war ended, the rocs were freed from giant domination and spread throughout the world.

Though cloud giants and storm giants sometimes tame these great birds, rocs treat even giants as potential prey. They fly great distances in search of food, soaring high above the clouds to reach their favored hunting grounds. A roc seldom hunts swift or small creatures, and it ignores towns and forests where prey can easily take cover. When it locates a large and slow-moving target such as a giant, a whale, or an elephant, a roc dives down to snatch its prey in its massive talons.

Remote and Alone. Rocs are solitary creatures that can live for centuries. They lair in nests made from trees, tents, broken ships, and the remains of caravans they carry off, placing these massive tangles in mountain clefts out of the reach of lesser creatures.

Sometimes a roc's nest contains treasures from the caravans or ships they raid, but these creatures are heedless of such baubles. More rarely, a nest holds eggs that are taller than a human, produced by the rocs' infrequent mating.

Roc
Gargantuan monstrosity, unaligned

Armor Class 15 (natural armor)
Hit Points 248 (16d20 + 80)
Speed 20 ft., fly 120 ft.

STR	DEX	CON	INT	WIS	CHA
28 (+9)	10 (+0)	20 (+5)	3 (−4)	10 (+0)	9 (−1)

Saving Throws Dex +4, Con +9, Wis +4, Cha +3
Skills Perception +4
Senses passive Perception 14
Languages —
Challenge 11 (7,200 XP)

Keen Sight. The roc has advantage on Wisdom (Perception) checks that rely on sight.

Actions

Multiattack. The roc makes two attacks: one with its beak and one with its talons.

Beak. *Melee Weapon Attack:* +13 to hit, reach 10 ft., one target. *Hit:* 27 (4d8 + 9) piercing damage.

Talons. *Melee Weapon Attack:* +13 to hit, reach 5 ft., one target. *Hit:* 23 (4d6 + 9) slashing damage, and the target is grappled (escape DC 19). Until this grapple ends, the target is restrained, and the roc can't use its talons on another target.

Roper

Living in caves and caverns throughout the Underdark, voracious ropers feast on whatever they can catch and seize. A roper eats any creature, from Underdark beasts to adventurers and their gear.

A roper has the appearance of a stalagmite or stalactite, which often allows it to attack with surprise. The creature can move slowly using thousands of sticky cilia beneath its base. It creeps up cave walls and along stone ceilings, finding the best position from which to attack.

Underdark Hunters. The roper is an evolved, mature form of piercer, with which it shares its rock-like appearance and hunting tactics. A roper can hold still for long hours, shutting its single eye to look like nothing more than a mundane formation of rock. Creatures that come too close are surprised when that eye snaps open and sticky tendrils shoot out to seize them. The roper then makes horrible guttural sounds as it reels in its struggling victims, drawing them close for the fatal bite of its stony teeth.

A roper can digest anything it eats with the exception of platinum, gemstones, and magic items, which can sometimes be retrieved from the creature's gizzard after death. A roper's digestive juices are also valuable, fetching a high price from alchemists who use them as a solvent.

Weakening Tendrils. A roper has six nubs set along its body, through which it extrudes sticky tendrils that bond to whatever they touch. Each tendril sends out hair-like growths that penetrate a creature's flesh and sap its strength, so the victim can struggle only weakly as the roper reels it in. If a tendril is cut through or broken, the roper produces a new one to replace it.

Roper

Large monstrosity, neutral evil

Armor Class 20 (natural armor)
Hit Points 93 (11d10 + 33)
Speed 10 ft., climb 10 ft.

STR	DEX	CON	INT	WIS	CHA
18 (+4)	8 (–1)	17 (+3)	7 (–2)	16 (+3)	6 (–2)

Skills Perception +6, Stealth +5
Senses darkvision 60 ft., passive Perception 16
Languages —
Challenge 5 (1,800 XP)

False Appearance. While the roper remains motionless, it is indistinguishable from a normal cave formation, such as a stalagmite.

Grasping Tendrils. The roper can have up to six tendrils at a time. Each tendril can be attacked (AC 20; 10 hit points; immunity to poison and psychic damage). Destroying a tendril deals no damage to the roper, which can extrude a replacement tendril on its next turn. A tendril can also be broken if a creature takes an action and succeeds on a DC 15 Strength check against it.

Spider Climb. The roper can climb difficult surfaces, including upside down on ceilings, without needing to make an ability check.

Actions

Multiattack. The roper makes four attacks with its tendrils, uses Reel, and makes one attack with its bite.

Bite. *Melee Weapon Attack:* +7 to hit, reach 5 ft., one target. *Hit:* 22 (4d8 + 4) piercing damage.

Tendril. *Melee Weapon Attack:* +7 to hit, reach 50 ft., one creature. *Hit:* The target is grappled (escape DC 15). Until the grapple ends, the target is restrained and has disadvantage on Strength checks and Strength saving throws, and the roper can't use the same tendril on another target.

Reel. The roper pulls each creature grappled by it up to 25 feet straight toward it.

RUST MONSTER

Most dwarves would rather face a squad of orcs than confront a single rust monster. These strange, normally docile creatures corrode ferrous metals, then gobble up the rust they create. In doing so, they have ruined the armor, shields, and weapons of countless adventurers.

A rust monster's body is covered in thick, lumpy armor, its long tail ends in a bony protrusion, and two feathery antennae sprout from its insectile head.

Underground Scavengers. Rust monsters roam subterranean passages in search of ferrous metals such as iron, steel, adamantine, and mithral to consume. They ignore creatures not carrying such metals, but can become aggressive toward those bearing steel weapons and armor. A rust monster can smell its food at a distance, immediately dashing toward the scent's source to corrode and consume the object.

A rust monster doesn't care if the rust it consumes comes from a spike or a sword. Adventurers can distract the creature by dropping ferrous objects behind them.

Subterranean Wanderers. Rust monsters are rarely found in large numbers, preferring to hunt alone or in small groups. They meander along tunnels, moving from cave to cave in their tireless search for ferrous metals to consume. Their wanderings often bring them into contact with other Underdark denizens that find them harmless or unappetizing. Thus, rust monsters may be found in close proximity to other subterranean monsters. If they are well treated and well fed, they can also become friendly companions or pets.

RUST MONSTER
Medium monstrosity, unaligned

Armor Class 14 (natural armor)
Hit Points 27 (5d8 + 5)
Speed 40 ft.

STR	DEX	CON	INT	WIS	CHA
13 (+1)	12 (+1)	13 (+1)	2 (−4)	13 (+1)	6 (−2)

Senses darkvision 60 ft., passive Perception 11
Languages —
Challenge 1/2 (100 XP)

Iron Scent. The rust monster can pinpoint, by scent, the location of ferrous metal within 30 feet of it.

Rust Metal. Any nonmagical weapon made of metal that hits the rust monster corrodes. After dealing damage, the weapon takes a permanent and cumulative −1 penalty to damage rolls. If its penalty drops to −5, the weapon is destroyed. Nonmagical ammunition made of metal that hits the rust monster is destroyed after dealing damage.

ACTIONS

Bite. *Melee Weapon Attack:* +3 to hit, reach 5 ft., one target. *Hit:* 5 (1d8 + 1) piercing damage.

Antennae. The rust monster corrodes a nonmagical ferrous metal object it can see within 5 feet of it. If the object isn't being worn or carried, the touch destroys a 1-foot cube of it. If the object is being worn or carried by a creature, the creature can make a DC 11 Dexterity saving throw to avoid the rust monster's touch.

If the object touched is either metal armor or a metal shield being worn or carried, its takes a permanent and cumulative −1 penalty to the AC it offers. Armor reduced to an AC of 10 or a shield that drops to a +0 bonus is destroyed. If the object touched is a held metal weapon, it rusts as described in the Rust Metal trait.

Sahuagin

Across fog-shrouded coasts or endless ocean swells, an ominous drone sounded on a conch shell chills the blood of all who hear it. This is the sound of the sahuagin hunting horn—a call to raid and battle. Coastal settlers refer to sahuagin as "sea devils," for sahuagin have no compassion in them, slaughtering the crews of ships and decimating coastal villages.

Devils of the Deep. Sahuagin are a predatory, piscine race that ventures from the ocean's black depths to hunt the creatures of the shallows and shore. Though they dwell in the deepest trenches of the ocean, sahuagin view the entire aquatic realm as their kingdom and the creatures in it as blood sport for their hunting parties.

The self-styled rulers of sahuagin ocean domains are massive mutant males that grow second sets of arms. They are terrible foes in battle, and all sahuagin bow down before these powerful barons.

Way of the Shark. Sahuagin worship the shark god Sekolah. Only female sahuagin are deemed worthy of channeling the god's power, and priestesses hold tremendous sway in sahuagin communities.

Sahuagin are driven into a frenzy by the smell of fresh blood. As worshipers of Sekolah, they also have a special kinship with sharks, which they train as attack animals. Even untrained sharks recognize sahuagin as allies and don't prey on them.

Elven Enmity. The sahuagin might control the oceans if not for the presence of their mortal enemies, the aquatic elves. Wars between the two races have raged for centuries across the coasts and seas of the world, disrupting maritime trade and drawing other races into the bloody conflict.

So intense is sahuagin hatred for the aquatic elves that the sea devils have adapted to combat their ancient foes. A sahuagin born near enough to an aquatic elf community can enter the world as a malenti—a sahuagin that physically resembles an aquatic elf in every way. Sahuagin are prone to mutation, but whether this rare phenomenon is a result of the wars between the sahuagin and the aquatic elves—or whether it preceded or even began the conflict—none can say.

The sahuagin put the malenti to good use as spies and assassins in aquatic elf cities and the societies of other creatures that pose a threat to sahuagin. The mere shadow of the malenti threat incites paranoia and suspicion among aquatic elves, whose resilience is weakened as the prelude to an actual sahuagin invasion.

"The village was empty, the seagulls were strangely quiet, and all we could hear was the surge of the sea."

—An account of the aftermath of a sahuagin raid

Sahuagin
Medium humanoid (sahuagin), lawful evil

Armor Class 12 (natural armor)
Hit Points 22 (4d8 + 4)
Speed 30 ft., swim 40 ft.

STR	DEX	CON	INT	WIS	CHA
13 (+1)	11 (+0)	12 (+1)	12 (+1)	13 (+1)	9 (−1)

Skills Perception +5
Senses darkvision 120 ft., passive Perception 15
Languages Sahuagin
Challenge 1/2 (100 XP)

Blood Frenzy. The sahuagin has advantage on melee attack rolls against any creature that doesn't have all its hit points.

Limited Amphibiousness. The sahuagin can breathe air and water, but it needs to be submerged at least once every 4 hours to avoid suffocating.

Shark Telepathy. The sahuagin can magically command any shark within 120 feet of it, using a limited telepathy.

Actions

Multiattack. The sahuagin makes two melee attacks: one with its bite and one with its claws or spear.

Bite. *Melee Weapon Attack:* +3 to hit, reach 5 ft., one target. *Hit:* 3 (1d4 + 1) piercing damage.

Claws. *Melee Weapon Attack:* +3 to hit, reach 5 ft., one target. *Hit:* 3 (1d4 + 1) slashing damage.

Spear. *Melee or Ranged Weapon Attack:* +3 to hit, reach 5 ft. or range 20/60 ft., one target. *Hit:* 4 (1d6 + 1) piercing damage, or 5 (1d8 + 1) piercing damage if used with two hands to make a melee attack.

SAHUAGIN PRIESTESS
Medium humanoid (sahuagin), lawful evil

Armor Class 12 (natural armor)
Hit Points 33 (6d8 + 6)
Speed 30 ft., swim 40 ft.

STR	DEX	CON	INT	WIS	CHA
13 (+1)	11 (+0)	12 (+1)	12 (+1)	14 (+2)	13 (+1)

Skills Perception +6, Religion +3
Senses darkvision 120 ft., passive Perception 16
Languages Sahuagin
Challenge 2 (450 XP)

Blood Frenzy. The sahuagin has advantage on melee attack rolls against any creature that doesn't have all its hit points.

Limited Amphibiousness. The sahuagin can breathe air and water, but she needs to be submerged at least once every 4 hours to avoid suffocating.

Shark Telepathy. The sahuagin can magically command any shark within 120 feet of her, using a limited telepathy.

Spellcasting. The sahuagin is a 6th-level spellcaster. Her spellcasting ability is Wisdom (spell save DC 12, +4 to hit with spell attacks). She has the following cleric spells prepared:

Cantrips (at will): *guidance, thaumaturgy*
1st level (4 slots): *bless, detect magic, guiding bolt*
2nd level (3 slots): *hold person, spiritual weapon* (trident)
3rd level (3 slots): *mass healing word, tongues*

ACTIONS

Multiattack. The sahuagin makes two attacks: one with her bite and one with her claws.

Bite. *Melee Weapon Attack:* +3 to hit, reach 5 ft., one target. *Hit:* 3 (1d4 + 1) piercing damage.

Claws. *Melee Weapon Attack:* +3 to hit, reach 5 ft., one target. *Hit:* 3 (1d4 + 1) slashing damage.

SAHUAGIN BARON
Large humanoid (sahuagin), lawful evil

Armor Class 16 (breastplate)
Hit Points 76 (9d10 + 27)
Speed 30 ft., swim 50 ft.

STR	DEX	CON	INT	WIS	CHA
19 (+4)	15 (+2)	16 (+3)	14 (+2)	13 (+1)	17 (+3)

Saving Throws Dex +5, Con +6, Int +5, Wis +4
Skills Perception +7
Senses darkvision 120 ft., passive Perception 17
Languages Sahuagin
Challenge 5 (1,800 XP)

Blood Frenzy. The sahuagin has advantage on melee attack rolls against any creature that doesn't have all its hit points.

Limited Amphibiousness. The sahuagin can breathe air and water, but he needs to be submerged at least once every 4 hours to avoid suffocating.

Shark Telepathy. The sahuagin can magically command any shark within 120 feet of him, using a limited telepathy.

ACTIONS

Multiattack. The sahuagin makes three attacks: one with his bite and two with his claws or trident.

Bite. *Melee Weapon Attack:* +7 to hit, reach 5 ft., one target. *Hit:* 9 (2d4 + 4) piercing damage.

Claws. *Melee Weapon Attack:* +7 to hit, reach 5 ft., one target. *Hit:* 11 (2d6 + 4) slashing damage.

Trident. *Melee or Ranged Weapon Attack:* +7 to hit, reach 5 ft. or range 20/60 ft., one target. *Hit:* 11 (2d6 + 4) piercing damage, or 13 (2d8 + 4) piercing damage if used with two hands to make a melee attack.

S

Salamanders

Salamanders slither across the Sea of Ash on the Elemental Plane of Fire, their sinuous coils and jagged spines smoldering. Intense heat washes off their bodies, while their yellow eyes glow like candles in the deep-set hollows of their hawkish faces.

Salamanders adore power, and they delight in setting fire to things. Outside their home plane, they play among the burning skeletons of charred trees as forest fires rage around them, or slither down the slopes of erupting volcanoes to linger in fire pits and magma floes.

Fire Snakes. Salamanders hatch from eggs that are two-foot-diameter spheres of smoldering obsidian. When a salamander is ready to hatch, it melts its way through the egg's thick shell and emerges as a fire snake. A fire snake matures into a salamander adult within a year.

Slaves of the Efreet. Long ago, the efreet hired azers to build the fabled City of Brass, but then failed in their attempt to enslave that mystical race when the azers' work was done. Turning instead to strike against the salamanders, the efreet had better luck in establishing a slave race, which they use to unleash war and destruction across the planes.

Salamanders despise the azers, believing that if the efreet had succeeded in dominating that race of elemental crafters, the salamanders would still be free. The efreet use this enmity to their own advantage, stoking the salamanders' hatred and pitting them against the efreets' former servants.

The efreet suffer salamanders to serve no other master; when efreet encounter salamanders dedicated to the cults of Elemental Evil, they slay them rather than taking them as slaves.

Domineering Nobles. Although salamanders follow the destructive impulses of their fiery nature, slavery under the efreet has impacted the culture of free salamanders. They rule their own societies according to the efreet model, in which larger and stronger salamanders claim dominion over their lesser kin.

As salamanders age, they increase in size and status, rising to positions of power as cruel nobles among their kind. Nobles rule wandering bands of salamanders, which move across the Elemental Plane of Fire like desert nomads, raiding other communities for treasure.

Living Forges. Salamanders generate intense heat, and when they fight, their weapons glow red and sear the bodies of their enemies on contact. Even approaching a salamander is dangerous, since flesh blisters and burns in its proximity.

This inherent heat is an asset to salamanders' skill as smiths, allowing them to soften and shape iron and steel with their bare hands. Although not as meticulous as azers, salamanders number among the greatest metalsmiths in all the planes. Powerful creatures summon them as warriors, but others enlist the salamanders for their crafting skills, or bind them to forges and ovens to generate limitless heat.

Fire Snake
Medium elemental, neutral evil

Armor Class 14 (natural armor)
Hit Points 22 (5d8)
Speed 30 ft.

STR	DEX	CON	INT	WIS	CHA
12 (+1)	14 (+2)	11 (+0)	7 (−2)	10 (+0)	8 (−1)

Damage Vulnerabilities cold
Damage Resistances bludgeoning, piercing, and slashing from nonmagical attacks
Damage Immunities fire
Senses darkvision 60 ft., passive Perception 10
Languages understands Ignan but can't speak
Challenge 1 (200 XP)

Heated Body. A creature that touches the snake or hits it with a melee attack while within 5 feet of it takes 3 (1d6) fire damage.

Actions

Multiattack. The snake makes two attacks: one with its bite and one with its tail.

Bite. *Melee Weapon Attack:* +3 to hit, reach 5 ft., one target. *Hit:* 3 (1d4 + 1) piercing damage plus 3 (1d6) fire damage.

Tail. *Melee Weapon Attack:* +3 to hit, reach 5 ft., one target. *Hit:* 3 (1d4 + 1) bludgeoning damage plus 3 (1d6) fire damage.

SALAMANDER

Large elemental, neutral evil

Armor Class 15 (natural armor)
Hit Points 90 (12d10 + 24)
Speed 30 ft.

STR	DEX	CON	INT	WIS	CHA
18 (+4)	14 (+2)	15 (+2)	11 (+0)	10 (+0)	12 (+1)

Damage Vulnerabilities cold
Damage Resistances bludgeoning, piercing, and slashing from nonmagical attacks
Damage Immunities fire
Senses darkvision 60 ft., passive Perception 10
Languages Ignan
Challenge 5 (1,800 XP)

Heated Body. A creature that touches the salamander or hits it with a melee attack while within 5 feet of it takes 7 (2d6) fire damage.

Heated Weapons. Any metal melee weapon the salamander wields deals an extra 3 (1d6) fire damage on a hit (included in the attack).

ACTIONS

Multiattack. The salamander makes two attacks: one with its spear and one with its tail.

Spear. *Melee or Ranged Weapon Attack:* +7 to hit, reach 5 ft. or range 20/60 ft., one target. *Hit:* 11 (2d6 + 4) piercing damage, or 13 (2d8 + 4) piercing damage if used with two hands to make a melee attack, plus 3 (1d6) fire damage.

Tail. *Melee Weapon Attack:* +7 to hit, reach 10 ft., one target. *Hit:* 11 (2d6 + 4) bludgeoning damage plus 7 (2d6) fire damage, and the target is grappled (escape DC 14). Until this grapple ends, the target is restrained, the salamander can automatically hit the target with its tail, and the salamander can't make tail attacks against other targets.

S

Satyr

Satyrs are raucous fey that frolic in wild forests, driven by curiosity and hedonism in equal measure.

Satyrs resemble stout male humans with the furry lower bodies and cloven hooves of goats. Horns sprout from their heads, ranging in shape from a pair of small nubs to large, curling rams' horns. They typically sport facial hair.

Hedonistic Revelers. Satyrs crave the strongest drink, the most fragrant spices, and the most dizzying dances. A satyr feels starved when it can't indulge itself, and it goes to great lengths to sate its desires. It might kidnap a fine minstrel to hear lovely songs, sneak through a well-defended garden to gaze upon a beautiful lad or lass, or infiltrate a palace to taste the finest food in the land. Satyrs allow no festivity to pass them by. They partake in any holiday they've heard of. Civilizations of the world have enough festivals and holy days among them to justify nonstop celebration.

Inebriated on drink and pleasure, satyrs give no thought to the consequences of the hedonism they incite in others. They leave such creatures mystified at their own behavior. Such revelers might have to scrounge for excuses to explain their disordered state to parents, employers, family, or friends.

Variant: Satyr Pipes

A satyr might carry panpipes that it can play to create magical effects. Usually, only one satyr in a group carries such pipes. If a satyr has pipes, it gains the following additional action option.

Panpipes. The satyr plays its pipes and chooses one of the following magical effects: a charming melody, a frightening strain, or a gentle lullaby. Any creature within 60 feet of the satyr that can hear the pipes must succeed on a DC 13 Wisdom saving throw or be affected as described below. Other satyrs and creatures that can't be charmed are unaffected.

An affected creature can repeat the saving throw at the end of each of its turns, ending the effect on itself on a success. If a creature's saving throw is successful or the effect ends for it, the creature is immune to these panpipes for the next 24 hours.

Charming Melody. The creature is charmed by the satyr for 1 minute. If the satyr or any of its companions harms the creature, the effect on it ends immediately.

Frightening Strain. The creature is frightened for 1 minute.

Gentle Lullaby. The creature falls asleep and is unconscious for 1 minute. The effect ends if the creature takes damage or if someone takes an action to shake the creature awake.

Twixt day and night the spirits goad me on
They pine for ages past when hearts were pure
Against all reason now they seem unsure
They laugh and scream between mine ears anon.
Now fill my cup not once, not twice, but thrice
With flagon's brim upon my lips I dance
Let unseen pixies toss their gowns askance
While I, the Carnal King, indulge my vice.
With folded boughs, the treants take their leave
As merry damsels' corsets come undone
My song doth stir them like a summer breeze
They fill mine empty cup without reprieve.
The sun becomes the moon becomes the sun
I while away the hours as I please.
— Sonnet of a Naughty Satyr

Satyr
Medium fey, chaotic neutral

Armor Class 14 (leather armor)
Hit Points 31 (7d8)
Speed 40 ft.

STR	DEX	CON	INT	WIS	CHA
12 (+1)	16 (+3)	11 (+0)	12 (+1)	10 (+0)	14 (+2)

Skills Perception +2, Performance +6, Stealth +5
Senses passive Perception 12
Languages Common, Elvish, Sylvan
Challenge 1/2 (100 XP)

Magic Resistance. The satyr has advantage on saving throws against spells and other magical effects.

Actions

Ram. *Melee Weapon Attack:* +3 to hit, reach 5 ft., one target. *Hit:* 6 (2d4 + 1) bludgeoning damage.

Shortsword. *Melee Weapon Attack:* +5 to hit, reach 5 ft., one target. *Hit:* 6 (1d6 + 3) piercing damage.

Shortbow. *Ranged Weapon Attack:* +5 to hit, range 80/320 ft., one target. *Hit:* 6 (1d6 + 3) piercing damage.

Scarecrow

At harvest time, when death revisits the twilit world and summer's blossoms bow their withered heads, eerie scarecrows loom in silent vigil over empty fields. With immortal patience, these stoic sentinels hold their posts through wind, storm, and flood, bound to their master's command, eager to terrify prey with its sackcloth visage and rend victims with its razor-sharp claws.

Spirit-Powered Constructs. A scarecrow is animated by the bound spirit of a slain evil creature, granting it purpose and mobility. It is this uncanny presence from beyond death that allows a scarecrow to inspire fear in those it gazes upon. Hags and witches often bind scarecrows with the spirits of demons, but any evil spirit will do. Although aspects of the spirit's personality might surface, a scarecrow's spirit doesn't recall the memories it had as a creature, and its will is focused solely on serving its creator. If its creator dies, the spirit inhabiting a scarecrow either continues to follow its last commands, seeks revenge for its creator's death, or destroys itself.

Construct Nature. A scarecrow doesn't require air, food, drink, or sleep.

SCARECROW
Medium construct, chaotic evil

Armor Class 11
Hit Points 36 (8d8)
Speed 30 ft.

STR	DEX	CON	INT	WIS	CHA
11 (+0)	13 (+1)	11 (+0)	10 (+0)	10 (+0)	13 (+1)

Damage Vulnerabilities fire
Damage Resistances bludgeoning, piercing, and slashing from nonmagical attacks
Damage Immunities poison
Condition Immunities charmed, exhaustion, frightened, paralyzed, poisoned, unconscious
Senses darkvision 60 ft., passive Perception 10
Languages understands the languages of its creator but can't speak
Challenge 1 (200 XP)

False Appearance. While the scarecrow remains motionless, it is indistinguishable from an ordinary, inanimate scarecrow.

ACTIONS

Multiattack. The scarecrow makes two claw attacks.

Claw. *Melee Weapon Attack:* +3 to hit, reach 5 ft., one target. *Hit:* 6 (2d4 + 1) slashing damage. If the target is a creature, it must succeed on a DC 11 Wisdom saving throw or be frightened until the end of the scarecrow's next turn.

Terrifying Glare. The scarecrow targets one creature it can see within 30 feet of it. If the target can see the scarecrow, the target must succeed on a DC 11 Wisdom saving throw or be magically frightened until the end of the scarecrow's next turn. The frightened target is paralyzed.

Shadow

Shadows are undead that resemble dark exaggerations of humanoid shadows.

Dark Disposition. From the darkness, the shadow reaches out to feed on living creatures' vitality. They can consume any living creature, but they are especially drawn to creatures untainted by evil. A creature that lives a life of goodness and piety consigns its basest impulses and strongest temptations to the darkness where the shadows hunger. As a shadow drains its victim's strength and physical form, the victim's shadow darkens and begins to move of its own volition. In death, the creature's shadow breaks free, becoming a new undead shadow hungry for more life to consume.

If a creature from which a shadow has been created somehow returns to life, its undead shadow senses the return. The shadow might seek its "parent" to vex or slay. Whether the shadow pursues its living counterpart, the creature that birthed the shadow no longer casts one until the monster is destroyed.

Undead Nature. A shadow doesn't require air, food, drink, or sleep.

Shadow

Medium undead, chaotic evil

Armor Class 12
Hit Points 16 (3d8 + 3)
Speed 40 ft.

STR	DEX	CON	INT	WIS	CHA
6 (−2)	14 (+2)	13 (+1)	6 (−2)	10 (+0)	8 (−1)

Skills Stealth +4 (+6 in dim light or darkness)
Damage Vulnerabilities radiant
Damage Resistances acid, cold, fire, lightning, thunder; bludgeoning, piercing, and slashing from nonmagical attacks
Damage Immunities necrotic, poison
Condition Immunities exhaustion, frightened, grappled, paralyzed, petrified, poisoned, prone, restrained
Senses darkvision 60 ft., passive Perception 10
Languages —
Challenge 1/2 (100 XP)

Amorphous. The shadow can move through a space as narrow as 1 inch wide without squeezing.

Shadow Stealth. While in dim light or darkness, the shadow can take the Hide action as a bonus action.

Sunlight Weakness. While in sunlight, the shadow has disadvantage on attack rolls, ability checks, and saving throws.

Actions

Strength Drain. *Melee Weapon Attack:* +4 to hit, reach 5 ft., one creature. *Hit:* 9 (2d6 + 2) necrotic damage, and the target's Strength score is reduced by 1d4. The target dies if this reduces its Strength to 0. Otherwise, the reduction lasts until the target finishes a short or long rest.

If a non-evil humanoid dies from this attack, a new shadow rises from the corpse 1d4 hours later.

SHAMBLING MOUND

A shambling mound, sometimes called a shambler, trudges ponderously through bleak swamps, dismal marshes, and rain forests, consuming any organic matter in its path. This rotting heap of animated vegetation looms up half again as tall as a human, tapering into a faceless "head" at its top.

All-Consuming Devourers. A shambling mound feeds on any organic material, tirelessly consuming plants as it moves and devouring animals that can't escape it. Only the shambling mounds' rarity and plodding speed prevent them from overwhelming entire ecosystems. Even so, their presence leeches natural environments of plant and animal life, and an unsettling quiet pervades the swamps and woods haunted by these ever-hungry horrors.

Unseen Hunters. Composed of decaying leaves, vines, roots, and other natural swamp and forest compost, shamblers can blend into their environs. Because they move slowly, they rarely attempt to pursue and catch creatures. Rather, they remain in place, sustaining themselves by absorbing nutrients from their surroundings as they wait for prey to come to them. When a creature passes near or alights upon a shambling mound, the monster comes to life, seizing and absorbing the unwary prey.

Spawned by Lightning. A shambling mound results from a phenomenon in which lightning or fey magic invigorates an otherwise ordinary swamp plant. As the plant is reborn into its second life, it chokes the life from plants and animals around it, mulching their corpses in a heap around its roots. Those roots eventually give up their reliance on the soil, directing the shambling mound to seek out new sources of food.

The Weed that Walks. The instinct that drives a shambling mound is its central root-stem, buried somewhere inside its ponderous form. The rest of a shambler consists of the rotting heap that it simultaneously accumulates and feeds on, which protects the root-stem and animates to smash and smother the life from any creature.

The dense mass of a shambling mound's body shrugs off the effects of cold and fire. Lightning reinvigorates the root-stem, strengthening the shambling mound and bolstering its consumptive drive.

Despite its monstrous form, the shambling mound is a living plant that requires air and nourishment. Although it doesn't sleep the way an animal does, it can lie dormant for days on end before rising to hunt for food.

A Resurgent Menace. If a shambling mound faces defeat before an overwhelming foe, the root-stem can feign death, collapsing the remains of its mound. If not subsequently killed, the root-stem beds down in the shambler's remains to slowly regrow its full body, then once again sets out to consume all it can. In this way, shambling mound infestations long thought destroyed can recur time and again.

SHAMBLING MOUND
Large plant, unaligned

Armor Class 15 (natural armor)
Hit Points 136 (16d10 + 48)
Speed 20 ft., swim 20 ft.

STR	DEX	CON	INT	WIS	CHA
18 (+4)	8 (−1)	16 (+3)	5 (−3)	10 (+0)	5 (−3)

Skills Stealth +2
Damage Resistances cold, fire
Damage Immunities lightning
Condition Immunities blinded, deafened, exhaustion
Senses blindsight 60 ft. (blind beyond this radius), passive Perception 10
Languages —
Challenge 5 (1,800 XP)

Lightning Absorption. Whenever the shambling mound is subjected to lightning damage, it takes no damage and regains a number of hit points equal to the lightning damage dealt.

ACTIONS

Multiattack. The shambling mound makes two slam attacks. If both attacks hit a Medium or smaller target, the target is grappled (escape DC 14), and the shambling mound uses its Engulf on it.

Slam. *Melee Weapon Attack:* +7 to hit, reach 5 ft., one target. *Hit:* 13 (2d8 + 4) bludgeoning damage.

Engulf. The shambling mound engulfs a Medium or smaller creature grappled by it. The engulfed target is blinded, restrained, and unable to breathe, and it must succeed on a DC 14 Constitution saving throw at the start of each of the mound's turns or take 13 (2d8 + 4) bludgeoning damage. If the mound moves, the engulfed target moves with it. The mound can have only one creature engulfed at a time.

SHIELD GUARDIAN

Wizards and other spellcasters create shield guardians for protection. A shield guardian treads beside its master, absorbing damage to keep its master alive as long as possible.

Master's Amulet. Every shield guardian has an amulet magically linked to it. A shield guardian can have only one corresponding amulet, and if that amulet is destroyed, the shield guardian is incapacitated until a replacement amulet is created. A shield guardian's amulet is subject to direct attack if it isn't being worn or carried. It has AC 10, 10 hit points, and immunity to poison and psychic damage. Crafting an amulet requires 1 week and costs 1,000 gp in components.

A shield guardian's solitary focus is to protect the amulet's wearer. The amulet's wearer can command the guardian to attack its enemies or to guard the wielder against attack. If an attack threatens to injure the wearer, the construct can magically absorb the blow into its own body, even at a distance.

A spellcaster can store a single spell within a shield guardian, which can then cast the spell on command or under specific conditions. Many a wizard has been rendered helpless by enemies, only to surprise those foes when its shield guardian unleashes potent magical power.

Magnificent Treasure. Because a shield guardian's ownership can be transferred by giving its matching amulet to another creature, some wizards collect exorbitant sums from princes, nobles, and crime lords to create shield guardians for them. At the same time, a shield guardian makes a mighty prize for anyone who slays its master and claims its amulet.

Construct Nature. A shield guardian doesn't require air, food, drink, or sleep.

SHIELD GUARDIAN
Large construct, unaligned

Armor Class 17 (natural armor)
Hit Points 142 (15d10 + 60)
Speed 30 ft.

STR	DEX	CON	INT	WIS	CHA
18 (+4)	8 (−1)	18 (+4)	7 (−2)	10 (+0)	3 (−4)

Damage Immunities poison
Condition Immunities charmed, exhaustion, frightened, paralyzed, poisoned
Senses blindsight 10 ft., darkvision 60 ft., passive Perception 10
Languages understands commands given in any language but can't speak
Challenge 7 (2,900 XP)

Bound. The shield guardian is magically bound to an amulet. As long as the guardian and its amulet are on the same plane of existence, the amulet's wearer can telepathically call the guardian to travel to it, and the guardian knows the distance and direction to the amulet. If the guardian is within 60 feet of the amulet's wearer, half of any damage the wearer takes (rounded up) is transferred to the guardian.

Regeneration. The shield guardian regains 10 hit points at the start of its turn if it has at least 1 hit point.

Spell Storing. A spellcaster who wears the shield guardian's amulet can cause the guardian to store one spell of 4th level or lower. To do so, the wearer must cast the spell on the guardian. The spell has no effect but is stored within the guardian. When commanded to do so by the wearer or when a situation arises that was predefined by the spellcaster, the guardian casts the stored spell with any parameters set by the original caster, requiring no components. When the spell is cast or a new spell is stored, any previously stored spell is lost.

ACTIONS

Multiattack. The guardian makes two fist attacks.

Fist. *Melee Weapon Attack:* +7 to hit, reach 5 ft., one target. *Hit:* 11 (2d6 + 4) bludgeoning damage.

REACTIONS

Shield. When a creature makes an attack against the wearer of the guardian's amulet, the guardian grants a +2 bonus to the wearer's AC if the guardian is within 5 feet of the wearer.

SKELETONS

Skeletons arise when animated by dark magic. They heed the summons of spellcasters who call them from their stony tombs and ancient battlefields, or rise of their own accord in places saturated with death and loss, awakened by stirrings of necromantic energy or the presence of corrupting evil.

Animated Dead. Whatever sinister force awakens a skeleton infuses its bones with a dark vitality, adhering joint to joint and reassembling dismantled limbs. This energy motivates a skeleton to move and think in a rudimentary fashion, though only as a pale imitation of the way it behaved in life. An animated skeleton retains no connection to its past, although resurrecting a skeleton restores it body and soul, banishing the hateful undead spirit that empowers it.

While most skeletons are the animated remains of dead humans and other humanoids, skeletal undead can be created from the bones of other creatures besides humanoids, giving rise to a host of terrifying and unique forms.

Obedient Servants. Skeletons raised by spell are bound to the will of their creator. They follow orders to the letter, never questioning the tasks their masters give them, regardless of the consequences. Because of their literal interpretation of commands and unwavering obedience, skeletons adapt poorly to changing circumstances. They can't read, speak, emote, or communicate in any way except to nod, shake their heads, or point. Still, skeletons are able to accomplish a variety of relatively complex tasks.

A skeleton can fight with weapons and wear armor, can load and fire a catapult or trebuchet, scale a siege ladder, form a shield wall, or dump boiling oil. However, it must receive careful instructions explaining how such tasks are accomplished.

Although they lack the intellect they possessed in life, skeletons aren't mindless. Rather than break its limbs attempting to batter its way through an iron door, a skeleton tries the handle first. If that doesn't work, it searches for another way through or around the obstacle.

Habitual Behaviors. Independent skeletons temporarily or permanently free of a master's control sometimes pantomime actions from their past lives, their bones echoing the rote behaviors of their former living selves. The skeleton of a miner might lift a pick and start chipping away at stone walls. The skeleton of a guard might strike up a post at a random doorway. The skeleton of a dragon might lie down on a pile of treasure, while the skeleton of a horse crops grass it can't eat. Left alone in a ballroom, the skeletons of nobles might continue an eternally unfinished dance.

When skeletons encounter living creatures, the necromantic energy that drives them compels them to kill unless they are commanded by their masters to refrain from doing so. They attack without mercy and fight until destroyed, for skeletons possess little sense of self and even less sense of self-preservation.

Undead Nature. A skeleton doesn't require air, food, drink, or sleep.

SKELETON

Medium undead, lawful evil

Armor Class 13 (armor scraps)
Hit Points 13 (2d8 + 4)
Speed 30 ft.

STR	DEX	CON	INT	WIS	CHA
10 (+0)	14 (+2)	15 (+2)	6 (−2)	8 (−1)	5 (−3)

Damage Vulnerabilities bludgeoning
Damage Immunities poison
Condition Immunities exhaustion, poisoned
Senses darkvision 60 ft., passive Perception 9
Languages understands all languages it knew in life but can't speak
Challenge 1/4 (50 XP)

ACTIONS

Shortsword. *Melee Weapon Attack:* +4 to hit, reach 5 ft., one target. *Hit:* 5 (1d6 + 2) piercing damage.

Shortbow. *Ranged Weapon Attack:* +4 to hit, range 80/320 ft., one target. *Hit:* 5 (1d6 + 2) piercing damage.

MINOTAUR SKELETON

Large undead, lawful evil

Armor Class 12 (natural armor)
Hit Points 67 (9d10 + 18)
Speed 40 ft.

STR	DEX	CON	INT	WIS	CHA
18 (+4)	11 (+0)	15 (+2)	6 (−2)	8 (−1)	5 (−3)

Damage Vulnerabilities bludgeoning
Damage Immunities poison
Condition Immunities exhaustion, poisoned
Senses darkvision 60 ft., passive Perception 9
Languages understands Abyssal but can't speak
Challenge 2 (450 XP)

Charge. If the skeleton moves at least 10 feet straight toward a target and then hits it with a gore attack on the same turn, the target takes an extra 9 (2d8) piercing damage. If the target is a creature, it must succeed on a DC 14 Strength saving throw or be pushed up to 10 feet away and knocked prone.

ACTIONS

Greataxe. *Melee Weapon Attack:* +6 to hit, reach 5 ft., one target. *Hit:* 17 (2d12 + 4) slashing damage.

Gore. *Melee Weapon Attack:* +6 to hit, reach 5 ft., one target. *Hit:* 13 (2d8 + 4) piercing damage.

WARHORSE SKELETON

Large undead, lawful evil

Armor Class 13 (barding scraps)
Hit Points 22 (3d10 + 6)
Speed 60 ft.

STR	DEX	CON	INT	WIS	CHA
18 (+4)	12 (+1)	15 (+2)	2 (−4)	8 (−1)	5 (−3)

Damage Vulnerabilities bludgeoning
Damage Immunities poison
Condition Immunities exhaustion, poisoned
Senses darkvision 60 ft., passive Perception 9
Languages —
Challenge 1/2 (100 XP)

ACTIONS

Hooves. *Melee Weapon Attack:* +6 to hit, reach 5 ft., one target. *Hit:* 11 (2d6 + 4) bludgeoning damage.

SLAADI

In the Ever-Changing Chaos of Limbo, bits of forest and meadow, ruined castles, and isolated islands drift through a tumult of fire, water, earth, and wind. The foremost inhabitants of this inhospitable plane are the toad-like slaadi. Slaadi are undisciplined and have no formal hierarchy, although weaker slaadi obey stronger ones under threat of annihilation.

The Spawning Stone. Long ago, Primus, overlord of the modrons, created a gigantic, geometrically complex stone imbued with the power of law. He then cast it adrift in Limbo, believing that the stone would bring order to the chaos of that plane and halt the spread of chaos to other planes. As the stone's power grew, it became possible for creatures with ordered minds, such as modrons and githzerai, to create enclaves in Limbo. However, Primus's creation had an unforeseen side effect: the chaotic energy absorbed by the stone spawned the horrors that came to be known as slaadi. Sages refer to Primus's massive creation as the Spawning Stone for this reason.

The slaadi wiped out every last modron enclave in Limbo. As creatures of utter chaos, slaadi loathe modrons and attack them on sight. Nonetheless, Primus stands by his creation and either doesn't perceive the slaadi as threats or chooses to ignore them.

Birth and Transformation. Slaadi have horrific cycles of reproduction. Slaadi reproduce either by implanting humanoid hosts with eggs or by infecting them with a transformative disease called chaos phage. Each color of slaad reproduces or transforms in a different way, with red slaadi spawning blue and green slaadi, and blue slaadi spawning red and green. Each green slaad undergoes a lifelong cycle of transformation into the more powerful gray and death slaadi. With each transformation, the slaad retains its memories.

Shapechangers. Some slaadi can transform into the humanoid creatures from which they were originally spawned. These slaadi return to the Material Plane to sow discord in the guise of their former selves.

RED SLAAD

When a red slaad claws a humanoid creature, it can inject an egg from a gland under one of its claws. The egg works its way into its host and gestates, eventually forming a slaad tadpole. Such a tadpole then eats its way out of the host's body, feeds on the host's remains, and then seeks any other fresh meat it can find. The tadpole transforms into a fully grown blue slaad—or green slaad if the host had the ability to cast 3rd level spells or higher—within 2d12 hours.

BLUE SLAAD

The bone hooks that protrude from the back of a blue slaad's hands inflict a terrible transformative disease on humanoids wounded by them. This infection, called chaos phage, transforms its victim into a fully grown red slaad—or green slaad if the host was a spellcaster able to cast 3rd level spells or higher.

GREEN SLAAD

Green slaadi are surprisingly intelligent and possess innate spellcasting ability. A green slaad can change its shape to appear as a humanoid. If it was born of a humanoid host, the slaad usually adopts its host's form.

At some unpredictable point in its existence, a green slaad unlocks the means to magically, instantly, and permanently transform itself into a gray slaad. Unlocking this knowledge can take years, even decades.

GRAY SLAAD

Outside of Limbo, gray slaadi act as living extensions of the will of their masters, the death slaadi. A gray slaad journeys to the Material Plane on errands of doom, often taking humanoid form. A gray slaad learns how to master the use of a greatsword and imbue it with its own innate magic.

A gray slaad that eats the entire corpse of a dead death slaad instantly transforms into a death slaad.

DEATH SLAAD

Death slaadi are suffused with energy from the Negative Energy Plane and exemplify evil's corruption of chaos, and they take sadistic pleasure in bringing harm to others. They propagate their race by dragooning mobs of red and blue slaadi and invading other planes. Humanoids who survive the incursion become incubators for new slaadi.

VARIANT: SLAAD CONTROL GEMS

As a slaad emerges from the Spawning Stone, the stone magically implants a fragment of itself in the slaad's brain. This fragment takes the form of a magic gem roughly the size and shape of a human child's fist. The gem is the same color as the slaad. Another creature can use magic to draw forth a slaad's gem and use it to subjugate the slaad. The slaad must obey whoever possesses its gem. If a slaad's gem is destroyed, the slaad can no longer be controlled in this way.

A slaad born from something other than the Spawning Stone has no gem in its brain, but it gains one if it ever comes into contact with the Spawning Stone. Slaadi on Limbo are attracted to the Spawning Stone, so most end up with a gem. A slaad with a control gem in its brain has the following additional trait.

Control Gem. Implanted in the slaad's brain is a magic control gem. The slaad must obey whoever possesses the gem and is immune to being charmed while so controlled.

Certain spells can be used to acquire the gem. If the slaad fails its saving throw against *imprisonment*, the spell can transfer the gem to the spellcaster's open hand, instead of imprisoning the slaad. A *wish* spell, if cast in the slaad's presence, can be worded to acquire the gem.

A *greater restoration* spell cast on the slaad destroys the gem without harming the slaad.

Someone who is proficient in Wisdom (Medicine) can remove the gem from an incapacitated slaad. Each try requires 1 minute of uninterrupted work and a successful DC 20 Wisdom (Medicine) check. Each failed attempt deals 22 (4d10) psychic damage to the slaad.

Red Slaad

Blue Slaad

Green Slaad

Gray Slaad

RED SLAAD

Large aberration, chaotic neutral

Armor Class 14 (natural armor)
Hit Points 93 (11d10 + 33)
Speed 30 ft.

STR	DEX	CON	INT	WIS	CHA
16 (+3)	12 (+1)	16 (+3)	6 (−2)	6 (−2)	7 (−2)

Skills Perception +1
Damage Resistances acid, cold, fire, lightning, thunder
Senses darkvision 60 ft., passive Perception 11
Languages Slaad, telepathy 60 ft.
Challenge 5 (1,800 XP)

Magic Resistance. The slaad has advantage on saving throws against spells and other magical effects.

Regeneration. The slaad regains 10 hit points at the start of its turn if it has at least 1 hit point.

ACTIONS

Multiattack. The slaad makes three attacks: one with its bite and two with its claws.

Bite. *Melee Weapon Attack:* +6 to hit, reach 5 ft., one target. *Hit:* 8 (2d4 + 3) piercing damage.

Claw. *Melee Weapon Attack:* +6 to hit, reach 5 ft., one target. *Hit:* 7 (1d8 + 3) piercing damage. If the target is a humanoid, it must succeed on a DC 14 Constitution saving throw or be infected with a disease—a minuscule slaad egg.

A humanoid host can carry only one slaad egg to term at a time. Over three months, the egg moves to the chest cavity, gestates, and forms a slaad tadpole. In the 24-hour period before giving birth, the host starts to feel unwell, its speed is halved, and it has disadvantage on attack rolls, ability checks, and saving throws. At birth, the tadpole chews its way through vital organs and out of the host's chest in 1 round, killing the host in the process.

If the disease is cured before the tadpole's emergence, the unborn slaad is disintegrated.

SLAAD TADPOLE

Tiny aberration, chaotic neutral

Armor Class 12
Hit Points 10 (4d4)
Speed 30 ft.

STR	DEX	CON	INT	WIS	CHA
7 (−2)	15 (+2)	10 (+0)	3 (−4)	5 (−3)	3 (−4)

Skills Stealth +4
Damage Resistances acid, cold, fire, lightning, thunder
Senses darkvision 60 ft., passive Perception 7
Languages understands Slaad but can't speak
Challenge 1/8 (25 XP)

Magic Resistance. The slaad has advantage on saving throws against spells and other magical effects.

ACTIONS

Bite. *Melee Weapon Attack:* +4 to hit, reach 5 ft., one target. *Hit:* 4 (1d4 + 2) piercing damage.

BLUE SLAAD

Large aberration, chaotic neutral

Armor Class 15 (natural armor)
Hit Points 123 (13d10 + 52)
Speed 30 ft.

STR	DEX	CON	INT	WIS	CHA
20 (+5)	15 (+2)	18 (+4)	7 (−2)	7 (−2)	9 (−1)

Skills Perception +1
Damage Resistances acid, cold, fire, lightning, thunder
Senses darkvision 60 ft., passive Perception 11
Languages Slaad, telepathy 60 ft.
Challenge 7 (2,900 XP)

Magic Resistance. The slaad has advantage on saving throws against spells and other magical effects.

Regeneration. The slaad regains 10 hit points at the start of its turn if it has at least 1 hit point.

ACTIONS

Multiattack. The slaad makes three attacks: one with its bite and two with its claws.

Bite. *Melee Weapon Attack:* +8 to hit, reach 5 ft., one target. *Hit:* 12 (2d6 + 5) piercing damage.

Claw. *Melee Weapon Attack:* +8 to hit, reach 5 ft., one target. *Hit:* 12 (2d6 + 5) slashing damage. If the target is a humanoid, it must succeed on a DC 15 Constitution saving throw or be infected with a disease called chaos phage. While infected, the target can't regain hit points, and its hit point maximum is reduced by 10 (3d6) every 24 hours. If the disease reduces the target's hit point maximum to 0, the target instantly transforms into a red slaad or, if it has the ability to cast spells of 3rd level or higher, a green slaad. Only a *wish* spell can reverse the transformation.

Green Slaad

Large aberration (shapechanger), chaotic neutral

Armor Class 16 (natural armor)
Hit Points 127 (15d10 + 45)
Speed 30 ft.

STR	DEX	CON	INT	WIS	CHA
18 (+4)	15 (+2)	16 (+3)	11 (+0)	8 (−1)	12 (+1)

Skills Arcana +3, Perception +2
Damage Resistances acid, cold, fire, lightning, thunder
Senses blindsight 30 ft., darkvision 60 ft., passive Perception 12
Languages Slaad, telepathy 60 ft.
Challenge 8 (3,900 XP)

Shapechanger. The slaad can use its action to polymorph into a Small or Medium humanoid, or back into its true form. Its statistics, other than its size, are the same in each form. Any equipment it is wearing or carrying isn't transformed. It reverts to its true form if it dies.

Innate Spellcasting. The slaad's innate spellcasting ability is Charisma (spell save DC 12). The slaad can innately cast the following spells, requiring no material components:

At will: *detect magic, detect thoughts, mage hand*
2/day each: *fear, invisibility* (self only)
1/day: *fireball*

Magic Resistance. The slaad has advantage on saving throws against spells and other magical effects.

Regeneration. The slaad regains 10 hit points at the start of its turn if it has at least 1 hit point.

Actions

Multiattack. The slaad makes three attacks: one with its bite and two with its claws or staff. Alternatively, it uses its Hurl Flame twice.

Bite (Slaad Form Only). *Melee Weapon Attack:* +7 to hit, reach 5 ft., one target. *Hit:* 11 (2d6 + 4) piercing damage.

Claw (Slaad Form Only). *Melee Weapon Attack:* +7 to hit, reach 5 ft., one target. *Hit:* 7 (1d6 + 4) slashing damage.

Staff. *Melee Weapon Attack:* +7 to hit, reach 5 ft., one target. *Hit:* 11 (2d6 + 4) bludgeoning damage.

Hurl Flame. *Ranged Spell Attack:* +4 to hit, range 60 ft., one target. *Hit:* 10 (3d6) fire damage. The fire ignites flammable objects that aren't being worn or carried.

Gray Slaad

Medium aberration (shapechanger), chaotic neutral

Armor Class 18 (natural armor)
Hit Points 127 (17d8 + 51)
Speed 30 ft.

STR	DEX	CON	INT	WIS	CHA
17 (+3)	17 (+3)	16 (+3)	13 (+1)	8 (−1)	14 (+2)

Skills Arcana +5, Perception +6
Damage Resistances acid, cold, fire, lightning, thunder
Senses blindsight 60 ft., darkvision 60 ft., passive Perception 16
Languages Slaad, telepathy 60 ft.
Challenge 9 (5,000 XP)

Shapechanger. The slaad can use its action to polymorph into a Small or Medium humanoid, or back into its true form. Its statistics, other than its size, are the same in each form. Any equipment it is wearing or carrying isn't transformed. It reverts to its true form if it dies.

Innate Spellcasting. The slaad's innate spellcasting ability is Charisma (spell save DC 14). The slaad can innately cast the following spells, requiring no material components:

At will: *detect magic, detect thoughts, invisibility* (self only),
  mage hand, major image
2/day each: *fear, fly, fireball, tongues*
1/day: *plane shift* (self only)

Magic Resistance. The slaad has advantage on saving throws against spells and other magical effects.

Magic Weapons. The slaad's weapon attacks are magical.

Regeneration. The slaad regains 10 hit points at the start of its turn if it has at least 1 hit point.

Actions

Multiattack. The slaad makes three attacks: one with its bite and two with its claws or greatsword.

Bite (Slaad Form Only). *Melee Weapon Attack:* +7 to hit, reach 5 ft., one target. *Hit:* 6 (1d6 + 3) piercing damage.

Claws (Slaad Form Only). *Melee Weapon Attack:* +7 to hit, reach 5 ft., one target. *Hit:* 8 (1d10 + 3) slashing damage.

Greatsword. *Melee Weapon Attack:* +7 to hit, reach 5 ft., one target. *Hit:* 10 (2d6 + 3) slashing damage.

DEATH SLAAD

Medium aberration (shapechanger), chaotic evil

Armor Class 18 (natural armor)
Hit Points 170 (20d8 + 80)
Speed 30 ft.

STR	DEX	CON	INT	WIS	CHA
20 (+5)	15 (+2)	19 (+4)	15 (+2)	10 (+0)	16 (+3)

Skills Arcana +6, Perception +8
Damage Resistances acid, cold, fire, lightning, thunder
Senses blindsight 60 ft., darkvision 60 ft., passive Perception 18
Languages Slaad, telepathy 60 ft.
Challenge 10 (5,900 XP)

Shapechanger. The slaad can use its action to polymorph into a Small or Medium humanoid, or back into its true form. Its statistics, other than its size, are the same in each form. Any equipment it is wearing or carrying isn't transformed. It reverts to its true form if it dies.

Innate Spellcasting. The slaad's innate spellcasting ability is Charisma (spell save DC 15, +7 to hit with spell attacks). The slaad can innately cast the following spells, requiring no material components:

At will: *detect magic, detect thoughts, invisibility* (self only), *mage hand, major image*
2/day each: *fear, fireball, fly, tongues*
1/day each: *cloudkill, plane shift*

Magic Resistance. The slaad has advantage on saving throws against spells and other magical effects.

Magic Weapons. The slaad's weapon attacks are magical.

Regeneration. The slaad regains 10 hit points at the start of its turn if it has at least 1 hit point.

ACTIONS

Multiattack. The slaad makes three attacks: one with its bite and two with its claws or greatsword.

Bite (Slaad Form Only). *Melee Weapon Attack:* +9 to hit, reach 5 ft., one target. *Hit:* 9 (1d8 + 5) piercing damage plus 7 (2d6) necrotic damage.

Claws (Slaad Form Only). *Melee Weapon Attack:* +9 to hit, reach 5 ft., one target. *Hit:* 10 (1d10 + 5) slashing damage plus 7 (2d6) necrotic damage.

Greatsword. *Melee Weapon Attack:* +9 to hit, reach 5 ft., one target. *Hit:* 12 (2d6 + 5) slashing damage plus 7 (2d6) necrotic damage.

SPECTER

A specter is the angry, unfettered spirit of a humanoid that has been prevented from passing to the afterlife. Specters no longer possess connections to who or what they were, yet are condemned to walk the world forever. Some are spawned when dark magic or the touch of a wraith rips a soul from a living body.

Beyond Redemption. When a ghost's unfinished business is completed, it can rest at last. No such rest or redemption awaits a specter. It is doomed to the Material Plane, its only end the oblivion that comes with the destruction of its soul. Until then, it bears out its lonely life in forlorn places, carrying on forgotten through the ages of the world.

Undying Hatred. Living creatures remind the specter that life is beyond its grasp. The mere sight of the living overwhelms a specter with sorrow and wrath, which can be abated only by destroying said life. A specter kills quickly and mercilessly, for only by depriving others of life can it gain the slightest satisfaction. However, no matter how many lives it extinguishes, a specter always succumbs to its hatred and sorrow.

Dwellers in Darkness. Sunlight represents a source of life that no specter can ever hope to douse, and it pains them. When night falls, they leave their final resting places in search of living creatures to slay, knowing that few weapons can harm them in return. At the first light of dawn, they retreat back into the darkness, where they remain until night falls again.

Undead Nature. A specter doesn't require air, food, drink, or sleep.

VARIANT: POLTERGEIST

A poltergeist is a different kind of specter—the confused, invisible spirit of an individual with no sense of how he or she died. A poltergeist expresses its rage by hurling creatures and objects using the power of its shattered psyche.

A poltergeist has a challenge rating of 2 (450 XP) and gains the following additional trait:

Invisibility. The poltergeist is invisible.

The poltergeist has the following action options in place of the specter's Life Drain:

Forceful Slam. *Melee Weapon Attack:* +4 to hit, reach 5 ft., one creature. *Hit:* 10 (3d6) force damage.

Telekinetic Thrust. The poltergeist targets a creature or unattended object within 30 feet of it. A creature must be Medium or smaller to be affected by this magic, and an object can weigh up to 150 pounds.

If the target is a creature, the poltergeist makes a Charisma check contested by the target's Strength check. If the poltergeist wins the contest, the poltergeist hurls the target up to 30 feet in any direction, including upward. If the target then comes into contact with a hard surface or heavy object, the target takes 1d6 damage per 10 feet moved.

If the target is an object that isn't being worn or carried, the poltergeist hurls it up to 30 feet in any direction. The poltergeist can use the object as a ranged weapon, attacking one creature along the object's path (+4 to hit) and dealing 5 (2d4) bludgeoning damage on a hit.

SPECTER
Medium undead, chaotic evil

Armor Class 12
Hit Points 22 (5d8)
Speed 0 ft., fly 50 ft. (hover)

STR	DEX	CON	INT	WIS	CHA
1 (−5)	14 (+2)	11 (+0)	10 (+0)	10 (+0)	11 (+0)

Damage Resistances acid, cold, fire, lightning, thunder; bludgeoning, piercing, and slashing from nonmagical attacks
Damage Immunities necrotic, poison
Condition Immunities charmed, exhaustion, grappled, paralyzed, petrified, poisoned, prone, restrained, unconscious
Senses darkvision 60 ft., passive Perception 10
Languages understands all languages it knew in life but can't speak
Challenge 1 (200 XP)

Incorporeal Movement. The specter can move through other creatures and objects as if they were difficult terrain. It takes 5 (1d10) force damage if it ends its turn inside an object.

Sunlight Sensitivity. While in sunlight, the specter has disadvantage on attack rolls, as well as on Wisdom (Perception) checks that rely on sight.

ACTIONS

Life Drain. *Melee Spell Attack:* +4 to hit, reach 5 ft., one creature. *Hit:* 10 (3d6) necrotic damage. The target must succeed on a DC 10 Constitution saving throw or its hit point maximum is reduced by an amount equal to the damage taken. This reduction lasts until the creature finishes a long rest. The target dies if this effect reduces its hit point maximum to 0.

Sphinxes

In sacred isolation, a sphinx guards the secrets and treasures of the gods. As it calmly regards each new party that comes before it, the bones of supplicants and quest seekers that failed to pass its tests lie scattered around its lair. Its great wings sweep along its flanks, its tawny leonine body rippling with muscle and possessed of forepaws powerful enough to tear a humanoid in half.

Divine Guardians. Sphinxes test the worth of those who seek the treasures of the gods, whether forgotten secrets or mighty spells, artifacts or magical gateways. Creatures that choose to face a sphinx's test are bound to that test unto death, and only those worthy will survive it. The rest the sphinx destroys.

Some sphinxes are high priests of the gods that create them, but most are simply embodied spirits, brought into the mortal realm by devout prayer or direct intervention. A sphinx maintains its vigil tirelessly, not needing to sleep or eat. It rarely engages with others of its kind, knowing no other life except its sacred mission.

Magical Tests. The secrets and treasures a sphinx guards remain under divine protection, so that when a creature fails a sphinx's test, the path to the object or knowledge it guards vanishes. Even if a sphinx is attacked and defeated, a quester will still fail to gain the secret it sought—and will make an enemy of the god that placed the sphinx as a guardian.

Benign deities sometimes grant a sphinx the power to remove supplicants that fail their tests, transporting them away and ensuring that they never encounter the sphinx again. However, those who fail a sphinx's test typically meet a gruesome end beneath its claws.

Extraplanar Beings. Mortals that encounter sphinxes do so most often in ancient tombs and ruins, but some sphinxes can access extraplanar realms. A conversation with a sphinx that begins between tumbled stone walls might suddenly shift to an alien locale, such as a life-sized game board or a daunting cliff that must be climbed in a howling storm. Sometimes a sphinx must be summoned from such an extradimensional space, with supplicants calling it from its empty lair. Only those the sphinx deems worthy gain admittance to its realm.

Fallen Sphinxes. Whether through the weariness of the ages, regret at the slaughter of innocents, or dreams of worship by supplicants that attempt to bargain their way to knowledge, some sphinxes break free of their divine command. However, even if a sphinx's alignment and loyalties drift in this way, it never leaves the place it guards or grants its secrets to any except creatures it deems worthy.

> Round she is, yet flat as a board
> Altar of the Lupine Lords
> Jewel on black velvet, pearl in the sea
> Unchanged but e'erchanging, eternally.
> —Riddle of the Gynosphinx
> of White Plume Mountain

Androsphinx

An androsphinx bears the head of a humanoid male on its lion's body. Outwardly gruff and downcast, it often begins conversations with insults or negative observations. Beneath this gruff exterior, however, an androsphinx has a noble heart. It has no wish to lie or deceive, but it doesn't give away information readily, choosing its words as wisely as it guards its secrets.

An androsphinx tests the courage and valor of supplicants, not only by forcing them to complete quests but also with its terrible roar, which echoes for miles as it terrifies and deafens nearby creatures. Those who pass its tests may be rewarded with a *heroes' feast*.

Gynosphinx

A gynosphinx bears the head of a humanoid female. Many have the regal countenances of worldly queens, but some are marked with wild, leonine features. A gynosphinx's eyes see beyond the present time and place, and penetrate veils of invisibility and magic. Supplicants who look deep into those eyes might find themselves magically displaced, banished to some far-flung plane where a difficult trial awaits them.

Gynosphinxes are virtual libraries of knowledge and lore. They ask riddles and present puzzles to test the wit of supplicants that come to learn their secrets. Some are willing to bargain with such supplicants for treasure or service.

A Sphinx's Lair

A sphinx presides over an ancient temple, sepulcher, or vault, within which are hidden divine secrets and treasures beyond the reach of mortals.

Lair Actions

On initiative count 20 (losing initiative ties), the sphinx can take a lair action to cause one of the following magical effects; the sphinx can't use an effect again until it finishes a short or long rest:

- The flow of time is altered such that every creature in the lair must reroll initiative. The sphinx can choose not to reroll.
- The effects of time are altered such that every creature in the lair must succeed on a DC 15 Constitution saving throw or become 1d20 years older or younger (the sphinx's choice), but never any younger than 1 year old. A *greater restoration* spell can restore a creature's age to normal.
- The flow of time within the lair is altered such that everything within moves up to 10 years forward or backward (sphinx's choice). Only the sphinx is immediately aware of the time change. A *wish* spell can return the caster and up to seven other creatures designated by the caster to their normal time.
- The sphinx shifts itself and up to seven other creatures it can see within in its lair to another plane of existence. Once outside its lair, the sphinx can't use lair actions, but it can return to its lair as a bonus action on its turn, taking up to seven creatures with it.

ANDROSPHINX

Large monstrosity, lawful neutral

Armor Class 17 (natural armor)
Hit Points 199 (19d10 + 95)
Speed 40 ft., fly 60 ft.

STR	DEX	CON	INT	WIS	CHA
22 (+6)	10 (+0)	20 (+5)	16 (+3)	18 (+4)	23 (+6)

Saving Throws Dex +6, Con +11, Int +9, Wis +10
Skills Arcana +9, Perception +10, Religion +15
Damage Immunities psychic; bludgeoning, piercing, and
    slashing from nonmagical attacks
Condition Immunities charmed, frightened
Senses truesight 120 ft., passive Perception 20
Languages Common, Sphinx
Challenge 17 (18,000 XP)

Inscrutable. The sphinx is immune to any effect that would
sense its emotions or read its thoughts, as well as any
divination spell that it refuses. Wisdom (Insight) checks
made to ascertain the sphinx's intentions or sincerity have
disadvantage.

Magic Weapons. The sphinx's weapon attacks are magical.

Spellcasting. The sphinx is a 12th-level spellcaster. Its
spellcasting ability is Wisdom (spell save DC 18, +10 to hit with
spell attacks). It requires no material components to cast its
spells. The sphinx has the following cleric spells prepared:

Cantrips (at will): *sacred flame, spare the dying, thaumaturgy*
1st level (4 slots): *command, detect evil and good, detect magic*
2nd level (3 slots): *lesser restoration, zone of truth*
3rd level (3 slots): *dispel magic, tongues*
4th level (3 slots): *banishment, freedom of movement*
5th level (2 slots): *flame strike, greater restoration*
6th level (1 slot): *heroes' feast*

ACTIONS

Multiattack. The sphinx makes two claw attacks.

Claw. *Melee Weapon Attack:* +12 to hit, reach 5 ft., one target.
Hit: 17 (2d10 + 6) slashing damage.

Roar (3/Day). The sphinx emits a magical roar. Each time it
roars before finishing a long rest, the roar is louder and the
effect is different, as detailed below. Each creature within
500 feet of the sphinx and able to hear the roar must make a
saving throw.

First Roar. Each creature that fails a DC 18 Wisdom saving
    throw is frightened for 1 minute. A frightened creature can
    repeat the saving throw at the end of each of its turns, ending
    the effect on itself on a success.
Second Roar. Each creature that fails a DC 18 Wisdom saving
    throw is deafened and frightened for 1 minute. A frightened
    creature is paralyzed and can repeat the saving throw at
    the end of each of its turns, ending the effect on itself on
    a success.
Third Roar. Each creature makes a DC 18 Constitution saving
    throw. On a failed save, a creature takes 44 (8d10) thunder
    damage and is knocked prone. On a successful save, the
    creature takes half as much damage and isn't knocked prone.

LEGENDARY ACTIONS

The sphinx can take 3 legendary actions, choosing from the
options below. Only one legendary action option can be used
at a time and only at the end of another creature's turn. The
sphinx regains spent legendary actions at the start of its turn.

Claw Attack. The sphinx makes one claw attack.
Teleport (Costs 2 Actions). The sphinx magically teleports,
    along with any equipment it is wearing or carrying, up to 120
    feet to an unoccupied space it can see.
Cast a Spell (Costs 3 Actions). The sphinx casts a spell from its
    list of prepared spells, using a spell slot as normal.

GYNOSPHINX

Large monstrosity, lawful neutral

Armor Class 17 (natural armor)
Hit Points 136 (16d10 + 48)
Speed 40 ft., fly 60 ft.

STR	DEX	CON	INT	WIS	CHA
18 (+4)	15 (+2)	16 (+3)	18 (+4)	18 (+4)	18 (+4)

Skills Arcana +12, History +12, Perception +8, Religion +8
Damage Resistances bludgeoning, piercing, and slashing from nonmagical attacks
Damage Immunities psychic
Condition Immunities charmed, frightened
Senses truesight 120 ft., passive Perception 18
Languages Common, Sphinx
Challenge 11 (7,200 XP)

Inscrutable. The sphinx is immune to any effect that would sense its emotions or read its thoughts, as well as any divination spell that it refuses. Wisdom (Insight) checks made to ascertain the sphinx's intentions or sincerity have disadvantage.

Magic Weapons. The sphinx's weapon attacks are magical.

Spellcasting. The sphinx is a 9th-level spellcaster. Its spellcasting ability is Intelligence (spell save DC 16, +8 to hit with spell attacks). It requires no material components to cast its spells. The sphinx has the following wizard spells prepared:

Cantrips (at will): *mage hand, minor illusion, prestidigitation*
1st level (4 slots): *detect magic, identify, shield*
2nd level (3 slots): *darkness, locate object, suggestion*
3rd level (3 slots): *dispel magic, remove curse, tongues*
4th level (3 slots): *banishment, greater invisibility*
5th level (1 slot): *legend lore*

ACTIONS

Multiattack. The sphinx makes two claw attacks.

Claw. *Melee Weapon Attack:* +8 to hit, reach 5 ft., one target. *Hit:* 13 (2d8 + 4) slashing damage.

LEGENDARY ACTIONS

The sphinx can take 3 legendary actions, choosing from the options below. Only one legendary action option can be used at a time and only at the end of another creature's turn. The sphinx regains spent legendary actions at the start of its turn.

Claw Attack. The sphinx makes one claw attack.
Teleport (Costs 2 Actions). The sphinx magically teleports, along with any equipment it is wearing or carrying, up to 120 feet to an unoccupied space it can see.
Cast a Spell (Costs 3 Actions). The sphinx casts a spell from its list of prepared spells, using a spell slot as normal.

Sprite

In secret groves and shaded glens, tiny sprites with dragonfly wings flutter. For all their fey splendor, however, sprites lack warmth and compassion. They are aggressive and hardy warriors, taking severe measures to ward strangers away from their homes. Interlopers that come too close have their moral character judged, then are put to sleep or frightened off.

Forest Protectors. Sprites build little villages in the boughs of trees and willing treants, in verdant glades brightened by moss, wild flowers, and toadstools. Wild nature thrives, and the sprites allow no trespassers. When intruders are spotted, the sprites lead them astray with ominous rustling from the bushes and distant snapping twigs. Creatures foolish enough to persist in intruding on a sprite's territory are stung with poisoned arrows and lulled into a senseless sleep. While they slumber, the sprites make good their escape, retreating to an even more secluded area of the forest.

Heart Seers. Sprites can sense whether a creature is good or evil by the sound and feeling of its beating heart. Weighing the balance of a creature's past actions, a sprite can tell whether its heart beats rapidly in love or flags in sorrow, or whether it is darkened by hate or greed. The sprite's power to perceive the heart always shows the truth, because the heart can't lie.

Poison Brewers. In their forest domains, sprites brew toxins, unguents, antidotes, and poisons, including the sleep poison with which they coat their arrows. They venture far into the woods to harvest rare flowers, mosses, and fungi, sometimes crossing dangerous territory to do so. If desperate, sprites even steal their ingredients from the gardens of hags.

Good-Hearted. Because they are judges of the heart and favor good creatures, sprites oppose the will of evil fey and pledge to thwart evil archfey at every turn. If they encounter adventurers on a quest to rid their forest of an evil fey creature or goblinoid menace, they will pledge their support and even come to their aid when the adventurers least expect it.

Unlike pixies, sprites rarely indulge in frivolous merriment and fun. They are firm warriors, protectors, and judges, and their stern bent causes other fey to consider them overly dour and serious. However, fey that respect the sprites' territory find them staunch allies in times of trouble.

> "THE TREE HAD A WEE VILLAGE NESTLED IN ITS BOUGHS, I SWEAR.
> NEXT THING I KNEW, I WAS LYIN' FACE-DOWN IN THE DIRT. MY
> HEAD WAS FULL OF STARS, AN' WHEN I STOOD UP AN' LOOKED
> AROUND, BOTH THE TREE AN' THE WEE VILLAGE WERE GONE."
> —TALE OF A HALF-ORC RANGER

Sprite
Tiny fey, neutral good

Armor Class 15 (leather armor)
Hit Points 2 (1d4)
Speed 10 ft., fly 40 ft.

STR	DEX	CON	INT	WIS	CHA
3 (−4)	18 (+4)	10 (+0)	14 (+2)	13 (+1)	11 (+0)

Skills Perception +3, Stealth +8
Senses passive Perception 13
Languages Common, Elvish, Sylvan
Challenge 1/4 (50 XP)

Actions

Longsword. *Melee Weapon Attack:* +2 to hit, reach 5 ft., one target. *Hit:* 1 slashing damage.

Shortbow. *Ranged Weapon Attack:* +6 to hit, range 40/160 ft., one target. *Hit:* 1 piercing damage, and the target must succeed on a DC 10 Constitution saving throw or become poisoned for 1 minute. If its saving throw result is 5 or lower, the poisoned target falls unconscious for the same duration, or until it takes damage or another creature takes an action to shake it awake.

Heart Sight. The sprite touches a creature and magically knows the creature's current emotional state. If the target fails a DC 10 Charisma saving throw, the sprite also knows the creature's alignment. Celestials, fiends, and undead automatically fail the saving throw.

Invisibility. The sprite magically turns invisible until it attacks or casts a spell, or until its concentration ends (as if concentrating on a spell). Any equipment the sprite wears or carries is invisible with it.

STIRGE

This horrid flying creature looks like a cross between a large bat and an oversized mosquito. Its legs end in sharp pincers, and its long, needle-like proboscis slashes the air as it seeks its next meal.

Stirges feed on the blood of living creatures, attaching and draining them slowly. Although they pose little danger in small numbers, packs of stirges can be a formidable threat, reattaching as quickly as their weakening prey can pluck them off.

Blood Drain. A stirge attacks by landing on a victim, finding a vulnerable spot, and plunging its proboscis into the flesh while using its pincer legs to latch on to the victim. Once the stirge has sated itself, it detaches and flies off to digest its meal.

STIRGE
Tiny beast, unaligned

Armor Class 14 (natural armor)
Hit Points 2 (1d4)
Speed 10 ft., fly 40 ft.

STR	DEX	CON	INT	WIS	CHA
4 (−3)	16 (+3)	11 (+0)	2 (−4)	8 (−1)	6 (−2)

Senses darkvision 60 ft., passive Perception 9
Languages —
Challenge 1/8 (25 XP)

ACTIONS

Blood Drain. *Melee Weapon Attack:* +5 to hit, reach 5 ft., one creature. *Hit:* 5 (1d4 + 3) piercing damage, and the stirge attaches to the target. While attached, the stirge doesn't attack. Instead, at the start of each of the stirge's turns, the target loses 5 (1d4 + 3) hit points due to blood loss.

The stirge can detach itself by spending 5 feet of its movement. It does so after it drains 10 hit points of blood from the target or the target dies. A creature, including the target, can use its action to detach the stirge.

SUCCUBUS/INCUBUS

Succubi and incubi inhabit all of the Lower Planes, and the lascivious dark-winged fiends can be found in service to devils, demons, night hags, rakshasas, and yugoloths. Asmodeus, ruler of the Nine Hells, uses these fiends to tempt mortals to perform evil acts. The demon lord Graz'zt keeps succubi and incubi as advisers and consorts.

Though legend speaks of them separately, any succubus can become an incubus, and vice versa. Most of these fiends do have a preference for one form or the other. Mortals only rarely see a succubus or incubus in its true form, however, for the fiend typically begins its corruption in veiled, insidious ways.

Beautiful Corrupters. A succubus or incubus first appears in ethereal form, passing through walls like a ghost to lurk next to a mortal's bedside and whisper forbidden pleasures. Sleeping victims are tempted to give in to their darkest desires, indulge in taboos, and feed forbidden appetites. As the fiend fills the victim's dreams with debauched images, the victim becomes more susceptible to temptation in everyday life.

Inevitably, the fiend enters the mortal realm in tempting form to directly influence a creature's actions. Appearing in the guise of a humanoid who has previously appeared only in the victim's dreams, the succubus or incubus seduces or befriends its victim, indulging all its desires so that it performs evil acts of its own free will.

A mortal bequeaths its soul to the fiend not by formal pledge or contract. Instead, when a succubus or incubus has corrupted a creature completely—some say by causing the victim to commit the three betrayals of thought, word, and deed—the victim's soul belongs to the fiend. The more virtuous the fiend's prey, the longer the corruption takes, but the more rewarding the downfall. After successfully corrupting a victim, the succubus or incubus kills it, and the tainted soul descends into the Lower Planes.

The succubus or incubus resorts to charming a victim magically only when necessary, usually as a form of self-defense. A charmed creature isn't responsible for its actions, so forcing it to behave against its will won't bring the fiend closer to the ultimate prize: the victim's soul.

Deadly Kiss. The kiss of a succubus or incubus is an echo of the emptiness that is the fiend's longing for a corrupted soul. Likewise, the recipient of the fiend's kiss gains no satisfaction from it, experiencing only pain and the profound emptiness that the fiend imparts. The kiss is nothing short of an attack, usually delivered as a final farewell before the fiend escapes.

Fiendish Offspring. Succubi and incubi can reproduce with one another to spawn more of their kind. Less commonly, a succubus or incubus reproduces with a humanoid. From this unholy union, a cambion child is conceived. Invariably, the fiendish offspring is as wicked as its fiendish parent.

Succubus/Incubus

Medium fiend (shapechanger), neutral evil

Armor Class 15 (natural armor)
Hit Points 66 (12d8 + 12)
Speed 30 ft., fly 60 ft.

STR	DEX	CON	INT	WIS	CHA
8 (−1)	17 (+3)	13 (+1)	15 (+2)	12 (+1)	20 (+5)

Skills Deception +9, Insight +5, Perception +5, Persuasion +9, Stealth +7
Damage Resistances cold, fire, lightning, poison; bludgeoning, piercing, and slashing from nonmagical attacks
Senses darkvision 60 ft., passive Perception 15
Languages Abyssal, Common, Infernal, telepathy 60 ft.
Challenge 4 (1,100 XP)

Telepathic Bond. The fiend ignores the range restriction on its telepathy when communicating with a creature it has charmed. The two don't even need to be on the same plane of existence.

Shapechanger. The fiend can use its action to polymorph into a Small or Medium humanoid, or back into its true form. Without wings, the fiend loses its flying speed. Other than its size and speed, its statistics are the same in each form. Any equipment it is wearing or carrying isn't transformed. It reverts to its true form if it dies.

Actions

Claw (Fiend Form Only). *Melee Weapon Attack:* +5 to hit, reach 5 ft., one target. *Hit:* 6 (1d6 + 3) slashing damage.

Charm. One humanoid the fiend can see within 30 feet of it must succeed on a DC 15 Wisdom saving throw or be magically charmed for 1 day. The charmed target obeys the fiend's verbal or telepathic commands. If the target suffers any harm or receives a suicidal command, it can repeat the saving throw, ending the effect on a success. If the target successfully saves against the effect, or if the effect on it ends, the target is immune to this fiend's Charm for the next 24 hours.

   The fiend can have only one target charmed at a time. If it charms another, the effect on the previous target ends.

Draining Kiss. The fiend kisses a creature charmed by it or a willing creature. The target must make a DC 15 Constitution saving throw against this magic, taking 32 (5d10 + 5) psychic damage on a failed save, or half as much damage on a successful one. The target's hit point maximum is reduced by an amount equal to the damage taken. This reduction lasts until the target finishes a long rest. The target dies if this effect reduces its hit point maximum to 0.

Etherealness. The fiend magically enters the Ethereal Plane from the Material Plane, or vice versa.

S

Tarrasque

The legendary tarrasque is possibly the most dreaded monster of the Material Plane. It is widely believed that only one of these creatures exists, though no one can predict where and when it will strike.

A scaly biped, the tarrasque is fifty feet tall and seventy feet long, weighing hundreds of tons. It carries itself like a bird of prey, leaning forward and using its powerful lashing tail for balance. Its cavernous maw yawns wide enough to swallow all but the largest creatures, and so great is its hunger that it can devour the populations of whole towns.

Legendary Destruction. The destructive potential of the tarrasque is so vast that some cultures incorporate the monster into religious doctrine, weaving its sporadic appearance into stories of divine judgment and wrath. Legends tell how the tarrasque slumbers in its secret lair beneath the earth, remaining in a dormant state for decades or centuries. When it awakens in answer to some inscrutable cosmic call, it rises from the depths to obliterate everything in its path.

Tarrasque
Gargantuan monstrosity (titan), unaligned

Armor Class 25 (natural armor)
Hit Points 676 (33d20 + 330)
Speed 40 ft.

STR	DEX	CON	INT	WIS	CHA
30 (+10)	11 (+0)	30 (+10)	3 (–4)	11 (+0)	11 (+0)

Saving Throws Int +5, Wis +9, Cha +9
Damage Immunities fire, poison; bludgeoning, piercing, and slashing from nonmagical attacks
Condition Immunities charmed, frightened, paralyzed, poisoned
Senses blindsight 120 ft., passive Perception 10
Languages —
Challenge 30 (155,000 XP)

Legendary Resistance (3/Day). If the tarrasque fails a saving throw, it can choose to succeed instead.

Magic Resistance. The tarrasque has advantage on saving throws against spells and other magical effects.

Reflective Carapace. Any time the tarrasque is targeted by a *magic missile* spell, a line spell, or a spell that requires a ranged attack roll, roll a d6. On a 1 to 5, the tarrasque is unaffected. On a 6, the tarrasque is unaffected, and the effect is reflected back at the caster as though it originated from the tarrasque, turning the caster into the target.

Siege Monster. The tarrasque deals double damage to objects and structures.

Actions

Multiattack. The tarrasque can use its Frightful Presence. It then makes five attacks: one with its bite, two with its claws, one with its horns, and one with its tail. It can use its Swallow instead of its bite.

Bite. *Melee Weapon Attack:* +19 to hit, reach 10 ft., one target. *Hit:* 36 (4d12 + 10) piercing damage. If the target is a creature, it is grappled (escape DC 20). Until this grapple ends, the target is restrained, and the tarrasque can't bite another target.

Claw. *Melee Weapon Attack:* +19 to hit, reach 15 ft., one target. *Hit:* 28 (4d8 + 10) slashing damage.

Horns. *Melee Weapon Attack:* +19 to hit, reach 10 ft., one target. *Hit:* 32 (4d10 + 10) piercing damage.

Tail. *Melee Weapon Attack:* +19 to hit, reach 20 ft., one target. *Hit:* 24 (4d6 + 10) bludgeoning damage. If the target is a creature, it must succeed on a DC 20 Strength saving throw or be knocked prone.

Frightful Presence. Each creature of the tarrasque's choice within 120 feet of it and aware of it must succeed on a DC 17 Wisdom saving throw or become frightened for 1 minute. A creature can repeat the saving throw at the end of each of its turns, with disadvantage if the tarrasque is within line of sight, ending the effect on itself on a success. If a creature's saving throw is successful or the effect ends for it, the creature is immune to the tarrasque's Frightful Presence for the next 24 hours.

Swallow. The tarrasque makes one bite attack against a Large or smaller creature it is grappling. If the attack hits, the target takes the bite's damage, the target is swallowed, and the grapple ends. While swallowed, the creature is blinded and restrained, it has total cover against attacks and other effects outside the tarrasque, and it takes 56 (16d6) acid damage at the start of each of the tarrasque's turns.

If the tarrasque takes 60 damage or more on a single turn from a creature inside it, the tarrasque must succeed on a DC 20 Constitution saving throw at the end of that turn or regurgitate all swallowed creatures, which fall prone in a space within 10 feet of the tarrasque. If the tarrasque dies, a swallowed creature is no longer restrained by it and can escape from the corpse by using 30 feet of movement, exiting prone.

Legendary Actions

The tarrasque can take 3 legendary actions, choosing from the options below. Only one legendary action option can be used at a time and only at the end of another creature's turn. The tarrasque regains spent legendary actions at the start of its turn.

Attack. The tarrasque makes one claw attack or tail attack.
Move. The tarrasque moves up to half its speed.
Chomp (Costs 2 Actions). The tarrasque makes one bite attack or uses its Swallow.

THRI-KREEN

Thri-kreen wander the deserts and savannas of the world, avoiding all other races.

Thri-Kreen Communication. Thri-kreen employ a language without words. To show emotion and reaction, a thri-kreen clacks its mandibles and waves its antennae, giving other thri-kreen a sense of what it is thinking and feeling. Other creatures find this manner of communication difficult to interpret and impossible to duplicate.

When forced to interact with creatures of other intelligent species, thri-kreen employ alternative methods of communication, such as drawing pictures in sand or making pictures out of twigs or blades of grass.

Limited Emotions. Thri-kreen experience the full range of emotions but aren't as prone to emotional outbursts as humans. Thri-kreen with psionic ability often demonstrate a wider range of emotions, particularly if they live near or interact with humans or other highly emotional creatures.

Isolationists and Wanderers. Thri-kreen consider all other living creatures as potential nourishment, and they love the taste of elf flesh in particular. If a creature might be useful for something other than food, the thri-kreen aren't likely to attack it on sight. Thri-kreen kill to survive, never for sport.

Sleepless. Thri-kreen don't require sleep and can rest while remaining alert and performing light tasks. Their inability to sleep is thought to be the reason why thri-kreen have such short lifespans, the average thri-kreen life expectancy being only thirty years.

THRI-KREEN

Medium humanoid (thri-kreen), chaotic neutral

Armor Class 15 (natural armor)
Hit Points 33 (6d8 + 6)
Speed 40 ft.

STR	DEX	CON	INT	WIS	CHA
12 (+1)	15 (+2)	13 (+1)	8 (−1)	12 (+1)	7 (−2)

Skills Perception +3, Stealth +4, Survival +3
Senses darkvision 60 ft., passive Perception 13
Languages Thri-kreen
Challenge 1 (200 XP)

Chameleon Carapace. The thri-kreen can change the color of its carapace to match the color and texture of its surroundings. As a result, it has advantage on Dexterity (Stealth) checks made to hide.

Standing Leap. The thri-kreen's long jump is up to 30 feet and its high jump is up to 15 feet, with or without a running start.

ACTIONS

Multiattack. The thri-kreen makes two attacks: one with its bite and one with its claws.

Bite. *Melee Weapon Attack:* +3 to hit, reach 5 ft., one creature. *Hit:* 4 (1d6 + 1) piercing damage, and the target must succeed on a DC 11 Constitution saving throw or be poisoned for 1 minute. If the saving throw fails by 5 or more, the target is also paralyzed while poisoned in this way. The poisoned target can repeat the saving throw on each of its turns, ending the effect on itself on a success.

Claws. *Melee Weapon Attack:* +3 to hit, reach 5 ft., one target. *Hit:* 6 (2d4 + 1) slashing damage.

TREANT

Treants are awakened trees that dwell in ancient forests. Although treants prefer to while away the days, months, and years in quiet contemplation, they fiercely protect their woodland demesnes from outside threats.

The Sleeping Tree Awakens. A tree destined to become a treant meditates through a long cycle of seasons, living normally for decades or centuries before realizing its potential. Trees that awaken do so only under special circumstances and in places steeped with nature's magic. Treants and powerful druids can sense when a tree has the spark of potential, and they protect such trees in secret groves as they draw near the moment of their awakening. During the long process of awakening, a tree acquires face-like features in its bark, a division of the lower trunk into legs, and long branches bending downward to serve as its arms. When it is ready, the tree pulls its legs free from the clutching earth and joins its fellows in protecting its woodland home.

Legendary Guardians. After a treant awakens, it continues to grow exactly as it did when it was a tree. Treants created from the mightiest trees can reach great sizes while developing an innate magical power over plants and animals. Such treants can animate plants, using them to ensnare and trap intruders. They can call wild creatures to aid them or carry messages across great distances.

Protectors of the Wild. Even after awakening, a treant spends much of its time living as a tree. While rooted in place, a treant remains aware of its surroundings, and can perceive the effects of events taking place miles away based on subtle changes nearby.

Woodcutters who avoid culling healthy living trees and hunters who take only what they need of the forest's bounty are unlikely to arouse a treant's ire. Creatures careless with fire, those who poison the forest, and those who destroy great trees, especially a tree close to awakening, face the treant's wrath.

TREANT
Huge plant, chaotic good

Armor Class 16 (natural armor)
Hit Points 138 (12d12 + 60)
Speed 30 ft.

STR	DEX	CON	INT	WIS	CHA
23 (+6)	8 (−1)	21 (+5)	12 (+1)	16 (+3)	12 (+1)

Damage Vulnerabilities fire
Damage Resistances bludgeoning, piercing
Senses passive Perception 13
Languages Common, Druidic, Elvish, Sylvan
Challenge 9 (5,000 XP)

False Appearance. While the treant remains motionless, it is indistinguishable from a normal tree.

Siege Monster. The treant deals double damage to objects and structures.

ACTIONS

Multiattack. The treant makes two slam attacks.

Slam. *Melee Weapon Attack:* +10 to hit, reach 5 ft., one target. *Hit:* 16 (3d6 + 6) bludgeoning damage.

Rock. *Ranged Weapon Attack:* +10 to hit, range 60/180 ft., one target. *Hit:* 28 (4d10 + 6) bludgeoning damage.

Animate Trees (1/Day). The treant magically animates one or two trees it can see within 60 feet of it. These trees have the same statistics as a treant, except they have Intelligence and Charisma scores of 1, they can't speak, and they have only the Slam action option. An animated tree acts as an ally of the treant. The tree remains animate for 1 day or until it dies; until the treant dies or is more than 120 feet from the tree; or until the treant takes a bonus action to turn it back into an inanimate tree. The tree then takes root if possible.

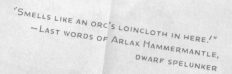
intelligent creatures weaker than themselves and show no mercy toward those they capture and drag back to their lairs to be devoured. The largest and toughest troglodytes lead the hunt and become the leaders of their tribes. However, if a leader shows any weakness or hesitation, other troglodytes attack and eat it in a frenzy.

Troglodytes make little and build less, scavenging their possessions from their prey. They understand the value of metal weapons and armor, and fight among one another for the right to have such items. A troglodyte tribe might be torn apart by battles over a single longsword.

Devotees of Laogzed. Some troglodytes venerate Laogzed, a demonic, monstrously fat toad-lizard that slumbers in the Abyss. Laogzed offers the troglodytes nothing in return except aspiration, for it is the dream of his troglodyte worshipers to become as fat, well-fed, and wearily content as he seems to be.

TROGLODYTE

Medium humanoid (troglodyte), chaotic evil

Armor Class 11 (natural armor)
Hit Points 13 (2d8 + 4)
Speed 30 ft.

STR	DEX	CON	INT	WIS	CHA
14 (+2)	10 (+0)	14 (+2)	6 (−2)	10 (+0)	6 (−2)

Skills Stealth +2
Senses darkvision 60 ft., passive Perception 10
Languages Troglodyte
Challenge 1/4 (50 XP)

Chameleon Skin. The troglodyte has advantage on Dexterity (Stealth) checks made to hide.

Stench. Any creature other than a troglodyte that starts its turn within 5 feet of the troglodyte must succeed on a DC 12 Constitution saving throw or be poisoned until the start of the creature's next turn. On a successful saving throw, the creature is immune to the stench of all troglodytes for 1 hour.

Sunlight Sensitivity. While in sunlight, the troglodyte has disadvantage on attack rolls, as well as on Wisdom (Perception) checks that rely on sight.

ACTIONS

Multiattack. The troglodyte makes three attacks: one with its bite and two with its claws.

Bite. *Melee Weapon Attack:* +4 to hit, reach 5 ft., one target. *Hit:* 4 (1d4 + 2) piercing damage.

Claw. *Melee Weapon Attack:* +4 to hit, reach 5 ft., one target. *Hit:* 4 (1d4 + 2) slashing damage.

TROGLODYTE

The savage, degenerate troglodytes squat in the shallow depths of the Underdark in a constant state of war against their neighbors and one another. They mark the borders of their territories with cracked bones and skulls, or with pictographs painted in blood or dung.

Perhaps the most loathsome of all humanoids, troglodytes eat anything they can stomach. They dwell in filth. The walls of their cavern homes are smeared with grime, oily secretions, and the debris of their foul feasting.

Simpleminded Brutes. Troglodytes have a simple, communal culture devoted almost entirely to procuring food. Too simple to plan more than a few days into the future, troglodytes rely on constant raids and hunting to survive. They take sadistic pleasure in hunting

Troll

Born with horrific appetites, trolls eat anything they can catch and devour. They have no society to speak of, but they do serve as mercenaries to orcs, ogres, ettins, hags, and giants. As payment, trolls demand food and treasure. Trolls are difficult to control, however, doing as they please even when working with more powerful creatures.

Regeneration. Smashing a troll's bones and slashing through its rubbery hide only makes it angry. A troll's wounds close quickly. If the monster loses an arm, a leg, or even its head, those dismembered parts can sometimes act with a life of their own. A troll can even reattach severed body parts, untroubled by its momentary disability. Only acid and fire can arrest the regenerative properties of a troll's flesh. The trolls, enraged, will attack individuals making acid and fire attacks against them above all other prey.

Troll Freaks. Their regenerative capabilities make trolls especially susceptible to mutation. Although uncommon, such transformations can result from what the troll has done or what has been done to it. A decapitated troll might grow two heads from the stump of its neck, while a troll that eats a fey creature might gain one or more of that creature's traits.

Variant: Loathsome Limbs

Some trolls have the following trait.

Loathsome Limbs. Whenever the troll takes at least 15 slashing damage at one time, roll a d20 to determine what else happens to it:

1–10: Nothing else happens.
11–14: One leg is severed from the troll if it has any legs left.
15–18: One arm is severed from the troll if it has any arms left.
19–20: The troll is decapitated, but the troll dies only if it can't regenerate. If it dies, so does the severed head.

If the troll finishes a short or long rest without reattaching a severed limb or head, the part regrows. At that point, the severed part dies. Until then, a severed part acts on the troll's initiative and has its own action and movement. A severed part has AC 13, 10 hit points, and the troll's Regeneration trait.

A **severed leg** is unable to attack and has a speed of 5 feet.

A **severed arm** has a speed of 5 feet and can make one claw attack on its turn, with disadvantage on the attack roll unless the troll can see the arm and its target. Each time the troll loses an arm, it loses a claw attack.

If its head is severed, the troll loses its bite attack and its body is blinded unless the head can see it. The **severed head** has a speed of 0 feet and the troll's Keen Smell trait. It can make a bite attack but only against a target in its space.

The troll's speed is halved if it's missing a leg. If it loses both legs, it falls prone. If it has both arms, it can crawl. With only one arm, it can still crawl, but its speed is halved. With no arms or legs, its speed is 0, and it can't benefit from bonuses to speed.

Troll
Large giant, chaotic evil

Armor Class 15 (natural armor)
Hit Points 84 (8d10 + 40)
Speed 30 ft.

STR	DEX	CON	INT	WIS	CHA
18 (+4)	13 (+1)	20 (+5)	7 (−2)	9 (−1)	7 (−2)

Skills Perception +2
Senses darkvision 60 ft., passive Perception 12
Languages Giant
Challenge 5 (1,800 XP)

Keen Smell. The troll has advantage on Wisdom (Perception) checks that rely on smell.

Regeneration. The troll regains 10 hit points at the start of its turn. If the troll takes acid or fire damage, this trait doesn't function at the start of the troll's next turn. The troll dies only if it starts its turn with 0 hit points and doesn't regenerate.

Actions

Multiattack. The troll makes three attacks: one with its bite and two with its claws.

Bite. *Melee Weapon Attack:* +7 to hit, reach 5 ft., one target. *Hit:* 7 (1d6 + 4) piercing damage.

Claw. *Melee Weapon Attack:* +7 to hit, reach 5 ft., one target. *Hit:* 11 (2d6 + 4) slashing damage.

"The wall caved in. That's the last thing I remember."
—A survivor's account of an umber hulk attack

U

Umber Hulk

An abominable horror from deep beneath the earth, an umber hulk burrows into cave complexes, dungeons, or Underdark settlements in search of food. Those lucky enough to survive an umber hulk attack often remember precious little of the incident, thanks to the umber hulk's mind-scrambling gaze.

Devious Delvers. Umber hulks can burrow through solid rock, forming new tunnels in their wake. The steel-hard chitin of its body can withstand the cave-ins, tunnel collapses, and rock falls that commonly follow it.

Burrowing into the wall of a cavern or passageway, an umber hulk lies in wait for creatures to pass by on the other side, its hair-like feelers sensing any movement around it. When it explodes out in a shower of earth and rock, its unsuspecting quarry turns to face the oncoming threat—and is entranced by the umber hulk's bewildering eyes, forced to stand helpless as its mandibles snap shut.

Mind Scrambler. Many survivors of an umber hulk encounter recollect little about the attack, because the monster's confusing gaze scrambles their memory of the event. Those who have fought and killed umber hulks recognize the signs. For other denizens of the Underdark, grisly tales of vanished explorers and wanton destruction speak of an unknown foe. Umber hulks take on supernatural status in these harrowing stories, many of which convey the same warning: once an umber hulk has been spotted, it is already too late to escape it.

Umber Hulk
Large monstrosity, chaotic evil

Armor Class 18 (natural armor)
Hit Points 93 (11d10 + 33)
Speed 30 ft., burrow 20 ft.

STR	DEX	CON	INT	WIS	CHA
20 (+5)	13 (+1)	16 (+3)	9 (−1)	10 (+0)	10 (+0)

Senses darkvision 120 ft., tremorsense 60 ft., passive Perception 10
Languages Umber Hulk
Challenge 5 (1,800 XP)

Confusing Gaze. When a creature starts its turn within 30 feet of the umber hulk and is able to see the umber hulk's eyes, the umber hulk can magically force it to make a DC 15 Charisma saving throw, unless the umber hulk is incapacitated.

On a failed saving throw, the creature can't take reactions until the start of its next turn and rolls a d8 to determine what it does during that turn. On a 1 to 4, the creature does nothing. On a 5 or 6, the creature takes no action but uses all its movement to move in a random direction. On a 7 or 8, the creature makes one melee attack against a random creature, or it does nothing if no creature is within reach.

Unless surprised, a creature can avert its eyes to avoid the saving throw at the start of its turn. If the creature does so, it can't see the umber hulk until the start of its next turn, when it can avert its eyes again. If the creature looks at the umber hulk in the meantime, it must immediately make the save.

Tunneler. The umber hulk can burrow through solid rock at half its burrowing speed and leaves a 5 foot-wide, 8-foot-high tunnel in its wake.

Actions

Multiattack. The umber hulk makes three attacks: two with its claws and one with its mandibles.

Claw. *Melee Weapon Attack:* +8 to hit, reach 5 ft., one target. *Hit:* 9 (1d8 + 5) slashing damage.

Mandibles. *Melee Weapon Attack:* +8 to hit, reach 5 ft., one target. *Hit:* 14 (2d8 + 5) slashing damage.

Unicorn

Unicorns dwell in enchanted forests. Unrelated to the horses it resembles, a unicorn is a celestial creature that wanders sylvan realms, its white form glimmering like starlight.

A unicorn's brow sports a single spiraling horn of ivory whose magical touch can heal the sick and the injured. Its ears catch the words and whispers of the creatures that share its domain, and it knows the tongues of elves and sylvan folk. Unicorns allow good-hearted creatures to enter their woods to hunt or gather food, but they hold evil ever at bay. Foul-hearted creatures seldom leave a unicorn's domain alive.

Divine Guardians. Good deities placed unicorns on the Material Plane to ward away evil and preserve and protect sacred places. Most unicorns protect a bounded realm such as an enchanted forest. However, the gods sometimes send a unicorn to guard sacred artifacts or protect specific creatures. When the forces of darkness strike against an individual the gods wish to protect, they might send that individual to a unicorn's forest, where evil creatures pursue at their peril.

Unicorns most often serve deities of the forest and woodlands, including the gods of benevolent fey. Although all unicorns have natural healing power, some serve the gods in greater capacities, performing miracles normally reserved for high priests.

Forest Lords. A unicorn's forest is a celestial realm where nothing that occurs beneath the sun-dappled leaves escapes the creature's notice. A unicorn hears each breathy tune sung by the elves that reside amid the treetops. It senses where every caterpillar spins its cocoon, each leaf and branch upon which a bright butterfly rests its tired wings.

In a unicorn's forest, a sense of calm pervades. From wolves and foxes to birds, squirrels, and tiny insects, the creatures of a unicorn's domain seem quite tame. Pixies, sprites, satyrs, dryads, and other normally mercurial fey loyally serve a unicorn when they dwell within its woods. Under a unicorn's protection, creatures feel safe from the threat of encroaching civilization and the insidious spread of evil.

A unicorn roams its domain constantly, moving ever so carefully so as not to disturb other denizens. A creature might catch a passing glimpse of the unicorn then suddenly see nothing but the wild woods.

Sacred Horns. A unicorn's horn is the focus of its power, a shard of divine magic wrought in spiraling ivory. Wands of unicorn horn channel powerful magic, while unicorn horn weapons strike with divine force. Wizards can work powdered unicorn horn into potent potions and scroll ink, or use it as a component in eldritch rituals. However, any creature that takes a role, no matter how small, in slaying a unicorn is likely to become the target of divine retribution.

Blessed Mounts. When darkness and evil threaten to overwhelm the mortal world, the gods sometimes see fit to pair a unicorn mount with a champion. A paladin astride a unicorn is a sign of the gods' direct intervention in the affairs of the mortal realm. It is a holy alliance made to cleave the heads from demons and banish devils back to the Nine Hells.

As long as the troubled times of darkness persist, the unicorn stays by the champion, its horn shining brightly to drive back the night. However, if the gods' champion falls from grace or turns from the cause of righteousness and good, the unicorn departs, never to return.

A Unicorn's Lair

A unicorn's lair might be an ancient ruin overgrown with vines, a misty clearing surrounded by mighty oaks, a flower-covered hilltop alive with butterflies, or some other serene woodland location.

Regional Effects

Transformed by the creature's celestial presence, the domain of a unicorn might include any of the following magical effects:

- Open flames of a nonmagical nature are extinguished within the unicorn's domain. Torches and campfires refuse to burn, but closed lanterns are unaffected.
- Creatures native to the unicorn's domain have an easier time hiding; they have advantage on all Dexterity (Stealth) checks made to hide.
- When a good-aligned creature casts a spell or uses a magical effect that causes another good-aligned creature to regain hit points, the target regains the maximum number of hit points possible for the spell or effect.
- Curses affecting any good-aligned creature are suppressed.

If the unicorn dies, these effects end immediately.

Unicorn

Large celestial, lawful good

Armor Class 12
Hit Points 67 (9d10 + 18)
Speed 50 ft.

STR	DEX	CON	INT	WIS	CHA
18 (+4)	14 (+2)	15 (+2)	11 (+0)	17 (+3)	16 (+3)

Damage Immunities poison
Condition Immunities charmed, paralyzed, poisoned
Senses darkvision 60 ft., passive Perception 13
Languages Celestial, Elvish, Sylvan, telepathy 60 ft.
Challenge 5 (1,800 XP)

Charge. If the unicorn moves at least 20 feet straight toward a target and then hits it with a horn attack on the same turn, the target takes an extra 9 (2d8) piercing damage. If the target is a creature, it must succeed on a DC 15 Strength saving throw or be knocked prone.

Innate Spellcasting. The unicorn's innate spellcasting ability is Charisma (spell save DC 14). The unicorn can innately cast the following spells, requiring no components:

At will: *detect evil and good, druidcraft, pass without trace*
1/day each: *calm emotions, dispel evil and good, entangle*

Magic Resistance. The unicorn has advantage on saving throws against spells and other magical effects.

Magic Weapons. The unicorn's weapon attacks are magical.

Actions

Multiattack. The unicorn makes two attacks: one with its hooves and one with its horn.

Hooves. *Melee Weapon Attack:* +7 to hit, reach 5 ft., one target. *Hit:* 11 (2d6 + 4) bludgeoning damage.

Horn. *Melee Weapon Attack:* +7 to hit, reach 5 ft., one target. *Hit:* 8 (1d8 + 4) piercing damage.

Healing Touch (3/Day). The unicorn touches another creature with its horn. The target magically regains 11 (2d8 + 2) hit points. In addition, the touch removes all diseases and neutralizes all poisons afflicting the target.

Teleport (1/Day). The unicorn magically teleports itself and up to three willing creatures it can see within 5 feet of it, along with any equipment they are wearing or carrying, to a location the unicorn is familiar with, up to 1 mile away.

Legendary Actions

The unicorn can take 3 legendary actions, choosing from the options below. Only one legendary action option can be used at a time and only at the end of another creature's turn. The unicorn regains spent legendary actions at the start of its turn.

Hooves. The unicorn makes one attack with its hooves.
Shimmering Shield (Costs 2 Actions). The unicorn creates a shimmering, magical field around itself or another creature it can see within 60 feet of it. The target gains a +2 bonus to AC until the end of the unicorn's next turn.
Heal Self (Costs 3 Actions). The unicorn magically regains 11 (2d8 + 2) hit points.

Vampires

Awakened to an endless night, vampires hunger for the life they have lost and sate that hunger by drinking the blood of the living. Vampires abhor sunlight, for its touch burns them. They never cast shadows or reflections, and any vampire wishing to move unnoticed among the living keeps to the darkness and far from reflective surfaces.

Dark Desires. Whether or not a vampire retains any memories from its former life, its emotional attachments wither as once-pure feelings become twisted by undeath. Love turns into hungry obsession, while friendship becomes bitter jealousy. In place of emotion, vampires pursue physical symbols of what they crave, so that a vampire seeking love might fixate on a young beauty. A child might become an object of fascination for a vampire obsessed with youth and potential. Others surround themselves with art, books, or sinister items such as torture devices or trophies from creatures they have killed.

Born from Death. Most of a vampire's victims become vampire spawn—ravenous creatures with a vampire's hunger for blood, but under the control of the vampire that created them. If a true vampire allows a spawn to draw blood from its own body, the spawn transforms into a true vampire no longer under its master's control. Few vampires are willing to relinquish their control in this manner. Vampire spawn become free-willed when their creator dies.

Chained to the Grave. Every vampire remains bound to its coffin, crypt, or grave site, where it must rest by day. If a vampire didn't receive a formal burial, it must lie beneath a foot of earth at the place of its transition to undeath. A vampire can move its place of burial by transporting its coffin or a significant amount of grave dirt to another location. Some vampires set up multiple resting places this way.

Undead Nature. Neither a vampire nor a vampire spawn requires air.

"I am The Ancient, I am The Land. My beginnings are lost in the darkness of the past. I was the warrior, I was good and just. I thundered across the land like the wrath of a just god, but the war years and the killing years wore down my soul as the wind wears down stone into sand."
—Count Strahd von Zarovich

Player Characters as Vampires

The game statistics of a player character transformed into a vampire spawn and then a vampire don't change, except that the character's Strength, Dexterity, and Constitution scores become 18 if they aren't higher. In addition, the character gains the vampire's damage resistances, darkvision, traits, and actions. Attack and damage rolls for the vampire's attacks are based on Strength. The save DC for Charm is 8 + the vampire's proficiency bonus + the vampire's Charisma modifier. The character's alignment becomes lawful evil, and the DM might take control of the character until the vampirism is reversed with a *wish* spell or the character is killed and brought back to life.

STRAHD VON ZAROVICH

A brilliant thinker and capable warrior in life, Strahd von Zarovich fought in countless battles for his people. When war and killing finally stripped him of his youth and strength, he settled in the remote valley of Barovia and built a castle on a towering pinnacle, from which he could survey his lands. His brother Sergei came to live with him in Castle Ravenloft, becoming Strahd's adviser and constant companion.

In his brother, Strahd saw everything he had lost. Sergei was handsome and young, while Strahd had become old and scarred. Resentment colored their relationship, eventually turning into hatred. Strahd's beloved, Tatyana, spurned him for Sergei, whom she pledged to marry.

In a desperate attempt to win Tatyana's heart, Strahd forged a pact with dark powers that made him immortal. At the wedding of Sergei and Tatyana, he confronted his brother and killed him. Tatyana fled and flung herself from Ravenloft's walls. Strahd's guards, seeing him for a monster, shot him with arrows. But he did not die. He became a vampire—the first vampire, according to many sages.

In the centuries since his transformation, Strahd's lust for life and youth have only grown. He broods in his dark castle, cursing the living for stealing away what he lost, and never admitting his hand in the tragedy he created.

A Vampire's Lair

A vampire chooses a grand yet defensible location for its lair, such as a castle, fortified manor, or walled abbey. It hides its coffin in an underground crypt or vault guarded by vampire spawn or other loyal creatures of the night.

Regional Effects

The region surrounding a vampire's lair is warped by the creature's unnatural presence, creating any of the following effects:

- There's a noticeable increase in the populations of bats, rats, and wolves in the region.
- Plants within 500 feet of the lair wither, and their stems and branches become twisted and thorny.
- Shadows cast within 500 feet of the lair seem abnormally gaunt and sometimes move as though alive.
- A creeping fog clings to the ground within 500 feet of the vampire's lair. The fog occasionally takes eerie forms, such as grasping claws and writhing serpents.

If the vampire is destroyed, these effects end after 2d6 days.

Vampire

Medium undead (shapechanger), lawful evil

Armor Class 16 (natural armor)
Hit Points 144 (17d8 + 68)
Speed 30 ft.

STR	DEX	CON	INT	WIS	CHA
18 (+4)	18 (+4)	18 (+4)	17 (+3)	15 (+2)	18 (+4)

Saving Throws Dex +9, Wis +7, Cha +9
Skills Perception +7, Stealth +9
Damage Resistances necrotic; bludgeoning, piercing, and slashing from nonmagical attacks
Senses darkvision 120 ft., passive Perception 17
Languages the languages it knew in life
Challenge 13 (10,000 XP)

Shapechanger. If the vampire isn't in sunlight or running water, it can use its action to polymorph into a Tiny bat or a Medium cloud of mist, or back into its true form.

While in bat form, the vampire can't speak, its walking speed is 5 feet, and it has a flying speed of 30 feet. Its statistics, other than its size and speed, are unchanged. Anything it is wearing transforms with it, but nothing it is carrying does. It reverts to its true form if it dies.

While in mist form, the vampire can't take any actions, speak, or manipulate objects. It is weightless, has a flying speed of 20 feet, can hover, and can enter a hostile creature's space and stop there. In addition, if air can pass through a space, the mist can do so without squeezing, and it can't pass through water. It has advantage on Strength, Dexterity, and Constitution saving throws, and it is immune to all nonmagical damage, except the damage it takes from sunlight.

Legendary Resistance (3/Day). If the vampire fails a saving throw, it can choose to succeed instead.

Misty Escape. When it drops to 0 hit points outside its resting place, the vampire transforms into a cloud of mist (as in the Shapechanger trait) instead of falling unconscious, provided that it isn't in sunlight or running water. If it can't transform, it is destroyed.

While it has 0 hit points in mist form, it can't revert to its vampire form, and it must reach its resting place within 2 hours or be destroyed. Once in its resting place, it reverts to its vampire form. It is then paralyzed until it regains at least 1 hit point. After spending 1 hour in its resting place with 0 hit points, it regains 1 hit point.

Regeneration. The vampire regains 20 hit points at the start of its turn if it has at least 1 hit point and isn't in sunlight or running water. If the vampire takes radiant damage or damage from holy water, this trait doesn't function at the start of the vampire's next turn.

Spider Climb. The vampire can climb difficult surfaces, including upside down on ceilings, without needing to make an ability check.

Vampire Weaknesses. The vampire has the following flaws:

Forbiddance. The vampire can't enter a residence without an invitation from one of the occupants.

Harmed by Running Water. The vampire takes 20 acid damage if it ends its turn in running water.

Stake to the Heart. If a piercing weapon made of wood is driven into the vampire's heart while the vampire is incapacitated in its resting place, the vampire is paralyzed until the stake is removed.

Sunlight Hypersensitivity. The vampire takes 20 radiant damage when it starts its turn in sunlight. While in sunlight, it has disadvantage on attack rolls and ability checks.

Actions

Multiattack (Vampire Form Only). The vampire makes two attacks, only one of which can be a bite attack.

Unarmed Strike (Vampire Form Only). *Melee Weapon Attack:* +9 to hit, reach 5 ft., one creature. *Hit:* 8 (1d8 + 4) bludgeoning damage. Instead of dealing damage, the vampire can grapple the target (escape DC 18).

Bite (Bat or Vampire Form Only). *Melee Weapon Attack:* +9 to hit, reach 5 ft., one willing creature, or a creature that is grappled by the vampire, incapacitated, or restrained. *Hit:* 7 (1d6 + 4) piercing damage plus 10 (3d6) necrotic damage. The target's hit point maximum is reduced by an amount equal to the necrotic damage taken, and the vampire regains hit points equal to that amount. The reduction lasts until the target finishes a long rest. The target dies if this effect reduces its hit point maximum to 0. A humanoid slain in this way and then buried in the ground rises the following night as a vampire spawn under the vampire's control.

Charm. The vampire targets one humanoid it can see within 30 feet of it. If the target can see the vampire, the target must succeed on a DC 17 Wisdom saving throw against this magic or be charmed by the vampire. The charmed target regards the vampire as a trusted friend to be heeded and protected. Although the target isn't under the vampire's control, it takes the vampire's requests or actions in the most favorable way it can, and it is a willing target for the vampire's bite attack.

Each time the vampire or the vampire's companions do anything harmful to the target, it can repeat the saving throw, ending the effect on itself on a success. Otherwise, the effect lasts 24 hours or until the vampire is destroyed, is on a different plane of existence than the target, or takes a bonus action to end the effect.

Children of the Night (1/Day). The vampire magically calls 2d4 swarms of bats or rats, provided that the sun isn't up. While outdoors, the vampire can call 3d6 wolves instead. The called creatures arrive in 1d4 rounds, acting as allies of the vampire and obeying its spoken commands. The beasts remain for 1 hour, until the vampire dies, or until the vampire dismisses them as a bonus action.

Legendary Actions

The vampire can take 3 legendary actions, choosing from the options below. Only one legendary action option can be used at a time and only at the end of another creature's turn. The vampire regains spent legendary actions at the start of its turn.

Move. The vampire moves up to its speed without provoking opportunity attacks.
Unarmed Strike. The vampire makes one unarmed strike.
Bite (Costs 2 Actions). The vampire makes one bite attack.

VAMPIRE SPAWN
Medium undead, neutral evil

Armor Class 15 (natural armor)
Hit Points 82 (11d8 + 33)
Speed 30 ft.

STR	DEX	CON	INT	WIS	CHA
16 (+3)	16 (+3)	16 (+3)	11 (+0)	10 (+0)	12 (+1)

Saving Throws Dex +6, Wis +3
Skills Perception +3, Stealth +6
Damage Resistances necrotic; bludgeoning, piercing, and slashing from nonmagical attacks
Senses darkvision 60 ft., passive Perception 13
Languages the languages it knew in life
Challenge 5 (1,800 XP)

Regeneration. The vampire regains 10 hit points at the start of its turn if it has at least 1 hit point and isn't in sunlight or running water. If the vampire takes radiant damage or damage from holy water, this trait doesn't function at the start of the vampire's next turn.

Spider Climb. The vampire can climb difficult surfaces, including upside down on ceilings, without needing to make an ability check.

Vampire Weaknesses. The vampire has the following flaws:
Forbiddance. The vampire can't enter a residence without an invitation from one of the occupants.
Harmed by Running Water. The vampire takes 20 acid damage when it ends its turn in running water.
Stake to the Heart. The vampire is destroyed if a piercing weapon made of wood is driven into its heart while it is incapacitated in its resting place.
Sunlight Hypersensitivity. The vampire takes 20 radiant damage when it starts its turn in sunlight. While in sunlight, it has disadvantage on attack rolls and ability checks.

ACTIONS

Multiattack. The vampire makes two attacks, only one of which can be a bite attack.

Claws. *Melee Weapon Attack:* +6 to hit, reach 5 ft., one creature. *Hit:* 8 (2d4 + 3) slashing damage. Instead of dealing damage, the vampire can grapple the target (escape DC 13).

Bite. *Melee Weapon Attack:* +6 to hit, reach 5 ft., one willing creature, or a creature that is grappled by the vampire, incapacitated, or restrained. *Hit:* 6 (1d6 + 3) piercing damage plus 7 (2d6) necrotic damage. The target's hit point maximum is reduced by an amount equal to the necrotic damage taken, and the vampire regains hit points equal to that amount. The reduction lasts until the target finishes a long rest. The target dies if this effect reduces its hit point maximum to 0.

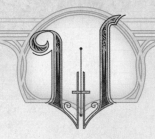

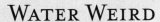

Water Weird

A water weird is an elemental guardian bound to a specific water-filled location, such as a pool or fountain. Invisible while immersed in water, its serpentine shape becomes clear only when it emerges to attack, using its coils to crush any creature other than its summoner and those its summoner declares as off limits. When slain, a water weird becomes an inanimate pool of water.

Good and Evil Weirds. Like most elementals, a water weird has no concept of good or evil. However, a water weird bound to a sacred or befouled source of water begins to take on the nature of that site, becoming neutral good or neutral evil.

A neutral good water weird tries to frighten away interlopers rather than kill them, while a neutral evil water weird kills its victims for pleasure and might turn against its summoner. A water weird loses its evil alignment if its waters are cleansed with a *purify food and drink* spell.

Elemental Nature. A water weird doesn't require air, food, drink, or sleep.

Water Weird
Large elemental, neutral

Armor Class 13
Hit Points 58 (9d10 + 9)
Speed 0 ft., swim 60 ft.

STR	DEX	CON	INT	WIS	CHA
17 (+3)	16 (+3)	13 (+1)	11 (+0)	10 (+0)	10 (+0)

Damage Resistances fire; bludgeoning, piercing, and slashing from nonmagical attacks
Damage Immunities poison
Condition Immunities exhaustion, grappled, paralyzed, poisoned, restrained, prone, unconscious
Senses blindsight 30 ft., passive Perception 10
Languages understands Aquan but doesn't speak
Challenge 3 (700 XP)

Invisible in Water. The water weird is invisible while fully immersed in water.

Water Bound. The water weird dies if it leaves the water to which it is bound or if that water is destroyed.

Actions

Constrict. *Melee Weapon Attack:* +5 to hit, reach 10 ft., one creature. *Hit:* 13 (3d6 + 3) bludgeoning damage. If the target is Medium or smaller, it is grappled (escape DC 13) and pulled 5 feet toward the water weird. Until this grapple ends, the target is restrained, the water weird tries to drown it, and the water weird can't constrict another target.

Shadow of the Grave. Wights flee from the world by day, away from the light of the sun, which they hate. They retreat to barrow mounds, crypts, and tombs where they dwell. Their lairs are silent, desolate places, surrounded by dead plants, noticeably blackened, and avoided by bird and beast.

Humanoids slain by a wight can rise as zombies under its control. Motivated by hunger for living souls and driven by the same desire for power that awakened them in undeath, some wights serve as shock troops for evil leaders, including wraiths. As soldiers, they are able to plan but seldom do so, relying on their hunger for destruction to overwhelm any creature that stands before them.

Undead Nature. A wight doesn't require air, food, drink, or sleep.

WIGHT
Medium undead, neutral evil

Armor Class 14 (studded leather)
Hit Points 45 (6d8 + 18)
Speed 30 ft.

STR	DEX	CON	INT	WIS	CHA
15 (+2)	14 (+2)	16 (+3)	10 (+0)	13 (+1)	15 (+2)

Skills Perception +3, Stealth +4
Damage Resistances necrotic; bludgeoning, piercing, and slashing from nonmagical attacks not made with silvered weapons
Damage Immunities poison
Condition Immunities exhaustion, poisoned
Senses darkvision 60 ft., passive Perception 13
Languages the languages it knew in life
Challenge 3 (700 XP)

Sunlight Sensitivity. While in sunlight, the wight has disadvantage on attack rolls, as well as on Wisdom (Perception) checks that rely on sight.

ACTIONS

Multiattack. The wight makes two longsword attacks or two longbow attacks. It can use its Life Drain in place of one longsword attack.

Life Drain. *Melee Weapon Attack:* +4 to hit, reach 5 ft., one creature. *Hit:* 5 (1d6 + 2) necrotic damage. The target must succeed on a DC 13 Constitution saving throw or its hit point maximum is reduced by an amount equal to the damage taken. This reduction lasts until the target finishes a long rest. The target dies if this effect reduces its hit point maximum to 0.

A humanoid slain by this attack rises 24 hours later as a zombie under the wight's control, unless the humanoid is restored to life or its body is destroyed. The wight can have no more than twelve zombies under its control at one time.

Longsword. *Melee Weapon Attack:* +4 to hit, reach 5 ft., one target. *Hit:* 6 (1d8 + 2) slashing damage, or 7 (1d10 + 2) slashing damage if used with two hands.

Longbow. *Ranged Weapon Attack:* +4 to hit, range 150/600 ft., one target. *Hit:* 6 (1d8 + 2) piercing damage.

WIGHT

The word "wight" meant "person" in days of yore, but the name now refers to evil undead who were once mortals driven by dark desire and great vanity. When death stills such a creature's heart and snuffs its living breath, its spirit cries out to the demon lord Orcus or some vile god of the underworld for a reprieve: undeath in return for eternal war on the living. If a dark power answers the call, the spirit is granted undeath so that it can pursue its own malevolent agenda.

Wights possess the memories and drives of their formerly living selves. They will heed the call of whatever dark entity transformed them into undead, swearing oaths to appease their new lord while retaining their autonomy. Never tiring, a wight can pursue its goals relentlessly and without distraction.

Life Eaters. Neither dead nor alive, a wight exists in a transitional state between one world and the next. The bright spark it possessed in life is gone, and in its place is a yearning to consume that spark in all living things. When a wight attacks, this life essence glows like white-hot embers to its dark eyes, and the wight's cold touch can drain the spark through flesh, clothing, and armor.

WILL-O'-WISP

Tiny undead, chaotic evil

Armor Class 19
Hit Points 22 (9d4)
Speed 0 ft., fly 50 ft. (hover)

STR	DEX	CON	INT	WIS	CHA
1 (−5)	28 (+9)	10 (+0)	13 (+1)	14 (+2)	11 (+0)

Damage Immunities lightning, poison
Damage Resistances acid, cold, fire, necrotic, thunder;
  bludgeoning, piercing, and slashing from nonmagical attacks
Condition Immunities exhaustion, grappled, paralyzed,
  poisoned, prone, restrained, unconscious
Senses darkvision 120 ft., passive Perception 12
Languages the languages it knew in life
Challenge 2 (450 XP)

Consume Life. As a bonus action, the will-o'-wisp can target one creature it can see within 5 feet of it that has 0 hit points and is still alive. The target must succeed on a DC 10 Constitution saving throw against this magic or die. If the target dies, the will-o'-wisp regains 10 (3d6) hit points.

Ephemeral. The will-o'-wisp can't wear or carry anything.

Incorporeal Movement. The will-o'-wisp can move through other creatures and objects as if they were difficult terrain. It takes 5 (1d10) force damage if it ends its turn inside an object.

Variable Illumination. The will-o'-wisp sheds bright light in a 5- to 20-foot radius and dim light for an additional number of feet equal to the chosen radius. The will-o'-wisp can alter the radius as a bonus action.

ACTIONS

Shock. *Melee Spell Attack:* +4 to hit, reach 5 ft., one creature. *Hit:* 9 (2d8) lightning damage.

Invisibility. The will-o'-wisp and its light magically become invisible until it attacks or uses its Consume Life, or until its concentration ends (as if concentrating on a spell).

WILL-O'-WISP

Will-o'-wisps are malevolent, wispy balls of light that haunt lonely places and battlefields, bound by dark fate or dark magic to feed on fear and despair.

Hope and Doom. Will-o'-wisps look like bobbing lantern lights in the distance, although they can choose to alter their colors, or wink out completely. When they activate their lights, will-o'-wisps offer hope, hinting of safety to creatures that follow them.

Will-o'-wisps lure unwary creatures into quicksand pits, monster lairs, and other dangerous places so that they can feed on the suffering of their prey and revel in their death screams. An evil being that falls prey to a will-o'-wisp might become a wisp itself, its woeful spirit coalescing above its lifeless corpse like a flickering flame.

Consumed by Despair. Will-o'-wisps are the souls of evil beings that perished in anguish or misery as they wandered forsaken lands permeated with powerful magic. They thrive in swampy bogs and bone-strewn battlefields where the oppressive weight of sorrow stoops even heavier than the low-hanging mist and fog. Trapped in these desolate places of lost hope and memory, will-o'-wisps lure other creatures toward dismal fates and feed on their misery.

Agents of Evil. Will-o'-wisps rarely speak, but when they do, their voices sound like faint or distant whispers. In the miserable domains they haunt, will-o'-wisps sometimes form symbiotic relationships with their wicked neighbors. Hags, oni, black dragons, and evil cultists work with will-o'-wisps to draw creatures into ambush. As their evil allies surround and slaughter creatures, the wisps hover above them, drinking the agony of a last breath and savoring the sensation as the light of life goes out in a creature's eyes.

Undead Nature. A will-o'-wisp doesn't require air, drink, or sleep.

and emotions become little more than faint impressions, fleeting as half-remembered dreams. A wraith might pause to stare at something that fascinated it in life, or it might curb its wrath in acknowledgment of a past friendship. Such moments come rarely, however, because most wraiths despise what they were as a reminder of what they have become.

Undead Commanders. A wraith can make an undead servant from the spirit of a humanoid creature that has recently suffered a violent death. Such a fragment of woe becomes a specter, spiteful of all that lives.

Wraiths sometimes rule the legions of the dead, plotting the doom of living creatures. When they emerge from their tombs to do battle, life and hope shrivel before them. Even if a wraith's armies are forced to retreat, the lands its forces occupied are so blasted and withered that those who live there often starve and die.

Undead Nature. A wraith doesn't require air, food, drink, or sleep.

WRAITH

A wraith is malice incarnate, concentrated into an incorporeal form that seeks to quench all life. The creature is suffused with negative energy, and its mere passage through the world leaves nearby plants blackened and withered. Animals flee from its presence. Even small fires can be extinguished by the sucking oblivion of the wraith's horrifying existence.

Vile Oblivion. When a mortal humanoid lives a debased life or enters into a fiendish pact, it consigns its soul to eternal damnation in the Lower Planes. However, sometimes the soul becomes so suffused with negative energy that it collapses in on itself and ceases to exist the instant before it can shuffle off to some horrible afterlife. When this occurs, the spirit becomes a soulless wraith—a malevolent void trapped on the plane where it died. Almost nothing of the wraith's former existence is preserved; in this new form, it exists only to annihilate other life.

Bereft of Body. A wraith can move through solid creatures and objects as easily as a mortal creature moves through fog.

A wraith might retain a few memories of its mortal life as shadowy echoes. However, even the strongest events

WRAITH

Medium undead, neutral evil

Armor Class 13
Hit Points 67 (9d8 + 27)
Speed 0 ft., fly 60 ft. (hover)

STR	DEX	CON	INT	WIS	CHA
6 (–2)	16 (+3)	16 (+3)	12 (+1)	14 (+2)	15 (+2)

Damage Resistances acid, cold, fire, lightning, thunder; bludgeoning, piercing, and slashing from nonmagical attacks not made with silvered weapons
Damage Immunities necrotic, poison
Condition Immunities charmed, exhaustion, grappled, paralyzed, petrified, poisoned, prone, restrained
Senses darkvision 60 ft., passive Perception 12
Languages the languages it knew in life
Challenge 5 (1,800 XP)

Incorporeal Movement. The wraith can move through other creatures and objects as if they were difficult terrain. It takes 5 (1d10) force damage if it ends its turn inside an object.

Sunlight Sensitivity. While in sunlight, the wraith has disadvantage on attack rolls, as well as on Wisdom (Perception) checks that rely on sight.

ACTIONS

Life Drain. *Melee Weapon Attack:* +6 to hit, reach 5 ft., one creature. *Hit:* 21 (4d8 + 3) necrotic damage. The target must succeed on a DC 14 Constitution saving throw or its hit point maximum is reduced by an amount equal to the damage taken. This reduction lasts until the target finishes a long rest. The target dies if this effect reduces its hit point maximum to 0.

Create Specter. The wraith targets a humanoid within 10 feet of it that has been dead for no longer than 1 minute and died violently. The target's spirit rises as a specter in the space of its corpse or in the nearest unoccupied space. The specter is under the wraith's control. The wraith can have no more than seven specters under its control at one time.

Wyvern

Travelers in the wild sometimes look to the skies to see the dark-winged shape of a wyvern carrying its prey. These cousins to the great dragons hunt the same tangled forests and caverns as their kin. Their appearance sends ripples of alarm through the borderlands of civilization.

A wyvern has two scaly legs, leathery wings, and a sinewy tail topped with its most potent weapon: a poison stinger. The poison in a wyvern's stinger can kill a creature in seconds. Extremely potent, wyvern poison burns through its victim's bloodstream, disintegrating veins and arteries on its way to the heart. As deadly as wyverns can be, however, hunters and adventurers often track them to claim the venom, which is used in alchemical compounds and to coat weapons.

Aerial Hunters. A wyvern doesn't fight on the ground unless it can't reach its prey by any other means, or if it has been fooled into a position from which aerial combat isn't an option. If forced into a confrontation on the ground, a wyvern crouches low, keeping its stinger poised above its head as it hisses and growls.

Aggressive and Reckless. A wyvern intent on its prey backs down only if it sustains serious injury, or if its prey eludes it long enough for another easier potential meal to wander along. If it corners a fleeing creature in an enclosure too small to enter, a wyvern guards where the quarry hides, lashing with its stinger whenever opportunity allows.

Although they possess more cunning than ordinary beasts, wyverns lack the intelligence of their draconic cousins. As such, creatures that maintain their composure as a wyvern hunts them from the air can often elude or trick it. Wyverns follow a direct path to their prey, with no thought given to possible ambushes.

Tamed Wyverns. A wyvern can be tamed for use as a mount, but doing so presents a difficult and deadly challenge. Raising one as a hatchling offers the best results. However, a wyvern's violent temperament has cost the life of many a would-be master.

Wyvern

Large dragon, unaligned

Armor Class 13 (natural armor)
Hit Points 110 (13d10 + 39)
Speed 20 ft., fly 80 ft.

STR	DEX	CON	INT	WIS	CHA
19 (+4)	10 (+0)	16 (+3)	5 (−3)	12 (+1)	6 (−2)

Skills Perception +4
Senses darkvision 60 ft., passive Perception 14
Languages —
Challenge 6 (2,300 XP)

Actions

Multiattack. The wyvern makes two attacks: one with its bite and one with its stinger. While flying, it can use its claws in place of one other attack.

Bite. *Melee Weapon Attack:* +7 to hit, reach 10 ft., one creature. *Hit:* 11 (2d6 + 4) piercing damage.

Claws. *Melee Weapon Attack:* +7 to hit, reach 5 ft., one target. Hit: 13 (2d8 + 4) slashing damage.

Stinger. *Melee Weapon Attack:* +7 to hit, reach 10 ft., one creature. *Hit:* 11 (2d6 + 4) piercing damage. The target must make a DC 15 Constitution saving throw, taking 24 (7d6) poison damage on a failed save, or half as much damage on a successful one.

Xorn prefer not to leave their home plane, where they easily eat their fill of gemstones and precious metals. When a xorn winds up on the Material Plane, whether by accident or from curiosity, it seeks sustenance and a way home.

Beggars and Thieves. Xorn scour the depths of the earth for precious metal and stones. Because they are unable to consume organic material, they ignore most other creatures. However, a xorn's ability to sniff out metals and stones often draws its attention to adventurers carrying coins and gems. Because a xorn isn't evil, it pleads or bargains in the hope of convincing owners to give up their treasure, offering up information it has learned from its travels in exchange. A xorn whose requests are ignored might resort to threats and bullying. If starving or angered, it resorts to force.

XORN
Medium elemental, neutral

Armor Class 19 (natural armor)
Hit Points 73 (7d8 + 42)
Speed 20 ft., burrow 20 ft.

STR	DEX	CON	INT	WIS	CHA
17 (+3)	10 (+0)	22 (+6)	11 (+0)	10 (+0)	11 (+0)

Skills Perception +6, Stealth +3
Damage Resistances piercing and slashing from nonmagical attacks not made with adamantine weapons
Senses darkvision 60 ft., tremorsense 60 ft., passive Perception 16
Languages Terran
Challenge 5 (1,800 XP)

Earth Glide. The xorn can burrow through nonmagical, unworked earth and stone. While doing so, the xorn doesn't disturb the material it moves through.

Stone Camouflage. The xorn has advantage on Dexterity (Stealth) checks made to hide in rocky terrain.

Treasure Sense. The xorn can pinpoint, by scent, the location of precious metals and stones, such as coins and gems, within 60 feet of it.

ACTIONS

Multiattack. The xorn makes three claw attacks and one bite attack.

Claw. *Melee Weapon Attack:* +6 to hit, reach 5 ft., one target. *Hit:* 6 (1d6 + 3) slashing damage.

Bite. *Melee Weapon Attack:* +6 to hit, reach 5 ft., one target. *Hit:* 13 (3d6 + 3) piercing damage.

XORN

Bizarre creatures native to the Elemental Plane of Earth, xorn sniff out gemstones and precious metals, then tunnel through earth and rock to consume those treasures. On the Material Plane, xorn must range far and wide through the Underdark to sustain themselves, becoming aggressive toward miners and treasure hunters when the valuable minerals of their diet are scarce.

A xorn's unnatural origins are suggested by its unusually heavy body and the large, powerful mouth sitting atop its head. Its three long arms are each tipped with sharp talons, and its three large, stone-lidded eyes see in all directions.

Elemental Travelers. Possessed of the power of elemental earth, a xorn glides through stone and dirt as easily as a fish swims through water. It doesn't displace earth or stone when it moves, but merges with and flows through it, leaving no tunnel, hole, or hint of its passage.

Y

"On your guard! That's not the wind howling!"
—Kelesta Hawke of the Emerald Enclave

Yeti

Large monstrosity, chaotic evil

Armor Class 12 (natural armor)
Hit Points 51 (6d10 + 18)
Speed 40 ft., climb 40 ft.

STR	DEX	CON	INT	WIS	CHA
18 (+4)	13 (+1)	16 (+3)	8 (−1)	12 (+1)	7 (−2)

Skills Perception +3, Stealth +3
Damage Immunities cold
Senses darkvision 60 ft., passive Perception 13
Languages Yeti
Challenge 3 (700 XP)

Fear of Fire. If the yeti takes fire damage, it has disadvantage on attack rolls and ability checks until the end of its next turn.

Keen Smell. The yeti has advantage on Wisdom (Perception) checks that rely on smell.

Snow Camouflage. The yeti has advantage on Dexterity (Stealth) checks made to hide in snowy terrain.

Actions

Multiattack. The yeti can use its Chilling Gaze and makes two claw attacks.

Claw. *Melee Weapon Attack:* +6 to hit, reach 5 ft., one target. *Hit:* 7 (1d6 + 4) slashing damage plus 3 (1d6) cold damage.

Chilling Gaze. The yeti targets one creature it can see within 30 feet of it. If the target can see the yeti, the target must succeed on a DC 13 Constitution saving throw against this magic or take 10 (3d6) cold damage and then be paralyzed for 1 minute, unless it is immune to cold damage. The target can repeat the saving throw at the end of each of its turns, ending the effect on itself on a success. If the target's saving throw is successful, or if the effect ends on it, the target is immune to the Chilling Gaze of all yetis (but not abominable yetis) for 1 hour.

Abominable Yeti

Huge monstrosity, chaotic evil

Armor Class 15 (natural armor)
Hit Points 137 (11d12 + 66)
Speed 40 ft., climb 40 ft.

STR	DEX	CON	INT	WIS	CHA
24 (+7)	10 (+0)	22 (+6)	9 (−1)	13 (+1)	9 (−1)

Skills Perception +5, Stealth +4
Damage Immunities cold
Senses darkvision 60 ft., passive Perception 15
Languages Yeti
Challenge 9 (5,000 XP)

Fear of Fire. If the yeti takes fire damage, it has disadvantage on attack rolls and ability checks until the end of its next turn.

Keen Smell. The yeti has advantage on Wisdom (Perception) checks that rely on smell.

Snow Camouflage. The yeti has advantage on Dexterity (Stealth) checks made to hide in snowy terrain.

Actions

Multiattack. The yeti can use its Chilling Gaze and makes two claw attacks.

Claw. *Melee Weapon Attack:* +11 to hit, reach 5 ft., one target. *Hit:* 14 (2d6 + 7) slashing damage plus 7 (2d6) cold damage.

Chilling Gaze. The yeti targets one creature it can see within 30 feet of it. If the target can see the yeti, the target must succeed on a DC 18 Constitution saving throw against this magic or take 21 (6d6) cold damage and then be paralyzed for 1 minute, unless it is immune to cold damage. The target can repeat the saving throw at the end of each of its turns, ending the effect on itself on a success. If the target's saving throw is successful, or if the effect ends on it, the target is immune to this yeti's gaze for 1 hour.

Cold Breath (Recharge 6). The yeti exhales a 30-foot cone of frigid air. Each creature in that area must make a DC 18 Constitution saving throw, taking 45 (10d8) cold damage on a failed save, or half as much damage on a successful one.

Yeti

A yeti's windborne howl sounds out across remote mountains, striking fear into the hearts of the scattered miners and herders that dwell there. These hulking creatures stalk alpine peaks in a ceaseless hunt for food. Their snow-white fur lets them move like ghosts against the frozen landscape. A yeti's icy simian eyes can freeze its prey in place.

Keen Hunters. Folk of the high peaks travel in groups and go armed, knowing that yetis can smell living flesh from miles away. When it finds prey, a yeti moves quickly over ice and stone to claim its meal, howling to the thrill of the hunt. Even in a blizzard, the scent of its quarry draws the yeti through the cold and snow.

Yetis hunt in solitude or in small family groups. When creatures flee from a yeti or engage it in battle, other yetis might catch the scent of blood and close in. The territorial yetis fight one another for the spoils of such battles, and yetis slain in the fight are also eaten, amid euphoric howls.

Terrifying Howlers. Before an avalanche, a blizzard, or a deadly frost, the yetis' howls sweep down the mountain slopes on the icy wind. Some people of the alpine peaks believe that the voices of loved ones killed in avalanches and blizzards sound out in the wails of the yetis, crying warnings of ill omen. More pragmatic folk attest that the yeti's howl is a reminder that, despite the great accomplishments of civilization, the civilized become the hunted in nature's untamed domain.

Brutal Rampagers. When mountain herds are abundant, yetis stay clear of humanoid realms. Driven by hunger, they attack humanoid settlements in waves, breaking down gates and stockade walls that once might have daunted them, then devouring the creatures within.

Devious mountain folk sometimes use the yetis as unwitting weapons. A warlord might lay down slaughtered sheep or goats to draw yetis into an enemy's camp, sowing chaos and thinning the ranks before battle. Mountain clan chiefs, wanting to expand their territory, overhunt local game to diminish the yetis' food supplies, inspiring attacks on humanoid settlements that are swiftly annexed in the aftermath.

Abominable Yetis. An abominable yeti is larger than a normal yeti, standing three times as tall as a human. It typically lives and hunts alone, though a pair of abominable yetis might live together long enough to raise young. These towering yetis are highly territorial and savage, attacking and devouring any warm-blooded creatures they encounter, then scattering the bones across the ice and snow.

YUAN-TI

Yuan-ti are devious serpent folk devoid of compassion. From remote temples in jungles, swamps, and deserts, the yuan-ti plot to supplant and dominate all other races and to make themselves gods.

Forsaken Humanity. The yuan-ti were once humans who thrived in the earliest days of civilization and worshiped serpents as totem animals. They lauded the serpent's sinuous flexibility, its calculated poise, and its deadly strike. Their advanced philosophy taught the virtue of detachment from emotion and of clear, focused thought.

Yuan-ti culture was among the richest in the mortal world. Their warriors were legendary, their empires always expanding. Yuan-ti temples stood at the centers of ancient metropolises, reaching ever higher in prayer to the gods they longed to emulate. In time, the serpent gods heard those prayers, their sibilant voices responding from the darkness as they told the yuan-ti what they must do. The yuan-ti religion grew more fanatical in its devotion. Cults bound themselves to the worship of the serpent gods and imitated their ways, indulging in cannibalism and humanoid sacrifice. Through foul sorcery, the yuan-ti bred with snakes, utterly sacrificing their humanity to become like the serpent gods in form, as well as in thought and emotion.

Serpent Kings of Fallen Empires. The yuan-ti view their physical transformation as a transcendent moment for their race, allowing them to shed their frail humanity like dead skin. Those that did not transform eventually became slaves or food for the blessed of the serpent gods. The yuan-ti empires withered or were defeated by those who fought against their cannibalism and slavery, and the serpent folk were left in the ruins of their great capitals, far removed from other races.

Cold of Heart. Humanoid emotions are foreign to most yuan-ti, which understand sentiment only as an exploitable weakness. A yuan-ti views the world and the events of its own life with such extreme pragmatism that it is nearly impossible to manipulate, influence, or control by nonmagical means, even as it seeks to control other creatures through terror, pleasure, and awe.

Yuan-ti know that the world they hope to rule can't be bound for long by brute force, and that many creatures will refuse to serve. As a result, yuan-ti first influence other creatures with the promise of wealth and power. Time and again, humanoid cultures make the fatal mistake of trusting the yuan-ti. They forget that a yuan-ti that acts honorably or lends aid in a time of trouble does so only as part of a grander design.

Yuan-ti leaders are cunning and ruthless tacticians who readily sacrifice lesser yuan-ti if potential victory justifies such losses. They have no sense of honorable combat and strike first in decisive ambush if they can.

False Worship. Yuan-ti life revolves around their temples, yet yuan-ti don't love the gods they worship. Instead, they see worship as a means to attain power. A yuan-ti believes an individual who attains enough power can devour and replace one of the yuan-ti gods. The yuan-ti strive for ascension and are willing to commit the darkest atrocities to achieve it.

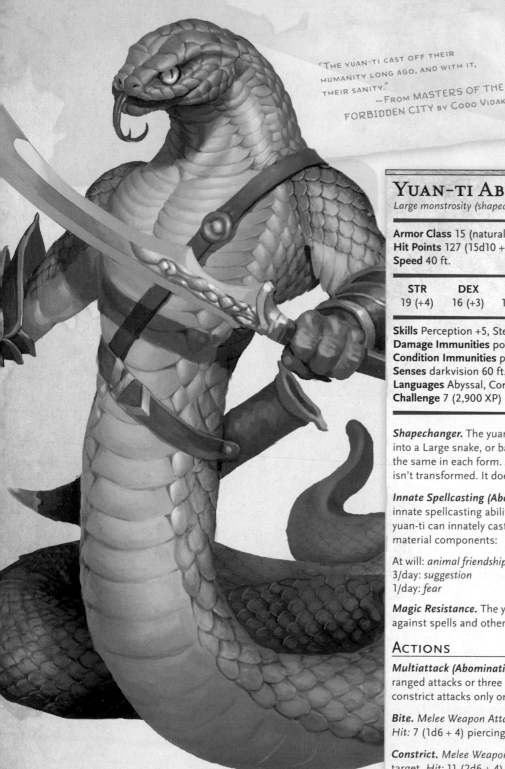

"The yuan-ti cast off their humanity long ago, and with it, their sanity."
—From MASTERS OF THE FORBIDDEN CITY by CODO VIDAK

YUAN-TI ABOMINATION

Large monstrosity (shapechanger, yuan-ti), neutral evil

Armor Class 15 (natural armor)
Hit Points 127 (15d10 + 45)
Speed 40 ft.

STR	DEX	CON	INT	WIS	CHA
19 (+4)	16 (+3)	17 (+3)	17 (+3)	15 (+2)	18 (+4)

Skills Perception +5, Stealth +6
Damage Immunities poison
Condition Immunities poisoned
Senses darkvision 60 ft., passive Perception 15
Languages Abyssal, Common, Draconic
Challenge 7 (2,900 XP)

Shapechanger. The yuan-ti can use its action to polymorph into a Large snake, or back into its true form. Its statistics are the same in each form. Any equipment it is wearing or carrying isn't transformed. It doesn't change form if it dies.

Innate Spellcasting (Abomination Form Only). The yuan-ti's innate spellcasting ability is Charisma (spell save DC 15). The yuan-ti can innately cast the following spells, requiring no material components:

At will: *animal friendship* (snakes only)
3/day: *suggestion*
1/day: *fear*

Magic Resistance. The yuan-ti has advantage on saving throws against spells and other magical effects.

ACTIONS

Multiattack (Abomination Form Only). The yuan-ti makes two ranged attacks or three melee attacks, but can use its bite and constrict attacks only once each.

Bite. *Melee Weapon Attack:* +7 to hit, reach 5 ft., one creature. *Hit:* 7 (1d6 + 4) piercing damage plus 10 (3d6) poison damage.

Constrict. *Melee Weapon Attack:* +7 to hit, reach 10 ft., one target. *Hit:* 11 (2d6 + 4) bludgeoning damage, and the target is grappled (escape DC 14). Until this grapple ends, the target is restrained, and the yuan-ti can't constrict another target.

Scimitar (Abomination Form Only). *Melee Weapon Attack:* +7 to hit, reach 5 ft., one target. *Hit:* 11 (2d6 + 4) slashing damage.

Longbow (Abomination Form Only). *Ranged Weapon Attack:* +6 to hit, range 150/600 ft., one target. *Hit:* 12 (2d8 + 3) piercing damage plus 10 (3d6) poison damage.

YUAN-TI ABOMINATION

Monstrous serpents with burly humanoid torsos and arms, abominations form the highest caste of yuan-ti society, and they most closely resemble the race as the serpent gods intended it. They mastermind elaborate schemes and perform dark rites in the hope of one day ruling the world.

YUAN-TI MALISON

A malison is a hideous blend of human and serpentine features. Three different types of malisons are known to exist, and other types are possible. Malisons form the middle caste of yuan-ti society and hunt with arrows tipped with their own venom. They use their magical powers of suggestion to force their enemies' surrender.

YUAN-TI MALISON

Medium monstrosity (shapechanger, yuan-ti), neutral evil

Armor Class 12
Hit Points 66 (12d8 + 12)
Speed 30 ft.

STR	DEX	CON	INT	WIS	CHA
16 (+3)	14 (+2)	13 (+1)	14 (+2)	12 (+1)	16 (+3)

Skills Deception +5, Stealth +4
Damage Immunities poison
Condition Immunities poisoned
Senses darkvision 60 ft., passive Perception 11
Languages Abyssal, Common, Draconic
Challenge 3 (700 XP)

Shapechanger. The yuan-ti can use its action to polymorph into a Medium snake, or back into its true form. Its statistics are the same in each form. Any equipment it is wearing or carrying isn't transformed. It doesn't change form if it dies.

Innate Spellcasting (Yuan-ti Form Only). The yuan-ti's innate spellcasting ability is Charisma (spell save DC 13). The yuan-ti can innately cast the following spells, requiring no material components:

At will: *animal friendship* (snakes only)
3/day: *suggestion*

Magic Resistance. The yuan-ti has advantage on saving throws against spells and other magical effects.

Malison Type. The yuan-ti has one of the following types:

Type 1: Human body with snake head
Type 2: Human head and body with snakes for arms
Type 3: Human head and upper body with a serpentine lower body instead of legs

ACTIONS FOR TYPE 1

Multiattack (Yuan-ti Form Only). The yuan-ti makes two ranged attacks or two melee attacks, but can use its bite only once.

Bite. *Melee Weapon Attack:* +5 to hit, reach 5 ft., one creature. *Hit:* 5 (1d4 + 3) piercing damage plus 7 (2d6) poison damage.

Scimitar (Yuan-ti Form Only). *Melee Weapon Attack:* +5 to hit, reach 5 ft., one target. *Hit:* 6 (1d6 + 3) slashing damage.

Longbow (Yuan-ti Form Only). *Ranged Weapon Attack:* +4 to hit, range 150/600 ft., one target. *Hit:* 6 (1d8 + 2) piercing damage plus 7 (2d6) poison damage.

ACTIONS FOR TYPE 2

Multiattack (Yuan-ti Form Only). The yuan-ti makes two bite attacks using its snake arms.

Bite. *Melee Weapon Attack:* +5 to hit, reach 5 ft., one creature. *Hit:* 5 (1d4 + 3) piercing damage plus 7 (2d6) poison damage.

ACTIONS FOR TYPE 3

Multiattack (Yuan-ti Form Only). The yuan-ti makes two ranged attacks or two melee attacks, but can constrict only once.

Bite (Snake Form Only). *Melee Weapon Attack:* +5 to hit, reach 5 ft., one creature. *Hit:* 5 (1d4 + 3) piercing damage plus 7 (2d6) poison damage.

Constrict. *Melee Weapon Attack:* +5 to hit, reach 5 ft., one target. *Hit:* 10 (2d6 + 3) bludgeoning damage, and the target is grappled (escape DC 13). Until this grapple ends, the target is restrained, and the yuan-ti can't constrict another target.

Scimitar (Yuan-ti Form Only). *Melee Weapon Attack:* +5 to hit, reach 5 ft., one target. *Hit:* 6 (1d6 + 3) slashing damage.

Longbow (Yuan-ti Form Only). *Ranged Weapon Attack:* +4 to hit, range 150/600 ft., one target. *Hit:* 6 (1d8 + 2) piercing damage.

SERPENT GODS

The yuan-ti revere a number of powerful entities as gods, including the following.

Dendar, the Night Serpent. Dendar's followers say that one day she will grow so large from feasting on the fears and nightmares of the world that she will devour it whole. Yuan-ti that serve Dendar terrorize other creatures in any way they can, growing and nurturing the fears of humanoids to feed the Night Serpent.

Merrshaulk, Master of the Pit. Merrshaulk is the long-slumbering chief deity of the yuan-ti. As worship of Merrshaulk waned, he went into slumber. Merrshaulk's priests are yuan-ti abominations that maintain traditions of living sacrifice and cause suffering in the god's name. With enough vile acts, the abominations believe that Merrshaulk will reawaken and restore the yuan-ti to their rightful place.

Sseth, the Sibilant Death. Sseth appeared to the yuan-ti of antiquity in the form of a winged yuan-ti claiming to be an avatar of Merrshaulk. Speaking with Merrshaulk's voice, Sseth vowed to pull the yuan-ti out of decline and build a new empire. Many of Merrshaulk's devout turned to the worship of Sseth. Some yuan-ti have long suspected Sseth as an usurper taking advantage of Merrshaulk's slumber to make himself a god. They believe that Sseth might even have devoured Merrshaulk, and now answers the prayers of Merrshaulk's followers, as his priests convert or consume Merrshaulk's more stubborn adherents.

YUAN-TI PUREBLOOD

Medium humanoid (yuan-ti), neutral evil

Armor Class 11
Hit Points 40 (9d8)
Speed 30 ft.

STR	DEX	CON	INT	WIS	CHA
11 (+0)	12 (+1)	11 (+0)	13 (+1)	12 (+1)	14 (+2)

Skills Deception +6, Perception +3, Stealth +3
Damage Immunities poison
Condition Immunities poisoned
Senses darkvision 60 ft., passive Perception 13
Languages Abyssal, Common, Draconic
Challenge 1 (200 XP)

Innate Spellcasting. The yuan-ti's spellcasting ability is Charisma (spell save DC 12). The yuan-ti can innately cast the following spells, requiring no material components:

At will: *animal friendship* (snakes only)
3/day each: *poison spray, suggestion*

Magic Resistance. The yuan-ti has advantage on saving throws against spells and other magical effects.

ACTIONS

Multiattack. The yuan-ti makes two melee attacks.

Scimitar. *Melee Weapon Attack:* +3 to hit, reach 5 ft., one target. *Hit:* 4 (1d6 + 1) slashing damage.

Shortbow. *Ranged Weapon Attack:* +3 to hit, range 80/320 ft., one target. *Hit:* 4 (1d6 + 1) piercing damage plus 7 (2d6) poison damage.

YUAN-TI PUREBLOOD

Purebloods form the lowest caste of yuan-ti society. They closely resemble humans, yet a pureblood can't pass for human under close scrutiny because there's always some hint of its true nature, such as scaly patches of skin, serpentine eyes, pointed teeth, or a forked tongue. Wearing cloaks and cowls, they masquerade as humans and infiltrate civilized lands to gather information, kidnap prisoners for interrogation and sacrifice, and trade with anyone who has something that can further their myriad plots.

Yugoloths

Yugoloths are fickle fiends that inhabit the planes of Acheron, Gehenna, Hades, and Carceri. They act as mercenaries and are notorious for their shifting loyalties. They are the embodiments of avarice. Before serving under anyone's banner, a yugoloth asks the only question on its mind: *What's in it for me?*

Spawn of Gehenna. The first yugoloths were created by a sisterhood of night hags on Gehenna. It is widely believed that Asmodeus, Lord of the Nine Hells, commissioned the work, in the hope of creating an army of fiends that were not bound to the Nine Hells. In the course of making this new army, the hags crafted four magic tomes and recorded the true names of every yugoloth they created, save one, the General of Gehenna. These tomes were called the *Books of Keeping*. Since knowing a fiend's true name grants power over it, the hags used the books to ensure the yugoloths' loyalty. They also used the books to capture the true names of other fiends that crossed them. It is rumored that the *Books of Keeping* contain the true names of a few demon lords and archdevils as well.

Petty jealousies and endless bickering caused the sisterhood to dissolve, and in the ensuing power grab, the *Books of Keeping* were lost or stolen. No longer indentured to anyone, the yugoloths gained independence, and they now offer their services to the highest bidder.

Fiendish Mercenaries. Summoned yugoloths demand much for their time and loyalty. Whatever promises a yugoloth makes are quickly broken when a better opportunity presents itself. Unlike demons, yugoloths can be reasoned with, but unlike devils, they are rarely true to their word.

Yugoloths can be found anywhere, but the high cost of maintaining a yugoloth army's loyalty typically exceeds what any warlord on the Material Plane can pay.

Being self-serving creatures, yugoloths quarrel among themselves constantly. A yugoloth army is more organized than a ravening horde of demons, but far less orderly and regimented than a legion of devils. Without a powerful leader to keep them in line, yugoloths fight simply to indulge their violent predilections, and only as long as it benefits them to do so.

Back to Gehenna. When a yugoloth dies, it dissolves into a pool of ichor and reforms at full strength on the Bleak Eternity of Gehenna. Only on its native plane can a yugoloth be destroyed permanently. A yugoloth knows this and acts accordingly. When summoned to other planes, a yugoloth fights without concern for its own well-being. On Gehenna, it is more apt to retreat or plead for mercy if its demise seems imminent.

When a yugoloth is permanently destroyed, its name vanishes from every *Book of Keeping*. If a yugoloth is re-created by way of an unholy ritual requiring the expenditure of souls, its name reappears in the books.

The Books of Keeping. When all four copies of the *Books of Keeping* disappeared, Asmodeus and the night hags lost control of their yugoloth creations. Each *Book of Keeping* still exists, drifting from plane to plane, where the brave and the foolish occasionally stumble upon them. A yugoloth summoned using its true name, as inscribed in the *Books of Keeping,* is forced to serve its summoner obediently. The yugoloth hates being controlled in this manner and isn't shy about making its displeasure known. Like a petulant child, it will follow its instructions to the letter while looking for opportunities to misinterpret them.

The General of Gehenna. Somewhere in the brimstone wastes of Gehenna, there roams an ultroloth so strong that none contests his power: the General of Gehenna. Many yugoloths search for this great general in the hope of serving with him. They believe that service with the General of Gehenna grants power and prestige among lower planar entities.

Whatever the case, no fiend finds the General unless the General desires it. His personal name is unknown, and even the *Books of Keeping* contain no mention of this powerful, thoroughly evil entity.

Arcanaloth

Arcanaloths are sly, jackal-headed beings with humanoid bodies, but they can employ magic to take any humanoid form. They do so to gain the trust of creatures with whom they negotiate, replacing jackal snarls with winsome smiles.

Regardless of its chosen form, an arcanaloth appears well groomed, clothing itself in fine robes. Highly intelligent spellcasters who hunger for knowledge and power, arcanaloths command units of lesser yugoloths and maintain the contracts, records, and accounts of their kind.

Arcanaloths speak and write all languages, making them cunning diplomats and negotiators. An arcanaloth properly paid can broker treaties or alliances with subtlety and finesse, just as an arcanaloth who changes sides can easily turn the best-laid peace talks into all-out war. What the fiend demands in exchange for its time and talent is information, as well as powerful magic items that it can trade for even more information.

Variant: Yugoloth Summoning

Some yugoloths have an action option that allows them to summon other yugoloths.

Summon Yugoloth (1/Day). The yugoloth chooses what to summon and attempts a magical summoning.

- An **arcanaloth** has a 40 percent chance of summoning one arcanaloth.
- A **mezzoloth** has a 30 percent chance of summoning one mezzoloth.
- A **nycaloth** has a 50 percent chance of summoning 1d4 mezzoloths or one nycaloth.
- An **ultroloth** has a 50 percent chance of summoning 1d6 mezzoloths, 1d4 nycaloths, or one ultroloth.

A summoned yugoloth appears in an unoccupied space within 60 feet of its summoner, does as it pleases (unless its summoner is an ultroloth, in which case it acts as an ally of its summoner), and can't summon other yugoloths. The summoned yugoloth remains for 1 minute, until it or its summoner dies, or until its summoner takes a bonus action to dismiss it.

Mezzoloth

The bulk of the yugoloth population is made up of mezzoloths, which are human-sized insect creatures covered in dense chitinous plates. Mezzoloths serve as foot soldiers in yugoloth armies, their wide-set eyes glowing red as the mezzoloths bear down on their foes.

Violence and reward are the fundamental drives of a mezzoloth, and powerful beings that promise one or the other can easily attract them into service. Although it has lethal claws on its four arms, a mezzoloth typically wields a trident in two of them. If surrounded by enemies, a mezzoloth exhales toxic fumes that can choke and kill whole groups of creatures.

Nycaloth

The elite airborne shock troops of the yugoloths, nycaloths look like muscular gargoyles. Powerful bat wings bear them swiftly aloft in battle, and the razor-sharp claws of their hands and feet cut through flesh and bone with ease. A nightmarish foe, a nycaloth strikes hard and fast without warning, then teleports away. It uses its innate magic to turn invisible or create illusory doubles of itself, further confounding its enemies.

Nycaloths are the most loyal of the yugoloths. When they find an evil master that treats them well, they are unlikely to break their agreement unless the reward for doing so is extreme.

Ultroloth

Ultroloths command the yugoloth armies of the Blood War. An ultroloth looks like a slender gray-skinned humanoid with an elongated head. Its face bears no features except for two ovoid eyes. These eyes can become sparkling pools of light that can transfix other creatures and leave them reeling and helpless.

Frequently at one another's throats, ultroloths continually scheme to enhance their own power. When not employed to fight in the Blood War, ultroloths lead yugoloth forces throughout the planes, acting as crime bosses or commanders of evil mercenary companies.

With a reputation for cruelty, ultroloths command their minions to fight while the ultroloths stay removed from combat themselves. Lesser yugoloths know their place when facing an ultroloth and respond to its summons without demand for payment.

Arcanaloth

Ultroloth

Nycaloth

"Power. We all crave it, but only a select few of us deserve it."
—Shemeshka the Marauder, arcanaloth in Sigil

Arcanaloth
Medium fiend (yugoloth), neutral evil

Armor Class 17 (natural armor)
Hit Points 104 (16d8 + 32)
Speed 30 ft., fly 30 ft.

STR	DEX	CON	INT	WIS	CHA
17 (+3)	12 (+1)	14 (+2)	20 (+5)	16 (+3)	17 (+3)

Saving Throws Dex +5, Int +9, Wis +7, Cha +7
Skills Arcana +13, Deception +9, Insight +9, Perception +7
Damage Resistances cold, fire, lightning; bludgeoning, piercing, and slashing from nonmagical attacks
Damage Immunities acid, poison
Condition Immunities charmed, poisoned
Senses truesight 120 ft., passive Perception 17
Languages all, telepathy 120 ft.
Challenge 12 (8,400 XP)

Innate Spellcasting. The arcanaloth's innate spellcasting ability is Charisma (spell save DC 15). The arcanaloth can innately cast the following spells, requiring no material components:

At will: *alter self, darkness, heat metal, invisibility* (self only), *magic missile*

Magic Resistance. The arcanaloth has advantage on saving throws against spells and other magical effects.

Magic Weapons. The arcanaloth's weapon attacks are magical.

Spellcasting. The arcanaloth is a 16th-level spellcaster. Its spellcasting ability is Intelligence (spell save DC 17, +9 to hit with spell attacks). The arcanaloth has the following wizard spells prepared:

Cantrips (at will): *fire bolt, mage hand, minor illusion, prestidigitation*
1st level (4 slots): *detect magic, identify, shield, Tenser's floating disk*
2nd level (3 slots): *detect thoughts, mirror image, phantasmal force, suggestion*
3rd level (3 slots): *counterspell, fear, fireball*
4th level (3 slots): *banishment, dimension door*
5th level (2 slots): *contact other plane, hold monster*
6th level (1 slot): *chain lightning*
7th level (1 slot): *finger of death*
8th level (1 slot): *mind blank*

Actions

Claws. *Melee Weapon Attack:* +7 to hit, reach 5 ft., one target. *Hit:* 8 (2d4 + 3) slashing damage. The target must make a DC 14 Constitution saving throw, taking 10 (3d6) poison damage on a failed save, or half as much damage on a successful one.

Teleport. The arcanaloth magically teleports, along with any equipment it is wearing or carrying, up to 60 feet to an unoccupied space it can see.

Mezzoloth
Medium fiend (yugoloth), neutral evil

Armor Class 18 (natural armor)
Hit Points 75 (10d8 + 30)
Speed 40 ft.

STR	DEX	CON	INT	WIS	CHA
18 (+4)	11 (+0)	16 (+3)	7 (-2)	10 (+0)	11 (+0)

Skills Perception +3
Damage Resistances cold, fire, lightning; bludgeoning, piercing, and slashing from nonmagical attacks
Damage Immunities acid, poison
Condition Immunities poisoned
Senses blindsight 60 ft., darkvision 60 ft., passive Perception 13
Languages Abyssal, Infernal, telepathy 60 ft.
Challenge 5 (1,800 XP)

Innate Spellcasting. The mezzoloth's innate spellcasting ability is Charisma (spell save DC 11). The mezzoloth can innately cast the following spells, requiring no material components:

2/day each: *darkness, dispel magic*
1/day: *cloudkill*

Magic Resistance. The mezzoloth has advantage on saving throws against spells and other magical effects.

Magic Weapons. The mezzoloth's weapon attacks are magical.

Actions

Multiattack. The mezzoloth makes two attacks: one with its claws and one with its trident.

Claws. *Melee Weapon Attack:* +7 to hit, reach 5 ft., one target. *Hit:* 9 (2d4 + 4) slashing damage.

Trident. *Melee or Ranged Weapon Attack:* +7 to hit, reach 5 ft. or range 20/60 ft., one target. *Hit:* 7 (1d6 + 4) piercing damage, or 8 (1d8 + 4) piercing damage when held with two claws and used to make a melee attack.

Teleport. The mezzoloth magically teleports, along with any equipment it is wearing or carrying, up to 60 feet to an unoccupied space it can see.

NYCALOTH

Large fiend (yugoloth), neutral evil

Armor Class 18 (natural armor)
Hit Points 123 (13d10 + 52)
Speed 40 ft., fly 60 ft.

STR	DEX	CON	INT	WIS	CHA
20 (+5)	11 (+0)	19 (+4)	12 (+1)	10 (+0)	15 (+2)

Skills Intimidation +6, Perception +4, Stealth +4
Damage Resistances cold, fire, lightning; bludgeoning, piercing, and slashing from nonmagical attacks
Damage Immunities acid, poison
Condition Immunities poisoned
Senses blindsight 60 ft., darkvision 60 ft., passive Perception 14
Languages Abyssal, Infernal, telepathy 60 ft.
Challenge 9 (5,000 XP)

Innate Spellcasting. The nycaloth's innate spellcasting ability is Charisma. The nycaloth can innately cast the following spells, requiring no material components:

At will: *darkness, detect magic, dispel magic, invisibility* (self only), *mirror image*

Magic Resistance. The nycaloth has advantage on saving throws against spells and other magical effects.

Magic Weapons. The nycaloth's weapon attacks are magical.

ACTIONS

Multiattack. The nycaloth makes two melee attacks, or it makes one melee attack and teleports before or after the attack.

Claw. *Melee Weapon Attack:* +9 to hit, reach 5 ft., one target. *Hit:* 12 (2d6 + 5) slashing damage. If the target is a creature, it must succeed on a DC 16 Constitution saving throw or take 5 (2d4) slashing damage at the start of each of its turns due to a fiendish wound. Each time the nycaloth hits the wounded target with this attack, the damage dealt by the wound increases by 5 (2d4). Any creature can take an action to stanch the wound with a successful DC 13 Wisdom (Medicine) check. The wound also closes if the target receives magical healing.

Greataxe. *Melee Weapon Attack:* +9 to hit, reach 5 ft., one target. *Hit:* 18 (2d12 + 5) slashing damage.

Teleport. The nycaloth magically teleports, along with any equipment it is wearing or carrying, up to 60 feet to an unoccupied space it can see.

ULTROLOTH

Medium fiend (yugoloth), neutral evil

Armor Class 19 (natural armor)
Hit Points 153 (18d8 + 72)
Speed 30 ft., fly 60 ft.

STR	DEX	CON	INT	WIS	CHA
16 (+3)	16 (+3)	18 (+4)	18 (+4)	15 (+2)	19 (+4)

Skills Intimidation +9, Perception +7, Stealth +8
Damage Resistances cold, fire, lightning; bludgeoning, piercing, and slashing from nonmagical attacks
Damage Immunities acid, poison
Condition Immunities charmed, frightened, poisoned
Senses truesight 120 ft., passive Perception 17
Languages Abyssal, Infernal, telepathy 120 ft.
Challenge 13 (10,000 XP)

Innate Spellcasting. The ultroloth's innate spellcasting ability is Charisma (spell save DC 17). The ultroloth can innately cast the following spells, requiring no material components:

At will: *alter self, clairvoyance, darkness, detect magic, detect thoughts, dispel magic, invisibility* (self only), *suggestion*
3/day each: *dimension door, fear, wall of fire*
1/day each: *fire storm, mass suggestion*

Magic Resistance. The ultroloth has advantage on saving throws against spells and other magical effects.

Magic Weapons. The ultroloth's weapon attacks are magical.

ACTIONS

Multiattack. The ultroloth can use its Hypnotic Gaze and makes three melee attacks.

Longsword. *Melee Weapon Attack:* +8 to hit, reach 5 ft., one target. *Hit:* 7 (1d8 + 3) slashing damage, or 8 (1d10 + 3) slashing damage if used with two hands.

Hypnotic Gaze. The ultroloth's eyes sparkle with opalescent light as it targets one creature it can see within 30 feet of it. If the target can see the ultroloth, the target must succeed on a DC 17 Wisdom saving throw against this magic or be charmed until the end of the ultroloth's next turn. The charmed target is stunned. If the target's saving throw is successful, the target is immune to the ultroloth's gaze for the next 24 hours.

Teleport. The ultroloth magically teleports, along with any equipment it is wearing or carrying, up to 60 feet to an unoccupied space it can see.

ZOMBIE

OGRE ZOMBIE

BEHOLDER
ZOMBIE

ZOMBIES

From somewhere in the darkness, a gurgling moan is heard. A form lurches into view, dragging one foot as it raises bloated arms and broken hands. The zombie advances, driven to kill anyone too slow to escape its grasp.

Dark Servants. Sinister necromantic magic infuses the remains of the dead, causing them to rise as zombies that do their creator's bidding without fear or hesitation. They move with a jerky, uneven gait, clad in the moldering apparel they wore when put to rest, and carrying the stench of decay.

Most zombies are made from humanoid remains, though the flesh and bones of any formerly living creature can be imbued with a semblance of life. Necromantic magic, usually from spells, animates a zombie. Some zombies rise spontaneously when dark magic saturates an area. Once turned into a zombie, a creature can't be restored to life except by powerful magic, such as a resurrection spell.

A zombie retains no vestiges of its former self, its mind devoid of thought and imagination. A zombie left without orders simply stands in place and rots unless something comes along that it can kill. The magic animating a zombie imbues it with evil, so left without purpose, it attacks any living creature it encounters.

Hideous Forms. Zombies appear as they did in life, showing the wounds that killed them. However, the magic that creates these vile creatures often takes time to run its course. Dead warriors might rise from a battlefield, eviscerated and bloated after days in the sun. The muddy cadaver of a peasant could claw its way from the ground, riddled with maggots and worms. A zombie might wash ashore or rise from a marsh, swollen and reeking after weeks in the water.

Mindless Soldiers. Zombies take the most direct route to any foe, unable to comprehend obstacles, tactics, or dangerous terrain. A zombie might stumble into a fast-flowing river to reach foes on a far shore, clawing at the surface as it is battered against rocks and destroyed. To reach a foe below it, a zombie might step out of an open window. Zombies stumble through roaring infernos, into pools of acid, and across fields littered with caltrops without hesitation.

A zombie can follow simple orders and distinguish friends from foes, but its ability to reason is limited to shambling in whatever direction it is pointed, pummeling any enemy in its path. A zombie armed with a weapon uses it, but the zombie won't retrieve a dropped weapon or other tool until told to do so.

Undead Nature. A zombie doesn't require air, food, drink, or sleep.

"After Beek died, we cast an Animate Dead spell on his corpse. It was fun for a while, but the zombie started to smell real bad, so we doused it in oil and set it on fire. Beek would've found that hilarious."

—Fonkin Hoddypeak, on friendship

ZOMBIE
Medium undead, neutral evil

Armor Class 8
Hit Points 22 (3d8 + 9)
Speed 20 ft.

STR	DEX	CON	INT	WIS	CHA
13 (+1)	6 (−2)	16 (+3)	3 (−4)	6 (−2)	5 (−3)

Saving Throws Wis +0
Damage Immunities poison
Condition Immunities poisoned
Senses darkvision 60 ft., passive Perception 8
Languages understands the languages it knew in life but can't speak
Challenge 1/4 (50 XP)

Undead Fortitude. If damage reduces the zombie to 0 hit points, it must make a Constitution saving throw with a DC of 5 + the damage taken, unless the damage is radiant or from a critical hit. On a success, the zombie drops to 1 hit point instead.

ACTIONS

Slam. *Melee Weapon Attack:* +3 to hit, reach 5 ft., one target. *Hit:* 4 (1d6 + 1) bludgeoning damage.

OGRE ZOMBIE
Large undead, neutral evil

Armor Class 8
Hit Points 85 (9d10 + 36)
Speed 30 ft.

STR	DEX	CON	INT	WIS	CHA
19 (+4)	6 (−2)	18 (+4)	3 (−4)	6 (−2)	5 (−3)

Saving Throws Wis +0
Damage Immunities poison
Condition Immunities poisoned
Senses darkvision 60 ft., passive Perception 8
Languages understands Common and Giant but can't speak
Challenge 2 (450 XP)

Undead Fortitude. If damage reduces the zombie to 0 hit points, it must make a Constitution saving throw with a DC of 5 + the damage taken, unless the damage is radiant or from a critical hit. On a success, the zombie drops to 1 hit point instead.

ACTIONS

Morningstar. *Melee Weapon Attack:* +6 to hit, reach 5 ft., one target. *Hit:* 13 (2d8 + 4) bludgeoning damage.

BEHOLDER ZOMBIE
Large undead, neutral evil

Armor Class 15 (natural armor)
Hit Points 93 (11d10 + 33)
Speed 0 ft., fly 20 ft. (hover)

STR	DEX	CON	INT	WIS	CHA
10 (+0)	8 (−1)	16 (+3)	3 (−4)	8 (−1)	5 (−3)

Saving Throws Wis +2
Damage Immunities poison
Condition Immunities poisoned, prone
Senses darkvision 60 ft., passive Perception 9
Languages understands Deep Speech and Undercommon but can't speak
Challenge 5 (1,800 XP)

Undead Fortitude. If damage reduces the zombie to 0 hit points, it must make a Constitution saving throw with a DC of 5 + the damage taken, unless the damage is radiant or from a critical hit. On a success, the zombie drops to 1 hit point instead.

ACTIONS

Bite. *Melee Weapon Attack:* +3 to hit, reach 5 ft., one target. *Hit:* 14 (4d6) piercing damage.

Eye Ray. The zombie uses a random magical eye ray, choosing a target that it can see within 60 feet of it.

1. *Paralyzing Ray.* The targeted creature must succeed on a DC 14 Constitution saving throw or be paralyzed for 1 minute. The target can repeat the saving throw at the end of each of its turns, ending the effect on itself on a success.

2. *Fear Ray.* The targeted creature must succeed on a DC 14 Wisdom saving throw or be frightened for 1 minute. The target can repeat the saving throw at the end of each of its turns, ending the effect on itself on a success.

3. *Enervation Ray.* The targeted creature must make a DC 14 Constitution saving throw, taking 36 (8d8) necrotic damage on a failed save, or half as much damage on a successful one.

4. *Disintegration Ray.* If the target is a creature, it must succeed on a DC 14 Dexterity saving throw or take 45 (10d8) force damage. If this damage reduces the creature to 0 hit points, its body becomes a pile of fine gray dust.

If the target is a Large or smaller nonmagical object or creation of magical force, it is disintegrated without a saving throw. If the target is a Huge or larger nonmagical object or creation of magical force, this ray disintegrates a 10-foot cube of it.

APPENDIX A: MISCELLANEOUS CREATURES

This appendix contains statistics for various animals, vermin, and other critters. The stat blocks are organized alphabetically by creature name.

APE

Medium beast, unaligned

Armor Class 12
Hit Points 19 (3d8 + 6)
Speed 30 ft., climb 30 ft.

STR	DEX	CON	INT	WIS	CHA
16 (+3)	14 (+2)	14 (+2)	6 (−2)	12 (+1)	7 (−2)

Skills Athletics +5, Perception +3
Senses passive Perception 13
Languages —
Challenge 1/2 (100 XP)

ACTIONS

Multiattack. The ape makes two fist attacks.

Fist. *Melee Weapon Attack:* +5 to hit, reach 5 ft., one target. *Hit:* 6 (1d6 + 3) bludgeoning damage.

Rock. *Ranged Weapon Attack:* +5 to hit, range 25/50 ft., one target. *Hit:* 6 (1d6 + 3) bludgeoning damage.

AWAKENED SHRUB

Small plant, unaligned

Armor Class 9
Hit Points 10 (3d6)
Speed 20 ft.

STR	DEX	CON	INT	WIS	CHA
3 (−4)	8 (−1)	11 (+0)	10 (+0)	10 (+0)	6 (−2)

Damage Vulnerabilities fire
Damage Resistances piercing
Senses passive Perception 10
Languages one language known by its creator
Challenge 0 (10 XP)

False Appearance. While the shrub remains motionless, it is indistinguishable from a normal shrub.

ACTIONS

Rake. *Melee Weapon Attack:* +1 to hit, reach 5 ft., one target. *Hit:* 1 (1d4 − 1) slashing damage.

An **awakened shrub** is an ordinary shrub given sentience and mobility by the *awaken* spell or similar magic.

AWAKENED TREE

Huge plant, unaligned

Armor Class 13 (natural armor)
Hit Points 59 (7d12 + 14)
Speed 20 ft.

STR	DEX	CON	INT	WIS	CHA
19 (+4)	6 (−2)	15 (+2)	10 (+0)	10 (+0)	7 (−2)

Damage Vulnerabilities fire
Damage Resistances bludgeoning, piercing
Senses passive Perception 10
Languages one language known by its creator
Challenge 2 (450 XP)

False Appearance. While the tree remains motionless, it is indistinguishable from a normal tree.

ACTIONS

Slam. *Melee Weapon Attack:* +6 to hit, reach 10 ft., one target. *Hit:* 14 (3d6 + 4) bludgeoning damage.

An **awakened tree** is an ordinary tree given sentience and mobility by the *awaken* spell or similar magic.

AXE BEAK

Large beast, unaligned

Armor Class 11
Hit Points 19 (3d10 + 3)
Speed 50 ft.

STR	DEX	CON	INT	WIS	CHA
14 (+2)	12 (+1)	12 (+1)	2 (−4)	10 (+0)	5 (−3)

Senses passive Perception 10
Languages —
Challenge 1/4 (50 XP)

ACTIONS

Beak. *Melee Weapon Attack:* +4 to hit, reach 5 ft., one target. *Hit:* 6 (1d8 + 2) slashing damage.

An **axe beak** is a tall flightless bird with strong legs and a heavy, wedge-shaped beak. It has a nasty disposition and tends to attack any unfamiliar creature that wanders too close.

> ### OTHER ANIMALS
>
> A book of this size can't contain statistics for every animal inhabiting your D&D campaign world. However, you can use the stat block of one animal to represent another easily enough. For example, you can use the panther statistics to represent a jaguar, the giant goat statistics to represent a buffalo, and the hawk statistics to represent a falcon.

Baboon

Small beast, unaligned

Armor Class 12
Hit Points 3 (1d6)
Speed 30 ft., climb 30 ft.

STR	DEX	CON	INT	WIS	CHA
8 (−1)	14 (+2)	11 (+0)	4 (−3)	12 (+1)	6 (−2)

Senses passive Perception 11
Languages —
Challenge 0 (10 XP)

Pack Tactics. The baboon has advantage on an attack roll against a creature if at least one of the baboon's allies is within 5 feet of the creature and the ally isn't incapacitated.

Actions

Bite. *Melee Weapon Attack:* +1 to hit, reach 5 ft., one target. *Hit:* 1 (1d4 − 1) piercing damage.

Badger

Tiny beast, unaligned

Armor Class 10
Hit Points 3 (1d4 + 1)
Speed 20 ft., burrow 5 ft.

STR	DEX	CON	INT	WIS	CHA
4 (−3)	11 (+0)	12 (+1)	2 (−4)	12 (+1)	5 (−3)

Senses darkvision 30 ft., passive Perception 11
Languages —
Challenge 0 (10 XP)

Keen Smell. The badger has advantage on Wisdom (Perception) checks that rely on smell.

Actions

Bite. *Melee Weapon Attack:* +2 to hit, reach 5 ft., one target. *Hit:* 1 piercing damage.

Bat

Tiny beast, unaligned

Armor Class 12
Hit Points 1 (1d4 − 1)
Speed 5 ft., fly 30 ft.

STR	DEX	CON	INT	WIS	CHA
2 (−4)	15 (+2)	8 (−1)	2 (−4)	12 (+1)	4 (−3)

Senses blindsight 60 ft., passive Perception 11
Languages —
Challenge 0 (10 XP)

Echolocation. The bat can't use its blindsight while deafened.

Keen Hearing. The bat has advantage on Wisdom (Perception) checks that rely on hearing.

Actions

Bite. *Melee Weapon Attack:* +0 to hit, reach 5 ft., one creature. *Hit:* 1 piercing damage.

Black Bear

Medium beast, unaligned

Armor Class 11 (natural armor)
Hit Points 19 (3d8 + 6)
Speed 40 ft., climb 30 ft.

STR	DEX	CON	INT	WIS	CHA
15 (+2)	10 (+0)	14 (+2)	2 (−4)	12 (+1)	7 (−2)

Skills Perception +3
Senses passive Perception 13
Languages —
Challenge 1/2 (100 XP)

Keen Smell. The bear has advantage on Wisdom (Perception) checks that rely on smell.

Actions

Multiattack. The bear makes two attacks: one with its bite and one with its claws.

Bite. *Melee Weapon Attack:* +3 to hit, reach 5 ft., one target. *Hit:* 5 (1d6 + 2) piercing damage.

Claws. *Melee Weapon Attack:* +3 to hit, reach 5 ft., one target. *Hit:* 7 (2d4 + 2) slashing damage.

Blink Dog

Medium fey, lawful good

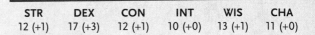

Armor Class 13
Hit Points 22 (4d8 + 4)
Speed 40 ft.

STR	DEX	CON	INT	WIS	CHA
12 (+1)	17 (+3)	12 (+1)	10 (+0)	13 (+1)	11 (+0)

Skills Perception +3, Stealth +5
Senses passive Perception 13
Languages Blink Dog, understands Sylvan but can't speak it
Challenge 1/4 (50 XP)

Keen Hearing and Smell. The dog has advantage on Wisdom (Perception) checks that rely on hearing or smell.

Actions

Bite. *Melee Weapon Attack:* +3 to hit, reach 5 ft., one target. *Hit:* 4 (1d6 + 1) piercing damage.

Teleport (Recharge 4–6). The dog magically teleports, along with any equipment it is wearing or carrying, up to 40 feet to an unoccupied space it can see. Before or after teleporting, the dog can make one bite attack.

A **blink dog** takes its name from its ability to blink in and out of existence, a talent it uses to aid its attacks and to avoid harm. Blink dogs harbor a long-standing hatred for displacer beasts and attack them on sight.

Blood Hawk

Small beast, unaligned

Armor Class 12
Hit Points 7 (2d6)
Speed 10 ft., fly 60 ft.

STR	DEX	CON	INT	WIS	CHA
6 (−2)	14 (+2)	10 (+0)	3 (−4)	14 (+2)	5 (−3)

Skills Perception +4
Senses passive Perception 14
Languages —
Challenge 1/8 (25 XP)

Keen Sight. The hawk has advantage on Wisdom (Perception) checks that rely on sight.

Pack Tactics. The hawk has advantage on an attack roll against a creature if at least one of the hawk's allies is within 5 feet of the creature and the ally isn't incapacitated.

Actions

Beak. *Melee Weapon Attack:* +4 to hit, reach 5 ft., one target. *Hit:* 4 (1d4 + 2) piercing damage.

Taking its name from its crimson feathers and aggressive nature, the **blood hawk** fearlessly attacks almost any animal, stabbing it with its daggerlike beak. Blood hawks flock together in large numbers, attacking as a pack to take down prey.

Boar

Medium beast, unaligned

Armor Class 11 (natural armor)
Hit Points 11 (2d8 + 2)
Speed 40 ft.

STR	DEX	CON	INT	WIS	CHA
13 (+1)	11 (+0)	12 (+1)	2 (−4)	9 (−1)	5 (−3)

Senses passive Perception 9
Languages —
Challenge 1/4 (50 XP)

Charge. If the boar moves at least 20 feet straight toward a target and then hits it with a tusk attack on the same turn, the target takes an extra 3 (1d6) slashing damage. If the target is a creature, it must succeed on a DC 11 Strength saving throw or be knocked prone.

Relentless (Recharges after a Short or Long Rest). If the boar takes 7 damage or less that would reduce it to 0 hit points, it is reduced to 1 hit point instead.

Actions

Tusk. *Melee Weapon Attack:* +3 to hit, reach 5 ft., one target. *Hit:* 4 (1d6 + 1) slashing damage.

Brown Bear

Large beast, unaligned

Armor Class 11 (natural armor)
Hit Points 34 (4d10 + 12)
Speed 40 ft., climb 30 ft.

STR	DEX	CON	INT	WIS	CHA
19 (+4)	10 (+0)	16 (+3)	2 (−4)	13 (+1)	7 (−2)

Skills Perception +3
Senses passive Perception 13
Languages —
Challenge 1 (200 XP)

Keen Smell. The bear has advantage on Wisdom (Perception) checks that rely on smell.

Actions

Multiattack. The bear makes two attacks: one with its bite and one with its claws.

Bite. *Melee Weapon Attack:* +5 to hit, reach 5 ft., one target. *Hit:* 8 (1d8 + 4) piercing damage.

Claws. *Melee Weapon Attack:* +5 to hit, reach 5 ft., one target. *Hit:* 11 (2d6 + 4) slashing damage.

BLINK DOG

CAMEL

Large beast, unaligned

Armor Class 9
Hit Points 15 (2d10 + 4)
Speed 50 ft.

STR	DEX	CON	INT	WIS	CHA
16 (+3)	8 (−1)	14 (+2)	2 (−4)	8 (−1)	5 (−3)

Senses passive Perception 9
Languages —
Challenge 1/8 (25 XP)

ACTIONS

Bite. *Melee Weapon Attack:* +5 to hit, reach 5 ft., one target.
Hit: 2 (1d4) bludgeoning damage.

CAT

Tiny beast, unaligned

Armor Class 12
Hit Points 2 (1d4)
Speed 40 ft., climb 30 ft.

STR	DEX	CON	INT	WIS	CHA
3 (−4)	15 (+2)	10 (+0)	3 (−4)	12 (+1)	7 (−2)

Skills Perception +3, Stealth +4
Senses passive Perception 13
Languages —
Challenge 0 (10 XP)

Keen Smell. The cat has advantage on Wisdom (Perception) checks that rely on smell.

ACTIONS

Claws. *Melee Weapon Attack:* +0 to hit, reach 5 ft., one target.
Hit: 1 slashing damage.

CONSTRICTOR SNAKE

Large beast, unaligned

Armor Class 12
Hit Points 13 (2d10 + 2)
Speed 30 ft., swim 30 ft.

STR	DEX	CON	INT	WIS	CHA
15 (+2)	14 (+2)	12 (+1)	1 (−5)	10 (+0)	3 (−4)

Senses blindsight 10 ft., passive Perception 10
Languages —
Challenge 1/4 (50 XP)

ACTIONS

Bite. *Melee Weapon Attack:* +4 to hit, reach 5 ft., one creature.
Hit: 5 (1d6 + 2) piercing damage.

Constrict. *Melee Weapon Attack:* +4 to hit, reach 5 ft., one creature. *Hit:* 6 (1d8 + 2) bludgeoning damage, and the target is grappled (escape DC 14). Until this grapple ends, the creature is restrained, and the snake can't constrict another target.

CRAB

Tiny beast, unaligned

Armor Class 11 (natural armor)
Hit Points 2 (1d4)
Speed 20 ft., swim 20 ft.

STR	DEX	CON	INT	WIS	CHA
2 (−4)	11 (+0)	10 (+0)	1 (−5)	8 (−1)	2 (−4)

Skills Stealth +2
Senses blindsight 30 ft., passive Perception 9
Languages —
Challenge 0 (10 XP)

Amphibious. The crab can breathe air and water.

ACTIONS

Claw. *Melee Weapon Attack:* +0 to hit, reach 5 ft., one target.
Hit: 1 bludgeoning damage.

CROCODILE

Large beast, unaligned

Armor Class 12 (natural armor)
Hit Points 19 (3d10 + 3)
Speed 20 ft., swim 30 ft.

STR	DEX	CON	INT	WIS	CHA
15 (+2)	10 (+0)	13 (+1)	2 (−4)	10 (+0)	5 (−3)

Skills Stealth +2
Senses passive Perception 10
Languages —
Challenge 1/2 (100 XP)

Hold Breath. The crocodile can hold its breath for 15 minutes.

ACTIONS

Bite. *Melee Weapon Attack:* +4 to hit, reach 5 ft., one creature. *Hit:* 7 (1d10 + 2) piercing damage, and the target is grappled (escape DC 12). Until this grapple ends, the target is restrained, and the crocodile can't bite another target.

Death Dog
Medium monstrosity, neutral evil

Armor Class 12
Hit Points 39 (6d8 + 12)
Speed 40 ft.

STR	DEX	CON	INT	WIS	CHA
15 (+2)	14 (+2)	14 (+2)	3 (−4)	13 (+1)	6 (−2)

Skills Perception +5, Stealth +4
Senses darkvision 120 ft., passive Perception 15
Languages —
Challenge 1 (200 XP)

Two-Headed. The dog has advantage on Wisdom (Perception) checks and on saving throws against being blinded, charmed, deafened, frightened, stunned, or knocked unconscious.

Actions

Multiattack. The dog makes two bite attacks.

Bite. *Melee Weapon Attack:* +4 to hit, reach 5 ft., one target. *Hit:* 5 (1d6 + 2) piercing damage. If the target is a creature, it must succeed on a DC 12 Constitution saving throw against disease or become poisoned until the disease is cured. Every 24 hours that elapse, the creature must repeat the saving throw, reducing its hit point maximum by 5 (1d10) on a failure. This reduction lasts until the disease is cured. The creature dies if the disease reduces its hit point maximum to 0.

A **death dog** is an ugly two-headed hound that roams plains, deserts, and the Underdark. Hate burns in a death dog's heart, and a taste for humanoid flesh drives it to attack travelers and explorers. Death dog saliva carries a foul disease that causes a victim's flesh to slowly rot off the bone.

DEATH DOG

Deer
Medium beast, unaligned

Armor Class 13
Hit Points 4 (1d8)
Speed 50 ft.

STR	DEX	CON	INT	WIS	CHA
11 (+0)	16 (+3)	11 (+0)	2 (−4)	14 (+2)	5 (−3)

Senses passive Perception 12
Languages —
Challenge 0 (10 XP)

Actions

Bite. *Melee Weapon Attack:* +2 to hit, reach 5 ft., one target. *Hit:* 2 (1d4) piercing damage.

Dire Wolf
Large beast, unaligned

Armor Class 14 (natural armor)
Hit Points 37 (5d10 + 10)
Speed 50 ft.

STR	DEX	CON	INT	WIS	CHA
17 (+3)	15 (+2)	15 (+2)	3 (−4)	12 (+1)	7 (−2)

Skills Perception +3, Stealth +4
Senses passive Perception 13
Languages —
Challenge 1 (200 XP)

Keen Hearing and Smell. The wolf has advantage on Wisdom (Perception) checks that rely on hearing or smell.

Pack Tactics. The wolf has advantage on an attack roll against a creature if at least one of the wolf's allies is within 5 feet of the creature and the ally isn't incapacitated.

Actions

Bite. *Melee Weapon Attack:* +5 to hit, reach 5 ft., one target. *Hit:* 10 (2d6 + 3) piercing damage. If the target is a creature, it must succeed on a DC 13 Strength saving throw or be knocked prone.

Draft Horse
Large beast, unaligned

Armor Class 10
Hit Points 19 (3d10 + 3)
Speed 40 ft.

STR	DEX	CON	INT	WIS	CHA
18 (+4)	10 (+0)	12 (+1)	2 (−4)	11 (+0)	7 (−2)

Senses passive Perception 10
Languages —
Challenge 1/4 (50 XP)

Actions

Hooves. *Melee Weapon Attack:* +6 to hit, reach 5 ft., one target. *Hit:* 9 (2d4 + 4) bludgeoning damage.

EAGLE

Small beast, unaligned

Armor Class 12
Hit Points 3 (1d6)
Speed 10 ft., fly 60 ft.

STR	DEX	CON	INT	WIS	CHA
6 (−2)	15 (+2)	10 (+0)	2 (−4)	14 (+2)	7 (−2)

Skills Perception +4
Senses passive Perception 14
Languages —
Challenge 0 (10 XP)

Keen Sight. The eagle has advantage on Wisdom (Perception) checks that rely on sight.

ACTIONS

Talons. *Melee Weapon Attack:* +4 to hit, reach 5 ft., one target. *Hit:* 4 (1d4 + 2) slashing damage.

ELEPHANT

Huge beast, unaligned

Armor Class 12 (natural armor)
Hit Points 76 (8d12 + 24)
Speed 40 ft.

STR	DEX	CON	INT	WIS	CHA
22 (+6)	9 (−1)	17 (+3)	3 (−4)	11 (+0)	6 (−2)

Senses passive Perception 10
Languages —
Challenge 4 (1,100 XP)

Trampling Charge. If the elephant moves at least 20 feet straight toward a creature and then hits it with a gore attack on the same turn, that target must succeed on a DC 12 Strength saving throw or be knocked prone. If the target is prone, the elephant can make one stomp attack against it as a bonus action.

ACTIONS

Gore. *Melee Weapon Attack:* +8 to hit, reach 5 ft., one target. *Hit:* 19 (3d8 + 6) piercing damage.

Stomp. *Melee Weapon Attack:* +8 to hit, reach 5 ft., one prone creature. *Hit:* 22 (3d10 + 6) bludgeoning damage.

ELK

Large beast, unaligned

Armor Class 10
Hit Points 13 (2d10 + 2)
Speed 50 ft.

STR	DEX	CON	INT	WIS	CHA
16 (+3)	10 (+0)	12 (+1)	2 (−4)	10 (+0)	6 (−2)

Senses passive Perception 10
Languages —
Challenge 1/4 (50 XP)

Charge. If the elk moves at least 20 feet straight toward a target and then hits it with a ram attack on the same turn, the target takes an extra 7 (2d6) damage. If the target is a creature, it must succeed on a DC 13 Strength saving throw or be knocked prone.

ACTIONS

Ram. *Melee Weapon Attack:* +5 to hit, reach 5 ft., one target. *Hit:* 6 (1d6 + 3) bludgeoning damage.

Hooves. *Melee Weapon Attack:* +5 to hit, reach 5 ft., one prone creature. *Hit:* 8 (2d4 + 3) bludgeoning damage.

FLYING SNAKE

Tiny beast, unaligned

Armor Class 14
Hit Points 5 (2d4)
Speed 30 ft., fly 60 ft., swim 30 ft.

STR	DEX	CON	INT	WIS	CHA
4 (−3)	18 (+4)	11 (+0)	2 (−4)	12 (+1)	5 (−3)

Senses blindsight 10 ft., passive Perception 11
Languages —
Challenge 1/8 (25 XP)

Flyby. The snake doesn't provoke opportunity attacks when it flies out of an enemy's reach.

ACTIONS

Bite. *Melee Weapon Attack:* +6 to hit, reach 5 ft., one target. *Hit:* 1 piercing damage plus 7 (3d4) poison damage.

A **flying snake** is a brightly colored, winged serpent found in remote jungles. Tribespeople and cultists sometimes domesticate flying snakes to serve as messengers that deliver scrolls wrapped in their coils.

FROG

Tiny beast, unaligned

Armor Class 11
Hit Points 1 (1d4 − 1)
Speed 20 ft., swim 20 ft.

STR	DEX	CON	INT	WIS	CHA
1 (−5)	13 (+1)	8 (−1)	1 (−5)	8 (−1)	3 (−4)

Skills Perception +1, Stealth +3
Senses darkvision 30 ft., passive Perception 11
Languages —
Challenge 0 (0 XP)

Amphibious. The frog can breathe air and water.

Standing Leap. The frog's long jump is up to 10 feet and its high jump is up to 5 feet, with or without a running start.

A **frog** has no effective attacks. It feeds on small insects and typically dwells near water, in trees, or underground. The frog's statistics can also be used to represent a **toad**.

Giant Ape

Huge beast, unaligned

Armor Class 12
Hit Points 157 (15d12 + 60)
Speed 40 ft., climb 40 ft.

STR	DEX	CON	INT	WIS	CHA
23 (+6)	14 (+2)	18 (+4)	7 (−2)	12 (+1)	7 (−2)

Skills Athletics +9, Perception +4
Senses passive Perception 14
Languages —
Challenge 7 (2,900 XP)

Actions

Multiattack. The ape makes two fist attacks.

Fist. *Melee Weapon Attack:* +9 to hit, reach 10 ft., one target. *Hit:* 22 (3d10 + 6) bludgeoning damage.

Rock. *Ranged Weapon Attack:* +9 to hit, range 50/100 ft., one target. *Hit:* 30 (7d6 + 6) bludgeoning damage.

Giant Badger

Medium beast, unaligned

Armor Class 10
Hit Points 13 (2d8 + 4)
Speed 30 ft., burrow 10 ft.

STR	DEX	CON	INT	WIS	CHA
13 (+1)	10 (+0)	15 (+2)	2 (−4)	12 (+1)	5 (−3)

Senses darkvision 30 ft., passive Perception 11
Languages —
Challenge 1/4 (50 XP)

Keen Smell. The badger has advantage on Wisdom (Perception) checks that rely on smell.

Actions

Multiattack. The badger makes two attacks: one with its bite and one with its claws.

Bite. *Melee Weapon Attack:* +3 to hit, reach 5 ft., one target. *Hit:* 4 (1d6 + 1) piercing damage.

Claws. *Melee Weapon Attack:* +3 to hit, reach 5 ft., one target. *Hit:* 6 (2d4 + 1) slashing damage.

Giant Bat

Large beast, unaligned

Armor Class 13
Hit Points 22 (4d10)
Speed 10 ft., fly 60 ft.

STR	DEX	CON	INT	WIS	CHA
15 (+2)	16 (+3)	11 (+0)	2 (−4)	12 (+1)	6 (−2)

Senses blindsight 60 ft., passive Perception 11
Languages —
Challenge 1/4 (50 XP)

Echolocation. The bat can't use its blindsight while deafened.

Keen Hearing. The bat has advantage on Wisdom (Perception) checks that rely on hearing.

Actions

Bite. *Melee Weapon Attack:* +4 to hit, reach 5 ft., one creature. *Hit:* 5 (1d6 + 2) piercing damage.

Giant Boar

Large beast, unaligned

Armor Class 12 (natural armor)
Hit Points 42 (5d10 + 15)
Speed 40 ft.

STR	DEX	CON	INT	WIS	CHA
17 (+3)	10 (+0)	16 (+3)	2 (−4)	7 (−2)	5 (−3)

Senses passive Perception 8
Languages —
Challenge 2 (450 XP)

Charge. If the boar moves at least 20 feet straight toward a target and then hits it with a tusk attack on the same turn, the target takes an extra 7 (2d6) slashing damage. If the target is a creature, it must succeed on a DC 13 Strength saving throw or be knocked prone.

Relentless (Recharges after a Short or Long Rest). If the boar takes 10 damage or less that would reduce it to 0 hit points, it is reduced to 1 hit point instead.

Actions

Tusk. *Melee Weapon Attack:* +5 to hit, reach 5 ft., one target. *Hit:* 10 (2d6 + 3) slashing damage.

Giant Centipede

Small beast, unaligned

Armor Class 13 (natural armor)
Hit Points 4 (1d6 + 1)
Speed 30 ft., climb 30 ft.

STR	DEX	CON	INT	WIS	CHA
5 (−3)	14 (+2)	12 (+1)	1 (−5)	7 (−2)	3 (−4)

Senses blindsight 30 ft., passive Perception 8
Languages —
Challenge 1/4 (50 XP)

Actions

Bite. *Melee Weapon Attack:* +4 to hit, reach 5 ft., one creature. *Hit:* 4 (1d4 + 2) piercing damage, and the target must succeed on a DC 11 Constitution saving throw or take 10 (3d6) poison damage. If the poison damage reduces the target to 0 hit points, the target is stable but poisoned for 1 hour, even after regaining hit points, and is paralyzed while poisoned in this way.

GIANT CONSTRICTOR SNAKE

Huge beast, unaligned

Armor Class 12
Hit Points 60 (8d12 + 8)
Speed 30 ft., swim 30 ft.

STR	DEX	CON	INT	WIS	CHA
19 (+4)	14 (+2)	12 (+1)	1 (−5)	10 (+0)	3 (−4)

Skills Perception +2
Senses blindsight 10 ft., passive Perception 12
Languages —
Challenge 2 (450 XP)

ACTIONS

Bite. *Melee Weapon Attack:* +6 to hit, reach 10 ft., one creature. *Hit:* 11 (2d6 + 4) piercing damage.

Constrict. *Melee Weapon Attack:* +6 to hit, reach 5 ft., one creature. *Hit:* 13 (2d8 + 4) bludgeoning damage, and the target is grappled (escape DC 16). Until this grapple ends, the creature is restrained, and the snake can't constrict another target.

GIANT CRAB

Medium beast, unaligned

Armor Class 15 (natural armor)
Hit Points 13 (3d8)
Speed 30 ft., swim 30 ft.

STR	DEX	CON	INT	WIS	CHA
13 (+1)	15 (+2)	11 (+0)	1 (−5)	9 (−1)	3 (−4)

Skills Stealth +4
Senses blindsight 30 ft., passive Perception 9
Languages —
Challenge 1/8 (25 XP)

Amphibious. The crab can breathe air and water.

ACTIONS

Claw. *Melee Weapon Attack:* +3 to hit, reach 5 ft., one target. *Hit:* 4 (1d6 + 1) bludgeoning damage, and the target is grappled (escape DC 11). The crab has two claws, each of which can grapple only one target.

GIANT EAGLE

GIANT CROCODILE

Huge beast, unaligned

Armor Class 14 (natural armor)
Hit Points 85 (9d12 + 27)
Speed 30 ft., swim 50 ft.

STR	DEX	CON	INT	WIS	CHA
21 (+5)	9 (−1)	17 (+3)	2 (−4)	10 (+0)	7 (−2)

Skills Stealth +5
Senses passive Perception 10
Languages —
Challenge 5 (1,800 XP)

Hold Breath. The crocodile can hold its breath for 30 minutes.

ACTIONS

Multiattack. The crocodile makes two attacks: one with its bite and one with its tail.

Bite. *Melee Weapon Attack:* +8 to hit, reach 5 ft., one target. *Hit:* 21 (3d10 + 5) piercing damage, and the target is grappled (escape DC 16). Until this grapple ends, the target is restrained, and the crocodile can't bite another target.

Tail. *Melee Weapon Attack:* +8 to hit, reach 10 ft., one target not grappled by the crocodile. *Hit:* 14 (2d8 + 5) bludgeoning damage. If the target is a creature, it must succeed on a DC 16 Strength saving throw or be knocked prone.

GIANT EAGLE

Large beast, neutral good

Armor Class 13
Hit Points 26 (4d10 + 4)
Speed 10 ft., fly 80 ft.

STR	DEX	CON	INT	WIS	CHA
16 (+3)	17 (+3)	13 (+1)	8 (−1)	14 (+2)	10 (+0)

Skills Perception +4
Senses passive Perception 14
Languages Giant Eagle, understands Common and Auran but can't speak them
Challenge 1 (200 XP)

Keen Sight. The eagle has advantage on Wisdom (Perception) checks that rely on sight.

ACTIONS

Multiattack. The eagle makes two attacks: one with its beak and one with its talons.

Beak. *Melee Weapon Attack:* +5 to hit, reach 5 ft., one target. *Hit:* 6 (1d6 + 3) piercing damage.

Talons. *Melee Weapon Attack:* +5 to hit, reach 5 ft., one target. *Hit:* 10 (2d6 + 3) slashing damage.

A **giant eagle** is a noble creature that speaks its own language and understands speech in the Common tongue. A mated pair of giant eagles typically has up to four eggs or young in their nest (treat the young as normal eagles).

Giant Elk

Huge beast, unaligned

Armor Class 14 (natural armor)
Hit Points 42 (5d12 + 10)
Speed 60 ft.

STR	DEX	CON	INT	WIS	CHA
19 (+4)	16 (+3)	14 (+2)	7 (−2)	14 (+2)	10 (+0)

Skills Perception +4
Senses passive Perception 14
Languages Giant Elk, understands Common, Elvish, and Sylvan but can't speak them
Challenge 2 (450 XP)

Charge. If the elk moves at least 20 feet straight toward a target and then hits it with a ram attack on the same turn, the target takes an extra 7 (2d6) damage. If the target is a creature, it must succeed on a DC 14 Strength saving throw or be knocked prone.

Actions

Ram. *Melee Weapon Attack:* +6 to hit, reach 10 ft., one target. *Hit:* 11 (2d6 + 4) bludgeoning damage.

Hooves. *Melee Weapon Attack:* +6 to hit, reach 5 ft., one prone creature. *Hit:* 22 (4d8 + 4) bludgeoning damage.

The majestic **giant elk** is rare to the point that its appearance is often taken as a foreshadowing of an important event, such as the birth of a king. Legends tell of gods that take the form of giant elk when visiting the Material Plane. Many cultures therefore believe that to hunt these creatures is to invite divine wrath.

Giant Fire Beetle

Small beast, unaligned

Armor Class 13 (natural armor)
Hit Points 4 (1d6 + 1)
Speed 30 ft.

STR	DEX	CON	INT	WIS	CHA
8 (−1)	10 (+0)	12 (+1)	1 (−5)	7 (−2)	3 (−4)

Senses blindsight 30 ft., passive Perception 8
Languages —
Challenge 0 (10 XP)

Illumination. The beetle sheds bright light in a 10-foot radius and dim light for an additional 10 feet.

Actions

Bite. *Melee Weapon Attack:* +1 to hit, reach 5 ft., one target. *Hit:* 2 (1d6 − 1) slashing damage.

A **giant fire beetle** is a nocturnal creature that takes its name from a pair of glowing glands that give off light. Miners and adventurers prize these creatures, for a giant fire beetle's glands continue to shed light for 1d6 days after the beetle dies. Giant fire beetles are most commonly found underground and in dark forests.

Giant Frog

Medium beast, unaligned

Armor Class 11
Hit Points 18 (4d8)
Speed 30 ft., swim 30 ft.

STR	DEX	CON	INT	WIS	CHA
12 (+1)	13 (+1)	11 (+0)	2 (−4)	10 (+0)	3 (−4)

Skills Perception +2, Stealth +3
Senses darkvision 30 ft., passive Perception 12
Languages —
Challenge 1/4 (50 XP)

Amphibious. The frog can breathe air and water.

Standing Leap. The frog's long jump is up to 20 feet and its high jump is up to 10 feet, with or without a running start.

Actions

Bite. *Melee Weapon Attack:* +3 to hit, reach 5 ft., one target. *Hit:* 4 (1d6 + 1) piercing damage, and the target is grappled (escape DC 11). Until this grapple ends, the target is restrained, and the frog can't bite another target.

Swallow. The frog makes one bite attack against a Small or smaller target it is grappling. If the attack hits, the target is swallowed, and the grapple ends. The swallowed target is blinded and restrained, it has total cover against attacks and other effects outside the frog, and it takes 5 (2d4) acid damage at the start of each of the frog's turns. The frog can have only one target swallowed at a time.

If the frog dies, a swallowed creature is no longer restrained by it and can escape from the corpse using 5 feet of movement, exiting prone.

GIANT FIRE BEETLE

Giant Goat

Large beast, unaligned

Armor Class 11 (natural armor)
Hit Points 19 (3d10 + 3)
Speed 40 ft.

STR	DEX	CON	INT	WIS	CHA
17 (+3)	11 (+0)	12 (+1)	3 (−4)	12 (+1)	6 (−2)

Senses passive Perception 11
Languages —
Challenge 1/2 (100 XP)

Charge. If the goat moves at least 20 feet straight toward a target and then hits it with a ram attack on the same turn, the target takes an extra 5 (2d4) bludgeoning damage. If the target is a creature, it must succeed on a DC 13 Strength saving throw or be knocked prone.

Sure-Footed. The goat has advantage on Strength and Dexterity saving throws made against effects that would knock it prone.

Actions

Ram. *Melee Weapon Attack:* +5 to hit, reach 5 ft., one target. *Hit:* 8 (2d4 + 3) bludgeoning damage.

Giant Hyena

Large beast, unaligned

Armor Class 12
Hit Points 45 (6d10 + 12)
Speed 50 ft.

STR	DEX	CON	INT	WIS	CHA
16 (+3)	14 (+2)	14 (+2)	2 (−4)	12 (+1)	7 (−2)

Skills Perception +3
Senses passive Perception 13
Languages —
Challenge 1 (200 XP)

Rampage. When the hyena reduces a creature to 0 hit points with a melee attack on its turn, the hyena can take a bonus action to move up to half its speed and make a bite attack.

Actions

Bite. *Melee Weapon Attack:* +5 to hit, reach 5 ft., one target. *Hit:* 10 (2d6 + 3) piercing damage.

Giant Lizard

Large beast, unaligned

Armor Class 12 (natural armor)
Hit Points 19 (3d10 + 3)
Speed 30 ft., climb 30 ft.

STR	DEX	CON	INT	WIS	CHA
15 (+2)	12 (+1)	13 (+1)	2 (−4)	10 (+0)	5 (−3)

Senses darkvision 30 ft., passive Perception 10
Languages —
Challenge 1/4 (50 XP)

Actions

Bite. *Melee Weapon Attack:* +4 to hit, reach 5 ft., one target. *Hit:* 6 (1d8 + 2) piercing damage.

A **giant lizard** can be ridden or used as a draft animal. Lizardfolk also keep them as pets, and subterranean giant lizards are used as mounts and pack animals by drow, duergar, and other Underdark dwellers.

> ### Variant: Giant Lizard Traits
>
> Some giant lizards have one or both of the following traits.
> **Hold Breath.** The lizard can hold its breath for 15 minutes. (A lizard that has this trait also has a swimming speed of 30 feet.)
> **Spider Climb.** The lizard can climb difficult surfaces, including upside down on ceilings, without needing to make an ability check.

Giant Octopus

Large beast, unaligned

Armor Class 11
Hit Points 52 (8d10 + 8)
Speed 10 ft., swim 60 ft.

STR	DEX	CON	INT	WIS	CHA
17 (+3)	13 (+1)	13 (+1)	4 (−3)	10 (+0)	4 (−3)

Skills Perception +4, Stealth +5
Senses darkvision 60 ft., passive Perception 14
Languages —
Challenge 1 (200 XP)

Hold Breath. While out of water, the octopus can hold its breath for 1 hour.

Underwater Camouflage. The octopus has advantage on Dexterity (Stealth) checks made while underwater.

Water Breathing. The octopus can breathe only underwater.

Actions

Tentacles. *Melee Weapon Attack:* +5 to hit, reach 15 ft., one target. *Hit:* 10 (2d6 + 3) bludgeoning damage. If the target is a creature, it is grappled (escape DC 16). Until this grapple ends, the target is restrained, and the octopus can't use its tentacles on another target.

Ink Cloud (Recharges after a Short or Long Rest). A 20-foot-radius cloud of ink extends all around the octopus if it is underwater. The area is heavily obscured for 1 minute, although a significant current can disperse the ink. After releasing the ink, the octopus can use the Dash action as a bonus action.

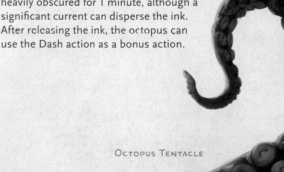

OCTOPUS TENTACLE

Giant Owl

Large beast, neutral

Armor Class 12
Hit Points 19 (3d10 + 3)
Speed 5 ft., fly 60 ft.

STR	DEX	CON	INT	WIS	CHA
13 (+1)	15 (+2)	12 (+1)	8 (–1)	13 (+1)	10 (+0)

Skills Perception +5, Stealth +4
Senses darkvision 120 ft., passive Perception 15
Languages Giant Owl, understands Common, Elvish, and Sylvan but can't speak them
Challenge 1/4 (50 XP)

Flyby. The owl doesn't provoke opportunity attacks when it flies out of an enemy's reach.

Keen Hearing and Sight. The owl has advantage on Wisdom (Perception) checks that rely on hearing or sight.

Actions

Talons. *Melee Weapon Attack:* +3 to hit, reach 5 ft., one target. *Hit:* 8 (2d6 + 1) slashing damage.

Giant owls often befriend fey and other sylvan creatures and are guardians of their woodland realms.

Giant Poisonous Snake

Medium beast, unaligned

Armor Class 14
Hit Points 11 (2d8 + 2)
Speed 30 ft., swim 30 ft.

STR	DEX	CON	INT	WIS	CHA
10 (+0)	18 (+4)	13 (+1)	2 (–4)	10 (+0)	3 (–4)

Skills Perception +2
Senses blindsight 10 ft., passive Perception 12
Languages —
Challenge 1/4 (50 XP)

Actions

Bite. *Melee Weapon Attack:* +6 to hit, reach 10 ft., one target. *Hit:* 6 (1d4 + 4) piercing damage, and the target must make a DC 11 Constitution saving throw, taking 10 (3d6) poison damage on a failed save, or half as much damage on a successful one.

> ### Variant: Diseased Giant Rats
>
> Some giant rats carry vile diseases that they spread with their bites. A diseased giant rat has a challenge rating of 1/8 (25 XP) and the following action instead of its normal bite attack.
> ***Bite.*** *Melee Weapon Attack:* +4 to hit, reach 5 ft., one target. *Hit:* 4 (1d4 + 2) piercing damage. If the target is a creature, it must succeed on a DC 10 Constitution saving throw or contract a disease. Until the disease is cured, the target can't regain hit points except by magical means, and the target's hit point maximum decreases by 3 (1d6) every 24 hours. If the target's hit point maximum drops to 0 as a result of this disease, the target dies.

> ## NOTICE
>
> Giant rats have been sighted throughout the city. Anyone bitten by a giant rat should visit a temple for ministration and prayer.
>
> The city hereby offers a silver coin for each giant rat slain within its walls. To receive payment, evidence must be delivered to the watch captain at the docks between highsun and dusk.

Giant Rat

Small beast, unaligned

Armor Class 12
Hit Points 7 (2d6)
Speed 30 ft.

STR	DEX	CON	INT	WIS	CHA
7 (–2)	15 (+2)	11 (+0)	2 (–4)	10 (+0)	4 (–3)

Senses darkvision 60 ft., passive Perception 10
Languages —
Challenge 1/8 (25 XP)

Keen Smell. The rat has advantage on Wisdom (Perception) checks that rely on smell.

Pack Tactics. The rat has advantage on an attack roll against a creature if at least one of the rat's allies is within 5 feet of the creature and the ally isn't incapacitated.

Actions

Bite. *Melee Weapon Attack:* +4 to hit, reach 5 ft., one target. *Hit:* 4 (1d4 + 2) piercing damage.

Giant Scorpion

Large beast, unaligned

Armor Class 15 (natural armor)
Hit Points 52 (7d10 + 14)
Speed 40 ft.

STR	DEX	CON	INT	WIS	CHA
15 (+2)	13 (+1)	15 (+2)	1 (–5)	9 (–1)	3 (–4)

Senses blindsight 60 ft., passive Perception 9
Languages —
Challenge 3 (700 XP)

Actions

Multiattack. The scorpion makes three attacks: two with its claws and one with its sting.

Claw. *Melee Weapon Attack:* +4 to hit, reach 5 ft., one target. *Hit:* 6 (1d8 + 2) bludgeoning damage, and the target is grappled (escape DC 12). The scorpion has two claws, each of which can grapple only one target.

Sting. *Melee Weapon Attack:* +4 to hit, reach 5 ft., one creature. *Hit:* 7 (1d10 + 2) piercing damage, and the target must make a DC 12 Constitution saving throw, taking 22 (4d10) poison damage on a failed save, or half as much damage on a successful one.

GIANT SEA HORSE

Large beast, unaligned

Armor Class 13 (natural armor)
Hit Points 16 (3d10)
Speed 0 ft., swim 40 ft.

STR	DEX	CON	INT	WIS	CHA
12 (+1)	15 (+2)	11 (+0)	2 (−4)	12 (+1)	5 (−3)

Senses passive Perception 11
Languages —
Challenge 1/2 (100 XP)

Charge. If the sea horse moves at least 20 feet straight toward a target and then hits it with a ram attack on the same turn, the target takes an extra 7 (2d6) bludgeoning damage. It the target is a creature, it must succeed on a DC 11 Strength saving throw or be knocked prone.

Water Breathing. The sea horse can breathe only underwater.

ACTIONS

Ram. *Melee Weapon Attack:* +3 to hit, reach 5 ft., one target. *Hit:* 4 (1d6 + 1) bludgeoning damage.

Like their smaller kin, **giant sea horses** are shy, colorful fish with elongated bodies and curled tails. Aquatic elves train them as mounts.

GIANT SHARK

Huge beast, unaligned

Armor Class 13 (natural armor)
Hit Points 126 (11d12 + 55)
Speed 0 ft., swim 50 ft.

STR	DEX	CON	INT	WIS	CHA
23 (+6)	11 (+0)	21 (+5)	1 (−5)	10 (+0)	5 (−3)

Skills Perception +3
Senses blindsight 60 ft., passive Perception 13
Languages —
Challenge 5 (1,800 XP)

Blood Frenzy. The shark has advantage on melee attack rolls against any creature that doesn't have all its hit points.

Water Breathing. The shark can breathe only underwater.

ACTIONS

Bite. *Melee Weapon Attack:* +9 to hit, reach 5 ft., one target. *Hit:* 22 (3d10 + 6) piercing damage.

A **giant shark** is 30 feet long and normally found in deep oceans. Utterly fearless, it preys on anything that crosses its path, including whales and ships.

GIANT SPIDER

Large beast, unaligned

Armor Class 14 (natural armor)
Hit Points 26 (4d10 + 4)
Speed 30 ft., climb 30 ft.

STR	DEX	CON	INT	WIS	CHA
14 (+2)	16 (+3)	12 (+1)	2 (−4)	11 (+0)	4 (−3)

Skills Stealth +7
Senses blindsight 10 ft., darkvision 60 ft., passive Perception 10
Languages —
Challenge 1 (200 XP)

Spider Climb. The spider can climb difficult surfaces, including upside down on ceilings, without needing to make an ability check.

Web Sense. While in contact with a web, the spider knows the exact location of any other creature in contact with the same web.

Web Walker. The spider ignores movement restrictions caused by webbing.

ACTIONS

Bite. *Melee Weapon Attack:* +5 to hit, reach 5 ft., one creature. *Hit:* 7 (1d8 + 3) piercing damage, and the target must make a DC 11 Constitution saving throw, taking 9 (2d8) poison damage on a failed save, or half as much damage on a successful one. If the poison damage reduces the target to 0 hit points, the target is stable but poisoned for 1 hour, even after regaining hit points, and is paralyzed while poisoned in this way.

Web (Recharge 5–6). *Ranged Weapon Attack:* +5 to hit, range 30/60 ft., one creature. *Hit:* The target is restrained by webbing. As an action, the restrained target can make a DC 12 Strength check, bursting the webbing on a success. The webbing can also be attacked and destroyed (AC 10; hp 5; vulnerability to fire damage; immunity to bludgeoning, poison, and psychic damage).

To snare its prey, a **giant spider** spins elaborate webs or shoots sticky strands of webbing from its abdomen. Giant spiders are most commonly found underground, making their lairs on ceilings or in dark, web-filled crevices. Such lairs are often festooned with web cocoons holding past victims.

GIANT SPIDER

Giant Toad
Large beast, unaligned

Armor Class 11
Hit Points 39 (6d10 + 6)
Speed 20 ft., swim 40 ft.

STR	DEX	CON	INT	WIS	CHA
15 (+2)	13 (+1)	13 (+1)	2 (−4)	10 (+0)	3 (−4)

Senses darkvision 30 ft., passive Perception 10
Languages —
Challenge 1 (200 XP)

Amphibious. The toad can breathe air and water.

Standing Leap. The toad's long jump is up to 20 feet and its high jump is up to 10 feet, with or without a running start.

Actions

Bite. *Melee Weapon Attack:* +4 to hit, reach 5 ft., one target. *Hit:* 7 (1d10 + 2) piercing damage plus 5 (1d10) poison damage, and the target is grappled (escape DC 13). Until this grapple ends, the target is restrained, and the toad can't bite another target.

Swallow. The toad makes one bite attack against a Medium or smaller target it is grappling. If the attack hits, the target is swallowed, and the grapple ends. The swallowed target is blinded and restrained, it has total cover against attacks and other effects outside the toad, and it takes 10 (3d6) acid damage at the start of each of the toad's turns. The toad can have only one target swallowed at a time.

If the toad dies, a swallowed creature is no longer restrained by it and can escape from the corpse using 5 feet of movement, exiting prone.

Giant Vulture
Large beast, neutral evil

Armor Class 10
Hit Points 22 (3d10 + 6)
Speed 10 ft., fly 60 ft.

STR	DEX	CON	INT	WIS	CHA
15 (+2)	10 (+0)	15 (+2)	6 (−2)	12 (+1)	7 (−2)

Skills Perception +3
Senses passive Perception 13
Languages understands Common but can't speak
Challenge 1 (200 XP)

Keen Sight and Smell. The vulture has advantage on Wisdom (Perception) checks that rely on sight or smell.

Pack Tactics. The vulture has advantage on an attack roll against a creature if at least one of the vulture's allies is within 5 feet of the creature and the ally isn't incapacitated.

Actions

Multiattack. The vulture makes two attacks: one with its beak and one with its talons.

Beak. *Melee Weapon Attack:* +4 to hit, reach 5 ft., one target. *Hit:* 7 (2d4 + 2) piercing damage.

Talons. *Melee Weapon Attack:* +4 to hit, reach 5 ft., one target. *Hit:* 9 (2d6 + 2) slashing damage.

A **giant vulture** has advanced intelligence and a malevolent bent. Unlike its smaller kin, it will attack a wounded creature to hasten its end. Giant vultures have been known to haunt a thirsty, starving creature for days to enjoy its suffering.

Giant Wasp
Medium beast, unaligned

Armor Class 12
Hit Points 13 (3d8)
Speed 10 ft., fly 50 ft.

STR	DEX	CON	INT	WIS	CHA
10 (+0)	14 (+2)	10 (+0)	1 (−5)	10 (+0)	3 (−4)

Senses passive Perception 10
Languages —
Challenge 1/2 (100 XP)

Actions

Sting. *Melee Weapon Attack:* +4 to hit, reach 5 ft., one creature. *Hit:* 5 (1d6 + 2) piercing damage, and the target must make a DC 11 Constitution saving throw, taking 10 (3d6) poison damage on a failed save, or half as much damage on a successful one. If the poison damage reduces the target to 0 hit points, the target is stable but poisoned for 1 hour, even after regaining hit points, and is paralyzed while poisoned in this way.

Giant Weasel
Medium beast, unaligned

Armor Class 13
Hit Points 9 (2d8)
Speed 40 ft.

STR	DEX	CON	INT	WIS	CHA
11 (+0)	16 (+3)	10 (+0)	4 (−3)	12 (+1)	5 (−3)

Skills Perception +3, Stealth +5
Senses darkvision 60 ft., passive Perception 13
Languages —
Challenge 1/8 (25 XP)

Keen Hearing and Smell. The weasel has advantage on Wisdom (Perception) checks that rely on hearing or smell.

Actions

Bite. *Melee Weapon Attack:* +5 to hit, reach 5 ft., one target. *Hit:* 5 (1d4 + 3) piercing damage.

GIANT WOLF SPIDER

Medium beast, unaligned

Armor Class 13
Hit Points 11 (2d8 + 2)
Speed 40 ft., climb 40 ft.

STR	DEX	CON	INT	WIS	CHA
12 (+1)	16 (+3)	13 (+1)	3 (−4)	12 (+1)	4 (−3)

Skills Perception +3, Stealth +7
Senses blindsight 10 ft., darkvision 60 ft., passive Perception 13
Languages —
Challenge 1/4 (50 XP)

Spider Climb. The spider can climb difficult surfaces, including upside down on ceilings, without needing to make an ability check.

Web Sense. While in contact with a web, the spider knows the exact location of any other creature in contact with the same web.

Web Walker. The spider ignores movement restrictions caused by webbing.

ACTIONS

Bite. *Melee Weapon Attack:* +3 to hit, reach 5 ft., one creature. *Hit:* 4 (1d6 + 1) piercing damage, and the target must make a DC 11 Constitution saving throw, taking 7 (2d6) poison damage on a failed save, or half as much damage on a successful one. If the poison damage reduces the target to 0 hit points, the target is stable but poisoned for 1 hour, even after regaining hit points, and is paralyzed while poisoned in this way.

Smaller than a giant spider, a **giant wolf spider** hunts prey across open ground or hides in a burrow or crevice, or in a hidden cavity beneath debris.

GOAT

Medium beast, unaligned

Armor Class 10
Hit Points 4 (1d8)
Speed 40 ft.

STR	DEX	CON	INT	WIS	CHA
12 (+1)	10 (+0)	11 (+0)	2 (−4)	10 (+0)	5 (−3)

Senses passive Perception 10
Languages —
Challenge 0 (10 XP)

Charge. If the goat moves at least 20 feet straight toward a target and then hits it with a ram attack on the same turn, the target takes an extra 2 (1d4) bludgeoning damage. If the target is a creature, it must succeed on a DC 10 Strength saving throw or be knocked prone.

Sure-Footed. The goat has advantage on Strength and Dexterity saving throws made against effects that would knock it prone.

ACTIONS

Ram. *Melee Weapon Attack:* +3 to hit, reach 5 ft., one target. *Hit:* 3 (1d4 + 1) bludgeoning damage.

HAWK

HAWK

Tiny beast, unaligned

Armor Class 13
Hit Points 1 (1d4 − 1)
Speed 10 ft., fly 60 ft.

STR	DEX	CON	INT	WIS	CHA
5 (−3)	16 (+3)	8 (−1)	2 (−4)	14 (+2)	6 (−2)

Skills Perception +4
Senses passive Perception 14
Languages —
Challenge 0 (10 XP)

Keen Sight. The hawk has advantage on Wisdom (Perception) checks that rely on sight.

ACTIONS

Talons. *Melee Weapon Attack:* +5 to hit, reach 5 ft., one target. *Hit:* 1 slashing damage.

HUNTER SHARK

Large beast, unaligned

Armor Class 12 (natural armor)
Hit Points 45 (6d10 + 12)
Speed 0 ft., swim 40 ft.

STR	DEX	CON	INT	WIS	CHA
18 (+4)	13 (+1)	15 (+2)	1 (−5)	10 (+0)	4 (−3)

Skills Perception +2
Senses blindsight 30 ft., passive Perception 12
Languages —
Challenge 2 (450 XP)

Blood Frenzy. The shark has advantage on melee attack rolls against any creature that doesn't have all its hit points.

Water Breathing. The shark can breathe only underwater.

ACTIONS

Bite. *Melee Weapon Attack:* +6 to hit, reach 5 ft., one target. *Hit:* 13 (2d8 + 4) piercing damage.

Smaller than a giant shark but larger and fiercer than a reef shark, a **hunter shark** haunts deep waters. It usually hunts alone, but multiple hunter sharks might feed in the same area. A fully grown hunter shark is 15 to 20 feet long.

Hyena

Medium beast, unaligned

Armor Class 11
Hit Points 5 (1d8 + 1)
Speed 50 ft.

STR	DEX	CON	INT	WIS	CHA
11 (+0)	13 (+1)	12 (+1)	2 (−4)	12 (+1)	5 (−3)

Skills Perception +3
Senses passive Perception 13
Languages —
Challenge 0 (10 XP)

Pack Tactics. The hyena has advantage on an attack roll against a creature if at least one of the hyena's allies is within 5 feet of the creature and the ally isn't incapacitated.

Actions

Bite. *Melee Weapon Attack:* +2 to hit, reach 5 ft., one target. *Hit:* 3 (1d6) piercing damage.

Jackal

Small beast, unaligned

Armor Class 12
Hit Points 3 (1d6)
Speed 40 ft.

STR	DEX	CON	INT	WIS	CHA
8 (−1)	15 (+2)	11 (+0)	3 (−4)	12 (+1)	6 (−2)

Skills Perception +3
Senses passive Perception 13
Languages —
Challenge 0 (10 XP)

Keen Hearing and Smell. The jackal has advantage on Wisdom (Perception) checks that rely on hearing or smell.

Pack Tactics. The jackal has advantage on an attack roll against a creature if at least one of the jackal's allies is within 5 feet of the creature and the ally isn't incapacitated.

Actions

Bite. *Melee Weapon Attack:* +1 to hit, reach 5 ft., one target. *Hit:* 1 (1d4 − 1) piercing damage.

HYENA

Killer Whale

Huge beast, unaligned

Armor Class 12 (natural armor)
Hit Points 90 (12d12 + 12)
Speed 0 ft., swim 60 ft.

STR	DEX	CON	INT	WIS	CHA
19 (+4)	10 (+0)	13 (+1)	3 (−4)	12 (+1)	7 (−2)

Skills Perception +3
Senses blindsight 120 ft., passive Perception 13
Languages —
Challenge 3 (700 XP)

Echolocation. The whale can't use its blindsight while deafened.

Hold Breath. The whale can hold its breath for 30 minutes.

Keen Hearing. The whale has advantage on Wisdom (Perception) checks that rely on hearing.

Actions

Bite. *Melee Weapon Attack:* +6 to hit, reach 5 ft., one target. *Hit:* 21 (5d6 + 4) piercing damage.

Lion

Large beast, unaligned

Armor Class 12
Hit Points 26 (4d10 + 4)
Speed 50 ft.

STR	DEX	CON	INT	WIS	CHA
17 (+3)	15 (+2)	13 (+1)	3 (−4)	12 (+1)	8 (−1)

Skills Perception +3, Stealth +6
Senses passive Perception 13
Languages —
Challenge 1 (200 XP)

Keen Smell. The lion has advantage on Wisdom (Perception) checks that rely on smell.

Pack Tactics. The lion has advantage on an attack roll against a creature if at least one of the lion's allies is within 5 feet of the creature and the ally isn't incapacitated.

Pounce. If the lion moves at least 20 feet straight toward a creature and then hits it with a claw attack on the same turn, that target must succeed on a DC 13 Strength saving throw or be knocked prone. If the target is prone, the lion can make one bite attack against it as a bonus action.

Running Leap. With a 10-foot running start, the lion can long jump up to 25 feet.

Actions

Bite. *Melee Weapon Attack:* +5 to hit, reach 5 ft., one target. *Hit:* 7 (1d8 + 3) piercing damage.

Claw. *Melee Weapon Attack:* +5 to hit, reach 5 ft., one target. *Hit:* 6 (1d6 + 3) slashing damage.

LIZARD
Tiny beast, unaligned

Armor Class 10
Hit Points 2 (1d4)
Speed 20 ft., climb 20 ft.

STR	DEX	CON	INT	WIS	CHA
2 (–4)	11 (+0)	10 (+0)	1 (–5)	8 (–1)	3 (–4)

Senses darkvision 30 ft., passive Perception 9
Languages —
Challenge 0 (10 XP)

ACTIONS

Bite. *Melee Weapon Attack:* +0 to hit, reach 5 ft., one target. *Hit:* 1 piercing damage.

MAMMOTH
Huge beast, unaligned

Armor Class 13 (natural armor)
Hit Points 126 (11d12 + 55)
Speed 40 ft.

STR	DEX	CON	INT	WIS	CHA
24 (+7)	9 (–1)	21 (+5)	3 (–4)	11 (+0)	6 (–2)

Senses passive Perception 10
Languages —
Challenge 6 (2,300 XP)

Trampling Charge. If the mammoth moves at least 20 feet straight toward a creature and then hits it with a gore attack on the same turn, that target must succeed on a DC 18 Strength saving throw or be knocked prone. If the target is prone, the mammoth can make one stomp attack against it as a bonus action.

ACTIONS

Gore. *Melee Weapon Attack:* +10 to hit, reach 10 ft., one target. *Hit:* 25 (4d8 + 7) piercing damage.

Stomp. *Melee Weapon Attack:* +10 to hit, reach 5 ft., one prone creature. *Hit:* 29 (4d10 + 7) bludgeoning damage.

A **mammoth** is an elephantine creature with thick fur and long tusks. Stockier and fiercer than normal elephants, mammoths inhabit a wide range of climes, from subarctic to subtropical.

MASTIFF
Medium beast, unaligned

Armor Class 12
Hit Points 5 (1d8 + 1)
Speed 40 ft.

STR	DEX	CON	INT	WIS	CHA
13 (+1)	14 (+2)	12 (+1)	3 (–4)	12 (+1)	7 (–2)

Skills Perception +3
Senses passive Perception 13
Languages —
Challenge 1/8 (25 XP)

Keen Hearing and Smell. The mastiff has advantage on Wisdom (Perception) checks that rely on hearing or smell.

ACTIONS

Bite. *Melee Weapon Attack:* +3 to hit, reach 5 ft., one target. *Hit:* 4 (1d6 + 1) piercing damage. If the target is a creature, it must succeed on a DC 11 Strength saving throw or be knocked prone.

Mastiffs are impressive hounds prized by humanoids for their loyalty and keen senses. Mastiffs can be trained as guard dogs, hunting dogs, and war dogs. Halflings and other Small humanoids ride them as mounts.

MASTIFF

APPENDIX A: MISCELLANEOUS CREATURES

Mule
Medium beast, unaligned

Armor Class 10
Hit Points 11 (2d8 + 2)
Speed 40 ft.

STR	DEX	CON	INT	WIS	CHA
14 (+2)	10 (+0)	13 (+1)	2 (−4)	10 (+0)	5 (−3)

Senses passive Perception 10
Languages —
Challenge 1/8 (25 XP)

Beast of Burden. The mule is considered to be a Large animal for the purpose of determining its carrying capacity.

Sure-Footed. The mule has advantage on Strength and Dexterity saving throws made against effects that would knock it prone.

Actions

Hooves. *Melee Weapon Attack:* +2 to hit, reach 5 ft., one target. *Hit:* 4 (1d4 + 2) bludgeoning damage.

Octopus
Small beast, unaligned

Armor Class 12
Hit Points 3 (1d6)
Speed 5 ft., swim 30 ft.

STR	DEX	CON	INT	WIS	CHA
4 (−3)	15 (+2)	11 (+0)	3 (−4)	10 (+0)	4 (−3)

Skills Perception +2, Stealth +4
Senses darkvision 30 ft., passive Perception 12
Languages —
Challenge 0 (10 XP)

Hold Breath. While out of water, the octopus can hold its breath for 30 minutes.

Underwater Camouflage. The octopus has advantage on Dexterity (Stealth) checks made while underwater.

Water Breathing. The octopus can breathe only underwater.

Actions

Tentacles. *Melee Weapon Attack:* +4 to hit, reach 5 ft., one target. *Hit:* 1 bludgeoning damage, and the target is grappled (escape DC 10). Until this grapple ends, the octopus can't use its tentacles on another target.

Ink Cloud (Recharges after a Short or Long Rest). A 5-foot-radius cloud of ink extends all around the octopus if it is underwater. The area is heavily obscured for 1 minute, although a significant current can disperse the ink. After releasing the ink, the octopus can use the Dash action as a bonus action.

Owl
Tiny beast, unaligned

Armor Class 11
Hit Points 1 (1d4 − 1)
Speed 5 ft., fly 60 ft.

STR	DEX	CON	INT	WIS	CHA
3 (−4)	13 (+1)	8 (−1)	2 (−4)	12 (+1)	7 (−2)

Skills Perception +3, Stealth +3
Senses darkvision 120 ft., passive Perception 13
Languages —
Challenge 0 (10 XP)

Flyby. The owl doesn't provoke opportunity attacks when it flies out of an enemy's reach.

Keen Hearing and Sight. The owl has advantage on Wisdom (Perception) checks that rely on hearing or sight.

Actions

Talons. *Melee Weapon Attack:* +3 to hit, reach 5 ft., one target. *Hit:* 1 slashing damage.

Panther
Medium beast, unaligned

Armor Class 12
Hit Points 13 (3d8)
Speed 50 ft., climb 40 ft.

STR	DEX	CON	INT	WIS	CHA
14 (+2)	15 (+2)	10 (+0)	3 (−4)	14 (+2)	7 (−2)

Skills Perception +4, Stealth +6
Senses passive Perception 14
Languages —
Challenge 1/4 (50 XP)

Keen Smell. The panther has advantage on Wisdom (Perception) checks that rely on smell.

Pounce. If the panther moves at least 20 feet straight toward a creature and then hits it with a claw attack on the same turn, that target must succeed on a DC 12 Strength saving throw or be knocked prone. If the target is prone, the panther can make one bite attack against it as a bonus action.

Actions

Bite. *Melee Weapon Attack:* +4 to hit, reach 5 ft., one target. *Hit:* 5 (1d6 + 2) piercing damage.

Claw. *Melee Weapon Attack:* +4 to hit, reach 5 ft., one target. *Hit:* 4 (1d4 + 2) slashing damage.

PHASE SPIDER

Large monstrosity, unaligned

Armor Class 13 (natural armor)
Hit Points 32 (5d10 + 5)
Speed 30 ft., climb 30 ft.

STR	DEX	CON	INT	WIS	CHA
15 (+2)	15 (+2)	12 (+1)	6 (−2)	10 (+0)	6 (−2)

Skills Stealth +6
Senses darkvision 60 ft., passive Perception 10
Languages —
Challenge 3 (700 XP)

Ethereal Jaunt. As a bonus action, the spider can magically shift from the Material Plane to the Ethereal Plane, or vice versa.

Spider Climb. The spider can climb difficult surfaces, including upside down on ceilings, without needing to make an ability check.

Web Walker. The spider ignores movement restrictions caused by webbing.

ACTIONS

Bite. *Melee Weapon Attack:* +4 to hit, reach 5 ft., one creature. *Hit:* 7 (1d10 + 2) piercing damage, and the target must make a DC 11 Constitution saving throw, taking 18 (4d8) poison damage on a failed save, or half as much damage on a successful one. If the poison damage reduces the target to 0 hit points, the target is stable but poisoned for 1 hour, even after regaining hit points, and is paralyzed while poisoned in this way.

A **phase spider** possesses the magical ability to phase in and out of the Ethereal Plane. It seems to appear out of nowhere and quickly vanishes after attacking. Its movement on the Ethereal Plane before coming back to the Material Plane makes it seem like it can teleport.

PHASE SPIDER

POISONOUS SNAKE

Tiny beast, unaligned

Armor Class 13
Hit Points 2 (1d4)
Speed 30 ft., swim 30 ft.

STR	DEX	CON	INT	WIS	CHA
2 (−4)	16 (+3)	11 (+0)	1 (−5)	10 (+0)	3 (−4)

Senses blindsight 10 ft., passive Perception 10
Languages —
Challenge 1/8 (25 XP)

ACTIONS

Bite. *Melee Weapon Attack:* +5 to hit, reach 5 ft., one target. *Hit:* 1 piercing damage, and the target must make a DC 10 Constitution saving throw, taking 5 (2d4) poison damage on a failed save, or half as much damage on a successful one.

POLAR BEAR

Large beast, unaligned

Armor Class 12 (natural armor)
Hit Points 42 (5d10 + 15)
Speed 40 ft., swim 30 ft.

STR	DEX	CON	INT	WIS	CHA
20 (+5)	10 (+0)	16 (+3)	2 (−4)	13 (+1)	7 (−2)

Skills Perception +3
Senses passive Perception 13
Languages —
Challenge 2 (450 XP)

Keen Smell. The bear has advantage on Wisdom (Perception) checks that rely on smell.

ACTIONS

Multiattack. The bear makes two attacks: one with its bite and one with its claws.

Bite. *Melee Weapon Attack:* +7 to hit, reach 5 ft., one target. *Hit:* 9 (1d8 + 5) piercing damage.

Claws. *Melee Weapon Attack:* +7 to hit, reach 5 ft., one target. *Hit:* 12 (2d6 + 5) slashing damage.

> ### VARIANT: CAVE BEAR
>
> Some bears have adapted to life underground, feeding on subterranean lichen and blind fish. Known as cave bears, these ill-tempered behemoths have coarse, dark hair and darkvision out to a range of 60 feet. Otherwise, they have the same statistics as a polar bear.

Pony

Medium beast, unaligned

Armor Class 10
Hit Points 11 (2d8 + 2)
Speed 40 ft.

STR	DEX	CON	INT	WIS	CHA
15 (+2)	10 (+0)	13 (+1)	2 (−4)	11 (+0)	7 (−2)

Senses passive Perception 10
Languages —
Challenge 1/8 (25 XP)

Actions

Hooves. *Melee Weapon Attack:* +4 to hit, reach 5 ft., one target. *Hit:* 7 (2d4 + 2) bludgeoning damage.

Quipper

Tiny beast, unaligned

Armor Class 13
Hit Points 1 (1d4 − 1)
Speed 0 ft., swim 40 ft.

STR	DEX	CON	INT	WIS	CHA
2 (−4)	16 (+3)	9 (−1)	1 (−5)	7 (−2)	2 (−4)

Senses darkvision 60 ft., passive Perception 8
Languages —
Challenge 0 (10 XP)

Blood Frenzy. The quipper has advantage on melee attack rolls against any creature that doesn't have all its hit points.

Water Breathing. The quipper can breathe only underwater.

Actions

Bite. *Melee Weapon Attack:* +5 to hit, reach 5 ft., one target. *Hit:* 1 piercing damage.

A **quipper** is a carnivorous fish with sharp teeth. Quippers can adapt to any aquatic environment, including cold subterranean lakes. They frequently gather in swarms; the statistics for a swarm of quippers appear later in this appendix.

Rat

Tiny beast, unaligned

Armor Class 10
Hit Points 1 (1d4 − 1)
Speed 20 ft.

STR	DEX	CON	INT	WIS	CHA
2 (−4)	11 (+0)	9 (−1)	2 (−4)	10 (+0)	4 (−3)

Senses darkvision 30 ft., passive Perception 10
Languages —
Challenge 0 (10 XP)

Keen Smell. The rat has advantage on Wisdom (Perception) checks that rely on smell.

Actions

Bite. *Melee Weapon Attack:* +0 to hit, reach 5 ft., one target. *Hit:* 1 piercing damage.

Raven

Tiny beast, unaligned

Armor Class 12
Hit Points 1 (1d4 − 1)
Speed 10 ft., fly 50 ft.

STR	DEX	CON	INT	WIS	CHA
2 (−4)	14 (+2)	8 (−1)	2 (−4)	12 (+1)	6 (−2)

Skills Perception +3
Senses passive Perception 13
Languages —
Challenge 0 (10 XP)

Mimicry. The raven can mimic simple sounds it has heard, such as a person whispering, a baby crying, or an animal chittering. A creature that hears the sounds can tell they are imitations with a successful DC 10 Wisdom (Insight) check.

Actions

Beak. *Melee Weapon Attack:* +4 to hit, reach 5 ft., one target. *Hit:* 1 piercing damage.

QUIPPERS

Reef Shark

Medium beast, unaligned

Armor Class 12 (natural armor)
Hit Points 22 (4d8 + 4)
Speed 0 ft., swim 40 ft.

STR	DEX	CON	INT	WIS	CHA
14 (+2)	13 (+1)	13 (+1)	1 (−5)	10 (+0)	4 (−3)

Skills Perception +2
Senses blindsight 30 ft., passive Perception 12
Languages —
Challenge 1/2 (100 XP)

Pack Tactics. The shark has advantage on an attack roll against a creature if at least one of the shark's allies is within 5 feet of the creature and the ally isn't incapacitated.

Water Breathing. The shark can breathe only underwater.

Actions

Bite. *Melee Weapon Attack:* +4 to hit, reach 5 ft., one target. *Hit:* 6 (1d8 + 2) piercing damage.

Smaller than giant sharks and hunter sharks, **reef sharks** inhabit shallow waters and coral reefs, gathering in small packs to hunt. A full-grown specimen measures 6 to 10 feet long.

Rhinoceros

Large beast, unaligned

Armor Class 11 (natural armor)
Hit Points 45 (6d10 + 12)
Speed 40 ft.

STR	DEX	CON	INT	WIS	CHA
21 (+5)	8 (−1)	15 (+2)	2 (−4)	12 (+1)	6 (−2)

Senses passive Perception 11
Languages —
Challenge 2 (450 XP)

Charge. If the rhinoceros moves at least 20 feet straight toward a target and then hits it with a gore attack on the same turn, the target takes an extra 9 (2d8) bludgeoning damage. If the target is a creature, it must succeed on a DC 15 Strength saving throw or be knocked prone.

Actions

Gore. *Melee Weapon Attack:* +7 to hit, reach 5 ft., one target. *Hit:* 14 (2d8 + 5) bludgeoning damage.

Riding Horse

Large beast, unaligned

Armor Class 10
Hit Points 13 (2d10 + 2)
Speed 60 ft.

STR	DEX	CON	INT	WIS	CHA
16 (+3)	10 (+0)	12 (+1)	2 (−4)	11 (+0)	7 (−2)

Senses passive Perception 10
Languages —
Challenge 1/4 (50 XP)

Actions

Hooves. *Melee Weapon Attack:* +5 to hit, reach 5 ft., one target. *Hit:* 8 (2d4 + 3) bludgeoning damage.

Saber-Toothed Tiger

Large beast, unaligned

Armor Class 12
Hit Points 52 (7d10 + 14)
Speed 40 ft.

STR	DEX	CON	INT	WIS	CHA
18 (+4)	14 (+2)	15 (+2)	3 (−4)	12 (+1)	8 (−1)

Skills Perception +3, Stealth +6
Senses passive Perception 13
Languages —
Challenge 2 (450 XP)

Keen Smell. The tiger has advantage on Wisdom (Perception) checks that rely on smell.

Pounce. If the tiger moves at least 20 feet straight toward a creature and then hits it with a claw attack on the same turn, that target must succeed on a DC 14 Strength saving throw or be knocked prone. If the target is prone, the tiger can make one bite attack against it as a bonus action.

Actions

Bite. *Melee Weapon Attack:* +6 to hit, reach 5 ft., one target. *Hit:* 10 (1d10 + 5) piercing damage.

Claw. *Melee Weapon Attack:* +6 to hit, reach 5 ft., one target. *Hit:* 12 (2d6 + 5) slashing damage.

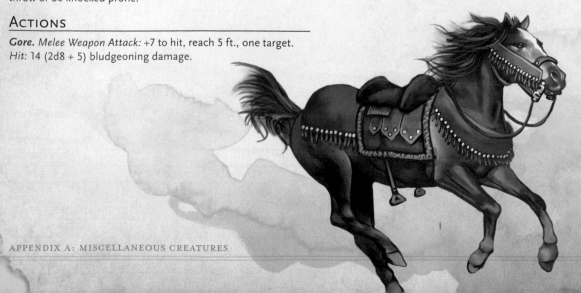

SCORPION

Tiny beast, unaligned

Armor Class 11 (natural armor)
Hit Points 1 (1d4 − 1)
Speed 10 ft.

STR	DEX	CON	INT	WIS	CHA
2 (−4)	11 (+0)	8 (−1)	1 (−5)	8 (−1)	2 (−4)

Senses blindsight 10 ft., passive Perception 9
Languages —
Challenge 0 (10 XP)

ACTIONS

Sting. *Melee Weapon Attack:* +2 to hit, reach 5 ft., one creature. *Hit:* 1 piercing damage, and the target must make a DC 9 Constitution saving throw, taking 4 (1d8) poison damage on a failed save, or half as much damage on a successful one.

SEA HORSE

Tiny beast, unaligned

Armor Class 11
Hit Points 1 (1d4 − 1)
Speed 0 ft., swim 20 ft.

STR	DEX	CON	INT	WIS	CHA
1 (−5)	12 (+1)	8 (−1)	1 (−5)	10 (+0)	2 (−4)

Senses passive Perception 10
Languages —
Challenge 0 (0 XP)

Water Breathing. The sea horse can breathe only underwater.

SPIDER

Tiny beast, unaligned

Armor Class 12
Hit Points 1 (1d4 − 1)
Speed 20 ft., climb 20 ft.

STR	DEX	CON	INT	WIS	CHA
2 (−4)	14 (+2)	8 (−1)	1 (−5)	10 (+0)	2 (−4)

Skills Stealth +4
Senses darkvision 30 ft., passive Perception 10
Languages —
Challenge 0 (10 XP)

Spider Climb. The spider can climb difficult surfaces, including upside down on ceilings, without needing to make an ability check.

Web Sense. While in contact with a web, the spider knows the exact location of any other creature in contact with the same web.

Web Walker. The spider ignores movement restrictions caused by webbing.

ACTIONS

Bite. *Melee Weapon Attack:* +4 to hit, reach 5 ft., one creature. *Hit:* 1 piercing damage, and the target must succeed on a DC 9 Constitution saving throw or take 2 (1d4) poison damage.

SWARM OF BATS

Medium swarm of Tiny beasts, unaligned

Armor Class 12
Hit Points 22 (5d8)
Speed 0 ft., fly 30 ft.

STR	DEX	CON	INT	WIS	CHA
5 (−3)	15 (+2)	10 (+0)	2 (−4)	12 (+1)	4 (−3)

Damage Resistances bludgeoning, piercing, slashing
Condition Immunities charmed, frightened, grappled, paralyzed, petrified, prone, restrained, stunned
Senses blindsight 60 ft., passive Perception 11
Languages —
Challenge 1/4 (50 XP)

Echolocation. The swarm can't use its blindsight while deafened.

Keen Hearing. The swarm has advantage on Wisdom (Perception) checks that rely on hearing.

Swarm. The swarm can occupy another creature's space and vice versa, and the swarm can move through any opening large enough for a Tiny bat. The swarm can't regain hit points or gain temporary hit points.

ACTIONS

Bites. *Melee Weapon Attack:* +4 to hit, reach 0 ft., one creature in the swarm's space. *Hit:* 5 (2d4) piercing damage, or 2 (1d4) piercing damage if the swarm has half of its hit points or fewer.

THE NATURE OF SWARMS

The swarms presented here aren't ordinary or benign assemblies of little creatures. They form as a result of some sinister or unwholesome influence. A vampire can summon swarms of bats and rats from the darkest corners of the night, while the very presence of a mummy lord can cause scarab beetles to boil up from the sand-filled depths of its tomb. A hag might have the power to turn swarms of ravens against her enemies, while a yuan-ti abomination might have swarms of poisonous snakes slithering in its wake. Even druids can't charm these swarms, and their aggressiveness is borderline unnatural.

Swarm of Insects

Medium swarm of Tiny beasts, unaligned

Armor Class 12 (natural armor)
Hit Points 22 (5d8)
Speed 20 ft., climb 20 ft.

STR	DEX	CON	INT	WIS	CHA
3 (–4)	13 (+1)	10 (+0)	1 (–5)	7 (–2)	1 (–5)

Damage Resistances bludgeoning, piercing, slashing
Condition Immunities charmed, frightened, grappled, paralyzed, petrified, prone, restrained, stunned
Senses blindsight 10 ft., passive Perception 8
Languages —
Challenge 1/2 (100 XP)

Swarm. The swarm can occupy another creature's space and vice versa, and the swarm can move through any opening large enough for a Tiny insect. The swarm can't regain hit points or gain temporary hit points.

Actions

Bites. *Melee Weapon Attack:* +3 to hit, reach 0 ft., one target in the swarm's space. *Hit:* 10 (4d4) piercing damage, or 5 (2d4) piercing damage if the swarm has half of its hit points or fewer.

Swarm of Poisonous Snakes

Medium swarm of Tiny beasts, unaligned

Armor Class 14
Hit Points 36 (8d8)
Speed 30 ft., swim 30 ft.

STR	DEX	CON	INT	WIS	CHA
8 (–1)	18 (+4)	11 (+0)	1 (–5)	10 (+0)	3 (–4)

Damage Resistances bludgeoning, piercing, slashing
Condition Immunities charmed, frightened, grappled, paralyzed, petrified, prone, restrained, stunned
Senses blindsight 10 ft., passive Perception 10
Languages —
Challenge 2 (450 XP)

Swarm. The swarm can occupy another creature's space and vice versa, and the swarm can move through any opening large enough for a Tiny snake. The swarm can't regain hit points or gain temporary hit points.

Actions

Bites. *Melee Weapon Attack:* +6 to hit, reach 0 ft., one creature in the swarm's space. *Hit:* 7 (2d6) piercing damage, or 3 (1d6) piercing damage if the swarm has half of its hit points or fewer. The target must make a DC 10 Constitution saving throw, taking 14 (4d6) poison damage on a failed save, or half as much damage on a successful one.

> ## Variant: Insect Swarms
>
> Different kinds of insects can gather in swarms, and each swarm has the special characteristics described below.
>
> ***Swarm of Beetles.*** A swarm of beetles gains a burrowing speed of 5 feet.
>
> ***Swarm of Centipedes.*** A creature reduced to 0 hit points by a swarm of centipedes is stable but poisoned for 1 hour, even after regaining hit points, and paralyzed while poisoned in this way.
>
> ***Swarm of Spiders.*** A swarm of spiders has the following additional traits.
>
> *Spider Climb.* The swarm can climb difficult surfaces, including upside down on ceilings, without needing to make an ability check.
>
> *Web Sense.* While in contact with a web, the swarm knows the exact location of any other creature in contact with the same web.
>
> *Web Walker.* The swarm ignores movement restrictions caused by webbing.
>
> ***Swarm of Wasps.*** A swarm of wasps has a walking speed of 5 feet, a flying speed of 30 feet, and no climbing speed.

Swarm of Quippers

Medium swarm of Tiny beasts, unaligned

Armor Class 13
Hit Points 28 (8d8 – 8)
Speed 0 ft., swim 40 ft.

STR	DEX	CON	INT	WIS	CHA
13 (+1)	16 (+3)	9 (–1)	1 (–5)	7 (–2)	2 (–4)

Damage Resistances bludgeoning, piercing, slashing
Condition Immunities charmed, frightened, grappled, paralyzed, petrified, prone, restrained, stunned
Senses darkvision 60 ft., passive Perception 8
Languages —
Challenge 1 (200 XP)

Blood Frenzy. The swarm has advantage on melee attack rolls against any creature that doesn't have all its hit points.

Swarm. The swarm can occupy another creature's space and vice versa, and the swarm can move through any opening large enough for a Tiny quipper. The swarm can't regain hit points or gain temporary hit points.

Water Breathing. The swarm can breathe only underwater.

Actions

Bites. *Melee Weapon Attack:* +5 to hit, reach 0 ft., one creature in the swarm's space. *Hit:* 14 (4d6) piercing damage, or 7 (2d6) piercing damage if the swarm has half of its hit points or fewer.

RAT

SWARM OF RATS

Medium swarm of Tiny beasts, unaligned

Armor Class 10
Hit Points 24 (7d8 – 7)
Speed 30 ft.

STR	DEX	CON	INT	WIS	CHA
9 (–1)	11 (+0)	9 (–1)	2 (–4)	10 (+0)	3 (–4)

Damage Resistances bludgeoning, piercing, slashing
Condition Immunities charmed, frightened, grappled, paralyzed, petrified, prone, restrained, stunned
Senses darkvision 30 ft., passive Perception 10
Languages —
Challenge 1/4 (50 XP)

Keen Smell. The swarm has advantage on Wisdom (Perception) checks that rely on smell.

Swarm. The swarm can occupy another creature's space and vice versa, and the swarm can move through any opening large enough for a Tiny rat. The swarm can't regain hit points or gain temporary hit points.

ACTIONS

Bites. *Melee Weapon Attack:* +2 to hit, reach 0 ft., one target in the swarm's space. *Hit:* 7 (2d6) piercing damage, or 3 (1d6) piercing damage if the swarm has half of its hit points or fewer.

SWARM OF RAVENS

Medium swarm of Tiny beasts, unaligned

Armor Class 12
Hit Points 24 (7d8 – 7)
Speed 10 ft., fly 50 ft.

STR	DEX	CON	INT	WIS	CHA
6 (–2)	14 (+2)	8 (–1)	3 (–4)	12 (+1)	6 (–2)

Skills Perception +5
Damage Resistances bludgeoning, piercing, slashing
Condition Immunities charmed, frightened, grappled, paralyzed, petrified, prone, restrained, stunned
Senses passive Perception 15
Languages —
Challenge 1/4 (50 XP)

Swarm. The swarm can occupy another creature's space and vice versa, and the swarm can move through any opening large enough for a Tiny raven. The swarm can't regain hit points or gain temporary hit points.

ACTIONS

Beaks. *Melee Weapon Attack:* +4 to hit, reach 5 ft., one target in the swarm's space. *Hit:* 7 (2d6) piercing damage, or 3 (1d6) piercing damage if the swarm has half of its hit points or fewer.

TIGER

Large beast, unaligned

Armor Class 12
Hit Points 37 (5d10 + 10)
Speed 40 ft.

STR	DEX	CON	INT	WIS	CHA
17 (+3)	15 (+2)	14 (+2)	3 (–4)	12 (+1)	8 (–1)

Skills Perception +3, Stealth +6
Senses darkvision 60 ft., passive Perception 13
Languages —
Challenge 1 (200 XP)

Keen Smell. The tiger has advantage on Wisdom (Perception) checks that rely on smell.

Pounce. If the tiger moves at least 20 feet straight toward a creature and then hits it with a claw attack on the same turn, that target must succeed on a DC 13 Strength saving throw or be knocked prone. If the target is prone, the tiger can make one bite attack against it as a bonus action.

ACTIONS

Bite. *Melee Weapon Attack:* +5 to hit, reach 5 ft., one target. *Hit:* 8 (1d10 + 3) piercing damage.

Claw. *Melee Weapon Attack:* +5 to hit, reach 5 ft., one target. *Hit:* 7 (1d8 + 3) slashing damage.

VULTURE

Medium beast, unaligned

Armor Class 10
Hit Points 5 (1d8 + 1)
Speed 10 ft., fly 50 ft.

STR	DEX	CON	INT	WIS	CHA
7 (–2)	10 (+0)	13 (+1)	2 (–4)	12 (+1)	4 (–3)

Skills Perception +3
Senses passive Perception 13
Languages —
Challenge 0 (10 XP)

Keen Sight and Smell. The vulture has advantage on Wisdom (Perception) checks that rely on sight or smell.

Pack Tactics. The vulture has advantage on an attack roll against a creature if at least one of the vulture's allies is within 5 feet of the creature and the ally isn't incapacitated.

ACTIONS

Beak. *Melee Weapon Attack:* +2 to hit, reach 5 ft., one target. *Hit:* 2 (1d4) piercing damage.

WARHORSE
Large beast, unaligned

Armor Class 11
Hit Points 19 (3d10 + 3)
Speed 60 ft.

STR	DEX	CON	INT	WIS	CHA
18 (+4)	12 (+1)	13 (+1)	2 (−4)	12 (+1)	7 (−2)

Senses passive Perception 11
Languages —
Challenge 1/2 (100 XP)

Trampling Charge. If the horse moves at least 20 feet straight toward a creature and then hits it with a hooves attack on the same turn, that target must succeed on a DC 14 Strength saving throw or be knocked prone. If the target is prone, the horse can make another attack with its hooves against it as a bonus action.

ACTIONS

Hooves. *Melee Weapon Attack:* +6 to hit, reach 5 ft., one target. *Hit:* 11 (2d6 + 4) bludgeoning damage.

WINTER WOLF

VARIANT: WARHORSE ARMOR

An armored warhorse has an AC based on the type of barding worn (see the *Player's Handbook* for more information on barding). The horse's AC includes its Dexterity modifier, where applicable. Barding doesn't alter the horse's challenge rating.

AC	Barding	AC	Barding
12	Leather	16	Chain mail
13	Studded leather	17	Splint
14	Ring mail	18	Plate
15	Scale mail		

WEASEL
Tiny beast, unaligned

Armor Class 13
Hit Points 1 (1d4 − 1)
Speed 30 ft.

STR	DEX	CON	INT	WIS	CHA
3 (−4)	16 (+3)	8 (−1)	2 (−4)	12 (+1)	3 (−4)

Skills Perception +3, Stealth +5
Senses passive Perception 13
Languages —
Challenge 0 (10 XP)

Keen Hearing and Smell. The weasel has advantage on Wisdom (Perception) checks that rely on hearing or smell.

ACTIONS

Bite. *Melee Weapon Attack:* +5 to hit, reach 5 ft., one target. *Hit:* 1 piercing damage.

WINTER WOLF
Large monstrosity, neutral evil

Armor Class 13 (natural armor)
Hit Points 75 (10d10 + 20)
Speed 50 ft.

STR	DEX	CON	INT	WIS	CHA
18 (+4)	13 (+1)	14 (+2)	7 (−2)	12 (+1)	8 (−1)

Skills Perception +5, Stealth +3
Damage Immunities cold
Senses passive Perception 15
Languages Common, Giant, Winter Wolf
Challenge 3 (700 XP)

Keen Hearing and Smell. The wolf has advantage on Wisdom (Perception) checks that rely on hearing or smell.

Pack Tactics. The wolf has advantage on an attack roll against a creature if at least one of the wolf's allies is within 5 feet of the creature and the ally isn't incapacitated.

Snow Camouflage. The wolf has advantage on Dexterity (Stealth) checks made to hide in snowy terrain.

ACTIONS

Bite. *Melee Weapon Attack:* +6 to hit, reach 5 ft., one target. *Hit:* 11 (2d6 + 4) piercing damage. If the target is a creature, it must succeed on a DC 14 Strength saving throw or be knocked prone.

Cold Breath (Recharge 5–6). The wolf exhales a blast of freezing wind in a 15-foot cone. Each creature in that area must make a DC 12 Dexterity saving throw, taking 18 (4d8) cold damage on a failed save, or half as much damage on a successful one.

The arctic-dwelling **winter wolf** is as large as a dire wolf but has snow-white fur and pale blue eyes. Frost giants use these evil creatures as guards and hunting companions, putting the wolves' deadly breath weapon to use against their foes. Winter wolves communicate with one another using growls and barks, but they speak Common and Giant well enough to follow simple conversations.

WOLF
Medium beast, unaligned

Armor Class 13 (natural armor)
Hit Points 11 (2d8 + 2)
Speed 40 ft.

STR	DEX	CON	INT	WIS	CHA
12 (+1)	15 (+2)	12 (+1)	3 (−4)	12 (+1)	6 (−2)

Skills Perception +3, Stealth +4
Senses passive Perception 13
Languages —
Challenge 1/4 (50 XP)

Keen Hearing and Smell. The wolf has advantage on Wisdom (Perception) checks that rely on hearing or smell.

Pack Tactics. The wolf has advantage on attack rolls against a creature if at least one of the wolf's allies is within 5 feet of the creature and the ally isn't incapacitated.

ACTIONS

Bite. *Melee Weapon Attack:* +4 to hit, reach 5 ft., one target. *Hit:* 7 (2d4 + 2) piercing damage. If the target is a creature, it must succeed on a DC 11 Strength saving throw or be knocked prone.

WORG
Large monstrosity, neutral evil

Armor Class 13 (natural armor)
Hit Points 26 (4d10 + 4)
Speed 50 ft.

STR	DEX	CON	INT	WIS	CHA
16 (+3)	13 (+1)	13 (+1)	7 (−2)	11 (+0)	8 (−1)

Skills Perception +4
Senses darkvision 60 ft., passive Perception 14
Languages Goblin, Worg
Challenge 1/2 (100 XP)

Keen Hearing and Smell. The worg has advantage on Wisdom (Perception) checks that rely on hearing or smell.

ACTIONS

Bite. *Melee Weapon Attack:* +5 to hit, reach 5 ft., one target. *Hit:* 10 (2d6 + 3) piercing damage. If the target is a creature, it must succeed on a DC 13 Strength saving throw or be knocked prone.

A **worg** is an evil predator that delights in hunting and devouring creatures weaker than itself. Cunning and malevolent, worgs roam across the remote wilderness or are raised by goblins and hobgoblins. Those creatures use worgs as mounts, but a worg will turn on its rider if it feels mistreated or malnourished. Worgs speak in their own language and Goblin, and a few learn to speak Common as well.

WORG

APPENDIX B: NONPLAYER CHARACTERS

This appendix contains statistics for various humanoid nonplayer characters (NPCs) that adventurers might encounter during a D&D campaign, including lowly commoners and mighty archmages. These stat blocks can be used to represent both human and nonhuman NPCs.

CUSTOMIZING NPCs

There are many easy ways to customize the NPCs in this appendix for your home campaign.

Racial Traits. You can add racial traits to an NPC. For example, a halfling druid might have a speed of 25 feet and the Lucky trait. Adding racial traits to an NPC doesn't alter its challenge rating. For more on racial traits, see the *Player's Handbook*.

Spell Swaps. One way to customize an NPC spellcaster is to replace one or more of its spells. You can substitute any spell on the NPC's spell list with a different spell of the same level from the same spell list. Swapping spells in this manner doesn't alter an NPC's challenge rating.

Armor and Weapon Swaps. You can upgrade or downgrade an NPC's armor, or add or switch weapons. Adjustments to Armor Class and damage can change an NPC's challenge rating, as explained in the *Dungeon Master's Guide*.

Magic Items. The more powerful an NPC, the more likely it has one or more magic items in its possession. An archmage, for example, might have a magic staff or wand, as well as one or more potions and scrolls. Giving an NPC a potent damage-dealing magic item could alter its challenge rating. Magic items, as well as adjusting a creature's challenge rating, are described in the *Dungeon Master's Guide*.

ACOLYTE

Medium humanoid (any race), any alignment

Armor Class 10
Hit Points 9 (2d8)
Speed 30 ft.

STR	DEX	CON	INT	WIS	CHA
10 (+0)	10 (+0)	10 (+0)	10 (+0)	14 (+2)	11 (+0)

Skills Medicine +4, Religion +2
Senses passive Perception 12
Languages any one language (usually Common)
Challenge 1/4 (50 XP)

Spellcasting. The acolyte is a 1st-level spellcaster. Its spellcasting ability is Wisdom (spell save DC 12, +4 to hit with spell attacks). The acolyte has following cleric spells prepared:

Cantrips (at will): *light, sacred flame, thaumaturgy*
1st level (3 slots): *bless, cure wounds, sanctuary*

ACTIONS

Club. *Melee Weapon Attack:* +2 to hit, reach 5 ft., one target. *Hit:* 2 (1d4) bludgeoning damage.

Acolytes are junior members of a clergy, usually answerable to a priest. They perform a variety of functions in a temple and are granted minor spellcasting power by their deities.

ARCHMAGE

Medium humanoid (any race), any alignment

Armor Class 12 (15 with *mage armor*)
Hit Points 99 (18d8 + 18)
Speed 30 ft.

STR	DEX	CON	INT	WIS	CHA
10 (+0)	14 (+2)	12 (+1)	20 (+5)	15 (+2)	16 (+3)

Saving Throws Int +9, Wis +6
Skills Arcana +13, History +13
Damage Resistance damage from spells; nonmagical bludgeoning, piercing, and slashing (from *stoneskin*)
Senses passive Perception 12
Languages any six languages
Challenge 12 (8,400 XP)

Magic Resistance. The archmage has advantage on saving throws against spells and other magical effects.

Spellcasting. The archmage is an 18th-level spellcaster. Its spellcasting ability is Intelligence (spell save DC 17, +9 to hit with spell attacks). The archmage can cast *disguise self* and *invisibility* at will and has the following wizard spells prepared:

Cantrips (at will): *fire bolt, light, mage hand, prestidigitation, shocking grasp*
1st level (4 slots): *detect magic, identify, mage armor,* *magic missile*
2nd level (3 slots): *detect thoughts, mirror image, misty step*
3rd level (3 slots): *counterspell, fly, lightning bolt*
4th level (3 slots): *banishment, fire shield, stoneskin**
5th level (3 slots): *cone of cold, scrying, wall of force*
6th level (1 slot): *globe of invulnerability*
7th level (1 slot): *teleport*
8th level (1 slot): *mind blank**
9th level (1 slot): *time stop*

**The archmage casts these spells on itself before combat.*

ACTIONS

Dagger. *Melee or Ranged Weapon Attack:* +6 to hit, reach 5 ft. or range 20/60 ft., one target. *Hit:* 4 (1d4 + 2) piercing damage.

Archmages are powerful (and usually quite old) spellcasters dedicated to the study of the arcane arts. Benevolent ones counsel kings and queens, while evil ones rule as tyrants and pursue lichdom. Those who are neither good nor evil sequester themselves in remote towers to practice their magic without interruption.

An archmage typically has one or more apprentice mages, and an archmage's abode has numerous magical wards and guardians to discourage interlopers.

ASSASSIN

Medium humanoid (any race), any non-good alignment

Armor Class 15 (studded leather)
Hit Points 78 (12d8 + 24)
Speed 30 ft.

STR	DEX	CON	INT	WIS	CHA
11 (+0)	16 (+3)	14 (+2)	13 (+1)	11 (+0)	10 (+0)

Saving Throws Dex +6, Int +4
Skills Acrobatics +6, Deception +3, Perception +3, Stealth +9
Damage Resistances poison
Senses passive Perception 13
Languages Thieves' cant plus any two languages
Challenge 8 (3,900 XP)

Assassinate. During its first turn, the assassin has advantage on attack rolls against any creature that hasn't taken a turn. Any hit the assassin scores against a surprised creature is a critical hit.

Evasion. If the assassin is subjected to an effect that allows it to make a Dexterity saving throw to take only half damage, the assassin instead takes no damage if it succeeds on the saving throw, and only half damage if it fails.

Sneak Attack. Once per turn, the assassin deals an extra 14 (4d6) damage when it hits a target with a weapon attack and has advantage on the attack roll, or when the target is within 5 feet of an ally of the assassin that isn't incapacitated and the assassin doesn't have disadvantage on the attack roll.

ACTIONS

Multiattack. The assassin makes two shortsword attacks.

Shortsword. *Melee Weapon Attack:* +6 to hit, reach 5 ft., one target. *Hit:* 6 (1d6 + 3) piercing damage, and the target must make a DC 15 Constitution saving throw, taking 24 (7d6) poison damage on a failed save, or half as much damage on a successful one.

Light Crossbow. *Ranged Weapon Attack:* +6 to hit, range 80/320 ft., one target. *Hit:* 7 (1d8 + 3) piercing damage, and the target must make a DC 15 Constitution saving throw, taking 24 (7d6) poison damage on a failed save, or half as much damage on a successful one.

Trained in the use of poison, **assassins** are remorseless killers who work for nobles, guildmasters, sovereigns, and anyone else who can afford them.

BANDIT

Medium humanoid (any race), any non-lawful alignment

Armor Class 12 (leather armor)
Hit Points 11 (2d8 + 2)
Speed 30 ft.

STR	DEX	CON	INT	WIS	CHA
11 (+0)	12 (+1)	12 (+1)	10 (+0)	10 (+0)	10 (+0)

Senses passive Perception 10
Languages any one language (usually Common)
Challenge 1/8 (25 XP)

ACTIONS

Scimitar. *Melee Weapon Attack:* +3 to hit, reach 5 ft., one target. *Hit:* 4 (1d6 + 1) slashing damage.

Light Crossbow. *Ranged Weapon Attack:* +3 to hit, range 80/320 ft., one target. *Hit:* 5 (1d8 + 1) piercing damage.

ARCHMAGE

Bandits rove in gangs and are sometimes led by thugs, veterans, or spellcasters. Not all bandits are evil. Oppression, drought, disease, or famine can often drive otherwise honest folk to a life of banditry.

Pirates are bandits of the high seas. They might be freebooters interested only in treasure and murder, or they might be privateers sanctioned by the crown to attack and plunder an enemy nation's vessels.

BANDIT CAPTAIN
Medium humanoid (any race), any non-lawful alignment

Armor Class 15 (studded leather)
Hit Points 65 (10d8 + 20)
Speed 30 ft.

STR	DEX	CON	INT	WIS	CHA
15 (+2)	16 (+3)	14 (+2)	14 (+2)	11 (+0)	14 (+2)

Saving Throws Str +4, Dex +5, Wis +2
Skills Athletics +4, Deception +4
Senses passive Perception 10
Languages any two languages
Challenge 2 (450 XP)

ACTIONS

Multiattack. The captain makes three melee attacks: two with its scimitar and one with its dagger. Or the captain makes two ranged attacks with its daggers.

Scimitar. *Melee Weapon Attack:* +5 to hit, reach 5 ft., one target. *Hit:* 6 (1d6 + 3) slashing damage.

Dagger. *Melee or Ranged Weapon Attack:* +5 to hit, reach 5 ft. or range 20/60 ft., one target. *Hit:* 5 (1d4 + 3) piercing damage.

REACTIONS

Parry. The captain adds 2 to its AC against one melee attack that would hit it. To do so, the captain must see the attacker and be wielding a melee weapon.

It takes a strong personality, ruthless cunning, and a silver tongue to keep a gang of bandits in line. The **bandit captain** has these qualities in spades.

In addition to managing a crew of selfish malcontents, the **pirate captain** is a variation of the bandit captain, with a ship to protect and command. To keep the crew in line, the captain must mete out rewards and punishment on a regular basis.

More than treasure, a bandit captain or pirate captain craves infamy. A prisoner who appeals to the captain's vanity or ego is more likely to be treated fairly than a prisoner who does not or claims not to know anything of the captain's colorful reputation.

BERSERKER
Medium humanoid (any race), any chaotic alignment

Armor Class 13 (hide armor)
Hit Points 67 (9d8 + 27)
Speed 30 ft.

STR	DEX	CON	INT	WIS	CHA
16 (+3)	12 (+1)	17 (+3)	9 (−1)	11 (+0)	9 (−1)

Senses passive Perception 10
Languages any one language (usually Common)
Challenge 2 (450 XP)

Reckless. At the start of its turn, the berserker can gain advantage on all melee weapon attack rolls during that turn, but attack rolls against it have advantage until the start of its next turn.

ACTIONS

Greataxe. *Melee Weapon Attack:* +5 to hit, reach 5 ft., one target. *Hit:* 9 (1d12 + 3) slashing damage.

Hailing from uncivilized lands, unpredictable **berserkers** come together in war parties and seek conflict wherever they can find it.

BANDIT CAPTAIN

COMMONER
Medium humanoid (any race), any alignment

Armor Class 10
Hit Points 4 (1d8)
Speed 30 ft.

STR	DEX	CON	INT	WIS	CHA
10 (+0)	10 (+0)	10 (+0)	10 (+0)	10 (+0)	10 (+0)

Senses passive Perception 10
Languages any one language (usually Common)
Challenge 0 (10 XP)

ACTIONS

Club. *Melee Weapon Attack:* +2 to hit, reach 5 ft., one target. *Hit:* 2 (1d4) bludgeoning damage.

Commoners include peasants, serfs, slaves, servants, pilgrims, merchants, artisans, and hermits.

CULTIST
Medium humanoid (any race), any non-good alignment

Armor Class 12 (leather armor)
Hit Points 9 (2d8)
Speed 30 ft.

STR	DEX	CON	INT	WIS	CHA
11 (+0)	12 (+1)	10 (+0)	10 (+0)	11 (+0)	10 (+0)

Skills Deception +2, Religion +2
Senses passive Perception 10
Languages any one language (usually Common)
Challenge 1/8 (25 XP)

Dark Devotion. The cultist has advantage on saving throws against being charmed or frightened.

ACTIONS

Scimitar. *Melee Weapon Attack:* +3 to hit, reach 5 ft., one creature. *Hit:* 4 (1d6 + 1) slashing damage.

Cultists swear allegiance to dark powers such as elemental princes, demon lords, or archdevils. Most conceal their loyalties to avoid being ostracized, imprisoned, or executed for their beliefs. Unlike evil acolytes, cultists often show signs of insanity in their beliefs and practices.

CULT FANATIC
Medium humanoid (any race), any non-good alignment

Armor Class 13 (leather armor)
Hit Points 33 (6d8 + 6)
Speed 30 ft.

STR	DEX	CON	INT	WIS	CHA
11 (+0)	14 (+2)	12 (+1)	10 (+0)	13 (+1)	14 (+2)

Skills Deception +4, Persuasion +4, Religion +2
Senses passive Perception 11
Languages any one language (usually Common)
Challenge 2 (450 XP)

Dark Devotion. The fanatic has advantage on saving throws against being charmed or frightened.

Spellcasting. The fanatic is a 4th-level spellcaster. Its spellcasting ability is Wisdom (spell save DC 11, +3 to hit with spell attacks). The fanatic has the following cleric spells prepared:

Cantrips (at will): *light, sacred flame, thaumaturgy*
1st level (4 slots): *command, inflict wounds, shield of faith*
2nd level (3 slots): *hold person, spiritual weapon*

ACTIONS

Multiattack. The fanatic makes two melee attacks.

Dagger. *Melee or Ranged Weapon Attack:* +4 to hit, reach 5 ft. or range 20/60 ft., one creature. *Hit:* 4 (1d4 + 2) piercing damage.

Fanatics are often part of a cult's leadership, using their charisma and dogma to influence and prey on those of weak will. Most are interested in personal power above all else.

CULT FANATIC

DRUID

Medium humanoid (any race), any alignment

Armor Class 11 (16 with *barkskin*)
Hit Points 27 (5d8 + 5)
Speed 30 ft.

STR	DEX	CON	INT	WIS	CHA
10 (+0)	12 (+1)	13 (+1)	12 (+1)	15 (+2)	11 (+0)

Skills Medicine +4, Nature +3, Perception +4
Senses passive Perception 14
Languages Druidic plus any two languages
Challenge 2 (450 XP)

Spellcasting. The druid is a 4th-level spellcaster. Its spellcasting ability is Wisdom (spell save DC 12, +4 to hit with spell attacks). It has the following druid spells prepared:

Cantrips (at will): *druidcraft, produce flame, shillelagh*
1st level (4 slots): *entangle, longstrider, speak with animals, thunderwave*
2nd level (3 slots): *animal messenger, barkskin*

ACTIONS

Quarterstaff. *Melee Weapon Attack:* +2 to hit (+4 to hit with *shillelagh*), reach 5 ft., one target. *Hit:* 3 (1d6) bludgeoning damage, 4 (1d8) bludgeoning damage if wielded with two hands, or 6 (1d8 + 2) bludgeoning damage with *shillelagh*.

Druids dwell in forests and other secluded wilderness locations, where they protect the natural world from monsters and the encroachment of civilization. Some are **tribal shamans** who heal the sick, pray to animal spirits, and provide spiritual guidance.

GLADIATOR

Medium humanoid (any race), any alignment

Armor Class 16 (studded leather, shield)
Hit Points 112 (15d8 + 45)
Speed 30 ft.

STR	DEX	CON	INT	WIS	CHA
18 (+4)	15 (+2)	16 (+3)	10 (+0)	12 (+1)	15 (+2)

Saving Throws Str +7, Dex +5, Con +6
Skills Athletics +10, Intimidation +5
Senses passive Perception 11
Languages any one language (usually Common)
Challenge 5 (1,800 XP)

Brave. The gladiator has advantage on saving throws against being frightened.

Brute. A melee weapon deals one extra die of its damage when the gladiator hits with it (included in the attack).

ACTIONS

Multiattack. The gladiator makes three melee attacks or two ranged attacks.

Spear. *Melee or Ranged Weapon Attack:* +7 to hit, reach 5 ft. or range 20/60 ft., one target. *Hit:* 11 (2d6 + 4) piercing damage, or 13 (2d8 + 4) piercing damage if used with two hands to make a melee attack.

Shield Bash. *Melee Weapon Attack:* +7 to hit, reach 5 ft., one creature. *Hit:* 9 (2d4 + 4) bludgeoning damage. If the target is a Medium or smaller creature, it must succeed on a DC 15 Strength saving throw or be knocked prone.

REACTIONS

Parry. The gladiator adds 3 to its AC against one melee attack that would hit it. To do so, the gladiator must see the attacker and be wielding a melee weapon.

DRUID

346

Gladiators battle for the entertainment of raucous crowds. Some gladiators are brutal pit fighters who treat each match as a life-or-death struggle, while others are professional duelists who command huge fees but rarely fight to the death.

GUARD

Medium humanoid (any race), any alignment

Armor Class 16 (chain shirt, shield)
Hit Points 11 (2d8 + 2)
Speed 30 ft.

STR	DEX	CON	INT	WIS	CHA
13 (+1)	12 (+1)	12 (+1)	10 (+0)	11 (+0)	10 (+0)

Skills Perception +2
Senses passive Perception 12
Languages any one language (usually Common)
Challenge 1/8 (25 XP)

ACTIONS

Spear. *Melee or Ranged Weapon Attack:* +3 to hit, reach 5 ft. or range 20/60 ft., one target. *Hit:* 4 (1d6 + 1) piercing damage, or 5 (1d8 + 1) piercing damage if used with two hands to make a melee attack.

Guards include members of a city watch, sentries in a citadel or fortified town, and the bodyguards of merchants and nobles.

KNIGHT

Medium humanoid (any race), any alignment

Armor Class 18 (plate)
Hit Points 52 (8d8 + 16)
Speed 30 ft.

STR	DEX	CON	INT	WIS	CHA
16 (+3)	11 (+0)	14 (+2)	11 (+0)	11 (+0)	15 (+2)

Saving Throws Con +4, Wis +2
Senses passive Perception 10
Languages any one language (usually Common)
Challenge 3 (700 XP)

Brave. The knight has advantage on saving throws against being frightened.

ACTIONS

Multiattack. The knight makes two melee attacks.

Greatsword. *Melee Weapon Attack:* +5 to hit, reach 5 ft., one target. *Hit:* 10 (2d6 + 3) slashing damage.

Heavy Crossbow. *Ranged Weapon Attack:* +2 to hit, range 100/400 ft., one target. *Hit:* 5 (1d10) piercing damage.

Leadership (Recharges after a Short or Long Rest). For 1 minute, the knight can utter a special command or warning whenever a nonhostile creature that it can see within 30 feet of it makes an attack roll or a saving throw. The creature can add

a d4 to its roll provided it can hear and understand the knight. A creature can benefit from only one Leadership die at a time. This effect ends if the knight is incapacitated.

REACTIONS

Parry. The knight adds 2 to its AC against one melee attack that would hit it. To do so, the knight must see the attacker and be wielding a melee weapon.

Knights are warriors who pledge service to rulers, religious orders, and noble causes. A knight's alignment determines the extent to which a pledge is honored. Whether undertaking a quest or patrolling a realm, a knight often travels with an entourage that includes squires and hirelings who are commoners.

MAGE

Medium humanoid (any race), any alignment

Armor Class 12 (15 with *mage armor*)
Hit Points 40 (9d8)
Speed 30 ft.

STR	DEX	CON	INT	WIS	CHA
9 (−1)	14 (+2)	11 (+0)	17 (+3)	12 (+1)	11 (+0)

Saving Throws Int +6, Wis +4
Skills Arcana +6, History +6
Senses passive Perception 11
Languages any four languages
Challenge 6 (2,300 XP)

Spellcasting. The mage is a 9th-level spellcaster. Its spellcasting ability is Intelligence (spell save DC 14, +6 to hit with spell attacks). The mage has the following wizard spells prepared:

Cantrips (at will): *fire bolt, light, mage hand, prestidigitation*
1st level (4 slots): *detect magic, mage armor, magic missile, shield*
2nd level (3 slots): *misty step, suggestion*
3rd level (3 slots): *counterspell, fireball, fly*
4th level (3 slots): *greater invisibility, ice storm*
5th level (1 slot): *cone of cold*

ACTIONS

Dagger. *Melee or Ranged Weapon Attack:* +5 to hit, reach 5 ft. or range 20/60 ft., one target. *Hit:* 4 (1d4 + 2) piercing damage.

Mages spend their lives in the study and practice of magic. Good-aligned mages offer counsel to nobles and others in power, while evil mages dwell in isolated sites to perform unspeakable experiments without interference.

VARIANT: FAMILIARS

Any spellcaster that can cast the *find familiar* spell (such as an archmage or mage) is likely to have a familiar. The familiar can be one of the creatures described in the spell (see the *Player's Handbook*) or some other Tiny monster, such as a crawling claw, imp, pseudodragon, or quasit.

NOBLE

Medium humanoid (any race), any alignment

Armor Class 15 (breastplate)
Hit Points 9 (2d8)
Speed 30 ft.

STR	DEX	CON	INT	WIS	CHA
11 (+0)	12 (+1)	11 (+0)	12 (+1)	14 (+2)	16 (+3)

Skills Deception +5, Insight +4, Persuasion +5
Senses passive Perception 12
Languages any two languages
Challenge 1/8 (25 XP)

ACTIONS

Rapier. *Melee Weapon Attack:* +3 to hit, reach 5 ft., one target. *Hit:* 5 (1d8 + 1) piercing damage.

NOBLE

REACTIONS

Parry. The noble adds 2 to its AC against one melee attack that would hit it. To do so, the noble must see the attacker and be wielding a melee weapon.

Nobles wield great authority and influence as members of the upper class, possessing wealth and connections that can make them as powerful as monarchs and generals. A noble often travels in the company of guards, as well as servants who are commoners.

The noble's statistics can also be used to represent **courtiers** who aren't of noble birth.

PRIEST

Medium humanoid (any race), any alignment

Armor Class 13 (chain shirt)
Hit Points 27 (5d8 + 5)
Speed 25 ft.

STR	DEX	CON	INT	WIS	CHA
10 (+0)	10 (+0)	12 (+1)	13 (+1)	16 (+3)	13 (+1)

Skills Medicine +7, Persuasion +3, Religion +4
Senses passive Perception 13
Languages any two languages
Challenge 2 (450 XP)

Divine Eminence. As a bonus action, the priest can expend a spell slot to cause its melee weapon attacks to magically deal an extra 10 (3d6) radiant damage to a target on a hit. This benefit lasts until the end of the turn. If the priest expends a spell slot of 2nd level or higher, the extra damage increases by 1d6 for each level above 1st.

Spellcasting. The priest is a 5th-level spellcaster. Its spellcasting ability is Wisdom (spell save DC 13, +5 to hit with spell attacks). The priest has the following cleric spells prepared:

Cantrips (at will): *light, sacred flame, thaumaturgy*
1st level (4 slots): *cure wounds, guiding bolt, sanctuary*
2nd level (3 slots): *lesser restoration, spiritual weapon*
3rd level (2 slots): *dispel magic, spirit guardians*

ACTIONS

Mace. *Melee Weapon Attack:* +2 to hit, reach 5 ft., one target. *Hit:* 3 (1d6) bludgeoning damage.

Priests bring the teachings of their gods to the common folk. They are the spiritual leaders of temples and shrines and often hold positions of influence in their communities. Evil priests might work openly under a tyrant, or they might be the leaders of religious sects hidden in the shadows of good society, overseeing depraved rites.

A priest typically has one or more acolytes to help with religious ceremonies and other sacred duties.

Scout

Medium humanoid (any race), any alignment

Armor Class 13 (leather armor)
Hit Points 16 (3d8 + 3)
Speed 30 ft.

STR	DEX	CON	INT	WIS	CHA
11 (+0)	14 (+2)	12 (+1)	11 (+0)	13 (+1)	11 (+0)

Skills Nature +4, Perception +5, Stealth +6, Survival +5
Senses passive Perception 15
Languages any one language (usually Common)
Challenge 1/2 (100 XP)

Keen Hearing and Sight. The scout has advantage on Wisdom (Perception) checks that rely on hearing or sight.

Actions

Multiattack. The scout makes two melee attacks or two ranged attacks.

Shortsword. *Melee Weapon Attack:* +4 to hit, reach 5 ft., one target. *Hit:* 5 (1d6 + 2) piercing damage.

Longbow. *Ranged Weapon Attack:* +4 to hit, ranged 150/600 ft., one target. *Hit:* 6 (1d8 + 2) piercing damage.

Scouts are skilled hunters and trackers who offer their services for a fee. Most hunt wild game, but a few work as bounty hunters, serve as guides, or provide military reconnaissance.

Spy

Medium humanoid (any race), any alignment

Armor Class 12
Hit Points 27 (6d8)
Speed 30 ft.

STR	DEX	CON	INT	WIS	CHA
10 (+0)	15 (+2)	10 (+0)	12 (+1)	14 (+2)	16 (+3)

Skills Deception +5, Insight +4, Investigation +5, Perception +6, Persuasion +5, Sleight of Hand +4, Stealth +4
Senses passive Perception 16
Languages any two languages
Challenge 1 (200 XP)

Cunning Action. On each of its turns, the spy can use a bonus action to take the Dash, Disengage, or Hide action.

Sneak Attack. Once per turn, the spy deals an extra 7 (2d6) damage when it hits a target with a weapon attack and has advantage on the attack roll, or when the target is within 5 feet of an ally of the spy that isn't incapacitated and the spy doesn't have disadvantage on the attack roll.

Actions

Multiattack. The spy makes two melee attacks.

Shortsword. *Melee Weapon Attack:* +4 to hit, reach 5 ft., one target. *Hit:* 5 (1d6 + 2) piercing damage.

Hand Crossbow. *Ranged Weapon Attack:* +4 to hit, range 30/120 ft., one target. *Hit:* 5 (1d6 + 2) piercing damage.

Rulers, nobles, merchants, guildmasters, and other wealthy individuals use **spies** to gain the upper hand in a world of cutthroat politics. A spy is trained to secretly gather information. Loyal spies would rather die than divulge information that could compromise them or their employers.

SCOUT

THUG

Medium humanoid (any race), any non-good alignment

Armor Class 11 (leather armor)
Hit Points 32 (5d8 + 10)
Speed 30 ft.

STR	DEX	CON	INT	WIS	CHA
15 (+2)	11 (+0)	14 (+2)	10 (+0)	10 (+0)	11 (+0)

Skills Intimidation +2
Senses passive Perception 10
Languages any one language (usually Common)
Challenge 1/2 (100 XP)

Pack Tactics. The thug has advantage on an attack roll against a creature if at least one of the thug's allies is within 5 feet of the creature and the ally isn't incapacitated.

ACTIONS

Multiattack. The thug makes two melee attacks.

Mace. *Melee Weapon Attack:* +4 to hit, reach 5 ft., one creature. *Hit:* 5 (1d6 + 2) bludgeoning damage.

Heavy Crossbow. *Ranged Weapon Attack:* +2 to hit, range 100/400 ft., one target. *Hit:* 5 (1d10) piercing damage.

Thugs are ruthless enforcers skilled at intimidation and violence. They work for money and have few scruples.

THUG

TRIBAL WARRIOR

Medium humanoid (any race), any alignment

Armor Class 12 (hide armor)
Hit Points 11 (2d8 + 2)
Speed 30 ft.

STR	DEX	CON	INT	WIS	CHA
13 (+1)	11 (+0)	12 (+1)	8 (−1)	11 (+0)	8 (−1)

Senses passive Perception 10
Languages any one language
Challenge 1/8 (25 XP)

Pack Tactics. The warrior has advantage on an attack roll against a creature if at least one of the warrior's allies is within 5 feet of the creature and the ally isn't incapacitated.

ACTIONS

Spear. *Melee or Ranged Weapon Attack:* +3 to hit, reach 5 ft. or range 20/60 ft., one target. *Hit:* 4 (1d6 + 1) piercing damage, or 5 (1d8 + 1) piercing damage if used with two hands to make a melee attack.

Tribal warriors live beyond civilization, most often subsisting on fishing and hunting. Each tribe acts in accordance with the wishes of its chief, who is the greatest or oldest warrior of the tribe or a tribe member blessed by the gods.

VETERAN

Medium humanoid (any race), any alignment

Armor Class 17 (splint)
Hit Points 58 (9d8 + 18)
Speed 30 ft.

STR	DEX	CON	INT	WIS	CHA
16 (+3)	13 (+1)	14 (+2)	10 (+0)	11 (+0)	10 (+0)

Skills Athletics +5, Perception +2
Senses passive Perception 12
Languages any one language (usually Common)
Challenge 3 (700 XP)

ACTIONS

Multiattack. The veteran makes two longsword attacks. If it has a shortsword drawn, it can also make a shortsword attack.

Longsword. *Melee Weapon Attack:* +5 to hit, reach 5 ft., one target. *Hit:* 7 (1d8 + 3) slashing damage, or 8 (1d10 + 3) slashing damage if used with two hands.

Shortsword. *Melee Weapon Attack:* +5 to hit, reach 5 ft., one target. *Hit:* 6 (1d6 + 3) piercing damage.

Heavy Crossbow. *Ranged Weapon Attack:* +3 to hit, range 100/400 ft., one target. *Hit:* 6 (1d10 + 1) piercing damage.

Veterans are professional fighters that take up arms for pay or to protect something they believe in or value. Their ranks include soldiers retired from long service and warriors who never served anyone but themselves.

INDEX OF STAT BLOCKS

Use this index to find a specific monster stat block.

FEB 0 6 2019

2-5-19

4-2-19

0